"THE RUNNER"

Lloyd Wendell Cutler

authorHOUSE®

AuthorHouse™
1663 Liberty Drive
Bloomington, IN 47403
www.authorhouse.com
Phone: 1 (800) 839-8640

Published by AuthorHouse   08/28/2015

ISBN: 978-1-5049-1477-2 (sc)
ISBN: 978-1-5049-1457-4 (e)

Library of Congress Control Number: 2015909466

Contents

Acknowledgements

"Nothing we do, however virtuous, can be accomplished alone; therefore we are saved by love."

Reinhold Niebuhr

Much thanks goes to Poet-historian, James McManmon, also known by his pen name, Seamus Cassidy. Jim graciously lent me his poetry, bits and pieces of which can be found spoken by character, "Wise Mac," throughout the book. You can find Jim's poetry online by Googling *"American Poet Seamus Cassidy."*

I would first and foremost like to thank my family for their undying support and tolerance during the long years and hours spent on this *pie in the sky* project. Today, when I need some privacy, all I have to do is start talking about my book and they scatter in every direction. It's not easy seeing loved ones burned out to the extent that they beg others not to ask him about "the book."

There is a special place in my heart for my editor, Bob Barnes, a native Las Vegan, editorial director of *The Las Vegas Food & Beverage Professional*, regional correspondent for *Celebrator Beer News* and he covers the LV restaurant scene for *Gayot.com*. If my narrative looks professional in any way, Bob was there to make it so. He spent tireless hours doing pro-bono work helping a friend realize a lifetime dream.

My gratitude goes out to Marsha Thiriot, lifetime librarian (retired), holding a Master's Degree in Library Science. She is a former member of the *Newbery Medal* and *Caldecott Medal Awards* committees. Marsha's insight into storytelling, structure, and other issues critical to a good read were insightfully poignant.

I would like to thank my lifetime friend, Lally Smith Barnes. She listened for hundreds of hours in restaurants while I tried out variants of the story. Her feedback was immensely valuable as I tried to construct entertaining characters who were both believable and superhuman at the same time.

Most of all I would like to thank you. If you made it all the way to Acknowledgements then you are about to read my book. Thanks. The greatest gift any storyteller can receive is the criticism that comes from someone who took the time to read what he or she had to say.

Prologue

I notice nine sweet toes touching eternity.

Wise Mac

December, 2078

    The pitch black of a silent room was disturbed by the alarm, warning the old woman that she would have to get out of bed and get moving soon, not right this minute mind you, but soon. When the alarm rang a second time just a few minutes later, she sat up, putting her feet to the floor, and then wondered why it was so difficult to wake up and get out of bed. Just a few hours ago sleep had evaded her, a cold and unfair fact of life. People her age should not have to wake to an alarm; they should just sleep until they didn't want to anymore. The vast majority of people her age were sleeping alright, pushing up daisies. Of the few that remained, most sat and stared blankly at Lord knows what. Some could walk, by and large with assistance, but were likely confined to one contraption or another and sadly most could not think coherently. Was it so bad that her albatross had been the battle of the bulge, fighting off weight gain all those decades? Her bones squeaked, creaked and ground together, but at least she could still move. Her face looked like it had survived the hundred year storm, but she could think and talk. "Gratitude, Trisha," spoken aloud. She turned off the alarm, used the restroom, sat back down, then rested her head on a pillow and fell into her deepest sleep of the night, though the day had found first light. The next time a bell rang it was the phone, the one she had with her at all times. The sun, now shining brightly through the hand-sewn curtains her sister had made more than 50 years ago, reigned its promise of the day to come. This time Trisha was fully rested, though now the 98 year old lady faced a more daunting problem: she was to attempt yet another milestone in her long and productive life. Trisha Jean Martin wanted to go in the books as the oldest female marathon finisher in history, at least according to Guinness, and because of the extra sleep, she was late, perhaps too late. She had not eaten, stretched, hadn't done anything to get ready but sleep some more. "Who cares," she smiled out loud to Buster, her old English bulldog, just rousting his head off of the bed himself. Buster had lost his companion and sister Tilda some months ago to old age. Now he and Trisha were alone . . . together. She answered the phone.

"Grandma, I was so worried. You were supposed to be out on the back patio almost an hour ago. You know, Great-Great Grandmother, when someone your age doesn't make an appointment, people wonder about things."

"I'm coming, Andrea. We still have plenty of time to make the run, uh, race that is. I am fine, just needed a bit of rest this morning. It's a prerogative for a tired old woman, you know. Tell them I am going to be stretching during the interview. I need twenty more minutes to eat and get ready."

"Not to worry, Grandma, they changed the start of the race. It won't begin for hours. A water pipe broke again and flooded the street. They are working on it right now. You have all the time in the world."

That little tidbit conjured a sense of relief. She had gotten away with it again. Hers had always been the best of luck. "Good, Andrea. In that case I will freshen up, put something comfortable on, grab a quick bite, and then be out back in a few minutes." She was true to her word. Her-now not natural-brunette waste-length hair had been braided into pig tails the night before. She dressed in simple but colorful clothing, and even took a few minutes to put on makeup. Her outfit accentuated a perfect figure for a girl of any age. Thank heavens she did not have to show them the leathered wrinkles that surrounded her still fit body. There was to be no tiny two-piece marathon outfit for Trisha on this run. Well, there was a famous running outfit she would wear, but with the addition of a white body suit, she would be covered properly. When she stepped on the scale, the same one she had used since she was a young woman, it read 103 lbs.

For her that was the accomplishment of a lifetime, literally. She went outside and immediately the film crew from ESPN, her family, other reporters, the Guinness representative and a couple of young world class runners started cheering . . . Public adoration was just as uncomfortable now as it had always been. Her life had never been her own, though she would not have traded it for anything.

"Ms. Martin, how does it feel to be the oldest person ever to run a marathon?"

"Get the question right, my friend. I am the oldest *woman* to try a marathon. Guy James, if he were here, would stand up and proudly state that he finished a marathon at the ripe old age of 101. Also, I did not say I was going to run a marathon; no, I am going to *attempt* a marathon." There was howling laughter. Well, she could at least still make folks laugh. "It feels terrible at my age." They laughed again.

"What is the best thing about being 98?" This time the question came from one of the runners. Young people who ran for a living always looked so good. Oh, how she wished to be young again.

"The best thing about it is that I enjoy being alive. Think of how dark and sleepy the alternative would be." If she'd had the time, Trisha could have been a stand-up comedian. They were laughing again.

"What is the worst thing about your age?," quipped the interviewer.

For just a moment, one that seemed too long, Trisha Jean Martin choked up and became melancholy, then a bit tearful. *I resent being old. It's no panacea. Even justifiable resentment can be tricky, though. Resentment slowly undermines our defenses against the demons we all struggle with.* "Almost without exception, the elderly are tortured with loneliness and most of us are plagued by a sense that we no longer belong. I am so lonely for my friends," again she had trouble controlling her voice. "Of course I'll never get over having to face life without my husband. Even after all these years I miss my father whom I lost just after high school. My mom and I had so much fun traveling the world together once the running thing took off. She was so much fun. Rachael was like a best friend and she's been gone for a long time now. I feel so lost without Michael, the guiding force behind everything I have been able to accomplish. David was more, much more than an agent. How could I have ever outlived him? He was younger than me. Running days are the worst since Stanley," she started crying again, this time not able to control herself and she became embarrassed, so she stopped talking.

"So many people still love you, Trisha. Does that replace lost loved ones for you?"

She is trying to make me feel better. "Yes and no. I'll admit that I am a people collector, and I keep going with a smile, sometimes a gritty smile, because I have so many wonderful family, friends and others in my life today. The great circle in the sky keeps on turning. Pain is a part of any living life. The pain I live with today is the curse of longevity. Remember, I am not interested in the alternative just yet, but race days are the hardest when it comes to the precious ones who are gone now, especially the ones who were there for me in the beginning. They literally saved my life."

This group was eager to hear more. "Care to tell us your story, Ms. Martin?" said the interviewer. "Now that the race is delayed we have time to listen. Please, tell us how it all began."

"One should not ask someone my age such an open-ended question, young reporter. It is the story of a lifetime, the grand design that almost never was . . ."

1

The Longest Day

I'd survived the horror of the slave ship,
so this beautiful place lent a measure of relief,
as I felt the chains of depression loosen
around my wrists and ankles.

Wise Mac

"Thank you very much, sir and have a nice evening. Be careful out there with those slick roads," she said. The man picked up his bags, smiled friendly-like, then walked out the door. Flickering house lights signaled the end of the day.

Rain, accompanied by a cold blustery wind, blew in sheets across the darkened empty parking lot, the crescent moon disappearing and reappearing intermittently beyond the vision of moving cloud formations just over the horizon south of Sunrise Mountain. It was a beautiful sight really, if one were a storm watcher. A very obese young woman, well, still young if you measured from the end backwards, not so young anymore if you were a college student, emerged from Target with her friend, April. Their next stop would be at Denny's for a huge after-work late night dinner. *I don't know what April wants, but I am looking forward to the Sampler, a Double Classic Cheeseburger with fries, and a Strawberry Shake,* thought the moonfaced woman as they trudged the rain-soaked parking lot to their cars.

Later that evening she made her way home via Circle K where fresh doughnuts and cold milk awaited. By the time she found her bed, she regretted the last meal she would ever enjoy, was coughing up acid, but headed straight for snacks and ate again anyway. It vaguely occurred to her that she may have already set herself a day back since it was after midnight. She felt a wash of fear set in with the realization that her promised day was on the horizon. A fitful night's sleep, made worse by a painful acid cough, was indicative of her conundrum, and yet soon enough morning arrived.

Trisha Jean Martin was faced with a cold reality. For her it was time to pick a plan, lay down a program, time for the lady to start her engines; day one was here. By virtue of the agreement she had made with herself she would have to pick something and get started today. Trisha was just plain out of excuses. The doctor said it was OK. In fact, he had been begging her for years to get moving. There would to be no relief in the exercise category either. Her doctor was mandating some sort of workout program and she had promised him—and herself—that today was D-day. *It is vital that you do not let him down*, she thought. At 30 years of age, Trisha Martin, who yesterday had weighed 279 pounds, was slipping not so gently into the longest day of her life and didn't even know it.

The phone rang. Her mother was on the line suggesting they meet at Lucille's for lunch and a nice stroll through The District flushing what little money or credit Trisha had right down the drain. *Perhaps*, thought Trisha, *I should start tomorrow, no?* NO! Cold sweat broke out on her forehead; her heart quickened, and she got a bit sick to her stomach, trying to think of something to say. The fatigue was terrible. To add insult to injury she was starving and it seemed as though she may not live to make lunch anyway. There was one person in the family who was even bigger than Trisha and that was her mother. She loved food. *Mom hates diets*, Trisha reminded herself.

"Mother, today is the first day of my new plan, the one I have been talking about; I promised my Doctor and do not intend to let him down. You know I can't go to Lucille's. There is nothing there for me. It is all fattening, plus, I have to start some sort of exercise program, Mom. I know you hate . . ."

"Oh, don't be silly, Trisha. I support you all the way. I am your mother, after all. I mean, diets aren't for me, they don't work, not for us anyway, but you need to find that out on your own . . ."

Trisha's mother rattled on and on the way she had for years. What seemed most offensive was that she should want this for her youngest the most, *but she doesn't*, or so Trisha thought.

Maybe Mom is trying to sabotage me. If I lose weight a man might want me and then she won't have me to go off gorging food with. Mother is so selfish she can't support me, the support that I desperately need today. First there was the resentment blossoming into doubt, and it was followed by a kernel of fear. Trisha slipped ever so gently into the trap she had been trying to avoid.

"OK, Mom. See you at 11:30 just outside Lucille's." She'd caved again . . . for the zillionth time. Good Lord, It was barely breakfast time on the first day. As Trisha walked away from the phone she thought of breakfast. Pop a few frozen waffles into the toaster, drench them in butter, drown them in syrup, swig a 32 oz glass of ice cold milk, eat a banana for health, and reload later—or not. Instead she poured a cup of coffee, black for the first time in memory, sat down on the couch and glanced at the television. *Oh gosh, a diet commercial.*

". . . With Hydroxycut you experience clinically proven weight loss thanks to a powerful, well—researched primary ingredient complex that can help you lose more weight than when dieting alone . . ." Click... "Weight Watchers is simple, satisfying and smart" . . . Click . . . . "Get maximum results for effective weight loss with Jenny Craig and Metabolic Max" . . .

What was going on here? *There is weight loss on every channel at the same time,* Trisha thought. Click . . . "Atkins is the most natural, easiest, tastiest, best long term way to achieve . . . ." click . . . "HCG triggers the body to provide a constant flow of "food" received from the fat that your body is breaking down" . . . Click, and off.

Trisha struggled up from the plush red sofa in her television room, leaving the remote to fall between squashed cushions. It took a swinging effort to heave her bulk up, and in the process she knocked over the reading lamp . . . again. After picking it up and setting it on the old English end table she waddled back towards the kitchen for a coffee refill, utterly miserable, hungry as hell, musing

3

twice about the waffles and she started to cry. It was a useless game she was stuck in, so disappointed in herself, her mother . . . and with her life. On her way to the kitchen she stopped by the family portrait taken many years ago when she was just a little girl excited for the great adventure ahead. Obviously, she regretted how the whole thing had turned out. She was alone, with no children . . . yet; she was still on this side of her birthing years—if just barely. Of course for her there would be no kids and no husband, except maybe for one of those freaky chubby chasers. Trisha would have none of that. What had gone so wrong? Everyone in the family reunion picture was thin, even her mother. They were so happy, at least that is the way she reminisced it. She fondly remembered what they ate that day.

Why does food control me? Is it at the root of emotional deformities, or is it just a symptom?

She remembered big bowls of chips, nuts, candy, and some bacon treat. There was a vegetable platter with dip, Coca Cola bottles iced up and ready to drink from, all before they sat down to dine. The fresh rolls were complemented by real butter, *oh I can still smell that smell*, and in the oven a huge roast beef readied itself. The giant iron pot of fresh gravy on the stove simmered.

There was corn on the cob bubbling in a milky-buttery broth and garlic mashed potatoes a plenty. The aroma of Grandma's homemade stuffing arrived through an open window as she and Grandpa made their way to the front door. There was a fancy salad with Thousand Island dressing already on the table along with Knott's Berry Farm strawberry jam for those rolls in case the butter didn't do the trick. No wonder everyone was so happy. Aunt Betsy arrived with fresh baked pies, Trisha's mother put out the hand-churned vanilla bean ice cream, and that young lady knew what heaven was like. Trisha winced with longing pain as she drifted back into reality. All of that was gone now, a memory, faded with lost chances at a normal life. *Things aren't right.*

When she reached the coffee pot she was sorely tempted to add heavy cream and sugar. *Will today end up as the first day or not?* Again she poured it black, sipping miserably as she went rummaging through the fridge looking for something to eat. Not much in the way of diet food to pick from. *Why not half rations?* I'll have half a loaf of toast, smothered in half a pound of butter, a half a rash of bacon, half of a dozen eggs, half a box of hash browns, half a gallon of milk, and finish it up with a half a box of Sugar Frosted Flakes with half and half. When she went small at lunch her mother would know that this time she was serious. *Just kidding*, she laughed to herself. There's humor in the game of trying to fight off a slow and slothful demise. *Great job, Trisha*; at the back of the fruit box was a honeydew melon. She had put it there for dieting protection yesterday.

She put one slice of bread in the toaster, cut the melon, continued sipping the black coffee and somehow made it through her first meal. It wasn't so bad, really. Trisha had not limited breakfast to something as simple as honeydew melon and a single slice of dry toast, perhaps ever.

Truthfully, it tasted sweet, kind of like magic, really. Fruit without sugar; sadly, once everything was cleaned up a new thought conjured a new red flag; *now what should I have for breakfast*? Dad-burn-it, she had forgotten to weigh herself in and now the scale would show even more. This was not going well, but then an epiphany struck. *Who cares how high the first number is? The higher the better so when I look back I can tell them all how much more I lost.*

She happily got on the old torture plate and took a reading . . . down four pounds from yesterday. *That is flat out impossible!* Yesterday, Trisha had eaten all day and culminated everything with a last supper that would have made Caesar himself proud. She was reminded again that this dieting business was tricky at best, and not altogether logical. Her body never did what it was supposed to.

For a moment her mind drifted into the past, to high school. She was once a long distance runner, a member of the track team. Trisha was skinny, real slender. She wasn't a chubby kid destined to grow enormous. Obviously Trisha had the 'fat' gene in her chromosomal make up, the propensity to gain weight, but it had not manifested itself in her life at that time. There was even some interest in her as a runner at the college level; that is, before she was injured at the end of her senior season. It didn't seem to be that big of a deal at the time, but, she never raced competitively again.

Trisha walked down the hall, an unusable cave except as a pathway to her room. The carpet was worn and frayed, there was nothing on the walls, and one of the two ceiling lights had not worked in some time, years perhaps. Her bedroom was a total mess.

5

The sheets were dirty and there were clothes everywhere. Behind where the headboard would be if she had one, there was an inch or thereabouts of open space to the wall. It served a specific purpose, a place to stuff fast food wrappers so she didn't have to get out of bed to throw them away. It was a sty. To the best of her knowledge, not another person had been allowed into her private space for years running. She didn't live in this hole; she just existed here, except for the kitchen. Everything in there was completely organized. You could sure tell what mattered to her in life. Pain medication in the form of food was what she lived on.

She took a shower. For the first time today Trisha felt better. No, it was the second time today. She felt a little better after she had eaten her breakfast, too. Somewhere deep inside of this troubled person there was a real human being, hidden yes, but she was still in there. That senior high school runner, the tiny little athlete who was fascinated by her many friends, was still a part of who she was. A different Trisha Martin was alive somewhere deep inside the wreckage of her present. Could that person ever come out again? Fantasy wishes of a delusionary, an obese person, one who lived in the past. She would have a great deal of trouble seeing that Trisha resurrected. It was painful to allow herself the luxury of daring that she could find that optimistic, vibrant, thin, running machine. Yet, one never knew the future. That was what her mother always said.

So that's where things stood that Saturday morning; it was still not yet 9:00. She decided to turn on the television in her room and watch news. *Do they still call that garbage 'news' these days? Who knows; who cares*, thought the onetime captain of the State high school debate team.

Instead of news, there was an informational program on— you guessed it—another dieting choice, Nutrisystem. Even Marie Osmond should be smart enough enough to know that garbage was dog food. How could anyone even consider eating that . . . that whatever it is? Click. "Dr. Sears Zone Diet burns fat faster . . ." Click. "Your alliplan helps your head learn healthy habits that stick; alli is all about eating . . . ." Click. Off. This was getting ridiculous. *Here I sit*, Trisha thought, *on the first day of my new life, I'm already overwhelmed, and every time I look at the TV all I see is one plan after another; it's surreal.* This had to be a message from God or maybe it's a nonsensical coincidence.

Trisha went to the dresser drawer and slid it open, the one with where she kept bedtime snacks. Inside there was a bag of chocolate covered walnuts, open and stale, three bags of chips, two huge Butterfingers, a partial tube of Ritz Crackers and more. She sighed, thinking of it as poison, not really, but for her today it was. She lost her wits and started to cry as she slammed it closed. Trisha Martin was literally stuck in a dreadful, horrible place. Her life was sinking into complete disarray. There didn't seem to be any way out of it. She flopped down onto the bed sobbing, collapsing too hard, and so dislodged the box spring from the frame. After a few minutes of extreme self pity, she drifted into a troubled sleep, not bothering to fix the tilting mattress. She dreamed.

It was a sunny day, a Saturday, and the high school senior was running like the wind. Racing had never felt better. The air was crisp and clean; she had reached the six mile mark, quickly hydrated with a lime drink and moved on. How Trisha Martin felt when running a race was as inexpressible as the inner workings of a horse's mind in the final turn at the Kentucky Derby. For some reason her body was responding like never before. Just three weeks ago she had finished a distant sixth at the Nevada State High School Cross Country Track and Field Championships. It had been her best time.

She'd been happy with it, but she knew there was more in her. Today, well, today was that more. There were over 1,000 runners in this race and she was near the lead pack. The kid picked up the pace, got back into rhythm, and began to pass runners, some of them experienced racers with credentials. One, a college sprinter on full scholarship at UCLA, seemed to be struggling as far as Trisha could tell. Not Trisha, not today. The course turned up into the hills and she pushed herself. Her reserves let her move on again. At the top of a sun-baked knoll the route took a sharp left, down through a shadowy dip, up a couple of hundred yards through a copse of evergreens and over the top. From there she could see the skyline of Los Angeles as if it were in a glass bottle, an amazing vista.

The dog jumped from the side of the road right in front of her, forcing an unnatural hop sideways. Trisha Martin stumbled, and then fell toward the pavement. She had her right foot on the ground when she felt the tell-tale snap in the back of that still grounded foot and . . .

"Trisha Martin. We have need of you."

Trisha woke up in a cold sweat. That same nightmare had haunted her almost as much as the loss of her father when she was away at school the following year. *Dad? Oh Daddy, I need you.* There she was, lying at an angle, sliding to the floor, crying again uncontrollably this time, and if she did not hurry and get going she would miss her mother and the free feast at Lucille's. Trisha did what she always did. She pushed herself up, wiped her face off in the bathroom, put on some makeup, hid her shame, her depression, and went to the closet to look for something to wear.

She had choices, lots of them. There were the green stretch pants, the red ones, the blue ones, or the black ones. *What color should I wear today? Hey, how can I know that without picking the top first, the size that fits either me or an elephant? Let's go with black. That way no one will be able to tell that I'm overweight.* The tears had turned to laughter. She was hungry. In spite of everything this gal was a fighter and would face this day as she had all others.

Something on the floor in the back of the closet caught her eye. Shoes, running shoes, not quite, but they were walking shoes. Trisha had purchased them four years ago when she'd made her last real attempt to do something about the mess she had become. *I wonder if they still fit*, she thought. *Will they go with my outfit? Oh good Lord, who cares about the outfit?* In order to reach them she had to get down on her knees, a workout in and of itself, *probably 100 calories or better,* she chuckled, counting the push up that would be required to get out of there, but she made it. *They most likely won't fit,* she scoffed at herself. *Feet get fat too.* Back to the dresser drawer she went, this time to look for some white *athletic socks,* and yes, there they were. *If the shoe fits, wear it. I'm a runner. My nose runs, my stockings run, hell, my butt runs, too. The jokes never end do they,* she mused. The shoes fit. One thing had gone her way, so, for whatever reason she labored and wheezed her way to getting them tied. It was a long way down to those feet when she had to tie shoe laces. Her flats were as complimentary to her style as the rest of her, um, wardrobe.

Something about the dream interrupted her, something troubling. Alas, dreams as they are, she could not remember what it was. She hated that dream. It always ended up the same way, but something was just a bit off. *Oh well.*

Trisha wondered how she would get through the meal at Lucille's and still be on the epic journey to skinnydom. It was very important to keep to the plan or the tiny breakfast she had eaten would be lost in yet another failed attempt. Suddenly she had an idea. *Where are all these great ideas coming from?* That much at least was different. She seemed to be at a loss regarding her newfound creativity, but hey, an idea was an idea. She walked down the hall to the office, the bedroom she set aside for business. The third bedroom was for her guests. It suddenly occurred to her that she had not had a guest in that room for at least five years. Her private life was very private. Trisha's inner sanctuary was not open to the public. Only her mother was allowed in the home. Even her sister and brother were never invited over. Once in a while they stopped by and she tried to be as cordial as possible, but she hated letting anyone see the way she lived. Hers was a secret life.

She sat down at the computer and used Google to get at Lucille's Nutritional Information. Perhaps there were options. For the first time today she found something interesting, something other than self pity, and suddenly she was infused with a bolt of positive energy. What she found blew her mind. *Oh my goodness,* she thought, *no wonder everyone is so fat. Now I know why those biscuits taste like heaven.* Wow! There were enough calories, fat, and sugar in most of what was on the menu to ruin any attempt at weight loss. Trisha had eaten at this restaurant so many times, yet she had no idea what she'd been eating. Suddenly she felt a bit stupid for not using the reach of her fingers on a keyboard to gain some knowledge. It felt like she had been hypnotized into a catatonic drone by others who would take her money and see her kill herself with food. She was getting a bit irate. This was turning out to be a very emotional experience. Like anyone might expect, this first day was a concoction of sorrow, shame, depression, fear, self loathing, humor, positive energy, and now anger filled her. Trisha had not even made it out of the house. *It's not a very healthy way to live,* she mused. In less than five minutes on the computer, Trisha found that she could indeed eat a healthy meal; one that she thought could be enjoyed, perhaps not by her, but by someone who had their act together. *How boring is that? Who would go to a place like Lucille's and want to eat healthy.* In that moment she experienced a fear as guttural as anything anyone went through. *My life is going to be so monotonous.* Like everything else she had lost, food was gone now, too.

Trisha got up from the desk and took a look around her office, a pathetic sight. The room was cluttered with junk. An old television in the corner was covered in dust; she could not remember the last time it had been turned on. The office-style trash container was, well, trashed. It was filled, no overfilled, with refuse, most of it from fast food bags too old for her to remember. In fact, she could not recollect the last time she had eaten in that room. Except for the keyboard and the screen, there were papers everywhere, piled at least three inches deep from one end of her desk to the other. It was a miracle that her bills were current; at least she thought they were. Perhaps she should look at her credit report. The entire home, not a home, just a house, a very dirty house, was a mess. There were pictures on the walls, some of her from years ago, living a different life. She still treasured the photo of her and her parents at the finish line of the last major competition she completed in high school. Her mood was quickly darkening again. *It's not possible to have any type of a positive outlook on life living like this,* she sadly admitted. As she took a final look around the office before leaving she noticed her trophies inside a dusty old curio cabinet next to the door, and for the hundredth time she looked at them, reminiscing what might have been.

Trisha Jean Martin picked up her purse, locked the kitchen door on her way into the garage, and got into her car. It was a nice car, a gift from her mother. It would have been a nice car if it wasn't full of garbage from one end to the other, if the maintenance promises she had made to her mother on her birthday three years ago had been kept. Good Lord. She started the engine, noticing the familiar red lights on the dash warning of needed service, backed out of the garage and rolled down the driveway. She noticed the porch light, the light bulb since its cover had shattered, still lying broken in the planter box below. Her lawn looked great. Another gift from her mother was front yard lawn service, including the water bill, which was sent directly to her mother's home so that the turf would stay green and clean for the neighbors and the Nazi Homeowners Association. She was 30 years old and her mother was still taking care of her as if she were a helpless child. Perhaps that is what she was, a 30-year-old stunted child.

On the way to Lucille's she decided that today's little adventure would include a stop at Smith's located diagonally across the freeway, perhaps a half a mile from the restaurant. Suddenly, Trisha had a new idea. Since this was going to be the first day of her new life, *yeah right*, she would park the car at Smith's Foods and walk on over to Lucille's, then back again after she and her mother had shopped. It would be tagged as her exercise for the day, the first she could remember in many years. Perhaps subconsciously she had planned something like that since she opted to put on those shoes. The drive from her home in Whitney Ranch took just a few minutes, driving past Green Valley High School, the site of her life's accomplishments, onto the 215, up one exit and then left to Lucille's in The District, oops, not left but right to Smith's. She had almost forgotten the decision to walk. She parked on the west side of Wendy's, one of her favorite places, got out, locking the car; *one must hope that my vehicle does not get broken into so that all those old bags of eaten food could be stolen*, and so began to walk, first one foot in front of the other. It seemed like two miles to lunch. The first thing she noticed was how nice it was outside.

Trisha made her way out to the Parkway, walking a bit more briskly than she had intended; in fact, there was a bit of a hop to her step. She didn't want to admit to herself that it felt good to be on the move, but in fact it did and her mood was improving. *Physical activity does good things to me, many things.*

* * *

A couple driving south on the Parkway noticed a very large woman walking vigorously. "Good for her," Carol pointed out to her husband. "Seeing people try to improve themselves . . . inspires me." They made eye contact and suddenly Carol felt bad for her. What a fix the woman was in, so she waved and smiled; it was her only chance to give some kind of encouragement.

* * *

Trisha knew that she would be a spectacle out in public, but there was no help for it. Humiliation took many forms in life and she had learned to dismiss it as part of the reality of being heavy. She tried to focus on something besides people in cars who may be laughing at her. The sun was up in the southern horizon, there were big puffy cumulous clouds floating along, and there was Trisha participating in the hustle and bustle of life. She had not experienced a day that way, except at work, for a long time. Most Saturdays were spent at home with her two best friends, food and television. Suddenly she was alive and well. For a minute, just a minute, she tried to forget that she was so big, and, well she started to move a little quicker, not running mind you, just more energy to the walking. It didn't take long before she broke out in a sweat, the nasty eye stingy kind not appreciated. It also became quite apparent that she had no stamina. Trisha was not even across the freeway and she was already out of breath. There was an athlete somewhere inside of her, because being out of breath was something she could relate to, and in a positive way, no doubt. Sweat suddenly became a blessing and a reward, even appreciated.

* * *

Becky Martin pulled from her driveway and headed out the west gate of her neighborhood to meet her daughter, Trisha, for lunch at Lucille's. She had made the appointment today in a latest attempt to jump start her deadbeat life. *Why can't Trisha be happy?* She had been worrying since waking. *She has so much, yet so little, never takes care of anything, her life is a mess; no matter what anyone tries to do to help it doesn't work, and she is depressed . . . ever since she'd dropped out of college after Roger's death.* It is like her verve stopped that day and all that had ever come of it was the misery of a totally disconnected life. Why couldn't she be more like Rachael or Mike? They seemed to pick up and move on just fine.

Michael had taken over the family business when Roger died. He was just a kid, barely four years out of college. Michael knew what he wanted and moved like a lion to keep things going. Becky hated business, loved money, loved the kids, and took the gamble that her son would make it. That was a good bet. When he insisted on buying her out in 2007 they had the papers drawn up and for Becky there was more money coming in now than ever; *good gracious Lord Almighty,* she thought, *Mike's payments to her, due for the next twenty years, was more money than Roger ever made.* The kid was a genius. When the economy tanked and restaurants dropped like flies, Michael cut expenses, went to war in order to save things, sought out people who were not going to fail in business, and grew stronger as everyone else slithered to oblivion around Las Vegas, the black hole of what had turned from the American dream into an American nightmare. *My son. I am so proud of him.* His wholesale food business would be alive long after she was gone.

Rachael on the other hand was an enigma. She didn't desire children of her own, and yet, she wanted to own and operate a day care center. *"Mother, so many of these kids are left behind by their busy parents. Have you seen how many of these children are just lost, shuffled around, and . . . well this is my mission. I don't have time to raise a family."* Truth is, Becky thought, *it's that selfish, immature, narcissistic husband of hers, Adam. She should have married, what was his name again? Oh well.* Her Rachael had always loved kids, always wanted them, and then, within five years from the time they got married it was announced that they had gotten together and chosen a different path, so to speak—come on. What kind of a yarn was that?

Trisha, on the third hand; she was a part time cashier at Target. When she was young and vibrant, Roger had said over and over again that this third child was no mistake; she had more going for her than all the rest of them combined, including her parents. *They were a team, those two.* When she was little and Roger would go out running, Trisha would race after him as hard as she could, once around the block and then it was back into the house for her and onto a lengthy run for him. Not too many years later he was chasing her, sometimes for 20 or more miles as she got older and had learned to love distance running. Running was something Becky could not understand. Why *would a human being run for no reason? Trisha, Trisha, Trisha, what is Mother going to do with you?* It was so troubling. Trish was locked into some emotionally based cerebral coma that she could never escape from. Becky took her 2010 Escalade south on Valle Verde, up the 215 to Green Valley Parkway, turned left, made her way over the freeway and looked at, oh good Lord, Trisha walking up the sidewalk. What was wrong? Had her car broken down again? Becky was stuck at the red light waiting to go and watching her daughter walk, a bit too fast. Something was very wrong and her heart sank. There was a lot of traffic that Saturday morning and she was in the wrong lane. When the light turned green she almost got into an accident speeding up and getting over to the right hand side so that she could pull over and pick Trisha up.

As she slowed and pulled alongside her daughter she noticed that Trisha was exerting breath and sweating all over herself. "Trisha, hop in. What happened? Where is your car? Did it break down again? Are you all right, sweetie?"

"Mom, I am fine. Just go on ahead and get us a table. You really want to help—then please have ice tea ready."

"Come on and get in the car, honey. There is traffic all around us. I am so worried. Trisha, hurry; that car almost hit us."

"Mom, you're not listening. I parked across the street. I WANT to walk. Go and order me some ice tea. I'll see you in less than ten minutes."

"Trisha, get in. It's dangerous to be stopped here. Please don't argue with me. I can't sit . . ."

"Damn-it, Mom, I am not getting in the car. I am walking for exercise. Go."

Becky drove on leaving Trisha behind, clearly frustrated. *I don't know why I try with her. She parked across the street? What does that mean?* Within five minutes Becky had parked the car over on the south side of the restaurant, walked around the front, in the door, and had a small booth ready to go. To settle her nerves she started her lunch with a glass of Chardonnay wine, Shafer Red Shoulder, her favorite. Who cares if it goes with fish? She liked it and she liked it cold. She was into her second glass and a bit relaxed when Trisha walked in and sat down across from her. "Hello, Trisha. How was your walk?"

"Mother," Trisha dug a smile out from inner turmoil.

"Mind telling me what was going on back there?"

Just then a quite young and energetic server stopped by, asking about drinks and whether or not Trisha wanted something from the bar. "Thanks for asking," she smiled. "I'd like ice tea please, lots of ice, make it two ice teas, with lemon, and if you can remember, an extra glass of ice. I am very thirsty." *Sitting in a full service restaurant and being waited on makes me feel better.* "So, Mom, do you know what today is?"

"Saturday, dear, happens every week about this time. Is your car broken down?"

There was another pleasant interruption. "Hi, I'm Kathy and I am going to be taking care of you today. Welcome to Lucille's. Have you dined with us before?"

Trisha smiled but it was her mother that responded. "More times than I can remember, Kathy. This place is one of my favorites. Don't you remember us, uh, me? You have waited on me several times. Can you do us a favor? I would like a Shafer please. Trisha dear, would you like me to order you a drink, maybe something from . . ."

"No thanks, Mom. I just ordered ice tea, and much as I would like to drink with you, with anyone right now, I am staying away from alcohol today, perhaps forever." Sensing tension between them, Kathy took her leave. "I parked my car over near Wendy's, Mom. It's running fine. Care to take a gander as to why I would do such a thing?"

"Oh, I don't know, Trisha. You want to get in some burgers and fries after we're done shopping, wanted to walk off lunch and warm up your thirst for a Biggie Ice Tea, no?" She was chuckling.

Trisha hated the smugness when her mother was drinking. Her timing was good. Kathy was walking up with a glass of wine when Becky finished her second drink in fifteen minutes. The server had set down two great big Kerr jars full of ice tea, loaded with lemons, and true to her memory she also set down a large glass of ice too. To tell the truth it looked absolutely thirst quenching. Trisha gulped the entire first glass in a single satisfying swig. Now she had one ice tea and two glasses of ice. "Mom, I know you don't need the money, but if you just had her open a bottle or two of your wine it would be a bargain the way you're dropping the ole lilac today." The look on her mother's face was murderous, but she said nothing.

"So, Mom, do you know what today is and I am not talking about the day of the week?"

"How about we forget the guessing game and I'll just let you tell me."

15

Kathy swung by the table. "Have we decided on appetizers?" She set down a cute little weave basket with a nice country pattern cloth. Inside of that cloth were three devilishly white steaming flakey biscuits and a cute little tub of Lucille's signature Apple Butter. Trisha's heart stopped and she defibrillated, panicking. There was no way she was going to make it through this meal, no way in hell. *Those things—buttered, are 600 calories . . . each!*

Becky jumped in. She was true to form and still had no clue. "We will have some Onion Straws, right, Trisha?"

Trisha, still quivering, somehow mouthed the words, "Go for it, Mom. I am having Flame Roasted Artichokes, a half order. Perhaps you should go with the half order on the Onion Straws." She was getting bolder.

Becky was completely flabbergasted. "OK." *Artichokes?*

Trisha eyed the establishment's comfortable surroundings. Lucille's was set up like a family home in some ways. There was plenty of color, old fashioned kitchen tables here and there, very interesting and thought provoking art, and she just loved the drinking glasses, old Kerr canning jars. She loved the atmosphere almost as much as the barbeque sauces. For today though, she was completely out of her element. *Why does the first day of a diet have to be so hard?* Couldn't they have just gone across the patio and eaten at King's Fish House, enjoying *that* atmosphere?

Her mother had to know what she was going through; it seemed as though she, Mom being Mom, was intent on making it as tough as possible. Perhaps Mother was testing her resolve. If she was looking for tenacity from her youngest daughter, well to the best of Trisha's knowledge, there was none. Perhaps she was living in her own world, not perceptive to what her youngest was really going through. Trisha was a bit obstinate though, and she would most likely be fighting for this no matter how much it hurt, no matter what. The only person she really had to face was the person in the mirror

Over at the bar, Trisha loved the bar here, there were televisions and all sorts of sports. On one TV she could see some sort of a long distance running competition. Ironically she had to strain to see; it seemed surreal and far away, a metaphor for a place in life she had wished for. Racing was such a big part of her life when she was younger, something like living on a different planet. There was plenty of color, what with the trees, grass, outfits, shoes, people, festivities, and competitive determination. She could only yearn for and dream of that life in a once- upon-a-time fantasy, now definitely sheathed in obesithy, shame, depression and . . . silent pain.

Becky Martin sipped wine, staring at her daughter, looking frozen in tense annoyance. Trisha wondered if her mother remembered what things were like before Dad died. Her mother was not overweight then and had a very different outlook on life. It wasn't just Trisha who gained weight as time wore on without Roger. Different people handle the tragic loss of someone as close as a husband or a father in different ways. *Is Mom's plight so different*? Perhaps Trisha should focus a bit on her mother's lonely journey. She never remarried, didn't date, kept to old friends and focused on the family as the source of her joy. And she got fat, very fat. She let herself go almost immediately. Trisha tried not to notice when her mother bit into the third biscuit without even offering it; perhaps not sharing this was a tiny peace offering. She decided, reluctantly, not to feel cheated, but to be grateful. Obviously, the first day of a diet was rent with mixed signals.

"Mom, do you ever think of Dad anymore?" The appetizers came. *Why is it in restaurants that the server never brings the food? They always trade that job back and forth to make it look like you were getting better service,* Trisha chuckled. She noticed Kathy taking someone else's food out to their table. The open ended question had her mother looking sad and Trisha was sorry she had asked.

"Only every day, child. When your dad died we were all taken by complete surprise. He was in good health, especially with all that physical fitness crap. Look at what good it did him!" Trisha burned with anger but held her tongue. Her mother looked horrible, her face twisted with resentment and helpless abandonment. "What can I say? He made himself indispensable to everyone, everyone except Mike who took the baton and launched a new future for himself almost immediately. I had no idea how to take care of myself. Maybe food would make it hurt less. I am still working on that part of it," she laughed, albeit sorrowfully. She drank again. Trisha's pain, now both physical and emotional, sucked the joy right out of that first workout walk, making her now very sorry she had brought her father up.

Kathy saved the day. "How does the food look? Are we ready to order lunch?" Trisha's mother was still motoring through Onion Straws, and lacked manners in trying to mouth an answer. She had poured the dip that came with the appetizer onto the plate and mixed in two different barbeque sauces conjuring a scrumptious treat that had Trisha sick with envy.

Trisha asked for a few more minutes and smiled at her mother who was eating herself to death. *She's just like me.* Her mother was no leader, never claimed to be, never had been, and she was thrown into a matriarch role with no warning and no help. At one time Trisha thought she herself was destined to lead, but time had written that lie out of her tool box. OK, for this one meal, Trisha would lead out in what to do. She felt a little better. Kathy got within eyesight, Trisha waived her over, and away she went armed with her research, knowing what to eat at this forbidden palace of decadence. "I am going to go with Pop's Beloved Fresh Pan Blackened Catfish, no potatoes, but let's add the Vegetable Medley to the Collard Greens. Please have the chef use the least amount of oil possible, none if he can do it." *What a waste of a nice menu,* Trisha thought sourly.

"Chef gets that request all the time," she smiled. "And for you?" Kathy smiled at Becky.

"I will have the Southern Fried Chicken." Trisha nearly fainted at the thought of eating diet prepared catfish across the table from that grand slam home run of a feast. For the umpteenth time today she would be swallowing the need for food. There'd be no relief, no relying on oldfamiliar patterns, not today. It was damnable D-day. The job was to somehow be grateful, by God. *Never happening,* she thought.

"Mom, it's like this," Trisha had worked up the nerve to open a real conversation. She scraped an artichoke leaf; they were better than she thought, that is as long as she stayed away from the mayonnaise looking dip. *The actual hearts are delicious,* she had to admit. "Today, February 6th 2010, is the first day of the rest of my life. I'm sick of being fat, of my life in the whole, and I am going to fix this."

"Sweetheart, there's nothing wrong with you. Such a beautiful girl as you should be proud of your body . . ."

"Mother, I'm fat, my home is a mess, and my car is a mess. Good Lord, you have to pay the water bill to keep me safe from those Nazi

HOA hound dogs. This is tough enough without you glossing over the obvious. You think you know me so well. I bet you called this lunch because you are worried sick that I have gone off of the deep end, right? Well I'm right aren't I? I know you too, Mother dear."

"Yes, Trisha Martin, you know me. What I was going to suggest is that you go and see Dr. Smith and have him refer you to someone who can help you get through your depression, maybe get you on some medication so that you can see the light of day again. Have you any idea how bright you are?" Unbelievably Becky almost ran her fingers on the plate of those greasy onion straws, but instead finished her third glass of wine and started looking for Kathy. That woman was a bottomless pit. Watching her eat made Trisha all the more determined to do something about her own situation.

"Not happening."

"You are even more stubborn than your dad was, Trisha Jean Martin."

"Thanks, Mom. I'll take that as a complement. Now as I was saying, and I will agree that I'm depressed, but I hate medication, I hate doctors. They're no better than Pablo the drug dealer. Are you aware of how many people die every year in this country from the side effects of prescribed pills?

"For goodness sake, Trisha, you are so paranoid." Just then Becky's phone buzzed. She had set it on vibrate but hearing it rattle around in her Gucci bag, the one more valuable than Trisha's car, was comical and the timing could not have been better.

"Better pick up on that, Mommy; it could be your hair dresser. Didn't you leave her a big enough tip when you were there this morning?" she laughed.

"Nice to hear you laugh, even at my expense. Hello. *Mike*, what are you up to? Rachael is with you? You found each other and are shopping together right here in The District. How lovely. No, Trisha and I are having lunch at Lucille's. Sure, come on over. Trisha, you don't mind if Michael and Rachael stop by, I hope."

Trisha had wanted do this one on one, but it was not to be, no; it never worked out her way.

What was she supposed to say? "Great. It will be good to see them. We'd better get Kathy to move us to a bigger table."

Becky hung up. She was all smiles. Whenever, wherever she could get everyone around the table together was a good day for her. Kathy walked by, got the bad news about a larger table and accommodated them. They started over and Becky celebrated by ordering wine. She should have bought the bottle after all. Soon enough they were seated again.

"Mom, let's cut this part of the conversation short, so perhaps you can just remember a year from now what I told you today. This time I mean it."

Mike and Rachael showed up at the host station, larger than life. Becky waved them over with a big smile and suddenly the meal had turned into a family dinner. Trisha couldn't help but notice how put together they both looked. Rachael's clothes were clean, conservative, expensive, and very well coordinated. She looked striking with a matching Coach bag in her left hand and several shopping bags full of treasure in her right. Michael looked like something of a race car driver on his day off. His trim, silk shirt was open at the collar with plenty of room for the Cuban Link gold chain around his neck. Very expensive looking pleated slacks, perfectly pressed, fell to just the right length onto polished shoes. Whatever style-king had put him together, Trisha swore that his pinky diamond ring matched the diamond rimmed gold Rolex on his wrist. His hair was well groomed, but what took the cake for Trisha was that his nails were manicured! To say that Trisha felt out of place with her well worn black 'hide the blubber' stretched K-Mart special outfit, just a bit of makeup, her $20 backpack purse, all augmented by broken nails, would be the understatement of the century. "Hi, guys," she peeped.

Mike and Rachael both tried to talk at the same time, each eager to visit with their reclusive sibling, but Mike won out . . . "Little sister, when I heard that you guys were here we just had to stop by. We never get to see you. What a miracle. I was speaking of you on the phone with Rachael yesterday, planning to make good on a bet I lost, which is why she and I are spending the day shopping. I wish we had more time together, with you that is. I hate going to malls, but here at The District at least I'll get to come up for air. I can sit outside on the bench and watch people. Getting lucky and seeing you, that makes the day. Even though I am definitely not a shopper, I wanted to get with Rachael, too. How great is that?"

He's trying to 'John Gray' me with that 'Venus and Mars' crap, Trisha thought. *Mike always knows what to say. I bet when he is with old ladies he tells them how young they look. He's as slick with the tongue as he is with the wardrobe.*

"Don't let him kid you," Trisha's sister jumped in. "I won the World Series bet and it has taken him this long to carve out a day for us, hasn't it, Mike." The look on his face plead guilty for neglecting his sister. He was a great guy, really loved his own family, was dead loyal to his birth family, but he was a guy after all. Guy time; it was a mystery that women let men live.

Kathy stopped by to let Trisha and her mother know that the food would be out in ten minutes and Mike asked about cooking time so that their lunches could come out together. "Oh, we're pretty good. First, let's get the drink orders." They both wanted ice tea, Mike went for the Corn Chowder, asked for biscuits with extra Apple Butter, and Rachael wondered aloud if the Smoked Salmon Salad would take too long. It wouldn't. Becky asked for a glass of wine.

"How many is that, Mom? How many has Mom had, Trisha," who sheepishly held up four fingers. Rachael said, "No. That's enough for one meal." She signaled to Kathy for another ice tea.

Becky spoke up, a bit put off by the troubling intervention. "Make that hot tea. Please don't forget the cute little honey bear. I'd like extra cream, too." Kathy smiled and walked away. The server had drinks on their table in less than a minute. *One of the great things about this place is the service,* Becky thought, grumpy now that her alcohol day was ruined. Maybe getting family all around the table came at too high of a price and she was not thinking about money. Rachael could be so bossy. *Why can't they be like Michael?*

Trisha was hungrier than when she walked in the place. The artichokes were good, very good, but for her it was like sucking on tea leaves. She had devoured the hearts as if they were the last food she would ever see. Biscuits and Apple Butter appeared in front of Michael and the aroma was unbelievable; the server pointed out that they arrived straight out of the oven.

Here we go again with fancy Southern-style feasting. Tsunami's of misery came and went with the food service. As she faded into the pang of food fatigue, it was Trisha's sister who came to the rescue. "Trish, it's so good to see you. I miss you; you never come over, never invite us over. Can we have lunch next Saturday, too?" Rachael sounded insistent.

"Sure. Tell me about this World Series bet you won from Mikey over here," she deflected. "I have never heard of him losing a bet before. You're not losing your touch are you, Michael?"

"She got lucky." Michael was obviously not ready to humble himself in front of mere women.

"Luck had nothing to do with it. I had a long conversation on the phone just before the Series began with my old high school boyfriend who was in town with his wife. Adam and I got together with them for dinner and he gave me all the inside juice as to why the Philadelphia Phillies would not be able to defend and how the Yankees always, or shall we say almost always, win when they get there. It was a no brainer.

Becky, perhaps a bit loose, opened an old wound, "I told you to marry him."

"Not so fast, Mother. He is a great guy and all, but do you know what Gary does for a living?"

"Gary, Gary Pullman," Becky mused. "That's his name. Gary Pullman; he was such a nice boy and he had great potential, too. I liked him better than Adam. Rachael, you should listen to your mother more often." She crinkled her nose into a facial frown. "You know what is wrong with hot tea? The water doesn't stay hot in that iron pot. Wine just mellows to room temperature and keeps on keeping on," she grumped.

"Like I said, not so fast, Mom. You make a much better Zsa Zsa than you do a fortune teller. Sure, Gary is a great guy. We're still friends, good friends after all these years. That is why I stay in touch with him. He himself would not agree with you. Gary and Adam are good friends. Adam has stayed at his place without me when he was in San Francisco. They even went deep sea fishing together. Our generation doesn't throw old friends away just because they're of the opposite sex and used to be in a relationship . . . ."

Michael piped back into the mix. "Gary sells bullshit information to suckers about all sorts of sporting events—like he has some angle on what may happen, Mom. He tells sucker A to take this team for this reason, then in the next call he'll tell sucker B to take the other team for a bunch of different reasons. After the event half of his "clients" think he is a whiz kid and they take him up again . . ."

"He's in the entertainment business, Mom; I will tell you this in his favor . . . ."

"I get that," Becky was in a mood. "What I mean is that if he and you had gotten together, given your strengths, you can sure chief your mom around, who knows how his talents could have been magnified with you in his life, and, he likes kids. I know Gary is married and has children. Adam doesn't like kids, so I get no grandchildren from your branch of the family tree."

Ouch. That casts a bit of cold water over the entire meal. Trisha was warming up to the party.

Dysfunctional family gatherings blossomed in special flavors. This one got her mind off of her own troubles.

"Stop! Mother, you are way out of bounds." For the first time today Rachael was angry, not able to hold her tongue. Usually she was pretty good about hiding negative emotions. It would take a very patient person to run a day care center and be respected by both kids and parents alike. Obviously, Becky had struck a raw nerve.

Trisha was grateful that the conversation had drifted away from her. She had no way to explain herself to the family, not with all of them so well put together. At least that's how the world looked from her point of view. Now things were getting juicy. She loved a good fight when she wasn't in it. This one could only get better. Trisha knew the big secret, had held it for years. She and Michael had never discussed it either. As far as Trisha knew, and she didn't really know, she was the only human being on the planet Earth that knew, outside of Rachael and Adam. *Here we go.*

Normally an interruption while a big family argument was brewing would have frustrated 'eager ears' Trisha, but not this one. The food was here at last. How did they do it? Rachael's salad was perfect. The Corn Chowder looked its usual— creamy and steaming hot, but it was the humongous fried chicken platter that had Trisha romanticizing Thanksgiving, her favorite holiday. The chicken was dipped in buttermilk, breaded, and then deep fried. It was to die for. Trisha loved the garlic mashed potatoes and the grilled asparagus looked scrumptious next to buttery corn on the cob. Wow. Her plate consisted of catfish, collard greens, and the vegetable medley. To be honest, it looked good, much better than how she envisioned it showing up. She was at least trying to look pleased. It was time to eat at last and for the first time all day Trisha felt a quiver of pleasure.

The mood improved at the table for everyone except Rachael, who was lost in thought, picking at her salad, and sadly, there were tears in her eyes. Something big was about to happen. Michael looked positively enamored by his lunch. Considering what he could have ordered, Trisha respected his restraint. Some people just had a way with food, ate just what they needed, seeming only to be interested in energy requirements. The pleasure of eating, the feasting gene she called it from time to time, came second to people like her brother who knew just what to put in their bodies. Unfortunately for her, it was all about the pleasure and never about the nutrition. Her mother was eating as if by tomorrow the earth would stand still.

The conversation lingered for long minutes while everyone was eating. Rachael was trying as hard as she could to hide the tears, but it was no use; she was breaking down. Becky looked like she had made perhaps the biggest mistake of her life in bringing up the "no children" thing, and she certainly wished she had kept her mouth shut. Michael was eating, slowly. He was a slow eater. You could see his brows burrowed together in an awkward form of consternation. Since the attention was on someone else, and because Trisha had done nothing to aggravate things, her attention was on the catfish. It was delicious. She could tell that the chef had limited the oil, and yet it was flakey, crisp, and seasoned perfectly. She had never eaten catfish in her life up until that moment. Catfish had such a terrible sounding name. Conceivably, southern folk were on to something. The fact was the vegetable combination of a medley and collard greens made the whole thing look just right for getting through a Lucille's experience on the first day of what promised to be a long and painful life ahead. All of this gave her a bit of hope. Perhaps if she educated herself properly there would be culinary delights that she was not aware of yet. *Oh boy—yippee.*

"Mom, I forgive you." Rachael was trying, but now tears formed and were causing her mascara to streak.

"I'm sorry, Rachael. I didn't mean to hurt your feelings. Once again my mouth got away from me. I feel terrible. Kids, your mother drinks way too much. This alcohol thing is shameful and sad. It is not an excuse; there are no creditable excuses for what I just did. I need to quit drinking, but I don't know how. I do know how to be more considerate. Please accept an apology for my boorishly rude comment."

Michael, the family leader, stepped in not wanting to waste an opportunity he'd been looking to take advantage of for quite some time. "Are you saying you're an alcoholic?"

There was dead silence at the table. What was fun just a few minutes ago had suddenly turned deadly serious. Everyone except their mother already knew the answer to that question; perhaps she knew, too. Becky had been in denial, though there had been many problems with her drinking for years, but like the pink elephant in the room, no one except Rachael had ever had the courage to confront her.

Rachael was energized. "Mother?" She was curt in the way that she used the word. "Look, Mom, if you admit it we can help you deal with this . . ." Mike was cut off in mid- sentence.

"Ok, yes. I'm an alcoholic, an overweight and lonely alcoholic. I have admitted it in the past, just not to you guys." Ashamed to say it out loud before, she now mouthed the words as best as she could. "I have been going to meetings, AA meetings, but I can't stop, still. I don't know what to do." She sipped her tea, forgoing any complaints about whether it was hot enough, choosing instead to look for escape in a healthy squirt of honey.

"Do you have a sponsor, and are you working the Steps?" Mike again, but this time he was smiling. "Rachael, all of us including your mother here respects your decision not to raise a family."

Trisha couldn't decide which was more delicious, her lunch or the fact that inquiring eyes were focused on someone else for a change. Her meal was turning out scrumptious. It would be enough food, she was already feeling full, well ok, satisfied, um, maybe not quite satisfied, but . . . Perhaps this dieting thing would be easy if she could just get a toe hold on it.

"Mother," said Mike, *time to press the issue,* "your son is asking a question. Let's try not to get too distracted from this. Remember that no matter what, there are no real secrets with us. Do you have a sponsor and are you working the Steps?" Mike was pretty sure she wasn't, but he needed her to acknowledge it. He had several friends, some of them good friends, in the AA program and was intimately familiar with how that game worked. A few of those friends were very successful in business and had great family lives, too.

"Not yet. I can't find the right one." She did sound a bit unconvincing.

"Mom, when you're drinking almost anyone would be the right sponsor. I suggest you get your lonely butt back into a meeting and ask the first person you see to be a temporary sponsor. Later when you meet someone you can really identify with, you can ask her to take you on. I know some people that do AA and they were much worse off than you. You can do this. My buddies tell me that relief is in the Steps; you need a sponsor to work the Steps, and don't you think it would be wise to get moving on this before you get a DUI, or worse? When is the next meeting?"

The restaurant manager stopped by the table to see if the food was cooked to everyone's satisfaction. Obviously it was and he moved on.

"There is a meeting tonight at 7:00 at a place called the Green Valley Group over on . . ."

". . . Post Street, Mom. I know the place. It's clean and the folks are mostly local. That would be a good choice for you. My question right now is about you driving today. Are you going to be OK to drive?"

"Trisha and I are going out walking around for a while after lunch. I'll be fine." Becky looked, well, not in her comfort zone at the moment. *Can there be anything worse than having to answer questions about my drinking?*

Mike pressed on. It was obvious he had been waiting for this opportunity. Perhaps he should go out with Rachael more often, using her as the door opener to get things done with his birth family. "Are you going to do it right this time, you know, get yourself a sponsor, like tonight?"

"OK. I promise. Tonight I'll head down there and jump into this thing fulltime. Mike, I know you only care about what's best for me." *I hope I say the right thing.* "Rachael, please really do forgive me. I'm embarrassed by what I said and about Adam too. He's a nice guy. I will never mention kids to you again. Your business is your business." She looked back into Mike's eyes, saying, "I hate to impose on people. It is hard to ask someone. I know I have to do something. This is my promise. I am going to commit to the AA life. Like I said, I've been there and I know it works . . . for me at least, that is if I put in effort on my side of the street."

Her mother had just admitted to everyone that she had a drinking problem. Trisha was ecstatic. *The problem at the table is not me for the first time in like . . . ever.* She started thinking about celebrating by having desert. She had earned it, had she not? *What a long day this is going to be.* Trisha, now emboldened because she was definitely not an alcoholic, ventured into the conversation. "Mike, thanks for being here. You know what I like about you? You have always been so well put together. I wish I could have turned out a little more like you, and just look at how handsome you are; Michael Martin is the perfect brother." She was trying to be real, truth be told, and she was being genuine. She secretly idolized her brother.

"Um," Mike cleared his throat, "Trisha, you're my favorite little sister."

"I'm your only little sister," she was beaming now. She also wished that she could lick the plate, but that was not going to happen at this lunch; perhaps if she were alone it might. *I wish I could be like them*, she thought, glancing over at the race on television in the bar area.

"You don't really know what a phony I am. My run of luck has been quite spurious when you consider what I have gotten away with since we lost Pops. Mike rolled his eyes, fingering the chain around his neck nervously. "It has been twelve years and in all that time I have not really told anyone what happened, have I? It seems there might be a secret or two at this table today after all. You guys want to hear the story?" Everyone was smiling and wagging their heads up and down. Rachael had composed herself and looked ready to rejoin the family lunch. Mom's ears perked up like radar. She loved good stories, most certainly wanting out of their last topic of conversation. She looked at Trisha who seemed to be watching television over everyone's head.

"Dad saved my bacon over and over again, just like he did everyone's. It was in his nature, after all. Don't think you're the only one, TJ. I have always thought that the difference between us was age. I was 28 and you were 18, just a kid. Dad was everything to all of us, but when you lost him you didn't have a career and a wife in place to lessen the pain. I did. We were grown up and off living our own lives. I can't speak for Rachael here, but you were still a kid. Dad always said that you were not a surprise, but someone destined to do something great, that he had earned the chance to help get you started on your way, and then wham-o; he's gone in a New York minute. Don't get all teary eyed, family, I might start to cry and ruin my motif for the day. I'll say this, Trisha; you were a surprise to me. There was Mom, getting with child like that after ten years. Your pregnancy came out of nowhere. He just couldn't keep his hands off of you, could he, Mother? No wonder you're so lonely. There simply is no way to replace Roger Martin in this world. He was a one-of-a-kind guy.

"Except for the business, that is; in that one category he absolutely had to have a contingency plan to replace himself should something go wrong. He had a plan alright, and my only part in it was to be there. I had absolutely no idea what it took to run the company or any type of a business. If you remember correctly, Pop was always frustrated with me. He often wondered whether I gave a damn or not about the wholesale food business. You guys trusted his judgment implicitly, and for good reason. He was right about that. Let me be honest without having to explain it to you. I hated the place, still do. For me it's a prison sentence. Oh, don't get me wrong, I enjoy life and my career, and that's why I am not going into what I mean by that today. Just remember, life is about perspective. You really don't know what someone is going through unless you walk a mile in their shoes. By the way, I have good company. Our fellow Las Vegas native, Andre Agassi, claims to hate tennis, and yet, several years after his competitive ATP playing days he can still be found out on the court from time to time. It is what it is.

"You remember the estate lawyer, Sam Giles. I not only remember him, but still see him on a regular basis. Before the funeral, *before* in case you missed what I just said, he called me down to his office and read me a letter from Dad. It was a rebuke of my immaturity, and it started off with the acknowledgement that there hadn't even been a funeral yet, so that I would not be angry with Samuel. He gave full power of attorney to Sam with a caveat. I was taking over the business, that is, if I had the balls. Giles gave me all of five minutes to decide, and I could be in charge as long as I did what he and two other business friends of his, Dad's really, told me to do in committee. It has been like that all these long years and although the five year window for power of attorney passed and I have taken full legal responsibility, that committee still meets. I continue to do what they say. You see, there are terms for this great advice I was so fortunate to run into, and it is great advice. I have to perform the same function for them when their kids take over their businesses, should something go wrong along the way. I am not a bit worried. Those old farts aren't going anywhere soon. In case you haven't heard, we entrepreneurs never retire, hence the prison sentence, life with no parole. You have no idea how many times I have wished for a government job. Do your thirty years and the fool public will send you checks forever, though you never have to go to the office again.

"The next time any of you see me as a wizard with a genius's knack for being put together just remember, and this is especially for you my running sister; today I'm the same kid that hated the place way back then. I just follow the dots from number to number as told. Dad still runs the Martin Wholesale Food Supply. You want to know how I know? He appears to me in dreams, and sometimes he still gets angry with me. I am a classic victim of a great father, stuck in a golden cage."

Kathy broke the interminable silence that followed and passed out a dessert menu. *Oh, not again,* Trisha thought. *It's only the first day and I have to be strong yet again.* She didn't want to argue with Michael, but the story he just told proved to her that he was indeed a genius. He could have screwed that up so easily. *No one has identified me as a runner for years; perhaps what he actually means is that I run from myself.* She was ashamed again. This lunch was turning out to be a very special lunch indeed. It wasn't too often that families, especially grown families, indulged in introspective with an objective mind. Everyone seemed to be getting something from this conversation.

"Michael, my genius son, I knew about the agreement. Your father and I had no secrets. He told me what he wanted to do and I signed the papers two years before he died. I told him then, and I tell you now. I would never have trusted anyone else with that horrible responsibility. Your little situation was on my mind within minutes once I got the call from the paramedics on the mountain. Thank you for growing up at just the right time. Now, I have narrowed my dessert choices down to three; either it is scotch and whiskey, hot brandy, or Lucille's Perfect Fruit Cobbler a la mode. Hmm," she smiled wryly, "I think I will go with the cobbler. How about you guys?"

Mike opted for the Red Velvet Cake, Rachael decided on the Snickers Ice Cream Pie, and everyone looked at Trisha. No one took their mother's bait at being cute with alcohol; for them it was not a laughing matter and hadn't been for some time. Trisha on the other hand was at a loss. The Big Chocolate Cake was one of her favorite treats and she always had it loaded with ice cream. She had never been able to turn it down. She was still hungry, but . . . "I am going to have a cup of black coffee and a fork. I would like a small taste of all three desserts since I just can't decide, and I am stuffed from the huge lunch we just enjoyed." Her mother didn't seem to even notice, but there was a perceptible beam on the faces of her siblings.

"So," she went on, "tell me about this bet you won, Rachael."

"It was beautiful, Sis. The Yankees won in six games. My smartass brother was so sure of the Phillies. For winning I was awarded a two-day date with yours truly here on my left. Last night we went to the beauty shop and got our hair done, both of us, and then to hammer his masculinity we had our nails done, too. You look so pretty today, Michael." He sarcastically held his hands out for everyone to see. "This morning we have been splurging on my $2,000 spending spree. We still have almost $1,500 to go, but only one more stop. He's taking me to Jared's," she said laughing. "I'm getting a fully loaded Pandora bracelet. Yes, I am living in the lap of luxury today." Her hands, held out for everyone to see, curled graciously upward, the fingers extending ever so slowly, like a ballerina. She did her best to emulate the glamorous smile of a professional model. Beautiful she was, Cheryl Tiegs she was not. It was entertaining to hear her tell it though, especially in the presence of Michael with that big 'you got me' grin on his boyish face.

"And what if you had lost?"

"I'd be on the hook for a trip to this year's Final Four college basketball tournament, and I would have had to go with him." She looked like she had escaped a trip to hell. The coffee came, everyone got their drinks reloaded, and yes, there was fresh hot tea for Mom to 'enjoy' with her dessert.

Rachael's mood turned very dark, like it had twisted on a dime. She sat there, turning white, looking for words she hated to speak, but wanted to come out right. The silence was deafening. She was projecting like a tearful teenager who had just been caught with a boyfriend in her room in the middle of the night, and then, "I'm barren." Trisha was beside herself. Rachael's secret of all those years was over and out of the bag. Trisha knew instantly that Mike was definitely not in on this one. He looked sadly shocked.

"What? What was that?" her mother squeakily mouthed.

"Barren, Mother, infertile, non-reproductive, sterile; you must have heard of this kind of a thing before, just not in our family." She started crying again and Mike took his right arm and squeezed her close, then with his other arm he held her like a small child. She put her head on his shoulder and cried real tears. Trisha felt, not sympathy, but empathy for her. Life is so hard, so damnably hard. Why did everything have to be so hard? Why was there so much pain in the world? If God had tagged anyone to be the mother of the year it would have been Rachael. She was so committed to kids that she built a day care center to make up for it. Where was the fairness in all of that?

Becky was thunderstruck. She looked truly hurt. "H-how long have you kno-known this dear, and w-why didn't you tr-trust me with this information? I am your *mother.* I could have helped you through this. Oh, I am so sorry I have been disrespectful of your husband. I never knew. Can you tell me what the diagnosis was?"

"It was a combination of cervical stenosis, and, as if that were not bad enough, I have, or had, distorted fallopian tubes, but it is all over and done with since the hysterectomy. Mom, I couldn't tell you; it would change nothing and since it was so close to when Dad passed we just, I just . . . Adam was totally supportive and would have had no problem with me telling people, but I did not want anyone to know. The only person I ever told was Trisha here. You have been great, Trisha. Nothing has ever come back. I trust you because of that." Trisha felt proud in that moment. Their mother looked so sad, but, hey, she was a Martin after all and she bit her lip on this one. In essence, she gave her oldest daughter a pass, probably because she had it coming after her boorish behavior.

Dessert has a way of smoothing over a bad mood and so when delicious little treats arrived at the table, everyone was instantly cheered up, well, everyone except Trisha. One is not supposed to be hungry in a restaurant setting when the meal was over, but she was ravishing, felt cheated, and wished she had ordered cake. If wishes were fishes, her mother had always said. They ate, Trisha got her little dabs of everyone else's delight, the bill came and Mom went for her purse even as Mike grabbed the check. "Lunch was part of the bet," he said. "Today is your lucky day, girls." Rachael held her thumbs upright at shoulder height while making the kind of a face that says something about who gets the credit. Trisha and her mother giggled.

In just a couple of minutes everyone had freshened up and was out on the patio in front of the restaurant. Trisha took a moment to gather her thoughts. "Family, I am happy to go eat with you anywhere-anytime, but not here, please. That was torture for me. I am off in a new direction with my life. Obviously I can get through a meal at Lucille's, but I am thinking that almost any dining experience may be more pleasant in different surroundings, so what I am actually saying is that it is OK to come here . . . but only on occasion."

Becky put in her two cents worth. "We hear you. Let's try King's Fish House next week." She looked at all three of her kids, proudly. "It seems as if Trisha is the one that's so well put together today anyway, doesn't it?"

"Yup," Trisha proudly strutted. "Except for a few things; the fact that my house is a total mess, the car needs servicing, I dropped out of college. I'm only a part time cashier at Target, my career as a long distance runner is stagnated at 5'6", 275 lbs. I'm looking great." Everyone laughed, including her. It was the defining point of the meal.

"You did great, TJ, really. I am impressed. Just from the looks of it, I like your chances this time," Mike was smiling and it was of the warm, loving type. He looked like his father in that moment. "I think it would be easier to get a good decent healthy meal in a restaurant if we just threw a dart at the yellow pages. Hey, I almost forgot. Tomorrow is the Super Bowl. Who's going to win?"

"I don't know. The Colts are a 4 ½ point favorite, and besides, this is the Saints' first time ever in the big game," Rachael was quick to share her knowledge. "Gary says to bet on Indianapolis. Want to make another bet, Mike?"

"Maybe, though I am not ready to make another bet with you. You have too much inside information. But I agree, in a squeaker it is going to be Indianapolis this year; the Saints will show up and win it next year. I have not laid down my wager yet, but I am going with Indianapolis. They are 14-2. The Saints are 13-3 and they barely escaped Bret Favre and the Vikings in overtime a couple of weeks ago. "How about it, Sis, you want to bet the game with me?" Michael was looking directly at Trisha.

"Sure, why not, Mikey. What do I get if I win?" "What do you want?"

Trisha was thinking of the big prize that Rachael had just racked up and it took her only a second to come up with an answer. "I want a $3,500 makeover at my home. That's new paint inside and out, new carpet, and everything repaired; that will do it for me."

"That's a big bet, even for me. What are you prepared to give up?"

"Oh, Michael, I didn't think of that. No way can I afford this bet. Let's just go for $10. I know it won't interest you, but it would be fun."

"Hold on, TJ. Let me think for a minute . . . I have it. If the Saints win, you'll get your makeover and I will super the entire job myself. All you have to do is pick out what you want and I'll take care of the rest. If Indy wins, and there's no point spread for family bets, they're straight up and down, win or lose, then you have to run four 10k's with me and the Las Vegas half marathon in December out on the Strip. You can afford that can't you, with your new life in place and all? I am talking about jogging fun runs, nothing competitive." This time when he looked into her eyes, he probed deeply. Michael wanted to get into Trisha's head and had found a way. The smug look on his face spoke volumes.

Trisha on the other hand went cold, frozen in a new reality. Real fear gripped her for the first time in many years about whom she was and just what she could *actually* do about it. She knew her brother. *If he wins the bet I'm screwed. My fat person life is over. On the other hand, perhaps I can outsmart the rascal.* "Ok, you're on Michael, except I want the Colts. It is a straight up game and if we go for this

I want the Colts." Trisha's smile let him know that she could make moves too, good ones.

"Not so fast, kiddo. We need to compromise. Tell you what; I'll flip you for the Colts . . ."

"Be careful, Trisha," Rachael cut in, "the reason he knows about Gary is because he is as shrewd a better as anyone out there. He hates to lose bets. I am telling you he's planned this from the moment he set eyes on you inside the restaurant. I am not sure I would let him get away with this."

It was too late for practical advice. Trisha's fear had turned to greed. She had never made a Super Bowl bet, not in all of her life and she desperately needed to get her home fixed up. It would be a great start to the year for her. *I can see myself jogging, exercising, and dieting all in my new home.* She smiled at her brother, a big confident smile. OK, so starting a diet was an act of desperation. Being forced to eat healthy in a place like Lucille's was in no uncertain terms a form of abuse. All of that negative stuff was moot compared to getting her home made new.

"Like I was saying, heads I get the Colts, tails you get 'em." Trisha smiled with anticipation.

Mike flipped the coin . . . It was heads. "Yes!" Michael blurted.

Before he could put the silver dollar back in his pocket Trisha noticed something. A shimmer of light flashed off of the coin and something wasn't right. "Hey, let me see that coin, you charlatan." He sheepishly, very reluctantly, handed it to her. "I'll be a monkey's uncle if this isn't a two headed silver dollar." Mike looked so busted, and Rachael started laughing, as did Becky.

"You tricked me. My own brother tricked me."

"I told you to watch out for him," said Rachael. "Good job, Trisha. He's a total scoundrel. Mike, you're busted and so you've lost the toss. You want the Colts, Trisha, they're yours. I can't believe you would take advantage of your own sister that way. I am ashamed of you. You know what, Mike. Perhaps a $500 penalty is in order for taking advantage of my younger sister."

He began to laugh too. "Forget it, Rachael. My bet with Trisha has nothing to do with you. I am not letting girls gang up on me." He turned to Trisha. "You are one sharp cookie, Kid. You want Indianapolis"?

"Yes." She was energized, bubbly, happy and ready to start shopping. Trisha Jean Martin couldn't remember feeling so in control in her adult life. She was going to skin her brother and get a do-over on her home. Now she was ready to absolutely straighten the place and get the ball rolling, itching to get home and clean the joint up. Oh, yes. This was going to turn out sweet. She no longer had any cravings to eat. *Am I full because I am so excited, or was the book right? If you wait just a few minutes, the hunger does go away, at least for a while. Maybe it's both.*

There were hugs, promises of love, and there was joy all around. The family luncheon had turned out much better than Trisha thought it would. Becky whispered something in Rachael's ear and then they both took off in different directions.

As they walked The District, mostly window shopping, Becky threw some reality on Trisha's dream come true fantasy. "Mike's in very good physical condition. He works out and plays tennis over at Club Sport several times every week. He'll have no problem running those races."

"That's true, Mom, and he may be, but, can he engineer the remodeling job I'll be shopping for in the morning? I think the Colts are going to win. I can feel it."

Becky smiled. It was a crooked smile, too. She could see instantly what Michael was up to. It was a 'no lose' bet for him. In any universe he would not be welcome in her trashed home, so if he lost the bet he'd be pulling a Roger on Trisha. He gets in, helps fix the place up, and strategically places himself in her transformative process. With him on her team, she'd be sure to succeed. If it went the other way, she was trapped into losing weight. That boy was the spitting image of his dad. She didn't have the heart to tell him how much his father loathed that place where their money came from. Like father, like son.

At last it came time for them to go their separate ways. Becky's phone rang again; she answered it and had a sobering minute with someone on the other end. "Who was that?" Trisha asked.

"God . . . in the form of my sponsor, who asked me to meet her tonight at the GVG so we could share in a birthday cake for her sponsor who is celebrating twenty two years of sobriety. Go figure."

"I thought you didn't have a sponsor, Mom."

"I lied. So have me thrown in jail." Trisha's mother was white as a ghost, but her youngest was beside herself with anticipation. For the first time in as long she could remember, Trisha actually had something to look forward to . . . the Super Bowl!

"See you, Mom. I'd thank you for lunch but Mikey took care of that. Thank you for inviting me and spending the afternoon of the first day of the rest of my life with me. Love you. Good luck in AA." She hugged and kissed her mother affectionately, then turned and walked away, stiff as a board and sore from head to toe. Her car was a hundred miles gone, she had to go to the store, get some things, and then it was home to start the humongous job of cleaning up the mess of her life. This day was never going to end.

As Becky made her way to the car she was deep in thought. Somehow she was sure that her life was about to change, too. She had laid it on the line with her oldest as they parted and now the job of cleaning up her act was directly in front of her. Was she happy? No. Was she satisfied that she would finally start to follow those pesky recommended Steps at AA? No. Was she passionate about following the lead of a real sponsor relationship? Hell no. What was she? She was terrified.

Trisha hiked the twenty minutes or so back over to Smith's. When she got there the first order of business was to get the car to a garbage bin and clean out the trash, a truly pathetic unloading of all that fast food paper. There was no food to worry about. There never was with the empty bags she threw over her shoulder. Yes, cleaning the crap out of her car made her feel better, a little. Inside of the store, she picked up things like trash bags, the large black ones, the white kitchen type, and some other paper stuff that was needed. She added Ziploc bags, Brillow Pads, soaps, cleaners, some candles, a mop and bucket, Pledge, Windex, and some other odds and ends. It took her only a few minutes to get back to the car, which she started and then drove to the Terrible Herbst up on Eastern just off the freeway a couple of exits farther up I-215. There she vacuumed her car, fueled it, got an oil change with other services, took pride in the fact that the red lights disappeared off of the dash, ran through the automatic car wash and was back on the freeway in less than another hour.

Trisha headed over to Fresh and Easy, a convenient fresh food store that specialized in fruits and vegetables along with a full range of groceries. Once inside she was amazed at how easy it would be to eat fresh foods. There were little bags of veggies, all types, and every kind of fruit. She thought about tomorrow's football game, knew she would be glued to the television this year, and thought about a personal Super Bowl party for one. As she walked down the aisle sporting the goodies, chips and cookies, her mouth started watering. She remembered some advice she had been given during one of her previous attempts to diet. "Stay away from the boxes and bags in the center of the store." Trisha moved on.

She decided that tomorrow morning she would have scrambled eggs; she picked out a small carton, a bagel without spread, and coffee. For a dieter that looked like a feast. The Super Bowl party would consist of a vegetable platter and she promised herself that she must, simply must, go easy on the ranch dip. Hey, that was better than the alternative, and she had determined not to go there. She decided on a simple chicken breast to go with a small salad and an orange for dessert later on when she would be celebrating victoriously. That was it then; tomorrow it would be lean protein, carbohydrate, and some fat in limited amounts. To hydrate it would be ice tea, diet soda, or hot coffee. Tomorrow's one day plan was set. She checked out at the automated cash register, bagged her own stuff, and was out the door and in her driveway by 6:00. Trisha was starving again.

She did not eat, but instead decided to eat later when the garbage was out of the house. *It's a sort of second workout of the day, two-a-days,* she thought, smiling inwardly. Moving as fast as she could, Trisha went from room to room pitching trash, stuff she didn't want or need, and generally straightening things up. What she found under her bed almost made her heave. The junk food in the dresser drawer got tossed, empty garbage cans were lined properly, and she did find the energy to vacuum. At 8:00 she called it a day and took her second shower, a new record for her. Trisha had parked in the driveway so she could throw the tied garbage bags into the garage until Tuesday when the trash was picked up. She looked into that garage and was astonished to see so many of those bags they would have to be separated in order to be counted. But, since they

37

did not need to be counted she just closed the door and headed for the kitchen, settling in for her next small meal, something she had been looking forward to.

It's funny how life can change on a dime. Unbelievably, she was not as hungry as before.

Trisha chucked one of the veggie bags into the microwave, added two small slices of ham, threw one slice of bread into the toaster, brewed fresh ice tea, and nourished herself properly for the third time in a single day, a new record. After she finished eating, Trisha cleaned the kitchen again. *Why ruin a good thing*, she decided. It did take all of five minutes. She didn't want to turn on the TV either. Somehow she knew it would be nonstop diet commercials. The gods had her number today and she was not capitulating. Instead she wandered into her office, still a huge mess, picked out the *Weight Watchers* magazine that had been sitting there and decided to thumb through it.

She had never really had an interest in *Weight Watchers* before. It was something she was thinking about tonight. The magazine had pictures of skinny beautiful women on the cover. *I'm not impressed*, she thought, but it did have what at first glance looked like good advice about food, exercise ideas, success stories, and other now interesting articles. Trisha was not ready to commit to any sort of a plan, but the Weight Watchers program made the cut for a second look. One thing Trisha Jean Martin was going to hold to was the advice given her by a friend a couple of years ago. "Do not get the information you trust from advertising. Do your own work and run things down. You will be glad you did."

Trisha wondered for just a moment how her mother fared this evening. She prayed that everything went OK. Contrary to what she had been thinking this morning, she truly liked her mother, who was in fact her best friend in the world.

Trisha went to bed. Just like the invaders at Normandy Beach in 1944 she had somehow survived "The Longest Day."

She fell into one of her deepest sleeps ever, and yes, she dreamed.

2

Stanley Burton

Well, do what you must;
I wouldn't miss this for anything.
I, too, have learned to remain teachable.
It's a dream come true, my friend.

Wise Mac

It was still very dark when she awoke in a cold sweat. Trisha Martin had no idea where she was, what time it was, or anything else as she stumbled into the kitchen to look for something to eat. She felt stiff, but could not for the life of her remember why. The back of her throat was scratchy and sore again; she had been snoring. She did sense that something was different though, because the place didn't stink; in fact, there was a pleasant smell throughout her home and the garbage was gone. *What is it?* When she got to the kitchen and turned the lights on Trish was amazed to find it clean. Perhaps she was still dreaming. Instinctively, she opened the door to the garage to check on her car, but there was no car. Instead there were at least fifty garbage bags all full and tied off. She came instantly awake and remembered yesterday; in fact, she remembered everything that had happened. Officially, she was in the second day of her diet, the new life she had bragged about at lunch yesterday with her family. She had been dreaming, but not about the cleanup job that was underway. There was a moment, just a couple of minutes before she drifted into sleep, when she had absolutely broken down emotionally. In a blaze of fear and regret, perhaps being subjected to a bout of loneliness for her father, maybe the realization that food as she knew it was gone, all combined to extract a toll of tears. Why? Perhaps in her lifeless life she had reduced herself to relying on the likes of the refrigerator for love, excitement, fun and comfort. She had no idea what a lonely future without even that soothing reassurance, the one thing she used to medicate her pain. She was aroused by the epiphany of the dream.

Trisha usually didn't remember dreams. Does anyone? This dream she remembered. She was at an amusement park with high school friends and they were having fun. Was it Disneyland, Six Flags Magic Mountain, or somewhere else, who knows? No matter how hard Trisha tried she could not place where they were. She chuckled for a second at just how deep-seated her mind must be to addiction. There was food everywhere, the kind of garbage chow only available at places like that, but try as hard as she could, Trish, in the mind trap of the dancing dream was not getting to any of it. Could one actually smell in dreams? She experienced smells in this one, and distinctly remembered corn dogs covered in mustard, her favorite theme park fast food. Her friends were laughing at her and yelling to make sure that she kept up with them as they ran from one ride to another. The day was bright and hot, a gift of summer's blazing sun. There were billowing cloud formations drifting by, the mechanical sounds of rides, the joyous screaming of happy and excited children, parents yelling at crying exhausted little ones, bells, sirens, chatter, colorful stores, vending kiosks, big top attractions, and of course a veritable sea of people. Her thoughts turned from dreamscapes to the snack at hand, a real one she could both feel and taste, not some sleepwalker's illusion.

By now the fat free, sugar free, hot chocolate mix she had put into the microwave oven was ready and she was sipping it, all for under twenty calories. It was the treat of a lifetime, the symbol of her new life. For once Trisha Jean Martin felt good about herself as she glanced at the big digital clock on the wall. It was 2:34 AM.

Pondering the dream again, she remembered the final ride and that only she had the courage to climb on, strap herself in, and zoom away. Everyone else stayed back. It had to be Six Flags because Disneyland or Knott's Berry Farm didn't have this type of a roller coaster. She wasn't fat either, and not scared like her friends, who seemed to be shrinking into the grayness of dissipating lost companions, slipping out of reach, fading in the wisp of a fallible memory. She smiled proudly at them even as they were sucked into a black vortex. The locking bolt of her seat belt clicked and she felt a surge of power as she was launched into darkness. Where had the blazing sun gone? Suddenly the fun had become a nightmare as the ride went too fast, out of control, upside-down, twisting, and she could remember sensing that something was wrong.

Faces had come directly at her in every turn, angry faces, threatening smiles, and there were swings with weapons that barely missed. In wild and out of control turbulent gyrations, she was looping around and around on the outside, dangling something like a rag doll at the mercy of the devil himself. It was in that terrifying moment Trisha noticed that she was the only rider. At full speed, on the outside top of the loop, upside down, her car was flung away tumbling over and over again into a steep fall with no bottom. Then she woke up and now she was here. It was weird, meaningful or not, and though she remembered the fear of imminent death, she also liked thrills and adventure. She marked it as her first 'no food forever' nightmare, garish and thrilling just the same. Within short minutes her vivid dream had dissipated into some sort of a subconscious chamber of darkness, because she was losing memory of the whole thing and just a few minutes later, the dream seemed to be gone forever.

Trish started the laundry. The rhythmic agitation of the washing machine was soothing her frayed nerves, and it was proof positive that her new life would yield a second day. She checked the driveway, saw her car, and looked for the newspaper. It was not there yet. She was not sleepy, so she meandered into the chaos of her office and picked up a diet book; there were plenty of those. Some author she could not remember, Eda LeShan, had long ago (turned out that it was 1979, she discovered when checking the copyright page) published something called *Winning the Losing Battle,* subtitled, WHY I WILL NEVER BE FAT AGAIN. *So, people struggled with weight issues way back in the 1970's,* she laughed. The table of contents introduced some very interesting subjects, but it was Chapter 4, "Getting Ready to Lose Weight," which jumped out for her and so she took a look at it. She skimmed pages, not awake or alert enough to read with any depth, but one thing did strike her as relevant: Recording Your Dreams. There were pieces of paper right there, hundreds of them, so she decided to write down her dream, what little she was still hanging onto, not quite gone forever as it turned out, so in three short sentences, just to remind herself to be open to suggestions while acclimating to this new life of hers, she wrote of the wild rollercoaster ride into Hell. She finished her drink and decided to go back to bed, except for one thing. The wash cycle had finished. She quickly moved the laundry to the dryer, started a second load, went back to bed and fell instantly into another deep sleep. Some hours later she dreamed again, a familiar and haunting nightmare, an apex of her passing from one life into the next, a box from which Trisha Jean Martin would not escape.

This time though, there were helpers out there trying to . . . well . . . help.

* * *

Somewhere on the other side of the veil, a very unreliable angel named Mac, and Roger Martin himself were set to go. It would be just a tweak this time, a tiny yet crucial pinch, all part of a big plan hatched at a much higher level than from where they operated in their misty and lofty paradise. Afterlife was nothing like mortal humans imagined it to be. Trisha's father was so energized he forgot for just a moment that his time in mortality was over. "Don't blow this, Mac," said Roger to his angelic buddy. The look that Wise Mac gave him was like a dagger to the soul of the unloved, something a Deceiver would do, so Roger threw him a bone. "Don't worry, my friend, I have the faith; you're going to get this just right; I know it."

* * *

Trisha's reminiscent dream played its awful hand. Somewhere in the middle of October, 1998, a beautiful young adult was a freshman at Saddleback College in Mission Viejo, California. *Her foot was healing. They, she and some of the other walk-on track types, were heading over to Laguna Beach to play volleyball. She was just winding* up a nice phone call with her dad. He was heading to Mt. Charleston to run the hill and wanted to make sure she was adjusting well to her new digs, her new friends, and that her Achilles heel situation was resolving itself. She rewarded his attentive call with all the right answers, wished him well and off they went, laughing and in a great mood. Laguna Beach was so picturesque when It was sunny, and today there were a few rolling clouds, the breeze was comfortable, and it was very warm; a kid might call it the perfect day. Trisha was riding shotgun and singing to radio tunes with her clan as they cruised down the winding road to the beach. The romance of the sand down at that beach was one of the special joys that made her new life so good. It was becoming apparent that she would soon get to race.

During the volleyball game at the seaside park, her phone rang again. She went ice cold. Although she could never resist during the spell, she tried to refuse the call, but despite yearnings to the contrary, as was the case that day in her real life she always answered, knowing the end of her world awaited hearing the dreadful voice on the other end. The phone kept ringing and ringing. Imaginings have a way of being so real and unreal at the same time. Although she was frozen in a paralysis of fear, her hand moved of its own volition and she pressed the phone's little green button, now hysterical.

"Hi, Trish; how is my little running girl?"

"Daddy?"

"There's a big problem, little one. We really need your help."

She dropped the phone, stared in shock at the sand beneath her feet, and the whole thing disappeared. She woke again, shaking and very confused. Her night's sleep was over. It was after 7am, she felt much rested, remembered the dream, some of it, but did not feel at all sickened as she usually did. She tried to remember why but couldn't. The dream was gone and there was not much worth putting to paper. It was frustrating to be able to remember advice, like recording dreams, but not be able to remember the dreams well enough to write something down. Trisha found an empty notebook and wrote these words. "Super Bowl Sunday, dreamt about Dad again last night but it didn't haunt me this time. Why?"

* * *

"You blew it, Mac," said Roger. He continued on, "I needed more time. We'll have to try again later." Mac frowned, and then laughed softly. He was clearly proud of himself, which Roger found confusing. "Dude, what are you so happy about?"

Mac just smiled. "Roger, I got it, the frequency pattern. You must understand it doesn't matter whether it is life or the afterlife; the laws of physics still apply. I have been trying to tell you this, but you are so excited to talk to that beautiful daughter of yours, you are not listening. I had to tap the resonance pattern of the dream waves at her exact cerebral frequency in order for you to initiate two way contact. I got it, got it spot on, Brother Martin. The next time she goes to sleep we are going in for the duration so you better get your story down pat. When you are totally connected it's a two way street and *you*'ll be the angel without wings . . . on the hot seat. Since Trisha will not be able to remember the dream properly, you will be imprinting her subconscious with the instructions and if *you* blow it, well, just make sure you get her pointed in the right direction. This is literally the stuff miracles are made of."

* * *

Trisha afforded herself a coffee luxury this morning, having picked up several flavors of Coffee-mate at only 10 calories per teaspoon. Additionally, she found flavored Splenda, in chocolate, hazelnut, and vanilla—sucralose—a derivative of natural cane sugar. Trish would run down the negative side of this stuff later, not today. There had to be something wrong with sucralose, had to be. For right now though, sipping chocolate coffee at 10 calories per cup was delicious, something to savor as she digested the morning rag.

The news was uncharacteristic as usual. Trisha remembered a day, way back in high school, when current events meant something to her. Not today, but still she could not resist the newspaper. The editorial board was exposing the 'secure our borders lie.' One thing interested her, a negative article on the HCG diet. She loved the comics every Sunday, there was a nude yoga post, plenty of advice on plenty of subjects, and then there was the Super Bowl. Today was her day to win the big bet. There was nothing in the way of that, except the remote chance that the Saints might somehow win. Not a chance.

Trisha scrambled eggs, ate an apple, toasted a very delectable bagel, brewed another coffee, this time flavoring it with a combination of hazelnut and vanilla; it was yummy. She ate, cleaned the kitchen again, she was turning into a respected homemaker, and then went back into the bedroom, laid down on the bed and picked up the diet book she had been reading in the middle of the night.

Eda LeShan's approach to the fat problem was very psychological, insisting that mental preparation and a full understanding of what went wrong in one's childhood played a huge role, but the part played by trauma fascinated her the most. She made the decision to read the book this week.

What the heck, it was Sunday and she allowed herself the luxury of nodding off, dozing into a morning catnap.

* * *

"Roger, she is going to sleep. Are you ready?" Mac was the one excited this time. Roger was ready, kind of, but he thought it would be a bit later and he was not allowing himself to be rushed.

* * *

Trisha thought of the football game in a hazy, misty, semi-snooze and was instantly awake. She jumped out of the bed, but did not make it up this time. Instead she put all of the whites into the washer after moving the laundry forward. Trisha was tired of dirty sheets—she was tired of a lot of things. Suddenly the thought of her father haunted her. He would not be pleased that she had fallen so far after he passed. Fact is, if she had to face her dad today, she would be ashamed for him to see her this way. The dried laundry had been folded and put away. Trisha brushed her teeth, freshened herself, jumped into the shower to rinse and headed for a walking workout. She quickly got dressed and bent over tying the shoes that she had dutifully filled with Desenex last night; you know what, it was no big deal this morning. The foot powder bubbled up as a good idea from a long ago lifestyle. *Uncanny.* She put an empty drink bottle into that trusty back pack, drank a full glass of ice tea, donned sunglasses and headed out the door. It was going to be a great day, a Super Sunday.

The walk over to Home Depot took less than thirty minutes. Someone honked and yelled a tasteless insult, making fun of her. Instantly Trisha Jean Martin became aware that all she ever was, she was still, because in her youth she could care less about stuff like that. She was not bothered. In fact, what she felt was pity for someone who was crass enough to hurl nonsense like that at a stranger. The actual thought that crossed her mind was . . . *what pain that sad person must be in.* She was not bothered in the least. Trish had been on her new plan, a plan not even very well thought out yet, for less than two days and already she could feel her inner self, a dormant person, taking command of her natural self. Hers was going to be a very remarkable journey. Trisha was just now beginning to sense that something special might be happening.

* * *

Michael Lee Martin climbed out of bed, found his way into the kitchen and brewed coffee. It was Super Bowl Sunday and one of his favorite days of the year. He was at the kitchen table drinking that coffee and reading the paper when his oldest daughter Rebecca came in and popped some toast into the toaster. She looked to be in a good mood. "Good morning, Dad? Who's going to win the game today?"

"Top of the day to you, Kid. I'm going on a hunch and picking the Saints. Want to go for a swim with me this morning?"

"Forget it, Dad. It's freezing out there. I know you hate the indoor pool and besides, I'm going back to bed." She washed down the toast with a small glass of juice and then disappeared back into her room.

Michael tossed out the paper, kissed his sleeping wife, jumped into his 2010 Nissan Leaf, an all electric car, and scooted over to Club Sport for a workout. He swam the outdoor pool for an hour in the chilly dawn air, rinsed off in the shower, put on some shorts, hit the weights for thirty minutes, cleaned up, checked his phone, and headed home again. It was barely 9:00 when he walked through the door. Michael had invited the family to Sunday brunch at Sweet

Tomatoes, but that wasn't until 11:00, so he left everyone right where they were and slipped into his home office to make some calls, the first one to his mother. When she picked up, the clarity of her voice confirmed that she had done as promised and went to the AA meeting last night. Good for her. Their conversation was pleasant and left him feeling like a good son.

* * *

Trisha was matching paint choices for the remodeling project that Mike was going to be starting tomorrow if all went as planned when her phone rang and suddenly there was Michael on the other end. "Go Colts," she blurted with a huge smile.

"Good mornin, TJ," he warmly responded. "I have been working out for our first 10k fun run since the crack of dawn. How about you?"

"I'm on my morning walk, a part of my new life but it has nothing to do with any fun runs, Mikey. Right this minute I am at Home Depot picking stuff out for the remodeling job you'll owe me before you go to bed tonight. We're going to keep the house the same color, I'm going easy with you on the carpet, since the best looking floor covering is also a very economical choice, and just to show good faith, I've decided to splurge and fix the porch light myself, before kickoff. Where are you watching the Super Bowl?"

"The boys and I are headed over to Samuel's. He is having a big party with lots of business types and it looks like most of the guys are bringing their sons, a kind of a stag football game bash. He is heating the pool, too. There is going to be a barbeque, a feast really. It should be a good show. Jan is heading to an arts and craft fair for sad Super Bowl wives and I have no idea what Rebecca is up to, yet. There is a reason I called this morning." For Mike the air became chilly.

"Trish, I have to defer to advice Dad gave me many times when we were growing up." He was fidgeting with a squeeze ball and really did not want to puncture her good natured optimism on a beautiful Sunday, but for him this bet had real consequences. He loved his younger sister . . . more than she could know. Getting into her home to fix the mess was his second objective, not a bad start in actuality, but he was serious about seeing her change, using his bet with Rachael to get something going for Trish. The plan was coming together perfectly and now it was time to seal the deal. "Dad taught me that it's easier to pay a bet; one shouldn't wager unless he or she was able to pay up, but the real consequence of betting was being willing to collect. Trisha, if I win, please be assured that I'll expect you to be ready to run with me. I've picked out the first race, a July 4th fun run in St. George, Utah. If the Saints win, I am not going to gloat, not going to call you at all. Just know that what's to happen becomes written in stone—that is unless you want out of it now. You can get out now if you are not committed." There was dead silence on the other end. Michael was wretched in pain thinking about how Trisha felt and the brutal price she would have to pay.

"I knew it yesterday, Mike. I know this about you. Your bets are famous. If the Saints win, my fat days are over for sure. I'll be ready. Now, I have to keep shopping because I am going to win. I love you. Don't worry about me. The real Trisha inside of me is busting to get out. I can feel it. I agree, no calls if I lose today. I will be ready." The thought of what it meant to run by July 4th made her blood run cold . . . again. This bet was real in every way. "Have fun today with the boys, Mike. You only get to be dad for a while and you're a good one." The call ended and tears stung her eyes. *How could a 275 pound woman get ready for a run in less than five months?* She blocked it out of her mind.

Trisha finished listing what she needed on her Android, and then purchased a porch light cover, put it in her backpack and hiked across the street to the Terrible Herbst-Chevron station. She bought and ate a banana, filled her drink, drank from it, filled it again, and made the thirty minute walk back home with a hop in her step, something unheard of just two days earlier.

Once home, she moved all of the laundry forward again, cleaned the broken glass up in front of her door with a new broom and dust pan, installed the new light cover and then started cleaning again, a job that would go on for quite some time.

Trisha went to work in her office, mowing through papers that needed to get filed or tossed, filling yet another bag with old garbage. Under the kitchen sink she went, wishing she had knee pads to cushion excessive weight. She found the furniture spot remover, grabbed a new sponge as well, and then attacked the furniture in the musky old office. There was a kernel of optimism in this work. Trisha's inkling was that this room could become central to 'event management' in a new, more exciting life, and so a measure of positive pride, an emotion she was not at all used to of late, replaced the tiny kernel of fear that she would lose the bet. Her heart rate quickened a bit as she set about dusting wood and shining the glass in the curio cabinet. Trisha took time to clean the trophies, too. It was a sad and sobering job inside of that cabinet, but it had to be done. In a way, those memories, the feelings generated by handling the trophies, were a boost of confidence. Could there really be a runner inside of her? Beyond hope, she prayed that today would not be the moment of truth in that category, forced by the loss of the Super Bowl bet. She needed to win. It was time for some lunch, the 'new way' kind of lunch and she was looking forward to it.

Trisha was prepared to indulge in a real Sunday dinner. The chicken noodle soup recipe included precooked skinned chicken, chicken stock, carrots, celery, parsley, some noodles, salt, pepper, and that was it. She allowed herself one small bag of soup crackers and in less than an hour she was so full it felt as though she had abandoned her diet. Although it was very hard to do, old habits have a way of nudging themselves from the back burner to the front; she cleaned up after herself, keeping things moving in the right direction. After showering and changing into something comfortable (this time she chose the blue and blue combination to support her Indianapolis Colts), she laid back on the couch, turned on the television, and fell asleep, drifting into the nods.

It was a festive day at the track and field championships. The event was televised, and there were media people everywhere. The announcers sounded familiar, yet she could not properly place herself. Just over the hill, a rock concert was taking place and the crowd was raucous. The runners were gathered at the start line, but Trish was only a spectator.

* * *

Wise Mac was trying to break into the dream but was having, shall we say, technical difficulties. Roger was with him. "What's the problem, Mac? I thought you had all the wavelengths and frequencies wired in."

"The television signal keeps getting in the way, Roger. Every time I get wired into her head, the show changes the way your daughter is dreaming. We are going to have to wait again."

* * *

Now Trisha was running, but over a hill all by herself into a meadow by a stream that flowed downhill into a crystalline lake at the base of the mountain, some distance away. She could see deer running with her, but off in the distance, shadowing her every move. The announcers were arguing about who would win, and no one was picking her. Suddenly, one of the announcers had a female voice, excitedly talking about the deer, which had swiftly turned into a herd of horses, colts she called them. The music changed again and a loud crowd of unruly folks were singing "When the Saints Come Marching In," a song she had learned as a child. She opened her eyes, now awake, and realized she had been dreaming along with the pregame show for today's competition, which was about to begin.

Trish broke out the vegetable platter, opened the salsa dip, set a couple of diet soda cans on the coffee table and listened with pride as the National Anthem, sung by Carrie Underwood, was performed. There was a flyover of some kind. She couldn't remember in her lifetime such an exciting buildup prior to a televised event. *It must be the bet*, she thought. She recognized Jim Nantz and Phil Simms from her dream. Emmitt Smith tossed the coin, won by the Saints, and they chose the football first. Trisha Jean Martin, sitting in the living room of her very modest home, one that had been cleaned for the first time in years, one that smelled like good food and was fresh with the scent of soap for a change, yes, the new Trisha, the sports betting enthusiast, was already nervous.

The Colts got the ball after the Saints could do nothing with it, then marched right down and kicked a field goal to take the lead. Trisha ate celery sticks in celebration. The Saints had to punt again, pinning the Colts on their own 4 yard line; they responded with a 96-yard drive and suddenly Trisha's bet had a 10 point cushion. Everything was going as planned. She sipped Diet Coke, ate carrots and started planning her week. It was going to be sweet, no doubt about it. At the commercial break, Trisha finished up he laundry. Her home was cleaner than it had been in years. She was determined to keep it that way, already imagining the smell of new carpet and fresh paint. She hadn't yet reeled in the bet so she started dusting furniture to ward away nervous energy. If all four quarters of the game went the same way, her Colts would win 40-0, a pasting. *But,* she thought . . . *but like Mom said, "if wishes were fishes . . ."*

Trisha, in an effort to reduce anxiety, kept polishing furniture. By the time she made it back to the couch the game had changed a bit. Her nerves were more than a little frayed when the Saints kicked a field goal and cut into the Colts' lead. The Saints almost scored a touchdown, but were held up at the goal line. The first half was almost over, yet, the Saints forced a punt, took the ball, and in just a short amount of time, made another field goal and so at the half the Colts were up, now only 10-6. *Now I remember the roller coaster dream from last night. Perhaps before I try and go to sleep tonight I'll be flung away from my remodeling plans after all.* Little did she know, but she quickly ran into the other room and wrote as much as she could remember about that dream.

* * *

Michael was outside by the barbeque, near the kids through most of the first half and had not paid much attention to the game. When he got stuck with the Saints he'd lost some interest, defending his bet half-heartedly at best. There were at least fifty people at Samuel's house for the big party, and like it or not, Mike needed to work the crowd. He had more interest in the halftime show than the game itself; *The Who* was one of his favorite rock and roll bands. Roger Daltrey and Pete Townsend were great and the kid on drums was none other than Beatle, Ringo Starr's son, Zack Starkey. Mike was once again outside where the boys were, over by the swimming pool, when the gang inside by the television went crazy. *What just happened, he thought*?

* * *

51

Trisha had stayed in front of the tube for the halftime show, a Who concert. She was in a good mood because, at the beginning of the second half, the Colts would take the kick off and possibly score first. When the Saints completed a successful onside kick and recovered the ball at the beginning of the second half, she began to feel a nauseating worm of fear creeping into the pit of her stomach. This betting business was a two bladed sword, a horrible mix of pleasure and pain. *Please, Lord, please help me today.* Trisha laughed at herself. *What kind of a person would make a football bet on the Sabbath, and then ask God to intervene so as to help the Sabbath breaker win the bet?*

Michael took a keen interest in the game, but for the moment he was still out back with the younger boys. There was no one to glad-hand because everyone was out of the pool and crowded into the large entertainment room inside of Samuel's house. No one had ever seen an onside kick in a Super Bowl like that and it had changed the game, maybe for good.

Unfortunately, Trisha's pleasure and pain mechanism shifted into numbed shock when Drew Brees threw a touchdown pass and the Saints took the lead. Even though the Colts scored a touchdown on their next possession, Trisha had lost confidence in them and knew there would most likely be trouble before the big-time bet was over.

The Saints were on fire. The field goal they scored in the waning minutes of the third quarter brought them to within one point of the lead. Trisha's stomach was turning not unlike her washing machine just a couple of hours earlier, suddenly thinking. *Wouldn't it have been easier to just save up for the remodeling job? Gambling like this isn't worth it, not at all.*

When the Colts blew a field goal opportunity and the Saints scored a touchdown Trisha went cold. *This cannot be happening;* yet it was, and right in front of her eyes. The Saints, bold today, went for the two point conversion, resulting in a disputed call ruled 'good' on the challenge and suddenly they had a 24-17 lead. Trisha cleaned up the area, washed all the dishes, put away the extra food and decided to pray. *"Dear Heavenly Father . . ."* She could not ask for touchdowns by the Colts, or to win a bet; it wouldn't be right. She giggled, nervously, and thought of asking forgiveness. *"Please help me do the right thing no matter what happens."* Tears stung her eyes. Inside of herself she wanted to have faith, Trish really did, but what she truly wanted was for the Colts to come back and win the game. That she could have hoped for some peace in the firestorm of an emotionally draining experience, one that would change her life forever, never cropped up.

* * *

"Roger, she's praying," said Mac. "This is great news for us."

* * *

Michael was inwardly smiling, though he was conflicted. Outwardly he was taking credit for having done the research necessary to know that the Saints were the team to beat today. He was high fiving all the other Saints fans, yet, the turmoil inside of him as he thought of his sister was the clash he knew his dad was referring to in teaching a mischievous son the lesson of collecting on bets. He knew Trisha was in pain tonight, at least for the moment. There was still time on the clock, but momentum was painting the picture. Oh well. There is nothing he could do about that. He had tried to pass the Saints off on her, well not really. He had made it possible that his sister had the chance to eye his two headed coin, catching him at the little trick which was sealing his fate today. Mike did not expect to actually win this bet, but here it was, and so it was to be. He wanted to fix up her house more than she did. Sadly, as game time slipped into the past, a remodeling contract would take a backseat to a new future.

Tracy Porter intercepted a Payton Manning pass and suddenly the Saints had the ball and the lead. Trisha sat in traumatized silence, as opposed to a raging male Colts fan that would likely be screaming and knocking holes in walls. When the Saints scored again to take a 31-17 commanding lead the game was effectively over. She had lost the bet. Not only would there be no home makeover this week, but Trisha Jean Martin, all of 275 lbs., would somehow have to muster the courage and meet a new obligation and be ready for a run of more than six miles in less than five months, a feat that on the surface did not seem possible. She turned off the television, turned off her telephone, took a long hot shower, ate an orange, brewed coffee and settled in to calm herself by glancing at a couple of books in her newly cleaned office. She did pause long enough to chastise herself about being so clever with Michael and that stupid silver dollar with two heads. *Why couldn't I leave well enough alone?*

* * *

Mac and Roger both smiled. Their day was going perfectly. Mind you, it was not possible to intervene in football games; fundamentally, manipulation of events was not how things worked in their neck of the woods. Deceivers practice the art of manipulation all the time, but they were terrible at having events turn out their way, at least on Earth. For Mac and Roger, their little project had just gotten markedly more manageable. Roger, a true football fan, noted that it was one of the most exciting Super Bowls ever. Mac would have played the harp for him, but he was not that kind of an angel.

* * *

Trisha would have to trust God this time. She had prayed, did believe, and did have faith, so this must be what was supposed to happen. *Perhaps I could start with liposuction surgery—not.*

She was an old fashioned girl and this was going to go down the old fashioned way. The dieter picked up one of her many motivational books, first covering her eyes and then turning her arm with pointed finger in a circle so as to land on the right one, perhaps one chosen by the hand of Providence.

There were so many diet books in her library she could not count them all. This one, *The Beck DIET Solution* was written by Judith S. Beck. It emphasized, not a particular diet, but the training of the brain so it would "think like a thin person." There was plenty of good information right in the table of contents. Cognitive therapy was something she could identify with. The book looked like a boot camp for weight loss, a process dedicated to changing the patterned behavior that obese people operate on, subliminal impulses they were not even cognitive of. Was there something in that book that could melt a mountain of fat in five months? No. Was she in need of changing the way she thought, about food, about everything?

Definitely. Trish decided, bowing to the hand of the Lord in these things, to read the book and at least give it a try. Right on the cover she read words a cynic like her could identify with: "Works with any Diet." *This author wants nothing from me. I like that*, she thought.

Trish then took a gander at another type of book, Stephen R. Covey's *The 8th HABIT*. Although of late it could not be seen in her actions, Covey's, *The 7 Habits of Highly Effective People*, was a book she had read and enjoyed. *Perhaps this one would be good, too.* She thumbed through some of the pages and unbelievably felt better. It suddenly dawned on her that Mike had done her a great favor. She was going home . . . home to the little girl and to the life she loved and missed so much. Trish was going to run again, and maybe, just maybe . . . better than ever. It was time to go to bed and get some rest. Tomorrow, day three, promised to be filled to the brim with a million things to do and she had to be at Target for the evening part-time shift. Trisha got on her knees, thanked the Lord for her life, climbed into bed and fell asleep. She dreamed.

The day was sunny, a Saturday, and the high school senior was running like the wind. Racing had never felt better. The air was crisp and clean; she had reached the six mile mark, quickly drank a cup of lime drink and moved on. How Trisha Martin felt when running a race was as inexpressible as how a racehorse might feel in the final turn at the Kentucky Derby. For some reason her body was responding like never before. Just three weeks ago she had finished a distant sixth at the Nevada State High School Cross Country Track and Field Championships back home. It had been her best time, she was happy with it, but she knew there was more in her. Today, well, today was that more. There were over 1,000 runners in this race and she was near the lead pack. The kid picked up the pace, got back into the rhythm, and began to pass runners-some of them experienced racers with credentials, and one a college sprinter on full scholarship at UCLA who seemed to be struggling, as far as she could tell. Not Trish, not today. The course turned up into the hills and she pushed herself, her reserves letting her pick it up again. At the top of a sun-baked knoll the route took a sharp left, down through a shadowy dip, up a couple of hundred yards through a copse of evergreens and over the top. From there she could see the skyline of Los Angeles as if it were in a glass bottle. It was possibly the most beautiful sight she had ever seen.

The dog jumped from the side of the road right in front of her. Trisha leaped, and in a burst of joyful laughter, cleared the four-legged furry friend as if it were a track hurdle, landing on her right foot first, then her left, and on she went down the hill. The road twisted back on itself in the first of a series of switchbacks and the dog was barking, running loose, its owner unable to get it under control. Trisha was horrified when the UCLA sprinter went down, screaming in pain and grabbing her right foot. It looked like her Achilles heel had snapped, but then the road turned right again leaving the unfortunate incident behind her for good. Sports injuries were a sad part of every athlete's life and no one liked for them to happen, even to their fiercest archrival. She felt truly sorry for the UCLA runner, hoping for her recovery. Trisha pushed on, clearing ten miles while the road was still switching back and forth. Most of the run was downhill at this point; there were upgrades of course, but the descent stress on her quads was proving to be quite challenging. Her strength was in climbing. The young runner managed to keep up, and in fact, passed more of the women and some of the more competitive men. She began to see today shaping up to be the race of her life. She had boundless energy.

The road leveled somewhat into a small decline that would eventually reach the valley floor. At the eighteen mile mark the course twisted through orange groves, Christmas tree farms, other fields of agriculture, and then up the hill to the marathon's final crest. At the top of the hill Trisha could see all the way to the front of the race below her. There were five or six men out in front, perhaps two miles ahead of her, thirty or forty runners between them, and then the lead pack of female marathoners. Trisha was shocked. They could not be more than five hundred yards out, and there were only four of them, taking turns in the lead role of a tightly knit formation designed to reduce the overall drag of the entire group. There was a helicopter above them focusing cameras on the ladies and two scooters with cameras leading them very closely. The camera operators were sitting backwards taking in the action. Trisha had never been in a race where there were television cameras that close. Just being able to see such a spectacle, the front of a race from within the race itself, was a very special moment in her running life. Trisha Martin had to be dreaming. This was not the kind of result she had expected.

The high school graduate measured her stamina, noting she had gas in the tank, took the hydrate again and then turned up the heat. The lead pack was now only about three hundred yards ahead. They had crossed the 22 mile mark without incident. As she moved forward, passing some very fast male marathoners, Trisha felt energized with almost superhuman power. At lower elevation smog was beginning to make its presence known. Trisha first noticed through palm trees and even sycamore bushes along the side of the road, but later it became even more pronounced, especially when viewed up against the hills, but it wasn't troublesome. The road course took a hard left at a street light in front of a Ralph's grocery store, and in less than a minute all hell broke loose. The crowds were cheering her on with urgency; she stepped on the go-pedal, hungry with the need for speed. Suddenly one of the little scooters slowed down, allowing her to catch up, sped up again to give her running room, and then settled in to see what would happen. For Trisha it was nerve racking to suddenly deal with the intrusion, both intimidating and exciting at the same time. She turned the next corner in the race and all at once one of the four runners in the lead pack appeared just a couple of hundred feet ahead of her; she had lost her wind, lost steam, and was now hanging on to even finish the marathon. Trisha had not lost anything, running past her and two of the three women ahead of her. Now she had moved into second place.

They had reached the 24 mile mark, just a bit over two miles left; it was, perhaps ten minutes to the line. She now had only one contender to pass, a world class runner from Africa. The boisterous crowd, the noise of the helicopter above, a scooter right there just a few feet ahead, and the lead runner not fifty feet away made this the biggest stage of her short life. She decided to use a strategy no one had ever told her about before. She strong-willed herself to run down the lead scooter and pass it like a dog at the racetrack chasing the proverbial rabbit. The dog could not catch the rabbit, but it could win the dog race. Trisha kicked.

It was obvious that the African had no kick. The tape was in sight, the African's dream of victory was dissipating, her energy exhausted; there was no reserve to call on. The high school runner's exuberance contrasted with real pain in the eyes of the world class distance runner from Africa. Trisha passed her at a steady pace she knew would support her all the way to the tape. It did.

The roar of the crowd was deafening, coming from both sides of the street and drowning out the little scooters. The helicopter was so low Trisha could feel the wind of the blades. There were two cameras poking out of its side and they were on her as she broke the tape, all smiles, and then she ran straight into . . . her father's arms. "Daddy!"

"Hello, Trisha, my favorite runner in the world. You looked great out there today." Trisha looked around and out of the blue she realized that this was all part of a very vivid dream. She had not run this race at all, she'd dreamed it, and was still dreaming. The walls of reality were closing around her and the finish line, which had disappeared. Yet she continued dreaming and talking to her father. She hugged him very close.

"I love you, Daddy. I've missed you so much. Please don't leave me. Are you OK? Are you happy? Are you in heaven? I have so many different things to talk to you about, Dad."

"Trish, I am fine. Time moves differently here and I have not missed out on anything. It is you, you and everyone else, mortals who are suffering the pain of so much trial and tribulation. For me it is yesterday when I was up on Mt. Charleston running and tomorrow when I'll welcome you home again. For you though, there is much to do, and that is why we have been allowed this conversation.

"And speaking of time, Trisha, we just happen to be a bit short on time right this minute. Not because of some limitation on this end, but you, you could wake up at any moment and this little conversation will disappear in a puff and go dissipating like a wisp of smoke from that cedar fireplace down the street from where your mother and I raised you. Do you remember that smell, Trish, blowing through those great big oak trees that lined our street?" She nodded with a warm smile. "First of all, I have to tell you that I love you, wish I could be with you, and I am by your side always. Even though you'll not remember this dream, your life is going to change in ways you could never think of and we need your help. Are you ready to get into the solution?"

"Who are they, Daddy?" Trisha was looking at the folks gathered around to enjoy the show. It was not very often that the dearly departed and mortal humans could have direct contact. In those rare moments, the curious always took a peek if they could.

"Wonderful folks, kid. See that man behind me? Listen, and listen carefully. If Mac can make 'Angel' you can get here with your eyes

closed, walking backwards, hopping on one foot, and with both hands tied behind your back."

"I heard that," Mac smiled.

"Mac is the engineer that facilitated this two-way dream. It is a good job well done for him. We have to move on, time is short. As I said, we need your help."

"What can I do, Dad? I will do anything for you."

"Good. First off, sorry about the football game. Michael is ruthless when it comes to a bet, but he got this one right. You need to train . . . hard—full time. You have to get the weight off, not some of it, or most of it, but literally all of it. We need you to run the Las Vegas Marathon at the end of 2011, and it needs to be the performance of your life, just like what happened today. Trisha, what happened today is in your potential skill set. You can be a world-class runner. You would have found it out that day if you had not hurt your foot. The race you ran today may have actually happened if you hadn't gone down. Moreover, that latent potential is still inside of you."

"You need me to run a race? I don't understand." Trisha noticed that the surroundings had changed—big time. They were on the side of a beautiful hill, encircled by different types of evergreens, white pine, ponderosa pine, redwoods, and a beautiful stream full of crystal clear water. The dirt was red, the pine needles carpeting the ground were yellow, and the jumping fish in the little pond looked like rainbow trout. The meadow they were in was just large enough for a small group of people, and now there were others. Trisha could tell that this was an 'afterlife experience,' her dad was in it, was happy and fulfilled, but they weren't wearing white outfits. They looked very normal, yet loving, too.

"Trisha, honey, the world, your mortal world, is a very dangerous playground. We cannot make anything happen. We can see things, can hope for things, and want very much for our friends and families to be well and safe, to come home to us when their lives are over. There is a vast, indeed an endless myriad of life out away from Earth. We are just a tiny speck of sand on an ocean of beachhead. You have, not by any design of yours . . . or of ours, placed yourself in the vortex of a very important conflict.

"In this situation, and it is complicated, we want you to be in that marathon. There is someone from your past, we cannot reveal who, *because you may actually remember too much and then it won't work out. The aim is for him to see you, to have him remember you, and perhaps show some sort of an interest. We feel that if you are a part of his life, and we are not saying you have to marry the guy, your influence may help him organize his life in such a way that he can move forrward and fulfill a purpose. Mac and I here are not all that aware of exactly what it is he is supposed to do, but, the reason for me getting to make this call, and believe me, kid, today's the biggest day of my eternal life, getting to be with you is a dream-come-true of mine, has to do with that purpose, which looks to be huge." The little group of listeners had grown significantly.*

There really must be something to this request. "Dad, what man cares about a 275 lbs. . . . . ?"

"Trisha, my little runner girl, the big you is not you. We are asking you to get prepared and actually try to win the race. You will have earned that on your own. We can't do it for you. The correct question would have to include you as the 105 lbs. race winner or something like that. What man would not be interested in that girl?"

"Oh . . . , I see."

"There is one thing we can do, and have granted you for this. The nightmares about my little brain hemorrhage, your Achilles heel, and your disappointment in how you have handled things are over. They're gone. I am almost gone now, too.

"I have this one more thing to say. Stop fretting about life. It is what it is. I didn't raise you to lie down and feel sorry for yourself. We, all of us, live with disappointments and setbacks. Even those of us in this realm deal with the same problems. Eternal life itself is no panacea either, Trisha. You've heard the story of the lion and the lamb lying down together. Did you ever think how that would work out for the lion? The lamb gets to eat grass, but the lion needs meat. What does he get for dinner if he can't have chops? Sleep soundly, get up, and get going. The way I see it you have much to do in order to protect your knees when you and Michael make the 10k race in July."

"I will, Father. I will. Thank you for being my father. I have the greatest dad on earth or in heaven. Is there anything else?"

"Yes. Much as I love Michael and laugh at his antics, I'd appreciate it if you would be ever so kin as to run his butt into the ground at the half marathon come Christmas time! Can you handle that for me?"

Everyone in the meadow started laughing. Trisha started laughing. She laughed in her father's arms until tears took the place of laughter. She had not experienced that love in so long she had forgotten that it even existed. She woke up, still laughing, but could not, for the life of her, remember why. Trisha instantly took the note pad and tried to write, but again there was nothing to write about. She must have had a sweet dream for a change. It was 7:30 in the morning. She had slept through the night, perhaps a byproduct of her diet and exercise plan. Trisha felt like a million bucks, and there was much to do, so she jumped out of bed and began a new life.

She started by figuring out that she had 147 days to do something about her weight and physical fitness prior to St. George on July 4th. In the bottom of the dresser drawer she found just what she was looking for, a small white magic marker board, about the size of a standard piece of paper. It had a loop hole in the back for mounting on a wall, and true to form, there was a small plastic bag containing nails stapled to the back of it. She quickly grabbed Covey's *8th Habit* and used it as a hammer to drive the nail into the wall in her bathroom; she was already using Covey to find her "voice" and hammer down a new direction in her life. She went into the office, found a magic marker with a small tip, a green one, and quickly wrote "147"; the countdown was on.

Trisha went back into the office, opened the front desk drawer and started looking through all the junk. She again found what she was looking for in the far back right hand corner of the drawer, stuck in dried chewing gum, laced with icky hair. She found a loose dime that was sitting on the desk, caught onto the gum and pried it out of the drawer. For the first time in years, her fingers rubbed up against a Club Sport Member Card. "I wonder if this thing will get me past the front desk," she laughed. She ate a small appropriate breakfast, collected some toiletries in a Ziploc bag, and decided on the green muumuu, which she bagged with some other clothes, put on her only swimsuit, then a very large Hawaiian t-shirt, and headed for the club. The card worked! Trisha prayed to the Lord that no one, not one person, would recognize her as she went to the indoor pool, got in, and started free-styling in what turned out to be a vigorous hour of exercise, way over the limit for a normal person this early in any fitness program, let alone someone as far out of shape as she was. The hour seemed more like a year.

On her way out of the locker room she could see into the tennis courts and, yup, there he was. Michael was out on Court 4, running back and forth on the baseline playing tennis. He saw her, but she quickly turned, hoping that he didn't notice her watching him. Was he laughing when he saw her? *Men are pigs; at least they can be,* she mused, perhaps a bit jealous. Trisha Martin felt so out of her element.

Trisha picked up two days worth of food at Smith's. For the time being she was going to emphasize fresh fruit, vegetables, lean protein, small amounts of whole grains, and lay off of the rest of it while she figured out what to. She went home, organized everything, and went to work in her office, continuing the process of turning it into something she could be proud to work in at least. No home makeover? She felt empowered, realizing that there were many things she could get done on her own, without much money, even without any money. This place required sweat equity and needed love just as much as she did.

After a very tasty lunch Trisha went for a walk, a very brisk walk, through her neighborhood. She wanted to test her knees and see what was there. In about fifteen minutes she covered a full mile. Back at the house again, she went to her computer and Googled, looking for tracking software, free tracking programs she could utilize to monitor her activities. There were so many choices; most cost money, but in the end Trisha decided to make something temporary on an Excel spreadsheet. She knew that she had to keep track of what was going on if she was to make sound, organized progress.

During her shift at Target that evening, Trisha decided that she was ready to bank the first week using what she had. She was tired of research for the moment, and wanted to settle into something that kept her going in the right direction, including the decision to read LeShan and of course, the recommendation of Providence, *Beck's DIET Solution.* And that is what she did. There was one thing that she could not get off of her mind. How come the card worked? Who was paying her bill at the club? She had absolutely no idea.

The next two days went like clockwork for Trisha, both the eating and the exercise. She kept her house clean, slept well, ate as she planned, went to the club and swam for an hour, took a brisk walk after lunch, and worked the evening shifts at her job. There was no way to tell how she was doing on the scale, as she had promised herself not to weigh more than once a week, if that. Thursday was a nightmare. She woke up famished and could not get rid of hunger pangs no matter how many fruits and vegetables she ate. Her bread choices tasted great, but went down like cotton candy, providing no help whatsoever. Trisha could barely finish the hour swim, and when she counted laps, the total was down significantly. What was wrong? She headed upstairs and almost, *almost* ate at the little café there. *Have I bottomed out*, she thought, feeling like she was going to die? Her plan now was reduced to a minute-by-minute excruciating practice in the art of self torture. She did eat at the café, but only ice tea and a banana. What happened next kind of reminded her of what it was like to hide and then someone sneak up behind you . . . She felt a tap on her shoulder.

"Trisha Martin? You aren't by any chance Trisha Martin are you?" The face looked familiar, but she could not place him. That he recognized her was, for her, a new and embarrassing source of pain. Trisha did not want to see anyone from her past.

"Stanley. You're. . . Stan Burton. How are you? I haven't seen you since you graduated from Green Valley back in, what was it, 1997? You were a year ahead of me if I'm not mistaken." The humiliation of being recognized by one of her fellow track teammates must have been easy to see, what with her blush, the way she twigged her hair and the complete look of shock on her face. How she had avoided seeing old athletes from high school at Target was a well guarded secret.

"Trisha, I've been watching you, not stalking you, be assured of that, since you came in on Monday. I would like to congratulate you for coming down here and getting started on what looks like a brand new plan."

"Stan, I hate you seeing me like this . . ."

"Don't go there, Trisha. Everyone fights things, personal demons and such. When it is weight, everyone else gets to enjoy your pain, but not me, and welcome back. I am very proud of you." He was genuinely glad to see her and now she felt something comforting. She could see that this man was sincerely genuine, and then he went on. "I am a personal trainer and a certified dietician. I am not looking for a new client this afternoon, but just wanted to say hi to you and let you know that someone, at least me anyway, notices what you are doing and is rooting for you. I see you are enjoying a banana with your ice tea. Good choice. You get hydration and nutrition, but don't waste calories."

"Not for long, Stanley. My next stop is Fatburger. I'm so hungry right now I could eat anything. I am not going to make it. See this banana? It went down like a single peanut, though it tasted great. I am missing something. It's like I haven't eaten a thing yet."

"Come over here and sit down for a minute. I need to hear what is going on with you right now. Since almost everyone who tries this on their own fails miserably, perhaps you have experienced that failure for yourself. Trisha, I want to see if I can help you through today at least." He led Trisha over to the secluded area on the west side of the café over by the window. It was quiet there, they had some modicum of privacy, and Stan ordered himself a bottle of green tea while Trisha had her ice tea refilled. "Now then old friend, what is going on here, other than the obvious?"

Trisha told him about her plan from last Saturday, the bet she had lost, what the consequence was, and how the week had been going so far. Everything had been going smoothly up until this morning when she turned up too hungry, craving fast food. She was trapped, she told him, because there was no way to go slow and be ready for a six mile run by July 4th. "Sounds like Michael Martin to me," Stan smiled. "Whatever are you going to do about it?"

"I am going to starve myself, get in shape, lose tons of weight, and make that race if it kills me."

"By eating a King Burger, skinny fries and onion rings? Oh, and let's not forget the milk shake with hand-packed ice cream." He laughed out loud. She laughed, too. Trisha was staring out the window and could see swimmers in the outdoor pool lapping. They were thin, beautiful, and moved like dolphins. By contrast she imagined herself looking like Shamu, floating back and forth with her black swimsuit and pearl white skin. "Tell me, what are you eating right now, this week, Trish? Maybe you need more. Perhaps you're in protein deprivation right this minute?"

Just then Mike walked into the café and purchased a health bar of some kind. Try as she may, it was impossible for Trisha to go unnoticed. He saw her and came by to say hello to them. "Trisha, Stan, how are you guys today? I'm proud of you, Sis, for getting the card out and coming down to the gym. What a great game Sunday, yes?"

"No more sports betting for me, Mikey. It was terrible. The whole day was a roller coaster ride through hell. I hated the game." Both Michael and Stanley burst out laughing. They were all smiles. Two or three heads turned their way from the counter, reacting to Trisha's comment. One uninvited guest raised his coffee cup and shouted a big *hurrah* looking directly at Trisha. He was obviously a Colts fan who was just as disappointed as she was.

"You hear the good news, Stan? Trisha Jean Martin is going to run again, in an official race come July 4th up in St. George at their 10k fun run. I will be there with her. TJ, you want to go to The Painted Pony for dinner after the run?"

"Never heard of the place, but, if the food is good . . ."

"It's the best food between Vegas and Salt Lake City. Would I ever lead you astray? Maybe we can rent rooms, enjoy the local fireworks show after dinner and make it a date, my treat."

Trisha smiled. She did love her brother, pig that he was. He was gloating right now. "Hey, are you thinking of letting Stan get you ready for the run? He is one of the best trainers around here."

"Whoa, Mikey, I can't afford a trainer right now. I haven't been made store manager yet; in fact, I'm only part time over there. Unless there is *manna from heaven* I'm stuck on my own here. Stan is just being an old friend catching up."

It was not hard to see that Stanley Burton was out of his element in this family conversation. He had no intention of imposing himself onto Trisha today, or ever. He did really like her though. They were the type of old friends that could find their way to becoming new friends, that is if the cards fell into place correctly. He felt very uncomfortable at the suggestion. It was too much, way too soon to put her on the spot like that, but then again, here he was in the presence of Michael being Michael. What else could he have expected?

* * *

Roger looked directly at Mac. "Now, one angel to another, push him with the 'endowment' intimation so he'll think of it." Mac made his move.

"I'm in, Roger. Now, I pinch just a little hypnotic sub hematoma suggestion and . . . bingo."

* * *

"TJ, speaking of *manna from heaven*, have you forgotten about Dad's endowment?

"What endowment are you dreaming about? Here comes another trick from my brother, I can just feel it."

"Dad left a sizable endowment that I am the Trustee of, well me and Samuel actually, that was intended to fund education, other worthy endeavors, and that includes hard training for races where you are concerned. I told you about it some time ago." Trisha was no longer hungry in the least. Somehow she didn't expect that to last, but her ears were up. "I would have to include what you are doing right now as the kind of training he was interested in, so, if you want Stan, and he is willing to help, you're free to make the deal." Trisha was shocked at the news. "Your monthly fee has been paid out of that fund for years now and you didn't even know it. Truthfully, it seems to me that you owe back dues, not in money, but in hard work. We don't want you to pay your bet by blowing your knees if you don't lose enough weight over the next few months."

"This is nonsense, Michael. There is no trust . . ."

"Oh, but there is. Just call Samuel; he'll tell you all about it." Mike made a mental note to call his lawyer as soon as he was out of earshot and let him know what was coming and what to say about it. She was technically right about the trust idea he just conjured up out of thin air. He could sense her hope, and the bright optimistic look of opportunity on Stan's face that had more to it than just some money. He wanted to guide this athlete back into the world of the living, no doubt about it. Mike patted himself on the back and let his ego whisper in his ear, *Michael my boy, you've done it again.*

* * *

Roger and Wise Mac high fived each other. No matter how this little episode worked out, it was a fun game for them to play.

* * *

Trisha looked out over the pool area. It was February, and though it was a sunny day, it was also windy and cold. Several of the lanes had swimmers droning through their workouts. The lifeguard was poised up in his chair, had an iPod plugged into his ears, was reading something, and was dressed in red. He looked to Trisha like his next stop would be the North Pole. In the summer on Friday nights that pool was a huge party, with music, food, and lots of people. There would be families, club members, the muscle hunks, pretty swimming suits on pretty girls, and a DJ to run the show. Club members looked forward to Friday nights at the pool. Today it was a very quiet workplace of the committed. Trisha was falling deeper into the life she had abandoned so long ago. She was beginning to feel like one of the committed. "You have room for a dangerously overweight marathoner in your busy schedule, Stanley?" The look he gave her, loaded with daggers, was well prepared, but not reassuring.

"No, I really don't, Trish. I would send a 'big fat marathoner' off to one of the ladies who specialize in workout gossip. You know, the kind of trainer who spends forty-five minutes of the hour in passive conversation. Sorry, Miss Martin. I am not able to help that person. Now you may be a different kind of person," Stanley said very seriously. Mike was all smiles. He knew what was going on here.

"I have to go, kids. You have your fun. Don't forget to call Samuel, Trisha. You can get his number if you don't have it from my front desk. You remember my assistant, Roberta? Give her a call if you need to consummate a relationship with either Samuel here or someone else if you want. I trust you. It makes no difference to me what direction you go as long as it is forward." When he was out of earshot he got Sam on the phone and told him everything, but when it came time for instructions, Samuel interrupted him with the shock of his life.

"Slow down, Michael. The trust exists. As of the first of the month it had over $2,000,000 in it and is in good shape. Roger made sure the investments were safe and secure." He went on to explain to Michael that his father had wanted to leave a protected and secret legacy, so that at some time in the future he would be in a position to help, though he himself was long gone. Mike was so dumbfounded he could hardly believe this. His dad had trumped him. *Good for Trish,* he thought. Then he was bothered by an epiphany working its way around between his ears somewhere. "You're screwing with my head again, aren't you, Dad?"

* * *

Roger smiled. Mike was so sure of himself that he had said the words aloud. He shouldn't be so hard on the boy. His son had been everything he had hoped for, and more, in the years Roger had been gone.

* * *

"Sam, she has the biggest road to navigate ever. It is an almost impossible task. You say I am a trustee, well here is my input. Give her anything she needs on any level; but, make her commit to training like it's for the Olympic Games. That's the price to be paid. Keep her feet to the fire." The attorney blessed the idea and the conversation was over.

"Trisha, I set aside time for serious people. When we work, we work, and we work more than you could know; well, you would know since you were an athlete once. If you want to play ball with me, and I don't care as much about the money as I do my reputation, then you have to do it my way."

"Stan, tell me what to do."

"Finish this day the way you had planned, except for the Fatburger part. Before we see each other tomorrow, at what, 11:30 am, you run a mile upstairs on the soft track, without stopping; that is, unless your knees can't handle it, or your doctor won't allow it, and then you hit the pool for an hour-long swim. Take a shower, get into your street clothes, and then meet me at Sweet Tomatoes at 11:30.

"Yes, sir. See you tomorrow." Suddenly, Trisha had no interest in Fatburger or anything else. She headed home to eat appropriately. When she pulled into the driveway, she considered all those bags of garbage that were put onto the street Tuesday, and it reminded her of the other garbage, stuff inside of her. It was about to go.

She called the Samuel Giles Law Firm while eating and it turned out that this time Mike had been right. There was an endowment, and according to Samuel, Trisha's plan could be a part of that endowment. He confirmed that it had never been used, but it was meant to perpetuate and was designed to be utilized in future generations. He agreed that at the very least she could hire a personal trainer, but that she had to come down and sign a contract to firm up the details. Trisha finished eating and was again attacked by relentless hunger. It was immediate, a defeating and debilitating pang, lined with the kind of panic that only a starving overweight person could identify with. She almost decided to go out and get something to eat. Instead she chose to brew coffee, add a small amount of chicken to her just finished meal, and then eat one of the diet cookies she had purchased the other day. It was the best she could come up with. Surprisingly, within thirty minutes she felt better, much better. Perhaps the chicken or more specifically the protein fixed things. Her current diet books both spoke of how protein could be used to solve hunger problems.

Thursday was becoming the second longest day of the new plan which was still less than a week old. Trisha went out for her afternoon walk, actually ran some of the way just to feel what it would be like, made it back to her home, cleaned up, ate a Healthy Choice meal, and made her way to the evening shift at Target. The popcorn smell from the snack bar was overwhelming, but something else startled her. Her supervisor Marsha Thompson paid her a compliment.

"Hi, Trisha," she opened. "You are looking, I don't know, like you have more energy lately. Is there something different about you?" Trisha smiled. Just then a customer came by to check out. His was a single item purchase, and then he was followed by another with several items. She was grateful that nothing needed be said at the moment, because she was very uncomfortable talking about what was going on. Trisha had failed at so many attempts in the past she had no confidence in telling anyone what she was up to. There was only one break during the evening part-time shift and when she sat down in the employee lounge there were the usual three or four people in there. One of them was her best friend at work, or so she thought. April, had similar weight issues, always complained about management, people here and there, and was the resident expert on the politics of the day at Target. Trisha stayed out of that kind of stuff, except to listen, which she did enjoy. One of the things they did have in common was food. They always seemed to be eating together during the break in the middle of the evening shift. Tonight it would be different, but the same. April was munching some little white doughnuts and, being the kind friend she was, offered some of them to Trisha.

"Not tonight, thanks." Trisha was starving. It had been a very long day and even the thought of losing weight at the moment seemed a million miles away.

"Oh, come on, don't make me eat alone. I've been here waiting for you. You're not going to believe what Miss Pilkington said to Greg in Sports tonight. She is such a, well, I can't use the word."

"I don't know, April, she has been very nice to me of late. I wonder what Greg did. It couldn't be that he screwed up or anything. He never makes bonehead decisions." She laughed sardonically.

After April put the doughnuts away they walked out front so April could smoke. Not even the employees were allowed to smoke inside the building, even during their breaks in the employee lounge. Trisha picked up a diet soda at the fountain and found herself out front looking out over the parking lot while April smoked. She looked longingly across the parking lot at Applebee's and decided to invite April to eat there next week. One of the things Trisha liked about Applebee's was their 'under 600 calorie' menu. She could actually get a steak dinner out of that place, and if she stayed away from the free food, drank no alcohol or sugar water, she could get out of the place on the low side. The good news for her was that there were a lot of places like that nowadays.

"Are you on a diet, Trisha?" One thing about April was that she would get straight to the point. Trisha liked that. "I have been noticing that you are not eating like usual. Do you get angry with me when I eat in front of you?"

"Yes and no. Yes, I am on a plan, but why talk about it during the first week? How many times have we tried something just to watch it go down the drain? We announce to the universe that we are going to lose weight, take credit for a phantom accomplishment, try something until it gets a bit rough, lose willpower, slip, slide down off of the plan, and eventually give up. I am not telling anyone this time. But since you asked, yes, I am in a complicated fix and have to lose weight. No, I do not mind being in front of you or anyone who is eating. I have my mother to thank for that. She forced me to go to Lucille's on the first day of my diet and then she pigged out right in front of me. I would mind it if those I were with relentlessly cajoled me into eating when I didn't want to, but I know you aren't into that kind of thing. Hey, we need to get back inside. Applebee's next week for you and me will be a great idea. Fortunately, I still get to eat a little."

"What's wrong? Is it medical? Are you diabetic or something? You don't have cancer do you?"

Trisha laughed. "Not. The short answer is that I lost a huge Super Bowl bet. I took the Colts and Payton Manning let me down." They were walking back to their work positions, and that popcorn snack-bar type smell hit her hard again, but she had a parting comment for her friend. "I lost the bet to my brother and he collects every time. I have to run four 10k races starting in July and I have to run a half marathon with him in December. I don't know about other planets, but on this one I am not aware of anyone my size and in my physical condition that can do that. He trapped me."

April was laughing out loud as they split up and went their separate ways. Trisha was glad she had confided in her friend, but did worry a bit since April was well known to be endowed with a loose tongue. Trisha wondered if April had not just conducted a de facto news conference.

When Trisha got back to the car after her shift she noticed the little red light on her phone blinking. It was a text message from Samuel Giles' office, requesting that she drop by tomorrow afternoon, perhaps around 2:00 for a short visit with the old man and his son David. Figuring that her lunch with Stanley would be over in plenty of time, she hit the reply button and confirmed the appointment. Good grief, her life was getting busy all of a sudden. That damned Super Bowl bet, a two edged sword at best, was playing havoc with her privacy.

Trisha had the hardest time at night, saving calories for bedtime, which helped her sleep. It was after 11:45 when she crawled into the sack; her house was definitely a more comfortable place. She ate an orange and two Ritz crackers, such a treat. Sometime after she fell asleep, after about what seemed like an hour or so, her alarm sounded and she was forced to get out of bed. There was simply no way she could show up at lunch and try to explain why she didn't follow Stanley's instructions. As tired as she was that would definitely not be the right way to start a new relationship with someone who seemed to be very serious about training and fitness.

The freezing wind had her shivering but she decided to try for the outdoor pool. Of course it might just be possible that the reason she went outside had something to do with the fact that the indoor pool was more than full at two swimmers per lane. Outside, she had a modicum of privacy, sharing that pool with only one other person. Quite quickly Trisha learned that there was an opposite effect when swimming in cold weather. In the summertime it was common to approach the pool hesitantly, then jump in and experience the refreshing jolt of a cold plunge on a really hot day. Out in the early morning cold though, she could not get into the warm comfortable water quickly enough, finding the experience to be an invigorating surprise. Trisha kicked off and started to swim. After just a few laps she was feeling loose and willing to push a bit, and so she did.

One of the peaceful aspects of a swimming workout was that it gave the swimmer time to think, to let one's mind wander about. It did cross her mind that if all those inside knew how nice it was to swim in a warm pool during cold weather, she may have had a hard time getting a lane out here. As big as she was, she didn't want to have to share a lane with someone else. It occurred to her that Mike would laugh at her for liking the outdoor pool in the morning during winter months and now she knew why. As she paddled from one end to the other, over and over again, it occurred to her that winners in life always seem to take the road less traveled. *Is it winning that gives people the joy they seem to carry around, or is it the little gains through sacrifice and work that set them apart from the grouchy grumps? Or is it something else altogether?* When Trisha swallowed water and started coughing she lost her train of thought. One other thing that her mind drifted to was an unrealistic grasp on how time works. She had slept more than six hours and that had seemed like minutes to her. This one-hour swim seemed to be going on all day.

She had pushed too hard early in the hour and was now barely treading water as her time to close out the swim approached. *I'm so out of shape.*

It was almost impossible to pull her tired, spent body up the ladder and out of the pool. She went into the showers, took a long hot sauna, climbed into her special K-mart type workout clothes and headed to the café for some breakfast. There was a one-mile run waiting. It dawned on her that she had conducted the morning's workout backwards from Stanley's instructions, and that perhaps he would be disappointed. How could she ever hope to run a mile today? It took an hour for her to find out. One mile on the inside was just over thirteen times around a very spongy track, which was a good thing, and she did not feel that her knees were at risk. The worst part of it was how she looked. There were several runners on the track, none in her size category, and in fact very few of them were overweigh at all. She felt very conspicuous. *There goes my privacy . . . and my dignity.*

The job was to 'run' the mile. She didn't think she could do it when she started out, aching all over from the swim; but, off she went. It was the longest fifteen minutes of her life; however, she got through the jog without stopping or walking. The other runners on the track were very nice and encouraging. One, who had lapped her several times, pulled alongside and introduced himself. Trisha was so out of it that she forgot his name within seconds, but the shoulder hug he gave her, the warm words of support, *that* made her day. She had run a mile for the first time in almost twelve years. This time when she went to the shower area, she took full advantage of the whirlpool Jacuzzi and sat there until her skin was wilted. Trisha Jean Martin was officially a runner. There it was again, that deep core feeling, kind of exciting, very scary. She'd entered a one way door and the only way out was forward.

On her way up the stairs to the café she again met the runner who'd hugged her . . . "Hi, Trisha. Joshua Sullivan, you remember me from out on the track."

"Hello, Joshua Sullivan; how nice to make your acquaintance again."

"Call me Josh."

"OK, Josh it is. Can I buy you a soda or something?

"Oh please, allow me."

"No, I insist. Barbara, please get this gentleman something and put it on my tab." My, wasn't Trisha feeling forward this morning. "Barbara and I are getting to be old friends now that I am an everyday member again, right Barb?" Barbara smiled back.

"So Josh, do you hug all the girls out on the track, or just the helpless ones like me?" Trisha liked this guy, who was no threat, seemed to be genuinely interested in conversation, and he was not too hard to look at.

"Now see, Trisha, can I call you Trisha?"

"By all means, please do." This conversation was kind of ridiculous, but she was having fun for a change. Enjoying the company of this fellow was much better than eating candy in bed.

"Trisha, I am not one to mince words and hide from the pink elephant in the living room. It is easy to see what you are up to, yet something intrigues me. On the one hand you are grossly out of shape, had no business running the way you did, and yet, you looked comfortable out there. Perhaps it takes a trained eye like mine," he was laughing at his own humor now, "but your running style does not exactly fit your physique."

"Are you one of those freaky chubby chasers, Joshua, because if you are, forget it. I may just be the only thirty-year-old virgin left on the planet, but I won't be giving it up to a pervert chubby chaser."

"Holding out for Prince Charming are you? Damn it. My day is ruined." He laughed, trying to look disappointed, but no matter how well he could run, he was a bad actor. "My wife will be in here in just minutes to catch up with me; she was downstairs lifting, and if she knew that I was a chubby chaser it would be over between us. Please don't let her know." Trisha was laughing, raising a single eyebrow and having a great time, in fact. She did like this guy, married or not. "Seriously now, you run with the grace of someone who knows exactly what you're doing. Have you run competitively before?"

Trisha was suddenly choking on the words, trying to hide unexpected tears. Her new friend, Josh, had struck a nerve she didn't know existed. She turned her head away, apologized, wiped her nose with the napkin, and, started to laugh again. What the hell. "Yes." She was so hoping that he couldn't see the pain through her smile. "I was a marathoner back in high school, many lifetimes ago."

Just then Joshua's wife came into the café, found them, got introduced to Trisha by Josh, sat down a minute or two for pleasantries, and they were up on their feet and needed to go.

"It was so nice to meet you, Michelle. Josh, I enjoyed our visit. You folks have a great day." "You as well, Trisha," said Josh's wife Michelle. "Welcome to Club Sport life. Good luck with what you are going to be getting done. I am here a lot, know most of the ladies, and if you need anything at all, just let me know," she genuinely responded.

"You have a nice day too, Trisha; I will be out on the track at the same time tomorrow. Hope to see you," said Joshua.

They were gone. It was time for Trisha to be gone. She had a lunch date with Stanley over at Sweet Tomatoes, one she had been looking forward to. She put her things in the trunk, got in, started the well maintained, clean, and clean-smelling car, a car that she was proud to drive today. Trisha headed out onto Olympic, east to Sunset Dr., then southeast to Stephanie. At Sunset and Stephanie she had to wait for an overweight wheelchair-bound woman being pushed across the street by a feeble man. The sight of it made her heart bleed. *Unless I can keep this thing turned around,* thought Trisha, *that is my future.* She made a right hand turn, trudged through three lights of heavy traffic, had to slow down for a couple of joggers, and in ten minutes found herself parked and ready for a Sweet Tomatoes lunch. Like clockwork, Stanley Burton was out on the front patio, sitting on the green park bench waiting for her. He seemed very happy that she was punctual.

"Trisha, it's good to see you this morning. Have a seat. Let's visit for a few minutes before we go inside and enjoy a very nice lunch." The workout was in the bank, Trisha was looking forward to seeing Mr. Giles in a couple of hours and she still couldn't believe her good fortune, literally. Her dad had set her up for this training, almost like he was watching over her—still. Trisha loved Sweet Tomatoes, especially the food in the back where the kitchen was. That was where they kept the soup and breads, desserts, pizza, the pasta . . . the yummy stuff. She had a bit of a sinking feeling that today the dining experience would be much more reserved, more of an educational experience and that was just fine with her.

"Did you get through the workout, especially the run? Did you run a full mile without stopping or walking this morning?"

"Yes and yes. You know, Stan, I am sore from head to foot after these couple of days, and I am tired, but the run was most satisfying. I haven't run a mile in twelve years. That was worth the whole week of work and yes, I'm excited to weigh in tomorrow morning. Will I get the day off for good behavior, especially if I lost weight?"

"I'm afraid not, young lady. I'll give you a day off when you bank a full month. There is so much to get done and if you rest and eat too much for a day, not only do you lose that day, but you go backwards a day, like a two day penalty. What have you been eating all week?"

Trisha was contemplating this accomplishment, the pain of self-denial, psychological battles she had been struggling through, and was proud of the fact she had held to her guns and denied the impulse to eat big every day— so far. "I have eaten a lot of fruit, apples, oranges, some bananas, strawberries, grapes, some other stuff, and oh, I remember eating some pineapple, too. I have eaten my share of veggies. I go to Fresh and Easy where you can get 110 calorie bags of all kinds of things. I have eaten chicken a couple of times, scrambled eggs in a no-stick pan so I do not have to oil the bottom first, and I have eaten fish twice. I have also had bread a couple of times, once at Subway where you can get a very tasty 6" sub for less than 500 calories. I am sure that I have lost at least 25 pounds," she snickered.

"Let's watch people for a while. I want you to see absolutely what you are up against in this noble quest of yours. Tomorrow when you come into the club, I won't be there, but Pam in the tennis shop can show you to where my office is. I want you to slip your food diary underneath the door so I can take a look at it."

"Food diary, uh, uh . . . I don't have one."

"I thought as much. That really wasn't a fair question. Almost no one with your history does. Trisha dear, you'll have to keep an accurate diary of what you're eating. Let me demonstrate. What did you eat just yesterday?"

"Let me think," she said.

"No thinking, Trisha. If you have to think, then you will not be prepared to eat the right portions and variations of food from day-to-day. There are several places to keep a food diary online, but I recommend the Nutrisystem diary. When you get into it you'll see why."

"Oh Stan, please don't make me eat that food. It, it's like dog food. I tried it once, years ago." Just then Stanley stood, leading Trisha up by the arm, and they started walking to his car. What could she do but follow? Lunch seemed a million miles away, based, if nothing else from the look on his face. She dreaded what he was going to do, and when they opened the trunk of his car, there it was—a big rectangular box, a Nutrisystem box . . . good Lord.

Stan proceeded to carry that box to her car, her clean car thank heavens, and he had her open the trunk so he could put it in. "Trish, you have to be open minded about this. Let me first give you the good news. You are not going to be on the Nutrisystem plan, per se, but you will be eating this food as you go along, at least while you're getting started. I insist." She almost puked right there on the spot. "I'll give you credit for doing all the right things this week. I just made your life much easier now whether you know it or not." They walked back to the bench and sat down, again. When were they going to get something to eat? Trisha didn't want to admit to Stanley that she was starving, that she wanted to go back into that kitchen and ravish the pasta, pizza and other bread. What could she do but suffer in silence with a smile on her face? It was terrible.

At least forty people had walked past them and into the restaurant. "Have you noticed anything unfortunate about the crowd, like how many overweight people have strolled right past us on their way in to eat?"

"I had never noticed so many," she admitted. "Is it like this everywhere, or is there something special about Sweet Tomatoes, or something different about Las Vegas, or anything that would make this an out of the ordinary anomaly?"

"There is so much access to food in our society, even a paperboy can get fat. Obesity is the single most debilitating aspect of our lives. Staying healthy now is harder than at any time since George Washington crossed the Delaware. We suffer from all kinds of food, in all kinds of places, and in all kinds of ways. I would lay money that when you open the box of Nutrisystem food, and try anything, you'll be surprised at how good it is. The reason I am throwing it your way has to do with portion control. Nutrisystem is a portion control *cut back* that is very easy to follow. I am not selling this one diet as the save-all for mankind. All of the different weight loss options get the job done just fine if the subject puts in the effort and does the work. The vast majority of successful weight loss candidates organize their own plan utilizing all sorts of tools. This is the one I picked for you because of the time problem you're facing, and I love their website. It's free. You do not have to buy any food from this company to get your own personal webpage set up. I want you signed up and recording your food intake daily beginning Sunday morning.

"OK."

"I will let you explore the different nuances of the site for yourself. It is very easy to navigate, fun if you get involved in the Nutrisystem community at large, and you will find it the most flexible way to manage what you eat. Like I said, there are other plans out there, and they are all good; this is just a choice for this year. Later, after you make the half marathon, if you want, you can move on to something else. One other thing; I want you to summarize each day in a Microsoft Calendar." He pulled a piece of paper out of his shirt to show her his. "On the top line you list the day as a number followed by a slash representing the relative number of quality days against the total days in your count. Then you track food and exercise. Underneath that you summarize the type of day you had, such as what you see here. Do you have any questions about that?" She didn't. "Today I will say 'Sweet Tomatoes with Trisha.' What do you say? Let's go eat. Remember this simple rule, Trisha: only track on days that you want to lose weight! Are you ready?"

"You're the boss," she smiled, overcome with relief. She had never sat in front of food like that before, another lesson in food addiction. Trisha could instantly see how the diary system he had devised would keep her on the straight and narrow. Knowledge is power; the one tool most dieters fail to take advantage of was a proper and easy-to-use tracking system so that they could know what they had eaten. Trisha had eaten at night many times only to remember, too late, that she had also overeaten during the day. This was something that, once mastered, would solve that problem—if she could stick with it.

As they picked up their trays, and surprisingly Stanley had suggested she take two large plates instead of one, he noted, "When you get your online page established I want you to email me the password and login codes so that I can track what you are doing from day-to-day. It'll be much easier than having you give me reports, easier for both of us."

This guy was smart. All she had to do was cooperate and perform; the rest would take care of itself.

Trisha loved the smell inside and Stanley was ready to teach proper eating the Sweet Tomatoes way. "Go with whatever leafy greens you like best, and be generous with yourself. Take advantage of all the different colors of the leafy types. You'll build a great salad without calories. On the other plate, load things in like cucumbers, tomatoes, celery, a nice serving of peas, just a touch of the corn for color and taste, and add if you like just the tiniest taste of potato or macaroni salad. If you want to hit a home run, sprinkle on some garbanzo beans, and on the other plate add some of the kidney beans. Don't be too generous with the carrots, but add a few. Be sure to enjoy the zucchini, beats, green peppers, radish, onions, cauliflower, broccoli and dill pickles, too." By the time they arrived at the dressings there were two very different looking low calorie salads to cover. "You won't believe this, but if you go with just a small ladle of the Creamy Italian or Bacon, you will be better off than with either of the Vinaigrettes, which are higher in sugar. Try the fat-free Honey Mustard, too. It is very low in calories. If you want any bread out back I recommend that you forget the croutons, but the choice is yours." Trisha decided to hold out for bread from the kitchen. Lunch was going to be delicious, she could see that, and this was an entirely new way to look at a full service salad bar. Stanley paid the bill, they got some water and ice tea and then found a nice place to sit and eat. The conversation turned to exercise, a new passion . . . but kind of like going back to the future.

"I spoke to Mike late yesterday and he is very excited to see what you are capable of, Trisha. We all seem to agree that there is, latent within you, the makings of a very good athlete. You can get it all back if you pay the price. Fortunately for you, the price does not include money. You are the luckiest girl in the world that way. So many people have no support when they attempt to get rid of the excess body fat; but you, you have what amounts to a professional team behind you. You are meeting with the money people after lunch, yes?" She nodded.

"Trish, I want you to just forget about your excess body weight. You are not that person anymore, so let the big Trisha go. You are eating less than 500 calories for this meal, by the way, and you need more, so I suggest we go get some soup, bread, and yes, today you get some dessert. Do you like chicken noodle soup?" She grinned, probably anticipating the noodles. When she went to fill her soup bowl, instinctively she drained the broth and filled the ladle with all the noodles she could get in it. "Whoa, not like that. You can load up on the chicken though, since we didn't put any on the salad. Do not underestimate the value of protein in the never-ending war on hunger. The chicken in the soup is much better tasting and it's hot."

Trisha ended up with a bowl of broth, ample chicken, and just a few noodles. "The other soups are OK too, except for a couple of them; you can go online to learn about them nutritionally. This is the type of meal that you can call a reward in your new life. I know, it's not a Double-Double from In-N-Out. That is a different type of reward. Before we pick the bread, tell me which of the desserts you are interested in."

"I think I'll try the Vanilla Frozen Yogurt."

"Good choice; it is only 140 calories if you do not put anything on it. Now you can pick your bread choice."

"I would like the Bruschetta Focaccia." Trisha was beaming with pleasure. It was like she had forgotten all about the Nutrisystem food—but she hadn't.

"That is another good choice, Trisha. You are getting out of this feast for about 1200 calories. It is a good meal for you, given that it is a reward, and the amount of work you're putting in. This restaurant has so many different choices it is no wonder people come here to eat healthy but never seem to get out of here without eating way too much. That will not be the case with you in the future." When they were seated again Stanley went back to visiting about her exercise program.

"The first thing I want to do with you is set a short term program that will get you ready for the first 10k run in July. If you follow my plan I expect it to be no big deal. The only thing getting in the way is possible damage to your knees because of your weight." For the first time in years Trisha was looking at a formal training schedule. She was so excited about it. Last night she had been reading Tres

Prier Hatch's *Miracle Pill* book and was trying to digest the advice regarding how one should take time to savor food and eat slowly. It was a good thing that Stanley was going over details and, perhaps without even being aware, allowing her a sound situation with which to practice the pace at which she ate. In her heart of hearts, Trisha was a gobbler, at least the current Trisha was. Now she was taking as much time as she could between bites.

"Trisha, we're going to break down the preparation for the December run into four phases.

First, we are going to acclimatize, get you comfortable with a solid training regimen designed to get you ready for the July 4th run. If everything checks out OK at that point, we will step it up a bit and intensify your program. What we will be looking for in the second race is solid progress. Mind you, your body weight will be changing dramatically. I have a feeling that the pounds will drop in much the same way, like a *Biggest Loser* contestant's does. In between the second and the third run, phase three will be an overall preparation period. That will continue to the fourth 10k which will take place in November, at least according to Michael. How would you like to have the bulk of your weight out of the way by Thanksgiving?"

"Is something that dramatic even possible, Stanley?"

"You watch television, don't you? I am planning on working you as if you are a contestant on television. I expect those kinds of results, but you simply must be on board for the journey. The fourth phase of this preparation will be known as the special preparation period where you will take what you have at that time and push as hard as you can. If all goes well, by December nobody who knows you now will even recognize you. I hate to talk about weight, but in just ten months, if you follow this plan, you will effectively be a normal sized person."

"Stanley, it's exciting to think about. I love training, I really do. It doesn't seem fair to me that I get all this help and so many others out there spend years getting their weight off."

"Be grateful, be happy, be dedicated, but do not be fooled. This is not the best or healthiest way to get weight off. I am not a fan of *The Biggest Loser* or of Jillian Michaels' crash diet strategies. There is hell to pay for this down the road, my dear."

Trisha looked worried. "Why is that?"

"The human brain is a very crafty foe, the center of one's being, and it is happiest when allowed to do things its own way. The brain, and that is where appetite is developed, is the master of all addiction. It, by virtue of the way it secretes hormones into your body and sends signals, will work overtime to get you eating and gaining weight. Once the half marathon is over, the need to eat will be overwhelming. Speaking of *The Biggest Loser*, have you seen the reunion shows for the years that all of the winners have kept their weight off? No. And you probably won't either. I am not so sure of their long term track record. If they were all sustaining their television success don't you think the show's producers would take advantage of that? Make no mistake about it; we are going to have to put a formal plan in place once this is over to protect you from that pesky brain of yours. It will have you eat yourself to oblivion by Christmas if we don't attack the problem. My point to you now is, not to worry about how good you have it, but like anything else in life, there is no true shortcut. The fiddler always gets paid. Trisha's hunger tsunami awaits us, but that is for another time. We can worry about keeping weight off later. My guess is that we will have a training schedule for you in the future, too. You are going to earn this on your own, no matter how much help you get from others."

They enjoyed the rest of their meal. Stanley gave Trisha specific instructions on what to do in the next week, and how that would play for the month. She was to weigh in tomorrow, log it on her Nutrisystem page, commit her food life to the tracking diary, work the schedule Stanley had put together, and meet with Stanley in two weeks.

Trisha couldn't help but notice how many of the customers were significantly overweight. Thinking back on it, she had blocked her mind to the problem society was facing, perhaps in a denial type reflex. Stanley was very smart. He was a hard worker, too. Trisha could not believe her good fortune. The next stop was to meet with Sam Giles and take a look at what the money situation was. There was her daddy again, still in the game. He had never left, really. Sometimes the veil between where he was, and where she was, seemed very thin when she consciously connected with him, like out in the pool or up on the running track.

She gave Stanley a hug, thanked him for being such an effective nutritional consultant, and headed for the car. Trisha was due at the attorney's office in just under an hour, which was about how long the drive clear across town would take in afternoon traffic.

While driving she could see the Las Vegas Strip very clearly and from that vantage point, it looked like a glass fantasy playground, even in broad daylight, akin to an adult version of The Emerald City. She loved Las Vegas; it was her home and she intended to spend the rest of her life here. The Friday afternoon traffic on I-15 was unbearable, so she decided to stay on the 215 and get off on Decatur, the next exit. The surface streets looked better, but they weren't. She arrived at the Giles and Associates Law Firm, located just off of Paradise Road on Howard Hughes Parkway, right on time.

Trisha was a bit surprised to find the Giles firm was such a small place. There was a double door entrance of dark mahogany, adorned with huge brass handles. Once inside she was led into a side room set in early American décor. All the furnishings were rich, lavish, and there were what looked at first to be original paintings on the walls, representations of all the wars, the Revolutionary, Civil, Spanish American, World Wars I and II, and a modern photograph of John F. Kennedy, America's 35th president. The suite was very small, but no expense was spared in developing a very impressive motif. Within minutes she was escorted into Samuel's office. It was also copiously decorated, but in his office, and it did seem a bit out of character since he was the elder statesman, the design was all modern.

"Good afternoon, Trisha Jean Martin. Welcome to our offices. If I am not mistaken this is your first visit here. It is really only my son David and I. We do have an intern who hopes to pass the Nevada bar, but one never knows what is to happen in the future. Let's go into the conference room. David will be joining us and Michael is here as well. You are the hot topic this afternoon."

Trisha gulped. She had not known that her brother would be here, but she was not altogether surprised. Off they went, down the hall and into the glass executive board-type room. Once inside everyone extended greetings, Mike gave her a big hug and a kiss, David flipped a switch and the glass went opaque.

Samuel started things off. "Trisha, this is a big day for us, for our firm, and we know for you as well. We have been sitting on your dad's money for a long time, and except to manage the growth fund, no one has qualified for it until now. Congratulations. Just so you know, we managed to keep the fund growing even during the past few years where most everyone's investments tanked. The reason for this has to do with the conservative nature of our money strategies, a slow grower, but safe. Now we are prepared to place a bet, on you, and if we are correct in this wager, by the time you move on there will be more money than ever to work with. Today we are offering you a contract as the trust's first beneficiary. The contract is very aggressive, more than you can even guess; but, should you do everything in your power to implement your end of the bargain, in the end, should you wish it, you could move from beneficiary to a trustee. This is to be a perpetual endowment designed to help selected people reach out and find success in achieving their goals and aspirations."

"Excuse me, Mr. Giles," Trisha said. "If I run four 10ks and a half marathon, by the end of the year, you will make me a trustee of this fund?" Mike started laughing out loud. Trisha smiled. "What's the joke, Michael?"

"Oh, Sis, I love you, more than you'll ever know. If you had any insight as to how special you are, and you will soon, this conversation would not be so funny. What if I confess to you that I had no clue about the endowment when I blurted it out the other day at the club in front of you and Stanley? In truth I did not have any idea, had never even thought such a thing existed. It's the ole man's doing. He set this up. You are going to work for him, not me. The Super Bowl bet is what it is. I imagine that you and I both will find the time we spend together this year to be enjoyable. They are going to be fun runs, for both of us, but the end game is deadly serious. I'm convinced that Dad planted that thought into my head. Like I said at Lucille's last Saturday, he appears to me in dreams and tells me what to do. When I called Sam and told him to cover my line and bill me for your training expenses, he blew my socks off with this outlandish, genius scheme of Dad's. The man never quits, even in death. His is the never ending story." Tears were welling up in Trisha's eyes. She was going to work for her father, after all these years?

"Your overweight life is over, TJ. It is over for good. Don't even bother to think of yourself as fat or even overweight again. It is utterly useless for you to see yourself that way. I imagine there will be a measure of discomfort as you transform into the person we think you were meant to be, but if you live as a runner, a runner you shall be. Show TJ the proposed agent contract, David. Trisha, David is taking control of your running career and for now he is to be your professional agent. It is your job to run, and it is his assignment to raise money on your behalf."

Trisha was in shock—a running contract, like a professional athlete. *Are these guys crazy? I am doing this to fulfill a dream of my father's?*

Trisha took a full twenty minutes to read the simple contract. David, on behalf of the firm and as a representative of Mr. Giles, trustee of the endowment, was authorized to seek funding on her behalf from just about anyone. The proceeds were to be split on a 70/30 basis, Trisha to keep 70% of the money, which would be utilized to reduce the liability of monies she took from the fund to train. Since the funds she took from the endowment were not a loan, or truly an advance, there were no guarantees from anyone, but, should things work out, there would be annual audits and adjustments as needed to ensure that everyone was treated fairly. What could she do? Trisha signed the contract. David signed on behalf of the firm, and both signatures were notarized by Sara Mead, who had appeared suddenly; she had been buzzed into the room by a button from underneath the table, and that was it. Trisha Jean Martin was officially a professional athlete, a laughable reality, at least up until she was handed the debit card.

"What is this for?" Trisha was definitely not used to being handed a debit card. She was used to being a part-time cashier at Target, and living day-to-day, kind of broke most of the time.

Samuel gave her the answer. "We put $10,000 on the card to get things started. Money is not going be your issue. When the bills come in, we'll recharge the account, then call you in and chastise you for wasting money, if need be; we shall see. As for now, you have total discretion, but keep focused on what you are doing. Be assured young lady, this is no gift."

"$10,000 dollars! You're kidding, right?"

"We're deadly serious, and so must you be." This time it was Michael that was bearing down. David just sat there with a grin on his face. After all, she was his first sports client. Perhaps he could land other athletes. He'd always wanted to be a sports agent. Granted, his client had much to do if she was to earn him anything. His cut came out of the money he raised. He was not a beneficiary of any endowment.

"What are you dreamers hoping that I'll do, win an Olympic gold medal?"

Michael started laughing again.

"TJ, you remember the two-headed silver dollar? Want to flip over your next signature?" Trisha noticed that Sara Mead was still right there. David had suddenly produced what looked like some sort of a supplemental addendum to their contract. "You still have time to give us back the money, Sis, but I am betting that you won't." Trisha could care less what was on that sheet of paper. There was no way . . . no way in hell that those millionaires were getting the card back.

David handed it over. It was a scope of requirements, training obligations, weight management schedules, and goals for her from the fund. Her eyes popped out at the master goal. She was to train for and give full attention to qualifying for the US Olympic Track and Field Team as a marathon runner for the 2016 Rio Games. *This is over the top.*

"This is what Dad wants? He wants me to try for the Olympics?"

"No, TJ, if Dad were here, he would tell you it is what he expects. All we are asking is that you try. You sign this and you work for him. We are just the management team. He gave me these instructions in a dream last night. I kid you not."

Trisha ignored his *bull-pucky* vision drama, signed the addendum, as did David, and Sara Mead notarized the document as well. Within minutes the assistant returned with the entire packet, and handed Trisha's copy to her. It was much thicker than the contract was. Perhaps she had not read things as thoroughly as she could have. *Who cares, they're never getting the card back. I'm rich!*

"One smidgen of good advice, Trisha; I assume you have some sort of a deal with Stanley?"

She affirmed by nodding. "Sign a training contract with him first, tell him you have the money to pay his normal fee, then, I repeat *and then* let him read our packet outlining what we expect of you. He'll know what to do. I have a great deal of confidence in his ability to get you through this year at a minimum. Have fun, Trisha. You are truly special and would not be sitting here otherwise. By the way, you cannot remodel your home with this money. That bet is yours and mine to resolve later."

When Trisha had made it back to her car, floating down the walkway as it were, she was so giddy with anticipation she didn't know truly how to feel. Even the box of Nutrisystem food in the trunk of her car could not dissuade her mood. She had money, a father again, a program that looked failsafe, and for the first time in years, many years, she acknowledged herself as a runner.

This team had faith in her, the kind of faith that sends people to places like RIO in 2016. *We shall see*, she thought. Suddenly she felt that it would not be a good idea to bet against her. For a minute, a short minute, she forgot that she was overweight.

Even though there was no plan, she had the time to head over to the club for another hour in the pool, and yes, another mile on the track. This time she pushed as if her life depended on it. That was twice in a single day. She had run two miles today. After a quick shower it was time to get to work. She was hungry, but didn't have the time to stop and eat. A thought occurred to her. Maybe there was something in that dog food box in the trunk she could force down without throwing up. She cracked the box, dug through the packages, and found what looked like a candy bar. It had a nice enough sounding name-MILK CHOCOLATEY DELIGHT BAR, so she worked up her nerve, ripped open the wrapper, and . . . ate it. It was delicious.

The evening at Target was uneventful. Trisha was grateful, she was exhausted, and when she got home at just after 11:00, she took the Nutrisystem food in, unloaded it, and put it away. She could not help but notice how attractive some of the packaging was. She was a bit hungry; in fact she was ravished, so she put the HAM AND BEAN SOUP in the microwave oven for a minute, ate an orange, then the soup and, like the candy bar, it was delicious too. This stuff was not half bad. Tomorrow sometime she planned to go on the website and establish her own personal home page as requested by her trainer. She put her laundry in the washing machine, took the garbage to the outside container, tidied up, took a quick shower and fell dead asleep into bed. She dreamed.

Trisha was on a jet airplane to a faraway place. It must have been some sort of a charter because there was noise everywhere and colors- red, white and blue. There were media types, small television cameras, people with microphones and recorders, and someone in the back was giving a news conference. The plane must have been double decked because there was a staircase.

Everyone was happy. When it landed in some foreign place with a huge airport, the people were mobbed as they exited the causeway into the terminal. There was loud cheering, a barrier to keep a way open for them to proceed, and police protection; it was a madhouse. When they got onto busses, after being hustled by concerned security types, the group was more sedated, even scared. What was going on? Eggs hit the side of the bus; it sounded like guns went off, and there were mobs of protesters all along the roadway leading from the airport. Soon they were in the countryside, traveling a peaceful highway to their destination.

She found herself in a luxury hotel inside of some safe zone where the mood was much more festive. Suddenly she was in a huge stadium with thousands of others, and many thousands more in the seats. It was the most exciting thing she had ever seen.

Trisha was running and running and running, endlessly chasing a white rabbit, up hills, down winding roads, through tunnels and over bridges. A stray dog jumped out in front of her, forcing an awkward sidestep; the dream was turning into a nightmare. Her foot snapped; there was a sharp pain that reminded her of some long forgotten tragic past. The bell was ringing. It wouldn't stop. When it did finally stop, she noticed that she was on a stretcher with sheets all around her, crying and pleading for the pain to stop. The bell started ringing again. Trisha snapped awake in a sweat, both hot and cold at the same time, to realize that the phone was the bell she had been hearing. She had slept right through the night. Instinctively, Trisha checked her Achilles heel and found that the dream thankfully was only that, just a dream. She answered the phone.

* * *

Roger was angry. "Mac, I said no more nightmares!"

Apologetically, Mac, said tepidly, "I know, Roger. I'm trying. Hey, if I were perfect do you think they would have me on this project? Sorry."

* * *

"Trisha, honey, why didn't you answer the phone? I called twice. It's almost 9:30." "Sorry, Mom, I was asleep. What's up?

"It's Saturday, that's what. How about King's Fish House? Can you meet me there at 2:00?

"Sure." Trisha was thankful for the change of venue. This would be a no-brainer compared, say, to Lucille's across the sidewalk.

"Sweetie, I have so much to tell you. I'm sober one week if I can make it to bed without a drink tonight! Sadly, Rachael will not be joining us as planned. She had to leave town on business."

"That's wonderful, Mom. I am so proud of you. See you then. I have to get moving. There is much to do if I am going to get there on time. Love you." She hung up.

Trisha was sore from head to toe and could hardly move. If she were on a traditional program, it would be an easy call to say she had overdone the week, but no, she was a professional athlete, and had a debit card to prove it. Today when she and her mother went shopping she intended to put it to use. She was going to enjoy the card for at least a month before the demon auditors caught up with her and shut down the impending spending spree. That was a fight for another day. Before she went to lunch, she was going to hit the pool hard, and then see if she could best the mile times she recorded yesterday. Yes, there was much to do.

She decided to scramble some eggs, and, oh yeah, the box of Nutrisystem waited, so she decided to see what they had in the way of breakfast. In a moment of reconciliation it was decided to cave and try to enjoy the food, with the eggs. Before going to the kitchen she stopped into the bathroom to freshen up. On the wall by the mirror, where she had left it, was the card where she was to record her weight. Her weight! It was time to weigh-in.

Suddenly terrified, Trisha got the scale out, set the arrow at zero and with trepidation she stepped onto the plate. The scale read 263 lbs. What? No way. She could not have possibly lost 12 pounds in the first week. She got on the scale again. She weighed 262 lbs. this time. There had to be something wrong with the scale. She got on the scale again—263 lbs. Nothing like this had ever happened in her entire adult life. Stanley was not going to have her weigh in again for about a month, well, March 4th . . . actually, the Saturday after March 4th, so this was it for a while. She wanted to laugh, or cry, or be humble, or exultant with pride. She did not know how to feel.

Suddenly buoyant with joy, Trisha Jean Martin said out loud to her great spontaneous surprise. "Daddy, I have just completed the longest week of my life. I am so happy to be working for you."

* * *

Roger smiled. Mac laughed out loud. The game was on.

3

It Takes a Village

I believed a shooting star
when he said that dreams don't lie.
Yes, one moment of burning beauty
to joy the dark night of another's soul.

Wise Mac

Saturdays were *the* day in the Martin family, what with Becky gathering up her Gucci bag, climbing into her big, just polished Escalade, rounding up the ladies to begin a day of eating, of fun, shopping, and yes, laughing. This particular Saturday was going to be a different kind of experience for Trisha Jean Martin; she had acquired a delightful, delicious debit card to help enhance the occasion for her, and so was on a mission with much to do. *Funny how life works out,* she thought, with a sense of satisfaction; just a week ago she was lonely, lethargic, in pain, emotional pain anyway, going nowhere, and generally depressed. Today, well today she was a busy bee.

She made three phone calls; one to REI, a sports equipment store up in The District, a second to Curves In Motion, a plus-sized option sports clothing outlet, and the third to her mother, asking for a ride from the Club at noon, a bit later today than usual. There was definitely something different about her mother and she was looking forward to getting to the bottom of her story once they got together.

Trisha had made a choice. From this point forward she would act as if there was no weight problem at all, she would exercise every chance she had, and internally visualize that she was in fact training to be an Olympic marathoner. That was why, after eating her breakfast, she organized herself as best she could, put what she needed in the trusty backpack, including some treats from the Nutrisystem box, and power walked the couple of miles up the hill to Club Sport. Walking in the chilly morning air was cathartic all on its own. The pace she kept was brisk, but there was still time to think about and ponder her situation, like how she had managed to digress so much. In a short week, Trisha wondered how she had ever let things happen the way they did. There were positives as well. The swirling cumulous clouds overhead were very beautiful in the morning sun and once recrimination had run its course, the budding runner remembered that she still possessed good technique, like the feeling a bike rider has when they climb up and ride for the first time in years. Southern Nevada had such a pleasant climate in the wintertime. There were black birds singing their morning songs, a few stray cats to greet along the way, and she saw a wild coyote on the loose up high on the Whitney Mesa. Walking had many pleasures to offer. Trisha notice something else that Saturday morning. There were people out and about exercising, some on bikes, some running, some walking dogs, and others too. As a group they looked physically fit. *Oh, the mind game that regular exercise plays on folks,* she thought.

Time was going to become an issue today so she was in the pool within short minutes of getting through the front door at the club, enjoying an exhilarating swim. The dread of getting workouts started was beginning to wane, though, like she was thinking, it was still there. Her body was responding to its new lifestyle. That, in and of itself, gave her fortitude, the boost that comes from positive change. An hour in the pool went at a quicker rate. The fifteen minute run, completed with more vigor than she thought possible, resulted in twenty of those indoor laps, a bit more than a mile and a half this time, a huge positive. Reliable Josh Sullivan was there again; he was obviously a dedicated running enthusiast, and quickly becoming a good friend as well. After the run Trish enjoyed a hot shower, spending plenty of time in the sauna pampering herself while getting ready for her mother, who was out front and right on time when she exited the club.

"Mother, it's so good to see you. I trust you have had an eventful and joyous week. Have you been busy?" Trisha's mood was trending positive because it was obvious the weather was going to hold for her long afternoon out and about spending money and having fun.

"Good morning to you too, Daughter. I have been hearing a lot about your new life from Michael. Did you lose any weight this week?"

"Just a couple of pounds," Trish lied. She did not want to give anything away just yet. There were so many pitfalls in her many sad attempts to lose weight, meaning of course that there was nothing to brag about at this early stage. "Mom, before we go into Kings Fish House, and did you know by the way, that it is almost impossible to get their nutritional information online or anywhere else, I need to stop in REI. I am purchasing a bike and want them to have it ready for me when we're done shopping."

"You're getting a bike? Good job on the weight loss, Trish. At that rate you will have it all off in less than two years," she beamed with a genuine smile, but also a comical wink.

If it had been just two pounds, after what I put myself through, I would have declared a disaster. "Yup, thanks for the compliment and about the bike, that's why I had you pick me up at the club, so I can ride out of The District later today. Because of that stupid Super Bowl bet, I now find myself in a huge conditioning program. Riding a bike is an effective way to cardio up without blowing my knees out. My trainer, Stanley Burton, suggested it when I was talking with him on the phone a couple of days ago. I love the idea. It's refreshing to get outside after sitting in front of the television for so many years. I intend to move around from now on as much as possible under my own power. Lord knows, I have enough "stored energy" to haul freight from here all the way to Bangor, Maine," Trisha chuckled, perhaps a bit sardonically. "By the way, Mother, how was that meeting you went to last Saturday night? You haven't mentioned it one bit during this past week. It was that bad, huh?"

They had just turned right on Sunset for Green Valley Parkway. Trisha was looking at the mountains in the distance, noticing patchy wind-whipped snow on top of Mt. Charleston. From this vantage point the scene reflected how her mother seemed, she had suddenly grown very still. For long minutes as they headed towards The District, Becky Martin just drove quietly, something her daughter rarely experienced. Becky Martin, her mother, was at a loss for words. If there was one thing that Trisha had learned early in this, her new way of life, it was that people's moods and other tendencies were hard to judge, easy to misjudge. She resolved to let her mom's story of the Alcoholics Anonymous adventure, perhaps her new lifestyle, dance to the tune of her voice before she decided what this unusual introspective silence meant. She let the issue drop.

"Is that a new dress, Mommy Dearest?"

"I thought you would never notice."

"You seem to have a new outfit every Saturday, Mom. If you wore the same thing twice, now that would be something to notice." Her mother smiled wryly when she heard the warm hearted cynical gesture. "I like new clothes too, Mother. I know you haven't seen me wearing stuff lately, but I think I'm going to be shifting in that department, though not much right now. Today it's about the bike." Trisha was, out of the blue, hit with the sudden desire to eat, didn't feel like waiting all the way to the restaurant, *no wonder why I am fat*, and so she opened her pack and pulled a Nutrisystem goodie out, a Chocolate Chip Scone. "Mom, I had it all wrong about Nutrisystem. This is the best food since buttered bread. I love this stuff. I used to think of it as horrible diet food, but not anymore. Did Michael tell you about my new debit card?"

"What do you mean a new debit card?" Becky Martin's radar went active whenever she was getting the goods on spending money. Mrs. Roger Martin loved to spend money, yes she sure did.

"I am under contract, to Dad, no less. I had to sign an agreement over at that lawyer's place, a ridiculous deal to be in training for the Olympics, and they gave me money. Of course I signed it. They gave me $10,000 for training funds. I would sign a ladies professional mud wrestling contract for that, so I am in training to become a representative of the USA in the 2016 games as a marathoner. How ludicrous is that? I am going to spend money like a drunken sailor, at least for a month until the auditors they have try to stop me. All I have to do is diet, lose weight, and put up a professional effort at fitness. You may not know this, but I love fitness. It's a no-brainer for me."

"Hold on just a minute, Trish. Are you talking about the trust that your dad set up to help people with potential? I remember that. I signed on to it quite a while before he passed. You're getting money out of that fund? This is fantastic news! Let's go shopping baby!"

There was belly laughing in that Escalade as they pulled into exactly the same parking space they had used a week ago. Somewhere deep inside of Becky she was thinking of Roger and the reflection of her late husband brought tears to her eyes. *Why is it that after all this time I dream of him?* Thank God the hold he had on her was a loving one. He had power she had never known in any other human being. *Those dreams were more than real,* mused Becky reverently.

* * *

Mac looked at Roger, who was crying now. He loved his wife so much. It would not be too long before they were together again, at least in his time line.

* * *

The walk over to REI is the beginning of a great afternoon, Becky was thinking. The District always had interesting people to watch; today was no different, and the sun was out. It was one of those warm February days in the Las Vegas Valley. Winters here were all over the place weather-wise. One day it was cold, by local standards, down in the 50's, sometimes even into the 40's, and the next day a warm front would roll in, usually from the south and it could be up into the 70's. Today was one of those days, which was always a good thing on a Saturday. Trisha seemed to be excited as they meandered into the outdoor goods store.

Inside there were all sorts of fascinating things: bikes, accessories, clothing, camping equipment, all different types of outdoor shoes, tools, helmets, and well, you name it they had it. Becky had never been in this place, ever. It was no wonder why. Her idea of outdoor fun had a decidedly different tone to it, something that began with a credit card and personal service. Except for the credit card part, this was definitely not her type of a retail outlet, but for Trisha, it was a different perspective altogether. She looked like a kid in a candy store. She also seemed to know exactly what she was there for. She went to the front desk and asked for one Kendall Bryant, the person she had talked to on the phone earlier. During the walk from the car Trisha had explained what was going on.

"Hi, I am Kendall Bryant. Can I help you?" He was a very handsome young man, perhaps in his early 20s. The calves on his legs, down under those long green shorts he was wearing, were inflated like balloons, not filled with water, but rock-hard muscle. You could tell just by looking at him that he knew from experience what he was talking about.

"Good afternoon, Mr. Bryant. I am Trisha Martin, the one who spoke to you just a couple of hours ago about a bike and some other stuff, and this is my mother, Becky." "Hello to both of you. Call me Kendall," he said smiling.

"Kendall then," she laughed. *He is also a gentleman*. The debit card was burning a hole in her wallet and she was itching to make something happen with it. Trisha needed to be very careful in making the proper selection. If all went as planned, this purchase would set direction for some major cardio work in the early months of her program and just may give her an advantage in the game she was playing with Mikey while getting ready for that first 10k run, come Independence Day. She was not interested in any *fun-run* jog, but instead wanted to push the whole way down the road and truly celebrate July 4th this year. "So, what have you lined up for me, Kendall? By the way, I love those shorts you are wearing. Are they for cycling in?"

"Absolutely, these are Cannondale Quick Baggy Bike Shorts. They sell for $60. If you are interested in some women's versions we have great product lines, like Novara Bonita Double Bike Shorts, and we do have larger sizes.

"Getting back to the bikes, I have picked two that you may want to consider seriously. Let's take a short walk over here." Trisha and Becky followed him through a very interesting array of outdoor products. "I have lined them up. First, take a look at this one. It is a Scott Speeder S50, the 2010 version. It is strong, will bear much more than your weight, and you can make this bike go very fast, that is if you like speed. It is yours for a bit under $900. The other one, priced just a bit higher, is a little over $1000. Did I mention that if you join REI's preferred customer membership club, you'll save 10%? Anyway, this other one is the Novara Strada Bike. It is a bit sturdier than the Speeder, but you cannot go wrong either way. If you'll trust me to narrow your choice down to these two, I suggest that you ride them both for an hour or so and then pick."

Although she did consider her feelings carefully, Trisha was never one to take a lot of time in deciding such things so she moved rather quickly in choosing the Speeder. By the time they left for lunch, she had the deal all set up, having them mount their sturdiest tires, fitting a matching helmet, *I hate helmets but this is the 21st Century after all,* some gloves, a small tool kit, riding clips for the new shoes she picked out, a mounted water bottle, and a pair of riding shorts with a matching nylon shirt. It blew her away that they fit, so she decided to keep them on for later. When they checked out, the young man assured Trisha that everything would be good to go right after lunch, and presto, she had spent $1,357.25 of the debit card money. *Let the bet tricksters eat that one,* she giggled to herself. It was time for some hot tasty food and she was hungry. If this were any other life she was in, the food would get gorged. As it was, she had to be very careful when she was hungry like this, even with the exercise. There was so much to do and a long way to go if she were to succeed in this monumental effort.

The problem with King's Fish House, for her, was that the food was not nutritionally published. She would be able to get it done, but it was not so easy when one had to guess at what was in food recipes. Some people, well-meaning or not, never learned. *Why conceal the nutritional content at a place like this?* Oh well, if she could not be careful in a sea food restaurant, where could it be done? This was not the last time she would be faced with the problem of not being able to dissect the menu to match her specific needs. She loved to eat, always would, and would make it work. Food for Trisha Jean Martin would never be an exact science.

Trisha and her mother were seated in the bar area and waited on by a guy named Henry. He was a funny man, rather stout. He was balding, and in fact, his head looked like a tan colored human bowling ball with a band of hair around his ears, and his mustache was curled at the ends like one of those old barber shop types from a hundred years ago. "Good afternoon, ladies. You look ready for some great food and spirits. Can I get you something from the bar to loosen the occasion up? My name is Henry, by the way. No, I am not Henry the Eighth I'm not, it's Henry the Ninth I am. I did get married, but not to the widow next door and she's not been married any times before."

Trish was laughing but Becky couldn't even hear him. She just realized that sitting in the bar was a bad idea. She was thinking wine, big time. Her hands started to shake, but then she got hold of herself. "Not for me, thanks. I'll have some ice tea, no, make that hot tea, with lots of honey and cream too," she said timidly. Trisha motioned for the ice tea. Thank God she didn't have to worry about alcohol.

"Are you OK, Mom? Do you want to move to the other side of the restaurant?"

"No. I like it here. Just keep the juice away from me, Henry the Ninth; I don't drink anymore. But, I do have a question." She was trying to change the atmosphere of her experience from wanting a drink, back to wanting to have fun with her special daughter, and thank the Lord for Montyne, her sponsor, whose image and strong advocating life of sobriety were playing its intended role—with the way her mind was supposed to function. One of the interesting things about her new way of life, which still sucked, was that it was hard to think of what a belly full of booze would feel like when one had taken to a head full of AA. Becky blurted out a sly thought, "If your wife didn't have eight Henries before you, how can you be Henry the Ninth?" Henry smiled, then turned away and took leave to be about his assignment.

It didn't take long before Trisha and her mother found their way into the lunch menu, *or was it the full menu, who knows*, and for Trish to go directly at her mother. "OK, Mom, now out with it. Tell me how your AA program is going. Have you really stopped drinking? What do they do at those meetings? Are they boring? Is it expensive? Are the men and women divided into separate meetings? What is a sponsor anyway? Do you have to pay a fee to have a sponsor? What are the Steps? Is it like church? Do you sing hymns?

"Slow down, Child. That's too many questions. Yes. Share. Not at all. Free if you're broke, $1 is traditional; some give $2. Sometimes yes, sometimes no. A person who helps you learn to stay sober. No. Twelve suggestions on good living. No. Definitely not." Becky was laughing out loud because she remembered all the questions and was able to give rapid fire answers. She had outwitted her daughter.

"What?"

"What do you mean, what?"

"What you said. It made no sense."

"Made perfect sense."

"Didn't make sense to me."

"Can't understand why; you asked the questions."

"I forgot some of the questions though,"

"Do you remember the answers?"

"No. Now I can't remember the questions right or the answers," they were both laughing. "I'm buying lunch today, Mother. My new card is working; I am busting my tail out there like never before, and I am running out of time." Trish looked deadly serious.

Henry's assistant stopped by and laid out the most incredible looking sour dough bread with butter, a generous heaping of honey, cream, some hot water with Earl Grey tea bags, a plate of lemon wedges, and ice tea for both of them. They thanked him for getting everything right; Trisha had pulled a little pencil out and had been marking the King Sushi sheet up. It did not look as though her mother had even noticed, or perhaps she wanted to be surprised at the appetizers. Here came Henry to make sure that they were having a good time.

"My dear ladies, I would like to apologize profusely for walking away from you in the middle of our very important conversation. When I was but a boy my father would always sing that stupid song, you know the one about Henry the Eighth, *I'm Henry the Eighth I am, Henry the Eighth I am, I am.*" He was actually singing, and pretty much on key, too. "It seems, although I never did the genealogical research, that for nine generations now, the first born son has always been named Henry. My son, Henry, has vowed not to marry any girl unless she lets him carry on with it."

"How old is your son, Henry, Henry, and did your father Henry have anything to do with this?" Trisha asked this while handing him the King's Fish House Sushi sheet. Henry was smiling with pride.

"He's nine. Now let's see here. You're going with the Costa Rican Whitefish, Kyushu Yellowtail, Halibut caught near Santa Barbara, and some Spicy Tuna Rolls, all Sashimi sized for two. This looks delicious."

Becky was beside herself and pale with what appeared to be true fear. "Whoa there, King Henry. Trisha, that is way too much. I never eat sushi. Forget it. It's disgusting. It will be hard just to watch you pretend to be a barbarian from the Orient." Trisha was definitely having fun this Saturday. Henry could not stop laughing, and walked away fast as Trish told him to get going.

"Now, Mother. Do not be so closed-minded at trying new things. That is what we are about now. You have your new program and I am up against it training for an Olympics that is only six short years away. We need to live a little. Plus, I want to push the envelope on those bastards who took my fat freedom away, enslaving me with this money card. Just try it. I have never eaten sushi either. It's now or never." Her mother looked like she needed to be transported up to St. Rose Dominican and checked into the hospital, and her smile was gone. Now she did look sober.

"So, Mom, can we try the AA thing again?" She dabbed the tiniest amount of butter on the heel of the half loaf of bread that was screaming at her, reminding her again that imminent death awaited if she did not start eating. In her case, and she knew this, the exercise program was brutal and way out of line for someone in her situation. She needed to eat. Whatever happened here would be long gone by the time she got back to the Nutrisystem food later. She was itching to get on the bike and ride.

"I have forgotten the questions and the answers, Dear, now that you have ordered up food poisoning for the weekend."

"Give me a break, Mom. When is the last time you heard of someone at King's Fish House getting sick off of the food? This is gourmet cuisine and you know it." Becky squeezed her nose up, turned heavily *made up* eyes down, and puckered a big frown. This was going to get fun. Ying, the assistant, stopped by and dropped off a couple of plates, some chopsticks, sauces, and a healthy dab of something green. What was that stuff? She tasted it. Wow! It's like horse radish or something not spicy, not hot, but spicy and hot both and then some. Just then Henry came by to see how things were going.

"You're not familiar with the wasabi and how to use it, I see. You guys really are novices at sushi aren't you? Here, now take just a dab of the wasabi, mix it into our special soy-based secret recipe sauce created just for you. Do you know how to use the chopsticks?" Both of them shook their heads no. It looked like it would take a court order to get Becky started, but she relented. "You hold them a bit like a pencil, well two pencils, using your thumb and first two fingers, and then you pinch down. Why don't you practice picking up some of the sugar packets for a while and see if you can get the hang of it before the food comes out. Just remember what Confucius say."

Trisha took the bait, no pun intended considering the appetizers that were on the way.

"What did Confucius say?"

"Confucius say, "Man with just one chopstick go hungry." They laughed; he left again.

Becky solemnly spoke up. "I will take one bite, that's it."

"Now, Mom, if you like the sushi, you may eat more than your share and then have to eat your words." Mom was looking pretty grim at the moment. They kept working on the mastering of their new eating utensils. It became apparent to Trisha that her mother had indeed used chopsticks before and was bluffing because she did not want to eat the sushi. Surprisingly, Trish got the hang of it pretty quickly too. Trisha didn't worry much about the bread and butter. Her mother was removing that temptation at a record pace, what with only a single bite of the appetizer to satiate her until they had their lunch, which they had not even ordered yet. Of course they could get more bread, but before that happened here came the sushi. It was the moment of truth.

Henry took charge of getting the food organized on the table. It was, he said, the least he could do since these fine daring women had bravely undertaken the culinary challenge of their lives.

"Ladies, I have tried and tried to help this establishment become more customer-friendly. It is so hard to change the spots on a leopard. In addition to the fact that we do not publish the nutritional information, we have a special rule here." Trisha was listening and looking at the sushi. It looked pretty good, she had to admit. Even her mother found the presentation attractive.

"What rule, Henry the Ninth?" Becky was not exactly in a cooperative mood yet.

"You see the chef over there, staring straight at you?" They nodded. He had his arms folded and also two huge knives, one in each hand crossed over his chest. He did look menacing, like some sort of a Samurai culinary warrior king. "He say tell you, no lunch order, till eat sushi *first*." Henry thought he was so cute. "At this establishment we require all virgin sushi cuisine adventurers to take a small bite of each sushi choice before we take the main course order."

"That's bull," snorted Becky. "I will take one bite of the Yellowtail." She expertly took some fish with her chopsticks, swabbed it in the wasabi-laced sauce, and down it went. It was impossible for her to keep the pleasant surprised look off of her face. At the same time, Trisha did likewise with the whitefish, and then they traded. That was before they both took one of the tuna rolls, and just like that they had sampled all of it. The chef never even smiled. He just turned and went back to his kitchen. "Oh my goodness, this stuff is great," Becky mused.

Henry was beaming with pride. "I usually never recommend a competitor but you ought to try this other sushi place. They cater primarily to lawyers. It is located downtown by the courthouse."

"What's the name of it? Maybe I have heard of it before," said Trisha.

"Sosumi." It never ended with this guy. "What can I get you for lunch today, ladies?"

Trisha went first. "I am going to start with Wild Newfoundland Bay Shrimp Cocktail, and then it'll be a cup of White Bean and Smoked Salmon Soup. If you please, for the main course I will go with Farm-Raised Idaho Rainbow Trout. Can you blacken that a bit?" Henry nodded. "For the sides I would like the special today, Ratatouille and the Sautéed Fresh Spinach." There was oil in the Ratatouille, but she guessed that is was the good fat and would help her maintain energy levels during the afternoon ride she was looking forward to.

"Excellent choices, if I may say so myself; and now for you, Becky?" He must have picked up her name in conversation. "Oh, Becky, may I please call you Becky?" she smiled the big *yes, you can.* "I think it is hardly fair that you eat the sushi all up just because your daughter here is taking her time ordering, no?"

"Funny," she smirked. "I will say, Henry, that I am shocked to have missed this food for all the years of my life. I have always thought of myself as . . . open to new ideas where food is concerned."

"I would like the King's Crab Cakes. Since I am hungry, and not on a diet today, I would please like a bowl of New England Clam Chowder. For the main course, don't you think the Wild Alaskan Red King Crab, the 1 ½ pound size, would go well with Garlic Mashed Potatoes and Sweet Buttered Corn?"

"That is the yummiest order of the day around here and I have served quite a few lunches. I have special crabs set aside just for you."

"OK, Henry, I will not get crabby at your lousy jokes. What is so special about these crabs?

"They are straight from prison."

"Prison! Whatever were they in prison for?" She was playing along.

"They were always pinching things."

"Go get us our lunch, Henry. Good lord." Trisha tried not to laugh, but instead to look annoyed, and failed. Henry needed an entertainment career. He sure did. She turned her attention back to the sushi. It was going fast. Her chopstick skills were holding her back too, in this competition anyway.

"Mom, I thought you were only taking one bite."

"Just being polite, Dear. One must always take care to show appreciation at times like this." It looked to Trisha as if her mother were making up for lost years at the art of eating sushi. "Trisha, dear, tell me more about your diet and exercise program."

"Sorry, Mom, I want to hear about the AA program first. You are sober a week?"

"Tomorrow, but we never look at more than today. This is day 7 for me."

"Mother, I take it the AA thing is going well for you so far."

"Well, as I said to Henry the comic over there, as of now I really have stopped drinking. The meetings are very entertaining to say the least. After some opening rituals where we read a little, people share the tales of their experiences, hence the sharing I was referring to. For me it is anything but boring. It is eerie how spending an hour with other alcoholics cures my drinking urge . . . for a bit. Some of the things they say are so awful, and some are so funny. It is the great tragic-comedy of my life story."

Henry showed up with the soup. It was delicious. Of course Becky filled her chowder with those tasty little oyster crackers but Trisha's only accouterment added to her bean soup was the freshly ground pepper. For once the waiter stayed out of the conversation, to everyone's relief.

Becky continued on. "It is not expensive in the least. Even a street urchin can afford this treatment. About half way through the meeting they pass a basket—according to tradition—and you throw something in, like at church. Some folks do not contribute at all, others give pennies, most put in a buck, and some put in two dollars, that kind of thing. Thank heavens both men and women are in the meeting I go to. There are ladies only meetings and also stag meetings; in fact, there are all kinds of meetings. I like what I have, though. You're not going to believe this, Trish, but I have friends there who are barely off of the street. One guy lived under a freeway pass for fifteen years!"

"Who is it? Do I know him?"

"Now, sweet Trish, if I said AA, and you know it is an acronym, what do you think the letters mean?

"Alcoholics Anonymous."

"You pass the test, Trish. It is an anonymous program. What is said there, who says it, it stays there. I am not telling, but you do not know that guy, I sincerely hope." They both laughed.

"Mom, last week you took a call from your sponsor. So tell me. Just what is a sponsor again?"

Becky's eyes filled with tears and her voice cracked. "First off, there is no fee. This is a pay it forward program. There are all kinds of sponsors in the Program, some good, some great, and some, well, maybe not so good. In the life and death business of getting sober though, even a *not so good* sponsor is better than the alternative. Having a sponsor is all about the Steps. Oh, and by the way, even though it is all about God, it is nothing like church. Though we have not sung yet, I would not be shocked if we did. I haven't been there for a birthday meeting, but I am told we sing "Happy Birthday" to celebrants who make a year or more. My sponsor is a wonderful person named Montyne C."

The afternoon luncheon was one of the best times Trisha Jean Martin could remember since the bad old days when they had lost her father and their lives had been turned upside down. The conversation took a decidedly more adult tone, they both had stories to tell of their life changing week, and it was very evident to Trisha that her mother was on a track that made her much more valuable to a daughter and to herself as well. She seemed to have a renewed purpose. Henry was a delightful waiter and the food was so tasty. For Trisha it was a huge meal, one she thought she would regret, but not really. When it was over Trisha felt very generous and added 20% to the bottom line of a $123 tab. You only live once, and she was not about to go easy with that new debit card. It was such a boon to have it in her purse. She had been broke for the many years of her adult life and now she had money. They shopped for a couple of hours in The District area; both of them spent money, on themselves, on each other, and on other family members. When it was time to go Trisha felt that in just the one week she had been in this new life, she had really been born again. She was working for Dad now, and as such was under new management. She could feel his presence. Little did she know.

The afternoon sun was beating down on them as mother and daughter prepared to separate for the day. Trisha exchanged her flops for the riding shoes, donned the helmet, fashioned her distinct look with new sunglasses, and was mounting her new 2010 Scott Speeder S50. As promised by the affable sales representative, Kendall Bryant, the shiny black bike was customized, adjusted to her leg length, and ready to go. Trisha was so excited. "Black on black, Mom, it is truly me."

"Let me get a photograph of you riding." Trisha hopped on, took it for a short spin and came cruising by slowly for the photo opportunity. When she saw the picture she was horrified and embarrassed. She had forgotten just how big she was. "Mom, delete that awful thing right this instant!"

"Sorry, Daughter. Father's orders here. I felt impressed just now to shoot an historical picture of a future United States of America gold medal winner. This shot is going to be heard around the world. Just think of the millions of people you are going to be helping when you try to explain this photo on worldwide television after your medal ceremony. I am going to have it framed, twice, once for you and once for me. My copy will be on the wall in my entrance hall within a week.

Don't you just love the pixel resolution on these new telephones, Dear?"

"Oh bloody hell, Mother. That was so sneaky. Now I know where Michael learned to be, well, Michael. Please don't hang that up in the entrance hall. You know what I look like there? I look like a giant panda cartoon movie character riding a mini bike. It is . . ."

"It's so you, Trish. Honestly, I think you are one of the most beautiful people, physically beautiful to make myself clear . . . anywhere. I love the new you."

Trisha Jean Martin was now a cyclist, a new updated person in a new updated life, a life to be savored, though not without a bit of sacrifice. She simply had an amazing ability to shut out of her mind what she must look like riding with traffic down a public street, huge as she was, on a bike. As she traveled east away from The District, she found herself enjoying the warm sun on her back. There, whistling in her ears was a refreshing breeze flowing through her *lighter than air* helmet. For the first time in years, Trisha was free. She could smell the desert all around. Even the scent from a runoff drain contributed to precious moments of solitude. Her legs were pumping speed into the bike, sometimes so fast that fear began to creep in on top of thrill. This was an amazing machine. Obviously, bikes had changed with the times, too. There was another aspect to this new workout, something unbearably discomforting to her, and that was the knowledge that she was going to have to deal with gnawing pains of a gluteus maximus nature. Her butt was going to be sore and there was no getting around it. *You knew this would happen.*

Trisha rode her new bike on and on for two hours that afternoon. It was a workout she had planned and it was necessary. The sky was bright, the billowing clouds beautiful, the traffic was light, and it was a perfect afternoon for a good extended ride. By the time she got home, Trisha had decided that the bike would become her main mode of transportation. She began to look ahead to work shifts at Target. Going to work used to be her means of getting money. Now, getting into Target was her diversion from living in the demands of a debit card. For most people, going to work was not something they genuinely looked forward to, but for Trisha it was. She loved her life there, had no intention of losing the roots of humility, or of abandoning valued friends. Target and Trisha were bonded in ways that had nothing to do with earning money.

The days started running together, one after the other and then one more after another. The routine was fairly simple. The runner would get up, eat, clean the house, eat just a bit more, and then hit the bike and ride to the club. She would always get into the pool as quickly as she could. Just like anyone else, for her the hardest part of any swim was getting into the water. She maintained the same schedule, spending about an hour in the pool, but she intensified the hour from week to week, pushing herself. Once she was out of the water, Trish would shower quickly, get comfortable, read the paper and enjoy a cup of coffee or tea. She would never eat before she hit the track. If Josh was there they would run together. Truthfully, for him it was social running at this point, but only for the 15 minutes that she was committed to. Those few minutes were hard running for Trisha. She was grateful that he was nice enough to run with her before he moved on at his own pace. It was of paramount importance that she protect her knees while she was still heavy. After the run it was back into the sauna, the hot tub and an hour of peace, time she spent mostly reading her novels. Trisha would eat a Nutrisystem snack before getting on the bike and riding to lunch. For her it was still always about the food. She still loved to eat, but now she paid a better price . . . in exercise, instead of a bitter price in fat and lethargy. She was not afraid to ride all over the valley in order to reach her favorite places. Since she was in weight loss she could not eat like she used to, but after a while she knew just what the right thing to eat in any establishment was, the right food for her at that time and on that day. It was a routine that was rooted in knowledge gained through work and sacrifice. As many times as not, she would eat alone. With the bike, once she got used to sitting on that little seat, the reward of solitude was among the most treasured aspects of any given day. On the other hand, she was always up for company too. Trisha had been a reclusive couch potato who had just spent the better part of twelve years sitting down. Sometimes chance (do you mean chance or change?) is radical. This lifestyle was an insane paradigm shift in behavior and attitude.

Trisha did not like riding at night, so it was a rule of hers to be home no later than 5:00 PM. During the next two weeks the weather held nicely, too. In the evenings it was either work or play. Her circle of friends was growing of late and there seemed to be no end of things to do. On one particular night though, there was nothing to do but eat and watch television, just like in the bad old days, the one difference being that of food choices. She turned on the news.

"We turn now to a human interest story unlike anything you may have heard of. Who are you talking to this evening John?" The reporter was none other than John King, the current big shot at that network.

The person being interviewed was Brad Peterson . . . . right there on CNN. There was a face from her long ago past. Trisha was astonished. She had not seen or heard from him since he left Green Valley High School after her sophomore year. He looked very good; Brad was brash and confident, just as she had remembered the one boy she had a crush on since she was fourteen years old. The old juices, perhaps surprisingly, perhaps not, stirred in her as she looked at him. If he saw her now she would be humiliated. Trisha was suddenly ashamed again of what she had become, feeling a sweep of anxiety, mortified embarrassment . . . hate fat. *I am such a failure.*

* * *

"Knock that crap off!" Roger threw the thought at her.

* * *

She felt the tinge of envy, of self-recrimination, slip from her conscious thought and let it go, almost as if she had been told to by some unseen presence in her persona. It was like a wisp from Casper the Friendly Ghost, her invisible protector.

"Dr. Peterson, tell us a little about you. How does a brilliant young pediatric brain surgeon, nationally recognized as one of the leading specialists in your field, just throw it up in the air and head off to a war zone, as a volunteer no less?"

Trisha could not believe what she was seeing. Where had she been not to know what Brad had been up to all these years? He was tall, dark, and handsome, just as she remembered. He still had that *boyish* look about him, though the little goatee on his chin gave away his age, at least to her. It had little streaks of grey in it, a very unusual trait for someone who was just thirty-three years old. In a dream filled past, from a long ago life, a place she could remember, but only when she needed to cry, they had run together, side by side. He was the fastest kid anywhere, and was the only one who could keep to her pace. As a sophomore she constantly challenged him for supremacy in distance running, laughing all the way. That he was a nationally ranked high jumper, his true talent, did not faze her at all. They never went on a date, never had a kiss, spoke romantically, nor was there any evidence that feelings of that nature could have been shared between them. He was too old, then. So she loved him in her heart, the secret place. Suddenly here he was, right on her television screen.

"Ever since I was a kid, my father drummed into my head the notion that getting outside of one's self and helping others was far more important than personal success. It may sound corny but this is a dream of mine. I am very proud to be allowed to participate at this level. One of my goals in life is to get married and raise a family, so it has to be now or never for this type of an adventure . . ."

Trisha lost track of the conversation for a minute. *He is not married,* she thought. There was no way on earth this guy was gay either. *Oh good lord,* she reflected, *I need to get this weight off, now!* It was not to win a man that she needed to lose the pounds. She was not the type to live in a romantic fantasy that would never be, but just the thought of him running around out there made her very uncomfortable in her skin. Suddenly there was a new sense of urgency, not to do more, because she was now doing entirely what she could; there just was.

"John, lest I sound like a phony do gooder, there is much to gain from this experience that will help in my career down the road . . . . . ."

The conversation lasted just a few more minutes. When it was over she felt as though she had lost him again. What fuddle butt nonsense was this? If he had thought of her name just one time in the past fourteen years, she would be shocked. *Oh well, time will tell the truth of all things*, she mused. She turned on the reading light, picked up the new Robin Hobb novel from the Old English end table and let herself slip into the world of Liveships, love, dragons, assassins, Rain Wild adventures, life in the Six Duchies, and the world of Bingtown Traders, real true to life experiences that she could wrap her imagination around. *There is nothing that heals my soul better than a well-written fantasy novel.* Even so, Trisha's eyelids grew heavy, the result of the day's fatigue, and she peacefully drifted into snoozing an hour or so later. She slept for some hours, and when she awoke, it was to a reading light shining in her face. There was more than a headache, she was sore all over from what felt like worthless sleep. By the time she turned the lights out and then did crawl into bed, deep sleep returned instantly. It felt wonderful, the kind of thing that sweet dreams are made of.

* * *

Roger and Mac went right to work.

Trisha Jean Martin, along with other athletes, climbed into the van outside of the hotel and began to make her way out of the heavily guarded compound. The area was very animated with people coming and going all over the place. She was in a festive—if guarded mood, riding on a wave of translucent flowing time and she knew not where. Everyone around her was an athlete of some type. Why would a person like her be in the company of all these amazing athletes? Then she noticed she wasn't fat, not even normal looking. Her body was a finely tuned machine, ready for the race of her life. From somewhere outside of the van a clump of dirt hit the windshield, obviously an unwelcome gift from a not-so-nice guy. There he was, jumped on immediately by police. Trisha looked around. There was more than just the race, a lot more. Politics and sports made for a very entertaining cocktail. The scene slipped from her grasp.

She fast forwarded to some place, out in the country. The crowd around them was very excited. It was race day. People were pushing forward to get a closer look at her and the others as they approached the starting area. Was that her father over there behind the pressing crowd? Impossible . . . or perhaps it was not impossible. The summer sun beat down relentlessly, though she could still smell and feel moisture from the night before. That beating sun was quickly turning the pleasant cool moisture into suffocating humidity. The many varied and multi-colored flowers were in bloom, the trees rich and leafy green, and the mud on the side of the road was still providing evidence of the rain that must have come in last night. As unremittingly hot as it was, which the humidity driven sweat running down the side of her neck demonstrated, she realized that this was a break in the weather from yesterday. Someone, he looked a bit like her trainer, what was his name? He was visibly animated and giving her advice. She could not make out a word he was saying, and then he thrust a telephone at her, her cell phone. He had it for some reason.

"Hi Honey, I'm home in front of the television, just got here a few minutes ago, have the coffee on, and can't wait for you get it done, for me, for us, for all of us, but for you the most of all. You would not believe what happened last night as we . . ."

Her phone rang. Suddenly she was so disoriented that she could not remember where or when she was. It was her cell phone. Where was it? Where was she? She was in bed, dreaming something that she could not quite remember, something about an athletic event and great excitement. She reached for the phone.

"Trisha, good morning." It was Stan. That was weird. She thought for a minute that she had been dreaming about him. Dreams were so weird, at least hers were.

"Hi, Stanley. How are you?"

"I am fine, Trisha, except for the fact that you blew the swim workout this morning, your run, and our scheduled meeting. Are you giving up on me?"

"No, Stan. I am sorry. I must have forgotten to set the alarm and slept in. What time is it?" "It is 11:37 on my clock. Don't worry, Trish; everyone knows how hard you have been working. I am sure it is just your body saying *hold on a minute*—that it needs some rest. In fact I want you to stay in today, relax. We are more than half way through your first month and you need a day off. We can reschedule

Lloyd Wendell Cutler

for tomorrow in the morning, same time—right after you clean up following your morning run, if that works for you."

The time was agreed upon and Trish drifted back into sleep, so tired and in seconds she was dreaming vividly . . . again. *She was out on her bike, riding the Red Rock Canyon Loop, and at a racer's pace. There were two riders with her on this run, and they were out in front, so she pushed the pedals harder to catch up. When she got there she discovered it was her father and that friend of his, the second class angel, Mac. They were smiling. "Daddy!"*

"So, my racing runner is a cyclist. You never cease to surprise me, little one, like the day your mother told me she was with child. We just kind of stared at each other for what seemed like minutes, and then we laughed at our bombshell-gift from God. After ten years we were going to have another baby."

"It's that stupid Super Bowl bet, Father. My knees will not take the pounding at this weight. Hey, all of a sudden I am not fat at all. How did that happen?"

"Trish, this is how you look to me. I do not see you as overweight. From the prism of my perspective, you are a well-honed athlete, a world class runner with a big future."

"Where are we, Dad? How can this be?"

"You have been working so hard these past few weeks that your body has shut down on you. You are in a deep sleep, which is why we finally have some time. For you this is a dream, a deep and insightful dream, Kid."

"Well then, let's keep this show going, Father. I like not being fat for a change. By the way, thank you for being so happy to have a late-life child. I really miss you so much. Michael says that I work for you now and that I have to become an Olympic runner, something even more far-fetched than this dream is, do you think? Hey, if you can make me a skinny person in the dream can you do other things too?"

"Trisha, my special one, the memories of our earliest runs together are among the choicest thoughts I hold dear. I just loved it when you would run around the block with me in the mornings. You were such a little firecracker. I knew before you were even born that yours was to be a very special life. We have much to talk about today and much to get done, but, we have the time. Do you remember the old movie

I would play for you when you were just a little girl? You called it the Heart Light movie."

"ET?"

"That's the one. Do you remember your favorite part?"

"I loved the part when E.T. took off with all the kids on their bikes. I think they were trying to help him get home."

"That is what I am trying to get done with you. I need for you to come all the way home to the person you were meant to be. Pull back on your handlebar." Mac seemed to do something and when she did they took off in flight, rising higher and higher over the beautiful desert near Red Rock Canyon out on the extreme west side of the Las Vegas Valley. It was a stunning turn of events and yet Trisha did not seem a bit ill at ease. She wondered if that secure loving feeling was a part of the dream. Of course it was. What a different dream this was turning out to be. Who would think about a dream, during the dream, in essence, dreaming about dreaming? The wind blowing through her hair was refreshing, the smells of the desert bloom so breathtaking, and the view was as beautiful as anything she had ever seen. She was flying like E.T. with her father and Wise Mac, who was no second class angel to her.

They circled south along the front of the Spring Mountains. Over her right shoulder she could see the snow-crested peak of beautiful Mt. Charleston. They flew even higher and she could see on the other side of the mountains all the way to Pahrump, the rural community in a vast desert valley west of Las Vegas. Trisha tried to burn this experience into memory, ensuring that this was one dream she would not allow herself to forget. They flew in silent companionship, a moment between father and daughter that no one could ever take away from her. Her dad was taking care of his little girl in a way that no one else could.

After a while they circled east and sailed past Black Mountain, the one with all of the antennas, and then on over the hill to Lake Mead. The sight of Hoover Dam with its new crossover bridge was magnificent and a memory worth savoring all on its own. The city view as they flew back, not far from a jet on the final approach to McCarran International Airport, would render any trip to the top of the Stratosphere Tower meaningless. They glided to a soft touchdown on her street in Whitney Ranch and rode up into the driveway. Just like that the flight was transitioning from the event of her life to a wonderful memory, hopefully somewhere inside of her head other than at the subconscious level.

"Come in, Dad."

"We can't, Child, but . . . we need to talk, so shut your eyes and then open them." She did and suddenly they were in a meadow, the same one she had seen in a previous dream. There were others there too.

Suddenly they were in front of their old Hillsboro home, the exact home, except it was out in the meadow near a brook, in the clearing by a copse of evergreen trees. Was this heaven? Dad got to take the whole house with him when he left? He put his arm around her shoulder and invited her in. Once in the entrance hall, she noticed the picture of her on the new bike right out in front of The District from just a few days ago. "I just love that picture, Trisha."

"I'm not so sure, Dad. What does it look like to you? To me it resembles a circus elephant riding a unicycle." Roger laughed.

"I agree with your mother on this one. To me it looks like one hell of a story that will have to be explained to the whole world when you win the Gold in Rio. Bob Costas is going to have a field day with that shot."

"What is it with you people and your delusion of my athletic endeavors? How is it everyone is so sure that a huge, overweight, out of shape 30-year-old, will impossibly reach that level of competitive fitness?" They had moved into the kitchen, the kitchen she grew up in, and Roger handed Trisha one of her mother's famous homemade cinnamon bagels. As she ate it, it donned on her that it just may be impossible to gain weight in a dream. She should eat everything she could get her hands on today. This fantasy now had a name. It was to be called the no-cal pig-out dream. Right on queue . . . her father gave her a huge glass of ice cold whole milk. It was so tasty in the chilled frosty glass that she considered the possibility that this may be more than just a dream.

"Trisha, take a walk with me through our home." They proceeded into the family room, the furniture was arranged just the way she remembered it, and then he led her out onto the back patio. "Ours was a wonderful home to grow up in, Dad, really—it was. I was never embarrassed to bring friends into this house. There was rarely ever any tension that I could put my finger on. It is a slice of heaven that you have carved out for yourself here. Are you lonely?"

"Never. I have friends over all the time and family, too. I am able to torment Michael whenever I want. Your mother sleeps right in this bed every night and doesn't even know it. I still have to live by the rules that govern the physics of life and life after life, but this is a great life for me. Today is very special as you must know. You have a long haul ahead and in the decades to come I hope that we will be in touch often. I am enthralled with what Rachael is accomplishing. It is sad that she cannot have kids, but it works out for her in the eternal perspective. All in all I have a huge life going, and from this side of the veil there is no end to it."

They moved to the back patio, the one she had shared with her father many a time during her growing years, for it was the place they mingled when it was time for him to parent in the one-on-one category. This was the place where things sometimes got very serious between them. On this day the view was beautiful. There were elm trees nearby, just like the ones they had when they had lived on Sepulveda before the move to Hillsboro Heights. There were spruce, white pine, and on the other side of the brook she could see flowers of every sort. The smell matched the view, fresh and clean, but it was the huge tall palm trees out in the front of the home, so high you could see them from the back patio, that took the cake. This was indeed a slice of heaven.

"Would you like to spend the night, Trisha? I can arrange that. Time flows very differently here and you do look tired. Flying is harder than you think, yes?" Trisha laughed.

"Sure, Dad. I would like that very much. I am getting sleepy." For him, the thought of his daughter sleeping in the other room was more than comforting. He had waited years to be with her.

"There is serious business at hand, Kid. It is far larger than you or I, yet our small part in the big game may prove pivotal. What did you think of young Brad Peterson when you saw him on CNN last night? I caught you feeling sorry for yourself in your current physical state. Did you hear me chase your self-pity away? I guess the uptick means that you like him, still. Who wouldn't? He is young, handsome, successful, a good-hearted man, seems to care for others, looks reliable, likes to run, loves kids, wants a family . . . ."

"I get it, Dad. Yes, I like him, even from this distance. What can I do about that? Just look at me."

"Normally I would leave that up to you. I have never pestered you about your situation until now. Mac here brought me in on the big picture and this whole affair was his idea. I am proud to sponsor your comeback. I have complete faith in your ability to obtain each and every thing we have talked about, even the Olympic medal quest, though that is not the relevant objective here, and as has been previously noted, we need your help. All you need now commit to is acceptance . . . having the faith necessary to give it your best shot. We need you to believe in you. Let me rephrase that need. From what I have been looking at, you already believe in you, isn't that so?"

"Promise, Dad that you won't tell. The fat is gone, just not yet. I have hated living like that and was primed to make the big change. It works out, that's perfect. Your money is in play, and I plan to take total advantage of that, you must know by now; the money only cements the process. Whatever I am to become in the athletic category, I am going to find out just where it takes me. Will I become the world class athlete others seem to be requiring of me? Who knows, but as long as someone is fronting me money I will pretend at least to be in training to run an Olympic marathon. You have me there."

Somewhere in the recesses of deep sub-conscious thought, Trisha Jean Martin knew she was already sleeping. Why then, or how then, could she go to sleep? And yet she was tired, very tired. Her father shared some hot cocoa and toast with her, led her to the bedroom she had slept in as a child, respected her privacy as she donned a cotton flannel night gown, and then prayed with her before she climbed into the soft single bed. She was immediately asleep and once again dreaming, a dream within a dream.

The darkness which surrounded her was suffocating. Something was not right. It was cold and humid, and there was a breeze accompanied by a stench which made the air barely breathable. Trisha felt claustrophobic and was afraid to move. She could not describe her feelings, but suddenly after such a wonderful experience, she was surrounded by a grating sadness, overwhelming was what it was, so evil in its origin. What place was this? She felt her way along the obsidian wall and made her advance upward, one step at a time. She crested the darkness and could suddenly see light down below, far below. In the purple haze, somehow lighted by an emanation from an unknown source she could see what looked like people, or zombies, *some form of human-like beings. They were moving about performing various mundane physical tasks, seemingly numb with inner pain and resignation that reminded her of the hopelessness she had seen depicted in the lives of American slaves she had studied during her first and only semester at Saddleback those many years and a lifetime ago. Were these the minions of some evil and its purpose that was forced upon them, for surely they did not want the path they were commanded to follow. They did not talk, did not smile, and did not reflect anything that she could see as the joy of life. Again she thought what place is this?*

"The universe is teaming with life, Trisha Jean Martin, all different kinds of intelligent life."

Trisha was so startled that she almost fell off the side of the overhang where she stood. It was Wise Mac, the so-called second class angel. His finger to lips—a universal message conveying the simple command to be still, compelled silence. "Do not give us away by allowing yourself to feel anything here. This is just a miniscule sliver of the huge pie which makes up the murky and terrifying malevolence we have been at war with since the beginning of all time. Be still, Child." If truth be told she was gripped with a fear she had never experienced, not even when she lost her father after the injury. She stood silent and petrified.

"Who are they?" Her whispers were barely audible, even to herself; she was gripped in terror stricken panic and did not want to give them away.

"We call them the deceived. Many of them are, or were, good folk who lost their way and were seduced into thinking the path they voluntarily chose was righteous and superior. Many of them did not believe in the reality that people can be caught between competing forces of good and wickedness, so unbeknown even to themselves, they chose the path of self-indulgence, immorality, a lack of value for the lives of others. They were looking to be free of the encumbrance of obedience. Instead they became consumed with the pleasures of flesh, without taking into consideration the consequences that are necessarily the result of those choices. It is a very complex place, this prison of the soul. Some, even here, live in the prism of denial and yet seek goals and objectives which are the unrealistic fantasy of their deluded minds. We do not have the heart to show you what happens

when they try to leave, or worse, find their way to punishment from the great and dreadful power which commands what is left of who they once were. They are the deceived. You were brought here to see for yourself and to find a way to remember, somehow keeping in mind these things when you are presented with forks in the road which we on the front lines of this grand cause are so familiar with. Unfortunately for you, having been kind of drafted into the service of eternal progression, you will get noticed. Count on it, dear. Don't you think we should move on to a more pleasant setting?"

"What do you mean, get noticed."

"When evil looks you in the eye, offers unbelievable reward, and does it with feigned love and respect you instinctively recognize, it will be the result of your role in the scheme, a far more dangerous place than the ordinary choices you would face if not directly a part of our cause. This risk is the awful price you are being asked to pay by engaging at the level we have need of. It is vital that you are aware of this. We do not control things that are attributed to us. We do not have say in all things. You are being recruited to get right into the line of fire, Trisha. We do not deceive in any way; we do not alter the flow of free choice. It is what makes us who we are, thus you get this glimpse of Hell, the permanent separation from God and His influence, and the fair warning that you will be noticed. I assure you that an intervention of some sort will make its way into the path of your evolution. We believe that you will recognize the truth and have faith in your unique goodness. Were it otherwise, there would be no calling for you in this. We love you completely. Pardon the obvious, but it is time to get the hell out of here. Close your eyes and open them." She did.

The snow was blinding in the wind, so different from where they just were. Mac and Trisha climbed up along a trail through a steep upgrade on the side of what looked like a huge mountain. "It's not very far," Mac was yelling to be heard over the wind and the blinding sideways snow. The cold was brutal and Trisha was sure that they would freeze, though it was less than twenty paces to the little hollow where there was some reprieve. Inside Mac found what he was looking for. He handed Trisha a pair of fur boots, of course they fit perfectly, and a massive overcoat that had to be from some type of polar bear. "Put on the goggles first and then the gloves," he said as she was given the necessary accouterments for the remainder of the hike. "I have loved this hike for more years than you could ever hope to count, Trisha. This is the most beautiful place in the entire realm."

In just a few minutes they were back out in the snow working their way up into the gap, a rocky outcropping so far above the tree line that Trisha felt a huge sense of vertigo. The goggles improved visibility and she could see that they were indeed high in a mountain range—with peaks everywhere. She was warm and snug inside of her protective clothing and was beginning to marvel at this great adventure, though she could not remember why or how she came to be in this fantastic place. She almost forgot that she was in a dream, almost. Dreams at this level were so new to her, to be able to cognitively recognize that she was in a lengthy dream, but not wake up.

Within an hour they approached a small bridge, handmade with rope and what looked to be laminated maple wood. Halfway across she looked down and could not see the bottom. There was a type of misty cloud far below, working its way through the depression between peaks that stretched way up into the sky. This was a most amazing place. On the other side of the bridge the trail widened and suddenly turned directly into the face of the mountain; no, there was a crease in the mountain which turned into steps, downward in-between what she thought may be solid granite facing. The steps led downward for at least the length of a football field and suddenly there was a huge door, made from the same wood as the bridge, with strong iron hinges and a large wooden handle that had no locking device. Mac opened the door and in they went. Their world changed again.

Having shed their gear, for it was warm and very pleasant inside, they strolled along and were met by others who seemed eager to greet the sleeping mortal one. It was not often that someone still in their mortal state was called in and Trisha was immediately set upon by some of Mac's friends. Trisha took one look back at the door they had come through, but it was gone.

Imagine that.

"Trisha, I would like you to meet Richard Polk, an old friend of mine, very old in fact. This is Dick's wife Nancy, and the gentleman on the left is none other than my father, McDonald Rhodes."

Trisha was beaming at the introductions, for they seemed to be very fascinating people, and she responded to each in-kind, but it was Mac's father who won her heart. He didn't look a day older than Mac, and yet, the wisdom he emanated accentuated his maturity. How old was old here anyway? The rocky tunnel they were in was well lit, albeit from an unknown source, and the way down the walk was very agreeable, with not much of a decline at all. The walls did seem to be a part of the mountain, but they also looked finished, something on the order of what detailed stonework resembled inside the Great Pyramid of Giza. A closer look revealed several appealing color variations and beautiful art engravings, which of course are not a part of Giza's four hundred and eighty-four foot monument to the Ancients who came to Earth from the stars. How did she know that? She felt at home here with Mac, his buddies and his father. After some time, something less than an hour, the four found the decline to be a bit steeper, and then the pathway led straight down a spiral staircase carved directly into the rock, a most unusual and creative work of art in and of itself. When they arrived at the bottom of the steps they walked outward heading for natural light and open air. They emerged from the mountain onto a large patio platform, and out into open sunlight, where the fantastic view overwhelmed her senses in a burst of joy and wonderment. Just a few minutes ago she had shed protective clothing from a blinding blizzard at high altitude and here they looked upon what could only be described as a piece of heaven. In this special place it was not cold at all. The valley below was lush and green; it was dotted with cottages, homes, small huts, and even a few mansions. There was running water throughout the valley, flowers of every sort, walkways, some finished in cobblestone and others looked to be just dirt. There were horses, riders, dogs and cats, open meadows with grazing deer, stags, moose, antelope, and even bison. Trisha thought she saw a wandering black bear alone at a higher elevation off to the south. In some areas there were tall pine trees, yet other places sported tropical vegetation. There were birds flying everywhere. It was a symphony of color, sight, and the sound of music—nature's harmony.

Nancy was the first to speak. "You like our little slice of eternity, Trisha?"

"Very much so, and who wouldn't? This place looks strangely familiar to me now that I think of it; I just cannot put my finger on it. I would like to live here."

Mac chimed in. "You never know, Trisha, but not today. There is much to do and we are beginning to run out of time again. Dad, why don't you fill Trisha Jean Martin in on why she is among us this morning?"

"It's that damned fool, Brad Peterson," the sage angel spoke like he was an impatient old man and suddenly looked a bit of his age, Trisha thought. "He's a good enough person, and we look forward to having him as part of our community, but we do not need him here at this time, and he has jeopardized a far reaching project that no live human could possibly grasp."

"Hold on a second, Mr. Rhodes. Is something wrong with Brad?" Trish was worried, though she could not even visualize her role in his life, not now so many years after they had played childish games on the running track.

"Father, didn't you try to get Joseph Kennedy to intervene in this misadventure young Brad Peterson has himself caught up in?" Nancy was smiling wryly at the idea. It may have been apropos, but presently an American bald eagle flew just overhead. The scene was majestic. Trisha had never seen such a creature up close. The wing span was enormous, and she could almost feel the flapping of the huge wings which she could definitely hear. This was the most unbelievable dream ever and it was getting more interesting in the here and now.

"You mean President Kennedy's father? You wanted to invoke J.F.K.'s father in Brad Peterson's current life? What is this all about, you guys?" Trish was astonished at hearing such a famous name, one she had rarely thought of in her secluded life.

Now it was Mac's turn to teach a bit of American history to the willing student. "No, Trisha Martin; my wife was referring to the President's brother, Joseph P. Kennedy. He is a classic example of why the committee has much trepidation in these types of direct intervention. Let me explain it to you.

"In the early 1930's, research that was leading to atomic physics, namely atomic power and the resulting calamity that new mass destructive weapons would reek on human civilization. The era of super modern man was in full swing. The consequence seemed inevitable; we needed someone to help prevent a global holocaust and for that person to be in a position to do something about it. We quickly decided that the Kennedy clan, led by none other than Joseph Patrick Kennedy, the same person you so eloquently mentioned, could be set apart and influenced to that end. It was believed by many, myself included, that his oldest son Joseph P. Kennedy, could be groomed to become the US President after World War II, and that he would make wise choices under intense pressure in a make-it or break-it moment, thusly preventing the end of our project on earth. The man responded with such flourish that he became too selflessly ambitious while serving in the war himself. At the time, Kennedy's tutor was none other than our own Harold Laski. Apparently, Brother Laski in his zeal was too effective.

"The US Navy initiated a very special and dangerous method of bombing heavily fortified German positions, an operation called Aphrodite. It involved creating remote controlled bombs out of B-24 Liberator planes that had to be flown to altitude where the pilots would bail out and the plane could fly on to its target under remote control. Unfortunately for us, Kennedy's plane exploded prematurely and he was sent on to this life instead of the Presidency of the United States, where he could have participated in the greater good."

"It was the Deceivers that did it," McDonald chimed in. "I am sure of it. Anyway, the burden fell upon his brother John Fitzgerald Kennedy, and subsequently the Cuban Missile Crisis, encouraged definitely by the Deceivers, did happen as planned and JFK did his job admirably. The world was saved. Please believe me when I tell you, young lady, that we were on the edge our seats just like everyone else in those days. We do not have the power or authority to choreograph events like some people who have blind faith believe. There is no predestination. This is not a high school play where everyone learns, rehearses, and performs their part. That you may not remember any of this when you wake up speaks to the truth of these things."

Trisha was pondering the little slice of eternity which Nancy was referring to, looking out over the peaceful and life-saturated valley. It was such a lovely place to be, something she could settle nicely into when some far future turn of events led her back, and she did have a heart swollen with hope. "Nancy, I love this place. I would live here if welcomed. Mr. Rhodes, why tell me any of this if I will not remember it when I wake? What's the point?"

"You pose a very good question, Child. We are deep in your subconscious mind now. Remember you are sleeping within a dream and the imprinting we do here can have a huge effect on your behavior. It is very rare that we go in this deep with someone, but the stakes are very high. If you were not receptive to our message, we could not be here at all. It is a testament of your faith that we even attempt this visit. Listen closely to this challenge and your life may be better for it, and ours as well.

"I have to confess that I once stood on the precipice of life as you do, for I was challenged to fulfill a destiny that I could not fathom. In my wildest dreams I never thought that day would morph into where we are today, and yet here we are. You must take tiny steps each day, looking forward to making a difference in the lives of others, thinking of ways to be a contributor in the great game of life going on out there. Everything you hope to realize in the future begins today with these special thoughts. The future is very uncertain, but it need not be a totally inscrutable and vague thing. In large part, where you end up will be shaped by the accretion of daily activities, small and simple things which end up as monumental accomplishments. In your hands we may be placing a great responsibility, but success in life, no matter how it is looked at, can only be completed in small bites, savored on a daily basis. For us, you included, the morrow is today, this one day. It is all you have to work with. I am reminded of an old religious hymn. 'Today, today, work while you may. There is no tomorrow, there's only today.'"

No dream could be this vivid, she was thinking. In just a millisecond, the bald eagle they saw only a few minutes ago perched on the pillar just in front of them seemed to be settling in, listening. Was such a thing possible?

Nancy, Richard's incredibly beautiful wife, was beaming with love and pride at her husband's wisdom. Trisha could see that in this, all things would make sense for her and the life she was living at this time.

"You want to lose all of that weight, get in shape, run marathons again, little one, isn't that so? I can see the dream lost in the great hole that fills your heart." Richard went on. "There are intangibles that you must consider if you want to have that elusive objective made yours. We all know that in your secret place, you dream of that Olympic adventure, that wondrous experience you will not publicly accept as possible.

Trisha could not keep the tears from streaking her cheeks. This was a dream she was sure to remember, somehow. Yes, she wanted the *impossible; doesn't everyone in their predicament, whatever malady besets their journey, want the impossible?*

Richard went on. "Let me give you three simple tokens that will guide you to this place. We need this for you more, much more than you need it for yourself.

"Make each day count with purpose, yet moderate that purpose with balance. This is the easiest of the three tasks we set for you, the generalities that become specific to meeting your destiny. Let me elaborate a bit here. The largest majority of our kind—human beings—validate work as a necessary evil, something to be avoided if at all possible. They view life in terms of enjoying the fruit of labor, rather than labor itself and the growth that it brings us. In learning the true purpose of hard work, the gratifying prize of productivity, it is incumbent upon you to balance the many demands placed upon you in the prospective of serving Him whom we all want to be more like. Keep the focus on that when you are working. You serve the Lord first and foremost. That brings us to the second objective.

"Live in the Spirit of your relationship with God. Everything you are granted will be part of your personal companionship with the Lord. Believe this; a personal relationship with God requires dedicated time and effort. Read about Him, learn His ways, follow them to the best of your ability and take time to pray, which reveals to one's self the soul's sincere desire. This form of spiritual exercise, much the same as what you are putting yourself through physically, will bond you to the greater purpose and make all things possible. If you are steadfast in this approach, you will not fail when it counts the most. The third thing is the most rewarding of all.

"Find ways every day if possible to be of service. When you serve the least of mankind you are serving Him. When you serve the greatest of all, you are yet serving Him, and Trisha Jean Martin, this task provides instant gratification, even when not reciprocated. It is through doing good in the world that you get relief from being so wrapped up in yourself. Your brother Michael is a good example of this trait. Study his example and be of service to others. That is what your father's foundation, the one you will one day lead, the Roger Martin Foundation is what we think you will call it down the road, is all about. It can be the vehicle which will set your eternal perspective. Remember, Child, what you do each day will become the groundwork for the next.

"Now it is time for you to go take full advantage of the great rest which has come upon you, but, it's incumbent upon me to give you a special gift. With just the slightest genetic touch, you are being given special talents of discernment. You will be able to see the truth of things when you look into the eyes of others." Wise Mac stepped forward and touched her forehead.

When she awoke, Trisha again found herself back in her father's mansion down in the valley.

She got up, stretched, felt so refreshed, and tried to remember where she had been in her sleep. She could not. Trisha wandered out into the kitchen, then onto the patio and looked up at the mountains in the distance. They looked so familiar to her, but she could not place just why. A beautiful, huge eagle flew overhead, circled around, and then flew horizontally across the meadow from the plaza she stood on. Unbelievably, its wings waggled as it flew away, high into the cloudless sky. If felt something like acknowledgement.

Her father approached from behind. "It's beautiful here is it not, Trish?"

"Oh, Daddy, I am so happy, happier than I ever remember. I wish I could stay here forever."

"In time, little one, in time. You slept hard. Was it as good as it looked? Did you dream?" He, of course, knew that she had. It was the purpose of her entire visit to this realm.

"I did. At first I thought it was going to be a nightmare, but it wasn't. I can almost remember, just not enough to put it to words. I recall a terrible place, a place that looked like Hades. That was the part that I thought was a nightmare. Then, I think I can place it, yes, Wise Mac was there. He took me on a journey and I met some other people, and there was someone special, I think it was his father."

"That would be Mac Rhodes, a good man. He had a nasty childhood and was a bit of a maverick in his youth. He did not get his head right until after he was fifty years old. Mac was one of those guys you'd think would never get here, but he did, and we are all better off for it, none more than Wise Mac, his son."

"I really love him, Father. He gives good advice, though I do not know what to make of it. He did not really talk about the running and losing weight or anything like that. His focus was on things that have to do with virtue, stuff like spirituality, purpose, and helping others. I *see why those things are a big deal in life, though just not how they relate to this monumental task ahead."*

"It is a simple thing, Trisha. Anyone out there can lose weight, get some exercise, and get in shape. To be the one person on the planet to win a gold medal in your sport at the Olympics, why that takes a special commitment, and so he armed you with special tools that will enable you to hone yourself in just the way you are needed. Remember, this project is not about you at all, the greater purpose is so much larger than that. As such, you will be tested many times along the way. It is vital that you have the tools in place to help you avoid pitfalls and meet those tests. There is so much at risk with your life, now. Sadly, though it need not be, you are in harm's way. The deceivers will be there testing you on every step of your journey. In actuality, they consider you a very easy target and so must be laughing at our simple plan.

"Give your dad a kiss and a hug, Trisha. It is time for you to go. This has been the most fun I've had since just before the little incident up on Mt. Charleston that day. I have total faith in you; this is the purpose you were born to fulfill. This calling was ordained before you even were to be, and such is the way of things from the eternal perspective.

Trisha hugged and kissed her father, (how? since he had no body) and dream or no there were real tears. Slowly he and the entire landscape faded away in the mist. At first the color was turning to shade, then to grey, and then to black.

She fell into the emptiness of the dreamless night. After some time, she knew not how much, her eyes opened to the darkness of her room, her home in Whitney Ranch. At first she felt a great loss, as though she had been abandoned by her family, but a sixth sense slowly made her aware that she had been sleeping for a long time, a very long time. When she climbed out of bed to relieve herself she could suddenly feel her enormous weight, the albatross of her life. It was then that she remembered dreaming, dreaming of things and places where she was not fat anymore. Trisha was back with her fat, and to add insult to injury she was famished. She suddenly decided that she deserved to eat, and eat big. The diet queen initiate intended, no matter what hour of the night it was, to head up to Fatburger and load up. She deserved it. Not only was her fat back, but the fat thinking, too, she guiltily moaned.

Her body was quivering with hunger, the likes of which she had not felt in some time. She was so hungry, she feared that she would starve to death before she could make it to the car. They took so long to cook at Fatburger she did not think she could wait that long and suddenly decided on Del Taco, where the food would come up quickly, then getting a hold of her senses, changed her mind yet again. She was weak with the pang of starvation. Trisha Martin felt real fear setting in. *What is wrong? Something is definitely wrong with me.*

* * *

Somewhere in the bowels of hell, Stump Killer, a loyal members of the Centex Charlatan Alliance, the CCA, was making a move. One of the things he could never understand about the human race was the need that renegade pious types exhibited for individualistic freedom, the poser attitude of choice. Life was so much easier when choice was not the issue, and he intended to help do his part. His conversion to the truth, the freedom of submission to the CCA, had been emancipating for him. Stump never was good at making choices, and now that he didn't have to think like that anymore he enjoyed the freedom of Centex, an existence where no one was any better or worse than anyone else, at least that was what they were led to believe. *But, then again, everyone else around here is an idiot, so I am still better.*

Trisha Martin, somehow a threat to the CCA, was driving towards Taco Bell. It was 3:30 in the morning. On the way, she decided that what she really wanted was Fatburger, even with the wait. Stump was pouring it on from a distance, laughing cynically. "This is so easy. All I have to do is tweak her weakness and poof, she will be out of the game on the first try. Those guys on the other side are losing it, wasting their efforts on such a weakling. I will have her sneaking food, a little at first, then more later on. In no time she will be all the way back to her starting point and beyond.

* * *

Trisha was famished. She had endured all different kinds of hunger in her life, and when she was out there big time the desperate hunger was overpowering, but for some reason this was different. Trisha drove up Sunset towards the back entrance to the drive thru, completely overwhelmed. Once in line another car moved in behind her. She was in line going through for sure now, succumbing to the excitement and dreading it at the same time. *Live a little, Trisha,* she thought. *I am still going to show a loss and no one will be the wiser, except you, of course.*

* * *

Stump doubled down his bet and suggested that she switch from a loaded Fatburger and go for the King Burger instead. *Why not add onion rings and a strawberry shake to go with the fries, too? You deserve this after all you've been through,* Killer sardonically suggested. He started laughing out loud, so loud in fact that his buddy, Imp Rogue walked over, caught wind of what he was trying to do, observed the helpless tub-a-lard sitting in the food line, and then he began to giggle. Soon they were both laughing.

* * *

By the time Trisha had arrived at the order sign her palms were sweaty, her heart was racing, and her purse was opening. There was no money inside, just the debit card. Suddenly it donned on her that the order would show up on the bill with the monthly expense report that was automatically downloaded at Giles' office. The debit card that signified her employment by, not only the Foundation, but her father—dead though he may be, was also very transparent. Her guts, stirring about, turned ice cold. Trisha would weather the storm before the calm, for suddenly she wasn't hungry like before. Somehow she had been rescued by the damnable debit card this time.

"Good morning. Welcome to Fatburger. Would you like to try some onion rings with your order today? We are having a half-off onion rings sale between now and 11:00 am."

Trisha asked herself what the "right" thing to do was, no matter how hungry she was. How did she plan to explain this to her team? *If I were advising someone else, not me, what to do right now, then what would I have them order?* Suddenly she knew. It just came to her.

"No thanks on any of that, though I must admit the deal sounds very tempting."

* * *

Stump, whose heart stopped, looked into Imp's eyes. They were done laughing and would have to wait for another day, bested by those pesky Eternals . . . for now. There would be other days.

* * *

"I am going for the Fat Salad Wedge with chicken, no dressing, and I will have a large ice tea, with lemon and extra ice." It was done. She felt empowered as never before in this line. *I can eat healthy anywhere, anytime, no matter what, and I feel good about it, yes, I do.* After eating in the car, she drove home, enjoyed a Nutrisystem Fudge Graham Bar, drank a cup of skim milk, walked out on the porch, picked up the newspaper and relaxed in her living room. She was not tired at all, nor was she hungry.

Stump got stumped this time and Trisha Jean Martin had no idea that malevolent forces were at play in her life. She was slipping into the vortex of the longest war in the history of the Universe.

When first light approached, Trisha ate again. She had not eaten in two hours and hunger was creeping once more. There was a big day on the horizon and she did need nutrition. She scrambled three eggs and combined it with Nutrisystem Pancakes to make a somewhat hearty breakfast. After finishing the newspaper, watching the morning news, getting ready for the club, and straightening up her home, she ate for the third time, a banana, an apple, and an orange. She was at the water's edge by the outside pool at 7:00 am sharp. It seemed like much longer than one day off as she began the monumental task of treading water, back and forth, back and forth. Her muscles were sore and tired this morning. *It's no wonder,* she thought, *that people abandon their exercise programs so easily.*

This was one workout that she hated and did not think would ever end. Thanks to the food she had consumed since waking, her new physical condition, and the biological consequence of raising her heart rate, cardiovascular circulation had its way, and when she turned to the backstroke she felt much, much better. Trisha decided not to count the first twenty minutes of this swim so by the time she had logged an hour and twenty minutes of pool activities, she felt great. The sun was out, it was a warm morning for mid February, the breeze felt good, she saw people she knew and enjoyed, and it now felt as though the extra rest had done wonders for her. Her body had responded properly.

As usual, Trisha took a relaxing shower before hitting the track. There was still so much weight on her that special care had to be taken to protect her knees at this point. Quite frankly, after just two weeks of running she wanted more than her body would allow. Trisha Martin was becoming impatient. She was beginning to feel better and her natural instinct was to push things, perhaps too much. She was allowed twenty minutes, and that was it. In the weight room it was all about reps, and so she focused on several rounds of light resistance repetitive movements, sometimes relying on light weights, and at others the resistance bands Stanley had shown her.

She enjoyed this part of the workout because it was possible to stress the whole body without putting herself in danger of the dreaded sports injury. Late last week, Stan Burton, her trainer, had given her the go ahead to put real time in on the Life Force 95xi Elliptical Trainer, as a supplement to running. Here was where she could go and go without endangering her knees. Today she put an hour in. After a good soak in the Jacuzzi, plenty of steam, another shower, and getting dressed, she walked into Stanley's office right on time, right into the lion's den. There was David Giles himself, the boss's son from the Law Firm, Stanley Burton, trainer extraordinaire, and a new person she had never seen. *What do these guys have up their sleeve?* It was still just a couple of weeks from the worst Super Bowl in history and the tricks just kept on coming. Oh the joy.

Reece Chartheart had known Stanley Burton for more than five years, and in all that time had never seen him act, either pretentiously or without substance to back up his ideas, but this was not just a tough sell, it was ludicrous. He was in Stan's office right now with some pencil sharpening lawyer, and being asked to make a $175,000 bet on what had to be the impossible dream. Just outside the office was the subject of the wager, a very nice looking girl, one who had legs, long legs, perfect looks, all with the exception of unmolded clay to the tune of some 175 lbs. if he had it right. She was huge. The young lawyer, one David Giles, with Stanley's support, was going on about a non-profit dedicated to helping gifted people reach their potential, a marketing campaign that Nutrisystem could take advantage of, and yet, not an exclusive arrangement.

It had been getting more entertaining by the minute this morning and now he was about to meet their victim, Trisha Jean Martin, the runner. What a joke. The traditional Nutrisystem platform with large folks was to have them sign up for one of their food plans, get them to use the website, set goals, and use their tools to reach those goals. The lucky few that really got something done were sometimes elevated to the "paid spokesperson" status, so that they could help promote the Nutrisystem way of life. This opportunity was quite different, perhaps a bit ass-backwards.

"Trish, come on in. I have someone I would like to introduce you to."

"Good morning, Stanley. What is *he* doing here?" She was looking right at the little boy lawyer, David, the kid who always left her feeling a bit uncomfortable. She saw him as unproven, a bit stuffy, and she didn't really like that he was able to 'officially' interfere with her use of the debit card, Trisha's newfound plunder of riches.

"Good morning to you too, Trisha," David interjected. "It is always a pleasure to see you." Stanley took quick control of the conversation. "Trisha, David is working, so let's let him work. I would like you to meet Mr. Reece Chartheart. Mr. Chartheart . . ."

"Hello Trisha, please call me Reece," and just like that they shook hands. Something about him left Trisha feeling warm. He was tall, dark, and handsome, had a warm smile, seemed personable, that sort of thing. He had managed to make her feel good without saying a word.

"As I was saying, Mr. Chartheart . . . I mean Reece, is with Nutrisystem, in their sales and marketing department, and he's reviewing a suggestion that David and I have made. He wanted to see just who it is we're talking about."

Trisha couldn't help but smile. "What is it that these scoundrels have up their sleeves, Reece? You must know not to trust a lawyer. I think Stan can be trusted, but . . . I am not so sure."

David tried to jump in but was cut short. "Perhaps I can explain, Trisha . . . ."

"Perhaps not, David, I have a different idea." Stanley gave it a shot but Trisha put the kibosh on that.

"I don't want your version either, loving trainer. I would like to hear Reece explain things, without interference from scheming backers of that evil brother of mine who tricked me into a bad Super Bowl bet. She looked directly at Reece and bid him to tell the story as best he could. This was going to be very interesting. Trisha had an hour to kill before lunch and the afternoon marathon bike ride. She was working tonight, too.

Reece Chartheart spoke for the second time. "It is a pleasure to meet you, Miss Martin."

"Oh please, Reece, do call me Trisha, or you can call me Trish. If you wish you can call me TJ like my older brother, the devil himself, but do not call me, Miss Martin. That's way too stuffy." She was staring out the window into the pool. There was Michael himself swimming laps. He looked to be working pretty hard too. Perhaps he wanted to be in better shape when they went running this summer; perhaps he did this on a regular basis. Who knew about him?

"In any event Miss, um . . . , Trisha, your team here has set some very ambitious goals for you, weight loss goals, physical conditioning achievements, and some rather unusual athletic objectives."

"Tell me about it. These clowns have me penciled in for the 2016 Olympic games and I am to win the Olympic Marathon gold medal." Reece barked out the most insidious laugh at that one, she joined in, Stanley started laughing as well, but the stuffed shirt, David Giles looked to be every bit as boring as he sounded when he talked, though this time he did not even squeak. "They bribed me with money, got me pointed in the right direction, and I'll have to admit some 'out of the gate' progress. At the rate were moving I will be in tip top shape faster than the Mars Rover, Opportunity, can climb a hill.

"There is one positive that I have to confess. I have been smitten by the Nutrisystem food that good Stanley gave me the other day.

I like your product. It is convenient, easy to prepare, very portable for when I am on the go, which is all the time these days, and, unlike Lucille Ball's vetavitagegamin, it taste good, too. There, I have just laid out the commercial for you. I am so fat that I could easily qualify for The Biggest Loser, and all I have to do is shed 175 lbs., which could make me your next poster child. That explains me, but what about you? Why would you want to talk to me, of the thousands of obese newcomers to your program? Why Trisha Jean Martin, Reece Charthouse?

Reece could not wipe the smile off of his face. "That brings us to the why of it, yes it does.

Mr. Giles here wants to commit you to a regimen within the scope of our program and get this, he is asking us to pay a thousand bucks a pound for your success, not to you, but to the Foundation you are indentured to. The contract is right there on Stanley's desk. I have already scanned it to our legal department for review, but I think they will give me permission to sign it right now before this little acquaintance session is completed."

Trisha was flabbergasted. Who paid that kind of money for weight loss? There was no way this company had that type of agreement with anyone else. She was sure of it. This had to be some kind of a joke. "I wouldn't sign it if I were you. These guys cannot be trusted. You will already owe me $12,000 just for the first week of work."

"I assure you Trisha Jean Martin, we are not fools. You see, there is to be no payment until you weigh in at 105 lbs. or less. No money unless you absolutely succeed. Not only do you have to lose the weight, but you have to adopt the program in its entirety."

Stanley piped in. "Just as you said, Reece, they have approved the contract and you are free to sign right now. I am not sure why they sent a 'happy smiley face that is winking' in the subject line.

Good Lord, she kept that little slur to herself. This life was getting more complicated by the day. Maybe the debit card wasn't worth it after all. "Please define the words 'adopt the program in its entirety' for me, Mr. Chartheart."

"Have you been to our website, Trisha?" He took a drink of water, loosened his tie, picked up the hard copy of the contract, and awaited her answer.

"Just once to look around, though I do not remember much of it. Can it be all that difficult?"

"The one out of pocket expense we are agreeing to is the food. We'll ship the food to you at no cost as long as you lose at least ten pounds each month, each and every month. You do not get to carry over excess loss, so if you lose twenty pounds in a month, you will still have to lose ten pounds the next month, or your Foundation gets charged back for the food that month. There are to be no secrets where your participation is concerned. This is strictly business for us. We want to make the payment to you, believe me. If you clear this weight and get anywhere near as good as everyone says you are, it will be a marketing boon for us.

"Let's take a look at the site." He had his trusty iPad turned on and open to Nutrisystem.com before she crossed over to where he was sittng by Stanley's desk. "Under the *My Program* tab you will be required to log all the food you eat, your weight, list your measurements, log your exercise, and keep a journal. You will be required to join our Community, which compels you to setting an *Overview*, keeping a My Page active, work out of our Inbox, *Blog* once a month under this contract, participate in our *Chat Room* once a month, join a *Discussion Board*, and set up *Tickers* to track you on a general basis. The good news here is that this stuff will help keep you focused all the way. The food diary is very flexible. You can add any food you want in any format, even the bad stuff. You just have to be totally honest. Is this something you think is possible to keep up on? We have people who will help you every inch of the way. Trust me when I say that we want you to succeed."

Trisha thought about what he had just said. She had not considered the work involved with this Roger Martin Foundation thing. It was just donning on her that this was going to be the never-ending story of her life from here on out. *If I succeed at this project with any degree of accomplishment, the commitment will wind up owning my life*, and she thought again, that once the running game took on a life of its own, her life would not really be her own anymore. Did she want that? But for the love of her father she absolutely did not want to become a public person. She did love her father though, and of late, she felt very close to him. It almost seemed as though she was with him from time to time. If she failed miserably at this little project, how would she feel then? She would feel dejected, sad and unhappy, that is how it would be, and for her that would not be acceptable either. What if she did what most folks did? What if she got physically fit, lost the majority of her weight, but did not go anywhere special with the running gig? That would be perfectly OK with her to say the least. Being normal again would be such a godsend. The idea that she could run competitively had not even occurred to her for many years. If racing stayed put in the little box of memories, she would be fine and who cares what others thought. What they were asking was impossible to say the least, but should she burst their bubble? She did like the money. How hard should she be willing to work for $120,000 a year, after taxes no less? She was hungry. "OK, Reece, I am in. I will sign you onto the ship of fools here and take your food, participate in all of the various dimensions of the Nutrisystem Program, do the work, work hard to get in shape, lose the weight, and force your hand in the end for the money. For you guys though, it has to be about the weighing in. I am not going to sign anything that lets you off the hook if it turns out that I cannot win marathons and such."

"I assure you, Miss Martin, I mean Trisha, your weight and health are all that matter to us. Even if you wind up anonymous with no public life, this accomplishment will benefit us on its own merit. You lose the weight, participate in the program our way, agree to appear on our behalf, and your end of the deal is made."

With that the contract was signed, notarized, sealed and implemented. Trisha was now an official spokesperson for Nutrisystem. There were hugs all around, one even for the boring stuffed shirt, David Giles, who could not wipe the smile off of his face. He spoke for the first time. "Did you know, Trisha, that I can see a little indentation in your face? You can see results in only two weeks. Imagine what a couple of years of this will do for you, for all of us really. Have you weighed in lately?"

"Not until the end of the first month, David. Thank you for the complement. I am out of here, guys. It is time for lunch." Trisha made sure a copy of the new contract had been emailed to her so she could study it later, picked up her backpack, straightened herself, hugged Stanley one more time, kissed him on the cheek, shook hands with Reece Chartheart, jokingly punched attorney Giles in the ribs, and headed out the door, looking to climb on her bike. Today she was going to ride all the way up Sunset Rd, past the runway at McCarran International Airport, cross Las Vegas Boulevard South, and get lunch at California Pizza Kitchen in Town Center. What she had on her mind was the White Corn Guacamole Chips, a cup of Dakota Smashed Pea + Barley Soup, and the Original BBQ Chicken Chopped Salad, all for fewer than 1,200 calories. There at the restaurant she could hide in plain sight, read her Robin Hobb novel, avoid dessert, then ride home the long way, and get a good nap before she went to work. Target was the one place where she felt safe from this new life of hers. That is exactly what she did.

* * *

The days passed, one at a time. Some mornings it was easy to get up and get going, others it was difficult, and once in a while it seemed impossible. One of the rules Trisha made for herself was to make the bed the moment she got up and started her day. It amazed her how such a simple task could be such a mountain to overcome. Each day she would climb out of bed, start for the bathroom, and then remember her promise to make the bed. The comical thought of a job that took less than two minutes reminded her of something her mother quoted from one of her Alcoholic Anonymous meetings, that people with problems would use a pole vault to jump over mouse droppings. She always smiled at that simple thought when she would walk away from a made bed not two minutes later. That simple task was a reminder for her of the promises she made, not to others, but to herself. One of those promises was to be helpful to others in little ways and whether they knew it or not wasn't important. Doing little things, clearing small objects out of the way of folks in need, made Trish feel good about herself.

It was beginning to don on her just how ominous a task the weight loss would be. For her it was like rowing a canoe across the Pacific Ocean. That thought made her smile as well when she remembered seeing a Discovery Channel documentary about Polynesians who had done just that, sailed small wooden craft across the ocean to the Americas long ago. Certainly, though the job at hand was enormous, it could not be considered as daunting as rowing a boat across the ocean. Even so, for her the shore she had left behind as she started to row was still in sight. She was just getting started, yet, *how can I fail in this?* The Nutrisystem food formula was easy to follow. One of the great lessons she had learned already was the truth about fruits and vegetables, just how good they tasted when one's diet did not consist of all that sugar and refined flour. The food itself may not have been the highest quality she had ever eaten, but it was good enough. It was easy to prepare, too. All she had to do was remove the box, crack the seal, put it, most of it anyway, in the microwave for a minute or so and presto, she was presented with hot tasty food, and in very balanced varieties.

As near as she could tell, she was consuming between 1,500 and 2,000 calories per day in food, nutritious food, and according to her Nutrisystem page, the mammoth workout regimen she was subjecting herself to was burning over 3,000 calories per day. It was huge, not normal, and she wondered if she should not be eating more to keep up. Trisha decided to venture onto the Nutrisystem Community page and test the waters of communication. For the first time she blogged a question. "If I bank more than 20,000 calories of workout time per week, how much more can I eat and still lose weight?" She decided that as long as she felt good, she would continue to eat the same way until she saw what came back from her blog, if anything. She also decided to visit with Stanley about it in their meeting at the end of the month. In the meantime it was becoming obvious to her that she was indeed losing weight—and fast. Was that a healthy thing? It certainly was as far as her knees were concerned. She could ill afford to damage her knees doing excess running while she was losing pounds, but the child still inside of her desperately wanted to get out and launch some real running.

Once again her routine of day after day workouts, Nutrisystem Program eating, part time shifts at Target, some time with her mother, reading, television; it all began to run together.

Trisha dutifully logged all program activities on her personal page at Nutrisystem.com. There were a few responses to her Community Page question, all of them telling her to slow it down and take it easy. She would burn out for sure. She agreed, but they did not have any idea what she was going through. After reading her contract, she found it a requisite even to document the water she drank. She found that accurately recording her food was as simple as one, two, three, and four. One, logging in Nutrisystem food was a simple click on the button under the tab associated with the exact product she consumed. Two, she had but to follow a list of recommended grocery foods, those things the Nutrisystem designers suggested as a complement to their own food so that the entire diet would balance nutritionally.

The third tab was a search of other foods, things that could not be resisted, but still needed to be listed. The fourth tab was a 'clear all' for her additions that could be manually entered right off of any product nutritional label. Those four things together consisted of more than 99% of all food consumed, so it was comprehensive and very easy to follow. That was the thing she liked the most about the Nutrisystem Program. It was convenient, easy, and most importantly comprehensive.

Getting involved in the Community aspect of the program was a bit more involved. There was so much available. She had asked a few questions, posted the dreaded picture of her on the bike that her mother had taken the other day, completed her profile, and surfed some of the other tools available. According to the contract, she would need to be proactive and get involved at all levels. It was not to be a secret that she was under contract to share her experiences and track her progress. At least going public would get her involved with others. As a Nutrisystem qualified weight loss candidate, Trisha wondered if the *naked* she felt when publishing her sad situation was anything similar to how an actress felt when having to appear nude in the movies for the first time. She felt totally exposed.

Trisha well knew that her program would be different from the norm. She was working out at a professional pace, pushing herself to the limit, and not headed to burnout because for all intents and purposes, this was her employment. Others should be so lucky. The invisible legions of overweight people faced enormous odds in trying to balance their jobs, husbands, wives, kids, money, and all the other demands of life into something that also left room for the work and sacrifice of a weight management and fitness program that made sense. Hers was a completely different animal. She was aware of that.

Sunday was usually Trisha's favorite day of the week, not for church, though she relied very much on God for direction, but she set aside time on Sundays, to simply relish her new life. One such particularly blustery day was spent at Target, a rare full shift that Trisha had to work. She made her way to the store on the trusty bike; Trisha always did nowadays, at least almost always, so she approached from the back of the building and went in through shipping. It was a very short ride from her house to the store and since it would be dark when the work day ended, she planned to ride straight home again. This was one day she wouldn't be working out and she'd slept a bit longer last night. One thing Trisha Martin was sure of was the need to get a good night's sleep, every night. A day at work was the real day off for her. She was in a very festive mood as she walked the bicycle in through the shipping door.

"Top**p**ada mornin to ya, Trish." It was Sean Keagan, the shipping guy. Trisha would have mistaken him for a troll since he was always there. It seemed to her that he lived in the back end of Target. To say that Sean was Irish, well, it'd be an understatement.

"Sean, is April working today? I'm hoping to get her for lunch at Applebee's."

"That she is, darlin'. Just remember an ole Irish saying. 'Who gossips with you will gossip of you.' On that note a question comes a callin' that me mum would say ta ask it as it were the next right thing to do, no matteh 'ow wrong it be. An believe it when I speak it as the compliment it is. How goes the big diet since you lost the Super Bowl bet?"

Trisha was already locking the bike up in its usual spot when she turned and gave Sean a wry smile. "I don't know for sure since I never weigh myself, but I feel much better, and thanks. Have a great day, Sean. You are right about the gossip thing. I am sorry I ever told anyone about it." With that she was off through the stock room and headed to the back wall door by the pharmacy. Once out on the floor she was fair game for customers who may have questions, and they did. Trisha made it a point to have a good working knowledge of where things were at Target. She prided herself on product familiarity, but it was the way she did it that impressed her managers. She always clocked in a few minutes early and took a walking tour of the floor before she reported in at the registers. While she floated around she took the time to make mental notes of where things were and showed pride in putting things back and straightening disorganized areas up. *Funny,* she thought to herself. *I have been organizing things around here for years, but left my own home such a mess at the same time.* It was never about the work. For her, it was about being able to be of service to customers who generally met her up front and asked things. She had a reputation for being sharp and many of the folks who had questions would seek her out. Whenever a manager or supervisor mentioned it to her, she would only say that she loved shopping and that Target was a good place to shop. She never wanted credit for this value added service. It was just who she was. She found April up front already at work and getting her cash register station organized.

"Good morning, April."

"Well, good morning to you, Trisha. You always come up from the back now. Rode the bike again, did you?"

"I did. Say, do you want to do lunch today? I have been looking forward to having some time with you. Remember, I owe you Applebee's." April smiled. "I am going to head over to the lounge and look at the schedule to see if we have the same lunch." When she got there she found that she was scheduled at 2:00, April at 3:00, and so it was off to where Marsha was to see if a trade could be accommodated. She walked back past April who told her that she preferred 3:00 because that left a shorter second shift, something she liked.

"Hi, Marsha," Trisha winked at her favorite supervisor. "April and I are planning on getting lunch together this afternoon. She would prefer late lunch with me, if that could be worked out, but I am flexible. What say you?"

"She is scheduled at 3:00, then?" Marsha was busy getting *Spring* front end specials out on the floor and was working very hard already. One thing Trisha knew about management was that she for sure had no interest in becoming a manager herself, *no way.* "I am going, or was going to take the late lunch, but as luck would have it I want to go early today, so tell her I will cover and you are all set. Just remember, there is always a price to pay," she wryly smiled and winked. I will get you guys back later. You owe me one, OK?"

"But of course. Marsha, how many is that? How many lunch trades do I owe you for by now? You say that every time, but you never call the debt. You're a push over. That's why I never try to take advantage of you." On her way to the register, she was now late and had to work fast to be ready for the first check outs of the day; she and April exchanged the knowing glance and when Trisha mentioned that it was the late lunch she just mouthed the word *'yes'* and pumped her fist. Whatever else the store-gossip person was, she was fun. Trisha could not wait for the chance to pump her for information.

Trisha loved watching people. Forget the money, everyone knew that Target didn't pay cashiers a living wage for a homeowner, but for her it was the secret pleasure of watching people. There were large people, Trisha was large, small people, shy people, loud people, nice people, jerks, men with an attitude, couples fighting, young couples definitely in love, mothers struggling to control their kids, teenagers good and bad, *but mostly good*, Trisha decided, old people, nasty people, smart people, and well, less than smart people. Some people were dressed nicely, even to the nines. For others, it would be a safe bet to say they needed help in deciding what to wear. Trisha, with her three stretch-outfits wardrobe, never judged people by their clothing choices. One of the things she decided to do when this diet thing ran its course was to frame her 'Target Tent' as she called it, the massive red Target shirt she wore while working. It was to be her trophy, the one symbol of her twelve years on the lamb from the life she had hoped for when she was young. She knew she was losing weight because that shirt was looking more and more like a knee length dress. It would not be long before she would graduate to something slightly smaller, a little non-scale victory she was looking forward to. The only people that ever offended her were the unkempt, the stinky reeking ones. You could smell them three aisles away.

One of the little games she played when not so busy was to watch people coming in the store, and then to guess what they would purchase and bring to the front when they were leaving, so when the three gentlemen and a lady came in together she knew something was up. These people looked like FBI agents, or DEA guys, some kind of official cops or something. Something was up, something big. They filtered out on different aisles and then met up with the General Manager on duty, Frank Zeppelin. At first they stood in a small circle over near Children's Clothing, trying not to look obvious, obviously. Cops, she laughed to herself, were terrible at looking incognito. They fanned out again and disappeared in different directions. Was someone in there stealing? She did not think so, this was bigger than that. Oh well, they were gone for now and she had customers waiting, so it was back to work for her.

It did not take very long for the story to get more interesting. She could see police, regular police gathering outside the front door. They spread out into a kind of a triangle . . . and drew their guns! Now she was frightened. From the back of the store she could hear yelling, "Get down – Now!" It was a male voice. She heard the big crashing sound of a display that went flying.

People were screaming, the fear grew inside of her gut, "Don't do it. No!" This time it was the female, and she could tell they were trying to stop someone. Suddenly, without warning there were people running all over the place. Out of the back section of the store she could see the police, the ones who had walked through the door just a few minutes ago trying to restrain a man whom she remembered when he entered the store just after it opened. He was not a large man, not poorly dressed; in fact, she had pegged him as a father in the store on a Sunday morning family errand to pick up something quick. Now she saw him in a completely different light. He burst into the front cashier area and bounded right past Trisha with all four cops in tow. Trisha ducked down low as he ran by and then he was out the door. Right behind them was the hero of Target, store manager Frank Zeppelin, though he was a safe distance behind the cops and his job was to help customers stay out of the way. So far no shots had been fired though all four of the police had their guns drawn as they ran to and through the front door.

The officers outside collapsed around the escaping man and hit him with several taser-looking weapons at the same time. And so, just as quickly as it had started, it was over. The gentleman they were interested in went down and begged them not to shoot anymore. He was quickly subdued, put on the ground, cuffed, and hustled into the back of one of the police cars. Within minutes they were gone, presumably to the Henderson Detention Center, and the only ones left were the four plain-clothes police who disappeared into the manager's office with Mr. Zeppelin. Life inside of Target quickly fell back into the Sunday morning routine that Trisha was used to. In just a few minutes, most of the customers in the store went their way, and those there now had arrived after the big event and the only ones the wiser were the employees who had become working zombies in a state of shock. This was shaping up as a day that Trisha would long remember, a people watching extravaganza.

Trisha often wondered what was wrong with her. She was intelligent, hard working, ambitious, liked a challenge, and yet she had no desire to be promoted or to change jobs the way career minded folks did. She lived for and loved the action right where she was, and in that moment she thought to herself, she decided that no matter what direction her new life took, she would always come back here and work shifts in the front end for as long as they would let her. She had never even asked for a raise. With the debit card she enjoyed, money would not be an object, not a problem that is if she lived up to her end of the agreement. After a short while, she realized that the emotionally disruptive bandit was no longer messing with her feelings, she was fine. The real problem was that she was hungry. That old popcorn smell from the snack bar was pulling at age-old longstanding inner need, the call for food.

In less than an hour, she had a visitor from Sporting Goods. It was Greg Simpson. She hardly knew him and could not guess what he wanted. "Trisha, I need to talk to someone, someone I can trust. I notice that you are scheduled for the late lunch. Can we get together then?"

"I am having lunch with April today, Greg, just a minute." She walked over to April, they visited for a few seconds and she returned. "Would you like to join us, or do you need to see me alone?" He looked very shook up. Trisha wondered why people in the store always came to her when they 'needed' to talk, but such was her life.

His head was lowered and he looked terrible. "OK. I just need some company for an hour. If you guys will let me, I will join you, thank you very much." With that he was off and back to his sporting goods. This was very bizarre. This day was getting weirder by the minute. Now she couldn't wait for lunch hour. Imagine how surprised

Greg would be when she paid for the lunch with her newfound wealth.

* * *

"Could you guys believe that? I mean, the guy ran right by me on his way out! It was unbelievable." Trisha was very animated as she described the story from her point of view. I saw the police out the front door with their guns pulled. When they shot him, all of them, my heart almost stopped. Those little electric thingies that shock people all seemed to hit him at the same time. I thought he was a dead man until he started begging for his life, and then I saw the wires and knew he had not been killed with bullets. I am still in shock over the whole thing, well, not so much now, and that's why I love this job. People are so crazy. I am going to have the 600-calorie steak lunch, April. Greg, what are you having?"

"The Cowboy Burger with fries," retorted Greg, who sullenly sipped his ice tea. He went back into silence which had Trisha wondering again, *what's on this guy's mind.*

"That sounds yummy," she was trying to cheer him up. "What about you, April, what are you going to have for lunch today?"

"Oh, I am going with the Grilled Shrimp and Island Rice. It's only nine points." April had her iPad out and was fidgeting with a little blue calculator thing, something she had never seen before. The iPad she had seen. April was on the internet looking at the Applebee's menu online.

"What do you mean nine points? What is that thing?"

"Oh . . . you're wondering about this little calculator? It's my Points Plus calculator, from Weight Watchers. I joined Weight Watchers. You have motivated me, Trisha Martin. I am finally doing something about my weight. There was a hopeful look in April's eyes as she started to explain her new diet.

Greg looked up; he was finally showing some interest in the conversation, and that made Trisha happy. She liked him, and knew him to be a good man in spite of the rumors about, shall we say, personal lifestyle issues. "My mother is on Weight Watchers," he said. "She has lost a bunch of weight. They convert everything to some kind of a point system. She goes to meetings every week, weighs in, and she tells me it is a lot of fun. Do you like it, April?"

"I do. I'm just getting started; I'm in my third week. I get twenty-nine points a day. The Plus is for bonus points I get weekly and extra points I get for doing exercise." She pulled something out of her purse, a little tiny notebook. "This is my weekly tracker. I write all the food down in this little booklet so I don't lose track of what's going on. I have already found out that I was eating far more than I thought before I started this new thing. The tracking is so easy, look." She wrote down her order and also the word vegetables next to it, but still only carded the nine points.

"Are you going to add veggies, April? Is that why you wrote the word *veggies* down?" Trisha looked like the canary that ate the cat, seeing the fun of having a real diet buddy from outside the world she was running in, and her Target life was in on the game. April was on a diet.

"Sure is, Trish. The good news is that fruits and vegetables, most of them anyway, are known at Weight Watchers as power foods with zero points, so I can bulk up any meal with some extra food as long as it is fruits and vegetables."

All good diets have an escape clause, Trisha thought.

When the food was ordered, the drinks refilled, and the bread almost gone from the table, Greg had snapped it up, the talk turned back to the big morning's excitement. Somewhere deep inside of Trisha she was experiencing one of those moments, the stirring of an inner need to help, and she could not identify for the life of her why she felt that feeling just now. Something was definitely going on here more than meets the eye, and her eye was focused on Greg Simpson. *This guy comes out of the back, out of nowhere really, and wants to have lunch? Then he sits and broods the whole time.* If she were a Catholic priest, hold it, a Catholic priest would not do, a Methodist priestess, she would be expecting him to start in on the confession session. She decided to cast some bait to get him talking. Now is the time for the juice, baby.

"So Greg, you were right back there in the thick of it. Surely you saw what happened. I thought they were going to kill him. I knew the minute those plain-clothed cops came in the door that something was up."

"It was exciting," Greg's response was less than exciting. He munched another roll, this one with butter all over it. Hopefully, eating would make him feel better. He was also pretending to watch the NBA game on the flat screen over by the bar, but Trisha could tell he really had no interest in that, either. *What is wrong with Greg?* "I saw the guy walking right toward me, then the police came in; there were two from behind him and one up the cross aisle. He was meandering as nonchalantly as if he were considering patio furniture in the back of the store and wanted to stop and look at music and movies on his way to the front end.

"I was helping the fourth guy look at bikes, truthfully had no idea who he was, when he turned away from me, asked me to stand back, and started walking toward their suspect, who then recognized what was about to happen. He got jumpy and ran, even after they told him to lie down. He knocked over a movie display, ran through lady's clothing, cut back to the center aisle, made it all the way to the televisions in the back of the store, at least that is what I heard. Then he bolted for the front end, and you know the rest. Whew," he exhaled unenthusiastically. To tell the truth, Greg looked scared, maybe a little buzzed or hung over, or even both, but he did not look well.

The subject changed back to April and her Weight Watchers diet as they worked their way through lunch. Trisha was very happy for her, so happy that she was trying to do something about her situation. She was genuinely supportive, and it made her feel much closer to the *gossip of Target,* as she was known. Trisha began to wonder just how much of that reputation was earned, and how much of it was nonsense. One thing Trisha never went in for was gossip, the garbage that one spewed about another. If you could not confront someone directly, you should keep your mouth shut. Trish was also beginning to see some purpose, a huge benefit that came from being of help to others, getting out of herself as the saying goes. She was so very tired of being a fat person who was always feeling sorry about things. It was a much nicer way of life to view one's self as a person who was there for others. In a strange way for her it was like a spiritual awakening.

Trisha had paid the bill, took a 'you're welcome bow' while the plates had been cleared, they were enjoying coffee and tea, and just about to get up from the table, with about ten minutes to spare, when Greg dropped the bombshell on them.

"I know him."

"Who? Who do you know?" Trisha asked, not sure if she wanted the answer. She took a sip of her tea, hot tea her mother would have loathed because it did not bear her signature of lavishly saturated cream and honey. Her curiosity was getting the best of her. April was absolutely lit up. Whether April was a gossip or not was yet to be seen for some, but she was an acknowledged expert at sucking out the facts, especially when the facts were scandalous.

"Him, the guy the cops were there for. I have never invited him to meet me at the store and had no idea he was coming in today. Also, I had no idea he was wanted by the police, but I know him. He sells me things."

This time it was April's turn. "Greg, you mean illegal things, like substances?"

"I have a drug problem," Greg broke down finally and for the first time in his life, a life he could see slipping away, he had told on himself, and in sort of a de-facto plea, was asking for some kind of help. Somewhere in the bowels of his bankrupt soul, he wanted to be saved. Now he had confessed the big secret right to the big gossip and he knew that things would never be the same.

They sat in stony silence, staring at each other, not knowing how to proceed, with time running out, needing to get back to the store, needing time to talk, knowing that walls were closing in on poor Greg; neither of them knew right off the bat what to do about it.

Trisha was thinking as fast as she could and came up with a temporary answer. "Greg, April, this conversation is confidential and cannot go anywhere for the moment. I want to help you Greg, but only if you want to be helped. Fortunately for you, April has kept many of my confidences over the years, just not the ones meant to have fun with. The serious stuff is right where it belongs. April, are you on board?"

"But of course. Greg, you have to promise not to inform others that I didn't tell on you. It would ruin my reputation," she smiled. "I like you, fool though you must be." *In a different life, I would see you in a different light, damn you. But then again, in a different life you would see me as . . . fat.* "Trisha is very smart, she knows her way

147

around the Target system, and if anyone can get you out of this mess it's her. You know your bad boy, a floundering criminal, drug buddy, is singing right now over at the police station, so I bet we have little, if any time anyway."

Trisha cut in. "This is going down today. We are to meet right back here in two hours when we go on break. Get ready to change your life, Greg, for better or worse. If we do not take this to management by tonight, the gig is up for you. You have to be ready to talk before the cops show up later. Now let's get back and act as if nothing has happened."

They were back at their stations right on time. For Greg the next two hours were torture. He was not sure from one minute to the next whether he would get arrested, confronted by management, shot and killed by one of Pablo's friends . . . who knew what was going to happen to him? True to her word, April did not talk. *Perhaps there is more to her than meets the eye, and perhaps the gossip tag laid on April is as they say, well, just gossip.* He was beginning to see stuff differently.

Trisha took the time to look at things from Greg's perspective. What would they do to him if he were confronted, if he turned himself in, or if there were some sort of deniability on his part? Now that she knew, was she at risk? Was she compelled to spill the beans on him? All of this was compounded by the fact that Greg was somehow connected to the incident in the store earlier.

It was 6 PM and they were right back in the same place, the same table even, where they had enjoyed lunch, well, at least Trisha and April had enjoyed it. Greg looked terrible then, now he looked even worse.

"OK guys, we have ten minutes. April, you're a part of this and will be a partner in our little adventure. You need to be available to help if possible. Are we good?" April nodded.

"Greg, your gig is up. The fun is gone and the game is over, over no matter what. Even if you wanted to go into denial, it would not work, not now that you have involved us. Company policy dictates that we report drug activity that we know about on premises. Your dealer showing up this morning and you're telling us of it, that involves us too now, so this is going down before we go home. You should not be bothered by this at all, Greg. We are soundly in your corner. I bet the cops are getting ready to come back to the store so I suggest we beat them to it, what do you say?

"OK."

"Greg," it was April's turn again, "everyone, even management, suspects you are a drug addict anyway. It is amazing that you freaking addicts think no one knows what you are up to, but I thought I would catch you up on the . . . gossip, as we say."

"I kind of knew that, too."

"Here is my idea, Greg. Just as soon as we go back to the store you are to report directly to Zeppelin and tell him the whole story. You must also tell him of our conversation at lunch, about both of us, and that we met here during our break and agreed that you would turn yourself in. You have been a good employee and I think you can survive this, but you will be going to rehab dude, and I bet you will be going tonight. Are you ready?"

"Yes for rehab, no for Zeppelin, but I will do it. I am so glad that it will be over. I have tried so hard to quit. This drug thing has been eating me alive for at least a couple of years. I have known it would all come to a head one day, but I never had any idea today would be that day. Let's move; I want to get this part over with while I still have a bit of courage, thanks to you two."

This time he paid, wonders never cease, and Trisha had very good vibes about how things might turn out for Greg, and she felt . . . satisfaction about being a positive contributor in a very negative situation. It was always better for her when it was the other guy in trouble. She had endured her share for far too long.

Things turned out very fortunate for Greg Simpson. He beat the cops by less than an hour, threw himself on the mercy of management, begged not to lose his job, prayed for the chance to go to rehab. The trip to a treatment center was granted, and he was on a plane for John Wayne Airport in Santa Ana, CA before he had time to even think about what he had done.

Later, just before her shift ended, Frank Zeppelin took Trisha aside and congratulated her for knowing what to do. He too liked the young man, Simpson, and wanted to give him a chance. "By the way, you are losing weight. I can tell. Everyone is talking about it behind your back. Keep it up, Trisha. You're worth so much to anyone blessed enough to be a part of your life.

A day in the life of Trisha Jean Martin came to a close. She rode her bike home in the dark, against her rules, but sometimes that was the way it had to be. Tomorrow she would be back at the pool, the track, the weights, the long hard rides, and the days would roll on into a very uncertain but exciting future.

* * *

Saturday, March 6th, 2010 rolled around just like all days do. Trisha wanted it to be as normal of a day as possible, but how could it? She was to weigh-in for only the second time since day one . . . this morning, and meet with Stanley at the Club after her workout.

After she had stepped on the dreaded scale, recorded the new weight on her personal page at Nutrisystem, cleaned up the house and prepared for the day, it was back on the Scott Speeder S50, her racing bike, and in no time Trisha was climbing the hill on Russell Road towards the Club and her first stop, the swimming pool. She hadn't been at Club Sport more than a couple of minutes before she was in the pool pushing harder than ever. It was cold and windy this balmy Saturday morning, but in the pool it felt like a warm bath. The water felt so good. Trisha made sure that she had plenty of time because she felt like ramping up the routine today. She had been working out for exactly four weeks and now she was strong enough to go hard for 90 minutes with no rest. First she free styled 10 laps, switched to the backstroke, turned to the breast stroke, and then actually went into a butterfly for 10 laps. It was exhilarating to be able to maintain a pace that strong for so long. In the end she sprinted the last laps at full speed in a freestyle which left her shaking, like low blood sugar fatigue, when she finally climbed out of the pool.

Trisha took a quick shower, dressed, went upstairs to the café and found Barbara Miller, who was eager to get her some energy food, this time in the form of a Chocolate Mint Promax Nutrition Energy Bar, one of her favorites. "Trisha, you're looking so good today," Barbara noted. "I can really see it this time. You must be doing very well." Trisha could only smile, thanking her for noticing and for saving the last Chocolate Mint Bar, since there was only the one left. "You're welcome, Trish. No one is working harder around here than you are."

Trisha left the standard $2 tip for the $5.49 charge, which by the way was left on the tab for a bill that she never saw, finished off the ice tea that came with her snack, and skipped back down the stairs, jogged across the basketball court walkway, took the stairs up two at a time and started running. She quickly fell in sync with Josh Sullivan and ran at his pace for two miles, the farthest she had run since that old heel injury just after she graduated high school way back in her first life.

"Trisha Jean Martin," Josh exhaled, "what has gotten into you this morning? You are running like I have never seen you run." She just smiled to herself. "Did Stan open you up to two miles or something?"

"Haven't seen him yet this morning, Josh. I just felt like pushing a bit harder today. There was a time in my life when running was my life. For some reason I just have more energy. I could keep going, but, well, you know the weight thing and protection where the knees are concerned."

"I was going to ask about that," he joked, "except it looks like you are losing weight big-time now. How is it going in that department?"

"You know I hate to weigh myself, Josh. Who knows? I just feel better today."

"You look great, Girl. Your hair is longer, too. You should see the way it flows when you are pushing it. You run like someone who knows their way around the track. I told you that before, didn't I?"

Speaking of around the track, they turned and could see down on the basketball court. There was a full court game going on and the men were playing hard, like there was something more to play for than just who bought the coffee afterwards. There he was again . . . Michael. He had been a high school basketball star, the kind who looks great on the floor in high school, but not the college level version. He did not look like he had lost his step either. She watched him grab a rebound, race the ball up the court, pass off to his teammate, take the pass back, and almost, not quite, but almost dunk the ball. Then the court disappeared as the track curved away and so it went, around and around they went a total of 27 times—two miles. It was time for Trisha to get off of the track.

She enjoyed what she called the "Saturday stroll," a fast paced run on the elliptical trainer for 60 minutes, lifted weights through her routine, went back into the locker room, showered, collapsed into the hot tub and pondered her morning workout. That was the most fun she'd had yet. She was beginning to get into good physical condition, and yes, the weight was coming off. She was looking forward to meeting her mother at The Elephant Bar over in The District for lunch, it was Saturday after all, but first she had a date with Stanley Burton, her loyal trainer. It was hard to keep the smile off of her face as she walked into the office, where she found not only Stanley, but Michael as well, none other than the demon brother who had changed her life with a two-headed coin just twenty-eight days ago. This was going to be good.

"Well, if it isn't Michael Martin, rascal betting rat, master of the two-headed coin flip, dressed to the nines, and it looks like you are hammering out there trying to get in better shape for these little fun jogs we are in for. Tell me you don't want to embarrass me this summer when we start running together."

"Not in a million years, Kid, or this year at least. TJ, it only looks that way to you because you have not been around. I work out like this all the time," he lied. Stanley laughed when he heard that. It was common knowledge that Mike was in a serious hunt to get ready for something, they just didn't know what. "I have, by the way, been keeping tabs on you, Sis, and it looks like you are walking the talk . . . so far. You look terrible, though. What looks so awful is your clothing. It doesn't fit anymore, except for the bike riding outfits you have on all the time. Have you been losing weight?" Michael was grinning from ear to ear.

"Not so fast, Mikey. If not for the serious training funds I would be so lost." In truth, she had spent money on anything and everything she could think of. The bike notwithstanding, she had personalized the training funds to mean training fun. Whatever else happened today, she needed them to keep on keeping on where the money was concerned. Once she became used to having money, the need set in like a fever dream. "Stan, do you think we can get Reece Charthouse on the phone?"

"I can always dial him up," Stan mused as he reached for the phone in the cradle, tapped the numbers, set the speaker into the on position, and then replaced the phone into its cradle. The phone rang.

"Stanley Burton, to what do I owe the pleasure of this touch? Nothing bad, I hope."

"Not at all, Reece. Thanks for taking the call. I have someone here who wishes to speak to you. Trisha Jean Martin, the phone is all yours."

"Good afternoon, Reece," Trisha smiled.

"You aren't backing out on the contract, Ms. Martin, I hope. There are serious . . . . ."

"Not at all, Reece, I'm not backing out at all here, and quite the contrary. The reason I had Stan get you on the phone was to let you know that the tab stands at $38,000 and running."

"What!" Reece snorted in *feigned* surprise. Michael was pleased as punch. Stanley sat there with his mouth open, aghast, *not really, since he had already checked Trisha's weight online,* at what he had just heard. Reece went on. "Are you trying to tell me that you," he shuffled papers, clicked some keyboard noise easily heard through the speakerphone, "that you have lost 38 lbs. in just four weeks! This is serious stuff. That is way too fast for anyone around here to be comfortable with. It is—supernatural. There has got to be some sort of a problem with your numbers. Perhaps it is that flimsy scale you are using. You need to shift to a better scale, and this has to be monitored officially. Stanley, look again at the contract. I want future weigh-ins to be handled by a third party and on a medical scale. We aren't buying any of this at all. I'll have to get input from our legal . . . . . ."

Michael put a stop to the emotional charade. "Chill out, loser. This is Michael Martin, humble brother of a professional athlete, and if you will recall, I reviewed the final contract with you directly. If you had wanted a medical scale you should have demanded it in writing. You and I both know it isn't in there. You'll disrupt the continuity of her program if you make her change scales. It's not happening."

"Mikey, it's OK with me if we have to change scales, but I would want an iron clad guarantee that we stick with the 275 lb starting weight, should some sort of an adjustment be necessary. If they will agree to that, then we can use the scale here in Stan's office." Stan had a medical balance weight scale right there that could be used. *I'll go along with these guys. They're just funning with me. I bet they were all on the phone together before I ever walked in here.*

"I rarely agree to that type of thing, Sis. It is a sucker's bet . . . but if you say so."

"We will agree to Stanley's scale," Reece cut in. We can have the amendment approved and scanned to you while we are on the phone. I won't get any arguments from legal."

They waited for what seemed like endless minutes before the email showed up in Stan's computer. Trisha signed it. Stan notarized the signatures, scanned it back, and received the signed and notarized amendment within minutes. This was exhausting, but a kill shot was coming.

"Stanley, you are the official weigh-in guy," Reece said. "Now young lady, if you would please step up on the scale for us, we can officially get this little misunderstanding settled."

Trisha slipped out of her riding shoes. She was no longer nude like when she weighed at home, she had rehydrated herself after the workout this morning, and had eaten a Nutrisystem Peanut Butter Lunch Bar. In spite of those facts, she was confident in what was about to happen. Her hatred of scales ruled her emotionally, and though she dreaded climbing up, she did anyway, because her life was no longer private business. Stanley slid the weights around, found the balance, and smiled at the new showing of 234 lb.

"Now the tab looks to be standing at $41,000," Trisha beamed. "Mr. Charthouse, once the contract has been fulfilled I want to make sure your company gets its money's worth. When we make commercials, can I keep my hair long or do you want it cut short?" Michael and Stanley laughed and there were hugs all around. On the other end of the phone Reece Charthouse murmured something about being set up by schemers who had it in for him. Trisha noted the sarcastic comedy in his voice and knew that he was as happy as everyone else was.

"I wish I could join you and mother for lunch today, Trisha, but alas, duty calls me in another direction. I can't believe what a start you have come up with, but then again, you are Trisha Jean Martin, the runner. Perhaps our little fun run in July will be a bit more competitive than we originally thought. We shall see," and with that he was out the door.

4

Going to War

Red-purple dawn
bruises mountain-pierced sky

Wise Mac

February 17th, 2010

Captain Brad Peterson had passed his own physical, been background checked in ways he did not think possible, been sworn into the United States Army, and had undergone training at the US Navy's Medical Support Command Center in San Antonio, Texas at Fort Sam Houston. He tried not to sleep through the classes, tried not to teach them either, though he could have. Now Brad was enjoying a walking tour of the Lockheed C-141B Starlifter he would be on this evening when it left for Baghdad, Iraq.

He was very impressed with the condition of the old bird, originally off the line decades ago during the Vietnam War. The aqua blue cockpit seats with their rich deep blue arm rests looked brand new. The instrument panel was in pristine condition and there wasn't even a scratch in the cockpit windows. It also looked freshly painted. To be honest, the entire plane looked as if it had just rolled out of the factory yesterday.

The drooping wings, slanted back at a 25 degree angle, high off of the top of the fuselage, painted white, held the four jet engines; they were painted grey just like the underbelly of the wings and fuselage where the landing gear was housed. The little American flag on the tail, underneath the rear stabilizer wings, combined with the big US AIR FORCE located on the front portion of the fuselage, just back of the cockpit windows, provided one hell of a patriotic thrill. This was a very emotional experience for him.

Brad was on his way. This flight, where he would spend 13 hours without a window to look out of, called to mind the great dream of his magical childhood. He wanted to go into a war zone and perform surgery. The dream, as vivid as if it had happened yesterday, was to this very moment the driving motivation for him to complete this mission. He had fantasized about it throughout medical school and had kept it in the back of his mind during many thousands of hours of post medical graduate study and specialization in surgery. He never forgot the dream during years as a resident in brain and neuro-surgical procedures, not even when he moved on to pediatric cerebral tumor treatment. It had all led to this moment. As a little boy he had heroes, just not the ones everyone else thought of. There was the great Surgeon, LaSalle Leffall. He was the first African-American to be elected **President of the Society of Surgical Oncology, President of the American Cancer Society**, both, and **President of the American College of Surgeons. He also admired a Russian from the early 1960's who performed an appendectomy on himself, Dr.** Leonid Rogozov. And then there was Dr. Christiaan Barnard, a South African, who performed the first heart transplant. These were the types of people that Brad loved and respected, not athletes or military leaders. He hoped to complete a book about surgical history someday using these and others little known outside of the medical community, people who inspired him.

"She is a beautiful old lady, is she not, Captain Peterson?" Master Sergeant Ted Hazelton, the young Air Force officer who was giving him the tour this morning was beaming with pride. "This very aircraft has served in many conflicts. During the Viet Nam War, it flew for thousands of hours on countless missions. It was a workhorse in Cyprus in 1974, and then the Bosnian conflict. Later she served during the Persian Gulf War from the early 90's and right up until this moment. These magnificent planes are due to be retired soon. It will be one of saddest moments of my career."

"She's all of that, Master Sergeant Hazelton," Brad complimented. "Your team has done an outstanding job of keeping her new for us, that's for sure. I'm impressed by the entire fleet here and the way this base operates. I cannot get over the size of that monster over there. What is that, a Galaxy C-5? That has to be the largest plane in the world. I cannot believe that thing will even lift off of the ground, no matter how powerful those engines are."

"It's our largest, commercial or military and I agree it's impressive. If big is what interests you though, you would have to see the Antonov 225, a Russian behemoth. It would be the world's largest. It has six huge engines, and get this, a Boeing 747 would fit under just one of its wings."

"Wow!"

"Getting back to our flight, I thought you would be glad to know that one of the more comfortable seats up front is reserved for you. We in the armed forces are grateful for your sacrifice and willingness to serve. I know you didn't have to do this, and personally, I wish you well as you go your way. The first time you look on one of our injured soldiers, counting on you to save his life, think of me. Thank you, sir."

"You're very welcome, soldier. This is not just a duty, but a great honor. I cannot tell you how satisfying this adventure is for me. I have looked forward to this time in my life since, well since about when this plane came off of the assembly line, maybe even longer than that; it is just about as old as I am." They both laughed and the "tour of respect and appreciation" continued for Captain Peterson a couple of hours more before they headed back to the Officers Lounge where his things were, where a hot meal waited, where he would shower and change in to his traveling uniform, and the last building he would be in before he left this world behind and set out on the great voyage that lay ahead . . .

* * *

The troop transport, out of Fort Bragg, North Carolina, was at cruising altitude sailing smooth skies over the Atlantic Ocean, carrying elements of the 182nd Airborne Division, a total of 186 soldiers returning to duty from home. These were some of the toughest kids Brad had ever seen. Mostly, they were asleep right now, although Brad couldn't see how they could possibly be comfortable back there. They were used to it, he guessed. His traveling companion was Colonel Robert Hankle and these were his guys. Hankle was very proud of them and of his command. Captain Brad Peterson was honored to be sitting next to him, found him to be very intelligent, though from Brad's point of view it was oxymoronic to be both intelligent and a career US Army guy going in and out of Iraq and other places in the Middle East for the past 20 years or so.

Brad was comfortable in the air, always enjoyed the adventure of a long flight, and though this trip was very different than flying first class, the seat was first class, the engines were quieter than he thought they'd be, though with the wings off of the top of the fuselage the blast was a bit louder than normal. So far it had been a smooth flight. He was listening to a collection of Turtles hits on his iPod and wearing the noise reduction headset he used when traveling. It wasn't like he was a real soldier or anything. This was going to be something like a yearlong military vacation with benefits, him a stranger in a strange land. He felt refreshed to be relieved from the pressure of his day job for the moment and had no inkling from one jiffy to the next what was going to happen. He knew that he would have to go through some rough spots helping injured fighters stay alive, but he knew triage and did not think he would experience any psychological problems. Brad wanted to help save these valiant kids. He was one of the few who really believed that it was possible to put Humpty Dumpty back together again. Yes, Brad Peterson, Captain Bradley Peterson, was living in the thrill of yet another big checkmark on of his bucket list. He felt a friendly tap on his right shoulder, removed the headset and smiled at the boss man of the flight.

"Want to check out a working cockpit, Captain Peterson?" It was easy to follow the sway of the Colonel's husky, powerful voice, which in its own way commanded a sense of loyalty just by how he used it and gestured as he spoke. His barrel chest was huge and he had to be at least sixty years old; this man was the true embodiment of a gritty lifetime soldier.

"You can do that? You can get me into the cockpit, Colonel? Ever since I was a kid, watching planes at Nellis AFB and McCarran International Airport, I wanted to be in the cockpit of a big jet while it was in the air. This is my first official flight in a military aircraft. They flew me commercial from San Antonio. I was hoping to hitch a chopper from the airport, but they picked me up in a shuttle bus, of all things. I rode over to the base with three of those brave kids back there."

"Call me Bob, son," the Colonel laughed. "Hell yes, I can do it. This is my plane. I can let you fly the thing were that my fancy. The Air Force guys up front will let you sit in the pilot seat if I wink at them just so. Come on, let's take a walk. It's stuffy back here with no windows and I need some fresh air. Now there is no way we can stick our heads out the window," the colonel cynically stated with intended humor, "but you will be amazed how refreshing going up front where there are windows will be. It'll help both of us get some sleep when we come back." With that they were moving forward past the latrine, a huge and well stocked galley, and up towards the cockpit door. The soldier on guard, a Private First Class if Brad had the insignia right, came immediately to attention.

"Colonel Hankle, sir," he saluted. "Captain Peterson, sir," he saluted to Brad who uncomfortably returned the gesture of respect, a part of military courtesy since the dawn of civilization.

"At ease, Private," Hankle barked. He moved right past the sentry, unlocked the door, he knew the combination, so in they went.

"Colonel Hankle, sir, welcome on deck." It was logical that they were not required to leave their post to greet the Colonel. The co-pilot was busy at the instrument panel and the pilot in command turned to greet Captain Peterson. "Captain Brad Peterson, the world famous pediatric brain surgeon, and our special guest. We are very proud to have you aboard with us this evening. You're in for a treat, Captain, as we are about to top off the tanks." Hankle looked surprised. "If you'll be still while we complete the task, I am certain that you will find this exercise a very interesting piece of work."

Brad was blown away by the sight of it all. The cockpit was dark except for the array of instruments which were outlined in a low glow sort of orange lighting. The sky outside was pitch black because there was no moon and the star field was brilliant. He could see the Milky Way Galaxy ribbon as he had never seen it before.

Suddenly, appearing out in front and above the C-141, was a massive jet with three huge engines, one in the tail, each with a billowing white contrail. It looked like they would hit each other. Hankle whispered, "It's a KC-10A refueling craft, part of the 305th Air Mobility Wing. It's about to drop **JP54 Aviation Kerosene** into our tanks. That baby holds over 360,000 pounds of fuel. You're going to love this, son."

It was so dark out there that Brad wondered how they did it. As the big boy approached closer and closer, he began to wonder just how dangerous this procedure was. The guys in the cockpit did not seem to be the least bit uncomfortable.

Unexpectedly, a boom with little wings dropped down from the back of the KC-10A's fuselage, a very big hose extended from its end, and within a minute or so it had audibly clanked down and locked onto the top of the C-141. While the planes were hooked, Brad was sure he could feel the tension in the cockpit; the refueling took around twenty minutes, plus a couple of minutes to get through the separation process, and it was farewell as the big jumbo peeled off and went its own way.

"Unbelievable, guys; you have just fulfilled a lifelong wish. If I never see anything else out here I'll have a great story for my family and friends. That was mind-boggling. How do you keep the craft in place? It looks very dangerous to me."

The co-pilot, a lieutenant, smiled. "All we do, sir, is get her ready, the right altitude, velocity, pitch, and they synchronize the flight. They are the magicians for this maneuver. Did you see the little window just forward of the Boom Extender? That is where the Boom Operator sits and guides the process."

Colonel Hankle spoke again. "That was smooth, boys. Care to let the Captain have a seat for few minutes?"

The co-pilot unbuckled his seatbelt, removed his flight headgear, and stepped back. "Have a seat, Captain Peterson while I go and utilize the lavatory services for a few minutes." Brad excitedly took the seat. When the pilot handed the headgear to him he carefully slipped it on and just like that he was connected to the pilot and flight control, wherever that was coming from. It was a surreal experience. He was a little startled when the incoming call came.

"US282 Alpha Zulu, this is Sat Com Bravo 4, do you copy?"

"S Com Bravo 4, this is 282AZ, reading you five, loud and clear," the pilot's voice responded, suddenly very formal, as would be expected. Brad sat as quiet as a mouse. He knew that for him, to touch nothing, say nothing; that was his job at the moment. Who knew if these guys would get into trouble for letting him play with their $77 million toy?

"282A, please confirm the status of your range."

"Say again." "282A..please..confirm..the..status..of..your..range."

"Just filled her up, S Com, full range, do you copy?"

"Copy that. Confirming a successful full load?"

"Copy, S Com, we are good to go."

"282A, turn right, heading 246 degrees northeast, climb to 44,000, increase airspeed to 550 knots and inform Colonel Hankle to stand by for new orders, do you copy?"

"Wilco, affirm 246 degrees northeast, 44,000, 550 knots, Colonel Hankle to be issued new orders. Over."

"Roger, 282A over and out."

"New orders," Hankle mused aloud. *What's going on?* Oh well, he would find out soon enough. Right now they were out over the middle of the ocean, hours from the implementation of any new command directives, so he had plenty of time to think on that one. He would wander back to his communications consul pad, located in his brief case, and get the message in a few minutes.

"Captain Peterson, would you like to do the honors for us?" The pilot, just off the mike in a very serious conversation, now had the casual smile that he had shown earlier.

"What kind of honors are you referring to, Captain?"

"Why, Captain Peterson, we are going to let you implement our new orders. Would you like to fly this big old bird?"

Brad's hands were shaking, quivering with anticipation; well, what the heck.

"Oh yes, please. I know you would not let us get into trouble. So . . . tell me what to do and I will do it."

"Fortunately, Captain Peterson, we have new avionics that make this a breeze. Even a ten-year-old Cub Scout could do it. Right now we're on autopilot and we will be staying that way. Look in the sleeve just to your right. See the small tablet-looking iPad there? Pick it up and hit the 'on' switch. Good, now touch the heading icon, tap the numbers 246 and then the NE icon, yes, and now punch in 44,000 on the altimeter icon. Good, thank you. Look on the forward dash, uh, the instrument panel, just under the front window, the yellow board there. See the knob just under the toggle switch, yes that one. Turn it two clicks to the right, thank you very much, sir. See the rolling tiny little flywheel on the forward dash, just north of the thrusters, yup, that's it; now move it until the window above it shows 550. There you go."

Brad quickly completed the little task. As far as he could tell nothing had changed at all. "Now, Captain Peterson, look at the iPad again. Down in the right hand corner you will find the red engage button. Go ahead and hit it three times. Brad did. Almost instantly, thruster controls edged slowly forward of their own power, the plane accelerated, started to climb, and began a right hand turn. *I did it!* Brad Peterson had flown a big jumbo jet. He swore to himself that when he got back the story would be embellished to the point that he had saved the lives of all aboard.

"Captain Peterson," Colonel Hankle said, "let's wander into the galley and see what there is to eat." Just aft of the cockpit was a kitchen galley that would be the envy of anything flying anywhere. It looked better stocked than the galley in the first class section of the flight he had made to Europe earlier in the year when he took two weeks off before reporting to Ft. Sam Houston for basic medical officer's training. After he had carefully removed the communications gear and climbed out of the seat, hopping over the thruster consol, Brad, squeezed past the returning co-pilot, followed his new friend, Bob, into the galley where the Colonel was busy rousting staff to get a general meal ready, a bit earlier than he had previously planned. Things were changing for him and that usually mandated getting the food taken care of more quickly. They had a very thick slab of roast beef on wheat bread with mayo and mustard, complemented with a heavy slice of American cheese, a large bag of Lay's BBQ chips, a full pint of cold, almost freezing cold milk, and a mammoth peanut butter cookie. It took them less than 15 minutes to eat and return to their seats.

Bob Hankle pulled an iPad out of his briefcase and looked for the incoming message. It was not there yet, so he put it back. It looked to him like Central Command was going to take its sweet time getting those new orders downloaded, but what bothered him the most about the delay was why they were taking so long. Usually, the longer it took to get him data, the more complicated the change would be. He knew by now that it was useless to speculate, so he changed the subject of his wandering thoughts, smiled and looked for a new conversation with his buddy, Brad. He really liked this kid. The brand new captain was smart as they came, very personable, loved adventure, had a good sense of humor, and he could hear tiny whispers of loud rock music trying to escape from the Bose Quiet Comfort 15 headphones he had linked up to his little iPod. It sounded like "Depeche Mode" if he was not mistaken. Bob rapped him on the shoulder and the headphones came off. He knew the boy was trying to go to sleep, but the Colonel's prerogative ruled the moment. Bob was wide awake, and he wanted to try out the conversation he had prepared for yesterday when he found out about the special guest who was hitching a ride with him and his kids.

"Peterson, why pediatric brain surgery? What in the world influences someone to specialize that much? From the looks of you, choices for your life were and are unlimited. Good Lord, son, if you like flying so much you could have been an astronaut."

"Bob, heck, it is hard to sit here and speak with a sitting colonel, one going back into harm's way again, frankly one that is quite a bit older too, and call you by your first name. I fell into the study of the anatomy of the brain through deduction. Pediatrics was always my focus. I see kids as so vulnerable, especially in these changed times. In my studies at the University of Utah Medical School I became very fascinated every time we were looking at the human brain and how it functions. It only seemed natural to tie the two together."

"I take it you like kids then. To me you're a kid still; I guess it's all relative. I love my kids here, and when we lose one occasionally, my gut aches for months. I know you are not a psychologist, but we are in a sense stunted here in the 182nd. We're the daredevils who get thrills the hard way. Apparently some aspect of our brains didn't properly mature the way they were supposed to. I guess our axons and dendrites didn't get insulated enough by the myelin matter where common sense is concerned, so the synapses are too far apart to get the signals straight. My prognosis is that the result is dysfunctions between the left and right hemispheres in communicating properly with the hippocampus. That is why we like to jump out of planes with guns and go shooting bad guys. We're crazy, right?"

"Now you have me wondering who is in the right profession, Colonel Hankle. Not a single person has ever articulated brain function on that level; that is, someone not involved in my field, but in a way you may be right. Have you ever heard of the thick-headed Guido soldier? In your case, the military seeks out those kids who would thrive in this environment, the same way a sports fan surfs television channels looking for the big game, and through the process of unnatural natural selection you end up here together. The maturation process of the brain, while physically complete very early in a young person's life, even before age 8, undergoes tremendous internal changes during the teen years and on into the early 20s. Some say it is an extensive remodeling, like a software upgrade, but I like to think of it as the building blocks of reasonable thinking. It is very fascinating. In surgery it is my job to protect that process and at the same time remove threats, like a tumor. If I do it right, the kid gets 70 years of life and therefore has the potential to live, not just a long life, but a productive one. If I screw it up, he is stunted forever, or worse. You might say I am kind of a daredevil too, but I see it as my contribution to the living.

Getting back to the thick-headed Guido soldier, the reason heads continue to grow physically, though the brain does not, is so the skull can develop and protect that little genius computer we have between our ears. In the case of crazy army guys the skull grows very thick, I think." Hankle burst out laughing, nodding his head up and down.

"What you are saying is that my soldiers missed the boat on emotional maturation, then?"

"I'm not saying that at all, sir. The physical changes inside of the brain that I mentioned just now, they naturally move from the brain stem, the part of the brain which is the oldest in our evolutionary journey, the place where basic functions like breathing, sight, and so forth originate, then onto the more recently developed cognitive centers through the corpus callosum which connects both hemispheres of the brain. This process takes years, many years during the life of young people. In the case of you mad jumpers, it just has not reached the stage yet where your reasoning would protect you from yourself and give you the wits to avoid this very strange and dangerous life. It is you, however, who is the enigma, as I see it."

"Why is that, Son?"

"What are you, 60?"

"I am 62, boy. Don't remind me."

"Bob, that is why you are the enigma, the one in a million people who never seems to learn the lesson. You should have forsaken this bizarre lifestyle decades ago, yet here you are, still jumping out of planes, I presume."

"And damn proud of it." The Colonel's pride was clearly visible on his wrinkled, but youthful expression.

"My point exactly; you are the adaptive adolescent who has yet to come to terms with life's scariest moments. You still go in for the big one, though your brain should have helped you learn not to walk across the blurry line of this high risk behavior. You have a family to be taking care of and yet you, once again, find yourself out here playing teenager. In this category your brain's frontal lobe myelination process has let you down, I'm afraid."

They both just looked at each other and then started laughing.

"Get some sleep, kid. I am afraid we are both about to get in a bit deeper than we had planned earlier today."

Brad fiddled with his iPod, spun the music, and changed from "Depeche Mode" to "Echoes of Nature," so that he could fall asleep on the beach listening to the peace and tranquility of ocean waves crashing on a remote shoreline. He put a mask over his eyes, got all settled in, and then realized he needed to make another stop. In spite of his vastly superior intelligence, Brad still forgot basic things and was never quite ready when he thought he was. It always annoyed him, this little human shortcoming which never seemed to improve. Soon he was settled back in that big first class seat, reclined into an almost level position, blacked out to the flight altogether, listening to the ocean and then drifting into a restless sleep. He dreamed.

Brad was in training at Ft. Sam Houston, remembering what he had been taught about captivity, the chance that the bad guys would get their hands on him; "cling to a moment from your childhood where you were happiest," a strange creature said. It was someone new whom he had never seen before. The moment was gone.

"Time," the test proctor bellowed. The American professor at Macquarie University in Sydney, Australia, where Brad had acquired his Master of Surgery Degree in pursuit of his apprentice work in Brain Surgery was an evil man who loved to kill careers. He sat in the back of the class where the test was being administered and was failing practicing surgeons in real time. He laughed an evil laugh . . . designed to humiliate. When the proctor handed him the test he licked his lips, waved his red glove in Brad's face and . . . the moment passed.

"He was at a track meet in Eugene, Oregon, all decked out in his UCLA Xterra gear, sprinting for the high bar, noticing his parents just a few rows up across the running track. He leaped, turned his back to the bar, and cleared his butt, then his feet . . . the moment passed.

"He was alone on the ocean, alone in a purgatory of pain, wondering where it all went wrong, and the waves were crashing endlessly on the beautiful pristine beachhead where he was consigned to spend forever with no one to love him. The blackness that settled within his soul was suffocating, the bright sky suddenly dark with billowing grey-black clouds, and an instant hurricane type storm, systematically wrenching any joy from his lost life, damned him forever. Oh the pain of his selfish deeds . . . the moment passed.

"Run, run, as fast as you can," she said. "You can't catch me or the Gingerbread Man." The little girl was laughing and making fun of him. Her giggle was so infectious. Her speed was uncanny, her endurance . . . . forever. He had never seen this one tired, ever. That kid, two years his junior, was the best runner in the world as far as he could tell. She was so pretty too, what with her skinny body, those magnificent long legs, and a brunette bouquet of thick straight hair all the way below her waste. Many times he had shaken his head, kinda wishing he was two years younger, or her two years older, which would be better for him. He had a rule about the younger crowd. Never date down. Never date anyone. You have too much to do, Brad. He ran harder. They were way out in front of everyone else. He always was, that is until this kid showed up at Green Valley High School, the fastest runner of all and just a freshman. He was a junior then, a senior now, and he had never bested her in any kind of a race.

"Come on, you goofball. You can't win if you don't run," she taunted. He ran harder. He was running harder than ever, trying to keep up with this jumping jack, but it was no use. The best he could manage was to be the best he ever was. *Maybe that was it? She made him better, better than ever. He loved that. He tried to remind himself that he was a high jumper, not a long distance guy, but when she was around that didn't matter one iota to him. Running from behind the little speedster was its own reward he reminded the carnal side of himself. She was so good looking and smart too. It was the legs. He loved looking at those long legs as they propelled her forward, faster and faster and . . .*

He was jolted awake. *Where am I?* He couldn't remember. "Captain Peterson. Wake up. We need to talk." *Hankle. Oh yes, I'm flying across the ocean, in the military now.* It was his choice. He thought that he remembered the dream vividly, but lost it in the bits and pieces he tried to put together. Now he was fully awake and there was hustle and bustle all over the place. Soldiers were moving about and seemed to be getting ready for, what the heck, combat. This was a transport flight, not a combat mission. What was going on here? The shouting over the aisles, command orders from one level to the next were disconcerting to Brad.

"Colonel Hankle, what is happening here? I thought we were headed to Bagdad."

"That is yesterday's news, son. We have had a change of orders; you have too." Brad was not paranoid, but could be considered a bit self conscious about what was usually going on around him. It looked like a number of the troops were watching him and the Colonel. "Captain Peterson," Hankle continued, "there is a terrible fight going on down on the ground, a surprise attack. It seems the Taliban and some Al-Qaida rushed one of our villages and the carnage is overwhelming. We are out over Afghanistan, down south of Kandahar, near the Pakistani border. You have been asleep for over six hours. That's a good thing, boy, because you are about to receive the proverbial baptism of fire. There is no safe place to land so we have to jump, you with us. You are needed at a makeshift hospital, very poorly equipped; it's just two clicks from the intense fighting."

"You're freaking kidding me! I've never jumped out of anything in my life, especially into a shooting war in the middle of the night, so far from our intended destination. I want to get on the radio and hear these orders first hand." Brad Peterson was terrified beyond imagination. Could they do this to him? Was the army that stupid to waste him like this? He would never survive the night. Good Lord, he was on a huge jet. What the hell were they going to do, open the damn door and jump out? Just then one of the officers on the plane worked his way towards the front where the conversation, if you could call it that, was taking place.

"Colonel Hankle, sir, we have been ordered to radio silence. It seems we are being picked up by Taliban message interceptors. All relays stand as delivered. We are to jump in 23 minutes. The Captain Pilot states that everything is ready."

Brad was paralyzed with fear, could hardly breathe, had no words, was about to piss his pants. "I need to use the bathroom." He sped away. Once inside he pretended to do his business and sat there thinking of a way out of the mess he had gotten himself into. He could refuse the order, but what would be the price of that? He had no idea what form of Catch-22 he was being forced to try and survive at that moment. He went back into the chaos of the readying troops and found other officers, one with a jumpsuit and a parachute just for him—all ready to go.

"Here, slip into this, Captain Peterson. You're going to save lives today, sir, and we are so grateful to you for being with us in this time of need." What could he do? He had been on his first assignment for only a few hours, had not even landed to begin his first hospital duty, and suddenly he was screwed by the pooch. He wanted to purge, felt the need to heave, but forced the bile back down his throat. He was cornered, still a man, and he did what any American soldier would do in that situation. Captain Bradley Peterson donned the jumpsuit, sat quietly sickened, in fear of his life, even as the parachute was tightened around his trembling torso like a straight jacket. He readied himself to die. *I'm going to die tonight.*

"Colonel Hankle, jump time, six minutes." sported an eager soldier; he was all ready to go.

Oh, goodie for him. Brad was numb, slipping into shock, and yet even as he prepared for death, he did not want the others to know that he was such a chicken. He quietly chuckled with resignation.

Colonel Hankle snuggled next to him. "Don't you worry about a thing, young hero. The suit will keep you plenty warm in the twenty below air out there, the parachute is set to go off by itself, and we have outfitted you with a GPS locater so we will find you within minutes once you hit the ground. You can do this. Can you do this?

"OK."

"I can't hear you. Scream it out loud. Can you do this? Say it. Say, 'I can do this.' Scream it."

"I can do this. I CAN DO THIS!" Brad was about to faint he was so weak in the knees.

"BOYS," Colonel Hankle bellowed at the top of his lungs. The hustle had temporarily come to a screeching halt. The only sound now was the throbbing of jet engines roaring through the night. One and all were geared up to the max for war. There were weapons everywhere, ammo strapped over shoulders secured for free fall, thick jumping suits, high altitude diving helmets ready to go, and they were all staring at Brad. "BOYS, is Captain Peterson ready? Is he good to go with us tonight?"

In unison they all responded, loud and clear, "SIR, HELL NO, SIR." Then there was dead quiet.

Suddenly raucous laughter erupted from one end of the cabin to the other.

The entire back end of the C-141 began to open. The cabin had been depressurized for the jump without any notice that Brad was aware of and just like that the night was a gaping window at the back of the big transport, and Brad could tell it was far warmer than the twenty below Hankle had mentioned, but still very cold indeed.

"The boys and I would never have conjured this little game if we didn't love you, Brad. The courage you have shown by coming out here to help us, what with the magnitude of your career, gives us hope for the real America, our fading free nation in these troubled times." Brad listened, numb from head to toe, the fear just beginning to recede a bit, and was suddenly aware that he was the butt end of some kind of ritual. In that moment he realized that he had bonded with these kids and their old man, and would never forget this crazy night.

"One minute to green light, Colonel."

"Brad, I'm sorry about that but I only take guys who are ready, and my boys say you're not ready. One good thing you can take from this little exercise though; it appears to me that you have a good working corpus callosum. It's keeping the connection

169

between both halves of your cerebral hemispheres well thickened, and therefore your hippocampus is directing traffic in a mature, experienced environment. Because of that, unlike me as you point out, you are able to generate good cognitive experienced thinking; it is balanced, complex, and of course sensible." He gave the doctor a warm, affectionate, and respectful hug. There were green lights everywhere and the crowd started moving quickly towards the end of the plane, departing out into the bitter rushing wind. "Goodbye, Brad. I look forward to seeing you again, just not in your office if you know what I mean."

"Understood, sir; please, may I never see you there, Bob. Thank you for the hospitality and for all the fun, though I am not so sure how much fun I am having at the moment. How is it you know so much about the human brain, biologically that is?"

Colonel Hankle smiled through the face plate, equipped with night vision, readying to fasten it shut and seal his hands into gloves. With all his cold weather gear, ammo and weaponry, the old warrior looked like a one-man-army, one of those oversized characters in a modern war video game. "I don't know jack, young Captain; I just looked up some terms in the dictionary so I could bluff my way through the conversation." He was laughing as he closed the mask, turned, made a running start for the rear towards the open ended fuselage, and as was custom, he was the last soldier to run off of the back of the jet, disappearing into the night and leaving Brad standing there, emotionally drained, almost alone, and suddenly very lonely. He watched the back of the plane close up, moved to take the silly outfit and equipment off, and then began to wonder what was next for him, but not until after he whispered a word of prayer for the safekeeping of his comrades, now forging directly into harm's way.

Things got quiet on board the big old jet, which had pressurized again, was climbing, accelerating and turning, probably to the north, him flying by himself and just a couple of others outside of the cockpit. The galley steward brought him a bottle of water, offered a full blown meal, recommended by the Colonel before he vanished into the late evening air. Yes, it was evening again. The length of the flight and the rotation of the earth made that seem logical. The food was a sound idea too, he was informed. His long day was to get longer yet and there was no need to go hungry; so he ate a huge breakfast of newly brewed coffee, fresh fruit, what was at least a 20 oz bone-in rib eye steak—perfectly cooked to order, a half a dozen scrambled eggs, three slices of thick Texas toast with a huge slab of melting butter, a generous bowl of strawberry jam, a king's portion of hash brown potatoes and a full quart of ice cold milk. He was stuffed when finished, made all the proper preparations this time, adjusted his iPod to new music, "Jungle Sounds," more from "Echoes of Nature," put on the headset, pulled the mask over his weary eyes and went back to sleep, for how long he did not know. He fantasized getting the dream back, but alas, he was not touched that way by the genie of subconscious adventures.

"Captain Peterson," Brad heard his name as if it were an echo off of a canyon wall, and from a far distance. There was the slightest tapping on his shoulder, but he could not figure why someone would tap his shoulder. Was it his father? No, it could not be. "Captain Peterson, it is time to wake up," this time the voice was loud and clear. Brad took off the headset, tired of the music anyway, and he was immediately engulfed with the sound and feel of the jet airplane he was still flying on after all this time. He removed the eye blinders, sat up straight, and found the co-pilot who had made room for him in the cockpit. "Captain Peterson, we'll be setting her down in just a few minutes. I was ordered to let you sleep as long as possible. You may think your day is over, but it is just beginning. I am afraid there isn't even time for you to eat."

"I am stuffed, Lieutenant. Where are we?"

"Approaching Oman, sir; we are now over the continent of Africa, about to land at Thumrait Air Base. You have new orders. I was told that your job in Baghdad is still waiting for you, but you are needed right now on the USNS Comfort, a Navy Hospital ship that is currently out in the Arabian Sea off of Karachi, Pakistan. You were brought here so you could hitch a ride out to the USS George Bush, from whence you will get a chopper lift over to the Comfort, situated less than fifty miles from the aircraft carrier. It looks like you are going to have another interesting day."

"It's hard to digest all this new information, Lieutenant. Is this normally how things go in the military? No, don't answer that. Let's just let it hang there." He was going to an aircraft carrier, to land on one? He . . . Good Lord. Going to an amusement park would never be the same again.

"We do have good news from the ground back along the Afghan border where we dropped the load a few hours ago. The Captain and I thought you would be happy to learn that our guys surprised the hell out of the enemy. They were cornered when Hankle and his boys plummeted in behind them. The operation was a complete success and we didn't lose a single guy, not even a scratch. The old man is laughing his booty off. He is a lunatic; you must have figured that out by now. Robert Hankle is more than ten years older than the next youngest Colonel who fills a similar role. He just loves field work. Anyway, they are out of harm's way again for the moment and wrapping things up there.

"Captain Peterson, you have just enough time to get a shower and freshen up. If you remember, there is a complete change of clothing for you hanging in the officer's wardrobe closet."

Brad felt the wheels touch down just as he was getting dressed and cleaned up. As becoming the officer he was, Brad was appropriately dressed in blue pressed slacks with a white belt, tucked in his army blue brass buttoned shirt; he then slipped into black polished shoes, and properly adjusted his white cap. Thank heavens he had slept so well. When the door opened for him he was instantly awash in bright sunlight, a brisk balmy wind blowing dirt. It was chilly, perhaps in the fifties, and there were huge cumulous clouds on the horizon, but what affected his senses the most was the smell. This placed reeked of a foul, filthy aromatic mixture of fuel, grease, grime and other nastiness he could not identify. He was instantly glad this would not be his home, he hoped. At the bottom of the stairs there was a military Hummer waiting. It was white and had a big red cross on the side, a medical vehicle of some sort. The soldier standing next to it with a big smile seemed very proud to be there.

"Good morning, Captain Peterson. I am Corporal Jonathan Milk," he saluted. Brad returned the salute and extended a handshake to the young man. He instantly took Brad's two duffle bags and hoisted them into the back seat of the vehicle. "Welcome to Oman, sir, and to the United States Army. We appreciate your service. I myself am a technician assigned to the base from the Blanchfield Army Community Hospital out of Fort Campbell, Kentucky."

"Good morning to you too, Corporal Milk," Brad stated as he took the envelope that the young technician had for him. As they drove, very fast he noticed, he shuffled through the papers and learned for the first time that there had been a huge terrorist bombing at a restaurant in Karachi, Pakistan at a hotel known as Avari Towers. Many of the wounded had been removed to the USNS Comfort, the ship that was his destination today. He was being called over to help with the injured and in particular head wounds on younger victims, something he definitely could get involved in right away. For the first time since he had decided to do this, his blood ran cold. *This is real.*

The Hummer drove right up to a very small funny looking jet; the engines were all warmed up and ready to go. The pilot was sitting in the cockpit; the one remaining seat for him was to his right. They were in a big hurry. As the Corporal loaded his bags into a small storage compartment, he climbed the ladder and sat down into the seat. The young technician waved them off, jumped back into the Hummer and drove away, much slower this time. Once again Brad Peterson found himself sitting in the co-pilot seat of a military aircraft. This one, however, was reserved just for him. He strapped himself into the seat, snapped on the helmet, and spoke with the pilot through the plane's radio system. They exchanged greetings; Brad found out that they were in a US Navy A-7 Corsair, one of the oldest and most reliable aircraft still in use. In no time at all they were in the air and out over the Indian Ocean, more specifically the Arabian Sea.

The pilot was a very busy man and did not socialize with Brad, a small thing for which he was actually grateful. If he was not worried sick about injured kids he would have found this little flight to be very adventurous. There was all kinds of air traffic about—helicopters, fixed wing radar planes, fighter jets, a refueling plane—and others too. After just an hour or so Brad caught sight of a small fleet of ships, all surrounding a tiny aircraft carrier in the center. His heart quickened when he realized that they were going to land on top of that thing. As it grew larger and larger, Brad was no more comforted by the little runway that loomed big in his immediate future. He wondered whether this was what a Japanese Kamikaze pilot saw in the last seconds of his life, flying full speed straight into something no larger than a postage stamp. With not a warning they seemed to slam into the deck, kind of like a controlled crash, and then the pilot did something that Brad could not believe; he gunned the engines, though they had hooked onto the catch wire and the plane came to an instant stop, all as the engine roared and then shut down. Navy personnel surrounded the jet, unloaded his bags, hoisted the ladder, helped him unbuckle, saluted him with a grateful smile, and then guided him to a small vehicle which had pulled up. He was whisked forward a couple of hundred yards in front of the bridge tower to the takeoff runway and welcomed into a red and white medical helicopter. In just a minute or two he had landed on the flat top of an aircraft carrier and was now back out over the sea in a helicopter. Still no one had talked with him at all.

The flight to the USNS Comfort took all of fifteen minutes. As they approached, Brad noticed that there were helicopters all over the place, many waiting in line to land, but his chopper must have been green-lighted since they flew directly to the helipad at the rear of the hospital ship. When he offloaded onto the Comfort, Brad was greeted hurriedly, though it was difficult to hear over the whining of the helicopter motor, which roared louder and louder as it took off and flew away, just as another one approached. "Captain Peterson, good morning," he yelled, and this time Brad was the first to salute. "Welcome aboard the USNS Comfort. My name is Commander Alfred Smitzer and this is my ship. We are so glad that you are here. What took you so long? No, don't worry about that. Look, we need you to scrub right now. We're in an emergency here. There was a terrible terrorist attack and we have some of the worst injuries. Minutes mean life or death in some cases. Come this way. The steward will stow your stuff. Everything you need to operate and professional help is right here." They were off, down the stairs and into the belly of a modern floating hospital. There was activity and urgency all around. For the next 18 hours Brad worked around the clock, operating, sometimes on two and once even three people at a time. He saved lives, fixed things, lost lives, in fact he lost count very quickly as he worked. It was an emotional roller coaster. When he would look back on this day later, he would realize that the events of today had changed his life profoundly. There was one American soldier who was injured. Brad remembered to think of Master Sergeant Ted Hazelton, whom he had met just a couple of days ago, the soldier who'd helped to keep that old C-141 looking new. The world was a very evil place and Brad was just one somewhat ordinary man in the forest of great men who worked to hold that evil at bay.

Over the next few months Brad finally found his way to the hospital he had been assigned to in the Green Zone of Baghdad, Iraq. He also traveled all over plying his trade and never turned down an assignment since he felt invincible, out saving lives in a war zone. He found great solace in his running time, a place where he could make sense of it all while jaunting, sometimes twenty miles or more. Brad felt it vital that he keep himself in crack physical condition because assignments like the ones he took rarely came with scheduled hours or days. Sometimes rest was a luxury he was not afforded. The time was passing quickly and although he came to know a new sense of numbness on his more sensitive side, all related to the trauma of his duty, he never regretted one minute of this work and all that it meant to him and his legacy. He even found himself sensing those chances to get into harm's way and make a difference. Yes, Brad Peterson was a thrill seeker. Perhaps if old Colonel Hankle could see him, he may revise those final statements he had made just before he ran off of the back of the C-141 on Brad's first day of duty. Brad loved danger, loved it. That was his secret. In pursuing these thrill rides to glory, Captain Bradley Peterson was developing quite a reputation.

* * *

Daily Grace . . .
huddles on amber horizons, dawn's unearned gift.

Wise Mac

May 7th, 2010

The alarm went off and she reluctantly rolled out of bed, lethargic, no energy, having emerged from dreaming nods, the pleasure of the nightmare, she called it, the drinking dream. Dreams are meant to be forgotten, but when she dreamt of the drink, and it happened often, she remembered them in vivid detail. *This time she had been hiding in the closet under the stairway. They were coming to get her. The Grim Reaper was there to take her away to the asylum on the other side of the veil where drop-dead drunks were sent after they had failed at trying to get sober. Before slipping into the closet she had been safely seated at the back of the bar trying to sip her wine, drink her wine, oh what the heck, she was gulping it, and it was cheap no-account wine at that, not the good stuff she was used to. The worst part of it, no matter how many she had, she never felt the buzz anymore. It was terrible. Now her sobriety was lost and she had to start over. Everyone would know and then she would be the fool, lambasted by all, sentenced to a life of shame and agony. Why couldn't the wine be worth something at least? No good wine is ever sold in gallon jugs with a screw-off cap. She was going down and it had been for cheap wine, the worst of it being that she could not even enjoy the euphoric feel that was the centerpiece of her drinking.* Then the alarm went off and she reluctantly rolled out of bed, lethargic, no energy, and yes, still sober. It had only been a dream. Her sponsor Montyne had told her to expect them, the dreams, that they were a fundamental part of getting and staying sober. "Our brains are wired different," she had told her more than once. "We are so addicted to alcohol that when we stop, the disease works its way out of us through dreams and other things." A great many women who went through the Program dreaded the dreams, but not Becky April Martin. She loved the dreams, the last bastion of her drinking life. It was fun to run and hide in your dreams, drinking your merry way down the highway of deceit, especially when you didn't drink. Yup, Becky loved the dreams. Today was a very special day—one that she did not think would ever get here. Becky hurried through the morning rituals, ate a small breakfast, yes, she was also trying to watch her weight like Trisha, though not at her maniacal pace, and then was off to her morning meeting. She would see Montyne at the 8:00 Sunkiss Group. Her mood was quickening into optimistic energy by the time she found her chair.

"Good morning and welcome to the Sunkiss Group. We meet here seven days a week from 8:00 AM to 9:00 AM. My name is Howard, and I am an alcoholic."

"Good morning, Howard," responded the group in concert, as was the custom in meetings of AA.

"Alcoholics Anonymous is a fellowship of men and women who share their experience, strength and hope with each other that they may solve their common problem and help others to recover from alcoholism . . ." Howard took them through the Preamble and did his duty as the secretary of the meeting. There were two newcomers who had less than 30 days of sobriety, a couple of visitors from out of town, several very unimportant announcements, *folks love to hear their own voices*, Becky thought, but then so did she. She was unique, just like them. This was her home.

"Is there anyone celebrating any kind of an AA birthday or milestone today?" Howard asked.

"Hi, I'm Becky, a grateful recovering alcoholic."

"Hi, Becky," in concerto the group matched her name, once again the way of things here. "I'm celebrating 90 days, today." The group roared its approval. Becky was beaming with pride and joy. She was popular with her fellow group members, perhaps because she insisted on enjoying life no matter what. She had to admit that life sober was more fun than the other way.

"Congratulations, that is wonderful. Would you like to take a couple of minutes and tell us how you did it?"

"Becky, alcoholic—I have been in and out of the program for many years, always trying to get sober without telling anyone around me. I just couldn't do it. Perhaps the 'half measures' approach is as fruitless as is foretold in Chapter 3 of the Big Book. Three months ago yesterday, I was enjoying lunch with my kids, all three of them for a change, and the conversation turned serious. Each of us spoke of personal challenges, things we were struggling with, mostly them and not me, since I very much dislike confessions of any sort. I was drinking again and the kids kind of ganged up on me. My oldest was counting the drinks and ordered me to stop drinking. She is so bossy. My youngest was starting a diet, and boy what a diet. She is losing weight at a phenomenal rate. My son it turns out doesn't like the career that his father set him up in, though he is a multi-millionaire, and my bossy oldest revealed that she cannot have children. I was blown away by all of that. In the spirit of the conversation I did mention that I had tried to stop drinking, couldn't, and was possibly an alcoholic. My sponsor, Montyne, was taking a chip that evening and had invited me to be there for her. That I could not quit surely wasn't her fault, I love her, and did not want to disappoint, so I agreed to go. That evening we talked for some time and she outlined a plan that I committed to, and so here I am. Truthfully, I did not do it at all. Because I decided to listen for a change and do as I was told, sobriety became mine. All I had to do was follow the instructions given me by my sponsor, turn things over to God, and *presto.* Thank you all for being here for me. I have not gone this long without a drink since before my husband died many years ago. With that I will pass." The group clapped and it felt just peachy to be in a position to say, all day, that she, Becky, was 90 days sober.

"Montyne, alcoholic—I have been Becky's sponsor for two years. For whatever happened that day at lunch I'll be forever grateful. When Becky came to me that evening, emotional to say the least, she looked different than she had since I've known her. Some say that you are ready when you are ready. On that day, she was ready. We opened up the tool box.

"In the past three months Becky has gone to a meeting at least 90 times, she has worked the first three steps, has called me almost every day, has completed each and every reading and writing assignment she's been given, is a greeter—giving service where asked—has developed relationships with many of us, become a part of who we are, and she has stayed sober. I wonder if all that legwork has anything to do with it." Everyone laughed. "Becky, I would like to present you with this 90-day chip in honor of your sobriety." She stood, walked over to where Becky was sitting on the other side of the room, gave her the chip and a big warm hug, then continued sharing as she returned to her seat.

"All any of us get when we work this Program is sobriety for a day. Just like the rest of us, if Becky wants to be sober tomorrow, she'll have to keep on keeping on. We have built-in forgetters that need to be stimulated on a daily basis. We need to be reminded of who and what we are. I like her chances now. Becky has also acquired a listening device that allows her to learn from day—to-day what she needs to do to stay sober. I can see a great difference in her. She is much more alert, is looking healthier, and her life's joy is infectious. Becky, it is a privilege and an honor to be your sponsor and friend. Thank you for being you. With that I will pass."

The rest of the meeting went along a very interesting line and when she left at 9:00 or so, Becky felt ready to meet the obligations of the day.

There was much to do. First she had to stop by and see if Michael was in his office. He wasn't. It turns out he was involved in a manager's meeting with the fast food people. Michael also had those Burger King restaurants down in Southern California. They brought in a tidy profit. People may be broke, but they still liked to eat hamburgers. She wanted to check on Trisha and find out what her clothing sizes were these days, wanted to surprise her with some new clothes on Saturday when they got together to eat and shop as usual. Michael's assistant, Roberta Ackley, had an idea, though. Sam Giles office kept all the numbers there and someone in that office could probably help her out. That turned out not to be true either—they did not include Becky on the confidentially list, something she would see to in short order. Becky was getting frustrated when her phone rang.

"Hi, Mom." It was Trisha.

"My favorite athlete, darling, how is my daughter today?"

"I'm fine, Mother. I just got a call from Giles office. They said you were there looking to find out how I'm doing but they couldn't tell you since you are not on the list. I took care of that and so you can get information anytime you want. There are no secrets here."

"How is it going, Trish? Where are you now? I almost couldn't recognize you when we got together last week, and then, I was reminded of how you used to look. Surly you have lost several dress sizes by now, haven't you?" *Sneaky me.*

"You know I hate talking about it, Mother. Yes, the weight is coming off, not fast enough for me, but who can argue about 66 lbs. in three months? I officially weigh 199 lbs. now, just broke one of the magic triple zeros; in fact it's the only one I have to cross. That is the good news. The bad news is that I am almost a hundred pounds overweight, but, it's a start. The exercise is what I am most happy with. It feels great to have some measure of physical fitness back. I still cannot believe I let it get so out of hand. Enough about that; I don't have to wear the super huge clothing anymore. I am a size 18 dress with a 41' waste. It is flat out embarrassing, Mother, but at least now I can shop for clothing in some of the regular stores, the one's that carry plus sizes. Never again will I dress like I used to. You know, there are some cute things even in my size. I don't want to be exactly like you, but I do like a bit of color nowadays. I go for the oversized tops and still like stretch pants. It's just that now they are a bit smaller than they used to be, and don't be shocked, I am more interested in shoes and purses, Don't tell anyone, please."

"I won't, dearest child. Your secret is good with me," *I can't wait to brag to Rachael about this*, "and I am so proud of your work ethic . . ."

"Oh, Mom, I have to go now. Love you. My appointment, you know him, Stanley, he's just walking up. Since I broke 200 lb he promised me a new, improved, more intense workout regimen. My evil brother's in serious training for our so called fun run in just under two months. Fun to him always leaves me embarrassed, but not this time. I'm going to shock him when we hit the road together. Will he ever grow up?"

"I hope not, Trisha. You have a nice day and thank you for including me on the list. I'd feel left out otherwise. See you Saturday." The line went dead. This was the year of change for the Martin family. *If only Roger could see us now.*

If she only knew. Roger was with them all the time, basking in his new assignment.

She went shopping, and boy was the shopping getting fun where Trisha was concerned. This new wardrobe wouldn't last very long so she went less expensive, but even so by the time she was finished she had dislodged over $500. You know how many clothes you can get for $500 at Kohl's?

* * *

May 18th, 2010

Rachael Austin, owner of Austin Day Care, was a very quiet person, especially quiet for a member of the Roger Martin family, but Rachael was moving and shaking today. She was eying a piece of land abutting Pecos on the east side of the street, between Warm Springs and Sunset Blvd. Here could be found land that still consisted of original desert landscape, an island in a sea of development. It was quite large, too. The weather outside was spectacular. It was sunny, warm and there was a slight breeze. She had done all the calculations, had a big plan, the property was a steal as listed and she was sure to get it at an even lower price if the right kind of offer were made. "Adam, I'm over at the Pecos property right now. I am sure this is where we want to build. There is plenty of land, it is in a quiet area, near countless homes, places where two income families live, and you know what that means. Since the economy tanked, the price is way down. I say it's now or never."

"How much of it do you think we ought to offer, Rachael? I have an idea that your big scheme is infected with the Martin grandiosity problem. So, let it out sweetheart. You want to buy the entire parcel, don't you?

"Of course I do. I may be conservative, may be known as the quiet one, but I am not stupid. If we control all of the property we get to develop the entire thing with our own objectives in mind."

"Just the zoning exceptions will drive us crazy," he pointed out. "You want to take prime rural land, currently zoned for ranch style living, including being utilized for the domestication of horses, and convert it into commercial mixed use so that you can build a daycare center there. If we can't get it on, and if the economy slips even further, we could take one heck of a bath on something that adventurous. Dear, it could even break us. You never take chances, except where your daycare vision is concerned. Are you blinded here by the love of kids, Rachael? Is that it?" Adam knew his wife and if she was calling him, he knew that she was as sure as could be this time. "Have you talked to Michael?"

"I wanted to get your approval first before I go to the big wheel about this one. If I have you in my corner, Mike is sure to help make this happen. I want to develop the property into something very special for kids—children from the cradle all the way through middle school— when it all comes together. The only other viable option in this area is Merryhill and since we will be centralized, know all the players, and have a much better plan, I don't think they will hold a candle to us. We've had that conversation, you and I."

"Ok, Rachael, I'm in. Give Michael a call and tell him you are ready to make the move, and then when you get off the phone, call me back and let me know what happened."

"You got it." She disconnected, called Michael on his mobile phone, was rewarded with his voice mail, and so she left a message.

This land would make her neighbors with Wayne Newton, whose ranch, Casa de Shenandoah, was right across the street and less than a block away. *I wonder what I could get done if I won the support of the entertainer and got him on my side.* Rachael walked back and forth up the fence line, making sense of the flood channel that ran down the south side of the property. Would that be a danger to the kids and could that hurt her chances? Now that she was taking a closer look at things, planning, scheming, hoping, dreaming, and looking forward, she could sense a future that was going to explode. She decided that the minute she got home, it was time to start sketching her first artistic impression of how the whole thing would come together. She could just imagine getting into an argument with the architects over the design of the childcare center, the pre-school, the elementary and middle schools, how the different playgrounds would work, what new and exciting things she could introduce that would attract parents to her vision. Who said Rachael Austin didn't have an imagination, that she was so stuffy? Somewhere in the moment she daydreamed a middle school basketball team playing a big game, the kids, parents, and others screaming them on to victory over Andre Agassi's Academy, when her cell phone rang. Michael was calling her back.

"Hi, Sis; sorry I couldn't pick up. I was down in the locker room at the club and mobile phones aren't allowed in there. What's up?"

"You live at the club these days, Michael. Are you afraid that Trisha is going to make you look silly in these little runs you have planned? You're pushing old age, aren't you?"

"Nonsense—that is not true, Rachael. I made the commitment to fitness way before the Super Bowl bet with Trisha. I haven't changed a thing."

"Yeah right, Mike, I am so sure of that. You always have something up your sleeve. You think she is going to perform way above expectations, don't you?"

"That would be impossible, Sis. The expectations she is living with are enormous. I don't think I could stand to go through what she's going through. That being said, you ought to come down here sometime and watch her do it. Her work ethic is beyond impressive. Everyone in the club that is anyone is well aware of what she is up to and they are all in her corner. She and Stanley, her trainer, are going at it like world class athletes. In my life I never dreamed she would perform at this level. Know what is so funny about the whole thing? She looks so happy. I think she can't believe that finally, finally after all these years, she is getting out from under all that weight, the depression of losing Dad, all the negativity of the dark time in her life. I also think she is a little embarrassed about letting herself go so far off course and is determined to put the whole thing behind her."

"How much weight has she lost?"

"Stanley has her weighing every Saturday now. As of last weekend she was down more than 75 pounds. She is but a shadow of her former self. I think she weighed in at 187 or something like that."

"Good for her. She's going to blow it all off in record time. Mike, the reason I called is . . ."

"Let me guess. You want to spend millions of dollars on a piece of property so we can get started on your new life, you have it all figured out, have won the support of Adam, that is if you can get me to go along, and we are all in for a big, risky, horrific new adventure." She was smiling. "You want the property on Pecos. You do know that those thirteen acres are listed for a tidy $4,000,000, a steal if you want my opinion. Are you aware that the zoning calls for residential homes, the smallest on ½ acre lots. That spot is not zoned as commercial property for your school, though I think I have an idea . . ."

The sun was shining bright that afternoon.

* * *

June 4th, 2010

Trisha had gone to bed very early last night in anticipation of today's morning bike ride. When she looked into the mirror, the person she saw was conflicted. At once she could hardly recognize herself. The only time she ever considered her weight was on Saturday mornings when she met with Stanley for the obligatory weigh in session and the counseling that surely followed. She looked more normal than obese now, still way too big; that was the conflict, to her she still looked enormous. One thing she admired though, and was grateful for—there were no stretch marks and her skin seemed to be keeping up with the weight loss. Was it possible that she could lose the weight and still have a nice looking body, one that did not droop with huge amounts of excess skin, all stretched out and hanging off of her like a burlap gunny sack? Stanley had said that anything was possible and showed her some research. It was too much to believe that she could escape the fate of huge weight loss and bad skin.

Trisha was headed to Hover Dam, a sightseeing destination; she wanted a look at the new Hover Dam Bypass Bridge which was almost completed and scheduled to open soon. Summer mornings were the best in the Las Vegas area. The weather was perfect today. It was still dark when she warmed up, stretched the muscle groups, ate a hearty breakfast of coffee, fruit, a Nutrisystem Cinnamon Bun and three scrambled eggs, all washed down with apple juice. She loaded her backpack with a couple of Nutrisystem breakfast bars, an apple, a banana, and a two quart version of what she had come to call 'Burton's Magic Drink,' vitamin and mineral laden no-calorie fluids. As first light, about 4:45 AM she set off on the adventure, keeping a moderate pace at first, and then ramping up to full workout mode for the duration of the journey, which took less than four hours to complete—round trip. The smell of the morning air was wonderful, it was quiet on the roads, and she felt free. Trisha always felt free when she was out riding her bike. By the time she arrived at the club for her regular morning workout, the temperature outside was well over 100 degrees, the hot scorching wind blowing in her face, made it feel like her skin was ripping away. She was drenched in sweat and looked forward to a cool shower, a huge mineral drink, and the newspaper before she hit the pool.

Once again the day was full of promise. Later, on the other side of an afternoon nap, after working hard and eating the right kinds of food, she would get the promised reprieve with another fun and interesting shift over at Target. *Am I the only person on earth who loves going to work?* It wasn't fair, but then as Trisha Jean Martin knew all too well, life was not fair. Tomorrow, it would be Stanley and the weigh in, usually a positive experience of late, and then on to a luncheon with her mother.

The scheduled installment with Stanley was getting a new twist this week. He had knee braces that would reduce the impact on her knees. She did not look forward to fitting them properly, but what promised to follow was what had her heart fluttering. On Sunday, she and Stanley were going to test them out on a 10k run, her first in many years. If everything went well, she would run 10ks several times between now and the July 4th event she had been living for.

* * *

June 30th, 2010

The scorpion nest buzzed along with the abundant life of a nighttime desert, its hunters looking for prey in bombed out buildings, often coming into contact with humans and other animal life who stumbled along, not unlike army soldiers out on a hunt of their own. This particular species, *Androctonus crassicauda*, was particularly nasty, having caused many deaths in the Middle East where they flourished. They were frightening just to look at, blackish brown, six inches long on average, thick and fat—they were as evil looking as they were poisonous, and they were smart, knew what to do and how to do it. What made them so dangerous, more so than the venom, was their chosen lair. They lived in dark places, in walls and other hollowed out edifices of human creation, and as horrific as they looked, at night when the nocturnal insects became active, because of their color, they were very hard to spot. Even the snakes were terrified of these little devils from hell.

* * *

The little boy, just 13 years old, had no idea what a fuss was going on about him, as he lay in an induced coma, fighting for his life on the operating table at Anadolu Medical Center in Istanbul, Turkey. He was being operated on to remove a benign brain tumor which had grown to the size of a golf ball. His parents, people of very meager means, had been told that an operation to save their son would not be possible, so they had tearfully praised God when they learned that a US Army captain, a soldier stationed in Baghdad, learned of their plight and had won permission to bring his team here and make the surgical attempt—at no charge. Because the surgeon was so well

185

known, a search of local facilities had turned into a competition to see who won the privilege of hosting the operation. Anadolu, one of the finest facilities anywhere, conveniently partnered with Johns Hopkins Medicine, had agreed to offer everything needed, including the full rehabilitation of the boy, pro bono, that is if their own staff could observe and record his work. They were just wrapping up, the operation had been a complete success, everyone was in great spirits, and surgeon Bradley Peterson was scrubbing down, getting ready to meet the parents and to inform them that they would be saddled with the normal discontented moodiness of a young teenager who was expected to fully recover and resume his life of mischief.

The chopper on the roof of the hospital had rotors turning as Captain Peterson enjoyed a moment with the family, all twenty three of them—parents, siblings, grandparents, cousins, and whatnot. They were cheering, crying, hugging each other, him—they knew him and would love him for life, though he did not even know their names. It didn't matter. It never did. He had done much more than give them hope. He, by the will of God, had given them all a new lease on life. There was a tear in his eye as he climbed the stairs out onto the roof, boarded the modified Blackhawk, situated himself, gave a thumbs up to the pilot, and watched out the door as the hospital, a six-story horseshoe building, slowly shrunk into his past, as did his view of Istanbul. The flight back had begun. Brad attached his now famous headset, clicked on a full set of Dire Straits, kicked back and enjoyed the ride. He was not even close to being sleepy, though he had just spent eleven hours in surgery. He was as high as a kite.

* * *

It was still quite hot, even many hours after sundown. Hammer Squad leader Germane Williams, 'Germ,' was rightfully concerned for his men. He didn't need anyone to pass out from the heat as they hunted down the elusive, vile thugs who, hiding behind the veil of Islam, were tormenting and killing people indiscriminately. Duhok, one of the very northernmost provinces of Kurdish-controlled Iraq, seemed to be targeted simply because they wished to live free, like most anyone would. Germ had a bead on the terrorist sett and really was confident that tonight would be the night. *Killing time has come.* They were patrolling the village of Zakho, a few miles south of the Turkish border, and had been tipped off by locals, ones they actually trusted, as to where the terrorist might be. *Yes, tonight . . . it'll be the night.* The surrounding area was a mix of rich farmland, desert oasis, industrial development, oil and fruits of the economy that oil brings—conveniences of modern life. It hardly seemed like a war zone at all when viewed from a distance. Williams had told his family that it looked more like Utah farmland. There were hard working people, families, education, and even religious tolerance, though Christians who had recently been attacked here by violent jihadists might not agree. Duhok Province represented the future of Iraq. Germ felt a wash of anger when thinking of the job ahead, digging out a swarm of evil insects and fumigating the vermin; these were poisonous scorpions that had to be dealt with in order for that future to be realized.

The ten-man squad, lead by Gunnery Sgt. Williams, was accompanied by a field medic and two four-man fire teams. As they moved through Zakho, stealth was their ally, meaty resolved steel their mojo, freedom their friend, and a primal fear that would not go away—until the shooting started. Being in Hammer Squad was not for the weak-of-heart. Zakho had Americans, civilian Americans living here too, so there was much to fight for. They were field equipped with 5.56 mm M249 light machine guns, standard issue M-16 rifles, grenades, one M4 carbine, night equipment, and many friends within shouting distance if things got out of hand and they needed help. Germ preferred the M4 carbine. It was smaller, had less punch than the M-16, but he was also an expert shot with it, having sent several of the Iraqi al-Qaeda to their paradisiacal reward in his three tours here. The first time he returned was because he had been *stop-lossed* back into action, an involuntary extension of his term. Later, he had decided his own fate by re-upping when he was offered a promotion. Unlike so many others, he did not regret it. There was nothing going on for him at home; now, this was his home. He loved the Army and was on the verge of dedicating his future in the Service as a *Lifer.* The small town was well lit at night, but not so well down by the Khabur River where they were, and for their purposes, the darker it was the better they liked it. They moved like alley cats, thinly spread over two streets, soft of feet, as they approached the property from both sides.

Germ whispered into his helmet-mounted microphone, "Panther, I see a light in the house just south of the target, and I see movement. It doesn't look right to me. Check it out from your vantage point and give me a run down."

"Looks like a rag-head bubble-up, Germ—not good. Maybe we got the wrong house. I'm beginning to see . . . ," and then all hell broke loose, from, not one, but two houses. Fighters poured out of both, shooting. It looked like they had just hit a hive of killer bees with a baseball bat. They were going to need help and fast if they wanted to stay off of the front page of tomorrow's newspapers—as the latest American KIA story. Germ was on the com blaring for help before he fired the first shot, which did hit its target. Help was six long . . . very long, minutes away. It was just possible that the *Lifer* status he was aiming for was going to be a much shorter career than he wanted.

* * *

The UH-60A Black Hawk was cruising along the southern Turkish border, an hour or so from home, at just over 16,000', some five hours out of Istanbul. They were not at the end of their range by any stretch, Peterson and his crew certainly didn't constitute a full load, but they were down to less than one third of their fuel before she had to set down; that was when the chatter started.

A couple of the guys were playing cards, three of them were dead asleep, the crew was working, and Brad was enjoying the night sky as they flew along at roughly 160 knots, the standard cruising speed of a Black Hawk. He was getting tired and wanted the trip to be over. Rules of engagement dictated that they fly battle-ready with fatigues and gear should something go wrong and they be required to land out in the middle of nowhere. Brad wanted to get out of these clothes and back into something more comfortable.

At first he did not notice how animated the crew had become, but after a few minutes it became clear that they were engaged in lively debate with each other. Brad put on a communications helmet—as

Captain of the team he had one issued every time they went out, but before he could say a word he was immersed in what he was hearing. There was a huge battle going on, a routine patrol had flushed out a swarming nest of enemy combatants; reinforcements were headed in from all over the place, drones had decimated the buildings, but apparently there were tunnels there and most of the fighters had survived by going into those tunnels—which were under attack. It was a mess and there were casualties.

"How far away is it, guys?" Bradley didn't want to jump into someone else's business, but it was kind of like he heard himself say it.

"Ten minutes, Cap. We should be over the battle zone in just a few minutes. We're going to skirt the fight, stay safe and move on. Our orders are to get you boys home safe and sound, so there is to be no monkey business for us tonight . . . Look! There it is. See the fires. Good hell, there are soldiers all over the place. They must have hit a hornets' nest or something. Look at the chopper activity going on. You know what this looks like. It looks like a scene from that Martin Sheen picture about Nam—what was that movie—*Apocalypse Now*? It's beautiful, man. We're getting them good tonight, Captain." By now everyone was alert and looking. These guys were a surgery team, not really suited to the battle front. Oh, they could do it; they were perfectly capable of working triage, more than capable—that is.

The call startled Brad just a bit. He needed to stay away from these communication helmets.

Apparently there was a shortage of onsite medical help. Two helicopters carrying extra medical personal had malfunctioned. Was it possible that Captain Peterson and his team could set up in the rear guard, a safe distance from the actual fighting, and give a hand to the medics onsite who were without their own Captain? Brad knew . . . *there is no way out of a request like that*. He and his guys weren't going home after all. He gave the nod to the pilot who banked towards the action. His team looked a bit shocked as he smiled that terrible 'here we go' face, and said, "Guys, I didn't volunteer for this. This time it is not my fault. Now get your game face on and let's show these kids a good time."

Like a scene playing out in a theme park, not denigrating the reality of the situation and what was going on, there was a preternatural underlying unreality taking place. The air was hot, it was humid down by the river, the smell of war was everywhere— gasoline, sulfur from propellants used in ammunition, a stench that Brad could only recognize from frequent visits to the morgue— the smell of blood, urine, defecation, and death. All of these things were filling his lungs in a new and horrible way. Of course, he was fascinated by the whole thing.

The sights and the sounds of war were mesmerizing. Black sky, dazzled with a spray of brilliant stars formed the background of a three dimensional moving picture. There were machines, vehicles, flying objects, manned and unmanned, whizzing about that made Brad wonder just how organized the military could be on such short notice. If someone had been caught by surprise this evening, and apparently they had, it was definitely not the Americans. And then there were the fires, flames flickering from several buildings in the area, a number of other buildings reduced to rubble in a fast moving conflagration. It was very loud. There was gunfire, a kind of a loud, popping, rapid zippering of bullets shot so close together that it was more of a violent hum than the rat-a-tat-tat he remembered from Hollywood type wars led by the likes of Clint Eastwood and John Wayne. There were also intermittent blasts ringing out every few seconds, bombs, ear crushing explosions, so close at hand that Brad's mood went from fascinated to shocked with the whole crazy-insane thing. He'd heard of bomb thump in the core of a soldier's body and had been told that it never truly went away. Now he knew. This was his first real up-close combat experience. What disturbed him most of all was the screaming, audible from quite a distance, reminding the young surgeon that war was more about tearing men asunder than what he did, which was to put broken soldiers back together again. This was the opposite end of what he was about, and yet, here he was with a vital purpose, one that would affect the future of many families, for better or worse, indeed, a number of them for the rest of their lives.

Brad was led to the safe-house, set back several hundred yards from the kill zones, where there was a triage set up and quite a few medical personnel already at work. In a field just behind the home, and that is what it was, a home, were helicopters, two medical Black Hawks and two old magnificent Boeing CH-47 Chinook twin rotor work horse helicopters. The smaller craft were to get the seriously injured who had been patched a bit, off the ground and to a hospital, while the larger Chinooks would take the less seriously injured in greater volume. Just like the fighters, the fixers were good at what they did.

Inside, Brad moved from patient to patient doing whatever was needed to get them ready for transport. Sadly, not everyone made it through the night, but most did, even some of the more severe cases. It was a proud moment to be in the lifesaving business. In what seemed like minutes, night disappeared and the light of a new day began to emerge on the eastern horizon. Unbelievably, the fighting was still going on, though casualties had diminished greatly and yet the battle was finally coming under control. Brad overheard one of the injured officers, not so badly injured, speaking to one of his soldiers, saying that so far they had counted 243 dead enemy fighters. He also said that there were even more down in the tunnels between the various houses they'd been operating from. Hammer Squad had opened a can of worms, initiating a killing operation among a pack of vermin the Coalition Forces had been looking to eradicate for quite some time.

Across the way, up in the center of town, morning brought a new day for the rest of the community as well. People were so used to war, so weary from hellish and endless fighting, that today was just another day, a microcosm of stunted humanity and the blunt loss of human sensitivity. If this were going on in the States, the world would be coming to a halt. Not here, though; Iraq was a playground in hell and the people who lived here knew it.

The human race is a funny breed. That eerie dynamic of how the community dealt with tragedy would form the nexus of stories from what had happened here this night. There were many dead and countless more injured, people who were making this neighborhood their home. Yet, life seemed to go on as if nothing much had happened.

Brad went back inside to see to patients and their needs, wondering if locals had any real connection to *these* particular thugs.

Maybe they were secretly as glad to be rid of them as the Coalition soldiers were. *Is it possible that we are actually winning this war?*

* * *

Imp Rogue, CCA conjurer, one of the best Deceivers in the Alliance, had been keeping an eye on surgeon Brad Peterson. He was looking for an opening to strike, intensely waiting for the chance to make a name for himself, to get noticed *and* to get reward for bagging one of the do-gooder suckers who got in the way. Now he sensed his chance. Ever since the high value target had set foot in the so-called safe-house, the one where soldiers were being saved from their deserved fate, he had been trying to influence the Iraqi al-Qaeda dogs into the underground tunnels where the fighting and flames would pressure the tunnel system and perhaps help to hemorrhage the trap he had set with his live contact on the ground. Rogue's plan was working. All of the terrorists would be killed, stupidly thinking that the Americans would not sense the vulnerability they placed themselves in by revealing their underground network—*so what, who cares about them anyway?*

* * *

Brad was overseeing the removal of several wounded to one of the remaining large helicopters when he heard the scream, recognizing the female voice of his lead assistant; she was in the back room so he ran in a desperate panic to check it out. First Lieutenant, Margaret Ross was slumped over one of the injured Americans and in excruciating pain. He pulled her off of the soldier, now obviously a dead man, and that was puzzling since his wounds were superficial and not life threatening. Ross was now unconscious. What was going on here? He carried her limp body to a nearby cot and laid her flat, examining her to see what could possibly be the cause of this when he felt something climbing his leg. *Oh bloody hell, it's a scorpion.* Further, he recognized it at once as one of the rare deadly kind. His panic turned ferociously to horror as the realization of danger set in. He tried to shake the little monster off but it clung to his pant leg, its stinger waving wildly in every direction. Now *he* was the one screaming. This was a threat he had not even considered, and yet, he had been trained to look for this little killer—warned about it. He hurriedly pulled the knife in his belt, awash in terrorized fright, and quickly flicked the scorpion to the floor. On the floor the little beast took off for the closet at the far side of the room. By this time several others had approached and Brad, who was following the scorpion to the closet, barked orders so his assistant would get medical attention that just might save her life. Brad was shouting above the noise all around, making sure that the team knew what they were up against. The scorpion slithered under the closet door and disappeared into the darkness. Brad opened the door. At least a hundred scorpions buzzed out into the room, every one of them with the power to kill. There were still almost twenty injured people in beds all over the place and staff working in every room. Suddenly Brad Peterson was in the middle of a frenzied, panic driven nightmare.

Sergeant Germane Williams and his second, Corporal Pantera Holt of Hammer Squad, had indeed survived those first six minutes last night when they pried open the can of worms that became the nexus of the fight. They, along with the rest of their squad, having not enjoyed even a minute of rest were guarding the safe-house for the injured, and were jolted by sudden screaming from within. "Panther, there is something wrong inside the house," Germ sounded aghast. Just as he spoke the words, people, healthy and injured alike, those that could walk or run, the rest carried in every conceivable manner, most spouting obscenities of a baser nature, came flying out of every opening that a human could fit through. They looked terrified.

* * *

Who says they don't have fun in Hades? Imp Rogue was having a great time. The pressure points in the tunnels had given way, the murderous insects had been driven to the hole in the closet floor, and the rest was left up to nature.

* * *

July 4th, 2010

The big day had finally arrived. It was July 4th, Trisha Jean Martin was entered into an official race, she and Michael were at the starting line, well, at least a hundred yards behind the start/finish line there on St. George Boulevard amongst several hundred runners of all shapes and sizes. Suddenly, the gunshot rang out and they were off.

It was hot, very hot—the morning sun was beating steadily down as they jogged at an easy pace. There was not a cloud in the sky, and the swirling wind was blowing what seemed to be a pneumatic dust of a reddish brown sort that was indigenous to the area, making it just a bit difficult to breathe. It did not help much that Trisha could not have slept more than a couple of hours the night before. This was supposed to be a fun run, and yet, Trisha was stupefied, sneaking about in a hidden reality, the quiet semi-awareness that this was the first of forever in her new life. She was a runner again. She had hated putting on the stupid braces, designed to protect her knees from damage, but soon forgot about them altogether. She had weighed in just yesterday, now down just less than 100 lb, and yet still almost 70 lb out from where she needed to be. The extra pressure on her knees could ruin everything. Stanley had insisted that she run this race for what it actually was, a slow jog just like any of the many she had experienced while training in the past couple of months.

Mike, who had chattered like a talk show host all the way up in the car, and who looked completely out of place in his brand new running outfit, was deadly silent now. Trisha felt very comfortable in her new outfit. She wondered if he was staying with her out of obligation and was feeling the frustration of holding back, or if his sullen languid demeanor meant something else entirely. He was a very complicated person. And so it went, a much quieter experience considering all the bravado and big-talk building up to the event. The course turned right on N. River Road, then there was another right turn on 7th Street, all the way back up to Bluff on the west side of town where they turned left for the first time. While many of the runners had stopped, some due to the heat, others because they were not physically fit enough for the run, and at least two because of dehydration, Trisha had hardly broken a sweat. She had taken every opportunity to drink along the way, but none of it was necessary. She was in excellent physical condition, remembering Stanley's comparison of her situation to that of an NFL offensive lineman who could be huge by choice, carrying an extra 75 lb or more, but in superb condition. Football players carried the bulk so that they could use the weight to their advantage. This was a no—brainer for her, in fact, a day off from what she was so used to. Today's run was a nice Sunday saunter.

Trisha began to daydream of the festivities they had planned for the rest of the day. She and Mikey would be shopping in little boutiques, strolling among the sites, and exploring the history of St. George. Later on they planned an early dinner at The Painted Pony where she had been given permission to eat a huge meal— the thought itself was intoxicating—and then they had reserved seats at the Tuacahn Amphitheater for a spectacular fireworks show when the sun went down. The backdrop of golden-red canyon walls promised a memorable July 4th extravaganza. Above all else, she had Michael to herself. Trisha so loved her brother. There he was, jogging lovingly at her side . . . or so she thought.

Just after the turn south onto Bluff, Mike picked up the pace. It was very subtle, a slow lengthening of stride, and yet his little push caught Trisha a smidgen off guard. *What is this?* Of course she kept pace, and in fact she liked the new rhythm, found it more comfortable. They began to pass runners, some looking at her like she was a freak—at least that is how *she* felt.

Mike looked at her and smiled—it was an evil smile. When the course turned again, a sort of a 'U' turn back north onto Main Street, Mike picked up the pace . . . yet again. *So this is how it's going to go for us, after all.* Trisha knew what the silence was all about. It had nothing to do with a frustrating slow poke sister companion slowing him down; instead this was all about a strategy.

He can't resist. Trisha easily matched his pace again. Now they were moving past runners and had become noticeable, a bit more out there. Trisha began to formulate a strategy all her own. *Oh, well,* thought Trisha, *so much for a loving fun run.* Today's was going to be a race after all. They approached a drink station. Trisha had feigned exhaustion and fallen just a few steps back, and when Mike slowed to take his drink, she bounded past him and took the lead. He cursed as he threw the cup down, finding that he had to work hard for the first time in the race to catch up. Trisha wasn't even thirsty. She looked at him and laughed out loud. This time she picked up the pace, noticing for the first time that Michael was having a bit more trouble breathing. She could easily have left him in the dust, the reddish brown stuff that was blowing around, but her strategy was all about the half-marathon in December. When the course turned back onto St. George Boulevard, Trisha kicked. She was passing runners as if they were standing still. Mike was falling back. Trisha had the wind to reach the finish line over a hundred yards in front of her brother, but chose instead to feign exhaustion again and let him catch up, which he did just before the finish, and they crossed the line together, her in much better condition than he. Oh what fun she had. Her first race was over.

The remainder of the day went as planned. While eating a full steak dinner, complemented by a large sweet potato, veggies, bread with butter, and apple cobbler a la mode with milk for dessert at The Painted Pony, Michael had asked how someone with her weight issues could have performed so well. She just smiled, but knew if he had attacked from the very start she would not have been able to hold him off. The fact she had only to push hard for a few minutes was the magic of that little run. They both knew that something special was yet to happen. Trisha continued to pay the debt incurred when she lost the Super Bowl bet that by now looked to be a lifetime ago. In the weeks to come, both Trisha and Michael worked a vigorous program, each in their own way.

* * *

Denial kept me alive
at the same time it was slowly killing me. I
was like a ghost ship's captain who doesn't
know where he wants to go, so no wind on
Earth could take me there.

Wise Mac

September 1st, 2010

Greg Simpson had spent 42 days at Pacific Hills Treatment Center in San Clemente, just a few miles south of Newport Beach, California, where he had been the perfect client. He never missed a meeting, always participated in group and individual therapy, enjoyed his time there, but was left wanting in the days leading up to his departure back into normal life. If he had taken the time to really digest the material he so willingly worked on, he would have learned over and over again that real recovery was an illusion without a sustaining Program. He would have bought into getting a sponsor and working the Steps. He would have understood that he should attend meetings, not because the court ordered him to, but because in his heart he knew that the path for him, a true addict, was grounded in following Program guidelines. Clean addicts learned stuff like changing playgrounds, playmates and playthings, listening, first obtaining and then listening to the inner voice of a Higher Power. They learned to pick up a phone and start calling people, not only a sponsor, but others in the Program who have similar challenges; these are the ingredients that make up Narcotics Anonymous. It was indeed a big project to adopt the AA/NA lifestyle. He had not been able to see the simple truth of this important fact.

Just before the completion of his institutionalized treatment, and while he was sitting outside by the campfire, he overheard one of the other clients ask one of the counselors just how they could tell if someone was going to make it on the outside. "We're never able to tell for sure," the answer came. "We can kick someone out of here for violating all the rules, he can walk into the Program, get a sponsor, work the steps, and be just fine. Then on the other hand, a wonderful client, the guy who on the outside seems to be just right, can go home and not last a week. This disease is truly cunning, baffling, and powerful, just like the Big Book says." In that moment Greg knew that he was still in a great deal of trouble. He didn't get it, he knew he didn't get it, though he had no idea what to do about his problem. Greg went home to a supportive family who wanted to celebrate the cure of his addiction. They didn't get it either. As he slipped the bonds of sobriety, Greg felt as bad for them as he did for himself.

The court had conditioned his probation on attendance at three meetings a week, staying gainfully employed, and that is what Greg had done. He sat in the back of the room at meetings, just long enough to get his court card signed, and then was out the door.

On a Wednesday early in September, his shift was almost over, and knowing there was no defense against what he was about to do, Greg called his connection. His body was vibrating in anticipation of what was to follow. Greg had to find a new source, but that would only take an hour or so, *and just this once I have to "chance it" and give in to the urge . . . just once to tide things over. Tomorrow I will get right back into sobriety.* Every time he thought of holding off, the pain was too great, like a monkey on his back demanding to be fed. It was not to be ignored. If he'd been invested in his program, perhaps Greg would have developed the tools necessary to meet the inevitable tsunami waves that were a part of recovery. Little did he know it at the time but for him it would be off to the races—again; it didn't even occur to Greg that his parole officer could call at any time for a drug test, even though he had been tested many times in the past couple of months. Greg wasn't thinking at all. Trisha was there that night. Perhaps he should go to her? She would know what to do, but he didn't, and why? The monkey said no.

Trisha had been keeping an eye on Greg Simpson for some time now and knew that his sobriety was in jeopardy. The conversations she had enjoyed with her mother over the summer had been very enlightening. She was learning a great deal about recovery from her mom, who had taken to her own program and was enjoying the fruits of a new life. She had been told about relapse, why so many had the problem, and how little could be done about it when the afflicted person was not able to listen and learn. Tonight, Greg Simpson looked entirely too forlorn and distant, so much so that he seemed to be existing in a different realm. She had no idea how to help him, wanted badly to try, and when she approached him, "Greg," as he walked out the door, he just turned away and jumped into a waiting car out front, one that did not look at all safe. In just a moment he was gone. Her heart sank. She would not see him at work again.

October 16th, 2010

Trisha was beside herself with anxiety. No one could have been working as hard as or harder than she, keeping to the nutritional guidelines set by Stanley, and working, working harder and working hardest, as if her life depended on it. She had not lost any weight for two weeks now, stuck at 142 lbs, again . . . and this time in tears as she faced her mentor. "What is wrong?"

"There is nothing wrong, Trisha. Your body is adjusting, like I said; it's just adjusting to the new you. Are you aware of what you have accomplished this year? In just over eight months you have lost, like 130 lbs. or something. That amounts to more than 15 pounds per month, a pound every two days. It's not natural. The only other place I have seen anything like this is on that television show. You're working like they do, but your nutritional requirements are so much greater. Remember, Trisha, that you are not working to a weigh-in on some television finale, but just getting started on the life of a finely honed athlete, one that shows world class potential. You must be patient. Here, look at this."

He showed her the picture he had taken on the day she first weighed in, and then showed her the picture he had just taken on his telephone. "Can you believe that?"

"Put that horrible picture away." Trisha softened into a smile. "Better yet, put it in the garbage where it belongs." He was laughing, which was putting her in a better mood.

"Remember the first run in July? Michael came to me shortly after that and asked how it was possible that someone so big could run like the wind on the tail end of a race that went on for more than six miles. Just look at what you have done for him, dear girl; his work ethic is like nothing seen around here except for you and still he cannot best you in these little runs. Your body just knows what to do. That is one of the little secrets that world class athletes, people like you I might add, just have over competition from others. Athletic muscle memory from your childhood is all still in there. Don't worry about the weight. I'm surprised you have not been gaining during this little stagnation. Give that running machine time to do its job and I'll promise you the moon. We're going all the way. Saturday, when you run again, Mike is going all out from the gun—determined to win at least once while you still have weight to lose. We have a small surprise for him. I am taking off the knee braces this time. You are in good enough condition, and have lost enough weight to pound those knees hard for the full race." Her heart leapt at the news. She hated the braces.

"You want some more good news? Reece Chartheart stopped by the other day and when I showed him your weight he almost purged all over my office. He knows now that they are going to have to pay up on the deal. He had been following your Nutrisystem Blogs, your Community Involvement, but wondered why you had not posted your weight in some time. When I informed him that we agreed to keep him, the slithering marketing guy, in the dark he just scowled. He wants you to post the weight immediately. Now get out there and go to work. Stop worrying about the weight loss and just stick to the plan. Your body needs far more than to just drop pounds. It is all about nutrition at this point."

* * *

November 5th, 2010

"Re/Max, Jenna Stone speaking, how may I help you?"

"Good morning, Ms. Stone. This is Michael Martin, is Denny available?"

"Just a moment—I think he is in . . . He is here sir, but is in a meeting right now. Can I have him call you back, or would you like to leave a message on his voice mail?"

"I'm more than happy to leave a message." She put the call through to voice mail.

"This is Dennis Keller, I am either away from my desk or on the phone right now, but your call is very important, so please leave me a detailed message and I will get right back to you."

"Denny, this is Mike Martin, long time no see—listen up. I want to buy that old dead piece of ground over there on Pecos. You know my number. Now, much as I would like to hear from you, you must know better than to think I am going to give you anywhere near the $4,000,000 price tag your dreaming client has it listed for. I have cash, but I'm not stupid, so if you want to play, give me a call." He hung up.

Rachael was sitting next to him in his office, the very same office she used to play in as a child when she went to work with her long gone father, Roger Martin. In those days it was a very simple corner workplace decked out with old furniture, a beat up chair, worn carpet, large overhead lighting, rotary phones, typewriters, green metal filing cabinets, boxes of stuff, and papers all over. Her father was not one for the fancy executive look. His assistant was a burley Polish woman who looked to be built for working and not much else, maybe arm wrestling. *My, my, how things have changed.* Michael's set-up was something else again. The furniture, matching natural cherry wood, was immaculate and well-coordinated with the natural stone flooring, and his executive chair she remembered as a gift from their mother from Relax The Back. The overhead lighting was gone, replaced by beautiful imported fan lamps, but the lamps were off and the fans twirled silently. The recessed lighting he used had to have been designed by some sort of an interior decorator. It was that good. Since he had expanded, the exterior glass gathered natural light in the mornings, but never reflected directly on the large flat screen HD television mounted on the wall, which was also bedecked with art from all over the world. On the wall behind his desk was a large oil painting of her dad, so lifelike that it almost had her in tears. There were no boxes or papers anywhere in sight. The electronics were all state-of-the-art, there were no filing cabinets, no files at all, and the only phone anywhere was his mobile, which he used exclusively. Michael's assistant, Roberta Ackley, was a bombshell. In truth she was known as one of the smartest, savviest, highly educated executives in town, the equal of Michael Martin, and she never let him forget it—the one person he in the whole place he could not intimidate. Perhaps Rachael should reveal Mike's secret about the committee whose advice he followed in running the business. No, that wouldn't be fair. Truthfully, someone that savoir-faire, that close to Michael, must know the whole story. She could tell that he loved her and most likely would not have any idea how to get along without her. When Michael hung up the phone Rachael spoke directly. "Mike, you said the property was a steal in this market."

"There is no way Denny is going to let us off of the hook here, Rachael. He knows what the property is worth as residential development. We won't have to pay the full price, and cash is king, so we do have an advantage. The key is to get it right. I do not want to take unfair advantage of the situation. After all, you're going to be a school, and we do have karma to think of."

"Since when did Michael Martin worry about karma in a deal? Am I now to think of my younger brother in the avuncular? Have you found religion since Trisha started kicking your butt all over the road?" she laughed.

"The karma is simple, my entrepreneurial wizard-sister. Yes, Trisha is unbelievable, unbeatable no matter how hard I work, and she is still losing weight. As a caretaker, a teacher of sorts, your primary purpose must not be to take advantage or solely turn a profit. Your mission is to try and make the world a better place, you know, make tomorrow a better day than today for countless youngsters," he intoned.

"What a crock. You're a scoundrel, Michael. This guy plays hardball for a living. That's it isn't it?"

"Sure is, Sis, and we need to take a very hard line just to not get taken advantage of ourselves." The phone rang. Was this him? Nope, it was his mother.

"Mom, how goes the battle this morning? "Yes—that's good to hear, Mother. It seems that she has all of us on our toes. You're losing weight, don't drink anymore; Rachael is about to grow her business, yes, I know . . . Unless she trips over another dog there is no way I will ever beat her in a race. My window of opportunity has closed, though I will not quit trying. I know. People do not even recognize her. She has regulars at Target who treat her like a new employee. No, Rachael is sitting right here beside me. We're working on the Pecos deal . . . Mom, don't worry. I have done the background work. It may take until the first of the year, but this plot is ours. Rachael? She is way ahead of the learning curve on that aspect of it. No, Mom. The Foundation is entering into a leaseback with the new Austin, LLC. Yes, we are taking all the risk. Come now, me, your son? This is an easier call than a flip of the two—headed silver dollar. The zoning— yes, I am confident in that. We do not want to play that card while the current owner is trying to maximize his leverage on the deal.

Oh, Mom, the phone is ringing again. Tomorrow, lunch—of course. Just a second." He looked over at Rachael. "Mom wants us all to get together tomorrow afternoon at, what's that, The Elephant Bar in The District. Are you in?" Rachael smiled. "We're both good, Mother. See you tomorrow."

His phone was indeed ringing. This time the call was from a client. During that call another call arrived, yet another client. During the second call Roberta walked some paperwork in and casually visited with Rachael while Michael digested the paperwork and finished up the call. When he looked up she was reminding him of his appointment across town with the city planner and one of the commissioners. He looked pleadingly at Rachael who was already collecting her things and moving towards the door.

"I loathe this job, Sis."

"More cockamamie from a BS artist, Mike—I can see that you love this place."

"Don't you worry your pretty little school teacher head off one bit. Together we will make a better day for your kids AND a nice tidy profit over the years. I love the game and am proud that you and Adam have included me in the grand scheme."

"Oh, the pleasure's all ours, Mike. You never lose, except to Trish," she laughed. "When is the next big race?"

"It's Thanksgiving Day, the 30th Annual Las Vegas Turkey Trot, out at Lake Mead, three weeks from now. You know, Rachael, I do not mind losing races to my little sister, and she is getting very little. It is not just that she is losing weight. Anyone can do that. I am beginning to really believe that she could compete at the highest levels. Her running mechanics are virtually perfect. According to Stanley Burton, she is very coachable. He has a running instructor meeting with her. I am thinking of turning her loose this time and just telling her to go for it. I'm holding her back. Can you believe that, holding her back, and by the medical definition of body mass index, she is overweight for this type of thing. I find myself trying to copy her body movement style, and by my standard I am getting away with it. I am in the best shape of my life, running farther and faster than since I was a kid, and she is slowing down on purpose out of consideration for my feelings. It is humiliating, except that it isn't. She is worth every penny we have put into her and in just a short time all that money and more is going to flow back into the coffers. That kid is money in the bank.

November 25th, 2010

Thanksgiving Day Nutrisystem Blog

By: Trisha Jean Martin

I cannot begin to express the gratitude in my heart tonight as I share innermost feelings which have flooded my soul. To say that I am losing weight this year is the understatement of my life. Last Saturday at the weekly strategy session with my trainer, Stanley Burton, I weighed just 137 lbs., now down so far from where it all started back in February, having lost just less than 140 lbs., more than half of my body weight—gone. I say this, not to brag or bang fists of glory on my chest for what I am going through, not different from you at all, but so different that I beg of you not to envy the accomplishment or to make any unfair comparison with your progress. We are on the same ship. If you are losing 1-2 pounds per week or less—so be it—for the nature of a thing is unique to each of us individually. I have discovered a proclivity to gain weight at the slightest alteration of my path. What this is telling me, and it has been affirmed by all those who advise me, is that my journey into weight loss and health will have to continue for the duration of my natural life, no matter the success of the moment, or it will fail utterly. In that we are all the same. Learn to live with the new you and your joy will be immeasurable, cast it aside and I fear your misery will be the same.

I should like to share a thing or two about my brother, Michael. I thought I knew the man before, before the Super Bowl bet which changed my life. If not for an errant pass thrown by the world's greatest quarterback, a mistake which sealed my fate, I may have enjoyed the spoils of a makeover of my humble home, a project that remains on the planning table to this day. Oh what I would have missed out on if I had won that bet, and all for some carpet and paint. Who was the large girl crying herself to sleep that night, facing a nightmare reconstitution of the essence of who she was?

Michael carries a flippant infectious persona that, without closer examination, would lead one to believe he is still a child who sees life only as an amusing playground. The fact that he played me with a two-headed coin on the flip for the bet would seem to bare the nature of what I say here. I have come to believe he tossed the coin in such a way that I would catch him and gain a measure of leverage, leverage he knew I needed but did not deserve at the time. That is Michael Martin. His depth of character is truly manifested by deeds rather than his demeanor, much the same as with other noble people I presume. In losing the wager I was conscripted to run four short races with him, followed by a half-marathon in December. Today we ran the fourth 10k race, the final tune up before the big one to follow.

Mikey is ten years older than I am, but has trained this year with the best of them. He is in the best shape of his life by what I see, yet, God given talent, and I mean that in the literal sense, gives me the edge in these little runs. He caught me slowing down again to keep him competitive, after all the agreement was that this was 'just for fun,' when I experienced another side of the man that acts the carefree boy. At first he urged me to press on. When I didn't he snapped at me, using his authority as my big brother, and let me know in no uncertain terms that it was my job to run the best race my body would allow. The last words spoken between us before the end of the run were, "Get lost—NOW!" and so off I went, albeit with a tear in my eye. As I pushed myself hard and competitively for the first time in years, passing runners at will, I sensed a new beginning to my life yet again; there have been so many this past year. Of course I did not win the race. In this universe I am still not there physically yet, but something inside of me has awakened, the small kindling of a dream, one I thought could never be courted again in this life, once again in exchange for some carpet and paint.

I know now that God loves me as He always did. This has been the best Thanksgiving Day since my final year of high school, the last one we shared with my father before he left us. As my life moves forward I see potential for a destiny to be fulfilled, not because I am different or better than others, but because I am in tune spiritually with greater forces for good. None of this would have been possible without the simple changes which set me, and you too I hope, off on this incredible journey of discovery.

For those of you who share Community space with me in the world of Nutrisystem, and for those of you who read my blogs and follow my progress, I will never leave you. No matter what happens in the future, I'm certain of the need to remain close to the herd in this program. I'm constantly reminded of the tendency to gain weight which is a cross those like us have to bear. I'll take that cross and be grateful for the chance to manage it, especially in lieu of other types of problems that folks suffer in the world, tribulations which seem to avoid me.

So, I sincerely wish everyone a Happy Thanksgiving Day. Stanley, my trainer, advises that should I lose more weight, early next year I will begin training for and running marathons again. Thank you Nutrisystem! With love, Trisha Martin.

* * *

December 1st, 2010

The full moon shone brightly in a star drenched sky, dimming the view of the Milky Way Galaxy, a bit, not much out in the blackness of nowhere, a freezing wind biting down the depression between cliffs which provided the cover for an encampment, army style. There was no campfire out here in the mountains of Afghanistan, northeast even of Fayzabad, almost to the Tagikistanian border, though the razor thin nylon tent blunted the worst of it. Heat and light, even suppressed light, was a bull's eye for modern weapons that even the Taliban had use of. Good Lord, something faint as a lit cigarette, the tiny red glow on the end of a modern day fire stick, could be all that an expert sniper would need, even from a mile or more distant, wind or no, to make his night. The specially coated tent blocked all light though and inside the warm glow of red night vision gave the men what they needed to function. There were more than 250 soldiers still out here tonight, scattered all over the place. Yet, to the naked eye one could discern nothing at all. These guys were experts at hiding in plain sight. The enemy had their cave networks to warm them. It was cold, very cold, yet Brad was warm, not just because he had the proper attire, but he was filled with a sense of purpose that these kids were his. He loved being with army regulars.

The ride out on the back, the very back of a Chinook CH-47 twin rotor chopper, was yet another spectacular experience; he, belted safely with his legs dangling over the rear edge of the troop release hatch, enjoying a breathtaking view of snow-striped desert mountains, the dawn breaking air, a clear turquoise firmament fading from dark to almost white at the horizon where the sun would soon make its appearance, and the helicopters droning along at 160 knots, not too far above the ground.

Now it was late, another battlefield secured from apparent danger, though things not perceptible to common sense did have a way of cropping up in these parts. He had escaped hospital drudgery by insisting he be allowed to go and play soldier just like any other field surgeon. Brad Peterson lived out on the edge of the game. In truth it was his desire to see the whole of it on this adventure and there was no good way to build proper war stories without leaving the safety of those who sought only to stay out of range.

Today, in addition to his personal egomaniacal desires, he had saved lives. Brad was getting quite a reputation among lower ranking soldiers. He liked them and they liked him. In one case earlier this afternoon Captain Peterson had saved, not only a life, but a leg. They had to helicopter the kid to a full service facility, but quick work by a knowledgeable triage guy, that would be Brad Peterson, had saved his leg. The last thing he said to Brad when they loaded him up was to thank him "for not leaving me eligible for the 'prosthetic-poster boy-of-the-year' award." They smiled at each other in their farewell. Officers were not supposed to fraternize with enlisted men, but Brad cared nothing at all for that rule. He was not that kind of an officer. After playing cards into the wee hours of the night, Captain Bradley Peterson, dug in with army enlisted fighters, curled up on the ground in a sleeping bag and slipped into a serene slumber as though he was on a Boy Scout outing. He dreamed.

* * *

In a peaceful forest valley, a kind of a Shangri-La, transcendent of earthly mortality, on the back porch of his home, Roger Martin, Wise Mac, and Tag Peterson carried on a quiet conversation as they waited for the young fool to finally go to sleep. "You've got to admire the boy," Roger said as he sipped at the hot spicy cider from his favorite mug. Roger still, after all these years, marveled at his new life, his life after life. He got to live in his own home, sleep with his own wife, enjoy her decorations as they came and went, though the house was never dirty for him, and he even got to use his favorite dishes. He never got tired of messing with the kids, especially Michael. This was much better than watching over them from behind some veil. The fact that this city-home for him existed in a pleasant rural forest setting was icing on the cake.

That they, he and his cohorts, were still saddled with earthly problems and those damnable Deceivers only made things interesting for him. "Perhaps he won't wind up like Joseph Kennedy after all. He seems to get the best of every world, even the dangerous parts, and he performs like the natural American hero that we predicted of him."

"Balderdash," retorted Tag. "No matter what lengths we go to in protecting this hoodwink, he outruns us right into the Deceivers' path. He better hope more than he thinks that he doesn't get his ass shot off. He'll go to Hell no matter what good deeds are on the list."

"How's that?" Mac cut in.

"If he's lucky enough to make it here, I'll make life an eternal living hell for him. We have worked generations to get the game-changer in place to set the human race up as accepted Eternals. Here is our best shooter wandering the around playing street ball with thugs, thugs who don't release prisoners, not ever. Blast this kid." He was on the edge of his seat, not looking at all heavenly right now. "There he goes—under finally. I want first shot."

"Hold on, Grandpa," said Roger. "We stick with the plan. Mac and I are getting pretty good at this. You'll get him, perhaps right here in the extra chair." The 'old' man snorted with little patience. No one here was really old, but if one could be, the old physician Tag would be.

Brad was soaring over the mountains on wings of silk, catching air in updrafts he could feel as if they obeyed his command. His pitch control was perfect, even with the surgical kit strapped to his back. He checked the GPS locater designed to drop him in just the right spot, utilizing a dolphin move to position himself with expertise known only to him in the entire world. He performed an asymmetric tuck, glided forward a full mile, followed by a full frontal tuck, maneuvered several spirals, went into a full stall, then spiraled safely to the center of his target, landing softly just outside the tent where the old man, still living, awaited his brand of surgical magic. The male protagonist had arrived. Brad unhitched the parachute and went quickly into the tent, ushered by two men, one whom he faintly recognized from his childhood, but could not place, the other a total stranger, and was confronted by the shock of his life. The man who needed him in that moment was none other than his own grandfather, Tag Peterson— How? "Grandpa, is that really you?"

"He can't answer you," said the complete stranger. Allow me to introduce myself. I am, Mac. This is my friend, Roger and we thank you for coming on such short notice, Dr. Peterson." For a second Brad was sure that his grandfather was spying out of one eye, then in a flash his eyes were shut and he looked all the worse, yet again. "Ole Tag Peterson," Roger said, the creature looked at least a hundred, "Ole Tag is slipping from the known universe into the realm of the long gone. Remember when he passed, leaving your grandmother, uh, what was her name, Sabrina, yes, his substantial dowager who funded your education beyond the scholarships so that you would enjoy comfort and lack nothing in those lean years. Now we are losing Tag forever. He is, if you can't find a way to help, dissipating to insubstantial mist." Incredibly, Grandpa started transmuting into thin air, if just a little bit.

"What can I do to help, Mac? I don't know what to do. Grandpa, please wake up. What's wrong with him?" Slowly, the ancient and frail man began to turn yellow, even as he was becoming wavy, losing substance. His yellow skin was blotching with horrific black and blue marks, little anomalies that sprouted purple varicose veins growing right in front of Brad's eyes. Was he smiling? No. Was his demoralized and sad countenance contrived? It looked that way to Roger, but not Brad, who was taken in hook, line, and sinker.

Roger looked as deeply concerned as he could in an attempt to muster the effect. "Perhaps if you bent low and told him you loved him? Take his hand in yours. Now put his other hand on your forehead and say sweetly, "There's no place like home, there's no place like home, and there's no place like home. Don't forget to click your boot heels three times."

"What?" He did as he was told. It was working. Suddenly the man came to life!

In his still wretched state he sat up full, looked his grandson in the eye, with all of the spook he could produce, and with a wicked smile, his eyes popping and bulging, his breath horrible behind yellow and rotting teeth, saying, "You're killing me, Boy!" The world around Bradley changed in an instant. Suddenly they were on the back porch of a home, a familiar dwelling which he could not quite place, yet in unfamiliar surroundings, out in a forested valley of sorts, a very beautiful setting. The two men standing were exactly the same as before, but his old and dying granddad, now sitting before him, suddenly looked in his prime, a young, vibrant and handsome man. Brad had never seen him like this before but recognized him instantly. The three men broke into uncontained laughter and the shocked, totally bewildered dreamer, who sat in their planned lair, now looked to be the one turning into a ghost.

* * *

At about the same time, in the bowels of Hell, the CCA spy reported to Stump Killer and Imp Rogue that he had located the careless hero, Dr. Bradley Peterson, and found him to be very vulnerable. It was time to strike. Stump looked at his cohort, smiling, and with a wink of his eye summed it up. "The last time we had a chance at this you booby-bumbled the whole thing playing with scorpions. This time we do it my way." Imp was not the least bit humbled. They put their plan into motion.

* * *

Colonel Sam Whitford was not someone you would want to have as an enemy, or even angry with you. His no-nonsense, matter of fact style of command, was perhaps unique in a hospital setting, though not so much here at *Bagram's SSG Heath N. Craig Joint Theater Hospital which was located within the confines of Bagram Air Base, out in the wilderness of Afghanistan, north of Kabul, where things got very serious on a regular basis. Witford's style appeared to be common from the perspective of professionals serving under his command. He* looked more like a battalion field commander, always carried a gun, dressed like a fighter, sported a scrubby beard, more like an unshaved face really, than a seasoned surgeon having performed thousands of operations himself during the decades of his long and illustrious military career. He had just completed a morning walk through the camp, proudly observing his staff transporting wounded soldiers from a helicopter on wheeled black stretchers towards an emergency room. They were under the kind of stress that only someone in the military would find normal. There were triage doctors, nurses, both male and female, various support personnel, and even a chaplain moving about in the well lit, state-of-the-art facility. If not out where the actual fighting was taking place, this was the front line on keeping casualties and injuries under control. They saved lives here every day, and yes, once in a while, they lost that battle, too, something that reality kept everyone on their toes.

When he was outside again, Colonel Whitford, breathing the pungent air, fresh to him, perhaps distinctively odorous to someone not familiar with a military air base in a war zone, enjoyed the wide open expanse of a blue sky, striped with high altitude clouds, pushed along by a winter wind. He thought of his family in Tucson, sensing déjà vu, regretting that he would miss Christmas at home—yet again. He was sure that his men would see the holidays through with him, knowing that they were involved in a great cause. He much preferred the day to the night here, with all the lights, the barbed steel mesh fences, and other accouterments that changed the environment for him from hospital to POW camp. It is what it is, he thought to himself.

He paused when he was back inside to visit with an injured soldier, a man of some 35 years, flat on his back, his long unshaven face spotted with blood; he looked forlorn and Sam wanted him to feel as though he would be cared for, cared for with tender but firm hands. There were all manner of injured soldiers being treated here, most looking much worse for the wear, wondering if this was their ticket home, back to war, or maybe to the morgue. It was not a pretty sight, yet in the midst of it all, Sam heard music, a very good voice coupled with exceptionally effective, almost professional guitar work. He followed the sound and found an injured army regular with a large cast on his right foot, entertaining anyone who cared to listen. This fighter looked to be in great spirits. On the next bed sat a very young *man who had been injured in an ambush, his head cocked to the right, following the rhythm of the music. Music is excellent therapy for these kids, the Colonel thought. In his visit with that young lad, he was told the story of how medical personnel had evacuated him right out of the middle of a firefight in the Tagab Valley, a desolate place where hardly anything abounded, except rocks. Never had the Colonel seen such a stirring sight. This soldier would live and return to duty.*

And so the day went. It was not the typical way the Colonel would spend his day, but there was not much going on in his office, he was lonesome for home, and if truth be known, it was they who were comforting him at least as much as he was them. Later that afternoon, he took time out for an Afghan military police officer, who'd had his leg amputated, the victim of a roadside bomb. After a very kingly dinner he spent the evening reading his Kate Elliott novel, The Burning Stone, a fantasy of war and swords, arrows and magic . . . his escape from the real world. Later still, with his iPod blaring, the old Colonel, a big fan of rock and roll music, was reminded again of the deep impression he felt when listening to The Door. This is the end, beautiful friend, Morrison sang. Lost in a Roman wilderness of pain—and all the children are insane. He loved the guitar melody of this song and wondered if the kid over in the hospital ward could replicate it, and then he slipped into a restless sleep.

It was not so unusual for an operations commander to get a call in the middle of the night, especially a call from Washington where it was not the middle of the night, but it was not something that happened on a regular basis to a hospital administrative commander. When the officer on duty woke Sam from a deep sleep, one in which he could vaguely remember an adventurous and colorful dream which he was now robbed of, he was startled and mind muddled. His throat was dry from snoring, his eyes were full of gunk, the refracted low level of the just lit light was banning the comfort of darkness, still too bright for his sleep deadened senses— confirmed that he was just not ready to communicate. As he swung his legs over the side of the bed, trying to stretch at the same time, he was overcome with cramping in his left calve. He jumped from the bed screaming, trying to ease the cramping in an effort to make the pain go away. The OOD, a young man, seemed to be shivering in fear at how his grumpy, sleepy, hopping boss would react to the news that the

Officer On Duty was ordered to wake the Colonel and see that he took the call. The damning look in Colonel Witford's eye did nothing to make him feel any safer. He patiently waited until Sam took a lengthy drink of the ice water from the mug at his bedside, slipped on his old worn out trusty robe, and used the restroom. Now he was fully awake. "What's this all about, Son?"

"It's the Warrior Transition Commander himself, Sir. He wants you on the line immediately. I think he has specific orders for someone or something here in our locale. He didn't say anything about it, just to get you on the phone at once. I told him you were sound asleep, but he had no interest in that. I'm very sorry to have to wake you, Sir."

"It's not your problem, Sergeant. Those fools in Washington think we all operate in the same time zone. I'd give this clown an earful, but, like you're beholden to me, I have to answer to him. He's my boss and that's what I hate about this man's army. It better be good. I'll bet he just wants to make sure that someone didn't forget to file their nails and blow their nose before they went to bed. Their idea of important can usually fit on a yellow sticky attached to the refrigerator for anyone to see. The closer you get to the Pentagon, the slower the thinking, the dimmer the wits. Hand me the phone." The young man handed him the phone. Sam wished he had kept the caller waiting even longer. "Colonel Whitford here, Sir—I am at your service, staying up all night waiting for calls from the brain trust," his greeting was spoken with tempered disdain, for he knew what would come next. "How can I help you?"

"Cut the crap, Sam. I can see you there now making fun of me. I would never have you woken unless something important came up, something that needs your immediate attention." He sounded very serious. *Perhaps this was going to be a little more interesting,* so Sam thought as he listened to his old friend, Brig. Gen. Gary H. Cheek. The General was current WTC Commander and an old Military Academy graduate from way back, way, way back, in 1980 or something like that, another lifer. In truth Sam respected his superior and liked him too. He had been all over the place; working for the Joint Chief's, teaching at West Point, training Gunnery above the 54-40 line in New Brunswick, had even commanded troops in Afghanistan, so he was a great deal more than a Pentagon brown-nosing specialist.

"We have a job for one of your boys. His name is Captain Bradley Peterson; he is well known around there so I am sure you have heard of him."

"I have, General Cheek. Captain Peterson is an amazing talent. He is fearless, loves to take a risk, has an almost perfect surgical record, saves lives, and with his arrogance is sure to get us all killed some day. What do you want with him?"

"I have a surgical team of Marines flying in right now on a VM-22 to pick him up. He'll be with us for assignment to an undisclosed location to perform surgery on a young boy. It is a diplomatic mission and it's black, all on the quiet, understand?"

"I do, sir. We'll have him ready. How much time do we have before he needs to be on deck? Does he need any equipment or supplies? Can I tell him what the destination is?"

"You need him ready at 09:00 hours, no equipment or help of any kind. He will have a fully capable team with him. We need just him. Even he doesn't get to know where he is going until the team is underway. Once in the air he'll get a full briefing as to his role in the mission."

"Six hours and twenty minutes, General. That should be more than enough time to suit the young genius for his next adventure as Superman. The kid will be more than eager for this one, just don't lose him. He is the best surgeon in the military, probably on the planet, definitely worth his weight in gold."

"Don't you worry one little iota, Colonel. This trip is as safe as a baby in mommy's pouch. He should be back in just a few days. Oh, Sam, I am going to be in Tucson next week. Marcy and I would like to drop by the house and deliver a gift to your wife if it would be okay. I know you would like to be there for her and we appreciate your efforts on behalf of the kids you're helping. Would that be okay with you?"

Sam got a bit choked up, hiding his emotion as best he could. He felt so guilty for the way he had allowed himself to be used at times like this and for the many years of his service, yet even he could not protect himself as he shed a tear and thanked his ole buddy.

He put down the phone, took another drink of that cold ice water, called for coffee, and wondered where the OOD was. He found him out in the front office, sitting in his little clerk's office chair, on the phone, frantic. "Sergeant Miller, get Peterson up. I have new orders to give him and they cannot wait until morning. What the hell is the matter with you, Miller? You look beside yourself, like a terrified ghost."

Sergeant Miller stayed on the phone, asking the Colonel for just a second, seemed to descend into himself, his eyes shutting, his face down; he was losing composure. Slowly he put the receiver in the cradle, looked up at his boss from across his worn oak desk, covered with papers, a computer, a bottle of pens with paperclips, an old lamp, and a table calendar. Only then did he compose himself, taking a sip of his own recently filled cup of black hot coffee and quite calmly stated, "I'm sorry, Sir, but Captain Peterson is not here at the time."

"What! Where in divinity's paradise is he, damn it?"

"Sir, he is up near Fayzabad, almost to the Tagikistanian border, with troops in the field on regular medic duty."

"You're kidding me, Son. This has to be some kind of a joke. We never send brain surgeons out on field medic duty. That's impossible. I want the officer who signed the papers assigning him to field medic duty in my office and I mean pronto . . . got that?" Sam was bristling. He had assured the WTC himself that in just about six hours he would have him ready for black ops and now he was learning that some fool let him out of the box and sent him on a frigging camping trip, and without him even knowing about it. Heads were going to roll, maybe his own. "Well, Miller, who sent him?"

"You did, Sir." Miller was ashen with fear. "When he arrived, if you will recall, he specifically requested regular rotation duty so that he could experience the full breadth of his role. Here is a copy of your slot assignment. His turn came up and out he went, just like anyone else." He handed the Colonel specific documents memorializing the duty roster rotation since he knew the wrath of what was coming when he overheard the Captain's name in the conversation. That was why he went to the phone to make arrangements to get him offloaded. He had thought that if everything went smoothly they could make the promised timeline anyway, but . . .

"Damn it all to hell. Let's get him back. I want someone over at the air base to heat up an AH- 1 Cobra or something fast, now!"

"Sir, there is another problem. I just got off of the phone with base command because I had a head start on what you would want done. That area just went hot. In the last hour they have come under heavy attack, rousted right out of their sleep, and they are in a fight for their lives right this minute."

Colonel Sam Whitford was caught. This Catch-22 could be his undoing. He had signed papers setting one of the world's leading surgeon's into harm's way, could not retrieve him in time, the young doctor may lose his life in the process, and there was a black ops mission flying into the base to pick him up. *I'm screwed now*, he sighed to himself. *What am I going to do?*

5

Willing to Live—Willing to Die

Far behind enemy lines he waits me out; then at the opportune moment, he causes a diversion: His true intent being to sabotage.

Wise Mac

Slybrain Thiefdemon had seen enough. Twice he had sent boys to do a man's work and twice he had seen them thwarted. On the surface their target looked to be easy prey, so full of himself—most likely due to gifts he was not aware of, talents crystallized by little sissy Eternals whose dreams of mammalian potential drove their passion. The mark walked into their traps over and over, and then walked out again with a smile on his face, never the wiser. So the young human doctor would march his self-aggrandizing ego through this little earthly skirmish and into the future to fulfill his purpose. *What objective could that be?* Slybrain knew that it must be pretty important or he would not be under boiler-level pressure from the Masters who relentlessly increased the heat here in Thiefdemon's little neck of the woods. He had no idea what the doctor's function was—wondered if they knew—though not enough to care much. Those blind Megadermatidae shouldn't have power over him anyway, and wouldn't soon enough if he had much to say about it. Thiefdemon summoned Stump Killer and Imp Rouge to his chambers with a mind to transform them into bats and hang them blind, naked and upside-down for all to see just what failure bought in Slybrain's realm. His own fear was the impetus behind a base need

---

to take control of the situation. As stupid and unimaginative as his masters were, their cruel knowledge of how to make him feel pain at their sufferance was without a doubt a great motivator. He did not want to face them with unhappy news.

Killer was sitting on a stone bench beside Imp Rouge's desk when the message on the viewboard 'requesting' that the two of them stop by Master Thiefdemon's chambers for refreshments and a short visit about the progress they were having with their assignment, the subtle threat flushing them to the bone with wanton fear.

"What does that brownnosing, Sly-no-brain want?" said Imp. "Refreshments, he says. I doubt that." Did bravado betray his fear? "The thief-demon wants our glory. He's going to take the credit for our great victory, which is what he always wants." The silicon in his veins, however, was running cold, his face sweating methane ice, and his knees were weak. Since his brain was on idiotic-autopilot, the only thing seeming to function at the moment was his running mouth.

"Shut up, you dupe. Thiefdemon has contacts all over the place. Did you even bother to think he could be listening to us right now? If he gets wind of your insolence we will both be skinned and used to lubricate the Great Machine. Let me handle this. I have dealt with the Masters many times and I know just what to say. You keep your mouth shut, hear me? Imp did as he was told, not because Stump was his boss, he wasn't, but because he realized that ears have a way of picking things up down here in Hell. He had made the mistake of talking too much and paid dearly for it in the past.

The Centex Charlatan Alliance was a network of beings, various intelligent life forms from all kinds of places. Right now they were recruiting on Earth to collect their first human draftees. There were legions of human dead they could make use of, but they were now looking for higher functioning types. Did the emotionally driven mammalian water-bags have what it took to serve the Great Lord? CCA operatives were scattered all over the galaxy in little known out of the way places, usually set up in subterranean caves on the dark side of otherwise uninhabitable planets. They had broken with the Eternals long ago, so far back in the past that no one could tell anyone else why. The consensus was that their original plan to control life forms had been rejected because they discouraged individual liberty.

It was too messy for them. Thiefdemon was boss man in charge of a very small outpost in an asterism known by humans as Ursa Minor, the Little Dipper as seen from Earth. They were underground on a planetoid orbiting Polaris, Earth's North Star, so they could have direct access to Sol III, planet Earth, where humans were being developed into a new breed of Eternals. Slybrain's mission was to terminate a single man. Whatever in hell could be the interest in one tiny life form— this Brad Peterson—and yet he seemed beyond the reach of anyone here. They just knew what they were told and that wasn't much. He had finished the last of his meal when the two boneheads approached. He had lied about offering them anything at all in the way of refreshments, the first of his rebukes.

"Well, if it isn't Fiddle-dee and Fiddle-dumb, come to whine about your failures. Is there anything at all about you two that shows promise? I ask you to ruin the life of a little girl and you screw that up. She is out running races again. I ask but a simple chore. Can you influence a few insane religious zealots into killing a single human? Not that either, I suppose. Have you heard of a game they play on earth called baseball? Let's play baseball, only this time I'll be both the pitcher and the batter. As pitcher I throw strikes. You have two strikes against you; you get one more and that's it, then I'm up to bat. Know what I plan to do? I am going to take my baseball bat and smash your heads into pulp. It's obvious you are not up to the task. What say you about your chances at getting a hit on the next pitch? You had better answer correctly for it'll be strike three and you are out! There is a place where dummies like you go from here and I assure you it is permanent."

"Master Thiefdemon, we won a significant victory in a great battle . . . the dead and injured."

"Silence your tongue, Killer—who named you anyway? I would like to award the Great Lord's Banner of State Service to whoever named you Stump. We set up the perfect opportunity for you in Fayzabad. You failed me again! Any worthwhile operative could have finished that without so much a flyswatter. Your earthborn cave worms did hit them in the middle of the night, had overwhelming superiority on the field of battle and he just flies away? He just up and flies out of there on the end of a rope. I could have taken care of that with a shooting straw and a loose bean, you incompetent buffoon!"

"Lord Slybrain, I told him as much," Imp's sheepish mouth was getting him into more trouble, and not just with his master. Stump's eyes flashed green with anger. "I said . . ."

"Shut it, you fool. You are rogue after all. Your father already lives, what is left of him anyway, at your next end. It'll be most pleasant to arrange a family reunion. I direct traffic myself, get helicopters disabled, drop the egocentric surgeon right into your lap and you attack him with SCORPIONS!" *Imp Rogue is an idiot.*

Rogue had been squirming like the little maggot Slybrain thought he was. Now it was obvious he was doing the best he could to keep a straight face, but alas, the Deceiver's countenance contorted into reluctant smile and he giggled, first just a little and then he could not stop himself.

"You think this is funny? If not for the urgency of this mission, and the need to show the Great Lord that I have control over my minions, I would end your role in this here and now, but I will give you clowns one more opening, only this time I am taking charge of the mission myself. We have another chance and I am not going to let you guys fail. My benevolence in this matter surprises even me.

Stump Killer and Imp Rogue, shrunk to peons with the kind of fear that causes even silicon innards to jam up. And then just as suddenly they found a morsel of hope where just a moment ago there was none.

* * *

The Sun's Midas rays turn me into a royal golden child of my Creator-King

Wise Mac

Saturday, December 4th, 2010

It was pitch black outside, a Saturday, though there would be no weigh-in today; the black limousine pulled into her driveway. Truthfully, it wasn't all that cold outside, the temperature was not down to freezing, but Trisha's was emotionally iced up. She was scared to death and had not slept at all during the night, save the hour or so before the alarm clock went off, and by that time she could hardly drag her tired, stiff body out of bed. Last Saturday she had weighed over at the club, a mere 113 lbs., skin and bones if you asked those close to her. By now she did have skin hanging about and wished it were not so, but such was the life of one who used to, in some other nightmarish reality, endure a different life. In those days she had been off of everyone's radar, save her mother and a friend or two over at Target where she still insisted on working a shift now and then, a personal refuge from the here and now. Such a private existence was no longer the case. Now everyone seemed to want a piece of her. Perhaps it was true that some dreams were better left unrealized, but not this one, not for Trisha Jean Martin. Race day had arrived.

Trisha took a slower than usual walk around her home, still not redecorated from what used to be a silly lost Super Bowl bet, unbelievably the turning point which would define her for the rest of her life. She knew that now. Her home itself was the manifestation of that defining moment in time. It was spotless. She glanced into what had once been a never used guest bedroom. Now it was loaded with exercise equipment courtesy of the Foundation and the perks of going back to work for her father. "Oh, Daddy," she spoke aloud, "here we go now. I promise to do the best I can, but these are real athletes this time and they've come from all over the world."

* * *

Roger and his friend, the now wiser and more seasoned angel, Mac, were out on the back porch, conflicted between satisfaction with the way his beautiful daughter had navigated this most turbulent year, and then there was the troubled Bradley Peterson who had finally found out the hard way that luck is a terrible friend. It always abandons at some point; his luck was now gone and this time it was not the result of anything he could have controlled. Brad's grandfather, Tag Peterson, was there as well. No one wanted to interrupt Roger's tears, which were flowing with great pride and

221

love for the kid who used to chase him around the block those decades ago.

* * *

Trisha noted with a sense of inner satisfaction that her home was in perfect condition, nothing out of place or any refuse anywhere. Every room was completely organized. She looked into her office and wondered if ever again she would have to find space for a trophy in the shiny polished curio cabinet, still staring at her from the past in the same corner of her office. That would not be today, she knew, but the stated goal was to keep the lead runners within sight all the way to the finish. Her office was all business now, new computers and communications electronics, a scanner, her mobile phone in its cradle, charged, which she picked up, a new chair, but she had insisted that her desk was fine and it had not been replaced. Her living room still brandished that comfortably squashed beautiful red sofa, coffee table, Old English end table and the same reading lamp, the only upgrade a large flat screen television mounted on the wall, now surrounded by new pictures and plants. Her favorite picture was the one taken recently with April Keller, a good friend from work, a shining star herself who had now lost over 40 pounds through her Weight Watchers program.

In the kitchen she went to the refrigerator and drank the last of Stanley's magic hydration drink, not because she was thirsty, but because she wanted none of his wrath, or to lie to him about finishing. With all those fluids in her body she felt as big as ever, bloated, though she well knew the difference. There was a knock at the door, the driver, and she knew that it was time to go. He carried her bag, though she tried to carry it herself, yet he insisted, and in just seconds she was sitting in the back seat with Stanley, Michael, and her agent, David Giles. My how things were getting more complicated as time flew by in the new life of the runner.

"Good morning, TJ. Did you get a good night's sleep?" Michael was all smiles. Of late he had been using Stanley to see if he could in any way improve his preparation for the half marathon, his first. Trisha could see new definition in his muscle tone, clarity in his facial expression, and the skin very tight throughout his neck. These were improvements which had defined his year of conditioning, an accomplishment in and of itself.

"I slept like a baby, Mikey," she had no qualms about fibbing to this one. No one could help her lost night of sleep no matter what she said, though she was coming awake now and feeling much better. "Good morning, Stanley. David, what gets you out of bed so early on a Saturday? I thought guys like you slept in and played golf on days like today."

"Top of the morning to you too, Trisha; I wouldn't miss this for the world. I don't care what happens out there today. In a million years I didn't think this would happen at all, let alone so fast." He handed her a bouquet, a nice spray of yellow roses. Trisha was both surprised and grateful. She had grown not only accustomed to her agent, but really liked him. "The Giles firm wants to thank you personally for allowing us to represent you. By the way, there is good news. I've secured a sponsorship from Target. For now it is a scaled investment based on your times and where you finish in early races, but it may grow substantially. Reece Chartheart is going to be there this morning with a film crew. They want to document your first real event. He knows that the inevitable is going to happen and he is ready to get into the action part of his contract with us. I am certain you will give him good material to work with." Trish had grown numb to the sideshow that now was a part of her daily life. It was hard to believe that a secret and concealed existence once held sway over her. Now her business seemed to be everyone's business. She could only smile and thank him sincerely for the flowers, also promising not to disappoint.

"You may not believe this, Trisha, especially with the loose handle you have on the debit card, but we have more money in the bank now than when you signed. You've paid all of the bills yourself up to this point, and we aren't even started." Trisha smiled. She was no longer frozen, but warmed inside. She was looking forward to the event.

What can I get done this morning? Anticipation started to worm its way in. She shivered. Abruptly, they had arrived at Mandalay Bay, she had checked in, been accounted for as a local running enthusiast with a "locals only" number pinned to her back, warmed up, stretched her muscles, tied her waist-length hair into a pony tail, took in some advice from Stanley, posed for pictures with Chartheart's people and was trying to push her way as far forward through the throng of thousands, getting as close to the front as possible. She made it to within about 100 yards of the start line; Michael was at her side. The place was a zoo. There were Elvis impersonators, people dressed in all sorts of costumes, even a couple of SpongeBob-SquarePants, yet still in the race, and quite a few who were to be married right during their run. The helicopters were buzzing about; there were film crews from the local news stations and from running organizations, too. Mike whispered into her ear. "Just take off and don't even think of me. I apologize about calling this a fun run back in February. You're to have fun alright, just not the kind we talked about." She turned, hugged and kissed him, then, just like that, the horn went off.

Trisha jumped to the side of the mob and sprinted as fast as she could to get through the mass of humanity which was keeping her out of sight of the leaders; they had their own privileged starting area. In less than a minute she jumped at least 500 people, had lost her wind, but found comfortable running room. She settled in for the event, recovered her breath, and set out again, this time to see what she could see. In less than 20 minutes she found herself alone between two groups, the professionals ahead of her, and the crowd behind. Now all she had to do was keep them in sight, the women that is. They were definitely fast. *How can they run so fast?* Slowly, inexorably, they pulled away, putting distance between them and anyone else who thought they could compete. The race was straight up and down the Las Vegas Strip, at dawn's early light, and with a reddened sky turning blue as they ran along, the sight was surreal. Trisha was flying. There were runners nearby, some passing her, but most were from other places, even other countries. She was in the zone with dedicated athletes where just under a year ago she lived a completely different life. She also passed runners, some world class athletes who had lost their gait, some of them men. One man she passed she did recognize, Josh Sullivan—from her own club. He smiled the biggest smile as she moved on ahead of him. "Trisha, if only polygamy were legal," he yelled out. "I'm in love with you!" She laughed. He was so sprung on that wife of his; she would have no chance with him in the real world. Still . . .

All of a sudden, the lead pack of men came barreling back up the road like cheetahs chasing their prey. The motorcycles preceded them with their cameramen sitting backwards. The sun was up, and it was warming nicely. *The turn must not be too far away.* Some short time later she saw the lead pack of women, and then suddenly, perhaps about a quarter of a mile out she found the turn. In just a minute or so she would be racing back up the Strip. Her body was responding well, there were no problems with conditioning, nothing was out of order, and the race had reached its halfway point.

The way back was nothing at all like the first part of the run. There was a veritable sea of people back there, thousands of them. At first she noticed that the runners were intense in a spirited drive. How was it that she was so far out in front of these great athletes? Josh waved at her when he approached and she waved back. Sometime later she saw Mikey approaching. He was definitely struggling, having not run a distance race before, but to her he looked great. When he spotted her, noting how far ahead she was, and how fast she was hurtling along, he looked startled. His smile was simple, warm, yet he was lost in his own cause. Competitive distance running was definitely harder than playing tennis.

Michael wasn't near the halfway point and yet today's run was something he never fathomed would prove this difficult. He had fallen into a rhythm and had adopted a running buddy, someone who wanted to go the same speed as him, slow and deliberate. They had been girl watching, first from behind, but now women were coming towards them.

"Look at that hottie. Her legs are perfect," said his newfound buddy. Wouldn't you like to get your hands on that one— yeah baby—she saw me. Look Michael, she waved at me and smiled too. What do you think about that?!"

"Mark, let me make this clear. As into girls as I am, and I love looking at pretty women, I would not want to put my hands on that one, OK. Secondly, she wasn't waving and smiling at you. It was me she was looking at."

"What makes you say that?"

"She's my kid sister and off limits to you, that's what."

"Oh, never mind," They both laughed. "Well, she runs like the wind."

"Doesn't she, though? She's an amazing person, too." They both trudged on.

There is a place deep within a person, a secret place where no one else has access, where a measure of greatness can be found, should it exist within that person and should they be willing to pay the price it takes to get to that place. There was no way Trisha should be able to compete at this level; it was so early in her new program. It did not seem possible, in less than one year, to go from where she once was to where she was now, but somehow for her it was there. She had the reserves for a kick and decided to pick up the pace a bit. In those last miles to the finish line Trisha Jean Martin thought of her father, whom she felt so close to of late, her brother, her sister who was building a new school for kids, her mother who had changed so much, not drinking anymore and losing weight, Stanley Burton, the person to whom she gave so much credit, and to God who had given her such a body to work with. It had to be Him. How was it otherwise possible to take up right where she'd left off so long ago? She passed only three more women between there and the finish line, not because she was losing steam, but because there were no more women out there except her and the professionals now about a mile and a half out in front. The end of the race was in sight. Soon female runners began to disappear past the finish line. One by one they and other men finished as she approached, kicking a bit faster in the final mile, if for no other reason than energy she had for the run to the line was still in the tank. Why not burn the gas? In just a few weeks Trisha would be training for and running marathons. She had, perhaps, a hundred yards of running space almost to herself now, a few sporadic males in front of her, everyone else behind. The course belonged to her and it felt good.

Something was happening that she could not understand. The crowd was roaring, screaming her name. How could they know her? She glanced up at the giant Jumbotron and saw herself on the screen, something inscribed below her name as she ran along. She almost tripped. A motorcycle fell in ahead of her and put the camera on. Why? At the finish line she could see the Nutrisystem team up on top of a truck with several photographers, their television camera, and then Trisha found Reece with his arms folded and a he sporting a huge smile. There was Stanley waiting at the finish line screaming with joy. Even David Giles was beside himself. Was this overthe-top stuff never going to end? She had done nothing but run a half marathon. Out of the blue they pulled tape across the finish line . . . for her. She couldn't understand what was happening. At least 30 women had already crossed the line ahead of her, many of those waiting at the finish for others. Oh well, through the line she went, pretending that she had won the race, and with a huge smile on her face. The clock registered 1:31:15; it was her best time ever. That chronometer couldn't be accurate. For the first time in the race she checked her running watch. The time was true. How could that be possible this morning? There was no way. She had to be dreaming. She wasn't. Unexpectedly she was surrounded by all sorts of people, Stanley and David both jumping up and down euphoric with her in between them, a newspaper photo journalist, several of the professional women runners, and finally a news crew from a local television station. The lady, with cameraman in tow, thrust a microphone in front of her. "Trisha Martin, who are you? You just won the Las Vegas Rock 'n Roll 'locals-division' women's half marathon." Suddenly for Trisha Jean Martin, that trophy case in her home, all shined up and polished, would be taking on new meaning in her very exciting life. She had an awards banquet to attend.

* * *

But deep within our mind's hallways we held our own counsel tightly as a leather glove embracing our knuckles—

Wise Mac

He wished himself dead. Not the kind of dead that a troubled teenager thinks of as the policeman approaches from the rear of the car to end his freedom because of the drugs all over the place. Not the kind of dead a man who loves his wife feels when she catches him with another woman. Not the kind of dead the head of household feels when he is terminated or laid off from the only means of support the family has. No, he wished himself dead, literally. This prisoner may or may not be the only suicide candidate who ever applied his personal knowledge of the human mind in to try and get his cerebral cortex to stop his heart from beating—just by thought control.

He shut his eyes again and commanded his brain to shut down. He needed the pain to end and this was his plan. "Die!" he screamed, again and again and again and again . . . until his voice ran horse and then empty. He had lost his tears and exchanged them for heart filled odium, a hatred he did not know was a part of who he was, or was becoming. He was tied to the stone floor, his hands and feet securely fashioned through iron rings. If he could have, he would have bashed his own head against that floor until he was dead. Had it been a week? Perhaps it had been a month, or a year. He saw no light, moved only by those who now owned him, always with a black bag over his head, and always to the same place . . . *the* room.

The first time they ripped the bag off of his head, he had been told that he was going home, the benefactor of an exchange between his captors and the Great Satan, America. It had been a lie, he found out, when he was told that first he just had to give correct answers to a few simple questions. When he surmised the lie, the vile nature of what they wanted, he had been strong but lately, not so much. "Captain Peterson, though we are not signatories, so you say, of the Geneva Convention, it is our policy not to inflict torture on guests. You may feel secure in that regard, Healer. We limit our methods to, what say the Great Satan . . . yes, extraordinary rendition, yes, that is it, extraordinary rendition." The chair he was tied into tipped back until his head was beneath his torso, tilted as far back as they could stretch it, a wet cloth was placed over his face and water was poured down his throat and nose. The suffocation was horrible, made worse because the water was being alternated, first very cold, almost freezing, then so hot it threatened to scald.

Brad was a genius when it came to self-control, among other things. When they learned that he had mastered the secret of how to survive extreme water-boarding, they simply opened the black box next to his chair and turned to a more innovative approach. The first thing they made sure of was that their prisoner could see into the box so that he would enjoy the compliments of their buffet. Could brain surgeons scream and sing at the same time?

When they put him back in the hole later, bolted to the floor, Brad Peterson tried to think his way out of the problem. He remembered a suggestion that came from Army training and tried to think of his childhood and how much he had loved it. He went to the school dances again, celebrated his birthdays with loving parents, family and friends, went on vacation to the theme parks, to Major League Baseball games, and watched movies in theaters he used to frequent. He high jumped to the State Championship. He ran. The escape into his mind worked for a while. He used to run with a girl, well not really, she was just a child, two years his junior, but she was fast, the fastest kid around. He liked her well enough, though she was too smart for her own britches and had no respect for the fact that he got an A in every class, every time. In here, deep in the recesses of his fantasy construct, they fell in love and got married, raised a family, made millions of dollars and lived the perfect *white picket fence* life. He had chosen Trisha to be his 'mind game' lover, not because she was so supportive, she made fun of him all the time. It was not because of her intellect. For all he knew she flunked out of school. No, he had to admit it. Brad chose Trisha Martin because of the way her body moved when he ran behind her. The only laugh he allowed himself in his dire hole was because in the darkest hour, he chose to marry the girl with the best butt in school. Would that she could see him now, begging to die; malevolent hatred flushed from within his heart into insane anxiety. *I'll kill these bastards with my bare hands.*

Hours crawled by, he gave up his quest to die, and instead went home to his wife and kids. She wasn't the best cook because there was never anything to eat, except a cockroach or two, and being bolted to the floor rendered even that little tasty meal out of reach. Brad continued to descend emotionally, losing complete touch with reality. Brad, if that was ever his name in the first place, knew his sanity was fragmenting into pieces. He would never be the same again. When finally he fell asleep, he did not dream at all, only floated in darkness until finally his nightmare came again.

"Cap, wake up. We gotta go. The base is under attack!" Brad had been sound asleep, dreaming sweetly about what, he could not remember— only that he was laughing and with friends in a far off fantasy of flight and fun. Now he was fully awake, grabbing what he could of his things and being rushed from the tent into the black of night, and suddenly jolted into the reality of a biting cold wind, with bullet tracers flying all aroiund. The sound of guns erupted

from defensive perimeters and flames shot out into the darkness up along the high side of the mountain. Flares lit up the peaks, casting eerie shadows of doom in every direction. There were, what looked like endless bugs crawling about up on the west side of where they were encamped. Not bugs; they were men, and they were not only shooting—but rushing the encampment. Brad looked over his shoulder and noticed that fighters were approaching from the east side of the make shift American position, too. They had been caught by surprise.

The wounded, some of them certainly dying, others dead already, were being brought in droves to the trench area where he and the other medics were setting up shop. It was a disaster and was getting worse. The fighting went on for hours. Thankfully, once the soldiers were organized, the hemorrhaging slowed to a trickle and finally stopped altogether. It didn't hurt that air support arrived within minutes and from that point on the tide began to turn in favor of the American forces, but the damage had been done. By every conceivable definition this little fight would turn out to be one of the worst days of the entire war effort. He dared not try and count the dead because he knew it would sicken him and make him unable to continue his work. He was shocked by what happened next.

"Captain Peterson, you've been ordered by Bagram's to be evacuated immediately," said the young officer who approached him.

"They're going to have to wait until this is wrapped up, Captain."

"Not happening, Captain Peterson. These orders are specific. They're dropping in another medic to take your place. You are leaving now—are going to get chopped out in five minutes. Follow me, NOW. No arguments." Captain Peterson knew when it was his turn to lead and also knew when it was time to follow. He snatched his backpack and followed. It was against everything he believed in to leave that trench and cross into the line of fire and away from his duty. What in hell's name was going on here? As they were running along, bullets struck rocks right next to where they were. His stomach lurched. It was the first time he had ever been shot at.

Just minutes later he was strapped into a basket chair, bundled and tethered to a sort of bungee cord. The cord was hung between two hook poles that stood about 20' apart. "It's way too hot for them to land so you get the wild ride. Try to have fun." The young soldier whose assignment this was had a smile on his face. "Oh, Captain

Peterson, before you go, several of the wounded wanted to pass along their sincere gratitude. You're the best." They had him and his backpack zipped into a black snowsuit, a one piece that included heavy gloves. They'd fastened a secure helmet over his head that had a one-size-fits all-kind of feel to it; the sky was beginning to grow from black to red, but still it was too dark to see much.

Shortly, two gunships appeared with multiple machine guns, and they were spraying fire in almost every direction. Perhaps it was their intent to get the enemy to lay low while the flight took place. Peterson was numb, sitting alone in a hole below ground level, protected by a metal overhang, waiting and watching the others who were still in his field of vision, when abruptly he was jolted straight into the air and found himself swinging uncontrollably. There was tracer fire all around him as he became the duck in a shooting gallery. He looked ahead and could see the helicopter, perhaps 200' above him, climbing at what felt like full throttle. He was safe from the bullets at least, but what he was going through, out in the frozen gale of night, riding in a little basket, swinging in the wind at what had to be more than 100 miles per hour—could only be described as hairy. As Brad was being reeled in his mood went from very dark, considering the work he had been doing, to incredible joy as he experienced the thrill of the wild ride, the ride of his life. This was even better than the landing on the aircraft carrier so long ago.

Once inside the helicopter, now blazing out over open desert, the sky beginning to lighten a bit more, even blue at this altitude, Brad discovered that relaxation would not be the objective, just yet anyway. They had hot water and a fresh change of clothing for him. Someone had even pulled his toiletries so he could brush his teeth and shave. Once he was cleaned up they fed him and then he was briefed. It took all of ten minutes. They would be setting down out in no man's land where he was to transfer over to another aircraft, a VM-22, sort of a helicopter and an airplane combined, so that he could take part in a top secret mission. They had no idea where he was going or what he would be up to, that knowledge would have to wait. The rendezvous would take place in about three hours. Now he could relax. It would take him some time to decompress from what had just happened, less time now that he was growing numb to the violence, the noise, horrible smells, sounds, and the blood of war. He ate again, dug though his back pack, found the iPod, put on the headset, set the music to a tranquil Dean Evenson "Tao Of Peace," pulled the mask over his eyes, and tried to go back to sleep. He had long ago decided to write a book detailing the greatest war adventure of all time. Today's chapter would be killer stuff. If only he knew.

Some hours later, the Blackhawk approached a stone outcropping up high on one of the nameless hills located in the wasteland of Afghanistan. The ferry team that had sprung him from the dissolute, insane fight, wished him well on his next journey, lowered the big whirly bird to the stone ground, and he exited the helicopter. He was totally alone as they swept away and returned from whence they came. In the silence of the desert morning, Brad had time to think. His feelings were changing, not only his outlook on life, but of what he was becoming. He again tried to reconstruct the dream he was dragged out of only hours earlier, but could not find any more than wisps and fragments, little tidbits of neuronal vision, dissipating no matter how hard he tried to remember. The thing is, he believed in dreams and their meaning, and for some reason, that one seemed to mean something. Oh well; instead Brad listened to the quiet of the wind, enjoyed the pleasant arid smells that crystal clean air brought to him on a very slight and balmy breeze. The morning sun brought a day of new promise, and he began to wonder just what could be so 'top secret' that he would be needed for.

The Crew Master on the Blackhawk had informed him his wait would be only a few minutes, they had just communicated with the Osprey, and he was perfectly safe. Presently he heard, rather than saw the plane first. It sounded like a giant vacuum cleaner only very far away and so he began to look around. When he saw it flying in it became apparent to Brad just why they would use this type of a craft, something he had never seen before. It had a stubby type body, very similar to the Blackhawk he had just flown in on, but had overhead fixed wings instead of rotor blades. Out on the end of the wings there were two large engines with huge propellers. The rear twin stabilizer tails completed the grey unmarked aircraft. For all Brad knew this could be anybody. What had he gotten himself into? As the plane approached something incredible happened. The engines on the end of the wings began to rotate into a vertical position, creating the mobility of a helicopter. When the propellers were pointed straight into the sky, fully vertical, the V-22 set down right beside him and a door, just aft of the cabin's huge windows opened.

Captain Peterson stepped out of the desert and into new surroundings.

The interior of the V-22 was huge, partly because there was no one else there, just him and the two person crew, USAF guys, both nice enough but very formal and quiet. Within a scant minute they were accelerating, climbing at a slow and steady pace, heading south and west. He tried to strike up a conversation, but all it seemed he could get were short direct answers to his questions. How high could they fly? The plane could make 26,000' with only him aboard. What was the range? He got no answer to that one, just that they would be in the air for several hours and would be refueling on the way to their destination. Which was? Again, he got no answer, but was instead handed a wax sealed manila packet with 'Top Secret' stamped in red across the face of it. He settled into a big, comfortable, first class style seat and opened the envelope.

"Captain Peterson," the letter on top started. "Welcome aboard. Please excuse the quiet nature of our crew this morning as they have been instructed to be very limited in their communication with you. I assure you they are the very finest officers and are totally dedicated to the mission. You are desperately needed, this minute, to perform surgery on a young child . . ."

Brad could not believe his eyes. He was being taken all the way to the Ivory Coast, now known as the Republic of Côte d'Ivoire, where he was to join a surgical team as lead surgeon in the attempt to save the life of a boy, the son of the Southern Leader. The Ivory Coast was in the middle of a brutal civil war, one sparked by Jihadist soldiers from hell, Boco Haram out of Nigeria. The USA wanted Brad to perform this service as a diplomatic strategy. That way they could win the South's support, a kind of a one-up-manship move to neutralize Chinese influence in the area. Even though Boco Haram was working with the rebels in the North. Good hell, what a mess this fight was. The surgery was to take place on the private grounds of the Leader, and the mission was black, never to be spoken of—ever. This operation, the letter said, was not, nor would it ever have taken place. He was sworn to the type of secrecy that, if it ever got out, would be denied all the way to the President. The flight was to take place in three phases;

Brad was in the first segment right now. He was to change planes at an undisclosed location, where he would board a Gulfstream G650 for the duration of the 5,000 mile flight. Two other team members would be on the jet with him. They would fly directly into Abidjan, Côte d'Ivoire's southernmost city, and then it was back into another Osprey for the hop over to the compound where surgery would be performed. When they wrapped up, the whole thing would be played in reverse, or so it seemed.

What's an army guy supposed to do? Brad decided that his focus would be on the surgery and not at all on the political intrigue he'd been drafted into. He opened the medical file and went to work. There was plenty of time.

The transfer to the Gulfstream happened at Thumrait Air Base in Oman, a place Brad was familiar with, having spent all of fifteen minutes there on the way over from the States; this time he was there for even less, switching planes at the end of the runway. These guys were in a big hurry. The surgeon was exhausted as he climbed aboard, weary of mind and spirit. For the first time since he had joined the Army, Captain Peterson did not feel good about this next assignment. His trepid instinct, the proximate cause of a sickening stomach had nothing to do with the surgery itself, except for the uncertainty regarding the team he would be working with and the quality of the facility. Surgery would take place in a private residence, in a city that could only be described as third-world Africa. His foreboding was about the clandestine nature of the mission and the politics that drove it. He felt extremely vulnerable. If it were possible, the two man crew of the jet made the guys on the Osprey seem like social butterflies. Brad noticed immediately that they were dressed in black business suits, a discomforting thing all by itself. They very stoically, almost curtly, welcomed him aboard, handed him a new packet, then disappeared into the cockpit and closed the door. He was all alone as the jet barreled down the runway and took to the air. Where were the other two guys?

According to the information provided in the envelope, they had been left off of the team at the request of the boy's father, a very powerful man. He would be on his own in surgery, but was assured that the surgical staff at his compound was fully qualified. Brad's sense of impending doom mounted. He decided to ask questions, moving forward through the cabin and knocking on the cockpit door. There was nothing on the plane identifying it as a military aircraft, the crew were dressed like characters from a Men In Black movie, and he definitely needed reassurance. The co-pilot opened the door, smiling this time, and offered Brad something to drink from the galley located aft.

"I would be happy to answer questions, Captain Peterson. First let me apologize for not introducing myself, as this mission does not allow us to fraternize with each other that intimately. It would be an insult to your intelligence if I made up a phony name, and since we're on the same side, I think we should be totally honest with each other. Our briefing states that the delicate nature of this undertaking mandates complete compartmentalization of each aspect of operations. Now, what can I offer in the way of reassurance?"

"What happened to my teammates? I know those guys; they're impeccably clean, have top clearances, one of them much higher than mine, yet, I'm here and they are not," Brad started.

"Sorry, sir; I have no idea."

"Are you guys military, CIA, NSA, what?" "I'm sorry, sir; that is classified."

"How do I know that the team I will be working with is truly qualified for the operation?"

"My apologies again, sir; we have no idea what your operation is. Our job is to ferry you in and out of Abidjan. Other than that, we have no specific knowledge of what you're up to. I'm assuming that you have been sworn to absolute secrecy and are not authorized to discuss your assignment with us either. You did notice that the packet of information we gave you was sealed."

"I did. Is there anything at all in the way of reassurance that you do have to offer?"

"Yes, sir; there is hot food in the galley, a bank of movies to choose from and you may want to get some sleep in the bed during the flight. If there is anything else we can do to make you feel comfortable, let us know."

Brad thanked him—thanks for nothing—he thought, watched him disappear back into the cockpit, and never saw the man alive again. He was sound asleep when he felt the plane lurch with a sudden loud pop. They were pitching and rolling all over the place and he was barely able to get seat-belted before they went into a flat spin, hopelessly out of control. When he looked out the window, Brad's heart sunk into sheer terror. The left side wing had been severely damaged and was on fire. One of the engines had to be on fire as well since they were spewing black smoke in all directions, spiraling downward towards what had to be certain death.

Brad could hear the crew, in calm demeanor, working to gain some control over the situation—true professionals functioning under extremely stressful conditions. His appreciation for their expertise gave him absolutely no hope at all, as his life flashed before his eyes. They had perhaps two or three minutes to impact. In a moment of creative genius, Captain Bradley Peterson reached into the pouch in front of his seat, pulled out and then pushed the play button on his iPod, put on the headset, then the face mask, and decided to try and think of something cheerful. It made no sense to try anything else. He also reached across the aisle, picked up a pillow and leaned forward, as he was told to do in training. He waited for the inevitable, singing a Simon and Garfunkel song, and enjoyed an epiphany. Today he would get to find out first hand if life after death existed . . . Impact . . .

That Brad lived through the crash was a miracle. That he did so without so much as a scratch was a phenomenon that would take space in his head for a long time. Check that. As Brad slowly emerged from the shock of what had just happened, he began to hurt all over. His ankle was twisted. He moved it, noting that it was not broken. His neck hurt, but he could move his head back and forth. From the way his shoulders felt, both of them, he bet that they were black and blue from bouncing around. There was a piece of metal sticking out of his right forearm. He pulled it out since it was superficial. He found out that he wasn't deaf after all; Brad learned that fact as the shock began to wear off, even as the stiffening ache and knowing pain permeated his entire body. That he was still strapped into his seat, though thrown from a broken, crashed jet, and still listening to Simon and Garfunkel, was more freakish than all that had ever taken place in his life. He finally recognized, that is saw, two things a few seconds after he had removed his sleeping mask and checked himself out. There was a fireball several hundred feet away, the cockpit was smashed into little pieces, the crew whose names he never knew—certainly gone, and *then there was the truckload of rambunctious soldiers bearing down on him like wolves after a little rabbit . . .*

* * *

A loud bang from somewhere in the building jolted the prisoner awake. Brad was shaking violently in the blackness of his dungeon, the chords around his wrists and legs were burning painfully, and then he remembered where he was. If only he had perished with the crew, then his nightmares would be over. Instead, Captain Bradley Peterson had been condemned to hell for his sins, whatever those were. He had no idea what was real and what was not. His purgatory, whether real or not, lay in what was behind the door. *What horror is that sound. Who cares?* Whenever he heard people-noises outside of that door, a nauseating terror and bile rose from within. Perhaps he was dead, a kind of a reverse flight of the Phoenix, where the causeway between life and death was a corridor through a castle of demonic evil. Once awake Brad tried to reconstruct his fantasy life, the one he subsisted on in his mind, to protect it from absolute insanity, but now his mind failed him. He could not remember any of it. If he could see all the way to his hands, those precious surgical instruments of salvation, he would see them shaking uncontrollably. Cognitively, he was in such emotional pain that he didn't even know he was quivering so badly. His mind was so far gone by now that he didn't even think of wanting to die anymore, and then he heard the noise, people-noises once more. "Oh no, not again, please, please, not again . . ." The words were spoken aloud. He regretted them immediately and promised himself to silence.

* * *

March 20, 2011

Running a marathon in Los Angeles meant many things to many people, and after all, there had been 7,839 women out on the course of almost 20,000 finishers. For Deba Buzunesh, who had won the race, it must have been a dream come true. When one considered the incredible sacrifice and work necessary to compete at the highest

237

level, the euphoric dream of victory must be the greatest 'high' known. Trisha sat alone at the hotel bar, eating chicken wings and fries, something considered completely off limits just months ago, but now a type of requirement if she were to sustain the energy commands made of her tiny 104 lb body. Getting to eat again was a significant reward for the lifestyle she lived. True to form, and as predicted by Stanley, she had gained weight over the holidays, her body reacting violently with famished hunger fatigue, the punishment for her very abnormal journey into weight loss. Stanley had laughed himself silly when she showed up a few pounds heavier, Trisha crying her eyes out, certain that she would get fat again. The episode was short lived and back to normal quickly enough, so here she was, living the dream of running marathons, and with money in the bank to boot. She snickered to herself about unrealistic expectations, having finished a 'disappointing' 22nd, logging a time of just under 3 hours, a new record for her. When Stanley put her on the plane yesterday, and asked her what the goal was, she merely stated that in LA, her goal would be to finish without snapping her Achilles like the last time she had raced here, vocalizing a bit sardonically. No one seemed to even remember her injury, except her, that is.

Now she was alone with her thoughts, enjoying junk food, the reward of race day recovery, sipping her cold iced tea and thinking of the dessert she would enjoy later that evening. Tomorrow would be another day and her nutritional requirements would be according to the plan established. She would be in training the rest of her life, no matter for her now that she had become a professional athlete. Training life was so much better than obese isolation—she had endured many years of loneliness. Trisha enjoyed the bar area here at the Westin Bonaventure. The lounge, located on the Registration Level of the hotel, sat smack dab in the middle of hustle and bustle, hotel style. She loved watching people, thinking to herself about what may be going on inside of their heads. She had worked a shift at Target just last week, now more of an annoyance to her managers since every time she came in the atmosphere became charged, a bit unruly, and though she begged to be ignored, that was impossible, just as impossible as it was for them to deny her the pleasure of working a check stand. She had become an official spokesperson for Target after the miracle in December at the half-marathon. Money was rolling in from all kinds of places these days. David Giles was a genius in his own right. Around the bar there were numerous televisions, some providing post-race coverage, but most were tuned in t college basketball. After all, March Madness was on everyone's mind. At first she hardly noticed when a news bulletin flashed about a press conference taking place in far off Africa, something to do with some prisoner of war, an American. Thank the Lord that Brad Peterson was stationed in Iraq, working in hospitals, not exposed to that sort of danger. She still thought of him, though she could not imagine why. Their time had ended so very long ago; all of it was just a whisper of a forgotten childhood puppy love. *Fantasy is a luxury best left in the box, rarely indulged in,* she thought. *At least if he shows up I won't be overweight and out of shape.*

For a moment she didn't recognize what was happening, did not make out the face of the poor man who was being led into the room to sit at a table with a microphone, only that he looked forlorn, sallow of face, so pale in fact that his ashen skin stood in stark contrast to the Africans who were leading him. He had a clean white open collared long sleeved shirt on; it did not fit properly, and the baggy pants were definitely not his, obviously given to wear at the meeting. *How sad is this?* His eyes betrayed a pseudo air of confidence; he was obviously in great pain. Something about him looked familiar, something troubling. She almost dropped her iced tea and . . . "Bartender, turn the sound up IMMEDIATELY," she screamed out. "I know him!" Trisha was struck with such a terrorizing wave of fear and shock, suddenly so disoriented she could hardly breathe . . . Brad was in big trouble. She started crying hysterically, composed herself again, then took a sip of her tea, and listened to the babbling captor as he spewed vile garbage.

* * *

The prisoner paid no attention to his owners, had not bonded with them as other POW's in American history had, was so far beyond the reason of any normal human being that he found himself wishing for an airstrike to kill everyone around, just as long as they didn't screw things up like those who had caused the jet to crash, and leave him alive. When they gave him the statement to sign and read, live on global television, he sounded as resigned and defeated as he could. He would read the statement. Was he a coward? Did he think they would treat him with respect if he did as they wished? Was the pain so great that he would do anything to make it stop, even betray his country? Perhaps in his last official act as a representative of life, liberty, and the pursuit of happiness, and in the most desperate place that any man could be found, Captain Bradley Peterson would play a game. It would have been more fun if he had better competition, *but sometimes you don't have control over who is on the other side of the board.*

His death would be the materialization of his cowardice, the felled king of bravado; he would trick these dumb fanatics into granting him the desire of his heart, a quick end. Only real cowards want to die so bad that they commit suicide. His would be a suicide by proxy. Their rage should do the trick. It was the middle of a hot humid winter night near the equator, some 10,000 miles from the home he loved, not a single friendly in sight; even the vultures with their cameras giving credibility to this charade sickened him. *How dare they seize this chance to further their own careers, pretending to be reporting news, these puppets of pretense?* He could see their eyes as he was led into the room, him wearing the clothing of his enemy, they feasting on their scoop. Now he did listen, for his turn was coming soon.

". . . the Great Satan gallops the world over, bearing death and destruction upon the poor and downtrodden, expanding their empire to swallow all that God loves. It is by the grace of Great God Almighty, goodness be his name, the one and only name of God who has delivered to us this minion of evil." All of his followers pointed their index fingers into the air, a show of unity and devotion. "He was sneaking into our sovereign nation when forces for good shot the eagle from the sky, sparing for us this marionette, this face of the wicked and Satanic invaders . . ."

That was enough for Brad. All of a sudden he was beginning to feel like himself again. In fact, he hadn't felt as well in about a hundred years, or since the crash, whatever was shorter. It was comical trying to listen to the man. Suddenly, Brad realized that his was not the biggest ego around for a change. He almost started laughing, using all of his strength to keep focused on his mission, the last chance he would ever have to be an Army guy. He could fix this with a single word.

The microphone was handed to another, who began to ask him questions.

"Are you Captain Bradley Peterson, of the United States Army?"

"Yes, sir, Captain Bradley Peterson, US Army, serial number 133825073, sir." Brad did it just like in a Clint Eastwood movie, a grimace on his face in attempt to hide a building sense of real joy, the first he had felt in quite some time. It looked to him like his owners were about to have an orgasm. After they had beaten the living hell out of him, drowned him among other unspeakable things, he could not imagine himself to be as pretty as all that.

"Are you of sound mind, Captain Peterson?"

"Sir, yes, sir. I have been watching television in the suite of rooms that my friends here provided me since the . . . untimely landing of our plane." The reporters laughed. The thing is, Brad would get himself spun into and out of his plan just by letting his ego compete with the smiling ass who was watching. He still had to be careful about how this went down. He tried to think of the wild ride. Oh what fun it was.

The big leader of the show grabbed the microphone back from his inquisitor. "Captain Peterson. Is, you say, what is the word, your sound mind well enough to tell us how, you say, you feel about the Great Satan and international crimes?" Brad nodded. "Please tell us you're American letters, the alphabet, and my friend, the press wants to be sure that you are, shall we say, of your own mind and spirit."

Game-set-match; there was no hesitation, no regrets, and it was time for the buzzer beater. He actually felt sorry that his war was about to be over. It had been such a great adventure.

"A, B, C, D, E, **F-U!**" His next act was to give the 'not so secret' American hand salute, palms up, finger extended; one finger from each hand, something bad drivers in his home country knew all about. Then he smiled. All hell broke loose.

* * *

By now almost everyone near a television had their eyes glued on the famous brain surgeon. It was no different around Trisha as she stood in shocked and horrified emotional trauma, watching her childhood idol dance the madness of his plight. The television signal suddenly went dark. It took several seconds for CNN to come back on with their commentary, a news story that would go on for some time. During those seconds the entire crowd, save Trisha, started the chant; "USA . . . USA . . . USA . . ." louder and louder; the reverberating sound was spreading all over the hotel lobby. Trisha could not stop the tears. She knew that he was as good as dead.

For everyone else, he was a hero, the man that stood up to terrorists on global television, but for her, the pain was just beginning to be felt. In her most secret place, the box that contained her fantasy, the new Trisha wanted for Bradley to see her. She knew in that moment that she had never stopped loving him, and now he was gone . . . forever. Within minutes she had retired to her room, preferring to suffer in silence and darkness.

* * *

Amidst the madness surrounding Brad's rebuke of his captors, something that would never be forgotten, guns came out, the press scattered as quickly as possible, Brad was shoved towards the door he had been brought in through, and he was sucker punched, kicked, slapped around, screamed at in a foreign tong, spit upon, and had his arms tied together behind his back.

Someone shot him in the back of his neck with a stinger of sorts. His presumption was that he had been drugged. It felt like wildfire spreading throughout his body. The black bag was over his head instantly. He didn't care a lick.

Hopefully in just minutes he would be spared further pain. Now that the objective, which was to taunt his enemy and to get the message out was in the rear view mirror. Brad could rest knowing that he had been a good soldier. He was at peace with himself, assured that he would never have to worry about his legacy or his patriotism, and that was the driving energy behind his volunteering in the first place. His next step was to draw deep within himself, head home to his wife and kids, and perhaps take in an old movie. He vowed never to speak to the pigs again, no matter what. In the end, they threw him back in the hole, bolted him to the floor, this time leaving the black bag in place, and promised one more television appearance, his online beheading for all to see. If he were speaking to them, he would have shown gratitude for their stupidity. *Please, cut off my head and unleash the dogs of war. Do it on television. Does your blood spill red?*

The beheading did not happen as quickly as the surgeon had hoped. He wanted this over in the worst way. Now when they approached him, except for a natural fear of dying, the good doctor was on the lookout for ways to prompt them to kill him, he anticipating their every move, hoping that some underling would wield his gun and end the pain. The problem with playing cards shorthanded, in his case trying to bluff with just a pair of deuces against a full house, was that things rarely went your way. He had been moved and moved again, several times. There was heightened anxiety amongst his captors, too. They seemed very unsure of themselves as they roughed him from place to place, always arguing with each other, never in English or any of the other western languages he was familiar with, and so he really had no idea what was going on. He was tempted to goad these guys, but did not want to break his vow of silence, the one weapon he could still use, so he just played zombie when they were with him, and yet he was always looking for a way to instigate the fatal violence that would complete his life story.

Several days had gone by since the news conference. It never occurred to Brad that a hurricane of death and destruction was building around him, just a single person—though well known, known by everyone everywhere these days. And Brad had no idea that he was a hunted man. Had he known that forces were trying to snatch him back he would have held a glimmer of hope, have something to work with. That would have been near impossible since he spent one hundred percent of his time tied down in some filthy hole, or he was being moved about with a black bag tied securely over his head. One thing he did know was that his current residence was out in the country; he was somewhere inside of a small village. Brad was able to surmise that because of sounds he could make out, noises of the jungle, and lack of noises from an urban area. Always—when they removed the head bag, he was in a black place with no light. His cell right this minute was at the bottom of a deep hole, his bed the muddy ground, the only light coming from atop the hole where the grate was locked. Fortunately, claustrophobia was not one of his problems. Brad tried so hard to stay sane, but that was proving to be an impossible task. He was filthy, still wearing the *news conference* outfit of baggy pants and white oversized shirt, though by now they were in tatters. He had lost his shoes and was barefoot, had at least a couple of broken ribs, compliments of his caretakers, a puffy swollen face, a gift of those same gentlemen, stripes on his back where he had been whipped before agreeing to read the statement they had given him, and no faith at all. His hope for quick death had turned into yet another nightmare. He fell asleep, not because he was tired, but because he could no longer stay awake. He dreamed, again.

My bright benefactor shines pure as grace,
leading me safely out of the house of death,
over the river of fate

Wise Mac

   "Cap, wake up. We gotta go. The base is under attack!" . . . and the whole thing started all over again, except this time he was jolted awake by the sounds of real gunfire. There was a firefight going on outside! Finally it could be over, no matter what. Either his captors would kill him quickly to keep their enemy from him, or he would be killed in the fighting by the enemy. It was almost over. Brad Peterson's sense of relief was overwhelming.
   The fighting raged above, and the ground was shaking violently from blasting bombs. Brad's insanity had acutely altered his sense of self and he realized it for the first time when the terror stricken screaming proved to be a comforting, even a very satisfying sound, for surely his captors had become the prey.
   Die, you bastards. Die . . . slowly for me—if you would, please. Don't die; no, I prefer that you live a long and painful life, perhaps several hours. Or just die, please hurt while you die! This was not at all the same Bradley Peterson who had audaciously entered the service to enjoy experiences that only those who save lives could empathize with. Now he was nothing more than a raging animal who wanted revenge; he had become just like any other dog of war. He

had come full circle, joined the dark side of humanity, and sought to unleash pain. If he could somehow get out of this damnable hole in the ground, he would find a bayonet and slash them to wherever people like that are supposed to go when they get their reward. It had to be almost over. He expected someone to open that grate and drop a grenade down upon his broken body, his soulless soul, and grant him the release he so desperately needed. Then the fighting stopped and there was silence above. He was insane, delirious, suffocating in a hellish place, unable to think coherent thoughts at all, waiting and waiting and waiting; what would happen next to the guppy hiding at the bottom of a tank of filled with angry piranhas? Brad shut his mind down, withdrew into himself, at first slowing down his heartbeat, calming himself to an inner peace, and then imagining the unimaginable, that of eating dinner late at night with the woman he intended to marry. They stared at each other in a romantic ogle through the flickering haze of table candles, enjoying crooked smiles of passionate love—mixed in with just a dab of wanton lust. She brushed her long, beautiful hair aside and stared directly into his eyes, licking her lips. Those eyes owned him. He could taste her feelings . . . , he was overwhelmingly reassured, then he actually heard her speak to him. *"I love you, Bradley. Don't worry. Everything will be all right in the end. It'll be over soon."* Tears stung his eyes. *Trisha.* Brad, ever so slowly blacked out once again, not really asleep, but definitely not conscious. He had escaped into the insanity of a love he had never known, and this time, amidst the chaos of violence, the surgeon drifted into a new dream, or was it a vision? *He was alone in the darkness, not a place of peace or joy, but not of evil either. He didn't hurt at all for a change and sensed goodness within. Perhaps he had passed and was moving into the realm of life after death—perhaps not—he didn't know. Brad felt safe enough, free at last and did not feel at all lost; in fact, he seemed to know the way, which was forward towards a small pinprick of light off in the distance. He began to walk towards the light which seemed to grow around him and did surround him with love he had not known for a while, perhaps ever. The way past a small bend in the tunnel revealed bright white light, the light of pure love, and at some point in the timeless walk did completely surround him. It was almost too bright to see anything, and then the tunnel opened and he entered into the most beautiful valley he had ever seen.*

This place did look familiar for he had been here before, though he knew not when. Three men walked towards Brad; he found himself smiling, and with great gratitude hugged his grandfather, then two of his friends, Roger and Mac.

"Welcome home, Bradley," his grandfather spoke. Roger and Mac seemed very happy to see him. "Would you like to stay? You are welcome to you know. We are so very sorry for what you have been put through. Life just isn't fair."

"Did I do OK, Grandpa?"

"You were valiant." Mac stepped forward and embraced the army captain. "You were simply valiant. Like I told you when you were here before, we don't always know the way of things and the future remains an uncertain domain. Let me also welcome you home. There is much to do here, and though your purpose remains unfulfilled, we have great need on this side of things for one such as yourself. We will make other plans, and there will be other times."

"Are you saying, Mac, that I did not do the job, fulfill the purpose set out for me?" Brad was suddenly very uncomfortable. The thought, growing deep within the essence of his core, was a bothersome tapeworm. Leaving things undone was not something this young man was accustomed to. He had to strike a balance between the undying joy he was feeling, the uncertainty of the situation, and an eternal perspective on what it would all mean. His mouth seemed to dance all on its own. "Can I go back and finish my work there?"

"Do you remember where you are on that side of the veil? We do not have the power to change that. If you went back you would find yourself right back in that hole. We would not ask that of you."

"I am going back . . . perhaps if only for a few minutes. I would not want to spend eternity wishing that I had finished what I was sent to do. That'd be worse than Hell for me, and you know that don't you, Grandpa?

Tag was shedding tears for the pain the boy was willing to endure . . . just to keep on and try to fulfill a job he did not know anything about. "Send you back into that hell hole? That we do have the power to do, boy. You may have the worst judgment of any hero in history, but cowardice is not a part of who you are. Just turn and walk back down into the dark. The good news is that you will most likely not remember this dream either."

Brad gave his grandfather a hug, a bear hug this time, smiled, shook Mac's hand and turned to Roger who had been silent the whole time. Roger had the biggest smile on his face. "What?" Brad laughed.

"Because of this unexpected decision on your part, I feel that our futures will be intimately intertwined for all of eternity in ways that you could never imagine. Of the three of us here, I was certain of your choice before you even showed up. Now turn around, my future son-in-law, walk back down into hell, fulfill your purpose, and climb back to heaven in the proper time."

"Who are you, Roger?"

"All things will be revealed in His time, Son."

Brad regained consciousness because someone was hammering at the grate above. It was time to die. In his dazed unconscious state he had been dreaming, but could remember nothing, except it was the first time he had felt like there were friends about. Now fully awake, he could hear voices, unrecognizable words from far away. The grate was off.

"Be careful with him," said the man with a gruff, aged accent, a vaguely familiar voice from up top as a younger man appeared at his side with a basket on the end of a rope. He spoke English, though Brad knew that meant nothing. He could be anyone and it was so dark down in the hole. He was in pain from head to toe, agonizing pain.

"He's bolted to the ground," shouted the man next to him. "Send down heavy iron cutters." They appeared instantly. Within a few minutes he'd been cut loose, gently placed into the metal basket, and was hoisted up and out of the hole. He was in excruciating pain, so glad that his life could finally end, almost gone now. Once outside of the hole they laid him on a cot, really it felt like a king-sized feather bed; but still he couldn't see, the daylight was too bright. Brad squinted up towards an old soldier, trying to surmise just who it was that now had control of him, be it his killer, someone to torture him even more, perhaps a compassionate enemy to deliver a quick end—which is what he was praying for, or someone else altogether. Though Bradley's face was intentionally shaded from the bright sun his eyes had no chance of focusing on the man's features, and yet he did his best to try and see who it was.

"Son, you make me feel like it is your axons and dendrites that didn't get insulated enough by the myelin matter where common sense is concerned. It turns out that your synapses are too far apart to get the signals straight. You're the one suffering from dysfunctions between the left and right hemispheres in communicating properly with the hippocampus. I told you on the plane that night that you are not ready for this. Good grief, kid, what am I going to do with you?"

"Co . . . Col . . . Colonel Hankle—is that you?" His heart lurched, and he tried as hard as he could to suppress any hope, long since knowing the way of his captors would use hope against him. *Could this possibly be my old friend?*

"It's time to go home, Brad and I told you to call me Bob. Do you have any idea the crap you stirred up with your little puppet show the other day? You are a lightning rod, son. Even so, as immature as you appear to be, I would never have bothered to come over here and dig you out of this grimy grave, except I love a good fight and this one seemed like fun." There were tears in the old man's eyes.

I'm going home. I'm going home. I lived. It's over. He came here, he found me . . . he saved me.

As they moved towards the helicopters, Brad's eyes began to take things in; they were just beginning to adjust. There were dead men everywhere. They were in a small village out in the jungle somewhere. Some of the troops had women and children cordoned off in one of the larger outbuildings. They were wailing and crying. He didn't recognize any of the terrorists who lay dead, but was certain that his tormenters were among them. He felt no pity, except for the women and kids, no other sadness or pain, nor did he feel the joy he had envisioned earlier when the fight was in full heat. He was completely numb. Someone had given him a shot to deaden the pain, once he had been secured, and the effect of the drug was making itself known to him; perhaps that had something to do with his lack of feelings, save the love he felt for Colonel Robert Hankle, the man who had saved his life.

Once they had him inside of his ride, Colonel Hankle directed one of his soldiers to take the Colonel's seat on the lead helicopter so that he could stay with the patient. Unbelievably, Brad also noticed an imbedded cameraman and a reporter shooting the scene as they moved out. Hankle would not let them on their craft, but did allow them to film the two of them together.

Brad smiled as he was told to, and together they gave the thumbs up sign. Suddenly they were airborne and moving very quickly just above tree tops, the high decibel flapping of multiple helicopter engines and blades were a symphony to his ears; it was a wholesome thundering herd of Brad's guys. He saved them in battle. They had saved him in battle.

"Bradley, normally we would have you to fix the patient, but today you're the patient. Should I let one of the medics take a look?"

"Why not?" The drugs were taking over now, but this time they felt good, very good. The medic moved in and began his work, in awe of the legend he had been called upon to help. Captain Peterson was well known around the world now, but before all the excitement, he was already well known throughout the corps. The stories told about his adventures, if only the good captain knew, were ridiculously embellished.

Brad looked at his friend, Bob. The pain had turned to numbness. Then it had turned into pleasure. Now he was as high as a kite. "How did you guys find me way out here in the middle of nowhere?" He had to shout in order to be heard, so Hankle put a communications helmet on the surgeon and then he asked again. "You found me. I have friends that would love to have you go deer hunting with them. You have the best kind of luck, don't you?"

"Luck had nothing to do with it, Son. Take if from this old soldier, if you look lucky all the time then you are most assuredly very good. We had two days to get a plant into the news conference. You remember young Andrew Thornton on the flight over from the States? He was the one counting down times before we jumped." Brad could not place him. "We got him Al Jazeera credentials out of their American branch where we have operatives, and he was there. He shot you with nana-bots, little GPS robots that are right now inside of you telling us where to find you. You must have felt something?"

"Hell yes, I remember. They stung big time. I thought they were drugging me. That was you guys? Wow." Brad was starting to get tired. He needed to sleep. In the few minutes before he passed

249

out they fed him, hydrated him orally and then had him hooked to intravenous tubes. He began shaking uncontrollably, washed over by fear and nausea, and then he settled down again.

"Brad, we have things that need to be discussed before we get you to the hospital, important classified things about your mission, but you can rest for now. Oh, I almost forgot. The boys and I went shopping and decided to give you a welcome home gift. We all went in on this together. He then handed Bradley a wrapped gift with a huge smile, which he opened. Inside he found a new Bose Quiet Comfort headset and an iPod with 10,000 songs already loaded for him to peruse. Never in his life had he felt as loved as in that moment.

"Thank you, old man. Thanks to everyone. Bob, would you like a hanky before your boys see that you're a softy after all? I really love you guys. It's kind of sad, but I think my war may be over now. I can't stop shaking and wouldn't be any good in surgery." It turns out that Hankle did need the hanky. In his decades of service he had never felt better. Not only had he rescued the most admired hostage on the planet, and would be rewarded for it accordingly, but he had saved his friend, the man who had saved so many others. They were now safely out over the ocean. Everyone could sit back and rest. As for Brad, he did peruse the playlist, and before he went to sleep, settled on "Our Time," a CD by *Eric Chapelle*. He fell into a dreamless sleep.

* * *

The runner ran and ran and ran, working the treadmill at the club with the steepest decline setting, emphasizing a long descent during a marathon run, her weakness. Her trainer, Stanley, had picked up the anomaly analyzing video produced during a descent off of Sunrise Mountain, well the Lake Mead highway on the east side of the mountain, when they were out just a few days ago. She had been at it for more than an hour without stopping. Stanley hit the buttons on the control panel and the running platform slowly leveled and then inclined, now going up at the machine's steepest ascent. Trisha took a drink without breaking pace and smiled. Her next stop was Madrid during the month of May, another of the Rock 'n' Roll series of marathons, and her first ever race overseas. She had picked this event herself, wanting to get out and see the world. The nine week interval between races gave her body time to recover, yet kept her focused properly. She was looking forward to the trip.

Something from the other side of the room distracted Stanley, and though Trisha was listening to music, she could see that he was very excited. He shut off the machine and she removed the ear plugs. "What's going on, Stanley?"

"We have to get to the television right now. I think they found Brad Peterson and maybe even rescued him." Trisha almost fainted. By the time they got to the big screen television over near the indoor tennis courts, the report was under way and there was quite a crowd gathering. Bradley Peterson was well known everywhere, but here in his home neighborhood he was considered citizen numero uno.

". . . would lead one to wonder just how the U.S. Military could keep the disappearance of someone that well known a tightly held secret for so long. Captain Bradley Peterson, it appears, has been gone since early in December, when he was kidnapped by Islamic terrorists of some unknown origin, secretly flown out of Afghanistan to be used as a bargaining chip in order to obtain the release of a number of Guantanamo Bay prisoners, this according to unnamed Pentagon sources. The aircraft they were using to transport their captive, apparently an old DC-3, experienced engine problems and tried to land on a dirt road near or inside of Ivory Coast, Africa, but crashed. There is currently a civil war being fought in that small nation. Fortunately, Captain Peterson survived the landing, but was taken hostage and had been held in several locations until he was freed earlier today. Undisclosed inside sources informed us, off of the record, that negotiations for his release necessitated the secrecy and was the basis for not releasing any information during the time he was held captive. We are going to go live to the Aircraft Carrier U.S.S. Nimitz, off of the western coast of Africa, right now where imbedded field correspondent Bing Thomas has the details," John King reported.

"John, this story gets more bizarre by the moment. Rumors are flying everywhere about a secret mission that Captain Peterson was on and that his jet was shot down, him the only survivor of the crash. Who knows what to believe? Here is something you can hang your hat on, though. Elements of the 182nd Airborne, led by Colonel Robert Hankle himself, the oldest active combat soldier in the Armed Forces, conducted a daring daylight raid on the small compound earlier today and rescued Captain Peterson, and killing 113 enemy militia guarding the prisoner. Peterson was being held captive deep in an underground cell, not much bigger than a refrigerator box. Take a look at the film we shot of the hole when we were there earlier. See Captain Peterson coming out in the rescue basket, exchanging greetings with Colonel Hankle. It's obvious they already knew each other, and in fact, if you look closely, you will see actual emotion on the face of the "ageless iron soldier," as he is known throughout the service. It was quite a touching moment, really. Here they are again, smiling and giving a thumbs up for the camera, this time a different finger than the one's Peterson used at his news conference when he had been put on display as a prisoner just days ago.

"Captain Peterson is in surgery himself now, broken bones being set, rehydrating his system, and undergoing evaluations to make sure that he is in good working order. He will be transferred off ship when he is healthy enough and sent to Landstuhl Regional Medical Center in Germany to recover. This is one story with a happy ending, Bing Thomas reporting."

It was all cheers downstairs at the club by the television. Brad was safe. Trisha could not wipe the smile off of her face. "You know, Stanley, if he showed up and asked me to win an Olympic Gold Medal, I wouldn't be able to turn him down."

"Perhaps you'll get lucky, Trisha. Oh, by the way, did you know the true definition of luck?" "Tell me, Stanley. I never get tired of your euphemisms."

"Luck is where preparation and opportunity get together. Where nearly everyone finds luck, the lucky are most likely very good at what they do. I say let's get back to work so perhaps one day you will get lucky and have some sort of an opportunity that would be worthy of a real hero."

* * *

Slybrain Thiefdemon was beside himself with anxiety. They had him! All those fool humans had to do was not be cute about the way they killed their prey. Everything had worked perfectly; they had his jet plane shot from the sky, and he lived. Surely it was the work of those pesky Eternals. He had been approached by a truckload of killers, yet they let him live and be captured. They worked him over for information, a bad idea to begin with, and true to form the quarry had not satisfied his captors, so they pushed their luck—parading him in front of cameras to amuse their egos. That had been a huge mistake, one that the Deceivers had not expected. Surely they did not imagine their prisoner would perform in front the crowd in the way they had hoped. He was not that kind of human, one driven by fear and paranoia. Instead his answer had brought down the wrath of many nations upon them, sending them running, scurrying from one hiding place to another, by then afraid to kill him. They had become the proverbial dog who caught the car and did not know what to do with it. Not only did they die, which was of no consequence to the Deceivers, but he lived and was rescued, ferried to safety and out of their reach again. The warlord whose son died because there was no one to perform surgery lashed out with an offensive strike, so intense that the entire country seemed now to be on fire. Good for them.

Now Thiefdemon sat quietly in his office with the two who had been charged with the task in the first place. Stump Killer and Imp Rogue didn't look all that worked up about the situation.

Slybrain knew why, too. They had a new ally in their assertion that the job of killing Brad Peterson was not as easy as it looked. The task of ruining the life of the girl, Trisha Martin, was no easier. There would be other days. This was a job that must not fail.

"It's those damnable mammals," said Imp. "They can't be controlled or managed properly. They're just too unpredictable. I think it's in their nature, being unrefined, disturbing, and emotionally based in decision making."

"I know that, bean brain. This goes to the core of why the Eternals and we never got along. They aspire to a universe full of free thinking, free feeling—emotional life forms that somehow collectively make correct decisions. They seek a utopia that is not possible. Their civilizations always end up a mess, disorderly and destructive, because the needs of one, the single fool who spoils it for everyone else, outweigh the collective good. But we should be able to kill a single person, even by proxy. There was no good reason for those bumbling idiots on the ground not to carry out the objective. If they had killed him as we predicted, it would be over, they would still be alive, and we could relax."

Stump Killer was deep in thought, thinking of some way to sell an idea that could advance his place in the Realm. "Perhaps, Master, we need to take direct action and send one of us to do the job. I would volunteer for such a mission."

"You have me stumped on that one, Killer." Thiefdeamon's face twisted into a sarcastic grin. "Great Lord's Banner, I think you have it. Of course you'll have to wear an environment suit since we cannot breathe oxygen, will have to hide the ship we let you use. That would be amusing since UFO sightings are such a fad there, oh, and you will tip off the Eternals when you approach the planet. Their response will short out your mission before you even get past Earth's big white moon. Once you arrive there, if at all, you'll still have to get close enough to carry out the execution. You will look just like an invading space monster, which is what you will be with your beautiful silicon body, almost twice the size of an average human. You are brilliant! When the Eternals track you back to this hiding spot, all of us will be in jeopardy. You know, with a think tank like yours and your buddy here, it's a wonder that we have not already taken over the known universe."

"It was just an idea Master," said Killer. "I see your wisdom now." Imp Rogue was pleased that he himself had not tripped on that one, since it had been his idea in the first place; and there was Killer jumping in front of him, still looking for credit he did not deserve. This time he did deserve the credit . . . for looking outright stupid.

"We go back to the drawing board, my foolish young troopers. First and foremost, nothing is to be said out loud about this recent failure. We do not need any oversight from Central coming down on us. I prey to the Great Lord that they were not watching this little escapade. If you guys are like me, you hate CCA command. It always comes with a terrible price."

Slybrain's minions readily agreed, having felt that wrath all by themselves recently.

Just then a message came through on the video board in front of them. They were too late and also wrong about the CCA and what they knew. Lurton Zama, a regional commander of the Alliance, their immediate boss, would be arriving via wormhole within days to review the project from top to bottom. He was bringing a couple of inquisitors along to make sure that they asked all the right questions, and he planned on staying for a while, so they best prepare for him properly. All three of them were frozen with terror.

6

Annie

His words
robbed their rest
of sullen silence
unearthing heroes
whose portraits he'd paint
in watercolors
dripping with his tears

Wise Mac

Lurton Zama, deep down was a very nice fellow, if you asked him—that is, if everything went his way—that is, if underlings and the mice that followed them around understood the natural hierarchy the Great Lord had established. That was back when rebels broke from the Eternals and set a new standard for how things ought to be. They formed Centex Charlatan Alliance. He was short, just under eight feet tall, sported stubby legs, his arms were too long, his snout a bit too short, was flat footed with too much webbing between his toes, and his skin color was not good. Zama's green reptilian exterior was not dark enough and the pink spots were exaggerated by his oversized stomach. He was not attractive at all. Perhaps that was why others feared him, and not just his underlings, but up the hierarchy as well. Perhaps they feared him because he was so smart. *Who knows?*

Zama, who had been called to the Great Lord's council, wandered the palace grounds outside the Crystal Throne, appreciating what was left of a glistening morning dew, enhanced by the bright binary suns, a small white dwarf and the shining yellow that showered light and warmth down upon the CCA home world of Didi, an oxygen rich planet bathed in water. Didi was not so unlike another planet he once served on in the outer reaches of the galaxy. Even from long distance he could feel the humming of the Great Machine, a tiny vibration, such a small disturbance. It was the one place in the entire known universe where wormholes could be manufactured and directed and it was those wormholes that the CCA relied upon to travel the galaxy safely, undetected by Eternals, their sworn enemy. It was still an amazing wonderment to the Draco native how this one place, this single invention, combined with a standard entangler could move objects, living or not, to or from almost anyplace, anywhere, any time. *How could a single machine do that*, he often wondered? Such things were beyond his comprehension, anyone's really since no one else had been able to replicate the machine in the eons since it was invented so long ago.

The day was beautiful. There were storm clouds on the horizon, the pleasant breeze was comforting, there were waves crashing against the rocks below, and he could smell the sea salt as he observed sailing vessels off in the distance. Lurton Zama was in a great mood this morning. He well knew the difference between appearing before the council as an invited guest and being summoned there for . . . other reasons. The Regional Commander of the outer arm of the galaxy had been called to the CCA home world because his special brand of talent and services were needed again. Perhaps this time when he completed the task there would be reward beyond his imagination. The inner confidence he was enjoying suffered a jolt of reality as the buzzer in his pocket let him know that it was his turn to go in and find out what was going on. In that instant a wash of fear, something he never allowed to show on his mottled face, reminded him that his was not the biggest stick on the block today, and that was something he would never get used to. He headed back, flashed his identification module to the guards, suffered the retina scan that matched his credentials and made his way to the second level of security. There would be no less than five checkpoints he would have to pass through before finding the inside of the chamber and learning his destiny. His fear was soon replaced by anticipation, an emotion that he savored as one of the few who still enjoyed a measure of personal freedom in the realm.

One thought did cross his mind as he progressed. *Just how eternal are those Eternals, the adversary?* He had served on that dusty, rocky, water world more than 3,000 Didi years ago; it was a globe called Earth. The planet Earth was now an exciting place in the CCA and, not coincidently, those same Eternals had a biding interest in events unfolding there. Perhaps this meeting had something to do with that. Zama, allowing boredom to be replaced by affectionate memories of his youth, thought fondly of his adventures on ancient Earth whenever he was on a similar planet, like this one. Those were the early days of a mammalian experiment, where CCA scientists dabbled with sentient evolution, using DNA taken from local primitive creatures, subject to the oversight of Draco leaders like Lurton Zama. Yes, of Earth he knew much. That it circled a medium-sized star in his quadrant was kind of a trophy for him to begin with, though he could not go there now, since their civilization had techno advanced and he would be found out immediately, most likely captured, or worse, but captured at least and stored in one of their hiding places where off-world types wind up. Draco natives were forbidden from stepping on-planet in this time. They could, however, influence events on planet Earth from a distance, using an entangler. The practice was an inexact science at best, since using humans to get things done was something less than reliable. The 'human' experiment as it was known to the Eternals, their baby, was to be short lived in any event. Human beings existed on the precipice of self-destruction all the time, were violent, paranoid, and could teach even the Draco a thing or two about evil intentions. Humans were a nasty breed. That was to be expected considering where they came from.

He had daydreamed his way past several levels of security, casually drifting into the central chamber, and when he looked up at the dais Lurton Zama nearly went into shock. There were only three Masters and none of them were on the Council itself, a Grey-man and two Annunaki, those same dreaded beasts that propelled intelligent life on Earth to begin with. It was their DNA that launched the local mammalian barbarian species on their way. He hated these guys more than anyone else, more than the Eternals themselves. Zama had been shocked when the Annunaki had formed an alliance with Eternals to try getting something done with mammals in the first place. What was this all about? In a short split-second his confidence was gone and he wanted to be gone too, but that was not to be.

"Where are the Council members? I was told . . ."

"Silence," the Grey softly intoned; his squeaky voice not so unlike his diminutive frame, his slimy skin was slippery and smooth, a direct connection to their own DNA project on that same Earth, *dolphins* they are called there. His eyes were pitching dark, slanted bubbles; he sported the inverse of Zama's snout, a tiny nose and an even tinier mouth. Zama, of course did not like the Greys, not at all. Things were going downhill in a hurry. How could Lurton not have seen this coming? If there was even a hint of things being kept from him back home . . . well, house cleaning would be in order, and it would not be pretty.

"Lord Zama, as you may have been informed by your knowledgeable field, how should I say it for I can barely accept the silicon oil monkeys as cognitively intelligent, uh . . . team, that the situation on Earth has become critical."

Lurton had been a fool to let those idiots take on the assignment. Further, he had no real idea what was going on there and had to think on his feet, lest his own ignorance bind him to a fate worse than death. Everyone feared the Greys. They seemed to take no pleasure in the sting they caused, but never missed a chance to inflict pain when it served their purpose, no matter how limited it was. The ugly little bodies they wore meant nothing. Their power was derived from ancient mind techniques held in great secrecy to this very day. He had to be dreadfully careful in how he chose to handle this situation. "Sire, we do know that they have achieved limited space travel . . ."

"Your inadequate understanding of the critical nature regarding them has nothing to do with their basic chemical rockets, not even their ion drive systems; it has absolutely nothing to do with any of their technology." The Grey went on as if he could see right through Lurton Zama. "You needn't fear us this morning, Lord Zama. We did not bring you here to make an example of you, but in fact are looking at you to jump in and add your expertise to a small project we have initiated there."

Zama was beginning to feel a little better, not much, but a little. He did allow himself to relax.

"Are you referring to the termination of the *one* man?"

"Yes, he has escaped your grasp once again, moving out of our reach for the moment, but we think you may be able to help. Here is the problem. Some time ago *these two* next to me, or the male I guess one should clarify, were on-planet developing a hybrid mammalian species, found them to be an attractive sort, and then began mating with their females directly. The DNA consequences were significant. The knowledge that humans possessed exploded exponentially and their civilization was off and running at unsustainable and uncontrollable levels. Now, barely three thousand years later, they may threaten the power structure for all of us, that is unless they're stopped. We have determined through the examination of the current timeline that this specific human plays a pivotal part in our undoing if he lives, something that cannot be allowed to happen. We cannot use our on-planet resources to directly interfere. Were our presence there to become common knowledge the consequences would be equally devastating. Humans are far too violent and individualized to be granted permanent status in the overall community of life out here. Were they to also be the first to develop the next Great Machine, and then to become aligned with Eternals, well, you must know where I am going with this."

"Sire, I know exactly what to do." Zama was smiling inwardly now. He was going to survive this little casting after all, though he couldn't shake the cold off from what he had heard.

*Yes, he has escaped **your** grasp once again. I own this, Lurton. Your life depends on it.*

"It is well for you that you do. Your performance will determine the quality of your next visit to our home world." Even though the ugly little Grey-man could barely form a smile with that smug little hole in his face, Lurton Zama could detect satisfaction in the way he delivered the threat. While retreating, Zama observed the two Annunaki, who had said not a word, had shown not the least amount of interest in their conversation, yet now were engaging the Grey angrily. It was apparent that they were not on the same page. The whole episode was troubling to say the least. When he made it back outside of the Chrystal Throne, the Draco inhaled fresh air as if it were the first time he had ever felt a pleasant breeze on his face. He was alive and still free . . . for now.

* * *

I realize I must,
for my own sanity,
enact term limits
on these warring members:
fear, false pride, resentment,
and self-pity—who've wasted my time.

Wise Mac

"Hello, hello, hello. How are y'all doing this morning?" Missy, the meeting leader was in her usual jovial mood. April loved Missy, she loved Weight Watchers. It was changing her life and she always looked forward to the meetings, except when she suspected that the weigh-in would yield an increase, one of the nasty realities anyone trying to lose weight experienced on their life altering adventure. Today was not that kind of a day. She was celebrating—big time. When April Keller stepped up on the scale this morning, her total weight loss had exceeded 100 pounds, a major accomplishment. Missy had eyes on her with a huge smile when she spoke the words . . . "OK, who has something to report?"

April said nothing. Trisha Martin was seated right next to her, taking it all in. The room was full of folks, people of all shapes and sizes, old and young, male and female, differing races and creeds, some large, some medium, and there were some small ones, too. One would never think it was a weight loss group based solely on the shape and size of those in attendance. The meeting was located at Central Christian Church in what looked like some sort of a multipurpose room. If you walked in and were listening to Caroline share, an elderly African-American, you may have thought you were taking part in a religious revival.

"Caroline, what is on that mind of yours this morning?" asked Missy, who after leading meetings for so many years could sense when someone wanted to talk.

"Missy, I know this is your congregation. I know you are the preacher here and we are your disciples," the group roared approval as she danced the words in an old southern accent, grinning from ear to ear. "The good Lord knows that I love everyone here from the bottom of this little ole heart beating inside my body. I do not have a loss to report today. I had a gain. There's a poison inside of me whispering in my ear that I should quit this business, but I tried that and gained back all those ugly pounds and more. Not this time. I'm in it to win it. My believer meter is in the red, baby." The noise from her approving fellow Weight Watchers rose to new heights.

"How many here have gained weight while on this journey?" Missy was addressing everyone now, and they all raised their hands, *even Trisha*, thought April. "Weight gain is a part of the experience. It's going to happen," she went on, producing the weight loss chart she carried outlining her own experiences, the ups and the downs, obviously more times down than up. She pointed out that we focus way too much on the scale, but not enough on the patterning that creates a person who can effectively manage fluctuating weight changes throughout his or her life, the development of good habits to replace bad habits. "Setbacks are going to happen along the way, folks. It's inevitable. Look at it as feedback. I'm a lifetime member, weigh myself once a week, and have had to step back into weight loss countless times. OK, who else has something for us? Adrian, what have you got?"

"Hi, Missy, it's good to be back. As you know I just rejoined. This week I lost 5.4 pounds." Everyone cheered.

She looked quite overweight, *but nothing like herself or Trisha had been*, thought April.

"I had a couple of bad weeks in a row and just gave up," continued Adrian. "That is why I have been gone for the past couple of months. I have been trying to do it on my own, but I seem to be the kind of a gal that needs the group. I missed the meetings. One thing I am going to do that is different this time is weigh myself only here at the weekly meeting. I had been weighing every day on my scale at home and it was driving me nuts."

"Welcome back, Adrian. We missed you, too. As we all know there are many different paths to success, and weekly Weight Watcher meetings are just one of them, but it works for us and for you, too. Folks, Adrian made a good point. Getting on the scale too often takes your eye off of the prize. Your weight is going to fluctuate every day, and what of it? That is what a body does. Many people make the mistake of rewarding themselves with food when their weight is down for the day and this is not so good. On the other hand, like in Adrian's situation, the discouragement of a weight gain can trigger one to eat inappropriately and give up. Nothing good comes of that type of a routine, for most of us, that is. There are some people who weigh themselves every day and use it to their advantage, but very few. I recommend that you limit your weigh-ins to just once a week. Your body weight is going to jump all over the place, sometimes higher due to retaining fluids, and once in a while it'll be lower because you may be dehydrated. Keep your eye on the prize, and what is that? It is the lifestyle changes that give you the control you need. Weighing yourself every single day reminds me of when I was a kid and we went on a trip. I asked over and over again if we were there yet or not. This journey needs to be fun. Take time to smell the roses. This is not a race. When you reach your goal you will still have to keep on keeping on to manage your weight if you do not want to join legions—like me by the way—who gain all the weight back and more. I had to lose my 30 pounds twice, since I couldn't keep it off the first time."

"Missy," one of the male members spoke up, "I brought a guest today," he said smiling. "My wife is in Hawaii with her sister on vacation so I brought along my son, Joey." April was beaming. He was a boy with Down syndrome and he was cute as a button. *Looks a bit like perhaps he should be in Weight Watchers, but good luck with that*, she thought laughing to herself.

"Welcome to our meeting, Joey. We are all very glad that you joined us this morning." Joey was a jubilant addition to the fun and reminded April of why she loved the Weight Watchers lifestyle. Stuff like this happened all the time. The boy, perhaps he was a young man, jumped up, danced around the room with his arms in the air, and hugged Missy, right in front of his obviously embarrassed father, much to everyone's delight, not the least of which was Joey's. He was an irresistible ham. How much fun was that?

"I'd appreciate it if all of our lifetime members would stand up so that others will know that this program does work," Missy spoke again. They did. Now Trisha could see why there were thin people at the meeting. They were the lifetime members. "How much longer will it be until you achieve lifetime member status, Mary Ann?"

"Three weeks," the middle aged woman in the back row spoke up.

"Guys, a lifetime member is someone who has achieved their goal-weight and kept if off for six consecutive weeks. Lifetime membership comes with many benefits. We're going to be talking about those next week. How much weight have you lost altogether, Mary Ann?"

"I have lost 36.6 pounds— total." *Everyone claps and cheers all the time at these meetings,* Trisha observed. Still, holding weight loss was quite an accomplishment for anyone, and her applause was very genuine. Trisha had plenty of experience gaining weight and not just from before. She had gained as much as 7 pounds in a single week—and that since she had lost her weight. If there was anyone more apt to gain weight than Trisha Jean Martin, she would like to meet that person.

"Mary Ann," said Missy, "can you give us three things that have helped you along the way? What would you say are the three most important tools that you have relied on in reaching your goal?"

"I would have to say my attitude. I believe in myself and do not let discouragement creep in, or I get rid of it as fast as it arrives. Secondly, I would point out that these meetings have helped me tremendously. It is wonderful knowing that I am a part of a group that cares about me and the success of my program. Third, and technically the most helpful tool for me, is that I track. If I eat it I record it, good or bad."

"Great job, Mary Ann. I am looking forward to awarding *lifetime status* just as soon as you are ready. So, who else has something? Wait! Let's get into a conversation about what it's like to go on a trip. Help me out here. Have you ever planned a vacation?" People were interested in finding out where she was going with this. She was working off of the big blank flip chart that she used every week.

"What do you need to do in order to have a successful trip? By the way," she said with a great big southern smile that accentuated her tiny frame, "planning your vacation is half of the fun, isn't it?" Everyone laughed, including Trisha who was in the midst of planning her next trip.

Answers came in from all over the room. Things mentioned included having a destination, budgeting money, what to pack, the planning of how food would play into things, and events that would be taking place along the way. Trisha still wondered where this was going when Missy jumped in again with her metaphoric journey of how a new lifestyle, in particular the lifestyle of the healthy and fit, was like a trip. She then went on to describe what the proper destination might look like when losing weight, what to look for in the way of food choices, how to shop correctly so that one could pack their home with the essential supplies, and how the budgeting process works, especially when utilizing activity points, power foods and good health guidelines. The journey to a new life is much the same as any other type of trip. *It's a great little lesson,* Trisha observed, one that she would take with her. Quite frankly, she did fancy, if just for a moment, that she was a fulltime member of the Weight Watchers community. Trisha wasn't the least bit disappointed in her Nutrisystem program, no, that wasn't a problem. These guys really were having a good time together. It did look like fun. *April always says it is more fun to have more fun,* thought the runner when she looked into her friend's eyes and saw how much fun she was having. *I'm glad she chose to share this moment with me. I'm having fun, too.*

Then it was another's turn, someone named Michelle. "Missy, I brought more 'I believe' charms. Remember a couple of months ago when I had some to give away. Today I have a few more if anyone would like one." She passed them out and they were taken quite quickly. Trisha got her hands on one of them. She needed to believe in her program. "Also, I have a food find. As everyone here knows I am addicted to muffins. I love all kinds. I found these," she held up a package of what looked like, or used to look like when they were in the bag, chocolate muffins, "And guess what. They're just one point each. They are to die for." She passed the empty bag around the room, and everyone enjoyed the good news, some more than others.

Now it looked to be April's turn. "April, do you have something to share with us this morning?" Missy's great big smile had returned. The meeting had come full circle from where it began, really just a few minutes earlier. These meetings were very fast paced. April looked up at the meeting leader, her voice choking with emotion, her face dripping with tears of joy. "I lost 4.6 pounds this week and have now lost 102 pounds altogether since I started Weight Watchers last February. It is a miracle." Trisha brushed a tear or two away. It was time for her to enjoy April's moment in the sun. The genuine love and support of this little group had really touched her.

"Now, April, tell us please; how did you manage to lose over a hundred pounds in less than four months?"

"It really isn't *that* much of a miracle," April said, "because by last February I meant 2010, not just four months ago and you know that." The place erupted in laughter. Trisha was astonished at how much had gone on in the past sixteen months, not just for her but for April and so many others too, including her own mother. It was a miracle.

"Yes, I knew that," said Missy. "In anticipation of today's miracle I brought you something." She was pulling a wagon from behind a small curtain and it had a huge sack of flour in it, a 100 lbs. bag if you believed the label, and April did. "I would like to award you this 100 lbs. sack of whole grain flour, just the kind of food that you are accustomed to. There's only one catch. You have to lift it yourself and carry it to the trunk of your car from here—that is, if you want to keep your gift."

April went over and actually tried to lift the sack. It was awkward, she could do it if she absolutely had to, but after barely lifting it she set it back down, noting out loud that she didn't want to chance throwing her back out.

"It's OK, April. We didn't really want you to try it, but to make a point; didn't you have to lift that much every time you got out of the chair before you started losing weight?" April had not thought of it that way, *but Missy is right!* "April, we do have a 100 lbs. medallion for you, this card signed by everybody, a dozen yellow roses for setting such a great example, and one big wish, that you keep going on in the direction you have so wondrously established. This is a program of new beginnings as I have said many times. You have a new life now. Tell us; what has changed for you?

"Hi, everyone. I am so proud to be an active weight losing member of Weight Watchers. The things I have learned here have changed me. I cannot possibly fathom my life without this program . . . and you. I'm a completely different person now. These little meetings are fun, they provide accountability for how I eat and exercise during the week, and it does work. I'm proof of that. Allow me to introduce my friend, Trisha Martin."

Missy interrupted her with a comment, "Hi, Trisha. Welcome to Weight Watchers. April has told me a bit of your story and you have to share it, you simply must."

"Good morning, Missy," said Trisha. "April and I are good friends. We work at Target together. I am here to support her today. It's her day and I don't want to take away from that." She genially smiled and clapped her hands before giving April a hug, imploring April to continue with her sharing.

April proudly continued. "Last winter I decided that enough was enough. One of my friends, a very good friend, started a plan of her own and seemed determined in a way I hadn't noticed before. I could tell that for her this time things would be different, and boy was I right. I wanted in on the game so I started to research ways that fit my personality and possibly something that would work for me. Weight loss can be contagious among friends and for us it was." There were nods of approval up and down each row. "When I came in the door weighing almost 300 pounds, I felt both hopeless and hopeful at the same time. One thing I have to admit. It was a very different experience to be starting an official program, something very real. The first thing I learned to do here was listen. Something Missy said gave me a boost—that I should visualize the process and see where it would lead without worrying about the pace of the journey. I was not in a race, like other people I know," she winked at Trisha.

I settled into a routine, religiously tracking all that I ate; it was shocking how much I had been consuming. Then I began the process of structuring my days around finding the right foods, the implementation of an exercise program, and dealing with the internal transition my body was going through. My body fights change and the changes that were taking place did exact a toll. In the first week alone I lost over 8 pounds. I know most of it was water, and that's

OK, but I also knew that I was off and running into a new life. It was exciting, heck it is still exciting. There have been many setbacks along the way, but the general direction, progress—not perfection, is now the way I live. My journey has just begun. I want to be a meeting leader myself one day, but by all current standards I am still obese. I have a long way to go and with your help I plan to make it all the way and beyond. Thank you very much for your support." The room erupted in applause. April and Trisha were both crying. Then April spoke again.

"There are two more things I want to say," she said with a smile. "I stopped smoking. I have not had a cigarette in more than eight months. I do not drink alcohol any more. It triggers me to eat junk food so I just gave it up and never missed it. The other thing has to do with my good friend, Trisha. This skinny little rail before you is the friend I told you about." Suddenly, Trisha Jean Martin looked embarrassed and it was obvious that she was hoping to avoid what was about to happen, but as usual that would not be the case today either. "Trisha was even bigger than I was. She is also very modest and does not like to brag. I brought a picture you may find entertaining and without asking her permission I am going to pass it around the room. That is what friends do to each other." She gave it to Missy, who winced. It was the photograph Trisha's mother had taken of her the day she bought the bike that was right now outside in the parking lot. People gasped and could not even recognize that the person on the bike was even her. "In case you do not believe me, Trisha is on a ride right now and that bike is right out front. She was a runner in high school, put on the shoes again, and is now a widely known marathon racer. Trisha Jean Martin is almost a household name in running circles. She is a world class runner, a professional athlete, and is ranked among the best 30 female marathon runners, not in America, but in the world. She accomplished this in less than two years! From the bottom of my heart, I am not here today without her losing a Super Bowl bet to her brother, I swear it on my life."

After another round of happy clapping Missy stepped back up and stated, "Trisha, you don't have to say anything if you don't want to. April took care of that, too."

"Thanks Missy. It has been a very informative time for me here today and I am grateful to meet everyone," the runner said.

"Friends," said Missy, "we are out of time. The example of these two should motivate each and every one of us to keep up the good fight. This week my challenge to you is to go back and read the materials we gave you when you joined the program. Go back and start again, no matter where you are at the moment. Like I just said a few moments ago, this is a program of new beginnings. For those of you who are staying to be a part of our orientation, we will begin in just a minute or so."

With that the meeting was over. It had all lasted less than forty-five minutes from the moment they had walked through the door.

Outside, the other class members gathered around the two as they made their way, April heading to her car and Trisha walking to her bike. They visited along the way; Trisha was able to answer the big questions about Nutrisystem food, exercise calorie allowances, activity points in Weight Watchers' lingo, and other things that made her journey unlike any others. She had to remind them that her type of transformation included a regimen that sent activity points off of the charts, and also that she had taken the time to use the Weight Watchers point counter and convert Nutrisystem food into points, a little trick that April had shown her. The programs were not all that different after all. When asked about the ride, Trisha told them that she would be heading out behind Sunrise Mountain via Lake Mead Blvd., and then along the North Shore Road all the way back around to Green Valley, where she was to meet with her trainer at the pool and swim for two miles. For her it was a very typical training day and something no one in her life could possibly understand. She also told them that gaining weight was a fact of life. Even with what she was doing, the weight started coming back when she took just a few days rest without limiting her food intake. Just like them she was in a lifetime program that took effort every day to properly manage. It was a sobering revelation, one that was not lost on some of those who may have been harboring thoughts of a finish line to the program they were on. Trisha could see the little steam engines in some of their heads churning out false hope. *If only they could get a do-over. It would be so easy to keep the pounds off. Oh, if they could just start at the right weight. I'm a mind reader. That's what my mind tells me. Let me tell it right back! You had your chance at Christmas—and I was betrayed with a huge gain in one week. My mind cannot be trusted, either.* It was time to climb back on the bike.

In just a few minutes of biking north to Lake Mead Blvd., and after hydrating and loading her pack with tasty things found at a convenience store—yes one could find nutritious snacks at 7-11—Trisha was climbing very comfortably up the hill towards the crest and then over to the back side of the mountain. It was simply a beautiful spring morning, not too hot and not too cold either. Once she had made her way east of Hollywood and past the interference of traffic signals, her ride became very desert-like in a rural setting. Except for some tumbleweed and other dry grasses, the primitive beauty of western lands, so magnificent in its own way, provided the perfect ambiance for allowing her thinking to shift into autopilot. One of Trisha's secret tricks was accomplished by not focusing on her workout so much, but allowing her subconscious brain its very own workout, learning and knowing how to push relentlessly all by itself. She was literally training her mind to push on its own, to control her breathing, the pace of her cycling or length of her strides, and even how hard she worked climbing hills, whether on the bike or not. Trisha could then let her mind drift in and out of all manner of things. There was very little traffic today as well, so she could enjoy solitude . . . most of the time.

There was one thing she had mentioned at the meeting that was still bothering her. On the way to the bike she had spoken of the two mile swim at the end of the ride. That was a little over the top for them to hear, since for the most part they were getting their activity points by walking with a pedometer on their hip. It was a good thing that she did not mention the high speed elliptical hour that she faced after the pool. Hers was definitely not an easy life, but to get paid for riding a bike out on a beautiful spring day, enjoying the purple mountains, the billowing cumulous clouds, *and oh my,* she thought, *there is a bighorn sheep up on the side of the mountain, no two, no several of them.* If she did not get her eyes back on the road, at her speed, even while climbing, she could crash. That could possibly spoil her European tour set to begin in just a couple of days.

As if the exercise wasn't enough, thinking of what lay ahead in Europe, especially Germany, got her heart beating even faster. Would she actually get to see him after all these years? That was the plan.

No one really knew where Brad was at the moment, or at least they didn't before Stanley got involved. After he had been rescued, the television said he was going to Germany, to some military hospital there to recuperate and recover from the ordeal he had been through.

There was quite a bit that she remembered of him from when they were kids. One of those things was his need to put on the shoes and run when his life was out of order. He used to tell her that when things got bad for him, he would run it off and then would feel better. Since she would be training in Europe for the Madrid marathon in May, Trisha had made the bold decision to try and find Brad Peterson, just to make sure for herself that there really was nothing there. Before she tried other options, it was her desire to see him—albeit possibly just curiosity, it felt more like taking a chance on another miracle in her life, and miracles didn't seem so beyond reach of late, and also because she wanted to nourish a seed of something that wanted to grow within her, Trisha would play high school kid and kind-a *bump* into Brad Peterson. She wanted to, she could, and so she would, try to find and get in front of war hero Brad Peterson. Even now, the thrill of the whole escapade was embarrassing, even to her. Stanley had found him. He was registered to run in a marathon in Germany, she couldn't remember where at the moment, and he had booked her to run there as well. The lump in her throat at the scheme jumpstarted her heart again with fear, the fear of failure. For someone who had never even had a real boyfriend, this move seemed so out of context. Perhaps it was perfectly in context. A more experienced person would handle this quite a bit differently, like, call him on the phone and ask if it would be OK to drop by. Nah, as hard as it was, she put the excitement of the game out of her mind and thought of other things. She had crested the hill. At the top she stopped, ate a snack, enjoyed a satisfying gulp of her magic drink, and took in the magnificent Las Vegas Valley from end to end. She loved her home. The man-made landmarks that were the icons of what her community was so famous for were spectacular from this distance, even in daylight. The rim of mountains around the valley was a splendor to behold. There was no place like Vegas in the whole world. Before two minutes had passed, Trisha was back on the bike and was speeding down the mountain at a furious pace. It was simply exhilarating.

Soon, Trisha turned the bike onto Lake Shore Road, beautiful Lake Mead shined blue to white, to rugged mountains, and then to the sky off to her left. On the other side the rock-strewn mountain she had just climbed looked lifeless. Trisha checked over her shoulder at open barren wilderness behind her and pretended to be on a terra-formed Martian expedition. She rode vigorously into the early afternoon, directly into the springtime sun, which was arching westward, and head-on into a stiff wind. There was forty miles of open road in front of her before she reached the swimming pool. Stanley didn't like her exposed like this, out in the middle of nowhere, a dodgy and treacherous, unsafe place for her to be. From her vantage point it was adventure, a grand way to push one's self to limits formerly only dreamed of. She had the satellite telephone on her hip should something come up, the pepper spray should someone need a suggestion, and Trisha could hit a speed dial button on the phone if she needed to summon help. Maybe her strongest ally was strength, the ability to ride sometimes as much as 30 mph for up to a half an hour, and there were other ways to limit the exposure. Still, Stanley didn't like it, not one bit. He wanted to be there or have someone there with a car to provide proper support services for a professional athlete. Trisha Jean Martin would have none of that, at least not today. Biking on the open road was one of the very few places she could be alone. This girl was one who truly valued her privacy, something that in her life was going the way of the dinosaur.

* * *

I glance up at fortune's star
low in the morning sky,
My bright benefactor shines
pure as grace.

Wise Mac

Annette Chappell did not need an alarm to wake up on workdays. No matter what time she went to bed, her own internal alarm clock went off at 4 am if she had the early shift. She was a morning person anyway, did not allow herself much of a nightlife on work nights, and was usually in bed before 10:00, not for the reason that she was boring and had no life, but because her career was the driving force of just who she was. Oh, she could be found nightclubbing all the time, liked dancing with strangers to jazz music, even took one home on occasion, the stranger that is, but that was the secret Annette, the bad little girl.

Once upon a time in a previous life her father had dissuaded her from settling down after obtaining a pre-med undergraduate degree at the University of Minnesota. *Parents can make that mistake if they're hoping for grandchildren, but want to see the career thing happen first,* Annie thought. *I wonder what Dad would want now,* she mused while going through her morning ritual. These days, the blonde bombshell, the little wild one, a spender who could churn through more money than a dairy could spin *cream into butter,* was looking beyond her Army stint and forward into a future that had no room for children and family.

Annette had credentials and opportunity. She had received a post graduate degree from the University Of Massachusetts Medical School's Graduate School Of Nursing, finishing almost at the top of her class, joined the United States Army, something expected of her, and was, at the ripe old age of twenty-nine, one of the most respected nurses at Landstuhl. As an officer in the Army, she knew her superiors were hoping that she would become a lifer, but an Army career was definitely not in her plans. No, she didn't want kids or a family either. What she wanted was to go back to UMASS where she hoped to complete medical school and become a doctor, perhaps specializing in pediatrics. She liked kids but was just not the maternal type. Annie had found that out during all the education years, mostly by watching and not envying the direction that lifelong friends were headed in. Once they married and had kids, the fun was gone. Professional growth? It was usually gone, too. Clubbing and the jazz scene . . . that was certainly gone. *Having kids is not for me. Sorry, Dad, but it's your fault,* Annie giggled.

These days Annette was taking care of the biggest prize of her career, the legendary Dr. Bradley Peterson, a wartime battle-tested triage doctor, a pediatric brain surgeon in his private life, a former prisoner of war, and now her patient. This guy was the rock star of the entire United States military, and getting close to him was not only a stroke of luck, but of genius. Annette was on call the day he arrived unannounced and in complete secrecy. He had been flown in directly from a Navy vessel, under cover of darkness, by helicopter. The lucky part was that she was there to receive him. The genius part was that she had a measure of control over her commander; *beauty has its privileges you know*, and she had managed the assignment. This case had become the single most important objective of her budding career. What she had not counted on was that he would walk off of that chopper . . . not just a screwed up basket case, *I can fix him*, but also that he was possibly the best looking man she had ever laid eyes on, that he had never been married, and that she would unexpectedly find him emotionally irresistible. There were risks associated with this but she wanted him badly . . . for herself; that was perhaps the most explosive part of the whole thing. Annette Chappell's feelings for Brad Peterson were definitely filed in that very private *secret life* department. Not even Captain Peterson himself would be allowed to know how she felt. On the one hand, she could fall in love. On the other hand, he could help get her into medical school, but on the one hand, she could be transferred from Landstuhl if she were found out, and yet on the other hand she could see a big future with this man once he had his head straightened out. It was all very complex.

* * *

The suffocation, the darkness, a perpetual darkness of hell the likes of which never ended, chased him minute by minute, down into everlasting seconds of anxiety, driven by intermittent sheets of cold and hot water being ruthlessly poured on his bound face and seeping through the black bag he lived his life in, downward into the Hades of insanity. His wrists, tightly cuffed behind his strained and pain-filled back, rocked into the dirty cement floor, buried under his own weight, assuring him that those instruments of healing were now ruined, never to be used again. The prisoner fought off the urge to scream out in pain. He would not give his captors that glory. The one last bastion of control that he exerted, suffering at the hands of the Prince of Darkness and his orks of evil, was that he would not give them the pleasure of hearing his voice, and so he maintained his vow of silence.

His ears still worked fine, though the constant ringing in his head also played games with him. He could hear the screaming and wailing of others, the laughter of tormentors as they amused themselves while playing with their toys, further degrading him, humiliating what little sense of self remained within a hidden soul that cried for help, help which never came. The music was the worst. Its evil intonation drummed into him the tune of his final dance, his only hope that it would end, that he would end, but he could not stop his heart from beating no matter how hard he tried. Then he heard them shuffling his way as they turned the lock on his chamber door, smugly enjoying themselves . . . Not again, please, not again. A hand gripped his shoulder. He lurched forward, teeth bared, and tried to fight back with a death howl, but instead came awake in a cold sweat.

Bradley Peterson looked into the face of the suddenly jolted nurse who had been trying to help him shift in bed, he having slept on his hands in an unnatural way. His nightmare wore its ugly mask upon his frightened countenance and he apologized profusely. "I am so sorry, Nurse Chappell. I was dreaming again."

"Now, now, Captain Peterson, you don't have to be sorry to me for having those horrible dreams." Annette Chappell had been there at the helicopter when Brad Peterson had been transported to Landstuhl, took an instant liking to him and had used her connections at the hospital to be assigned the duty of attending the renowned surgeon during his treatment and recovery. Her biggest secret in the world was kept by masking how her feelings for him had grown in the time he had been there. She was unexpectedly feeling true affection for him in a very personal way. What wasn't a secret at the hospital was the fact that he was not recovering. Captain Peterson, for unknown reasons, was not getting better, but instead was getting worse . . . again. It broke her heart to watch him digress from day-to-day. "Would you like some breakfast this morning?"

"Annette, I would, thank you. How about some coffee, you know how I like it, whatever fruit you can scrounge up, and if you can get your hands on a loaf of that sourdough bread that they were serving last night, perhaps a slab of butter, a jar of strawberry jam, and meet me out back at our favorite spot; we can enjoy a pleasant morning together."

Every time he makes any kind of a suggestion, my professionalism goes right out the window, my heart starts beating again, and I melt like a little puppy, she inwardly smiled, also not able to hide her joy and the twinkle in her eye as she responded in the afermative, and then she moved away from him, not able to contain the telltale swagger instinctively meant to convey something she dare not reveal, even to her hero, the world's greatest medical doctor, still so young and handsome.

Bradley was enjoying the view as his caretaker walked away from him. Her blonde hair was flowing out from under a very stylish cap. How she got away with the short, tightly worn nurse's outfit, was beyond his imagination. *She doesn't dress like any of the other nurses here. Her outfit borders on the word 'costume.' Watching her walk is my favorite way to wake up.* Annette Chappell not only had a great figure, but she kept herself very clean and presentable. She even took time to curl that blonde hair and wear a knockout combination of just the right amount of makeup. He crept out of bed, and then began shaking violently again. He could not seem to control his nerves, but still got through a shower and all the essentials, dressed himself, and began the long walk to a grove of trees on the east side of the complex.

Seen from the air, Landstuhl, with its Army-style box-like construction, looked to be a giant white ladder laying on the ground with a center strut supporting rows of buildings that formed the different wings of the facility. It was your basic garden variety hospital, serving all branches of the Armed Forces, treating every type of injury any soldier could encounter, all the way from addiction to neural surgery. It was perhaps the largest U.S. hospital outside of the United States. Lansdtuhl, Germany itself was a rural, small town, traditional European village, set in southwest Germany on the northwestern edge of the Palatinate Forest, a very beautiful place in the springtime. When he could hide the shakes as he called them and not make a spectacle of himself, Brad would walk the hospital visiting the wounded, trying to do anything to be productive, and then make his way to the edge of the trees where a table had been set up for him to read the paper every morning and have his breakfast. It was obvious that they were trying to do whatever they could to help him overcome the ordeal of his capture, his maltreatment, and it was also painfully obvious that he was definitely not responding to their help. He was at a total loss as to why.

There were soldiers at Landstuhl who he had helped in the field, still recovering from their wounds. He enjoyed immensely visiting with these guys. The inside of the facility was very plain, not all that pleasing to the eye, and when he entered any hall, the men were cheered up just by his presence. Captain Bradley Peterson, the miracle surgeon was in the neighborhood. The kids loved him. During these morning visits, Brad was again reminded, if only for a few minutes, that so much could be said about the quality of his wartime experiences before being captured. It always took him at least an hour to make the outside of the hospital where Annette Chappell would meet him. They had developed a good working relationship, her always giving him ninety minutes before appearing outside at his table and today was to be no different than any other. The weather was spectacular, mostly sunny with only very high stratospheric clouds to dampen the brightness. A slight breeze only enhanced the crisp mountain air. Brad loved the trails around the rural hospital campus, taking in the lush vegetation of the hilly area, admiring the ash trees, the evergreens, the bush, and the knowledge that man had occupied this area of the planet forever. The most attractive site of the day was Annette herself. He had really taken a liking to his nurse, perhaps too much. Brad was contemplating settling down and the qualities this lady possessed were the equal of her looks. She was definitely hiding her feelings too, he could sense it with the best of them. If only he could get control of his central nervous system, those damnable shakes that would not go away, and of course the nightmares haunting his sleep several times a week. He was in no shape to begin anything serious with a member of the opposite sex. He knew that, but didn't care. That was the intriguing part of the whole thing. *It's when you do not care,* he thought, *that you had better be very careful. You may just about be ready to slide over the falls and into the abyss of love.* She approached him now. The loaf of bread was obvious, as was the coffee thermos. He was pretty sure what was in the bag. Brad had not lost his appetite through this ordeal and he was grateful for that.

"I have a great idea, Nurse Chappell," he said as she walked up and set his little table. "What do you say we hike to Neuscharfeneck Castle? I was reading about it the other day, saw some pictures, and think we could make a nice day of it. Do you like hiking?"

In concealing her true feelings, she thought, *I really like this guy. I have never met someone so good looking and he is very charming too. I hate hiking.* "I can hike and would love to, Bradley," she replied. Perhaps she would like it once they got going, but she didn't think so. What she would definitely like is the time spent with him. *Oh well, if you want to corral the bull, you have to get a bit muddy,* she contemplated.

"Tell me, Annette," he spoke again as he began to devour the bread smeared with butter and jam. "What are your favorite things to do?" Brad washed down an oversized bite with a sip of his coffee. *Whoever brewed the coffee needs lessons,* he mused, *but throw a bit of cream, some sweetener in just the right amounts and presto, I find myself alive and well.* The service isn't half bad either. If Brad were on his game, he would have noticed her flattered expression, and a twitch of deception in her voice, but then again who cares? She was everything he was looking for in a girl.

"Well, Brad," she started, "I like taking care of brave soldiers. My family has served in the military for generations, so it was kind of expected of me, especially since I am an only child."

"My family is military, too!" Bradley was getting excited. They had a great deal in common, these two.

"I like to shop, Captain Peterson. When I'm at home, my mother and I shop until we drop. So, I guess you might say that I am an experienced hiker. We have hiked miles inside of the Mall of America, in Bloomington where I'm from. Over the years I've acquired a world class collection of Barbie Dolls. By the way, Bloomington is not Minneapolis. We always make sure that people know that much about us."

"I've been there. I actually know the difference between Bloomington and Minneapolis," he said proudly. He had finished his breakfast and wanted to get up and move around. "Care to take a walk with me, Nurse Chappell?"

"Oh, Captain Peterson, I would love to go walking with you, by all means." She put her hands to her mouth as they walked toward the forest's edge, along the path, and pointed excitedly up in the tree, where a huge raven sat watching them.

The old bird looked like a spy. *Everyone looks like a spy to me.* Brad slipped his arm around her shoulder and they walked right under the tree occupied by the creature, which did not even flinch. It obviously felt perfectly safe among the higher reaches of the evergreen tree. "Caaaw, caaaw, caaaw," squawked the black giant, seeming to greet the couple as they took their first romantic steps into the unknown. Brad's heart was racing. *I have been alone for so long,* he wasn't even sure if he could have any sort of intimacy with a woman, especially one as magnificent as Annette Chappell. He was clearly out of his comfort zone, but found this sort of thing to be feverish, exciting, and packed with boundless joy. Suddenly, another raven landed next to the other one and they began some sort of a bird-type conversation, making funny sounds, quite different from what he would have expected. Brad was beginning to feel much better. *Perhaps I can beat this thing after all.*

"I really enjoyed the Sea of Life Aquarium when I was visiting the Mall," Brad said as he took her hand in his, and found the smell of her hair, the warmth of her closeness, her perfume, but mostly the smile to be intoxicating. "I've been on every ride at the Nickelodeon Amusement park, too. Have you been on the rides, Annette?"

"It's funny, Brad. Those are the only two places at the mall I have not tried. Why don't you come there with me and show me around," she giggled.

They had come to a stream which crossed right in front of them, and the bridge over it was not accessible, gated shut on both sides. Brad noticed that there were stones across the stream that others had used in its place. "You want to try and cross with me?" he quested. *Let's see if this one likes adventure,* he thought to himself.

"Oh, I don't know," *he's testing me,* she feared. "OK," spoken with too much uncertainty, "I am game for this."

The stones were strategically placed, kind of anyway, about three feet apart, a few farther, and there was a huge tree out in the middle of the stream. It was like an island in the ocean for Annette, who was completely out of her element. Brad led her across the water, step by step. She almost fell down a couple of times. When they reached the tree, well almost reached the tree, there was a jump of at least four feet to its sloping base. Brad went first, effortlessly mastering the little distance. Annette froze.

"You can do it," he said. "Just leap into my arms. I won't let you go."

Annette took a leap of faith and jumped. She almost made it too, her feet slipping in the mossy area underneath the tree, but Brad did catch her, holding on to an under-hanging branch with one hand, and her with the other, his free arm snugly around her torso. They would both have slid into the water had he not been holding the branch. They gained solid footing at the base of the tree and he let go of the branch, looking into her eyes, those beautiful eyes. His free arm slipped around her other side as she leaned against his chest feeling the security of possibly the most popular soldier in the free world, the man of her dreams. She slipped her arms around his neck and when their lips touched . . .

* * *

Brad spent the next two days trying as hard as he could to get to the bottom of just what was wrong with him. He had an appointment with Dr. Brainsworth the following morning and he really wanted to make progress. Perhaps he could force himself to discover the core of pain that was agitating his mental stability and be ready for the good doctor this time around. So far they had accomplished nothing together as far as he was concerned. Though he had physically healed, Brad was suffering emotionally, tormented, and he still hadn't regained even partial control of his hands, the instruments of his craft. It was beyond belief to him that he may never be able to perform surgery again because of those monsters who had taken him, but deep down inside, he knew there was an underlying reason, something more than just emotional damage. He could feel it. There was more to this problem than met the eye. If he could just root it out, perhaps he would have a fighting chance.

His recovery, most especially his interest in getting well, had taken on new energy and Brad wanted to take advantage of some newfound zest. He had tasted something a day or so ago that had not been a part of his life for some time. He was very fond of a certain person and wanted to take advantage of a budding relationship.

Fortunately, Annette was an officer, a graduate of medical school, and someone he could identify with. If the powers that be actually found out about this little fling in the making though, he was sure they would move her from his case, perhaps even take her from the base altogether. He did not trust his superiors anymore. Brad didn't know if it had to do with the trauma he was suffering, or whether his concern was legit, perhaps based on secrets that were related to his final failed mission. One of the more troubling aspects of his service now was that as far as he could see, military life had secret tentacles that played with, perhaps even compromised his idealism, the basic nature of why he wanted to serve in the first place. Every time that dark kernel of mistrust manifested itself, conflict within him grew. He loved the kids he had helped. It had been immensely rewarding to aid them and no one could take that away no matter how fouled up the Armed Forces were. *These kids are just pawns in grand games of power,* he knew that now, but as pawns, and really he was no different than they were, anything unworthy of American goodness and idealism was certainly not their fault.

Brad had been held to absolute silence about what he was doing that day. Bob Hankle had debriefed him personally. If he needed to talk about it with someone, Colonel Hankle was the only person on the planet Earth he could go to, and Brad was not about to go there with his friend. This burden was his and his alone. He was resigned to the fact that those men who had put that mess into play, Americans who had inadvertently at best, and possibly not with the best of intentions, helped to start a raging civil conflict in a war-torn country, would remain forever nameless and faceless to Brad Peterson. For now it was absolutely essential that he keep his feelings for Annette Chappell to himself. He hoped that she understood the urgent privacy of their newfound *romance*—if that was what it could be called—to just themselves. He was not so paranoid to think that they were being followed or anything like that, and the two of them were looking forward to a hike in a few days away from the hospital. Brad liked the excitement of taking risks, too. He still had that about him. Playing hide and seek with a pretty girl was good therapy for the gamesman.

Later that evening, in an effort to somehow get a good night's sleep, without dreaming of the horrors of his war, Bradley donned his running gear, put on the headphones and ran almost ten miles through the small community that surrounded the hospital. Running felt so good, the burning of the air in his lungs, the rhythmic nature of moving under one's own power, the increased heart rate, and of course the music, his music. His broken ribs had healed enough. Ironically, if he could only run all the time, twenty-four-seven, his problem would be solved. When he was out running, Brad felt absolutely no lingering effects from his days as a captive. There was no uncontrolled shaking . . . nothing at all—as long as he was out running. He was going out five times a week now, considered himself in training for a marathon he had entered, and each time he went out, he wasn't a nervous wreck, and then when the run was over . . . it was uncanny. Brad had told no one. Perhaps if he absolutely had to perform surgery, he would put a treadmill up by the patient and run along as he worked, where even his hands could be trusted, sure and true. He was thinking of sharing that aspect of his situation with Dr. Brainsworth, but was not really sure he wanted to. *The truth is, I don't trust him either.*

When he finally fell asleep a few hours later, he had one of his worst nightmares yet. Brad wasn't getting better, he was getting worse.

* * *

"I don't understand, Trisha," Becky said. She was dressed very stylishly, all decked out in an exceptionally nice Amanda Strap Overlay Top, meant to enhance her newer, more slender look. She also had on a pair of black zipper crop slacks, accentuated with very comfortable, yet fancy, sandals. Of course her perfect hairdo was in top form. "Tell me once again why we are here. Lately, you are acting more like your brother than my sweet little girl. There always seems to be more about what is going on than you're telling me. You are not racing competitively until the Madrid event in May. It is the middle of April. We have been running, well you have been running. I have been walking all over Europe for almost two weeks, and now you are getting ready to run in the Frankfurt Marathon but want to train here, in of all the strangest places, Landstuhl, Germany. I don't get it. What gives, Trisha and tell me the truth?"

Trisha and her mother had just checked into the Hotel Goldinger in Landstuhl. It was a quaint little place and very nice. The white plastered buildings, covered in red tiles, much like almost every other structure around, were connected by an atrium common area adorned with glass walls designed to emphasize the beauty of the surrounding area. I guess one could identify it as a tourist attraction, but not Becky. She did like it, though. They had all of the amenities and there were not many people around. The atmosphere was very quiet. The rooms were very nice; the bedding was like new, the cherry wood furnishings first class, and she loved the look of the little café with its wicker chairs, the real foliage, and the red tile flooring. Becky had to admit to herself that this little out of the way place was a memory in the making. What she was not so sure of was just how this was to become a memory—from her youngest child's perspective. Becky, who had lost almost 40 pounds in the last year and a half, had not had a drink in the same amount of time, found herself looking a bit too longingly at the mugs of ale being delivered to thirsty customers. It had become obvious to her that the alcohol thing would never really go away. It would always call, just like her sponsor, Montyne had warned. She had been to several AA meetings on this trip and had found them to be delightfully entertaining. Maybe it was time to go to a meeting again. Trisha was not at all interested in allowing her mother to get to the bottom of the 'Brad Peterson' conjuring, not today anyway. She felt foolish enough as it was, out trying to finish high school like this, chasing boys like a little girl.

"Mom, I have been looking forward to working out at the Landstuhl Cross Fit and Combativeness Facility almost as much as the Madrid Marathon. It is a military based cross training center, one that has not been open to the public before, and it will help me acclimate to local competitive running conditions without being a part of an actual race. In Frankfurt I am going to start from the back of the field and take it easy. For me it is just another training run," she lied. "Moreover," *I want to change the subject,* "we need to get going since we have reservations in less than an hour. I can't wait to eat at Grumbeer. According to David Giles," *David, to the best of my knowledge, you've never even heard of the place. Agents also function as a solid lying board. When I need to lie, I just quote you,* she inwardly smiled, "it's the best German cuisine in all of Deutschland. You will love the food. It has potatoes in almost everything. You love spuds don't you, Mom?"

"I have to admit it, Trish. You do pick them right for someone who has never set foot in Europe. So, let's get going. I am as hungry as a bear. Do you think I have lost more weight since we have been on this trip?"

"You look thinner, Mom," Trisha lied again. Becky Martin had been eating her way across the continent since they got on the plane back in Las Vegas. Her mother, well Trisha either, had not gotten used to Euro style first class service and although Trisha had maintained her own strict nutritional guidelines, her mother had no such defense against travel fare. They set off on their dining adventure. Trisha looked pretty good, too. She had come a long, long way since the days of oversized tops and matching stretch pants. Now that she sported a sleek racer's body she could wear anything she wanted. Today she complimented a perfect body with a white Cara sleeveless tank top, conservative, yet very seductive reptile crop slacks, a slick black pearl bead necklace with hanging gold rings, and a brand new pair of sandals she had just purchased yesterday with a training debit card. Her hair was free-flowing all the way to her tiny hips and Trisha loved loud red lipstick, exquisitely balanced with just the right touch of makeup. These two would turn heads today.

* * *

"Annie, excuse me, um, Nurse Chappell, it is above and beyond the call of duty for you to go out on a run with me. Thank you for taking time out of your very busy day." They had changed clothing, cleaned up and were out to lunch.

"You are most welcome, Captain Peterson, um, um, I mean, Brad." They both laughed, he for taking leave of formalities and accidently calling her Annie, something he had overheard at the base, and she for calling him Captain, when she wanted them to be a bit more familiar with each other. "I may take up running full time," though she did not think it would ever happen. Annette could not fathom why people would go off running with no place to go, but she had places to go, with Brad Peterson. *Is this what it feels like to really care for someone else,* she thought? She knew herself to be a good person deep down inside. It's just that no one had ever taken her by surprise the way this guy had. They had run a mile together, a long and tortuous mile of painfully planting one foot in front of the other. She also noticed that he did not even break a sweat. For him it was obviously the chance to see if she had that outdoorsy type of personality. She also knew that people who fell in love didn't necessarily have to enjoy everything together. What was becoming obvious to Annette Chappell was the need to have this man as a part of her life. She had no clue as to how to go about it though. For her, men had always been a means to an end, not the end itself. Now she was unable to completely control her emotional involvement. For the first time in her life someone else meant more to her than she did to herself. It was wonderful.

Brad was sitting next to Annette at a corner table where they were lunching and he looked great, except for the *basket case* part. Both of his hands would start shaking on a moment's notice. It is not that the nervous twitching was unbecoming; it did not diminish his attractiveness at all. What was so bothersome to her was that he should be getting things under control after all this time. When the shaking started he would look forlorn and quietly slip his hands under the table. He was very self-conscious about the problem. Annette wondered how it affected the rest of him. *Does the anxiety carry through to other unseen parts of his body?* She bet it did. Her heart went out to him. She did not know how to help him. If only she could make it go away. It was a selfish thought, really; wanting to fix him was something she hoped would win his love. When Annie was with Brad away from the hospital, she could care less if he ever performed surgery again. She just wanted him. Her feelings for him went deep, deeper than she cared to admit, even to herself.

"Running is the ticket for me these days, little girl. Perhaps you should think a bit about running regularly, just to keep up with your patient and all. Besides, I like running behind you, if you know what I mean."

"Ha! That's what you tell all the girls you run with, isn't it?" She was giggling and having fun. "I'll have to admit, Annie. By the way, Annie, I like calling you Annie. Is it OK to call you Annie, Annie?

"Yes," she returned his compliment, giggling again, the compliment being that he wanted to get to know her even better. "But, what can I call you?"

"First the confession; I have told every girl I went out running with since I arrived at the hospital, you know, that I like running from behind them. I didn't want you to find that out in the rumor mill. That place is a chitchat factory and you know it. My mother used to call me Omar, after the World War II general, Omar Bradley, but no one else has. I guess I am just a boring old Brad. I had a friend when I was a kid. She used to call me 'goofball' all the time. She would taunt me by saying, "Run, run, as fast as you can. You can't catch me or the gingerbread man." Bradley allowed himself a reminiscent chuckle. Don't worry about her. I haven't seen Trisha Martin in many years, since we were in high school to be exact. She was never my girlfriend or anything like that. Oh, and by the way, you are the only girl I have been running with since I arrived. See, I am no good at games, either."

Annette covered his hand with hers. It started shaking and he tried to take it away, but she wouldn't let him. "I'm your nurse, Captain. I am also the only girl you have been out running with, or so you say, unless you are sneaking someone out at night when you go on the big runs." He smiled, he winked, and he put his other hand on her thigh. That hand started shaking, and this time he suffered the nervous twitch with a smile.

"Hey buster, hands off the merchandise. I know the real deal with your shaky hand and that is not it!" He laughed, she leaned in and kissed him on the cheek, and then her faced turned, their eyes met, their eyes closed, and the moment they shared there at Grumbeer, the nicest place in Landstuhl, was passionately tender, and filled with thoughts of what may be. They were very close to the hospital, but for some reason neither of them cared at all about the gossip, which by the way was beginning to make its way around.

* * *

"All right, smarty pants. I am going to leave it to you to get us the table, Mother." They had arrived at the restaurant and Becky was determined to try out her German. Before they left the States,

Becky had downloaded Rosetta Stone software and had decided that German and Spanish were languages she could learn to speak quickly. Now she was touting herself as fluent in German.

"Watch this," she bragged to Trisha as they made their way to the hostess. "Gooter Natchmittag. Were . . . mockten . . . einie . . . tabella . . . fur . . . zwee . . . nitch-tracher-zimmer . . . bitty." The hostess definitely looked confused. Becky had a very dim-witted looking smile on her face and Trisha was laughing out loud.

"Go ahead, Mom, try it again." Trisha was already sure they were going to have fun this afternoon no matter what the Grumbeer had in the way of food and service.

"Guter, natch my tag. Weer . . . mocki . . . ninny . . . fours . . . weench . . . tracker . . . simmer . . . . bitty." Now her kinda-dumb smile looked crooked. This time the hostess seemed to get it as she smiled in recognition. She spoke very quickly now.

"Ja! Guter nachmittag. Wir mochten eine tabelle fur zwei, Nichraucherzimmer bitte, Ja." She smiled, and then continued. "Willkommen in Grumbeer und den besten restaurants in Landstuhl, vielleicht in ganz Deutschland. Es besteht rauchverbot im gesamten speisesaal und wir haben fur sie in tabellen fidern durch das fenster. Genau in dieser weise bitte."

Becky just stared back at her. Trisha said, "Well, Mother, are we all set?" She had started laughing again. Becky looked forlorn, like they were not going to get to eat or something.

The hostess, a very stout middle aged woman crossed her arms, leaned back on her heals, and said, "Perhaps we should speak English, yes?" Trisha was practically rolling on the floor. "Welcome to Grumbeer, not only the finest establishment in Landstuhl, but possibly the best in all of Germany. We are very happy to have you here today. There is no smoking in the main dining area. I have a nice quaint little table for two right over by the window. Come this way please."

"Thank you very much. I sure do hope the food is as good as your reputation. If you ask my daughter here, we came all this way just to eat at your place," as she nodded a crooked eye in the direction of Trish. They were seated very comfortably and in just a few minutes were enjoying their iced tea. One plus was that, unlike most places they had been to, there was ice here, along with coffee and tea. The meal was off to a good start.

* * *

"You know, Mac, this is serious business." Roger and Mac were in the middle of meddling with affairs on Earth, technically a violation of the noninterference rules established long ago amongst Eternals. He looked over his shoulder at Tag Peterson, a constant figure of late in this game of Eternals and Deceivers, now dominating affairs on the humanoid planet where Eternals were trying to successfully develop sentient humans into Eternals.

It was Tag who spoke next. "Don't worry, Roger. My grandson will not go for the new girl in the end. She is a good person, deep down inside, but she's not his type. This little affair is nothing more than the romance of two people entwined by circumstances."

"It's not Brad that I am worried about at this delicate moment. It's Trisha," Roger said. "If she gets wind of the other girl I'm afraid that she'll shut down and walk away from him. The last thing she ever wants to be is embroiled in a love triangle and fighting over a man, especially since she is so out of place halfway around the world. The kid has never even had a boyfriend, let alone been up against someone as experienced in the art of attraction as this other young lady. We have to keep them apart now." He turned back to Mac. "Turn the love potion off, Tag. We are in way over our heads here."

"You wimps have no confidence in your own kids," replied Mac. "I have seen so many years, have watched so many kids stumble and fumble their way to the right choice, and I have a deeper, more objective take on this. Trust them and it will all be okay. Besides, I cannot undo what we have done here. We have to trust the process. At best this is a messy business."

Roger and Tag looked at each other. It was obvious they didn't have very much confidence in the second class angel that was messing with history right in front of their very eyes. Just then, that big omnipresent owl stopped by and perched very near them on the roof of Roger's back porch. It seemed to Roger that every time he sat out on his back porch and enjoyed the incredible serene view that was now his home, he would see the owl. *Is it always the same one*, he thought? *Is the giant bird a watcher of some sort?* Back in the real world, well the afterlife version, there was an additional complication the meddlers were just becoming aware of. They were not the only ones playing with human beings. At first it was just Mac who noticed, and then Roger, but shortly Tag also felt the presence of other powers as well, evil ones whom they had hoped would be unaware of what the three were doing. The Deceivers were on to them and were making moves of their own. It was naïve of them to think they could match Prince Charming and the Princess without the dad-burned Deceivers becoming involved. After all, they were obviously out to do Brad Peterson in . . . permanently.

* * *

Lurton Zama was furious. He could not believe his bad luck. He had been tweaking the budding relationship between Brad Peterson, the target, and the nurse, Annette Chappell, for some time now. When he had arrived at the North Star outpost and invaded the domain of the oil monkey, Slybrain Thiefdemon and his stooges, Stump Killer and Imp Rouge, his command of the situation had them terror stricken. He was the last Deceiver in the realm they wanted to see and he needed to win the day, lest they all get called back to Didi together. The Draco had a style, all their own, of projecting fear. He was just as petrifying to them as the Grey men were to him. Zama had a reputation to live up to and now those damned Eternals were getting in the way.

They had somehow managed to get the pretty little runner girl inside of the same establishment where his two lovers were right at this very minute. *How could this be?* For the first time since he had arrived and taken control, Lurton Zama was feeling pressure. He was furious. He remained calm and did not show them the uncertain nature of their predicament. Instead, he welcomed the mother and daughter into the equation as if it was a part of the overall plan. "You see, fools like you are not equipped for this mission." As Draco go he was not tall, and as Silicone go, they were tall, but Zama towered over them and he used his height advantage to make a point. "I should never have trusted you bumble-heads with this assignment. Now watch me work. If all goes according to my plan, and it is unfolding perfectly, you may just be spared from having to face the Great Machine, that is, if you please me and do what you are told." They sat frozen in silence, looking like the un-oiled Tin Man from an Earth movie filmed many decades ago. When they moved a little and tried to talk, they sounded like Tin Man, too.

* * *

"Brad, tell me the story of how you came to be in the military. The rumors that fly around you are all over the place. My family kind of expected me to serve, and I have not regretted my military life, but in your family the history runs strong, I am told. I cannot remember a single medical officer who left the lofty perch of a brain surgeon to go into the field and do triage work. Did you have some sort of a death wish?"

"Not at all; no, I had no death wish. It all started, like a hundred and fifty years or so ago with an ancestor of mine, Alvin Peterson. He is the one who set the Peterson standard that I have aspired to live up to. When I was a little boy out camping with my father and grandpa Tag, they produced a Civil War era journal of the true Peterson legend, General Alvin Peterson. The stories they told of him were amazing."

Does she look bored or is she truly hanging on my every word? Brad couldn't tell if this was one of those conversations that girls pretended to listen to, or if she really wanted him to go on. Women were very unpredictable that way, or so he had noticed over the years. Many of the girls he had grown close to in the medical business had bragged about being able to fool a guy into thinking his stories were interesting. They would also pretend to like camping, hiking, bowling, football games; they feigned interest in all sorts of things, and then when you married them . . . they changed. If there was an even bigger ego to get in the way of real communication, not named Brad, in the restaurant today, he would like to meet that person. He went on, pretending that she was not pretending. *I'm just Brad being Brad,* he smiled and felt power behind his fascinating tale.

"In actuality, the story of General Alvin Peterson goes back even farther than that. He was a Constitutionalist who favored the abolition of slavery and supported women's rights. He served on the Indiana Supreme Court, was the US Attorney under President Pierce, and a host of other things, too. But it was in the Civil War that he earned his reputation. He led Union troops directly into battle many times, as a front line regiment commander, and at places like Shiloh in 1862, the Siege of Corinth under the celebrated General Lee Wallace, and the Battle of Champion Hill. General Ulysses Grant praised him for that adventure. He was the general whose army won the Siege of Vicksburg and gave the Union virtual control of the Mississippi River. He commanded troops at the front line in the Atlanta campaign, the stuff books were written about, you know, books like *Gone with the Wind*."

"So Brad, you followed in your ancestor's footsteps because of his military life?"

"Yes and no. We have had family in all the wars. We Petersons fought in the Mexican American War, my great grandfather served in WW I, and my grandfather Tag was a colonel during WW II. My father fought in Vietnam and so here I am. I am the first member of the family to serve in a medical function, though and wouldn't you know it, also the first member of the family to become a prisoner of war. Go figure. From the moment I read those journals on that camping trip and listened to war stories around the campfire, this is what I wanted to do. I never thought it would happen, yet, like I said, here I am. The experience is surreal. I just wish I could get better and somehow get back into the field. The truth is they will not let me go back now that everyone knows my story. I am over the resentment of that. There are plenty of stories in my book to tell the next generation of kids. For the most part it has been a lot of fun and I am very happy that I did it. What about you?"

Just then he smelled something, something hauntingly familiar, though he couldn't quite place it. It was perfume, not too weak, not too strong, but in just the right amount. *Where did that fragrance come from?* All the tables were full. He could not tell which person had it on or even remember where he had experienced it before. Of one thing he was certain. That vague familiar scent was distracting; a lovely sort of distraction, granting him the wisp of something long forgotten. He decided not to mention the pleasing scent to Annie. There was no reason for this fine lady to even think he could remember the scent of a woman's perfume. In any event the déjà vu bouquet was gone in a moment and forgotten a moment later.

"My father, like yours, is a Viet Nam veteran. Unlike yours, I presume, he is also a veteran of the Gulf War. He spent twenty-seven years in the Air Force. All three of my uncles served in one branch of the Armed Forces or another. My cousins, the male ones at least, all served too. I am an only child and my dad always hoped that I would find my way into the Service, which I did. I cannot say that being here is the highlight of my life, but I never look back. If I had not joined, we would not have met and I would not be sitting here today. There have been plenty of good times for me since I entered the Service and I cannot say it has been a bad experience. I like helping people. They are hoping that I find my life's work here and there is no way that is going to happen."

"Nurse Chappell, what then do you see as your life's work?"

"I want to go back to medical school and get a medical degree. I want to continue my education and become a doctor. Is that so bad?"

"That's not a bad thing at all, Annie. If there's anything I can do to help, just let me know. Lord knows you've helped me."

He smiled and his hands were resting on the table, calm for a change. What Brad tried to hide was an uncertain twinge of what that might mean for them, though. Oh, what the heck, the kind of thinking that generated insecurity was way out in front of where they were. Anything could happen. The future was an unwritten book.

* * *

The conversation taking place across the dining room was just beginning to heat up and the food was incredible. Trisha was enjoying a fruit drink whose name she could not pronounce. As usual her mother was sipping hot tea sweetened with a very interesting German honey. Trisha had eaten the Cucumber Salad while Becky chose a traditional Green Salad. The big difference in their salads had to do with the dressing; Trisha had a spicy mustard sauce mixed in with a tomato based salsa, and Mom flooded hers with some creamy Italian. They had shared something known in this part of the world as Potato Pizza for an appetizer, and for the main course they split schnitzels and a small steak. Trisha had eaten more than she wanted but she would still allow herself the pleasure of dessert, you only live once. Her eating requirements of late were hard to keep up with since her training regimen was extreme. There was a time in her life when she could not stop eating, a time in her life when she had to watch every little bit she ate, and now she was in a time where her nutritional requirements forced her to eat. These days though, she was far more intelligent about what she would put into her body.

"Maybe when we get to Spain, Mother, you'll do better with the language," Trisha giggled. "You have to admit it, you were funny back there, and that old German battle ax seating people didn't give you much of a break. Did you see her when she ran you through the language gauntlet? That was priceless."

"It's all true, darling. But, remember one thing. This ole gal hasn't finished trying new things yet. I still like learning. I'm going to keep working on my German for the time being. You have yet to really tell me why we are here. So, as if it is the real truth, just what is the Landstuhl Cross Fit and Combativeness Facility? Why did you pick it again? I don't mind being here. We're having a great time and the hotel looks absolutely adorable, but there's something else on your mind. I know it. I know you."

"I like being free, Mother. I am my mother's daughter. Exploring new places and concepts is what this running thing is all about right now. Imagine this; you have nothing, go nowhere, and spend your time sitting in the room, when suddenly someone puts a bottomless debit card in your hand and tells you to go around the world having fun. When I found out about this cross training facility and that it would be open to the public I just had to try and get on the course. We're not very far from Frankfurt either. I have always wanted to visit that city, too."

"I remain very skeptical, Trisha. I knew you before you knew you. Come on, spill the story. There is intrigue written all over your face. I will get to the bottom of this. On the other hand, I love the food here. Isn't this little café the greatest?"

"It sure is, Mom. My favorite was the Potato Pizza dish. I don't think you can get that anywhere else in the world, but we will travel the planet from side to side and from top to bottom trying to find it again, OK?

"You got it, dear. By the way, what is so special about Frankfurt?"

"In addition to the timing of the run, giving me plenty of space to recover in time so that I can actually compete in Madrid, Frankfurt is an incredible place all on its own. The marathon itself is like the oldest one in Germany. The first year they had it was in 1981, so it has history. You know how much I like music, too. I have us scheduled for one of the biggest concerts of the year at the Old Opera House. We also just have to get to the Frankfurt Romans, their seat of government since the 1400s, and we will also be touring the world famous Cathedral of St. Bartholomew. They used to crown Holy Roman emperors there."

Dessert had come during the conversation, they had eaten it, paid the bill, and it was time to go. "You can be very convincing, Trish. You really can. Let's get out of here. I want to stop by some of the shops we saw on our walk over, and then I want to visit the spa in the hotel. I bet you have to get ready and go to work. Are you running this afternoon?"

"Later. I plan on logging about fifteen miles in a while when the food has settled and I can push things a bit. There's a gym not too far from the hotel and I have already registered online to go there and lift. As is usually the case, I have much to do. Perhaps we can go out again tonight."

They made their way through the dining room and walked out of the front door. As was customary for Trisha, a generous tip was left on the table, and they said a special goodbye to the hostess, this time in English. She responded very gently in German and wished Becky good luck in learning the language. They actually hugged each other. Trisha's mother promised to return and speak more fluently the next time and with that they were out the door.

*   *   *

Annette Chappell and Brad Peterson, conveniently located just three tables away from where Trisha Jean Martin and her mother, Becky had enjoyed their lunch, were visiting about Annette's chances of and desire to become a doctor. "I like your idea, Annie," Brad said. "First of all you finished so high up in the class when you got your nursing degree. Your experience out here can do nothing but further your opportunity and you know people . . ." *There it is again! Who's wearing that scent? It was unmistakably familiar.* Where did he remember that from? He looked around wildly hoping to notice something. Brad wanted very badly to see who was wearing that perfume. He did not recognize anyone in the room.

"What's wrong, Brad? You seem distracted. Are you having an episode? Is there anything I can do to help?"

In spite of Annette's concern, what Brad saw in her eyes was a hint of disappointment that he had abruptly become distracted, and all of a sudden he couldn't even remember what they were talking about. It took him a moment or two, the perfume had wafted and he smiled at his date, all the time searching his brain, trying to remember the conversation and then he had it. Brad had been talking about Annie and her plans to become a doctor. As usual, for a guy, the topic in his head egomaniacally slammed back into first person; it was always about him. He did not want to give that away, so he dared not ask her what they had been talking about. He could see that she already suspected the worst.

"It's none of those things, Annette, nothing of the sort. I was running a list of people in my mind that could be of help to you in achieving this goal of yours. I might be able to be a bit of help myself." He took credit for the save, but could see right through her countenance and her skeptical . . ." *Who is that out the window?* Brad noticed a couple of women as they walked past the front window. They had just been in here eating, but he didn't remember seeing them and she looked straight at him. He could not place her and really didn't make the connection between that tiny fraction of a second that they saw each other and the scent that had floored him, twice now. Just like that she was gone. "As I was saying," he would get busted big time if he kept allowing himself to become sidetracked, "you know a lot of people and so do I. If you play your cards right and stay on track, you will be getting anything you want in life. The world is your oyster, Annie." She was all smiles. Brad was getting better at this girl romancing thing. He needed her to go to medical school like he needed a hole in the head, but . . .

* * *

"Mother, let's go to the movies tonight. The German version of *Soul Surfer* is playing at the Odeon . . ." Just then she looked into the window where they had eaten and . . . *NO, it can't be. Was that him?* Trisha quickly averted her glance away. They had both looked into each other's eyes.

For a second, for just a second, she thought that it may have been him. *My mind has to be playing tricks with me,* thought Trisha. Since she did not get a second glance, the image quickly drifted away and she wrote it off to being a bit jumpy about Brad Peterson. Of course she would think that anyone would be him if there was even a remote resemblance at all. Thank the Lord that her nosy mother didn't notice what had just happened. The last person in the world she wanted to answer questions about was the man who was the real reason they had made the journey to this little backwater place in Germany in the first place. "Anyway, Mom, I want to see that movie. It is about a female surfer who was attacked by a shark and how she recovered from the ordeal. She surfs again with only one arm, even on the same beach. Are you up for it?"

* * *

"You guys have absolutely no faith at all," said Wise Mac to his long dead buddies, Roger Martin and Tag Peterson, two meddlers who were trying to put their families together. "Did you see that? This is more fun than I've had in all the time I have been here. What was the name of that movie? Match maker, match maker, make me a match, find me a find, catch me a catch . . ."

"It was *Fiddler on the Roof,*" answered Tag. "I loved that movie. On the one hand it was about a tragic time in human history. On the other hand it was a great love story. I mean on the one hand the Fiddler's daughters were so beautiful and so different. On the other hand they were attracted to such dissimilar men, the youngest to a soldier not even of the Jewish faith. If you look at that movie and take things in their proper perspective, you have to look at it both ways, for on the one hand it was an incredibly in-depth depiction of Russia during the tumultuous early 20th century, but on the other hand it was a display of great strength of family and love, especially love. Just look at this situation here. On the one hand . . ."

"Enough already," said Roger. "Remember when the youngest ran off with the Red soldier? The old man ran out of hands. For that there was no other hand. So, Mac, does this work down the road or something? What has you smiling?"

"You didn't see it?"

"See what?"

"You tell me, Roger."

"OK, Bradley and his female friend, Nurse Chappell, were sitting in the establishment enjoying their date when my wife and daughter came in, sat down, and ate? Then they got up and left. What did I miss?"

"You're slowing down in your no-body afterlife, Roger," said Tag. He was looking much smarter than his friend. "First off, I was very impressed with your wife. She is absolutely adorable. I can see why you fell in love with that one, Roger. Is it true, Mac, that Trisha has not worn that perfume since she was a kid?" Mac nodded. "Was that your magic potion?" Mac nodded again. "That was brilliant. You took my grandson right out of his game with the other gal. I'm surprised Trisha's mother didn't notice the fragrance, especially since she is curious as to why they are there in the first place. I am guessing that what Roger missed happened to be our two little lovebirds making eye contact as they left, yes?" Mac nodded yet again. "Down the road when they do meet, this little episode will pay off. Is that what you intended, Mac?" He nodded, for the fourth time in a row this time with a huge smile.

* * *

Meanwhile, down the drain in the land of the insane, Lurton Zama was all smiles, though in that big pink spotted belly of his, he was experiencing something quite unexpected, an emotion that could only be described as terror-stricken fear. He was beginning to lose control of the situation. Zama had been so sure of the role Nurse Chappell would play in his scheme and now his confidence had dwindled to basic insecurity. Damn those Eternals, wannabes— really since the human race had not been accepted as Eternals yet, and they were tripping him up.

"We have begun the process of disposing of the little girl who would wreak havoc with the bloated-ego war hero. Humans cannot control their primal desire for sexual conquest and Trisha Martin is no match for Annette Chappell, no match at all. You oil monkeys have a rare opportunity to learn, perhaps more than you are capable of, how a Draco takes the bull by the horns, as they say on Earth, and disposes of enemies. This minute human is no competition for me, even though I have to work from so far away. My power is great. Before she leaves Europe, the game will be over and I will be basking in the glory of my reward. I may keep you dummies on board as my slaves, or perhaps the Great Machine will need to be lubricated by silicon . . . yours. Who knows what I will do with you after all the trouble you three have caused?"

Slybrain Thiefdemon, Imp Rogue and Stump Killer were a little mixed in their feelings about the whole thing. They knew the score, were watching the lizard squirm; they loved it. There was a downside to his problem though, and that they feared. If he were to fail at getting rid of the man, their future would amount to the fulfillment of his threats. If he succeeded though, well, being a slave to a Draco was not the worst predicament. Many of the silicons had risen to great wealth in the realm as servants of higher orders. They had no desire to submit to Annunaki masters and the only life worse than serving the Great Machine would be to find one's self indebted to a Grey.

"Master Zama," said Slybrain, "it is brilliant that you could arrange to get them all together for this little meeting, and in furtherance of your plan to destroy the man. In order that I may better assist you moving forward, may I please ask what was accomplished? He could barely contain a smile, but dared not laugh out loud. Unfortunately, Stump Killer was not in that much control of his faculties. He burst out laughing. Imp Rogue, who was sitting nearby, trying as hard as he could to contain himself looked like a bleeding oil pump as the pressure in his face grew. In the end he started to laugh as well. Slybrain looked at the two idiots, coldly casting doubt on his choices for this project, and looked like he was ready to strike. Soon enough Lurton Zama, the Draco native, started laughing out loud as well. Apparently, Zama was not as serious as the Silicons previously thought. Master Zama could be a good guy after all.

"Gentlemen, let's go for a short walk," and now they were getting nervous again. They were at present inside a rocky dead planet in the Ursa Minor star constellation, in an arm among the outer reaches of the Milky Way Galaxy. Polaris, as the star they were orbiting was known on Earth, or better yet the North Star, was a medium-sized yellow planet builder, much like Earth's Sol. The surface of the globe was not conducive to life, not Silicon, Draco, Annunaki, and especially not human life. It was either too cold, too poisonous, or too exposed to Polaris' flaring magnetic storms, since there was no rotating iron core to create the necessary magnetic protective shield, like the one created for Earth itself so long ago. Down a few hundred feet where the Deceivers were, the story was completely different. They were located in methane rich, temperate conditions with excess room for the small contingent of realm defenders. The artificial environment was very efficient. They were well stocked with the necessary provisions and comforts needed to sustain their purpose. Why then did everyone here want to be somewhere else? The reptilian had a very clear voice when he spoke. "Have you genius types studied much of Earth's history? Do you even know who you are dealing with? They are a very crafty lot, these mammalians. Have you taken the time to learn about them through their television programming?"

The three were now petrified . . . again. Oh, they wished this guy would go away, go back to where he came from. Stump Killer spoke, very sedately, "We know of human television programming, Master." The other monkey nodded in-kind, but not Thiefdemon, who looked ready to strangle his errant subordinate for speaking out of turn. He well knew the tactics of the Draco. They would take your hand and walk you down to the river, then on down to the falls, where you would be unceremoniously thrown on the rocks to be devoured. His calm demeanor did not betray an inner dread, knowing as he did what Master Zama was up to.

They walked into a large cavern and there, not too far from the wall, were three curtains, all colored in red and green stripes, each with a large black number in the center. "Have you munchkins ever seen the American television show, *Let's Make a Deal*?

This time it was Imp Rogue who spoke out of turn. "Oh! I have. I saw that show. It is so funny."

"Shut up you idiot," said Slybrain. "Don't either of you say another word; do you hear me? From now on, when Master Lurton asks a question I am the one to speak, not you, not at all. Do you hear me?"

Stump could not help it. "But, he asked all of us . . ."

"I said shut your ugly trap, you fool. He is standing right here. You work for me. If you want to live you will shut up, NOW!" This time they understood, choosing to perch quietly, back a few steps from where Lurton Zama was at present clearly addressing Slybrain Thiefdemon.

"Slybrain, you'll need to wear a costume to play this game. You and your, *team* shall we call them, can pick from the ones provided. Hurry now, don't make me wait all day."

Thiefdemon found a gorilla suit that was just his size. It was purple, hot and stuffy. Gorillas were a common DNA source in the galaxy and he knew them well, in fact he loved the beast. Imp Rogue found a huge sponge-like costume with the face of an idiot. It was the one that Slybrain picked out for him, and for Killer, it would be a clown suit, conveniently matching his specific size.

"Who wants to make a deal?" shouted Lurton Zama with a huge crocodile-like smile. In that instant the entire area went totally dark except for the curtains. Slowly the light began to come back, except this time they found themselves on the set of an old American television show, and amidst a howling, cheering, studio audience, the ones down close were all wearing costumes. *It must be some sort of a realistic holographic projection*, thought Slybrain as he sweated out the ordeal inside of his gorilla suit. There was one last trick to make the magical moment complete. Their foul smelling fearless leader morphed into a projection of the actual game show host. He looked human now. It would've been a very entertaining moment, had Slybrain and the others not been in such a perilous situation. Imp Rouge, the fool, looked to be enjoying himself.

"Step right up, guys. Folks," and the crowd cheered even louder, "I have, ready to play—the brothers, Great Grape Ape, Sponge Bob, and R-r-r-r-r-r-r-Ronald McDonald! Welcome to the show, guys. Who is going to make today's deal for you?" Slybrain, um, Grape Ape, indicated that he would make the decisions, whilst Sponge Bob and Ronald McDonald stupidly looked on.

"Good. Jay, bring out the table with our gift item." An entertaining human man, answering to the name Jay walked over, set down a black table with a gift-wrapped box on top, topped by a beautiful, huge lime green bow with pink spots on it. "Grape Ape, I'll offer you this lovely gift or you can have what's behind Curtain No. 1. What's it going to be?"

"I'll take Curtain No. 1."

"Oh, goodie for you. Let's see what is behind Curtain No. 1." The curtain opened and a very pretty human female, elegantly dressed, walked across the area behind the curtain with her arm extended to lovely fingertips; she was elegantly dressed and proudly displaying some sort of a view box.

It was Jay who spoke for the first time. "It's a new color television. You are looking at the latest in television technology from Zenith, it has a 25" diagonal screen, is set in brilliant mahogany, and comes complete with a remote control! This beauty retails for $1,436." The crowd responded enthusiastically at the gadget.

"Now, Grape Ape, we're not done with you yet. I'll offer you $500 to give up the television for what is in the box."

By this time Slybrain had noticed that Zama's character was named Monty Hall, so he decided to go along with the gag and try out the name. "No thanks, Monty. I am going to stay with the television."

Unfortunately, his response was not as excited as it could have been. Monty did not look enthused. "OK, Grape Ape, are your two partners in agreement with you? Sponge Bob and Ronald McDonald indicated that they had complete confidence in their boss man. "Perhaps then, you would be interested in trading your television for what is behind Curtain No. 2."

"I really love the TV," said Slybrain Thiefdemon, aka Great Grape Ape, "so, no thanks."

"It is a beautiful set, isn't it? I would have a hard time giving that up myself. Let's have a look at what is behind Curtain No. 2."

The curtain opened and another pretty female danced around what Jay described as "a BRAND NEW CAR! You're looking at the new 1970 Cadillac Eldorado, two door, vinyl roof, including white wall tires; and it's is powered by the new 500 cubic inch V8 400 horse power engine. This vehicle, which could have been yours, is fully loaded and retails for $21,585."

"Oh, my," said Monty Hall. This time Grape Ape and his friends looked just a bit disappointed. "It is still a beautiful television, friends. I have one final offer for you this afternoon. First, I must reveal the secret." A welling of fear began to form a knot in the stomach of the big gorilla. The Sponge Bob character and his buddy, Ronald McDonald, didn't catch the phrase, or were caught up in the game by now. "There is more right behind the television. Knowing that, and knowing what you just gave up. Would you like to trade for what is behind Curtain No. 3?"

"I'm not so sure about this one, Monty." Slybrain was on his game now and did not want to get caught in a trap. He was confident for the first time since this little charade started. "We're going to stick with the television set. We are not greedy and are happy knowing that there is more, too," he spoke not a word of truth and tried as hard as he could to hold the wall of terror from their Draco Master that was engulfing him.

When Curtain #3 opened, instead of the beautiful music that accompanied the two previous scenes, this time there was a descending horn noise—Urrump!, followed by a banging drum—boom!, and concurrent symbol—srrringggggggg. Inside was yet another beautiful lady, this time wearing very short jean overalls, a checkered shirt, and sporting a straw hat. She stood laughing next to a wooden cart laden with bales of hay being pulled by a donkey.

"You guys made a great deal," said the game show host. "You almost got zonked that time. I am so happy for you. Before we reveal what is behind the television we need to take a look at what you missed out on when you passed up the chance to take the box on the table. Jay, would you do the honors please?"

Jay lifted the box and inside of it were bananas, several bundles of bananas. "You beat that zonk too, men. You are very good players," said Monty Hall. "Lana," the very first lady, still modeling inside of Curtain No. 1, pushed the television, which was on some sort of slider, revealing a large poster on some sort of an easel. Monty looked at Jay.

"You're going on an all-expenses paid vacation, a tour of the galaxy!" Monty simply looked beside himself with glee as Lana wheeled out what was obviously an entangler. Monty shoved them forward to the stage and into the glass chamber. They were horrified. Where were they being sent? The entire mirage dissipated into thin air, the illusion gone, Monty Hall gone, the curtains, gone, and the studio audience; they were gone too. The only things left of the amusing charade were the costumes worn by the three Silicons. "Take those silly costumes off, you dumb idiots, and get into the entanglement chamber. You must learn not to make fun of other people, nor to take lightly what we are doing here. Now get in!"

There were times when climbing into an entangler chamber was about the most exciting thing one could do, but not this time. The three had no idea where or when the settings had them going. They were frozen in the cold reality that their lives were over, or that an eternal nightmare had just begun. They had worked so hard on the plan, had been so inventive, and had even snared the target into the right hands. What could they do? How was it their fault that the unpredictable humans would not kill the mark? Standing up to the massive Draco bully was not an option. He laughed and walked away from them as the telling familiar white smoke filled the chamber, electrifying the space they occupied, lifting them skyward through a new hole in the ceiling of the chamber and into the wormhole that warped its way inward toward the center of the galaxy. In a nanosecond they folded space and were gone from the plane of their reality. They could not see out. They could not even see each other. They did observe a kaleidoscope of twisting and gyrating colors, well-known to all who traversed wormholes. They were in the recognizable vortex of interstellar space travel . . . but to where? The trip didn't last very long. When the smoke cleared and the door latch automatically released they walked out into the very same spot they had departed from. Stump Killer looked in an uncanny fashion at Imp Rogue, who was just as flabbergasted as his buddy. It was Slybrain Thiefdemon who spoke, though. "Something went wrong. The entangler must have malfunctioned. We are right back where we started from."

"Not quite, you aren't," said a now cynically humorous Lurton Zama, lounging on a chair off in the dark. "Lucky for you pound puppies that I decided at the last minute to use you again. It has been three days since you left my graces, ostensibly headed to oil the Great Machine, but conditions have changed. My little lovebirds are going on another date. I have an idea that may rid us of the runner child . . . permanently."

* * *

"Colonel Hankle, Brad Peterson here," said the surgeon on the telephone to his old friend. Had it still been less than a year since that amazing night on the Starlifter when Bradley had met the crusty old fighter at the beginning of his own 'longest day' adventure? He had begun the flight from Ft. Bragg, North Carolina to Baghdad, which was already the second flight of the day for him, the first being a red eye from San Antonio where he had completed training at Ft. Sam Houston upon entering the military. Things got a bit crazy when Hankle's troops had been called directly into action, the flight had been diverted, and he was sent to the hospital ship initiating his own active duty. It would be quite some time before he made it to his official first assignment within the Green Zone in the American sector of Baghdad, Iraq.

"How many times do I have to tell you to call me Bob, *Captain*?"

Brad laughed. Some things never change. *He wants me to call him Bob and I always feel the need to call him Colonel Hankle.* "Bob, how goes it out in the field? I miss being with the actives out there. The rush is gone, if you know what I mean."

"That's why I paid those yokels off in D.C. to leave me alone. I never get tired of being out here. That's too bad for you. Do you still have the shakes?"

"I do. Even worse than that, they wont let me back into the theatre no matter what. It's a conspiracy I tell you. The word is that they want me for a show dog now. I am to parade around as the image of what this man's army is all about, just what I hate. Secretly, I think they are going to cut me loose, too. For me the war is over. There is something I want to tell you. I have met someone. The trouble is, she's my personal nurse and I think the uppers don't like it. At first we tried to keep it confidential, but you know keeping something like that a secret around here is impossible. It's all over the place and it is starting to get in the way. They better not move on her."

304

"You want to know how hard it is to keep a secret, Bradley? I already knew it too. Her name is Annette Chappell, and she is a brainy nurse from Minnesota, right?"

"You have got to be kidding me. You must have better things to do with your time than worry about which girl I am dating, Bob. I just don't want shenanigans from her superior officers thinking they know better than we do about how to handle our own personal affairs. I like her taking care of me right now. I think she is helping me get better. Isn't that why I am here?"

"Have you noticed, young Captain, that she has not been given any marching orders, or even a change in her case load? Perhaps your old buddy already made the phone call and told those nincompoops to stay out of it."

"You really have my back don't you, old friend?"

"Bradley, I've been working on my brain matter, trying to get the hemispheres lined up right and mature, finally. I wonder which one of us will get better first?"

"Me, I hope. Your case is lost forever. I expect to read about you in the paper one day, getting killed in action because your wheel chair malfunctioned when you found the enemy infiltrating the old folks home," he smirked.

The colonel was sitting shotgun in a fully loaded Humvee crossing a muddy rock-strewn river out in the sunbaked desert of Afghanistan. Looking out the window at the volcanic outcropping behind him, he measured his situation, which he considered to be nominal. In less than an hour his troops would be in combat, hoping to surprise the Taliban in a village they had taken over. He didn't think a single soldier under his command wouldn't rather be somewhere else more comfortable, and yet he was in his element. The Captain was right. He was never going to change. His biggest fear was that they were going to take it all away from him because of his age. He blocked that out of his mind. Having a secure satellite phone was one thing. Talking with Brad Peterson, one of his favorite soldiers in the Army, was another thing altogether. "You're a smart ass, kid, but I'll have to agree with you. I hope you do get better before I do, since I am never going to change." At that very moment incoming mortar fire grabbed his attention. "Gotta go, Brad; over and out." The Colonel hung up and went to work.

Brad brooded silently when the phone went dead. He well knew the sound of action and Hankle had just engaged. A tremor of fear moved from the pit of his stomach up and down in a tiny wave of terror. If he were Bob's wife, the fear would be different. She would be terrified for his wellbeing, and that was understandable. He, on the other hand, suffered the pang of wishing he were there to help his buddy. He wished that he could go back into action.

Suddenly, his hands started shaking violently and he was overcome by nausea. Brad Peterson was a mess.

When Annette walked into the room she noticed immediately that he was having another episode. This time it was not a dream, but something that had come upon him while he was wide awake. It was worse than ever. Her forehead furrowed with concern. "Is there anything I can do to help, Bradley?"

Brad had not told his nurse, his friend, his girlfriend or whatever she was, about his relationship with the Colonel. His bond with Colonel Bob Hankle was something he kept to himself and did not feel ready to talk about. "You already have, Annie. Just by walking in the door and brightening my day, you're making me feel better." *And she is, that's the truth of it. Every time I see her I feel better. Am I falling in love with Annie, or am I in love with love.* "Thank you." He took her hand in his, kissed the back of it, pulled her down onto the couch and then on to his lap. Even though they were in a private room, his personal space, they were, in fact, inside of a hospital. Someone could conceivably walk right in on them.

"Brad," she giggled, wiggled, and tried halfheartedly to escape his grasp. She also noticed that the shaking had stopped. In an instant he stopped twitching altogether. *I think he loves me.*

"It's therapeutic treatment, girl. See, I'm better already." When he pressed his lips to hers, she melted into his arms, feeling the secure comfort of real love; now it was her protection, not only his shield, to be sure of things. His problems went too deep for that, but any fool could see that the heat they made when they were together—it made them both better people.

When she finally squirmed away, Nurse Chappell opened her bag and took out a thermometer. "I have to take your temperature. It looks like you have a fever and it is rising."

Medical tools always made Brad queasy. He didn't mind using the bag on others, but hated being the patient. "I don't trust you. You could get my body reading with the ear plug thermometer. What is that thing for?"

"I need to do a rectal reading this time. Now be a big boy and let me do my job."

"Forget it. You're not touching me with that thing," he said as she was waving it in his face and laughing. Instead she kissed him on the nose.

"Just this once I will let you off the hook." She kissed him again, and there was the giggle he had been waiting for. "Has anyone ever told you what a horrible patient you make?"

Brad looked around the drab hospital room, wishing he were away from the place; in fact, he felt the need to get away. Honestly, he wasn't making any kind of progress with his therapist, the worthy Dr. Ralph Brainsworth, that his treatment team had hoped for. He was physically fit, the nervous system issues notwithstanding, and there wasn't much anyone could do to make that problem go away. He was not really ready to tell Annette that it may be time for him to move on though. What would that mean for them and any future they may have with each other? One thing he did have a grip on was the help he was getting from Colonel Hankle. If he said that he had made calls to leave him and the girl alone, then he surely had. Brad felt empowered by that.

"Annie, I have been thinking. Let's stop worrying about whether anyone knows about us or not. I have a feeling that it won't matter. What do you think of that?"

"I have been meaning to tell you this, Bradley. My supervisor already told me that it is common knowledge all over the hospital about us. She wants to take me off of the case, but is running into trouble. It seems that her boss received a call from some big shot colonel out there who told them to keep their hands off of us. How some commander in the field found out I'll never know. Did you say anything? Oh, and by the way, I'm fine with everyone knowing that I have the most handsome, smartest, hero in the United States Army, as a close personal friend, or whatever you want to call us." She had shifted positions, gotten up from the couch and sat in the apposing chair so she could face him.

307

One of the things Brad noticed about the good nurse was that she was dressing a bit more conservatively lately. He was not altogether unhappy about the new style. "No matter where I am there are going to be rumors and stories floating about," he said. "I don't know why either."

"Could it be that you are just one of those *larger than life* types. It's a personality trait. You command the atmosphere when you walk into the room, even if it is a room full of total strangers, and so the mood in the room changes. In other words, everyone around, just because of the aura surrounding you, notices. Pretty soon people start talking. Since they do not really know very much, the talk turns to rumors and stories. It must drive you nuts, or at least bother you somewhat."

"I never think about it, Annie. Here is something I have thought about. I would like to go on a three-day driving tour." It was time to change the subject again. Brad wanted to take a risk with this woman and see where it led. The time for them to cement something had come and was going to disappear quickly. He wanted out of this place, even if it meant going home. "Since for now you are still my personal guardian, I would need your permission, but what I am asking is if you want to go with me. Here is the idea. We can scratch Neuscharfeneck Castle. That is quite a hike. We can get back to that later if you really want to go up there." Just the relaxing smile told him that he was on the right track. Going off on a big hike was not going to do the trick with Annette Chappell. She was not the outdoorsy type. "We will pick up the tour in Munich and travel the Romantic Road, exploring castles that way. One of the castles we will look at is Linderhof, a fantasy place that will take us back to our childhoods and enchanting things. In Frankfurt we'll visit Sleeping Beauty's castle. It is called Neuschwanstein. I am running a marathon there. There is one other thing I like about this little adventure, and that is the walking tour of Rothenberg, maybe the best example left of how medieval life on this continent used to be. Is that something you would enjoy?"

"Oh, Brad. I would love to go with you," and this time she really meant it. Perhaps they had more in common than just attraction. "Can we pick the days tomorrow after I've had a chance to clear the dates. Also, since we're not to be a secret anymore, would it be OK with you if I mentioned that this was to be a personal trip?"

"Of course, dear; I wouldn't have it any other way. The only real date that matters is the day I'll be running the Frankfurt Marathon." He wanted to leave the hospital, true, but he planned on taking her with him when he left. That was his goal. His plan was working perfectly.

Creatures from another realm were also very happy with how things seemed to be working out.

* * *

Payden Cooper pulled his Mercedes Benz E-350 over to the right in heavy traffic on the Autobahn, the 7 to be exact, just before the road traveled south into Austria. It was a shorter drive to the castle through Austria, and the winding rural roads that way were very scenic, but the hassle of crossing borders made traveling those rusty, country roads a poor choice. The young and handsome psychic had the top down on his grey and silver convertible, the wind was blowing through his jet black hair, western style classic rock music was blaring louder than ever thanks to the twin 10" subwoofers he had mounted in the tiny back seat of his luxurious race car, and yet he could not keep his mind off of business.

Ever since he was a little boy, Payden knew that he was different from others. Many times he would speak of something that seemed obvious to him, something he could 'see' and was sure that everyone knew about, only to be told to mind his own business. After a long time, the boy had made adjustments and had learned to keep his knowledge a secret. It seemed to him that when he was right, everyone scorned that, too. No one liked a smart mouth kid, especially when it turned out that he somehow knew what he was talking about. By the time little Payden was an early teenager though, he had mastered the art of taking little advantages of his prescience. He had tried his first séance when just eight years old and that had earned him a resounding spanking from his very conservative Christian father. It had also earned him some fame with his friends, especially the girls, for they had felt his psychic touch, something he himself was not yet aware of. By the time he was a teenager, Cooper was earning money conducting readings for teenage girls. For him it was a joke, for them it was anything but a joke. His reputation for knowing things was spreading far and wide among the young people in his life.

There is a certain amount of intelligence that goes with psychic powers. Cooper was far from slow. That he got straight A's in school earned him great praise from his parents. That he had quality friendships with both boys and girls also pleased them. That they could not get him into church was among the disappointments that plagued their relationship, even to this day. Payton had never married. He was not gay. He loved women. He did not relish the idea of marriage. For him, marriage was about two very good people trying to make a magic moment last a lifetime.

His years at Cornell were anything but boring. Payden loved his life. He had explained to his parents that the scholarship he'd been awarded at Cornell was better suited to his academic needs, and though he had plenty of offers elsewhere, that was to be his home for the next phase of his remarkable journey. He spent just thirty months there, the time it would take him to earn a bachelor's degree in metaphysical science. What he did not reveal to his mother and father was his desire to take advantage of Cornell's approach to psychic studies since they had never bought into his special condition. Payden wanted to know why this had happened to him. It was a question that had never been answered and he had given up trying. He just accepted the fact that he possessed psychic powers.

These days the tall, slender, confident, wealthy young entrepreneur was living in Frankfurt and conducting psychic readings for an array of clients. This evening he was headed to Neuschwanstein Castle where he was to conduct a sundown séance, earning a substantial fee. His clients were from Transylvania of all places and wanted to contact ancients about their history. Essentially, these were college students with too much money who thought they had some idea about the relevance of Transylvania, werewolves, vampires, and other creatures of the paranormal. One even claimed to be a direct descendent of Count Dracula, someone Payden thought to be a mythical legend and not a real vampire. He was very skeptical about vampires to begin with, but had agreed to do the séance anyway, since they had agreed to his upfront fee and the reality that no contact was guaranteed.

The reservation for the top chamber in the tallest spire had assured him of a spectacular setting for this event, something he considered as mere entertainment, but also an experience that should satisfy these kids and not leave them feeling let down after forking over $5,000 American for the privilege of spending less than three hours with the boy wonder. Cooper could perform a genuine psychic reading in a bathing suit out on a sundrenched beach, but for a show like this he utilized both costume and props. In addition to his long mustache and goatee, Payden would sport a pair of black leg tight sharkskin slacks, a red velvet vest, a black jacket with bat wing arms so that he could spread his wings at just the right time, and it featured a huge blood red collar. He would also use a cane to walk about. The toy box he had with him included many of the sights and sounds one would expect when gaining contact with the afterlife, especially an evil afterlife. He considered himself a fraud with the entire getup, but laughed it off as great fun. What harm was there in appeasing young foolish kids? If he did not take their money, someone else would. Perhaps he would finally get to know the real Count Dracula. Stranger things had happened.

He drove the winding road into the forest nestled in the foothills of the Alps, where the castle stood. It was a Bavarian picture postcard whether in the spring, like now, or in the winter, all covered in snow. He would arrive at his destination with more than three hours to stage the show, setting his little traps everywhere, sure to create just the right kind of atmosphere. Payden's outfit also featured hidden buttons and bells to be sprung at just the right time. Even if they caught him in the act, he would be able to talk his way out of the conundrum by lecturing them on the creation of a spiritual pathway that ancients would recognize and respond to. Yup, he was a fraud. Tonight he was going to get paid handsomely, but it was all just to have a good time.

* * *

311

"Mom, look over to the right. I think that's it, cropping just over the horizon. See, up on top of that sharp peak? I think it is one of the spires."

Becky could see where her daughter was pointing and perhaps she had caught first sight of Neuschwanstein Castle, or as she liked to call it, Sleeping Beauty's Palace. They had been driving the rental car; well, Trisha was the one doing all of the driving, alongside a picturesque lake out in the beautiful forested countryside. The bright and sunny spring day had held much promise and they had made the best of it. There were a few clouds high in the sky, and the backdrop of foliage was incredible. Now they were going to tour Sleeping Beauty's Castle and watch the sunset from high atop the old palace where they would enjoy a true Bavarian feast, at least she would. Who knew what Trisha would eat? Sometimes she did, sometimes she did not. Her daughter had not eaten much of late so perhaps she was saving up for tonight. Lord knows she had been looking forward to this part of the journey for some time. "I see it, dear. The anticipation builds," she smiled wryly. Perhaps they would bump into some kind of a medieval ghost from the past.

At that moment a fast little Mercedes sports car passed them on the road, a convertible with the top down, driven by a very handsome young German fellow. He smiled and waved at them while driving by. "See, Trisha. Even Germans like American music."

"Mother, the world gets smaller by the day." These two were becoming familiar international nuances now that they were world travelers. When they finally made it to the castle parking lot, some twenty minutes later, that convertible was sitting right there, though now the top was up, so they parked right next to it. "I hope we get to meet that guy, Mother. He seemed real nice when he waved at us. This is a pretty big place though, so I am not going to worry about it. If you see him, let me know." Trisha's mother smiled reassuringly and nodded, letting her daughter know that she would keep an eye out for the handsome young lad.

The ticket booth was on the far side of the parking lot and once they had paid the price of admission, they began the short hike up to the castle. They had been told that the evening tour was a rare occurrence there. Normally they closed at 5:00 PM, but were accommodating a special group this evening and decided to add two evening tours to their normal schedule. They would be one of the very few who had the opportunity to witness sunset, Neuschwanstein Castle style, along with their group of twenty-five and another group of twenty-five. They had chosen the Bavarian feast option over the wine and cheese party. The evening promised to be very enchanting. Just the hike up the Poellat Ravine on the way was interesting. They walked over a brook on a steel bridge mounted to the side of a cliff. The view was picturesque to say the least. The castle itself was set in a backdrop containing kaleidoscopes of color and foliage, all of which the two immaculately dressed women took in while crossing the ravine on a wooden bridge. In just a few minutes they had arrived in the courtyard of the captivating palace. Both groups were to congregate at different points, but not for a couple of hours, and so they had time to mill about the outside and take in the view, which they did. During their explorations, they found their rallying point and when it was time, they made their way to the small group. Trisha and Becky were both very excited for the evening's festivities to begin.

* * *

Lurton Zama, Slybrain Thiefdemon, Stump Killer and Imp Rogue had gathered at the cauldron wormhole entangler and were preparing themselves for the little project that lay ahead. Zama had made a bold decision, one he felt confident would rid them of the runner forever. They were going to risk exposing themselves to the Eternals by attempting to direct a particle beam via a holographic image weapon that lay dormant on the surface of Earth's moon. Zama test fired it into space and it was working perfectly. They had located the girl, sighted the entangler on her position and needed only the solar star shining down on Earth to fade into twilight at that location for their gambit to succeed. Lurton would then lean into the cauldron, project his own image, speak to get her attention, and then fire the weapon.

The particle beam would destroy her instantly. This was the advantage of the Great Machine and the one hedge they had against the Eternals. Unfortunately, if the Eternals found out what they were doing before it was too late; they could conceivably interfere with the process, protect the girl, and ultimately find their hiding place. The chance was remote, and so Zama had made the decision to give it a go. The reward for success was immeasurable; the consequence for failure was equally devastating. At this point they only needed the earth to turn towards the darkness that lighted their way.

*   *   *

"The Neuschwanstein Castle, perhaps the most popular of European medieval destinations is truly a Bavarian paradox. You see, it only looks medieval. The palace was actually constructed by Bavaria's *Fairytale King*, Ludwig II, and not opened until 1896 after he died, and long after castles served any strategic purpose as a stronghold. Take note of the modern, by late 18th century standards anyway, restroom facilities. It was also fitted with central heating . . ."

The tour guide's voice faded into the background as Annie and Brad, arm in arm, her head on his shoulders, were strolling through the halls and rooms of this historic edifice. "This is the kind of a place where a girl would want to have her wedding, Bradley. I have never seen anyplace so beautiful. Just look at all the colors and wood variations, I mean, look at the exacting cement work and the pillars. I just cannot believe this, this monument to luxury and tradition. Did you see the paintings in the music room? The poor king never even lived to move into his retirement home. Instead it is us and others like us who get to enjoy its beauty."

Brad was speechless and in awe of the way the day had unfolded, really how the entire trip had gone. He had enjoyed many women in various roles during his adult life. He had been with some of them in a more intimate setting, but nothing was like this. He had been all over the world, enjoyed the cultural beauty of uncounted places, the adventures of his military experiences, but nothing had prepared him for the way he felt about this lady.

Annie spoke again, "The cat got your tongue, soldier?"

"Yup, I . . . , I . . . ," and then he turned and embraced the woman he was so sure of. Their lips met in passion and that, coupled with the bonding of something new was too much for words. "I am just so happy today," he said. "I don't know if it is the intoxicating romance of being in Europe with a beautiful gal like you, or what it is. I just . . ."

She put her fingers to his lips, kissed him again on the neck, and they turned hand in hand, now a bit back of the pace of their group. "I'm hungry, Brad. We are almost to the drawing room for the wine and cheese part of the evening. They're even going to have live music. I overheard one of the guests saying that in addition to all of the different kinds of German breads, the desserts are incredible here. Thanks for making this such a special trip."

They were not disappointed. The music room was decorated with huge candle chandeliers, and they were lit, casting a magical sparkle all over the lavishly styled area. The west wall, which was enclosed by huge glass panes, happened to be the perfect portal for the settling of day into night. Through the windows one could enjoy the fading twilight as the sun disappeared behind the Alps, leaving a red sky adorned with billowing white clouds ringed by the fire of evening light. The band played softly as the wine was poured, and the refreshments played their part in what was turning out to be the perfect evening. *Is this what heaven is like?* Brad asked silently to himself. In the symphony of mind melds, Annie spoke, "It is heaven on Earth." They joined in spontaneous dancing to a live orchestra.

* * *

Everyone is better at something. Deceivers had their wormholes and entanglers, all manipulated by the Great Machine, hidden on some world closer to the center of the galaxy. They, so far at least, were the only ones who could travel the wonders of interstellar space while in their mortal state. It was a huge advantage for them.

The Eternals, on the other hand, had mastered the art of traveling in a different way. They were the All Seeing Eye, able to go places instantly, projecting their presence, through the fabric of space. Once beyond their mortal existence, Eternals lived forever, sentient beings no longer bound by the constraints of flesh. The addition of a Great Machine, or similar technology, would grant them an exponential increase in their abilities, something they had never been able to master.

Humans were the wild card in a grand scheme to further interstellar civilization. They were both talented and unpredictable. Their post mortal existence, the sphere where their souls went, was created to allow them to guard their own mortal descendants. They were the ones who kept an eye on things, had been provided a partial glimpse of their own potential, and folks like Wise Mac, Roger Martin, and Tag Peterson were a part of this group.

It was Tag who noticed what happened on the moon, a green laser that flashed into space. "What was that?" he queried.

Roger and Mac had been in the house playing chess. Oh, they were aware that Trisha and Brad had once again found common ground at the castle in Germany, but for now the situation looked stable and they were not paying attention. "What was what?" Roger called back. They walked out onto the patio where their friend was.

"Something just happened near earth on the moon. It looked like some green flash of light. It shot out into space for about ten seconds then shut off again." Tag was more curious than concerned.

Just then three American Bald Eagles, huge beautiful birds, flew in from the mountains south of the valley where Roger lived; they circled about and then landed in the yard just behind his porch. Immediately other creatures began to mill about. Birds landed in trees, dogs and cats looked on, and even a horse in the neighbor's field walked to the fence and appeared very interested in the unique scene that unfolded in front of their very eyes. Only Mac seemed to know what was going on. The beautiful creatures looked so intelligent, and so at peace with themselves. Mac smiled a welcoming that sent a clear message in any language. When the image of the birds began to waver and change, in what seemed only natural, Roger finally got it. For the first time in any life he had ever lived, Roger Martin was being granted, along with his good friends, a direct visit from Eternal beings. These were the true Masters of the Universe. To what did they owe this honor?

* * *

"I can't believe how much food I've eaten," said Trisha. "Here I am supposed to run a full marathon in just two days and I am stuffed like a Bavarian pig. If Stanley could see me now he would shake me down big-time, Mom." The mother and daughter world travelers were seated in the dining room of the Neuschwanstein Castle, enjoying the feast of Trisha's life. She did not doubt that her mother had enjoyed things like this many times. She herself had once been a huge eater, but not these days. Everyone else was tipsy from all the wine and lager that was served. Trisha and her mother did not drink, so they ate to make up for the lack of alcohol. It was not the first time, nor would it be the last.

Becky was enjoying the ambiance of the whole setting, and having fun in front of all these drinkers was something she did not think possible just a couple of years ago. *How my life has changed*, she thought. Trisha had ruled the roost in food choices since they had started this journey which had made them so much better. Becky admitted it, even to herself. This eating adventure was on her, though. She had set up the perfect banquet. The meal began with simple cheeses, bread sticks, vegetables, and a dipping sauce. It was followed by traditional liver dumpling soup, a Bavarian delicacy. Then came a local salad, some sort of a concoction of marshmallows, strawberry gelatin, nuts, pineapple, all drizzled in a creamy sugar sauce. It would have been the perfect dessert had not the main course followed. There were three different kinds of meat and a special Bavarian potato salad, served with rolls drenched in a honey butter mixture.

It was impossible not to eat. Trisha was looking ill at having eaten all that food when they brought out the desserts. That barrage of fat-laden calories included things like Bavarian chocolate cake, little molded chocolates, a creamy Bavarian pastry, strawberry mirror cake, Bavarian cream with kirsch cherries, a chocolate raspberry cake, Bavarian apple cake, and other choices as well. There was no way just twenty-five people could eat that much. Becky wanted to support the cause, though, and did her best. At her daughter, she simply smiled.

Has the day turned stormy? A crashing bolt of lightning struck, and very close, too. The light and the sound were simultaneous. *It may have struck the castle*, thought Trisha for a second. The entire building seemed to shake right to its foundation. That was weird.

* * *

Payden Cooper, a true psychic, a good man who truly had the best interests of others at heart, a genius too smart for his own

317

britches, and also an entertainer and a fraud, was to perform the séance of his life. He had been doing these ever since he was just a kid. He used the séance trick to get girls when he was in high school. In college he would woo the sorority sisters late on a Saturday night from time to time. He was a legend in his own mind. The one thing he had never accomplished in his entire life, the one thing, was to contact the dead. He had tried so many times he could not count. It had all amounted to practice sessions designed to earn money, because that was what people wanted and were more than willing to pay handsomely for.

It turned out that this evening's group of kids, males and females who were just now filing into the chamber tower room at the top of Neuschwanstein Castle, were members of the Transylvanian Society of Dracula, an enthusiastic Dracula club formed after the fall of Romanian Communism back in 1991. This particular minority, or sect within the group, was a bit on the geeky side, thinking that they could actually contact the mythical legend, someone who never actually lived in the real world, or so Payden thought. He was about to grant their wish.

The room was hauntingly set with lit candles. Payden had planted his little tricks in order to entertain and draw in the spirit of the vampire, which is how he would explain things if he were caught, something that hadn't happened. The murals on the wall were perfect for the occasion, deeply rooted in medieval lore, which is why he had picked this particular location. They had only agreed to let him use it for this event because they were testing out the idea of hosting small parties in the evening when the castle became dark and quiet.

The seven college students, who were dressed mostly in jeans and short sleeve shirts and sporting American sneakers, curiously walked into the chamber, all eyes and ears. "Come in," said Payden, his arms spread wide and in English using an eastern European accent. He confirmed with them that none, (except him that is), had eaten today. In his mind's eye he could feel the presence of their souls, the beating of their hearts. Payden took the time to shake each person's hand, using the opportunity to obtain a prescient reading of each person's feelings. It was after all his talent, and the reason he was worth the money. This was why he always knew what to say.

Their hearts were beating as one; their long awaited moment with the dead Count himself had arrived.

He arranged them around the table in order of their sensitivity to psychic connection waves. The table was of cedar wood, laminated in a brilliant red finish. Each of the cherry wood chairs had a high back and was cushioned with period embroidered art. They were stiff and designed for alert posture. In the center of the table was a crystal ball, about the size of a bowling ball. It was mounted on a black obsidian base, so dark it was almost invisible. There were large candles in front of each seat, centered on a red velvet cloth about the size of a personal table mat. The candles lighted each and every face, and the reflection of the candles on the crystal ball created a startling effect. The incense burning near other scented candles completed the mood.

"Now let us join hands and call forth spirits who no longer inhabit our realm." They took each other's hands and formed the completed circle. "Let us first pray," he spoke so quietly the sound of his voice was almost inaudible. "To the God of all life, we are ever grateful for thy holy bounty, and thy abiding forgiveness of our sins." His voice rose now a bit. "We have entered the land that God hath given us and seek seemingly detestable things from the nations of those who have gone before us. There is found among us, those who would pass through the fire of damnation and into the eternal abyss, calling forth one to answer for his deeds and crimes, oh Lord, oh God of justice. We hereby invoke this divination through the practice of witchcraft, omens and sorcery, casting a spell on Count Vlad Tepes, the one Dracula. Come forth, Count Dracula and reveal yourself to your countrymen, who have come to seek you out!"

Surprisingly the air in the room began to change. Payden wiggled his toe and a vent of smoke began to drift in the window, and with it a silent and disquieting sulfur-like aroma. It was truly evocative. And then the young imposter began speaking in tongues, an unintelligible babble of ancient languages. After some minutes of this he raised his hands, causing the hands of all there to rise up and as one they called forth, once again the spirit of Count Dracula to enter into their midst. This time even Payden was shocked out of his wits. The doors opened and then closed again, this time with no help from the psychic. The candles extinguished in concert. After a few seconds they lit again in the same fashion. At this point Payden Cooper was as much of an observer as the next guy. He had no idea what was going on.

* * *

"Mac, they are about to make their move," said Roger. "We have to help the kids. Their lives are in danger. Be ready to invoke the countermeasure when they ignite the laser weapon. I wish I knew where those scoundrels were hiding. At least the Eternals showed us what to do, thank the Lord."

* * *

Lurton was set to fire the opening salvo. First he would use the entangler to project an image of himself right in front of the girl, there in the castle eating her dinner. Once he could get her to look straight into his eyes, he would fire the weapon and destroy her. He would achieve his long awaited victory over the first of his two targets. He looked over his massive scaly shoulder at the three stooges behind him and smiled. It was time. Zama ignited the enabler and projected himself forward. That something had gone terribly wrong was immediately evident to both him and the underling Silicons. Lurton Zama raged in anger as his particle beam was directed to another place by a kind of psychic interloping attraction. What evil could this anomaly be? Zama became almost insane, raging in blind fury at what he would do when he discovered the truth.

* * *

There was a vortex of wind in the upper chamber of the tower where the séance was being held. The candles were out, the room was pitch black, and suddenly the crystal ball came to life. Payden Cooper was terrified. He was at a complete loss as to just what was going on. *Have I actually found the old vampire? Does stuff like that really exist? Are our lives in danger somehow by his little stunt? Who could know?*

Presently a tiny beam of yellow light slipped through the open window near the ceiling on the north side of the tower. The beam of light went directly into the lighted crystal ball, spreading upward into the room, and then into the vortex of wind. A grotesque looking creature appeared. Behind him were three others. The personage resembled some kind of a monster that not one person in the room could place, some kind of a hideous thing. Its eyes were the picture of anger and rage. "How dare you insolent humans interfere with my plan! Who do you think you are? You have hijacked me from my purpose! You—!" The angry monster was looking directly into Payden's eyes. "Look at me NOW, you foolish human, and I will give you the message you called on me to give. Look directly into my eyes." Every single person in the room heard the Count speaking in their primary language. It was as if he were speaking several different languages at the same time. Payden was drawn into the vortex of wind, stood silently like a puppet and stared directly into the figure's eyes. He slowly began to rise from the floor and float towards the hideous apparition, and the monster's hands encircled his neck and began squeezing the life out of him.

Something else happened next. A separate beam of light, very faint, bluish, and just as focused, entered the room from the window at the south side of the tower. When it descended into the crystal ball, Count Dracula and his three . . . Gargoyles, yes that is what they looked like, Count Dracula's Gargoyles, immediately changed countenance and fled in terror. Three new personages appeared. They had replaced the vision of the ugly monsters, and these men looked very gentle and loving. The séance had moved from the bizarre to the sublime. "Brad, Trisha, you must leave. Your life is in danger. Hold it. Who are you? Roger, Tag, something went wrong, we are in front of the wrong people." Mac looked again at the confused kids, though his gaze was anything but threatening. "Sorry to bother you folks. Have a nice evening," and then they were gone, just like that. The wind stopped, the room went silent, and there the séance ended in total darkness.

It took a few seconds for the opportunistic psychic to take advantage of the situation, especially since he was just as shocked out of his wits and in the dark as everyone else. "Folks, I'm afraid that Count Dracula and his minions will not be taking questions today and so that is the end of our time in the nether world." He had pulled a lighter from his pocket and lit the candle in front of him. The room, still dark, suddenly erupted in spontaneous applause. He had delivered to these kids the adventure of their lives. The story of how psychic Payden Cooper had contacted Count Dracula and his Gargoyles would quickly spread throughout all of Europe and even to the USA. He would contacted again and again to conduct séances. But Payden Cooper, for the rest of his mortal life, would never be able to repeat the performance.

7

Frankfurt

Sands of time had gradually covered my inner gifts,
entombing them under a dusty layer of denial.
Her creative archeological genius
allowed her to excavate with sensitive tools
all that years of sand storms had hidden.

Wise Mac

The day before Trisha and her mother departed Las Vegas on the first leg of their journey, Stanley Burton, Trish's trainer, mentor, kind-of best friend, and pseudo public relations guru, had her in the track team's classroom at Green Valley High School. It was a privilege for Trisha to visit her old stomping ground, somewhat of a tour down memory lane; she was fielding questions from kids on the track team.

"Ms. Martin, can you remember what kind of things you'd think about before you competed in marathons, you know, like when you were just starting out?" The inquisitive runner was a tiny, lanky little girl whose muscular physique, though not boney, came sculpted with sharp edges and curves.

"Thanks for the courtesy, my friend, but please call me Trisha. Soon enough, all too soon if you ask this old woman, we'll all be alumni of this great school. I have always loved running. Before I ever ran competitively, my interest in marathons was as a spectator. It seemed beyond my grasp, but you must remember, I was barely a teenager back then and much younger than you are now. I liked to run with my father, and we did quite a bit at distance, but a marathon was just a dream for me. I used to fantasize about it. Do you fantasize about running more than twenty-six miles in competition?" All of the kids thought that was funny for some reason. *If the running thing doesn't work out*, she thought, *I really am going to try standup comedy.*

Another student-athlete spoke up. "None of us have ever run that far in competition, Ms. Martin, uh, Trisha. What kind of training would you recommend?

"First of all," and Trisha suddenly felt the weight of having the ears of kids whose futures she held in her hands, "there is only one qualification for undertaking a project like this, and it's motivation. You have to be motivated. To be successful there has to be purpose to the madness, things like the improvement of your self-esteem, a conscious effort at fitness and weight management, or even international fame, it really doesn't matter. One thing you must know, and be sure of this to your very core, you cannot accomplish something like marathon racing if you are running for your parents, the school, or for anyone else except yourself. You must be the author of the purpose. Do you really want this?" Heads were wagging up and down, though her experiences taught a different lesson. For most, it would never happen, *and that's OK, too.* "Set short term goals as you train. Take the necessary time to get yourself acclimated to long distance training. Slowly build on things as you become more fit. I'm emphasizing the word *slow* here. As you close in on the last four months of training, and I recommend that you take a year to get ready for the first marathon, I suggest that you intensify gradually in the preparation phase and then in the weeks leading up to the race, you go into what I like to call the special preparation phase. It is quite a life changing experience . . ."

* * *

That was then and this was now. *What in the heck am I doing in Frankfurt, Germany, running a marathon from the back of the pack?* It was a ridiculous notion to begin with. Just a couple of days ago Trisha had pigged out just like in the bad old days with her mother at that castle. *What is the name of that place? Oh yea it's Sleeping Beauty's Castle.* For the life of her she could not remember the German name.

Trisha was beginning to feel normal again, not stuffed and constipated, really for the first time since she had worked out at the Landstuhl Cross Fit and Combativeness Facility almost a week earlier. That experience was worth coming to Germany for all by itself. It'd been quite a day, wearing and carrying all that military gear— running, climbing, jumping, crawling and huffing like an army soldier. She wondered if that was what basic training was like, and then it occurred to her that basic training's crazy workouts are repeated every day for weeks, or something like that, maybe even more than once a day.

Secretly, Trisha had hoped that she may run into *him* there. He had to be working out, and so she gave that place a try. *I'm an idiot,* she would think later. Alas, she did not get the *accidental* meeting. In the end though, she was very satisfied with the way things went. There were fifteen separate basic movements that one had to master in order to be set free on the course. The runner proudly made it through each skill set all in one day; she was just as motivated to excel as those kids she had lectured . . . all for a chance visit with Brad Peterson. She had to face it. The harebrained idea that she would get to meet up with the famous Army surgeon was totally 'high school' of her. It would be so embarrassing if it ever got out that she was still just a little girl virgin, looking to catch the high school boy she had admired. *Good Lord.* The week went by; she continued to prepare for Madrid.

And here she was at the starting line of a full marathon, except not exactly. The kind of starting line she had grown accustomed to just happened to be a white line painted across the road. That line was somewhere up ahead and off in her future this morning. There were thousands of runners ahead of her. She was so far back it may be possible that the race had started already, though she would not know it for some minutes. Trisha, the little runner girl and novice romantic, felt so foolish, and then the gun sounded. She did hear it. Off she went running through the crowd looking for one person. After some time her face was flushing red, not from exhaustion or stress, but from humiliation. *This is so stupid.* Trisha was weaving and crossing the running area from side to side, not even caring about the race. She did concede to herself that this would, in the end qualify as the workout she had planned. After weaving all over Frankfurt, Germany, by the end of the event she was sure to have run at least fifty miles. Then again, Stanley had assured her that the good Captain was indeed registered to be here. Just the thought of that, the notion that today was her big chance, sent the shame packing . . . to be replaced by the thrill of chasing a boy. Trisha Jean Martin was reaching out for love.

* * *

Annette Chappell felt like a stranger in a strange land. From a satellite, if you could find her in the big picture, she would be a tiny dot, one of 300,000 tiny dots, which in reality were people's heads. In a funny sort of way she was a spectator at the Frankfurt Marathon. In addition to the legion of racing fans, of which she was definitely not one, it was somehow her job to find Bradley zooming along with the 15,000 or so running idiots who were contestants in the race. *Why would someone run for fun?* At first they came galloping by at mind numbing speeds. Throughout the day she was sure to see slower runners, trotters, joggers, walkers, crawlers and an ambulance or two. What she was not sure of was whether she would be able to find her boyfriend or not.

For the first time since she had begun with Brad Peterson, the day did not look so bright.

Really, things had flattened out a couple of days ago once they had left Neuschwanstein Castle. Something had happened that night; it was a very special experience, something truly romantic. Annie was a bit out of her element in trying to establish a real relationship. *Is this something I really want?. How would I even know what I want? If there is anyone here less interested in watching a foot race than me*, she mused, *I would like to meet that person. We could go shopping, get something to eat, and laugh at the idea that we should stand in a throng of hundreds of thousands, watching other thousands running along.*

Just then her phone rang. Annette tried to answer the call but it got dropped. Since she didn't recognize the number, there would be no call back. *If they really want to talk, well then, they'll call me back.* She turned her attention once again to the race. In the three hours or so that she would be there, at the agreed upon spot so that they could kiss right during the race, something Annie thought a bit corny, there would be plenty of time to ponder that future. She stood next to a statue known as The Large Reclining Figure, and she was admiring sculptor Will Schmidt's masterpiece of a fat nude lying on her stomach with head held high. Though the lady was plump, she was also beautiful. Annette was not in a bad mood, not at all. Perhaps she was just too self-centered. Something was bothering her and she couldn't seem to pinpoint what it was.

Her plan was to get something to eat at the outdoor café there behind the statue, once Brad came by, took his kiss, and moved on. Her *not so bad* mood brightened a bit when she recognized the music from across the way. It was one of her favorite jazz musical acts, the Bajofondo Tango Club, right there in the flesh singing one of her favorite songs, "Hoy," off of one of her favorite CD's, Mar Dulce. That was something she could get into, and so she wandered as close as she could get, almost forgetting that she may miss the appointed moment, should her lover come running by. When the song ended, the group took a break and she returned to her waiting post. This love business was tedious work at best. It was worth it though. *You never know*, she thought, out loud this time, "perhaps my new man will recover completely, become a surgeon again, and carry me to heights I've never thought possible, and then again, perhaps not."

* * *

Trisha Martin had been chasing the boy she wanted for over an hour now, but had seen nothing and no one that reminded her of him. Today was, however, shaping up as a very nice workout. She was getting all that gunk from the huge meal processed, the crowds were vast and festive, the smells and sounds fun and exciting, and Frankfurt itself was simply beautiful. She had long since given up any hope of finding Bradley. There were just too many people in the race. She had all but forgotten what a race like this looked like from the back of the pack. As a professional runner she could have started up front like the others, but nope, not today. Today she was a lost little girl from Henderson, Nevada, chasing some ridiculous fantasy. That tidbit of truth would forever be, of course, her little secret.

When Trisha's mother had decided to shop all day instead of attending the race, her jogging daughter was more than gracious about her going off and having a good time. Trisha's mother was twice as nosy as her sister and knew that there was more to the story. Once this race was over, Trisha would forget about seeing Bradley Peterson and get back to the business of seriously preparing for Madrid, the public reason for her European adventure. It would all be over in just a few . . . *is that him?*

Up ahead she spied someone who looked just like Brad Peterson. *Have I found him! He moves just like Brad did, at least when we were kids*, she thought. Her already elevated heart rate increased again with anticipation. She closed in behind him—moving ever so tenderly. *What should I say? Oh no.* Trisha had given not a single thought as to what she would say. Now, with her heart racing, and a teenager love-struck dizziness settling in, her palms began to sweat. That was a first in any race she'd ever entered; Trisha could not think of what she was going to say. *Hold it*, she thought. She had all the time in the world to think of what she would say, because all she had to do was stay behind him for a while. He edged around the corner on a turn and she got a look at his profile. *It really is him.*

After a short time Trisha came up with a plan. Here is what she would say. *Brad, how nice it is bumping into you like this. Did you know I am still a virgin? I have been falling all over myself for a long time since I saw you on CNN that night before you went off to war. In the meantime I have lost 175 pounds and become a world-class marathoner hoping to catch you, marry you, and live happily ever after. I even schemed up this trip so I could stalk you right here in Frankfurt at this race. I didn't exactly find you entered to run here, I had my trainer go online and learn where you are. Even though I've not even seen you in all these years, I'm in love with you. Can we get married now?* What a joke. *I have no business in this man's life*, the thought horrified her. Perhaps she should fall back, or better yet move to the far side of the road and pass him, never to see the guy again. It was quite likely that he didn't even remember her. For the first time in quite a long time, Trisha Martin felt fat and ugly. She had absolutely no confidence, and yet she seemed to have found the reason for her trip. She had become the proverbial dog that actually caught the car. What would she do now?

It's funny how things work out sometimes. While she was fretting about passing him, she had lost her way and moved past him unconsciously. He was behind her now. In order to see him again she would have to let him see her. *Oh, this is so embarrassing.* Still, she could not resist the temptation and so she turned around. It wasn't him. In a huge release of nervous energy, as if a racer in a race needed someplace to dump unneeded energy, she started laughing out loud. *The games fools who think they are in love play. What kind of a fool am I to carry on with this nonsense?* She had to admit she was having fun, though. No matter how this day turned out, she was having a good time.

Trisha ran on, a bit faster than before. She decided to let fate play its role and quit looking so hard. The pace she had set was uncomfortably slow. While others in the race, most all of the others, were having trouble keeping pace, slowing down, and some were even walking, she needed to increase tempo, at least a little bit, to get into a comfortable running mode. She took time to enjoy the ambiance of the event, grinding past the Opera House her mother and she had enjoyed, looking on in awe at the Hermes Fountain, a nude male messenger from the gods, and then she slowed down to view the Johannes Gutenberg Monument which had been in place for more than a hundred and fifty years. *I thought Germany was bombed into oblivion during World War II*, she inwardly chuckled. Finally, she spotted the one monument that appealed to her the most, the Large Reclining Figure; it was just up ahead. She wanted to see the stature of a fat lady that was celebrated and picked it up a bit to get there. From behind her there arose a rogue gust of wind.

* * *

Brad Peterson had been running at a pretty good clip. This was his first attempt at a marathon in more than three years. His *running man* iPod, a tiny little thing that held about ten hours of music, was clipped onto his shirt, and Bose IE2 Headphones securely implanted in his ears blaring Steve Miller's "Wild Mountain Honey." It was just what the doctor ordered for an ideal day. The young captain had not suffered a single shaking experience while running along and that meant he felt perfectly normal. It was uncanny how running calmed the beast that would not release him. For a short second he reverted to thinking about those horrible days, and just as fast he quickly decided to dismiss the thought. It was too nice out. Soon he would be at the statute to get a kiss from the girl of his dreams. He was almost there. *Is she proud of my running abilities? Does she admire me?* He loved performing for Annie. Guys liked to perform feats of greatness for their women and Brad Peterson was a normal guy, yes he was.

From nowhere there came a gust of wind. It had not been windy all day . . . *There it is again! There's that perfume smell.* He could not mistake that fragrance. It overpowered him, casting away all thoughts of where he was or what he was doing. He turned around to see if he could recognize who it was . . . *Trisha Martin! It was Trisha Martin,* the kid he ran with so long ago from Green Valley High School. He could not hold back a huge smile as she came alongside and then passed him. He reached up and pulled the earphones out.

"Hi, war hero," she giggled, and then she turned back and ran on.

Oh my Lord, look at her, look at the way she moves. Oh, bloody hell that has got to be the prettiest sight I have seen since losing all those races to her so long ago. And she was still running. *Just look at Trisha Martin.* "Trisha, wait up!"

"It's a race, you goofball."

She was laughing at him, just like when they were kids. He sped up, trying to catch her, just like when they were kids. His heart was racing. There, right in front of him was Trisha Martin, the real Trisha Martin. Did he get that right? That was Trisha Martin. *Say the words again,* he told himself, running as fast as he could, *Trisha Martin.* She is so beautiful. Brad raced to try and catch her. *She's still pretty fast, that one.*

* * *

Annie was waiting at the statue, as promised. It had been a long morning but for her at least the race was almost over. She felt relief at the sight of her man, Captain Bradley Peterson, the legend of the U.S. Army, there to give her the promised kiss. She loved him in that moment, forgetting that she was hungry, really wanting to get over by the live band, sip some dark German beer, get something to eat, and then do some shopping before the end of his race. She had made it. He didn't seem to notice her though. He was yelling at someone right in front of him, and he was right in front of her.

"Trisha, slow down. I need to talk to you!"

Just then a very attractive lady came by, and just a few seconds later Brad ran right past her, not even noticing that she was where they had agreed to meet up. The lady giggled as if she were toying with him. "Run, run, as fast as you can; you can't catch me or the gingerbread man," she sang out the words, laughing solicitously. She giggled again and took off, and there went Bradley chasing right behind her, looking like a silly fool with a smile on his face, a twisting smile she had never seen. Suddenly she remembered the words, *"Run, run, as fast as you can; you can't catch me or the gingerbread man."* Annette Chappell froze, nauseated. It had just occurred to her who that was out in front of Brad. It was the girl he ran with in high school . . . Annie's heart sank.

Fortunately, it didn't take but a few seconds for Bradley Peterson, genius basket case, to realize what he had accomplished, running waggle tongued after an old friend and right past his appointed meeting place with Annette. He quickly yelled forward to Trisha Martin, "Wait for me at the finish line, Trisha." She turned, smiled, and waived an acknowledgement. Bradley put the brakes on and turned for the statue, so that he could collect his promised kiss, not sure that it would still be his to savor. There she was—all smiles.

"Brad, honey, and here I sit at the statue to kiss the love of the day, but what does he do? In the very flash of our long anticipated moment, the crescendo of his mighty run, and what a run it is turning out to be, he blows right by me, what with that bombshell pulling him along. I am not sure . . . what was longer— those legs or her hair? What do you think?" She kissed him . . . passionately.

It was obvious to the good captain that he had a fighting gal on his hands. He knew what she had seen . . . knew it. "Who do you mean?" he timidly said. "Annie, that was Trisha Martin, the friend I told you about the other day when we had lunch back near the hospital. I had no idea she was here, not until less than a minute ago. I can't wait to introduce you to her. She was always just a friend. You'll like her, I think. Meet us, I mean me, at the end of the race, just like we planned."

"Oh, I'll be there, Casanova. So, she was just a friend? I've always wanted to meet someone from your childhood. It'll be fun." *It's time for the old Annette Chappell to go to work. There is no way I am going to let that floozy onto my turf.* "Now get running, Brad. You are losing ground. Perhaps we can all have dinner or something together?" She kissed him again, this time a quick peck, and sent him off on his running way. *Keep your friends close, but keep your enemies even closer.* Annette was not an athlete, nor was she an expert in body language, but one did not have to be in order to see what this Trisha Martin had on her mind. The smile on her face as she passed Annie's Bradley could not have been mistaken. *I bet she came here to see him,* she thought as she began making plans to eliminate the threat.

* * *

Trisha crossed the finish line at a nice easy pace. It had been an exhilarating workout. If there was something out there known as a relaxing marathon experience, that was it. She never pushed herself even one time, had seemingly burned the excess garbage out of her system just like she had hoped, and beyond hope had found Brad Peterson. Her heart was racing as she milled about, wondering how long it would be before he crossed the line and they could talk. She would like to have cleaned up, *but at the end of a long race, people aren't supposed to suddenly show up wearing seductive makeup with their hair spun into innocent pig tails held together with lacy bows and wearing fancy little dark sunglasses. They wouldn't suddenly be wearing a tiny pleated miniskirt, glittery white socks, elegant mid-heeled shoes, and a midriff accentuated by a sheer tie-front top, like a high school girl in heat,* she giggled, looking around.

The day had found sunshine, a bright and optimistic promise filled with adrenalin-laced hope. The start/finish area was a madhouse of activity. There were all kinds of people everywhere. The downtown area of Frankfurt was ablaze with helicopters, television cameras, race officials, sponsors, fans, friends, and family. The colorful tents and ribbons added a festive touch of color to the circus-like atmosphere. Fortunately for Trisha, she had arranged for her mother to be, well, not here. *It's just a normal running workout and nothing to celebrate*, she had convinced her nosy mom that could herself be considered a helicopter, always hovering around trying to get at details that were none of her business. Trisha glanced back through the finish line to see Bradley Peterson just down the road. The time had come to make her play. She had absolutely no idea how to proceed. When he crossed the line his genuine and friendly smile calmed her immediately. They hugged. She was directly in front of a man she had secretly fantasized about for long years of prolonged absence. He did seem a bit distracted, though. Perhaps this was a bad idea after all; then she noticed his earphones, which he quickly removed and there he was, all smiles.

"Hello, Trisha Martin. It's wonderful to see you. I can't believe how you look; you haven't aged a day in all these years." His eyes welled up a bit moist, which was a surprise to both of them. This time when he hugged her, he held her close to his heart, a heart she could literally feel since he was just now beginning to cool off from his long run. Then he squeezed her tight against him and kissed her on the cheek. He stood back from her for a minute, holding both of her shoulders with his big strong hands, and smiled again. "This is too much," he said. "Here we are thousands of miles from home, strangers in a foreign land, and we meet. It is . . . uncanny. I just can't believe it. What are you doing here?"

"Well, first of all it's great to see you, Brad. I'm also very happy to see you doing so well; you're looking pretty good considering where you've been and it's such a coincidence, us running into each other like that. The last time I was around you, you hadn't even left to go to college and now look at you, a brain surgeon. I must admit when I saw you on the news that day, the day your captors paraded you in front of the television, you looked pretty bad, almost beyond recognition. Everyone went bonkers, you know, chanting 'USA-USA' type of thing when you defied them too, but me, I thought you were a goner, so I just went back up to my room to be alone. Brad, you look great. What a coincidence. *Am I actually going to get away with this charade?*

"Trisha, where were you that day?"

"I was in LA at the Los Angeles Marathon. The race was over and I was sitting at the bar eating chicken wings and fries when the television began to play it out for all of us. I thought you were in some hospital working far from that place, so when they dragged you in there, I had not a worry in the world, for you at least. That lasted for about three seconds."

"You look great. I mean, Trisha, I don't want to get too personal, but you're dressed to the nines for a marathon. You look like you have an endorsement deal with Adidas."

She did, but wasn't about to go there.

He continued. "Do you run a lot?"

"The only times that I run are in the morning, afternoon, and sometimes at night. Thanks for the compliment, by the way," she giggled. *This is going better than planned*, she thought. "My mother and I are touring Europe right now, so I am running here all the time." It was a fib, *but that is the way of things when you don't want to play your cards right off the bat*, she strategized. He was having trouble taking his eyes off of her. If he were a tailor, by the way he measured, he already knew her shoe size, the length of her pants, her waist, what size of blouse she wore and could accurately purchase her a hat. There was a real man inside of that veneer-shrouded nerdy brain of his after all. If only she knew what to do about it. *I'm so lost in this game* . . . and the realization of her inexperience made itself known with a jolt of fear that slid down the back of her neck into her upper body, and then settled in her gut, because just then another woman approached and stood right next to Brad.

"Hi, Annie," and he greeted her with a kiss on the lips. "I have someone I would like to introduce you to. This is my long lost friend, Trisha Martin, from Las Vegas, or more accurately, Henderson, Nevada. Do you still live in Green Valley, Trisha?"

"Hello, Trisha Martin. It is so nice to meet you." *Now I can size you up and deal you into the ditch, woman. You can't have him. He's mine. Can you read my mind telepathically, little running girl?* "Believe it or not, Brad has told me of you and how you used to run together in high school. I'm excited to hear about him, you know, things like when he was just a school boy."

These two are going to hit it off great. I can feel the synergy here. One of the things I like about Annie is that we are so compatible, Brad

Peterson was thinking. "That was so long ago, but I still consider ours to have been a great childhood, Trish. I hope you remember the good stuff and not just how boorish I was back then. You know what they say," he said laughing, "girls grow up, but for boys, once a kid always a kid."

"Oh, I would worry about me big time if I were you, goofball," said Trisha. "I could tell Annie here a hundred stories about the little nerdy boy who was too smart for his own britches. When he was in the sixth grade, Brad Peterson took two jars of some chemical mixture to school and nearly . . ."

"Slow down now, Trish," Brad was smiling. We wouldn't want to give Annette here the impression that I was in trouble all the time, now would we." *If truth be known, I really want her to keep up with that story. I just don't want them to know that.* At just that moment Trisha looked ashen. He could read her by looking into her eyes just like when they were kids. *Isn't it funny how resuming a friendship is like riding a bike,* he mused. In less than five minutes Brad had won back an old friend, someone who was very important to him. He didn't know why she was important, but just that she was. His public life had made him very weary of "out of the woodwork" types, showing up and wanting something, but in the case of Trisha, well . . . for her there was a different set of rules. The reason for the white face was quickly obvious. Her mother had just walked up behind them, then came around and handed Trisha a warm up suit, a towel, and some more comfortable shoes to put on. Trisha Martin, with puckered lips, looked as thrilled at seeing her mother as if she'd been caught doing something wrong. *Oh, boy.*

"Mother, I am happy to see you and thanks for bringing my stuff by. Do you remember Brad Peterson? He was a couple of years ahead of me at Green Valley High School and this is his friend, Annette Chappell. Brad was in the race today and we just bumped into each other." *I'm toast. I would rather have frozen or fried out here without my things than let you in on this conversation, Mother;* Trisha inwardly scorned the unwelcome intruder. *Go away, Mom.* The thought was delivered with an exuberant smile.

"Why, hello, Captain Peterson, which is if you are still a captain and have not been promoted to major since you took on those bad guys all by yourself. It was such a stir you made when you stood up to them. I've never been so proud in all of my long life. It's wonderful to see you." She gave the young and handsome surgeon a big bear hug, kissed him on the cheek, and then rubbed his head. You kids have all grown up. I remember when you were just a young pup and now here you are. I see you are still running like my youngest, Bradley. I've never figured out why people run and race all over the world, but to each his own." Next she turned to Annette Chappell. It's a pleasure to make your acquaintance, Ms. Chappell. Are you in the Army too?" *And now the truth comes out. I knew it!*

So, I get to meet mother and daughter in the same fell swoop. She is quite a lady. It is easy to tell that Mrs. Martin has been around. Her outfit reminds me of something my own mother would be wearing today, especially the cuffed black and white op-art styled jacket, something that matches perfectly with the blouse, slacks, jewelry, shoes, hair style, the works . . . really. If they had planned to impress Brad Peterson in some sort of a conspiracy today, Trisha's mother could not have come better equipped. I wonder. "It's nice to meet you too, Mrs. Martin. Yes, I'm in the United States Army. I am a nurse, stationed at an armed services hospital in Landstuhl, not very far from here."

Trisha, in the meantime had excused herself, walked into a public bathroom, put on the clean clothes, changed into the more comfortable shoes, straightened her hair into a loose ponytail and returned to the conversation, all in less than two minutes. She felt much better, actually happy that her mom had shown up. The question of how to handle her mother later when they were alone was pressing on her mind, but the real issue was this other woman. She could feel the tension and it was obvious that the man she had come so far to be with was, in fact, with someone else. It would have been silly of her not to think that a person of his stature would not have choices. Now Trisha slipped into a defensive mode, working to hide disappointment, pull herself up by the bootstraps, and make this work out as well as it possibly could. The truth was, she did not dislike this woman who seemed to be a very engaging personality. She rejoined the conversation just in time to learn that Annette Chappell was a nurse, stationed at Landstuhl with Brad and as the conversation developed, the picture solidified, tweaking itself and casting a dark shadow where just moments ago it was something else entirely. Their relationship was just the natural progression of young people like her who were trying to find some sort of a life together. Trisha was the problem, perhaps she was getting in the way, and maybe she needed to simply walk back out of this the same way she had walked, no run, well not run really—jogged into it— alone and lonely, but dignified.

Trisha noticed that Annette was whispering something into Brad's ear; *did she just bite him on the ear lobe? You have to be kidding me.* The overtly sensual nurse turned, mostly to Trish's mother, which was kind of a strange thing, considering, but Annette's subsequent remarks were for herself as well. "Mrs. Martin, would you and Trisha like to join us for dinner this evening? We're going to supper over at Brighella tonight at 7:00. Please join us." *Trisha Martin, I like you and beg your forgiveness for what I am about to do.*

"I'm very sorry," apologized Becky with a hint of a wink in her smile. Then she turned and faced her daughter. "A gentleman caller has enticed me away from you tonight, Trisha, at least until bedtime. I'll be back at the hotel in time to save my chastity," she was laughing with just the right amount of charm to take command of the situation. "I met him this morning just after I dropped you off. We had fun talking, mostly in German." Then to Brad and Annette, "I am trying to learn to converse in German right now." And back at Trisha, "He invited me to dinner with him; do not worry, child, we're to meet in a very public place. So guess what? I accepted. You're on your own. You're not the only one who gets to have fun."

Is Mom lying, speculated Trish? *I bet she is, but I'm going to play along with her . . . for now.* The last thing in the world Trisha Martin wanted to do was go out to dinner with this, this, this couple of love birds. It went against the grain of her nature, but she had to speak up. "If the offer is still open, for my mother is ever so much more entertaining than I could ever be, I would be happy to join you guys. It'll be fun to catch up with you, Brad, and to learn more of the enchanting lady that seems to have smitten my childhood buddy. Believe it or not, I think I saw the place you're talking about. It is over on Eschersheimer by the railroad tracks. Is that it?" *No matter how this goes down, I'm going to play the game with this woman. I can see the ice in her veins.*

"You nailed it, Trisha," said Brad. *I cannot believe my good fortune. The good Lord has blessed Annie and me. My fine friend, Trisha Martin, will see what a great lady this is. Trisha is so easy to like and she's even easier to look at, too. That amounts to two good women for the price of one very happy man.* Just then his hands began to shake and he desperately put them behind his back and made sure that no one was behind where they could see him stgruggling. *Damnation . . . not now*, he fumed.

"That's wonderful, Trisha," said Annie. We will see you at 7:00 sharp." *Please be late. It'll be great if you show up late and we have to wait. I . . . am a poet.*

They said their goodbyes and went their separate ways.

"So, Mother, I have two things for you. Number one, you don't really have a date tonight, do you? Number . . ."

"Oh, I am here to let you know, little girl, that you are not the only person out on the hunt during this trip. No ma'am, my little daughter; Trisha Jean Martin is sorely mistaken if she thinks that she is the only person interested in the opposite sex. Now I must admit. I didn't pick the world's most popular bachelor to go after, like a subtle hawk I must add, but yes, I am actually going out and you get to meet him—right now." Trisha and her mother had just exited a cab in front of their hotel, the Streigenberger, and they were walking up the steps of the old beauty, a tan brick edifice exuding German history, now more than one hundred and thirty years old. It was still perhaps the centerpiece of social life in Frankfurt. Trisha liked the magnificent landmark for its spa and fitness facilities; maybe the best in all of Europe.

Presently, Becky Martin escorted her daughter through an outdoor café, past linen covered tables that were also sheltered by large red umbrellas towards a side wall, where sat a truly handsome, if elderly fellow; his smile only grew as they approached. He looked to be in his early sixties, wore a close cropped beard that was the perfect match for his silver laced black hair, and he was dressed very nicely. That he was taller, slender, and physically fit became obvious when he stood to greet the mother and daughter. He was wearing a grey blazer, fashionably buttoned, over a brown tweed sweater that coordinated very nicely with smart looking casual beige pants. The only thing that looked different were the high top brown lace dress boots he had on, but hey, this was Europe after all. He stood politely.

"Guten tag, Becky Martin. Ist dies ihre schöne tochter, die ein sie über den ganzen nachmittag damit geprahlt haben, die läufer?" (Good afternoon, Becky Martin. Is this your lovely daughter, the one you have bragged about all afternoon, the runner?)

"Ja ist es (Yes, it is), Ebner. Trisha, I would like to introduce you to Ebner Hartmann, my date this evening. He and I struck up a very interesting conversation and he has been helping me speak fluent German. We are going to have dinner tonight while you are out chasing down the love of your life."

"Mother, don't be silly. Just like I told you in the cab on the way back to the hotel, it's a total coincidence that I saw Brad Peterson at the race today. I had no idea he was going to be here. By the way, how did you two meet?"

"Oh, that is so silly, child. You're playing me for a fool if you think that I don't know you planned the whole thing. I have been trying to figure out what this part of the trip was all about and now I know. What I am thinking is that this entire journey was about your getting that cute little body of yours in front of him. Go ahead and admit it."

Trisha could not hide the smile on her face. "I'll never admit it, Mom."

Handsome Ebner Hartmann could obviously speak English since he was laughing with a knowing grin. He was a gentleman, clasping both of his hands around hers and kissing the back of her left hand. "Ve met dis morning ven your muzzer approached me out of za blue and asked me some kvestions about za German language. I vas only most obliged to help. One ting led to anuzzer, ve had a great afternoon, and so here ve are. Ve are za best friends zat friends can be ven dey have only known each uzzer for a few hours," he said laughing. "Vezza vat your muzzer iss speculating iss true or not, young lady, it looks to me az zough gut fortune has found its vay into your blessed life. I do not mean to barge in on za conversation, but you are happy to have seen zis Brad Peterson, are you not? Ladies, please have a seat at za table. Trisha, vud you please join us for dinner?"

"Oh, how I would love to Mr. Hartmann, but I am meeting with Bradley and his lady friend for dinner. He is obviously with someone else and not in play, as we say over in the States." Trisha and her mother, along with this very good looking gentleman, who seemed to be a very nice person, seated themselves at the table.

"I vud most happily offer you a cocktail, but your mother says you and her do not drink. Za truth iss I don't like alcohol ezza. Let me put it another vay. I like alcohol too much. Zat is vy I am a friend of Bill's," he happily nodded, winking to Becky, who knowingly winked back.

"I am so happy to hear that, Mr. Hartmann. I know what a friend of Bill's is. How long have you been sober?"

"Twenty years, it has been since I last took a drink of any kind. You're muzzer and I plan on attending a local meeting before ve go out and enjoy dinner dis evening. I assure you zat she is very safe vit me. I say ve all haff coffee and tea or zumzing on za approved list, and perhaps small appetizers." He flagged down the waiter, they ordered, and then Mr. Handsome immediately returned his attention to Trisha. "Pleasse now, you must tell us of your adventure. Vat is it you plan to do dis evening? Let's assume, for just a minute, zat your muzzer is right. How do you plan on taking advantage of dis . . . opportunity, as ve say?"

Trisha felt totally disarmed. Not only was this man a gentleman, and good looking, but he could break down barriers easily. He almost had her speaking the truth. *All is fair in love and war. I'm going to war for love.* "I am planning to catch up with an old friend, one whom I have not seen for many years and who I have never been on a date with. I am genuinely happy that my friend, Brad, has a good lady to be with. He has been through a lot lately. If they are engaged and need help planning their wedding, I would be more than honored to be invited to help them along on their way." Trisha did not sound convincing, even to herself.

Ebner's smile looked entirely convincing. She was convinced he did not believe her either.

Her mother laughed out loud. "Oh, it is getting thick in here. This I know, Trisha. You are good, very good at this game, and to the best of my knowledge you have never even tried for this kind of a thing in the past."

Trisha held her ground anyway. This whole—adventure—as Mr. Hartmann had put it, was getting more convoluted by the minute.

"Believe what you will, you two. I know the truth." *So do they,* she thought. Trish had just met the man and was already referring to her mother and him as, *they. Life is so delicious, that is as long as it is properly seasoned.*

"Sie lügt, Herr Ebner. Meine tochter ist voller stolz. (She's lying, Mr. Ebner. My daughter is full of pride.) Becky was using an iPad to translate things she wanted to say. Her pronunciation and accent had been improving, too. Suddenly, she realized that it may be possible to carry on two conversations at the same time, right in the presence of two people—and keep one of them in the dark. *What a titillating concept,* the brilliant linguist giggled to herself.

"Dieser kann den stolz eines löwen, scheint aber sein herz sowie zu haben." (This one may have the pride of a lion, but seems to have its heart as well.) Becky read the translation on her little iPad, nodded knowingly and smiled. He went on. "Ich mag sie. Sie ist sehr smart. Trisha Martin aufnehmen sollte poker." (I like her. She is very smart. Trisha Martin should take up poker.)

This time Becky laughed out loud, knowing what her date had said without looking at the translator. In just that moment, the waiter showed up with a tray of vegetables, crackers, assorted berries, some pineapple slices . . . and an order of American style French fries. At the exact same time coffee, hot tea, a pither of iced tea, fresh lemons, cream, and various sweeteners landed on the table. Trisha was starving. She realized that she had not eaten anything except some fruit along the way during her *training* run, so she started in on the vegetables.

"You ought to meet Trisha's brother, Michael, Ebner. I am beginning to think they came out of the same womb; in fact, that is exactly what happened. Ihr vater war der schlimmste von allen. Er ist so anal, dass er aus dem grab arbeitet, machen die kinder dinge tun." (Their father was the worst of the bunch. He is so anal that he operates from the grave, making the kids do things.).

Ebner Hartmann laughed deliciously from the gut, roaring his approval. Trisha sat there staring at them . . . like an outsider. She had eaten all the vegetables and handed the waiter an empty platter, asking for a refill. That, plus the hot coffee, was working wonders. She moved on to the fruit and a slice of nut bread, while the senior citizen German Casanova peppered the celebration with yet another one-liner, the easiest way to speak German to an American with a translator.

"Ihre familie erinnert mich an meine eigene, all frech und stolz, das unschlagbare sort." (Your family reminds me of my own, all brash and proud, the unbeatable sort.). Trisha was getting suspicious now, perhaps a bit perturbed at the whole German thing. If her mother were going to keep this up, perhaps she would have to learn the languages right along with her. That seemed to be an ominous task right now with the university work she was involved in, her efforts with the Foundation, and not to mention the workout regimen that made all of the other things possible.

Becky Martin's response was so quick and flowed so easily off of her tongue that her daughter found it to be an astonishing accomplishment in such a short amount of time. *How could that be?* "Sie wissen nicht, die Hälfte davon, mein Freund. Wenn Sie jemals, sie zu treffen . . ." (You do not know the half of it, my friend. If you ever get to meet them . . .)

Trisha made a grab for the iPad. She wanted to see what was going on. "Mother, let me see that thing." Her tone made it clear to everyone that this was not a request.

Her mother jerked back, holding the translator to her chest. "I don't think so. Nope, not right now; I . . ."

Trisha stood over her mom and tried to take it away. Her mother, laughing now, leaned away belching out, "Nicht, it's mine. Go away, now. This one's not yours. Get your own!" The mother-daughter tag team wrestling match for control of the special little computer had turned into a spectacle, what with the grappling, bumping, and suddenly a broken dish on the floor. They looked at each other, staring in shock with their mouths stuck open, and each with just a bit of a smile. It took the busboy about two seconds to get working on the cleanup detail and so the ladies went back into action.

Their host, tall and handsome, well groomed, energetic, and so sophisticated, stood up, reaching across the table to his not so sophisticated escort for the evening and suggested, "Perhaps I can hold it for you vile za little vild one settles down."

They were making quite a scene for such a high class restaurant, though it was all in good fun. The outdoor plaza where they were seated, or at least used to be seated, was promoted as having a lively atmosphere to begin with. There were several loud conversations taking place. At the far side of the establishment the sounds of a German brass band played, quietly by some standards, but loud enough to be heard clearly all over. It was hustle and bustle hour at the Streigenberger Hotel, and all the fun as advertised was alive and well. The resort was measuring up to its reputation this afternoon. During the mêlée their waiter returned with more vegetables, placing them on the table as if he were invisible.

Trisha's attention turned back to the intruding gentleman whom they were sharing a table with. "Stay out of this, Frankenstein. Mom, hand it over. There is no way you know German that well. Just the other day . . ."

"Oh, take it then. But I want it back, Trisha." She handed the tablet to her daughter, who looked at it closely and there she was able to read the transcript of their entire conversation, scrolling up and down with her fingers on the view screen, the whole thing. It was an amazing toy.

"Mommy, you are so clever. Where did you get this thing?" Trisha was not the least bit offended. She had been a member of the Martin family far too long to be surprised by anyone's bag of tricks. Her mother had been spot-on about calling her a liar too. On that point she would not be budging, however. *If you stick with the con long enough,* she thought, *you'll even begin to believe it yourself.* Trisha went back to the vegetables, knowing what was good for her and what waited later this evening.

"I picked it up in Landstuhl after we had lunch at that nice potato restaurant. Don't you remember that I went shopping while you were working out? It cost a pretty penny, but it's working far quicker than I'd ever hoped. Do you like it?"

"I want one. Does it work in other languages?"

"According to the manual that came with it, the settings can accommodate more than a thousand different languages."

"How does it work?"

"Well, Trish, It broadcasts the words to the two-way receiver in my ear." Trisha noticed, for the first time, that there was a tiny, almost invisible attachment in her mother's right ear, away from where she was seated on her left side. It also had a tiny microphone. *When did she put it in?*

She was with me the entire time and I can't remember her putting the little ear thingy in. "I read the translation on the tablet, and it also broadcasts the words to me simultaneously. I softly whisper the response in English and the German pronunciation translation appears on the tablet. Then I mouth the words out loud. It is—fantabulous."

"My apologies to your gentlemen friend, Mom; Ebner, I did not mean to insult you by calling you Frankenstein."

"Zere vas no eensult taken, Miss Martin. I luffed Dr. Frankenstein. He vas a genius to create life, even if it vas just a movie monster." They all laughed.

He's funny. I do like Mom's new friend. What a great time they were having, even if the time had come to move on. "Mom, Ebner, I must take leave if I am to be on time to my dinner appointment. Thank you for introducing me to your new friend. Mr. Hartmann, please take good care of your date this evening. If I am not mistaken, my mother has not been out with another man since my father died thirteen years ago. I expect you to be a true gentleman, respectful in all ways, and modest in your expectations, though she is a very beautiful woman." She gave her mother a loving smile.

"Trisha, I am most honored to be vis your muzzer zis evening. I'll admit zat, in my old age, and vis my own Betlinde gone—four years now, perhaps it's time for me to allow my heart to vander, if just for some wholesome fun. People get lonely, you see. I understand zat ve do not really know each uzzer, but my character is vell respected and I hope to convince your muzzer zat our friendship should be allowed to grow in any direction zat fits our lives."

"You needn't worry at all, Trisha," said Becky. "Mr. Hartmann knows that he will not get even a peek inside of my clothing, where things have gone horribly wrong in recent years." They looked at each other and laughed. "If all goes well I am going to go to his AA meeting in the morning where I intend to improve on my German linguistic talents."

With that, and with hugs all around, Trisha walked away from the table and on into the hotel, still worried for her mother. She decided to take a leap of faith that the man was who he said he was, and with that she dropped it.

Trisha was light headed as she made her way through the hotel. There were people milling about in the luxurious registration area, some of them were good looking, well dressed couples happy to be about their business. There was an old man with a black long-coat and a top hat. He had a long white beard. At first she thought he was with the hotel, but then some children came running to him and he squeezed each of them, all smiles. The white marble floor and elegant gold laced walls seemed heavenly, especially with the large vase in the center of the room which was decorated with yellow and red roses. They were as fresh as her mood.

Against all the odds, the young and beautiful runner had indeed found the man she had planned the entire trip around. Tonight she would be having dinner with the famous Captain Brad Peterson and . . . his lady friend Annette Chappell. She wished she could have him to herself, but dealing with that little fly in the ointment was not to be the disappointment it seemed to be. She was going to put on her best face, force herself to have a good time, and leave possibilities where they should be, to the future. No one ever knew what would happen tomorrow, or next week, and Trisha had spent her entire life being optimistic, even when her life was on the downswing. By the time she had made it to the room, having meandered past the lounge, a piano bar, and even looking in on a wedding party that was in progress, Trisha had surmised that she had an hour to rest before getting ready.

The room she was sharing with her mother was elegant and nicely festooned. It had a king size bed, She and her mother both slept in the same bed on this stage of the trip, and it had been thoroughly cleaned. Trish drew a nice hot bath and slipped into the pink marble tub, lit two scented candles, and allowed the aches and pains of the day's run to drain from her tired body.

The snack she had eaten earlier with her mother and Ebner Hartmann turned out to be just the ticket in providing her the comfort and nutrition she needed, and so while relaxing she drifted into sleep rather lucidly right there in the tub, and though her rest could best be described as a very light siesta, she dreamed.

* * *

345

Trisha came alert, finding herself in her mother's bed, the one she slept in back home, and it was the home she had grown up in. How was this so? Her field of vision drifted to the large picture window. Outside it was daylight and slowly she began to remember that this was not exactly her childhood home. This was a different place, it was a wonderful place. It was where her father lived.

"Hello, Trisha." Her father was sitting on the other side of the room and she had not seen him until he spoke. When she heard his voice it was possibly the choicest sound in the entire Universe, the voice of a loving and caring father who had suddenly left her so long ago. She began to remember, to remember it all. She had dreamt of him several times in the past couple of years, but did not remember those experiences when she was awake. He had cheered her on as she won a marathon. That was a fantasy. It was the real life version of that race where she had destroyed her Achilles heel and the long slow degradation of her adult life had begun. They had also ridden bikes up in the air like E.T. did in the movies. He was always ready to have a good time, even in this reality. She sat up in the bed, tearing up and smiling at the same time, overcome with joy, comforted by the pajamas she wore when she was just a teenager, and then Trisha climbed out of the bed to walk to her father.

"Hi, Daddy, you have come to me again. I hope you're pleased with how things are going. It's Brad, isn't it? I am supposed to help Brad."

"Yes, Child, we need you to help Bradley. I have never doubted you, not since the day you were born. In all things you are a Martin. We have very little time before you wake up so we have to work fast."

"You're the boss, Dad. I work for you now."

Her father smiled broadly. "So you do, Kid. The way things are going you'll be the chair of the Roger Martin Foundation, helping me help others all the days of a very long life. Nothing pleases me more. Even though you don't remember the dreams, you always seem to be up to exactly what we need. It is . . . uncanny. Remember our bike trip, and you were shocked that in the dream you weren't fat anymore. I told you that you weren't an obese person and you didn't believe me. How do you feel about that?" There was nothing for her to say. She looked like . . . Trisha Jean Martin was supposed to look, all fit and trim. "Do you remember when I told you that it was within your special reach to obtain any goal in life that you could dream of? Today you're a world-class marathon runner. How do you feel about that?"

This time she did have something to say. "I feel blessed, Dad." He smiled at words that rang true. They had all been blessed.

"In spite of what you're telling your mother, and we agree that you need not admit things, we also know the desires of your heart, Trisha. We support you." "Who is 'we,' Dad? Is it Wise Mac, your friend?"

"Yes, it is him, and at least one other. There's a new person who's anxious to meet you." Her father turned to the door. "Tag, come on in." Presently, a man she had never seen walked into the room. He looked friendly and caring, and also a bit familiar, though she could not place that familiarity. "Trisha Jean Martin, my daughter, I would like to introduce you to Tag Peterson. Tag is Brad Peterson's grandfather."

"I am pleased to make your acquaintance, young lady. You are very impressive."

Trisha smiled and hugged the man who looked not like anyone's grandfather, in a weird sort of way since he was young. "The pleasure is all mine, Mr. Peterson."

"Since time is so short I am going to get right to the point. You have a biding interest in my grandson. It's OK with me, with all of us as your father has said. We would love nothing more than to see you two together, but that's not something we, or perhaps even you, have much control over. It is simply beyond us to match people up that way, though you wouldn't think it by watching Mac make a magic potion and stir things up with it. He sends his greetings and is sorry that he is not here to give you the hug you deserve. He is so proud of your work on our behalf."

"I do have a word of advice for you, though. Do not try to impress him with your accomplishments or how you can serve him. That won't work . . . she disappeared.

Tag looked at Roger. She was gone again and he did not have the chance . . .

* * *

Trisha was jolted from sleep by her mother; "Trisha, wake up. You'll be late for your dinner appointment." Her mother had come in and woken her from a deep bath-nap or she would have slept right on through and missed her supper with Brad Peterson and his . . . *oh what the hell, girlfriend*. It was senseless to think otherwise. She didn't even want to go now. Unfortunately, that was not the point. She hopped out of the tub, hastily threw some rags on, painted her face, dried her hair, letting it fall straight away, grabbed some loose jewelry, fastened her watch, and was out the door, in a taxi, and at the front steps of Brighella, an Italian 'ristorante' located in Frankfurt, Germany at precisely 7:00. Just as Trisha made the front door, a handsome couple, arm in arm, walked up the sidewalk and greeted her with smiles . . .

* * *

The afternoon had been warm and filled with of a sense of purpose for Brad Peterson. If he were not so tired from the marathon, his first in three years, well then he would have preferred to run all day. The reason his body functioned normally, calm, and with no symptoms of his time in captivity—during running activities— was a complete mystery to the Captain, but such as it was, he had enjoyed the day. With the small exception of a tiny shake earlier this afternoon, his nervous condition had presented no problems either and because of that he felt full of promise. For once the battle-tested soldier felt normal and he loved it.

"Annie, what did you find out about her?" Annette had suggested that they do some background research on Trisha Martin, not to investigate what she was up to, but to make it easier to spend time with a childhood friend; it would be like Brad had kept up throughout the years. Oh, he had thought of his childhood friend often. She was more than just some sort of a schoolmate. There was something intangible about this girl whom he had always been drawn towards. The truth was, he could not put a finger on just what it was.

Annette called back from the other room. "I found her, Brad. She's very interesting." *What do I tell him and what do I leave out?* "Like I said, she is a very nice person. It seems as though you pick your friends well, Bradley, even when you were young." That made him smile. "Would you like something from the bar before we go out?"

"I'm not drinking tonight, Annie. I'll have a Diet Coke though, if there is one in there." They were staying at the Westin Grand Frankfurt, not too very far from where they had made plans for dinner. Brad had gone for a *warm down*, in the gym and a swim in the hotel's fabulous pool. The great thing about the Westin, a five-star resort, in addition to its many amenities, was the fact that they could pay for their room with SPG points. By the time they had readied themselves for the short walk over to the restaurant, Brad was quite sure he knew more about his childhood friend, Trisha Martin, than she would have ever expected of him. She was still in college, attending school online, had become involved in some kind of a public relations position for Nutrisystem, and was a cashier at Target back in Henderson, Nevada. *Trisha has never married. What is that all about? I had her pegged for family life all along,* he thought. It was obvious she was still taking care of herself physically, something to be expected, but he saw one picture of her where she had gained weight. It was going to be interesting to fill in the blanks, but it was quite obvious that Trisha, though insanely attractive, was not the complete person he would have needed for a real relationship. She was definitely a good friend and would be again. *I would like to help her if I could.*

They were on the short and romantic stroll to Brighella and walking past a boutique that specialized in puzzles and games when Brad suddenly had an idea. "I would like to give Trisha a gift. Would that be OK with you?"

"Of course, darling," replied Annie. The air was pleasant, though a bit crisp for a spring evening and Annette was, shall we say, conflicted. She had not revealed all that she knew about the girl and was beginning to question her strategy. Trisha would surely want to speak of her accomplishments, for by now Annette Chappell was certain that the encounter was not a coincidence. Oh, it was somewhat of a needle in a haystack that she had found her man, but to run right past him, directly in front of her was, to say the least, a bit disconcerting. One of Annie's strengths, however, was the ability to think on her feet, something that gave her confidence. When the time came she would know what to do and what to say, she was sure of it. *I bet she will fall all over herself trying to impress Brad. It will be so sad that in the end I will be the one propping her up from minute-to-minute. I don't foresee a problem here at all. If I play my cards right, she will fall into place as a platonic third wheel in our lives. She is an appealing person and I really do not want to have to hurt her. On the other hand all is fair in love and war . . .*

Brad emerged from the little store with a wrapped gift box and caught up with Annie, who had been so lost in her thoughts that she did not see what he had purchased, and so decided not to ask. She would instead play possum, be a bit coy about it and see how long it took him to tell her instead. *The game goes on.* When they at last approached the restaurant, having navigated the last few blocks under the enchanting ambiance of trees lining a glimmering park, she found that her *third wheel* competitor was approaching the front door at the exact same time. Annie's first impression of the cleaned up Trisha Martin was surprising. She was, quite simply, beautiful. It was obvious that she had spent the entire afternoon getting ready for her move on Bradley Peterson. It was time to play. *So, the thin little runner girl is on time . . . drat!*

* * *

Trisha noticed that they had brought a little wrapped gift, probably for her. Right off the bat that small token had her feeling insecure. *I'm terrible at this. Why do I always feel fat in social settings,* she silently panicked? "Hi, Brad and Annette," she smiled, feeling awkward and out of place. *Am I really supposed to be here?*

Annette extended her hand and they enjoyed a courtesy hug. "Hello, Trisha. Once again, it was nice to meet you today. We are very glad to see you. Bradley has told me so much about you. I'm really looking forward to getting to know you better." *Brad does like you . . . more than I thought. Tonight we'll be setting the ground rules on where we all stand with each other. I am his, he is mine, and you are our friend, that is it and there is nothing more.*

Brad was next in line. He wrapped his arms around Trisha, squeezed her tight and then kissed her on the lips. It was just a small friendly kiss, nothing that would embarrass his girlfriend, though it sent an electric wave of emotion throughout her tired and aching body. There were emotions deep inside of her that had never made it to sunlight. He whispered in her ear, "Trisha, thank you so much for catching up with me today. I've really missed you. I am so glad to see you, you could never know." *I really hope Annette likes Trisha. She may not have accomplished much in her life but she is still Trisha Martin, my friend. She could be one of my best friends.*

Trish looked up into his eyes, trying not to tear up, and replied, "It's great to see you too, Brad. I'm just happy that you're safe and sound. Let's have some fun tonight." *He kissed me, Nurse Chappell.* The awkwardness dissipated, the fear subsided, and the self-loathing melted away; Bradley had touched her with his magic.

They opened the door and went inside. The place was buzzing with activity. It was the dinner hour, the establishment was part of a small hotel, and all the tables, well almost all of them, were full. The atmosphere was loud with lively conversation, not so unlike the level of energy Trisha had enjoyed with her mother earlier. *What's his name? Yes . . . . It's Ebner Hartmann. Now that is an interesting fellow,* thought Trisha. Here at Brighella the spindle candlelit simple tables were sheathed with white linen, embroidered with lacy floral patterns. The chairs were wooden and painted white, the utensils looked to be sterling silver as were the candle holders, and the art up on the wall looked to be original. It was a cozy place to renew friendships. This promised to be an evening to remember no matter what happened. The trio of Americans were seated, the refracted light up on the walls was comforting to tired eyes and a waiter instantly appeared ready to pour house wine, either red or white.

"I'll have the red wine," said Annie. "I feel a bit like something with meatballs or . . . oh, I just don't know yet. What are you drinking, Trisha?" *Are you going to show us how sophisticated you are and get the food and wine mixed up?* The waiter poured her wine and she took the first sip immediately. "It's delicious. This is your house wine?" He nodded. "Perhaps you could bring us a bottle. Brad, this is very good."

Trisha answered. "Oh, no thanks, tonight. I don't usually drink. What is that tea drink they are all having at the table across the way? Trisha was eyeing a table of four across the aisle. It was a family with children and they all had the same thing, which made it non-alcoholic, at least she hoped so. *People are very different about alcohol in Europe.*

"You know, madam, that we are in an Italian eatery, but what you ask of is a special German tea, blended with green apple juice, known here in Germany as Gluehwein," said the waiter. "Would you like to try some?"

"Yes, thank you. I would very much like to try it. I enjoy trying new things," smiled Trisha. *I could have gone with the wine. I would have had the white, but I want to be different than Annette.*

"And for the gentleman?"

"Thank you, sir. I am going to have some of that special German tea, too. Is there anything else in the Gluehwein other than apple juice and tea?" *I am surprised that Annie is drinking alcohol tonight, but, it's her choice.*

"Not so much, but the difference is in the type of tea and the apples. Some of the other ingredients are a small amount of grape juice, some sugar, and different kinds of spices and syrup. It is quite tasty. We serve it both hot and cold. They are having it on ice over there. Would you like yours served hot?

Trisha mentioned that she wanted it served cold, Brad agreed and off the waiter went. By the time he returned with the drinks and a bottle of wine for Annie, the table had a spread of breads, some olives, and different types of crackers; Trisha's mouth was watering. She knew that this meal had to be properly measured. For her, the trick would be to limit her eating in such a way so as not to bring attention to the fact. She took one of the rolls, spread it thinly with the restaurant's homemade churned butter and tried her first sip of the drink. She loved it. When the bar attendant came with the bottle of wine, Annie had thought better of her choice and changed her order to the special drink, too. She didn't want to be the only person drinking alcohol and had forgotten that Brad had told her that we wasn't.

"Trisha, in honor of our renewed friendship, we got you a little something on the way over.

It's a gag, really, but we can have some fun with it tonight," said Brad, handing her the little wrapped box. *I am not so sure about this idea. It is a bit corny. I hope she doesn't take it the wrong way.*

"This gift is from Brad, Trisha. I don't even know what it is yet. I waited outside the little store watching some people across the street while he shopped. I'm as interested to see what it is as you are. He never told me what was in the box." *If it is any kind of jewelry, Brad, you're a dead man walking.*

"There is no sense in keeping the mystery a secret." She unwrapped it and found to her surprise a . . . Rubik's Cube. Trisha started laughing. "Oh, Bradley, that is so sweet. You remembered."

Annette looked puzzled. Brad was grinning. He had scored points with his childhood friend. *I remember more than you'll ever know.* "Annie, when Trisha was in middle school she wrote a paper about the history of the Cube and why it was so hard to solve. If I remember correctly, Trisha became addicted to the three dimensional brainteaser, but like all of us, she never got one put back together. Tonight is the night for you, Trisha. Can you solve the Cube while we're eating dinner and still carry on a lively conversation while you work?"

"You guys are very well educated, even for the really well educated. I am just a junior college dropout. How can you expect me to function with such brainy types and work this unsolvable toy at the same time? Now you are putting me at a disadvantage." *I have an idea.* Trisha unwrapped the Cube, and then put it under the table where they could not see her hands and started twisting and turning. She wanted the puzzle to be in total disarray before she gave it back to them.

It was Trish's turn to ask a question. "Annette, where are you from?"

"I'm from Minnesota. I received my nursing degree at the University of Massachusetts, and then joined the Service." Annie went on and gave quite a bit of flattering information about herself. *You see, Trisha, you really do not belong here with Brad and me.* "Trisha, tell us a little about you. What have you been up to all these years?" *Here comes the story of her running career. This is something I will have to deal with. Let's get it out on the table right now.*

"What was that," asked Trisha? "I am having trouble carrying on a conversation with this thing in my hand. Annette, would you care to give it a try?" She handed the Cube to her new friend, who tried not to look taken aback, which she was, and suddenly Annie was presented with the unsolvable puzzle. *I really don't feel like being full of myself right now. I'm going leave that to the genius nurse with the advanced degree. I want to be different, not the same.* "I have taken it easy for the past years, and I'll have to admit that from the length of my resume I do not look like a promising mental protégé. I work at

Target as a cashier, you know the one, Brad. It is over on Stephanie and Sunset. It's not much, but I love it. I live in a small home in Whitney Ranch not too far from there and I like to work out. I have never been married. I'm a pretty boring person, really. There just isn't much to go on. I admire you guys and all that you've accomplished. Truly, I wish I had done more, but the past is the past. I am uh, taking some classes online right now and will get a bachelor's degree within a year or so. I am proud of that much."

The waiter came by and took their orders. Annie was eating quite a bit of food, Bradley was a bit more conservative, and Trisha focused on ample fruits and vegetables, a small pasta dish which was complimented with salmon, and she nibbled on another roll. Everything was going to be fine with her food choices. She would take in reasonable amounts of post-running nutrition, and keep it portion controlled, unlike the pig-fest she had indulged in a few days ago with her mother at that castle. What was the name of that place? She could never remember. Yes, it was Sleeping Beauty's Castle.

Annie was busy working the Rubik's Cube and appeared to be distracted. She was spinning the little colored blocks back and forth, around and around. She got a bit excited when three of the six sides were lined up, but from that point every time she tried to align the other color, something came undone. She may have been a whiz at school, a high achiever in the field of medicine, and she was certainly beautiful from head to toe, but her patience was wearing thin with the puzzle. *Is that what this is about,* thought Trisha. *Is Bradley testing us?* "Annette, what are your plans after you leave the military?" said Trish.

Annette replied, leaning close to her boyfriend, and she was actually snuggling. "I would like to go back to UMASSS and complete medical school. I will be out of the Army and can enroll there in the fall semester, that is, if I am accepted. "We," and it was obvious she was referring to Brad by the way she moved her head under his shoulder and smiled up at him, "completed the paperwork just before we left on this trip. Brad is helping me. I am hoping that he'll be well enough to be released in time to join me there. Perhaps he can find something at the University that suits his level of professionalism." Brad was smiling and enjoying the attention. Trisha's heart sank a bit and she had to work hard not to convey disappointment. "It would be my goal to get into pediatrics down the road." *Brad needs someone far more intelligent than a cashier to help steer him into the future, Trisha.*

She is gloating. "I think the medical profession is about the highest possible level of service that one can aspire to, Annette. I know I could never do that." *I am going to play along with you, Nurse Chappell. My guess about Bradley Peterson, and it is kind of a guess since I have not seen him since he was a kid, is that he could care less if the girl he ended up with was a doctor. He may even find that to be a boring choice. I am not at all intimidated by you.* "Brad, are you thinking about moving to Massachusetts?"

"I have given it some thought, Trisha. I'd like to help Annie get to where she wants to go, and if it all works out, turns out to be the right thing for me professionally, then yes, I would consider moving there. The future is an open book. Speaking of Annette Chappell, how are you doing with that puzzle, honey?" *Trisha, we are always going to be friends, you and I. In just the little amount of time that we have had today, I could not imagine not having you in my life. It is so comforting to me that you and Annie are getting along tonight. I can see that she likes you a lot.*

The food arrived and the conversation continued while they enjoyed their dinner together.

The atmosphere was pleasant and the food was great. Annie, however, was not getting any closer to solving the Cube. "I am not getting anything other than three sides. I can make any three sides come together, but after that the puzzle breaks down. If I make some progress on another color, then something else falls apart. Why don't you give it a try, Brad?" *I wish he hadn't bought this stupid thing. Puzzles are not my strong point.*

Brad accepted the Rubik's Cube and started twisting it around. *I am a smart guy. Perhaps I can get this.* "Trisha, by any chance do you remember the history of this toy? You wrote the report."

"Rubik's Cube, originally called the Magic Cube, was created in 1974 by a Hungarian professor of architecture named Emo Rubik. The man didn't even know it was a puzzle at the time. He was trying to help his students understand the dynamics of structure. Ideal Toy Company marketed it and that's why they changed the name from Magic to Rubik's, to patent and protect their intellectual property rights. I haven't had one in my hand since I was a little kid, until today that is." Trisha could tell that Brad was getting flustered already. What surprised her the most was how clumsy his hands were. *I thought a surgeon would have had surer hands than that.*

"Well, Trisha. This is our gift to you. It is obvious that we aren't getting anywhere with it. Perhaps you will have better luck," and with that, he handed the cube back to her.

Trisha took the little toy into her hands, folded them into her lap, and considered whether she could remember the algorithmic pattern she had memorized all those years ago. To the best of her knowledge, she did not think that Bradley was aware that she had spent uncounted hours working with a Rubik's Cube when she was in the sixth grade. She had solved it. That was why she studied its history and had written the report. She was the only one around where she grew up who'd ever put that Humpty Dumpty back together again. By the time she was in high school, Trisha had pretty much cast the toy aside for other things . . . like running on the track team. Now, after all these years, it had found its way back and she began the slow methodical twisting, counting, aligning and matching. It was like riding a bike. In order to keep the conversation focused she kept the entire process under the table.

The evening progressed cordially. They carried on a detailed conversation about medicine, brain surgery, what patients could expect to have happen when they recovered from different types of brain surgery . . . and about Annette's plans to attend medical school. It was all a little bit heady for Trisha, but she stayed in the conversation. She realized as the evening wore on just how much she had missed Brad. She would be missing him again . . . soon. He was totally in love with Annie and she had no interest in trying to break them up for her own sake. That was not the type of person who Trisha was. She focused on being happy for them and in reorganizing her own thoughts.

"I see the process of protecting the pathways of cerebral senses: sight, hearing, smell, touch, and taste in cognitive confluence through the surgical technique as being what brain surgery is all about. When we are inside of someone's head, literally, the essence of who that person is becomes the domain of the surgeon. If he gets the tumor out, or corrects whatever the problem is, but leaves the patient mentally or emotionally crippled, then one could agree that the operation was not a success . . ." Bradley Peterson had answered quite a few of Trisha's questions. What amazed him was how focused and pointed they were. It was as if she had prepared for a professional interview. *There is definitely more to this person than meets the eye. If she didn't even go to college, then where did she get this education?* "Trisha, that's enough about the medical profession. Let's change the subject. Your past is a total mystery to me. I have had many conversations with people our age, people who did receive college degrees, and none of them sound like you. What's up with that?"

Trisha's hands got a bit sweaty. They were still twisting and turning under the table with the Rubik's Cube and she provided a measured response. "I proudly admit to being a bit more cognitive than my level of formal education. I'm not very proud of my scholastic track record, and I am trying to make up for it right now. I am enrolled in college, still at Saddleback, but I take advantage of their online programs, and should have a four year degree in less than a year. Who knows what will happen after that? *This is the part of the evening that I dreaded. They are both so far along and I am so far behind. Look at Annette. Could it be more possible for her to enjoy my misery?* "Oh well, perhaps I am . . . just a late bloomer. As far as any street smarts I might have, I'm still well read. A few years ago I turned a corner, but I always read things. One day I woke up and added three rules to my daily approach, an overhaul of the training that makes my brain work. One, I learned to count my blessings. I have a great life. Second, I make time for myself. I want more out of life than I have earned to date, and so I invest in myself. Third, I push myself to see how far I can get beyond my comfort zone. Ever since making those small adjustments, I have kept a positive attitude and there have been results."

"I'm sure of it, Trisha. I still know you." *She is very smart. What more is there to this story? I have a charmed life, I have Annie, and now I am going to have Trisha Martin. Look at my girlfriend smile warmly. They really are taking to each other.* "How is your father, by the way? You used to run with him. Are your parents still together? Your mother kind of described herself as going on a date tonight. Does your dad still get out and run? I know you were close."

357

Trisha was stunned. Brad Peterson didn't know that her father was gone. Her fingers slowed on the puzzle under the table. The room dimmed perceptibly as she emotionally began to shut down. She hadn't had to tell her father's story in years. The inner pain began to well up inside of her and tears formed in her eyes. She fought valiantly to hold them back, especially in front of Brad's lady-friend, but the longer she took, the worse it got. "I lost my father just after high school. He passed away while running up on Mt. Charleston, of a brain aneurysm.

He was just . . . larger than life, and for me it was a tough thing to get over. I sure could have done a better job handling that part of my life, Brad." *Hold on, Trish. You can do it. You can handle this. You do not need to break down like a little girl. You are not confessing that the tail spin lasted more than a decade. Oh, Daddy.* "Life's not fair. I still miss him, but we all move on."

Brad understood. *When we were just school kids everything with Trisha was 'my dad this and my father that.' Trisha fell apart after she lost her father and who could blame her. I hurt for her, even now.* "I am so sorry to hear that, Trisha. I know how important he was to you. I wish I had been there to help. I wish I knew. Please accept my condolences."

"I accept, as long as we do not have to dwell on it, Bradley. It is to the future that we are headed, all of us." *I am so glad that you never knew what happened to me.* "Now, before the evening ends I want to hear some war stories, the good ones, and no embellishments either. It is true that you single handedly defeated ten thousand scorpions?" Brad started laughing . . .

As the evening wore on toward its destiny the real ice breaker for their reunion had to be Brad's experiences. His adventures had the makings of a movie. As he told of his times spent with real boots on the ground, the kids he was there to serve, she was again reminded of why she came to this place at all. He had turned out to be the kind of man that she would have wanted. It was time for Trisha to switch tracks no matter how dismal the reality of her place in Brad's pecking order was. She would have to somehow adjust her thinking of him, and now see their relationship in a platonic context, noting irony in that reality. They had never been together in the first place. Trisha still lived in the immature fantasy of things not real. Perhaps the fact that she had lost her father so young in life played into how she saw herself when men she was interested in came along. *Love and pain.* Soon, in about a million years there would be no pain, or not as much anyway, and romantic delusion would then be replaced by the practicality of reason. Yeah, right.

She decided that in spite of the obvious tension between her and Annette Chappell, his love interest, she liked the very intelligent and extremely beautiful woman. If she were not in love with Brad herself, she would have been happy for him. Perhaps in some future she would be. Two oft-repeated words in the English language, love and pain, were in fact synonyms as far as Trisha could see. The runner had picked correctly. She did not idolize Bradley Peterson because he was a true American hero. She wanted him for reasons that went way, way back. It wasn't to be. The race in Madrid suddenly looked a thousand leagues away. Trisha wanted nothing to do with it, and even considered going home. That, of course would blow her cover. Instead she decided to dedicate the next month to preparation and run the race of her life. That intense training would further her personal ambitions and cement the cover. It was obvious that Brad wanted her back in his life and so something positive had happened, no matter how barren and unpleasant the future looked tonight. She spent the rest of her time with them in an accommodating and supportive demeanor, working continuously to keep her disappointment hidden from view. She fumbled the Cube and dropped it to the floor and so leaned under the table to pick it up. Apparently she wasn't the only one hiding something. Brad's hands were shaking violently. There was something terribly wrong with Brad.

When Trisha came back up, the Cube still hidden from view and set to her side, she looked plaintively into his eyes. He couldn't hide the pain of having been found out. "Brad, what's wrong? Are you really OK?" Suddenly, Annette shrunk from the conversation and the tragic case of Brad's dilemma became the focus of conversation. Brad's face had turned white, his eyes downcast, and suddenly the shaking got even worse. Trish could see real fear in his eyes and suddenly knew that Bradley Peterson, the war hero, her idol, her friend, was in real trouble. He was suffering. Slowly and surely the shaking subsided and he returned somewhat to normal.

Brad told Trisha everything, well, everything that he could. He stayed away from the jet crash, no one but him knew much about that, about why he was where he was in the first place. He spoke of isolation and trying as hard as he could to limit the nature of violence committed against him by his tormentors. He spoke proudly of his rescue by the same troops he flew with that first night on the C-141. Because it would have made him uncomfortable, he decided to leave out the part of how he had fantasized a marriage and family life with Trisha Martin, the very girl he was with tonight, in order to avoid going totally insane. With each new twist of the tale, Trisha and Annette shivered away inward anguish, not able to even imagine what their friend had been through.

"Brad, what are they doing to help you? Are you on any medications? Are you going to have to undergo surgery?"

"That's the funny thing, Trisha. No one knows what is causing this. I would go to the ends of the earth to get rid of this condition, but I have no idea what to do." His voice began to shake a bit, and as the trepidation of his next revelation began to gurgle up and out of his mouth, Brad actually began to cry, something Annette had never seen him do. "If I can't find a way out of this, my career is finished."

"Don't talk like that, Brad. There is a long way to go," said Trisha. "Obviously I am not a doctor, not even a college diploma to hang on the wall in my tiny cluttered office, but have you given thought to attacking the problem from the inside out?"

"Hold on just a minute," said Annie. "We have the best minds in the world working on this problem. Brad doesn't need . . ."

"I want to hear what she has to say," Bradley had jumped right in and defended Trisha's interest in making a suggestion.

The uneducated runner went on. "I have found that there is much truth to the idea that our body is a manifestation of our thoughts. The nature of the way we think and how we control our emotions can play a pivotal part in how our bodies work. I am no expert and the challenges I have faced in the past couple of years are nothing compared to this, but have your treatment specialists invested in the theory of healing yourself directly through belief in the power of the mind?"

"I have a therapist who is helping me think my way through this problem, and yes he has mentioned that my attitude and the way I think can play a huge part in my recovery. I am beginning to believe that traditional medicine is not going to help much. That is why I am thinking of moving on from the hospital."

"I'm sure that he has emphasized that healing through the power of what is inside of that genius noggin over those handsome shoulders of yours can work in harmony with medical science. You can't give up, Bradley, it just isn't in you. I still know you that much—at least."

"I won't, Trisha. I'll try to stay positive and avoid negative thinking about this. To tell you the truth, when I shut myself off with negative thinking, that is when I feel it the most. The reason I decided to start running in public races again is the direct result of that approach. It is uncanny to me, though, that you would be the one to bring that approach up." *There is way more to you than meets the eye, little girl.* "I think it is destiny that we found each other in my very first race. No matter how sore I am physically from the run, and this little shaking episode notwithstanding, just getting to catch up with you is like a new pill for me. Do not ever, ever, let us get so far away from each other again . . ."

Just then Trisha's telephone rang; she looked at the number and recognized her mother's intrusion, and so she picked up. "Yes, Mother . . . You're kidding!" There was an animated look on Trisha's face, not one of panic or shock, but instead something that bordered on unbelief. When she put the phone down and returned to the conversation with her dinner-mates, expressing a wry smile, Trisha spoke. "Guys, I am going to have to call it a night. It appears that my crazy mother has found her way to the police station. As you know, Mom went on a date tonight with a new person she just met this morning. I met him this afternoon when we returned from the run. He seems like a nice enough guy. To make a long story short, he got in a fight with an off-duty policeman. It had something to do with honor, some sort of an insult to my mom, or whatever. I need to go over there and help her get him out of jail. It's a mess." She was laughing, and then the inbound text alert followed with the address and directions Trisha needed to find her way to the station.

"Annette, Bradley, it has been a wonderful evening. Brad, keep working. You are way too valuable to let this thing end your surgical practice. I know you can do it. I don't know how or why, but I just do.

Here is my phone number." She handed him a small piece of paper with her name, phone number, and home address. Feel free to call me anytime. "I'm paying for dinner tonight. Thank you for inviting me, but let's just call this my small contribution of gratitude for the sacrifice you two have made in the service of the good ole USA." *I love my debit card.*

"Trisha, Annie and I'd like to thank you for paying for dinner tonight, but we invited you. You simply must agree to let us take care of the bill next time." He handed her a business card with his contact information on it. "Call me anytime, too."

They chatted for a few more minutes while the waiter took care of the tab, Trisha signed the check and found that she was out of questions. For her the trip was over. Brad was with a very beautiful and intelligent, supportive woman, who certainly understood his needs. He was very happy, too. She was very concerned for his situation. The single draw she felt towards being with him would have been to explore patterns of behavior that could restore him to health. Her mothering instinct wanted access to Brad's condition.

Brad, on the other hand, had nothing but questions left in his mind. He had met up with the real life version of someone he had once fantasized being married to. He had met up again with a childhood relationship and this much he realized: he was no closer to figuring this girl out than he had ever been. He still didn't know anything about her.

When Trisha Martin disappeared out of the front door, the restaurant suddenly seemed empty and quiet. Her presence had filled the room with memories of home for Bradley. There was suddenly a big hole where an evening's entertainment had been. She had left him wanting more. He daren't let Annie know that. A couple of hours ago he was bragging to his inner self of having two special women in his life. Now he was back to one. He and Annie shared a glass of wine, their first alcohol of the entire evening. She could sense his abandonment, he knew it. About a half hour after Trisha had left them, they stood and began to make their way to the front door when Annette noticed something. It was the Rubik's Cube. Trisha had forgotten it, or had she? The Cube sat there on the chair next to where their hostess had eaten her supper, and it was back together again. Trisha Jean Martin had solved Rubik's Cube.

8

Olympiad

August 19, 2016

"Throughout the modern era, memorable Olympic moments have helped to define who we are as people. One needn't look further back than the 1968 games and the infamous black power salute, or to the horrific events that ended in tragedy during the Munich games, to see Olympic moments bleak in human history. The bright side of the coin can only be described as extraordinary; these are the achievements where Olympic contributions to society helped to shape our greatness as a civilization. Who could ever forget Jesse Owens's rebuke of Arian supremacy at the Berlin games in 1936 before the start of World War II? Were you alive in 1976 when Nadia Comaneci of Romania scored the first perfect 10 in gymnastics? In 1980 a band of American college kids came together to dethrone the mighty Soviet Union's hockey team at Lake Placid, the Miracle on Ice; can't you remember where you were when you found out what had happened that evening? History prioritizes these incredible moments in time, but one can now argue that the 2016 games in Rio will forever be enshrined by what happened today in the Women's Marathon. We go now to Jim Lampley and to the one and only time you will ever see this medal ceremony live."

"Thank you, Bob Costas. Folks, the atmosphere is electric here at the Olympic Medal Pavilion. In more than forty years of broadcasting sports, I have never seen anything quite like this. Throughout the Pavilion, enthusiasts who have made their way in are embracing in reverent silence. There are tears flowing freely, lit candles, lighters, and cell phone lights providing an ambiance of togetherness in these troubled times as we prepare for the Turkish national anthem . . .

* * *

July 20, 2016
The battalion passes by
the sentry without noticing
how he's subverted the divine order
of their universe.

Wise Mac

Shalane Flanagan wondered which ordeal would challenge her more, the news conference she was enduring or the race itself. "I have trained very hard for this Olympics. In London the cramping ate me alive during the more technical part of the run and I still finished 10th, about two minutes behind the gold medalist, if I remember correctly. Kara Goucher spoke of her pain that day as something akin to having a baby. I couldn't agree more. Rio promises to be even more difficult. Thank you very much for all of your support. I have a plane to catch, so if you'll allow, I will beg your pardon and take leave." The credentialed sportswriters applauded enthusiastically and wished her well. Abruptly the podium was empty and the room went quiet. Then the anticipation began to build for the last of America's three female marathoners.

The entourage began to file in. The first person to walk through the door was a well-known sports agent. David Giles was, perhaps, the most respected athletic agent of the day. He had clients from all over the world representing just about every sport, and a reputation that exuded shrewd loyalty. Behind him the entrepreneur who was the runner's manager and brother entered stone faced and all business. He looked to be on a mission. Just behind him, Stanley Burton, trainer extraordinaire, was known as the master genius for his work in bringing back to life the athletic career of a hopelessly overweight and out of shape long distance runner. The room erupted in applause for him alone. Next through the door was an elegant and beautiful senior citizen. Her flashy style and the smart, fashionable outfit that adorned her were outdone by the glorious smile that only the mother of an Olympic athlete could identify with. She looked the part, physically fit and trimmed to the max. This woman took great pride in looking good.

Suddenly there she was, America's best long distance runner. For what seemed like a full minute, but in fact was only a few seconds, she was the recipient of a standing ovation. Trisha Jean Martin was going to the Olympic Games, having fulfilled the contract she had signed those many years ago.

"Thank you, thank you very much . . . Enough already; you'd think I'd just won the race and yet we haven't even climbed aboard the plane for the flight to Rio." The crowd busted out in spontaneous laughter. Trisha could command a room with a wink. Her personality was absolutely infectious. Her meteoric rise as an international athlete had captured the attention of a nation. Maybe it was her natural beauty or the rich full waste-length hair, so unusual among the athletic community. Perhaps she was one of the few, the very few, that lived up to a larger-than-life reputation. Possibly it was because she was so lovable and talented at the same time, but had never left her humble roots. She was the sunshine on a cloudy planet with troubles abounding around every corner. Trisha Martin was an old fashioned truth, justice, and the American way kind of gal. "Obviously I have spoken repeatedly of my gratitude to represent my country in this Olympics. It's a dream come true, literally, brought to life with the undying support of the entire team, many who are here with me now . . ." Trish let the silence brew, looking about the room, which was packed and very hot with television lights, cameras clicking, sound booms, and a podium with enough microphones to intimidate almost anyone, almost. "Are there any questions?" she timidly smiled as the roar of many voices lent chaos to the moment of peace.

"Trisha, good afternoon, I'm Robbie Blakeley, with The Rio Times. If you had to define your long distance running career with a single word, what would that word be?"

"The word that comes to mind is *hope*. Here is the thing about hope and just how it leads to the fulfillment of potential. Hope gives all of us the time to unlock discouragement, to accept and understand our limitations, and then to move on and improve our lives. I have always enjoyed hope." *Please ask me oration style questions. I feel like trying to help others today.*

"Just one more question," said the senior reporter from the English newspaper published in a nation where Portuguese was the native tongue. "No one had ever heard of you and your potential to run at this level. Was it in Madrid, back in 2011 when you placed third and emerged onto the scene or was it in Las Vegas at the end of the year when you won your first marathon?"

She contemplated the amazing story of her transformation and chose something else altogether. "I would have to say it was in Las Vegas the year before at the half marathon when I won the locals version of the race. I had no idea that was going to happen, not until after I crossed the finish line. Shortly after that Stanley altered my schedule and intensified our project, saying that it would be a waste of time not to move up and turn professional. At the time I was just learning how to live again. Stanley taught me how to capitalize on mistakes that were being made and turn them into real growth." *Where would I be today without you, Stanley Burton? I am so lucky to have you in my life.*

"Trisha," shouted out the writer from Sports Illustrated. For the life of her, Trisha could not remember his name. "Who do you see as your major competitors in Rio? Will it be the Ethiopians, the Kenyans, or perhaps one of your own teammates?"

"None of the above." *What is your name? Jon . . . uh . . . Wor . . . um . . . Wertheim. That's it!* "I have to give you credit for the question, Mr. Wertheim. For me it is a critical one. My number one competitor is myself, but not in the way you think. There are any number of incredible athletes who will challenge for the gold in this race, all of them deserving. I do not see myself as the favorite by any stretch of the imagination. My problem remains me. I have absolutely no power over how the others perform. I can't compare myself with anyone, but who I am and what I expect of myself. If I go out there and give it all I have, and on my best day cannot win, then I can only hope for one of my teammates to get the job done. In the end I am still a fan of the race."

By the end of the press conference, Trisha Jean Martin had been given just what she had asked for, and that was the chance to encourage others. On this stage and at this level, she had been granted the unprecedented opportunity to help. She was able to turn answers into positive things; like the new meaning that life takes on when one helps another to recover from setbacks, how gifts like concern, compassion, and consideration fuel personal achievement, how miracles are bred through following the right kind of an example, how self-esteem improves when one follows a spiritual pathway, regarding the destructive emotion of omnipotence, the role that putting judgments onto others plays in self-recrimination, and why demanding the impossible when striving for emotional balance puts the cart before the horse and the wisdom of pulling back from seeing one's self as the center of the universe.

Trisha thought she could outlast the inquisition, but finally had to step away from the microphone, excusing herself. They were to board the jet for Rio in less than an hour, she and Stanley.

* * *

The headquarters of the US Olympic Committee in downtown Colorado Springs was abuzz with activity as the athletes began climbing, one by one, onto the buses for a short ride over to the airport where they would board and then fly to Los Angeles, meeting with other athletes from around the country for the flight to Rio de Janeiro and the expectations of dreams come true.

Each of the finely honed athletes had dedicated themselves to unimaginable amounts of work for the once-in-a-lifetime opportunity to represent the United States of America. They ranged in celebrity from the virtually unknown all the way to elite Tennis stars and NBA basketball players. Superstars like that arrived at the games in luxurious fashion. Most of the team, Trisha included, flew together on a charter flight, this time out of LAX.

Trisha and her group were still inside of the Center, given some privacy together in their final moments behind the glass that separated them from the pageantry of pandemonium taking place just outside where ribbons of red, white, and blue adorned street lights. American flags were everywhere. The cordoned off busses were at the center of attention as thousands of Olympic fans cheered, television cameras with spotlights glared, and civic leaders pontificated with broad smiles. The broadcast trucks churned away. There were last minute interviews taking place. Everyone was so excited.

Trisha hugged David and thanked him yet again for all he had accomplished on her behalf, and then took a moment to cry in her mother's arms. The microcosm of the macrocosm was in how her mother's life had changed in the years since the runner had resumed her career. Becky Martin had lost all of her weight, stopped drinking and started living again at full speed. Trisha could not for the life of her understand how her journey had brought about so many positive changes in others. Stanley stood quietly off to the side, waiting patiently, as Trisha shared a few moments with her brother, Michael.

"Mikey, I just don't know what to say." She leaned into his chest with her arms securely around his waist and her head bowed downward. Tears of gratitude welled up and dripped onto his solid muscular chest. In the years since the miracle in Las Vegas where it all began, Michael Martin had himself taken up long distance running, if for no other reason than to get a glimpse of what Trisha had to go through on a daily basis. "You brought me back from the dead."

They held each other in silence. There were no words worthy of what passed between brother and sister in that moment. Her brother was her hero. He was the closest thing to a father she had and had performed his role in developing her courage to undertake the impossible. Under his tutelage, Trisha Jean Martin had been transformed from a depressed 275 lbs. nobody into the American woman's marathon record holder. She had won several races outright, including a record-setting performance in the Olympic trials to earn the spot on the team. When she looked into his eyes to say goodbye, he smiled, pulled away and put a reassuring hand into his pocket and pulled something out. "I have a gift for you, TJ. I'm placing a bet on you to win your race and I want you to have this." He put a small velvet bag into her hands and folded them shut. "I want you to keep this with you and remember who you are. You are Trisha Jean Martin, my sister. I don't want to put any more pressure on you than you already have, but just think of this.

Is getting there really enough? I am betting on you to win." Michael kissed her forehead and then turned to walk away. He looked back one more time as she started to laugh, and he followed suit. Inside of the small bag was the two-headed silver dollar that got her into this pickle in the first place. She had won ownership of the famous two-headed silver dollar. She well knew what that coin represented. The pressure on her to perform again had made its presence known in a new and exciting way.

* * *

The flight to Rio had an uncanny sense of déjà vu, like she had been there before. After all the pomp and pageantry in Colorado Springs and a quiet flight into Los Angeles, the huge chartered flight south was crazy, because there was noise everywhere and colors, red, white and blue. There were media types, small television cameras, people with microphones and recorders, and someone in the back was giving a news conference. The plane must have been double decked because there was a staircase. Everyone was happy. When the plane finally landed in Rio, the team was mobbed as they exited the causeway into the terminal. There was loud cheering, a barrier to keep a way open for them to proceed, and police protection; it was a madhouse. When they got onto busses after being hustled by concerned security types, the group was more sedated, even scared. What was going on? Eggs hit the side of the bus she was in; it sounded like guns went off, and there were mobs of protesters all along the roadway leading from the airport. Soon they were in the countryside, traveling a peaceful highway to their destination.

Eventually she found herself in a luxury hotel, inside of the Olympic Village, where the mood was much more festive. Trisha had endured the torturous process of getting accepted into the Olympic Village, the security checks, the body scans, having all of her luggage opened and searched, and it had turned out to be a very good idea. Somewhere along the way, three athletes had been arrested and hauled away as terrorists. Now she was a free tourist inside of a very beautiful place among the greatest athletes in the world. She had had her picture taken countless times, had signed endless autographs, and had been asked to share her story over and over again, this all within the confines of a small city of athletes. Other Olympic athletes had sought *her* out.

The Opening Ceremonies were set to begin three days after they arrived. It was so exciting. *I can't believe I am actually a part of this*, she thought with a non-contradictory smile through tears of joy. The entire team was assembled in a large convention style room for the big announcement. They all wore the US Olympic Opening Ceremony outfit designed just for this one event, a loose fitting light jacket designed to breathe, cast in blue with white stars across the front on the right hand side, bejeweled in red and white diagonal stripes, all hand stitched. The matching slacks were blue with an inlaid American flag on each pocket. In so many other ways though, the athletes differed. Some had the jackets open in the front, others carried cameras, and a few had on oversized sunglasses. Tonight, the Americans would continue the tradition of a wild and rambunctious group of 600 athletes of all sizes, races, and backgrounds. They would be a sight to behold.

Larry Probst, the head of the Committee, was speaking, but Trisha could not hear a word he said. The atmosphere was electrically charged. Every athlete was there, save the few who could not attend due to training prohibitions. There was just too much going on. ". . . and so with obesity as the calamity of the modern era, we have chosen one special athlete to carry our flag into Maracana Stadium tonight. Trisha Jean Martin, please come forward." Trisha never even heard him and was completely taken off guard when those around her, friends that had already grown to more than just an acquaintance, became animated. Everyone cheered, staring at her and she didn't even know what for. When it dawned on her what had happened, she nearly fainted.

Later that evening as the US Olympic athletes waited their turn in line to enter the pageantry of the Opening Ceremonies, an interminable wait for the athletes, most of whom were partying with friends, the lone marcher of the bunch, the American Flag Bearer, stood alone in front of the red, white, and blue mob of participants, pondering just how fortune had played its part in her most unlikely life . . .

* * *

. . . The 2011 Las Vegas Marathon burst into her mind. Since finishing third in Spain some months earlier, Trisha had intensified her training into something unimaginable, pushing herself to beyond any limit or barrier that restricted belief in her potential. She was hungry to win again, knowing that what was once unthinkable, had become the mandate. Gone was any self-pity from the bad years. Now what she wanted was to make up for lost time. There had been more than 44,000 participants in both races, the half and the full marathon.

By many standards, the race had been a mess. There were complaints all around about how the race was handled, but for Trisha it had been a blur from the front of the pack. She won in 2:47:34, her first outright victory in fourteen years. In less than two years she had completed the comeback of the century. The win, just a year removed from the Miracle in Las Vegas, had absolutely nothing to do with why she thought of that particular race while waiting to enter the stadium as the American Flag Bearer. In all the delirium at the finish line, amidst all the attention, surrounded by television cameras, microphones, screaming fans, the Las Vegas media, her team going crazy, there was one, a lone man at the edge of the crowd capturing her much divided attention. It was so chaotic at the end that day. The wind was blowing December cold, creating a biting chill, coupled with the aroma of December in Vegas out on the Strip. Even now she could smell the food, the brews and also an arid smoke wafting through the loud scene. A rock and roll band was blaring away close by. Trisha had to force herself not to look at the handsome gentleman, for to do so would give away her advantage in a conversation sure to follow. He stood back, allowing a guarded smile on his face, drawing every ounce of energy from the moment. He did not look the least bit surprised. Trisha had not seen or heard from him in some time. Was she with him?

"Trisha, we are almost ready . . ." Poof, the daydream was gone. "We need to make sure the harness is properly set. It'll be a jungle behind you as your unruly teammates hurtle themselves to glorious idiocy. You, however, will be marching like an English Royal Guardsman, well, something like that," the choreography specialist giggled. "You can smile, in fact, we insist that you do. You're allowed to have fun." Again, the runner was caught up in the excitement of the moment.

Flag bearer, can you believe that? I get to carry our flag.

The spectators inside of the stadium were cheering as each of the countries presented their athletes. Trisha took time to relish the moment. She was more than just an athlete. She was a flag bearer in the Parade of Nations at the Olympics. Up ahead she could hear the names of those just in front the American team. "The Republic of Turkey," the announcer bellowed in quiet respect. You could hear the Turkish athletes in jovial fashion express their joy as they entered. Pride welled within Trisha Jean Martin and they inched just a bit forward. This was surreal. How could this be happening to her? Was this really real or was she dreaming. "Turkmenistan," and they inched forward again. The night breeze was hot, considering August was one of the cooler months down this way. There was also some moisture in the air and it was not the rainy season either. Additionally, anyone could feel the electricity in the air. "Tuvalu," the voice rang again. Trisha had never heard of them and didn't notice their flag, but there they were, all three athletes marching together, the one in the middle carrying the oceanic island's national flag. "The Republic of Uganda," and their fifteen competitors started a jumping and celebrating frenzy. It was amazing to see. Trisha, by now could see into the festive capacity-filled stadium. She would be the first American to enter and knew that all eyes would be on her. "Ukraine . . . United Arab Emirates," and then, and then, well, they were marching through the tunnel into the Opening Ceremonies. "The United States . . ."

* * *

He was a very busy man, succumbing to the demands of his profession above almost everything else. There were a couple of exceptions to the rule, but not many. Summer, his favorite time of the year, had been both fulfilling and lonely, satisfying because of the time he had spent with his twin daughters, alone because his wife and best friend was off on very important business. She was currently out of the country. The short drive home from his comfortable offices had been akin to walking through molasses. He seemed to catch every red light. The humidity added an unbearable accent to the heat during the desert monsoon season and the air conditioning in his car had gone out on the way in this morning. He just wanted to get home to the television set. His daughters were out of town in the care of his sister-in-law at Disneyland. He had the house to himself. By the time he had showered and changed into something comfortable, the Opening Ceremonies were well underway. He turned on the television just in time.

* * *

Trisha's heart was racing a thousand miles an hour. This flag bearing business had changed the scope of the experience and she was smiling from ear to ear. Again the public address announcer's voice shook the air with thunder. "The United States of America!" She did not expect the eruption of noise and ovation reserved for them. It was deafening. Chants of U..S..A.., U..S..A.. echoed from around and around as the spectators made their presence felt. American flags popped up in the most patriotic scene she had ever witnessed. Trisha had listened from outside as the Brazilians entered, but now wondered if the crowd had been even more vocal for the USA. America was still a very popular place, at least among Olympic sports enthusiasts. She took just a moment to look over her shoulder at the team and notice how even NBA basketball players were caught up in the spirit of what was happening. It was a sight she would never forget.

* * *

"Here come the Americans and it is time to reveal the secret that only I have known outside of the team itself." The host, Bob Costas went on. "The American Flag Bearer is Trisha Jean Martin. The choice of the long distance runner is based on overcoming adversity. As many of you have known, Trisha Martin has fought a battle with her weight and won it to become the current American record holder in the marathon. The US Olympic Committee chose her to be an example to others . . ."

Brad couldn't believe what he was seeing. He was hoping to get a glimpse of her somewhere in the throng of Team USA's athletic contingent and all he had to do was watch her carry in the flag. The woman was simply amazing. From the moment he had laid eyes on her back in Germany those years ago she had surprised him at every turn. To this day he had never seen the Rubik's Cube solved, except by her and now this. His memories flooded with the blur of the past . . . back to 2011 when his life changed again.

"Brad, do you remember when you came here and how we met?" For some special reason, Annie seemed to be very serious as they visited out where they had developed a tradition of eating breakfast together. He had a big surprise for her. Of late things had become a bit strained, but Brad thought everything was fine. They loved each other and could work anything out. "Do you remember, Captain Peterson? Tell me what you know of our meeting."

"Well," he smiled, thinking back about the trip in from the hospital ship on a chopper. "It was the middle of the night. You were there along with others from here at Landstuhl. What I remember most was your smile and how you looked to be interested in me as a person and not because I was a celebrity."

"That's correct, Bradley." What came next were the hardest words ever to come out of her mouth, a total lie, every word. "Unfortunately, that wasn't the truth. I have no interest in you as a person. All I ever wanted was to advance my career. I do not love you; in fact, I never did . . ."

"That's crap. Who put you up to this? I am so tired of all this Army nonsense. I volunteer myself to help others and all I get for it is a bunch of garbage. I'm not stupid, Anne . . ."

"Don't be silly, soldier. I don't care who you used to be. You're a cripple now. I am not throwing my career away on the life of a has-been." She began to laugh, wickedly. Suddenly, out there in the grass behind the hotel, though summer was upon them, the wind whipped chilly, the leaves fluttered in the air, a cloud floated in to cover the sunlight and darkness fell upon Captain Bradley Peterson. Everyone gets theirs. This was his. His fall had been as meteoric as his rise to fame had been and he was no longer the man he thought he was. He was no longer a man at all.

"Don't call me, Brad, not ever. I think you should check into the psych ward of any loony bin that takes charity and shake your life away," she laughed again. Then she turned and walked away. What had once been a promising day, accentuated by the ring in his pocket

that now weighed as much an elephant, had become the numb shock of a new reality. He was totally alone. As Annette Chappell disappeared into the building and out of his life, Brad's hands began to shake violently, tears of abandonment welled up within him, and he began again to sob in self-pity . . .

As Bradley watched Trisha carry in the American Flag, his thoughts once again turned to the past . . .

How did I know she was lying? I stood back in the trees and watched her leave. The forlorn look on her tear-reddened face and the way she moved gave her away. Why, though? The answer to that question had come in a dream never to be forgotten. *For the longest time after I had been in that dream I could not let go of the amazing experience. My grandfather, Tag Peterson, had told me of her damaged soul, how it had been taken advantage of by strange creatures, and how she had been used by a former lover to break her free of what was really the love of her life. My heart goes out to her this very day, wherever she is. I hope she has found true happiness.*

Bradley had been the recipient of a wakeup call just short weeks after the dream. He was still numb and lost, but had moved on to Walter Reed in Bethesda, Maryland for further evaluation. The national medical center was his home for that unforgettable summer. He well remembered sitting in the waiting room of the psychologist he was seeing and noticing the *Runner's World* magazine on the coffee table. There on the front cover was, yup, Trisha Jean Martin. The lead story jumped right off the page. Trisha had finished third in Madrid and was the fastest American woman in the race! He was both surprised and confused all at the same time. The woman was incredible. If she was that good, what the hell was she doing lumbering along in Frankfurt? The surge of adrenalin had the hair on the back of his neck standing up. Who was this creature from his childhood? What was Frankfurt all about? He wanted to call her right then and there, but, alas, he had lost her number. From that moment his thoughts turned away from the past he had with Annie and to getting back in front of Trisha Martin. It would take him the rest of the year to make that happen.

Bradley was jolted from those memories when his phone rang. He considered not taking the call so he could finish watching Trisha and the Americans enter the Olympic Stadium, but the call was from his office. They would not bother him this late unless they had a good reason so he let go of the television, muted the sound, and answered the telephone.

"Dr. Peterson, I have a potential case on the other line and he needs to be seen tomorrow. I see your schedule is booked solid . . ." Apparently a young teenage boy was in need of his special brand of medicine. If what he was hearing on the other end of the line played out as he feared, his plans for the next two weeks would be thwarted. His heart sank.

* * *

"Time out USA, and there is just 16.4 seconds to go in the game. The heavily favored Americans are down by two points to the hometown hero Brazilians. The basketball arena is going wild right now. You can barely hear yourself think in here. Brazil has never trailed in this game. Every time the Americans mount a comeback, they have responded to the challenge. This matchup was billed as the game of the Olympiad ever since the pairings were released and it has not disappointed."

The announcers had to yell into their microphones to be heard over the screaming throngs. This was Olympic basketball at a fever pitch, an upset in the making, and with the exception of a couple of thousand USA fanatics waving flags and yelling at the top of their lungs, it was all Brazil all the way around the court, a sea of yellow, blue, and green. From any standpoint the mob mentality inside looked like an ambush.

"OK, here we go. Paul inbounds to Blake Griffin over the outreached hands of Tiago Splitter. He dribbles down low and then throws the ball out front to Irving. Irving passes the ball inside to Paul who feeds it along the baseline to Anthony Davis. Nine seconds to go. Davis launches the three. No good! LeBron James gets the rebound and races out past the three point line. His shot is blocked. There's just 3 seconds to go in the game. Harden races to the ball just ahead of Anderson Varejao and puts up a prayer from twenty-five feet as time expires, GOOD! TEAM USA WINS! The Americans have escaped with a wild three thrown up by James Harden. Oh my, folks. If I ever see another finish like this again they'll have to check me into the hospital. My heart is down under the table somewhere. The crowd is sitting in shocked silence and the Brazilians are wandering around the court, dazed as they have surrendered their lead for the first time at the worst time. The USA team is celebrating on the floor along with those few American fans that somehow got their hands on tickets for this game. We'll be back for a recap of this afternoon's contest, but first we need to check in with Bryant Gumbel at Olympic headquarters for a look around at what is happening elsewhere. Oh, my, what a game. I'm Mike Tirico for Jeff Van Gundy. So long for now from HSBE Arena where twelve American basketball players have just stunned Brazil and about 15,000 basketball crazies. I am exhausted, Jeff."

"Thanks, Mike. Wow, what a game. The irony in the Olympic movement has been the spirit of competition, from arenas, both large and small. Contrast to the stage others use to prey upon the civilized world. These games have certainly had their share of both, but so far this basketball contest takes the cake. Do you need a breather? I do. Let's check in for a moment at the archery range where as usual the Koreans are dominating the competition.

"Good afternoon, folks. We are watching Seo Hyang-Soon obliterate the field. Today it is the Americans who get to schooled by the very best in the world as . . ."

* * *

The runner was working out for the last time before the race. Trisha Jean Martin, along with several runners from various countries, had taken a short flight down the coast to Florianopolis and were working out on its marathon route, a very similar experience to the coastal course they would be competing on in Rio. Stanley was in front of her on the back of a motorcycle facing to the rear so he could keep an eye on his protégé. She felt physically fit and ready to go, was running at a pretty good clip, and so let her mind drift into the past, thinking once again of how her life came together after she won her first marathon . . .

The Las Vegas Marathon, at least for Trisha Jean Martin, had been over for more than an hour. She had put on a sleek Adidas warm up, dismissing Stanley and telling him that she would find another way home. *He winked and then went his way. Stanley's fiancé, just a few feet away, looked like she wanted him to herself and was pleased. Finally the attention had waned and still he just stood there. Trisha had done everything in her power to ignore the fact that she knew Brad Peterson was waiting patiently for his chance to visit with the victor, and now there was no one left to buy her more time. She was terribly nervous. He looked a bit smug. There were others milling about as runners passed through the finish line, all decked out in multi-colored running outfits, most looking terrible at the end of their ordeal and hardly able to keep moving. Their families and friends cheered as each one made it through. The band played on and the loud speaker chimed in and out with announcements every few seconds. Brad had not called, sent an email, or in any other way tried to communicate with her since they'd been in Germany together. She was certain that he had moved forward with Annie, and so had allowed their moment together to slip gracefully into the past. Once time started to go by, she had quietly dismissed her scheme and had moved on with life, burying the pang of loss into hard training, the type of work that had paid off for her in a huge way. All of a sudden he had shown up and was visible again. As she approached, Trisha smiled in the way a friend who had not seen that special someone for years would, and began the long walk to where he was standing.*

"Why, Bradley. It is so nice to see you . . ." Trish started with an edgy and nervous voice. He picked her up and squeezed the life out of her, then held her close and whispered in her ear. "That was the most incredible performance I have ever seen, Trisha Martin. Who are you?"

He seemed very comfortable for a chap, supposedly a best friend variety, who was looking like the type of man who communicates with females in guy-time. "Just Trisha." That was pretty weak.

"I've never known anyone personally who has actually won one of these things at this level. Is there anything you can't do?"

His body was pressed close to hers, the heat of it providing comfort against the December cold of a Las Vegas night. His arms were still around her waist and his breath, just inches from her lips, had an intoxicating effect. Trisha had just accomplished the impossible with energy to spare. When she crossed the finish line, running through the tape, she was certain that her life was complete and whole. Now her knees had become wobbly. She had to admit that having a man hold her felt very good. She kissed him this time. "There are a lot of things I can't do, Brad. It just so happens that running isn't one of them. Before I turned professional I hadn't met any winners either. It is so good to see you. I'm having trouble sorting this out. Why are you here?" *That was lame. I am coming off like a ditz.*

"By here, do you mean at the race? I'm a running fan in case you forgot. Here at the finish line? I have a childhood friend who forgot to tell me that she is a professional runner the last time we got together. Ever since I wandered in front of a Runner's World magazine with her picture on the cover I wanted to see her cross the line. Fortunately, since it's a bit cold out, I did not have to wait long since she won the frigging race." Trisha started laughing. *Brad was still funny, too.* "Perhaps you mean why I am here in Las Vegas. It happens to still be where I'm from and I wanted to come home for Christmas."

"Oh, I see. Well, welcome home for Christmas, Captain Peterson, or can I call you Brad?" They were walking away from the finish area. Every few feet someone would approach and ask for a photograph or an autograph, or both.

"By all means, feel free to call me Brad, Trisha. By the way, I have something here. Can you please autograph my very own copy of Runner's World, the edition with you on the cover for the first time? Later on when I'm flat out of money, I can sell it for a few thousand bucks and get myself a new start in life." He actually went into his back pocket, producing the magazine and a sharpie he'd retrieved from his left front pocket, smiled in that not so genuine fashion and handed them over.

She obliged him. "How would you like this addressed, Sir?"

"Well, you could write 'to Brad from Trisha,' or maybe something more formal like 'to Captain Bradley Peterson, US Army.' Then there is the more intimate, 'to the love of my life' if you are so inclined."

When she looked into his eyes, reading his mind as if they were still kids, she began to wonder if he had given himself away, or if she had? Some things, like riding a bike, never change. They were starting right up where they left off as high school kids again. Sweat began to bead on her forehead even though it was cold out. Trisha tried as hard as she could to hide her real feelings. Her palms grew sweaty. She felt the loss of energy as her body flushed into weakness, an emotion quickly followed by a surge of powerful hope. *Is this what love feels* like? "Ha!" She had to think fast. They were walking into the hotel and Brad still had no idea where they were headed. "I need to think of just the right words, Bradley." Slowly, slowly but surely, the little high school girl in the 31-year-old body began to regain her confidence. "You haven't even invited me to dinner. You are engaged to one of the most beautiful women I have ever met. How presumptuous of a man are you?"

"How about dinner for the winner, Trisha? Is that a fair price for an old friend to get your autograph?"

Was there a race today? Didn't I just win my first marathon? If not for the need to hydrate more and the soreness, I would have forgotten the day since this man walked back into my life. Be careful, Trish. "Tell you what; I am going upstairs to clean up. Stanley has a staging room that has my stuff in it. I'll autograph your magazine, Bradley, if you think of just the right place for us to get a simple bite to eat. I'm starving and have no ride home, so you'll have to drop me off after we eat. Deal?"

"It's a deal, Trish." In that moment he looked like the cat's meow.

Trisha walked into an elevator; her hair was snugly tied into tight pigtails that were wrapped together for competition. What little makeup that remained had run its course. Her baggy warm-up suit was sweaty, and she needed a shower, not just to clean her body, but to wash away the pain of running more than 26 miles. Since she had just won a professional race, Trisha Martin was feeling much better than she looked in spite of the aches and pains of the day. She reappeared in just thirty minutes, a completely different person.

Brad was elegantly dressed in a casual, but very smart pair of stove pipe dark blue, belted jeans, a cream colored shirt, with a two-shaded blue striped tie. His sport jacket, which was brightl green, complemented his skin color and hair perfectly. He wore no socks underneath his brand new looking brown suede shoes. Trisha felt the need to choose something nice, too. Her well stocked room left her with good choices. She picked out an off-white heavier wool dress with a ruffled front section buttoned tight to the waist, and then flaring all the way to the bottom. The long cuffed sleeves included large matching buttons, and simple jewelry marked her as tasteful but not gaudy. The dress was conservative, warm and yet it accentuated her figure perfectly. Tight black ankle length leggings, visible from about *four inches above the knees clung perfectly and highlighted her silver greyish high top laced three inch heels. Trisha knew how to put on makeup. The stylish outfit was completed by a lavender Louis Vuitton Artsy shoulder bag. With her hair now flowing to a tiny waist it was possible to walk right past her and not recognize that she had just finished a marathon. When she next saw him, the smile of her ruby lips coupled with a refreshing but sexy fragrance, presented Bradley Peterson with the formidable task of behaving himself in the presence of true beauty.*

"Well, taxi driver, where am I taking you to dinner? I have a check in my purse that is burning a hole in my desire to spend money tonight. I won the race!"

"Congratulations; you're not taking me to dinner, Barbie. It's my turn to pay if you remember correctly. You got away with that the last time we shared a table." Brad slipped his arm around her waist, tugged her to his side, kissed her on the cheek, and began walking her to the back of the hotel where his car was self-parked.

Trisha Jean Martin was dizzy with expectation. Where's Annie?

* * *

Stanley Burton, Trisha Martin's running coach and trainer chimed in on the tiny microphone in the runner's ear, jolting her from a perfectly wonderful daydream. "Trisha, be careful with your foot plants. We don't want to risk an injury today now do we? It also looks like you are running a bit too far forward. Just because we are here doesn't mean you don't have to pay attention to technique. In addition, you can circle the legs just a bit to increase stride if you know what I mean. Are you daydreaming again back there? Come on, now—focus. We're not on vacation like everyone else, you know.

Just then Stanley's voice was gratefully drowned out by the roar of a low flying helicopter, now making pace just off of the road out over the ocean beach. Trisha didn't have to wonder who that was, what with the NBC insignia on the tail shaft and two television cameras jutting out of its side.

* * *

"Welcome back to your headquarters for Olympic coverage on NBC. We hope that you enjoyed the diving competition this afternoon. Remember to tune in later this evening when Greg Louganis and Cynthia Potter bring you the finals in both the men's and women's divisions.

"By way of announcement, Team USA will take on Spain in the next round of Olympic Basketball. It is something we can all look forward to after this afternoon's thriller. We are about to head next to the *Barra Velodrome* where Todd Harris and Jamie Bestwick are all set to go with Indoor Cycling Team Sprints. The favorites for gold today are Belgium, France, and Germany. The UK and Team USA both think that they'll have something to say about the outcome. We'll see.

"Right now it is time for a little fun. Check out Randy Moss. He's been flying around in a helicopter trying to find our Olympic Marathon hopeful, Trisha Jean Martin. She's practicing down the road a bit on the coast. Randy, what have you got for us?"

"Good afternoon everyone; welcome to our *'lookout'* segment. As you may know by now, each day, someone here at NBC takes a closer look at one of our athletes as they train for their event. Today we are spotlighting Trisha Martin. When Martin runs her marathon in just a few days, you will not see her hair flowing freely like it is right now. As is the case with any serious athlete, Trisha's locks will be tied down and out of the way. I know, I know. This is frivolous stuff folks, maybe she would be offended. We think not. Trisha Jean Martin just signed a multi-million dollar endorsement contract with Vidal Sassoon. The beneficiary of her contract is the Roger Martin Foundation, a non-profit dedicated to helping gifted and yet disadvantaged the world over. I find it amazing that these very special people, and on a far larger scale than anyone really knows, take the time and effort to reach out to those in need. I am going to try and get her to wave for us.

* * *

There was Randy Moss hanging out of the helicopter with a Vidal Sassoon sign asking for a wave to the home crowd. He had on a funny harness as he leaned forward, drifting ever closer to the road where Trisha was running along. Stanley was howling in her ear to get them away so that she could continue her workout unabated. Even if Trisha could hear him, she would not have done that. *Why can't I have some fun, too? Watching Stan jump around all agitated is amusing.*

He looked silly and so she started to laugh, not for the camera, but at Stanley Burton. Trish looked up at Moss, started mouthing USA, USA, USA, first pounding on her heart and then waved while she continued to laugh at her trainer.

"There she is, folks. Trisha Jean Martin, the American marathon record holder, waving and smiling for all of us. That about wraps things up from here, Bryant. I'll see everyone for track and field preliminary heats in several events later this evening."

* * *

"Mom, I'm scared of that place, it is so creepy looking. You know what it looks like? It's like a melting wax building. Truthfully, Mom, that's a stupid place. I should know, too, since I get all A's, even in spite of my headaches." Young Billy Dace was with his mother on their way in to meet with Dr. Brad Peterson, the famous war surgeon. Billy had studied all about Captain Peterson and what he did during the war. Billy always knew about everyone; he was sometimes known as the obnoxious genius, the little kid with all the answers, and most of the time his answers were right. He was up half the night preparing for his conversation with a true American hero. Everyone knew Dr. Bradley Peterson. Once they had made their way into the building and found his office, they were waived back into a comfortable patient's room. Instead of an aseptic white cloth table jutting out from the wall, there was a small desk, backed by a very comfortable office chair and with a modern computer on top. The patient, and this time his mother too, were seated in a plush, blood red leather loveseat. The coffee table in front of them provided many entertaining and informative reading choices. There was also a remote for changing the channel of an oversized HD-3D flat screen television mounted on the wall across the little office room and even several of the special eyeglasses that were used when viewing 3D television.

Young Mr. Dace went for the computer on the desk. "Billy, get away from the doctor's computer. Sometimes I wonder just how smart you are, and sometimes I wonder something else altogether." William Dace's mother had been chasing him for fourteen years. He was an unquenchable knowledge-seeking machine. Perhaps one day he would harness his genius, learn to stop crossing lines and grow up, but that day was certainly off in the future.

"Mom, how long will it be until Nurse Janis gets here? I feel another headache coming on. Now that I know what's wrong it is only a matter of time until they give me the right medicine and the pain will go away. Mother, it is starting to hurt again. Oh, Mom, please have them help me."

In just a matter of moments, right there in the doctor's patient room, the boy was slipping into another episode. Though he could see love and concern on her face, and knowing that they were in the right place, he also knew that she had no idea how to help him. When the pain started up again, always on its own, he would go from feeling normal to wanting death in just minutes. Though it seemed like hours, in fact the nurse came through the door just five minutes later. The very serious looking lady was not Nurse Janis as he expected, but someone totally different. "Where is Nurse Janis? She is always the one who sees me first," the young man worried aloud. He was obviously in great pain.

"Hello, young man. My name is Margaret Ross. I am a special physician's assistant to Captain, um, Doctor Bradley Peterson, who is seeing you today. Is it OK if I work with you? I assure you that Nurse Janis knows I am here and she completely trusts me to get today's visit started."

She was very reassuring, and a very pretty nurse. Billy Dace started to cry. He tried as hard as he could to hold the tears; he was embarrassed to be seen crying in front of a total stranger, but the pain was becoming unbearable. "My head hurts again. It really hurts. Can you give me something for it?"

Nurse Ross smiled comfortingly, "I'll be right back." She was gone, perhaps one minute or less and came in with two pills and a small cup of water. "Take these right now. The doctor has approved them and has read your chart."

"What, specifically are they, Nurse Ross?"

She was caught completely off guard. This was the type of a question usually asked by someone knowledgeable and interested in medicines, but never from a young teenage boy.

"Nalbuphine. It is a pain medication . . ."

"You're going to give me a potent narcotic? Normally I would avoid something so strong, but my head really hurts." He took the pills and swallowed them with the drink of water. Even though it would take minutes for the cause to become the effect, the knowledge that relief was coming seemed to settle him a bit. "I'm sorry. I didn't mean to interrupt you. I also heard you refer to Dr. Peterson as Captain. Do you know him from when he was in the Army?"

"That's where I met the doctor. I worked with him there and he also saved my life when I was stung by a very dangerous scorpion."

"Tell me the story, please, pretty please. I want to hear one of his stories. Wow, you knew him in the Army. You're so lucky." He looked pleadingly into her eyes.

Suddenly the boy seemed to forget his headache and so she obliged him. "We were out in rural northern Iraq, set back from a battlefield in a little makeshift medical area . . ."

"You had set up a triage?" Billy was very excited now.

"Yes, actually it was already set up. We were the last ones to arrive." She was taken back again. This kid was very intelligent. "How old are you now, Billy?" She leaned back, put her right foot forward and began tapping her toe with both hands firmly planted on her hips. If she were not fighting a sarcastic smile, he may have thought her serious. "Are you telling us the truth about your age? It is very important that we have accurate biographical data on who you are and your vocabulary is way stronger than it should be." She read the compliment from the countenance on his face. Margaret had won herself a friend. Telling the story of how Brad Peterson had worked through that night, her last in combat duty, had been whittled to a science. First Lieutenant Margaret Ross never got tired of telling Brad Peterson stories. She hated to admit, even to herself, that in this one area, she had a tendency to embellish, so when Brad walked in the door right in the middle of the story, she got a bit tentative.

"Oh, by all means, Nurse Ross. Please finish the lie for us," he laughed as he walked into the room, all smiles. Dr. Peterson was sharply dressed; he didn't really look like a doctor, but he did hold a file folder in his left hand.

Young William Benjamin Dace simply stared at him; he eyed both of them really, in awe as one might feel in the presence of heroes. For someone who had a splitting headache, or did have just a few minutes ago, Billy was sure he was the luckiest person on earth. His mother sat there and let him have all the ground he wanted. Her son was so smart that she relied on him to handle the doctors. It wasn't that she thought he was capable enough, just that he was far more capable than she was. In the manner of one genius to another, the boy gathered his wits, stood, extended a hand and introduced himself. "Hello, Doctor Peterson. I'm Billy Dace. It is a pleasure to meet with you today."

Brad gave the boy respect due any man, shaking his hand firmly and looking directly into his eyes. *Never be fooled by age. Intelligence is its own breed of humanity.* "The pleasure is all mine, son. My wife is out of the country right now. I had planned on joining her, but it looks to me like I will be getting to know you instead. My understanding of your situation has more to do with your diagnosis of the problem. I have read the file, updated the data, and think we should get started by moving onto the same page. Someone of your intellect must have heard somewhere that a doctor who treats himself has a very bad patient. In the interest of fairness, young Doctor Dace the Ace, do bring me up to speed if you will. Please, by all means, help me dispel the myth. Patient, heal thyself." Brad smiled, Margaret stood behind the boy, with hands reassuringly resting on his shoulders, now assuming the role of protecting the child from the master. Billy's mother sat quietly on the couch looking as if the conversation had gone completely over her head, and Billy himself took the bait.

"I'm suffering from cluster headaches." Billy Dace sounded quite confident. Brad listened, paying close attention, pulled a pen from the pocket of his jacket, and then opening the file as if to add specific data to the existing chart. He jotted little notes down as the boy went on. "The pain is always on the left side of my head. First, it starts in waves and intensifies for a couple of hours, then suddenly without warning the throbbing comes and goes like pitching machine shooting baseballs into my head. After a couple of hours, the ache goes away and I feel normal for a while." The boy then turned to his mother and asked her to hand him his file. He actually had his own chart. "You see, Doctor Peterson, I have a thorough record of what is going on for you to review. It includes dates, the intensity of the pain for each bout, how long they lasted, what I think triggers them, a list of all medications I have tried and whether they worked or not This pain medication I am on right now seems to be working very well, so perhaps we should move to the stronger narcotics. What do you think?"

Brad studied his work, admitting to himself that this kid was better prepared than almost anyone he had ever seen. "I am very impressed, son. Based on what you have had to work with so far, I would be inclined to agree with your diagnosis. Have you considered any other type of conclusion? Do you know what I do for a living?"

Billy smiled up at the surgeon. "You just happen to be the world's leading expert in pediatric brain surgery. I haven't thought of anything else. If there were something big wrong in there, wouldn't my cognitive development be stunted?"

"Perhaps it would, Billy, and maybe not. Why would your doctor, who could treat cluster headaches perfectly well himself, schedule an appointment for you to meet with me?" Brad always hated breaking the news to a kid, and the young man did look concerned all of a sudden. His mother looked positively ashen. Her countenance had gone completely white. She remained silent, knowing now that her fears were about to turn to nightmares.

"That's the one thing I haven't quite figured out yet, Doctor. This condition is always treated with medicine, diet and exercise."

Brad went on. "Perhaps objectivity, or the lack of it, is one of the foremost reasons that physicians do not diagnose themselves and prescribe their own treatment. Even I have doctors who I go to. You wish for something and cannot objectively analyze reality. Here, let me show you something further." He opened the file and pulled x-ray sheets from the scans taken just yesterday. "OK, Dr. Dace." Brad smiled inwardly every time he referred to the boy as a doctor. The kid loved it. "Tell me what you see."

"Wow, Doctor Peterson. Is that a scan of my brain?" The youngster was excited and had completely forgotten that he had been suffering an episode just a few minutes ago. The narcotic had taken full effect. Billy's mother looked interested too, but she was just beginning to understand what was taking place now. In just a few seconds she would learn the awful truth. He seemed to have forgotten completely and had not put two and two together. The full color scan was very clear and simple for him to read. "The big squiggly area is the left hemisphere of the cerebrum. That is where conscious thought takes place. When looked at closely, I can see the different lobes. There in the back at the base of the brain is the cerebellum. It's connected to my spinal cord. This stuff is so cool. When I look into the center of my brain I can spot things like the hippocampus, the pituitary gland, the hypothalamus, and the medulla oblongata glands. I studied all of this on my own so that we could fix the problem together."

Brad was very impressed with this kid. He felt, if for just a moment, the enormous responsibility of protecting Billy Dace's future. This boy had so much potential. In truth, he valued all children the same. The chance to help kids like young Dace was what led him into this field. "That is a very professional and accurate look at how your mind works, my boy. Can you tell me about the dark spot, about the size of a ping pong ball, just above cerebellum?"

"No. I don't know what that is."

"Come on, Billy; take a guess."

"It doesn't look like it belongs there."

"Go on. Why doesn't it look like it belongs there?" Brad was ready now to drop the bombshell on his patient, and just as importantly on the young man's mother.

Billy began to look sullen. "I'm not suffering from cluster headaches, am I, Doctor Peterson? That's a tumor. I have a brain tumor. I'm going to die, aren't I?" Billy's mom began to sob openly.

Brad ignored her for the moment. "Not if I can help it, young Mr. Dace. What do you say we take a good look at the alternatives? You are doing a great job so far. What kinds of treatment do you suggest, Doctor Ace-man. You happen to be the smartest kid I have ever worked with. What choices do we have then at our disposal?"

"We have to decide whether it's malignant or not."

"That is the right first question, Billy. If it were malignant I would have you on the table already. We will be performing a small noninvasive biopsy at the end of our meeting today and will know the results by tomorrow. I am about 99% certain by the look of it that we are not dealing with a malignant tumor. That being said, we know this tumor needs to go. Do you have any other ideas?"

"We may want to try steroids, chemotherapy, radiation treatment, and proton therapy. I have read about some of those." The youngster's voice was cracking. There was a tear in his eye.

The boy was beginning to falter. He didn't want to say the word and Brad felt that the time had come. "What do you think about direct surgery, Billy?"

"Is that what you are recommending, Dr. Peterson?" Now young Billy Dace had grown white, just as his mother turned when she had seen the direction the conversation was heading.

"We might make progress with some of the other ideas, many of which you so eloquently mentioned. The tumor may also break open and cause problems that could go out of control. I hate to make a young lad like you man up at such a vulnerable time in life, but circumstances dictate the course of events here. We need to protect your future. If I go in now, or in three days to be more succinct, I can get it all, Lord willing, and you can hope to move on and become the doctor you show such great promise of becoming. Maybe I will last long enough to practice with you. How about it, William Benjamin Dace? I want to go in and fix this thing, permanently. Do I have your permission?"

Billy looked across the room at his mother. She looked far worse off than he did. Her body was quivering with fear. All of her dreams for this kid were now wrapped into the hands of a brain surgeon. Billy smiled, disarming his own mother's dreadful trepidation. "It's alright, Mom. This is Captain Bradley Peterson. I wouldn't let just anybody go inside my head. He is the greatest war hero ever." He looked up into the eyes of the good doctor, and then over at the nurse who had listened to the entire conversation without uttering a word. "Will you be assisting Doctor Peterson in surgery, Nurse Ross?" She nodded affirmatively, never wavering from the reassuring smile that adorned her from the moment she had walked through the door. "Doctor Peterson. Let's get that damned thing out of my head. I have a life to live and am not about to get beaten by a ping pong ball-sized tumor lodged in my brain. You go in and remove it. I promise to be a force for good all the days of my life and to never forget what you did for me. Sadly though, we will never be able to practice medicine together. I am destined for a life of politics. One day I am going to be President of the United States of America."

*   *   *

Trisha relaxed, shifted the seat back into a reclining comfort zone and stared out of the window of the bus. They had flown down from Rio in the morning, but were taking a scenic ride back up the coast on a luxury bus. The Federal Republic of Brazil was an amazing place. Trisha had been all over the world in recent years, comparing one place to another. She and her mother had taken stock of all the different nuances that any country they visited contributed to modern life.

In just the short time she had been here for the Olympics, Trisha had seen famous landmarks such as The Christo Redentor and Sugarloaf Mountain where she had the privilege of riding the tram all the way to the top. After the Olympics she was looking forward to touring Iguazu Falls and hiking Mt. Roraima. She slipped back into thought, once again reminiscing . . .

Just two hours ago, Trisha had never won a marathon of any kind, hadn't really been on much of a date, and certainly had no real plans for this evening. Tomorrow, she was expected to give a speech at the awards banquet, but tonight she was free. The year 2011 had been very good, even better than 2010 had been. She was earning substantial money, garnering attention that she didn't really want, and now was walking to the parking lot of the hotel with Brad. How could all of that happen so fast? Why was he seemingly courting her? Wasn't Brad engaged to Annette Chappell? She was so pretty and they had so much in common. Trish had casually mentioned her a couple of times, but Brad did not seem interested in talking about his fiancé. What was that all about? One thing was certain. Come hell or high water, she would get to the bottom of the Annie story before this little 'date' was in the bank. She would not be letting Brad Peterson off of the hook, not after the three of them had spent an entire evening together in Germany. What she had to consider was the how of it. There was no way that Brad Peterson was going to get the upper hand in this relationship, not tonight anyway. They walked on through the back of Mandalay

Bay and into the parking garage. Brad's car was on the top level. Trish wondered what he was driving. Men were so into their cars. She could understand quite a bit about a man just from the car he drove and how he kept it. Michael had taught her that, though they had never spoken of it. There was something else on her mind too, as they moved through the parking lot. He sure was cozy about the way he held her as they moved, especially for a man who was supposed to be engaged to get married. She wondered for the umpteenth time about Annie and what part she played in this picture, but had decided not to speak of it for the moment. It felt good to have him close, providing of course that he tried no funny business. She giggled at the sight of his ride. "You have a thing for old Chevys, Brad. This one is gorgeous."

"You remember my old '57 Chevy from high school." She could see that he felt her admiration, though the thought of it was perplexing. "This is the exact same car. I have kept it all these years."

"No way . . . this is not the same car. That one was old and rusty. It was green and white if I remember correctly."

"It's the same car, Trisha. I just kept improving it over the years as kind of a hobby. You have no idea how proud I am that you remembered."

"How could I forget? You drove it everywhere. I can still remember when you drove it to school right after you got a driver's license."

"Not that my ego needs to be stroked by a beautiful lady, one who is a professional athlete that just won a major race. I love your hair, by the way." Trisha could not hold back the smile that brought to her face. "Can you tell all the things I did to it? Care to take a try?"

"Sure, I'll try. I remember the old rust bucket better than you think. I only got to ride in it one time and my brother warned me about older boys. He told me to be careful around guys like you, though I'm not sure what he meant. Let's see; it is illusion blue for one thing. Let me be the first to compliment you on how incredibly shiny it is. There is chrome from one end to the other. Back then it had standard wheels with regular hub caps. Now the chrome includes those immaculate wire wheels that house perfectly scrubbed wide white wall tires. The trim looks brand new. Go ahead and pop the hood." Brad proudly obliged her. "Good Lord, the engine looks brand new. Even the underside of the hood looks new. There isn't any grease at all on that block. I'm going to take a leap of faith and say that this is a whole new engine.

Is it blue printed?" He nodded. "The matching upholstery is new in the inside too. You must have spent a fortune. Tell me, Brad. Does it still have the same VIN number? No, don't tell me that. I know it does and do you know why?"

"Why is that, love?"

Trisha was feeling very confident. "Because, Captain, those are the same license plates. I like that. It means that you're sentimental. You could have put "classic" plates on this beauty. It is most certainly an historic vehicle. It looks completely restored to original condition throughout."

"Well, not quite. There is one very distinguishing difference." He popped the trunk open and revealed a giant subwoofer. I went all out on the sound system. It is almost the only thing that's not original. Let's go."

The gentleman opened her door and she climbed into the seat. "Hey, Brad. I didn't know that the '57s came with seat belts."

Bradley had walked around the vehicle and was climbing into the driver's side. "They didn't. I got these from a place called Retro Belt U.S.A. No one is comfortable riding in a car without getting belted anymore. They look original though, don't they?"

Trisha, a little flabbergasted, was having trouble with hers and could not get it to work.

"There's something wrong with mine. It tries to work, and even clicks, but it just comes loose again."

Brad worked very hard at keeping a straight face. He put his best doctor's look on and reached over. "Here, let me have a look-see at it." His face was down in Trisha's lap and he was fiddling with the latch. Trisha's body heat was intoxicating, a mixture of her perfume, the unnatural intimacy of his proximity and angle. It was all he could do not to . . . "Trisha, I'm sorry to tell you that the latch is broken. I'll get it fixed just as soon as I get a chance. Um, well, see now, it looks like you have three choices. We can put you in the back seat. I assure you one of those belts work, or you can trust me not to get into an accident and just go without. I do not recommend that. The third choice is to scoot over and use the middle seat belt here next to me," he grinned devilishly.

"Is this some kind of a trick? Guys! You always seem to have something up your sleeve, don't you? Did you disable that belt just to get me next to you? You want me to sit there like someone's girlfriend in the old days?"

Brad laughed. "I wish I could take credit for it. You have to admit it; that's a great idea," he kept up with the horsing around while Trisha sheepishly slid next to her escort and buckled that belt smoothly. "I'll say one thing, Barbie. You look terrific tonight. If we added a matching retro scarf and put on some oversized and modified cat eye sunglasses, you'd fit the part perfectly." He slid his arm around his friend, kissing her on the cheek, and then chuckled at his good fortune.

This would be a night that Trisha would never forget. Dinner that evening at Brio was perfect. The atmosphere was quiet in the bar area where they ate. The food was fantastic. Catching up with Brad Peterson had been all that she had hoped. Once or twice she had looked for an opening to find out about Annie, but it was fruitless. He did not want to talk about her and so she left it alone.

Brad told her the reason he was in the old Chevrolet was because there were people living in his home where his other car was parked in the garage. He didn't want to go by the house. The Chevy was commercially stored and so he had gone there instead.

For the first time she began to wonder if he had a place to stay. There were two duffle bags in the back seat. "Bradley, where are you staying tonight?" She decided to bring it up since he would be dropping her at home in just a few minutes. It was nearly midnight already. After dinner they had strolled Town Center and ended up at Yard House for coffee and dessert. One of the things she enjoyed the most was that neither of them had wanted any alcohol.

As for Brad's sleeping arrangements he said, "Well, um . . . um . . . to be honest I hadn't decided yet. I am not looking for anything. It's just that I was running late and didn't think about it. Don't worry about that right now. There are a couple of buddies from the old days that aren't married. I was thinking of waking one of them up and imposing . . ."

"Would you like to sleep at my place?" Her date almost gave himself away. Men are such pigs. Did he want to sleep with her? There was no way that was happening. "You'll be sleeping on the couch, Mister. It's old and it is comfortable. My room is already occupied to the max . . . if you know what I mean."

393

His answer had been so weak, she almost started laughing out loud. "I wouldn't want to impose . . . but if you insist."

Thankfully the place was clean. Fortunately it was a couple of years later. Trisha would never have told him how hard it was not to invite him into her room, but with Annie in the picture . . . and the fact that she had never been with a man, which was her big secret, there was just no way for her to let him in like that. They arrived at her home in Whitney Ranch, back in Henderson. Within just five minutes she had outfitted the couch the best she could, provided him with towels, showed him how to operate the big flat screen television, and then disappeared into her own room with the door shut. For Trisha Jean Martin, hope had arrived in full bloom. Maybe Annie was out of the picture. That seemed like more of a possibility. Her status was something that would have to come out on its own. It was hard to go to sleep, and why not? The formerly down on her luck lady had just won a professional race and had the love of her life tucked away just down the hall. Finally, after an hour or so of quiet music from her television set, Trisha fell into a dreamy, peaceful sleep. It would not last for long.

At first, Trisha was startled by the sounds coming from her living room, a kind of muffled groaning. Was Brad dreaming? Was something else at play here? Perhaps he was not the person she had hoped he was. Then the groaning grew into whelps of pain and agony. He began to plead, "Not again, please, oh God, not again . . ." and then silence. By now, she was awake and concerned. Was he alone out there? She listened intently. He started up again; "Ah, ah, no, no, stop." Then he screamed at the top of his lungs. "Trisha, help me . . . please! Oh, God help me, please let me die. Trisha, where are you? Ahhhh! Oh, God help me. Nooooo! Trisha, help me, PLEASE HELP ME!"

Trisha quickly put on a robe and ran out into the living room, ready for anything. She found Brad asleep on the couch, right where she had left him. He was shifting and turning, all the while talking in his sleep . . . . . to her. She leaned forward and held him. "Brad, wake up. You're having a nightmare." Brad was sweating profusely. He was soaking wet.

He started screaming again. "Trisha, help me, oh God, help me. Help me die, please. Oh . . ."

"Bradley, wake up." Now she was shaking him, trying to wake him from the dream he was having. What do I have to do with his terrible

nightmare? He opened his eyes, looking into hers. At once the fear turned to resigned embarrassment. "Brad, what's going on? You were having such a bad dream that you were screaming for death. What is it, Brad? Tell me."

"Trisha, I am so sorry. I haven't had one of these in a long time, almost a month."

"What do you mean, Brad? What's going on? Are you plagued by bad dreams?"

"Yes, uh, yes, I am. I cannot make them go away either. They come and go on their own. Sometimes I have them every night for days on end and at other times they go away for a while. I thought that when I came home, I could be rid of them. I guess not, though. I am so sorry that you had to see this. Trish, I am so sorry."

"You're soaking wet, Brad. Do you have any other pajamas that you can change into?"

"I do." He reached into his duffle bag and pulled out a fresh pair and some underwear. "I'm going to make some coffee while you get more comfortable. We need to talk." With that she disappeared into the kitchen. When she returned about ten minutes later, Trisha brought in a fresh pot of brew, some flavored Coffee-mate, Splenda, along with radishes, carrots, and a couple of tubes of crackers with a nice hunk of cheese. Brad had changed clothing and cleaned up. Now he looked hungry. Together they stirred their drinks, one eating radishes, the other crackers and cheese. Quietly, they peered into each other's eyes, Brad looking a bit foolish and Trisha very curious. "Start talking, Doctor hero, and do me a favor. Just this one time, please don't hold back. I want to know what is going on with you."

"You'll remember the shaking episode I suffered in Frankfurt back in May . . ."

"I don't mean to interrupt you, dear. Would you indulge me and go back a bit further. What happened to you? The news said you landed on a dirt road . . ."

"All lies, it's a pack of lies that the media were told about my crash. In fact the whole thing about what happened to me in the first place is a bunch of crap!"

"Go on." Trisha noted a profound sense of disillusionment just from the tone of his voice. This man was totally conflicted.

"The story I am about to tell you is so classified that you can never repeat it. I don't know why I am telling you, but I just have to get it out. I have never told a soul what happened to me. I was out of Bagram's hospital on field duty, caught in a huge firefight up in the mountains, when I was extracted and sent on a black ops mission that went terribly wrong. I should have died in the jet crash. We were shot out of the sky and I was the only survivor. That is how I was captured. The story about the rough landing was a cover, a total fabrication. Someone higher up than anyone I know made a deal with the devil to have me operate on a kid, the son of a brutal dictator. Instead of getting to perform the surgery, we were shot out of the sky and I was captured by rebels. In and of itself, that ignited a civil war that is raging to this very day. You know how many people have died because of that one fact? I have nightmares about it, but while I was in captivity . . ."

Bradley went on to tell the story of his captivity and torture. He had even tried to provoke his captors into killing him in order to end the pain. It hadn't worked. The one sweet spot in the tale was of his rescue, engineered by Bob Hankle, his best friend in the military. *"You see, Trisha, I am a total mess. I have healed physically, but inside I am so screwed up that I don't think I will ever be whole. My life seems over in so many ways."*

"You're pretty young to be totally washed up for life, Brad. We'll have to see about that. I am betting on you making a full recovery and not just because I love . . . uh, like you so much. No matter what happens, you still have to live life one day at a time. Each twenty-four hour period has its own possibilities. I don't want to sound preachy, but for me life is meant to be lived by facing challenges. Otherwise, we don't really live; we just exist. I know you are facing yours. We just haven't figured it out yet. Notice how I said, we. I'm here for you. There is obviously not an easy or soft way to the bottom of this, but for now knowing that a solution does exist is what matters. I'd like to ask you a question about your dream. You don't have to answer if you are uncomfortable, but are you aware that you were calling out my name in your sleep? You were begging me for help. What was that all about?"

Brad looked completely caught off guard. He allowed his eyes to roam the room, glancing about this way and that, not able to look Trisha in the eye . . . *"Well, uh, Trisha . . . there is a bit more to my story."* Brad coughed nervously. He clearly didn't want to go into *what, if anything, Trisha Martin had to do with nightmares about his war service. "It has to do with how I handled my captivity. You see, Trisha, they drive you insane there. You're isolated, blindfolded, beaten, electrocuted, water-boarded and more. It's so unbearable."*

Brad started to shake and then to cry openly. She did empathize with his pain. She sympathized with the horrible nature of his unbelievable predicament. Why then did the cry show up looking like crocodile tears? "Here, here now, Brad." Trisha held him close to her chest. He just had enough time to munch down another cracker with cheese and take a sip of his coffee before she kissed his cheek and comforted his bared soul. "Don't worry, dear. Trisha is here to make it all better. It's a good thing you remembered that you were sleeping on my couch while you were dreaming so that I could come to the rescue and give you the help you needed, isn't it?"

Brad seized the opportunity to get out of this conversation alive. Was it possible? "That's it, Trish. In my dream you were trying to save me from the bad guys. I was reaching out to you. I think it was because we were together tonight . . . and . . . uh . . . I am so very comfortable in your presence. That has to be it." He spoke with a tiny but wry smile. The twinkle in his eyes, the hope that betrays, let him down this time.

Trisha wondered whether to push it . . . or not. It isn't like she had all kinds of experience dealing with men. On the other hand, what could be so hard about the truth? As much as she loved him, he was the love of her life; still he was lying. There was more to this story than met the eye. She intended to get to the bottom of things, and this time she was a bit more dramatic. "I'm sooo happy that you are comfortable in my home, Bradley Peterson. Can you remember the dream . . . vividly?"

"Well, it's a bit sketchy. I can remember it pretty well, though." Brad loaded another Ritz cracker with hard cheese, popped it into his mouth, and then took a deep breath before sipping his piping hot chocolate-flavored coffee. He had regained some confidence. The dream was over and he was worming his way out of a difficult situation. "I was blindfolded, with both arms and legs bolted to the ground. I was lying on my back, which was pinned to a crude wooden bench. My head was hanging over the edge. First they hit me with the electricity. I refuse to tell you how they applied it."

Trisha seemed grateful. That would have been too much information. "They spoke in broken English, telling me that I had to renounce my service as evil and predatory. When I would refuse they'd put hot and cold alternating soaked towels over my face while tipping the bench back. It was like drowning."

Trish was truly moved. The thought of those things happening to her guy was in and of itself unbearable. She felt the horror, though it was a bit tempered by his try at drama. There was another side to this story, though. She was aware, kind of anyway, of what he had been put through. That he was coy enough to use his sad story to hide behind something proved that he was a, a . . . , a man! This was an easy read.

"There, there, now. As long as you are under this roof, I'll let no harm come to you, poor Brad." She held him close; his head was close enough so that he could feel her heart beating. Thankfully her resting heart rate was very low. It had risen quickly while she held him, but she didn't think he'd notice. Trisha was rocking him back and forth, like a mother reassuring a suckling baby. He was eating the attention up. "So tell me again how I play into these horrible dreams."

His lying denial almost provoked her into a burst of empty laughter, but she held her tone, barely. "I'm having trouble understanding, Brad. Are you saying that this is the first time you have ever spoken my name out loud in a dream?" He nodded and she decided to take a risk. "Oh, that's funny. Annie called me a week ago and said it happens all the time."

Brad broke firmly from her grasp; there was fear from one end of him to the other. It almost looked like he had slipped back into the dream. Did he suffer from more than one kind of a nightmare? "What's wrong, Bradley? Does the cat have your tongue?" Still, he didn't say anything, but instead returned to nervously looking about Trisha's living room. Trisha smiled and kissed him on the forehead. "I'm lying, Brad. I haven't heard from her since the night we met for dinner, but the look on your face tells volumes. Where is she and what's going on? I'm tired of dancing around with this. Why are you being evasive every time I bring up your fiancé?"

"Ann is enrolled in medical school. She is out of the Army and is in training to become a medical doctor. I helped get her admitted and am very happy for her."

"Are you going back there for Christmas? I'm assuming she's somewhere back east right now. That's great. I am happy for her too,

for both of you really. Or is she going to join you out here for the holidays? Maybe we can all get together for a fun dinner again?"

"Neither."

"What do you mean, neither? Don't lovers spend the holidays together?"

"Neither means not either one; we are not spending the holidays together. We are not doing anything together. Annie and I are no longer an item, Trisha. She, uh, uh, well, I don't quite know how to say it. She dumped me." For a long moment he stared up into her eyes trying to look hurt. "I haven't seen her in many months. She did call me once in September and asked if we could think about things. By then my heart wasn't in it. I didn't like the way she left. Right or wrong I felt a bit used. I knew at the time she had been coerced into ending the relationship for reasons known only to her and someone else, but for me it was over." Silence followed.

There in the middle of the night, inside of Trisha's home, two young people, both very talented and accomplished in their own way, sat there looking at each other and not knowing what to say or do next. Finally Brad broke the silence. "Try to wipe the smile off of your face, Trisha. It doesn't become you in my hour of grief." She actually tried not to smile, albeit with no success. There was magic brewing in the air. The time had come for truth or dare. "I couldn't marry her in any event. I'm already married."

That wiped the smile off of her face in an instant. The change in her countenance was so dramatic that it was Brad who had trouble looking serious. "You're married!" She wondered if Brad could sense her profound loss of balance. The flush of defeat and the feeling of her stomach sinking were impossible to hide. Trisha just had absolutely no experience dealing with this type of a situation. What did he mean? How could he be married? The evening they had just spent together now presented her with very conflicting signals.

"I've been married for quite some time. We have two children."

"OK, OK. Why didn't you tell me this before? Good heavens, Bradley. You get around. Tell me about her. What is she like?" Now I want to be dead!

The girl he went on to describe sounded like someone very familiar. She was an accomplished professional in her field, stood about 5'6" and had long beautiful hair. She was very pretty, was honest and truly *liked to help others, and she was very smart. His wife had a perfect body, was incredibly sexy, and yet carried herself in dignified modesty. She was an excellent mother in spite of her very busy life. The kids were the joy of their lives . . .*

Trisha was jolted out of her daydream by the sound of a familiar voice. "I'm looking for a 14-letter word, starting with 'P' that describes a concept where the latter part of a phrase or a sentence is surprising or unexpected." The voice belonged to Jerry Schumacher, the running coach. Jerry was a nice enough guy. His group, OTC Elite, included some of the greatest runners in America, including Kara Goucher and Shalane Flanagan, Trisha's running mates at this year's games. Trisha had immense respect for Jerry, and though she had stayed with Stanley right there in Las Vegas, he had always been willing to give her pointers and provide the support of a good loyal colleague. Stanley and he were friends, too. In fact they were sitting across the aisle from each other right now working separate crossword puzzles. Trisha looked out over the ocean to her right. They were cruising rather serenely up the coastal road towards Rio and the Olympic Village, having earned the right to a relaxing touristy afternoon, once the long morning workout, their last before race day, was finished. The bus driver was pointing out this and that; it was just like they were on a tourist bus. Trisha had not been listening, though. *I know the answer, but I'm not saying.* She could see some of the others on the bus looking in their electronic dictionaries; *they most likely won't find it in any of those,* she thought. Jerry was getting flabbergasted. "There is something wrong with this puzzle; the word does not exist." Everyone was talking at once. Insults were flying back and forth, shielded by laughter and the good time everyone was having. It was great to be out of training for a change. Stanley accused Jerry of cheating because he was asking everyone for help. If anyone else gave him the answer, according to him, they would be in big trouble. He went back into his own puzzle, now trying to close the game and win it.

Sometimes Trisha wondered who was more competitive, the training coaches or the athletes.

"Trisha, you haven't said anything. Do you know the answer? I bet Trisha knows the answer. She knows everything. I heard that Trisha Martin can solve the Rubik's Cube in just a few minutes. What do you say, Trisha? Help me beat your boy Stanley over here. Be a good girl for once on my side."

"I'll bet you a hundred bucks that Trisha doesn't know the answer," said Stanley. He winked at Trisha. His wink betrayed a worried countenance, as he knew that the one thing everyone recognized about Trisha Jean Martin was that she hated lying; she didn't tell everything about herself, but she never told lies. It was a trademark of her personality that everyone agreed on. The group looked at her quietly. The driver had stopped his diatribe about local points of interest and had turned up the music, now blaring out Alan Parson's "Turn of a Friendly Card."

Jerry was the next to speak, and he was looking directly into Trisha's eyes, searching for an answer to his own question of whether or not she could produce the long word. As hard as it was to hide her knowledge, something she did must have given herself away as he smiled. "You're on, Stanley. Trisha, turn the card for me. What word, starting with the letter 'P' and lasting a whopping 14 letters, produces a sentence or a phrase with a surprise ending? Oh, and Trisha, not only will I have your trainer's hundred dollar bill in my pocket, but this word will unlock several other words and most likely give me the game. Now, what is the word?"

"I love you, Stanley. You know that. I was just daydreaming about something from my past. I also remember something from my very distant past, but I'll not be telling that story. Trisha was not comfortable making fun of herself because of obesity problems. She would not want to hurt anyone's feelings, but there was not a single overweight person on the bus, not even the driver. "That word, my fellow teammates, is paraprosdokian, p-a-r-a-p-r-o-s-d-o-k-i-a-n, paraprosdokian; I'm sorry, Stan."

The laughter was a roar and Stanley smiled as he handed the bill over to his friend. He grinned and shook his head. "Every time I underestimate that girl I lose something."

Kara Goucher jumped into the fray. "You know, Jerry, most of the time I don't agree with you. In fact, usually when I do agree with you, that only makes both of us wrong." Folks on the bus that got it chuckled. "But this time, I agree with you about Trisha. She's not only smart, but witty. I just think sometimes she runs too fast, like when I am trying to beat her in a race." This time everyone laughed . . .

Trisha stared satisfyingly out of the window, eying a beautiful sailing vessel out on the water, and then allowed herself to slip back into thoughts of Bradley.

"Go on, Doctor. Tell me more about this family of yours. Hold it, I have a specific question. Why would you be seeing another woman when you're married? Why would you take time out of your life to be with another when you are not only married, but have two adorable kids that are the joy of your life. It doesn't make sense." Trisha had turned as cold as ice. An hour ago she was asleep wondering about Brad's girlfriend. Then she was jolted awake with one of his nightmares. After that she learned that Annie was out of the picture, opening the door for her to finally find love in her long and lonely life. Now he was married and had two kids. Trisha was being put to what she commonly referred to as the fellowship test, and it was not fair. She was a person, too. She wanted him to continue because he was obviously in trouble. Her job, no matter what, was to leave all of the credentials at the door, forcing her to deny selfish needs and recognize that every human being has a right to a healthy soul. What about my health, damn it!

"We were separated at the time, but we're back together now, Trisha. I didn't want there to be any misunderstandings between you and me about this. Our friendship is way too important for me to be anything but clear tonight. I am married. I'm not separated or getting a divorce. I am not at liberty to see other women, and I am very happy about it. Please forgive me if I took you in any direction that wasn't appropriate."

Could the news get worse? This idea had been a bomb from the very beginning. All at once Trisha wished she had never seen this guy leaving for Army duty at just the same time she was changing her life. In that moment she wished many things, all of them negative. Was God trying to test her resolve to be a better person? Was she a bad person at heart? Her heart was so heavy it was all she could do not to pucker her lips into a tear-filled sourpuss-like expression. She fought the urge to let him see that. Trisha dug down deep, swearing off all men forever. This was so painful. On the very eve of her first marathon win, Trisha Martin was totally miserable. She was not capable of feeling right, but perhaps she could at least put up some sort of a fight to act right. She immediately began constructing a ladder designed to pull her out of this emotional abyss. She would find sunlight somehow. What Trisha could not understand, even as she began to lose the battle to hide her emotional distress, was the smirk on his face. She also detected a bit of uncertainty in his eyes. He wasn't being entirely truthful, wasn't a very good liar, and it looked as though this humiliation had at least one more turn to it. Trisha started to cry even as Brad started to laugh. "What is wrong with you . . . you, you . . . thoughtless monster!"

"Oh, dear; please don't cry. I didn't mean to hurt you in any way. There is more to the story, Trisha. Haven't you ever played these games with any of your boyfriends over the years?" "Boyfriends! Who needs them?" Now Trisha was a woman scorned. She was bouncing emotionally all over the place.

"What are you saying, Trish? Are you a bit unfamiliar with how men think?" Bradley was growing a bit more concerned and comfortable at the same time. He had decided to end the charade and give her a break. "Haven't you ever heard of a paraprosdokian?" He was putting on his best smile, had turned on the couch and slipped an arm around her shoulder. She didn't seem much interested, but he wanted to be affectionate.

"A what, what was that word . . . , para . . . dork?"

"A paraprosdokian, it's the word of the day. You should know this since you use them all the time. A paraprosdokian is a phrase or a sentence designed to mislead and surprise the recipient with an explanation that they did not expect. That is what this is, my love." In that moment Bradley turned to Trisha, brushed the tear from her eye, slipped both arms around her waist and drifted closer. When their lips touched, Bradley felt as though he had arrived at destiny's doorstep, but it was his pounding heart, driven by the softness of her lips that defined him. Without knowing it, Bradley Peterson had lived for that moment; at least that is how he later described it to Trisha.

She was utterly confused. She had no idea what that big long word meant. Suddenly a married man had slipped his arms around her and kissed her in a way she was sure would never happen in her life . . . but, he was married. "I thought you were married," she croaked in a weak and flimsy voice, bereft of any real resistance. "Where does she live?"

"She lives here."

"Do I know her, Brad?"

"Actually," he wryly smiled, "you may and you may not. We ask ourselves these things all the time."

"How long have you known her?"

"Oh, I have known her somewhere between fifteen and twenty years."

"What's her name?" Trisha was ready to concede the future, and his inappropriate kiss had only made things worse for her. The dread of knowing him and him being involved with someone they both knew was unbearable.

"Her name . . . it's Trisha; Her name is Trisha Jean Martin. I told you I was crazy, or did I forget to tell you?"

The sound of the words rolled nicely off of his tongue. Was he trying to wiggle out of more . . . more and more like he did before? The surgeon has the slickest way of wiggling out of the truth. "Unless I married you in my sleep, that tale could not be possible. Shall I go in the other room and check on the kids, honey? We are definitely not married. You are a bit of a loony, Bradley, but I have decided to play along. How is it that we are married, with children no less? Listen carefully. Don't fib. I hate lying. Just be honest and tell me what you are up to, even if you are only having fun."

"I know this is news to you, but for me it is the real deal. I never forgot you, Trish. I never looked seriously at starting a family or anything like that, either, but still I thought of you from time to time. When I was in that hole trying to hang on to my sanity I searched my mind for something that would give me a place to go. I tried taking college classes, going to ball games, driving my '57 around; I tried a bunch of things. Eventually I settled on what it would be like to have a family." Bradley's hand started shaking a bit, but he grabbed hold of it and told it to stop. I picked someone from my youth who most interested me in different ways. When a picture of you crossed my mind, it was like a bolt of electricity had struck harp strings. It was one of the few times that I laughed while I was under their control."

Trisha was interested now. She was . . . all of a sudden in another place altogether. There was a fire brewing down below. For the first time in . . . forever, Trisha Jean Martin was being guided by forces beyond her control. What had she done? "Did you pick me because I am so sassy?

I am flattered that you remembered me, but was it just about a picture in the yearbook your senior year, you know the one where I won the 1,500 meters at a track meet? They used my picture because of my hair. Was that the reason?"

Brad looked a little sheepish. "Not exactly, but I do remember that photo. Sometime when we are over at my place, I'll dig it out and show it to you. You're a little smart-alecky, I have to admit it, but that wasn't the entire reason. No, hold it a bit. Yes, it was. You were so engaging and didn't fear me in any way back then. I would never go in for a girl who was afraid of me, intellectually or otherwise, so I have to say your attitude did play a part in why I picked you; it's just not the main reason." Brad's tongue was in his cheek. He was looking side to side, up and down. His toes were tapping on the floor. He looked uncomfortable all of a sudden.

Trisha on the other hand, seemed to be getting the upper hand. She was gaining control over the situation. "OK, clue me in, Doctor Peterson. Why little ole me? You could have picked a Playboy Bunny if you had wanted to."

"I know you're not going to believe this, Trisha, but even a Playboy Bunny wouldn't take you out of the game in this one category, and believe me, I'm being objective here."

Trisha looked Brad straight in the eye. "This I have got to hear. Spit it out, Doctor Kildare. And before you do, remember I am well versed in the writings of John Grey. I may be from Venus but let me tell you, I speak fluent Martian. Only a guy would still lie after he was told not to. So... goofball, let's hear it. What is it that I have over, even a Playboy Bunny?"

Bradley Peterson smiled; yes, he smiled a yummy kind of smile. "I really don't mean to be so shallow. Our relationship in all of its nuances is more important to me than you could ever know. I am not sure you're even aware of what happened back there in Frankfurt at the race when you came running by and changed my life. Remember when I came chasing you like a little boy after his mother? Annie was right there. I had to circle back around just to keep the meeting I had planned with her. From that moment on, Trisha, Annie was obsessed with you. She saw it right there and then, so I assure you this is not a shallow comment, but I promised to tell the truth and so I will. It's the buns, baby. I can't get over the look. Every time I see you from behind my head starts spinning. I lose all control. That is why I picked you, Trisha. I imagined you and I together . . . in a biblical sense. Now *that I see you in person, tonight for the second time, it's obvious that I made the correct choice, too. You are exactly the same size as you were when we were kids; in fact, you look better now than you did even then. Perhaps we should read the Bible together?"*

"Hmm," said Trisha, clearly not used to being prized and even desired by someone, especially someone that she loved and wanted herself. "Brad, you're lying. You have to be." Even as knots were untied by the knowledge that he wasn't really married, other knots were tying themselves in kind. She didn't know what to say or do. "I, I'm, uh, Bradley, I am happy that you thought of me and that it gave you some sort of comfort, but my bottom? It's a good thing you didn't get to see me before a couple of years ago. That would have been a different kind of torture. In all seriousness, thank you. I am not . . ."

He kissed her again, holding her tightly, clinging with his heart, moisture in his eyes, this time putting it all on the line. For the longest time they stood there in Trisha's living room, outlined in soft recessed lighting, ignoring whatever was on the television set, and with Trisha's head cradled against Bradley's chest. Every few minutes she looked into his eyes and they allowed the magic of the moment to consume them. It was a lover's embrace and for the first time they were able to get just a small glimpse of how each one made the other whole. The measure of their understanding was emotionally telepathic; they could read each other's hearts and minds. They were becoming one. After a moment that seemed to want to last forever, Brad was the first to speak up. "I'm so sorry, Trisha. Even as I allow myself to fall in love, really for the first time in my life, I know that I'm not up to the task. These dreams and episodes are just as bad . . .

"Shhhh," Trisha put a finger to his lips. "You do love me, don't you? I can see it in your eyes. You've earned a confession. I saw those eyes on me way back in high school and I tried to encourage you . . . subtly." She was giggling now. "The things we do for attention when we are kids. Bradley Peterson. I am not in love with a brain surgeon, a war hero, or anyone famous. I am in love with a high school heart throb. I don't care what your problems are. You want me on board? We can get through anything together. I have an idea. We both need a good night's sleep, dear. I do not think you will fall into another bad dream if you are closer to me . . ."

Trisha was leading a puppy dog down the hallway to the back room, her room, her bed, his future. When they entered the room, there were two wonderfully scented candles burning on the dresser. Brad looked around and noticed several photographs of Trisha, some which were completely unrecognizable. There were photographs of others there too, including one of him when he was crossing the finish line at a race in high school. He had given it to her himself. A humongous flat screen television was mounted on the wall. There was quiet music coming from the simple Bose sound system that accompanied the TV. The bed was not a king, but an oversized queen with a very thick mattress. The bedspread, pulled down because Trisha had been sleeping when Brad woke her up, was thick and soft, cream colored with deep red Asian floral patterns. The ornate romantically red pillows were still pretty much in place. Trisha was ever thankful in that moment that the sheets were fresh and clean. Simple white end tables were the support for crystal lamps which added atmosphere when lit by the reflection of the candles from across the room. Her conservative, but stunning satin aqua-colored Natori Shangri-La robe was very easy on the eyes, but not enough to turn the heat up too high. Unfortunately, as she removed the robe, what was left made for a very complicated moment between lovers crawling into bed for the first time. In and of itself, Trisha's cotton night shirt wasn't revealing, but what could not be seen commanded all of Brad's attention.

"I have two more confessions, Brad, before I allow you to get into this bed and sleep. One, I have never been with a man in spite of the fact that you say we have two children." Trisha smiled both deliciously and warmly; her lover didn't even flinch. "Two, I promised to save myself for marriage. The nuptial you conjured between us, I'll have to admit is alluring, but it doesn't count . . ." Brad removed his shirt and threw it into the corner, then fell into the bed, pulling her down on top of him and pressing his lips softly against hers, ending the confession session . . . for good. Her lips parted ever so slightly. It began as a tiny worm of pleasure, unraveling knots which had tied her love in for all of a decade and a half, then exploding uncontrollably when her eyes were stung by his tears. Trisha was rendered helpless by Brad's magic, not physical technique, but in the language of commitment and love. "Oh, my," the inexperienced girl said, even as she thought to herself that some things just could not be planned . . . Then he respected her *nuptial admonition, curled her up, snuggled close and they tried to sleep. The nightmare was gone.*

Trisha drifted back into the here and now. There was quiet conversation on the bus, the music was playing, and the added benefit was that the driver was silent. She looked over her shoulder and noticed that Stanley was sound asleep. The runner shifted her attention to the traffic, which was heavy. The clouds were rolling in from the mountain side of the highway, and yet the wind was blowing debris across the road the other way. The entrance to the Olympic Village was just ahead. The dusk was dark as usual, since the sun had long since disappeared behind the mountains to the west. What always disturbed her were the protesters. Why did people have to try and destroy the Olympics? They were so selfish.

Trisha pulled her cell phone from the bag and checked for messages. There was an email from Brad. *Has he changed flights? Is he coming in tomorrow or perhaps even tonight with the kids?* It was neither. Her heart sank. In spite of the fact that both partners in this marriage and family had danced around their very busy lives, it had worked out. It wasn't a perfect marriage, but it was a good one. They supported and trusted each other. In her biggest moment, Bradley was not coming for the race. He had to perform surgery on a kid. If everything worked out, they still planned on joining her after the Games. *"I am so disappointed, Trish. I hope you'll take a call just before the race. I'm going to watch it on television. Everyone around here is planning on watching your race. It is being billed as the biggest thing around Vegas since Andre Agassi won the Grand Slam . . ."* A wave of nausea, the reality of her situation settling once again in the pit of her stomach, could only conjure a single one word thought, *great.* Trisha closed the email without deleting it and in that instant she put her family on the back burner and started to focus on the evening ahead, which included having dinner with Annika Langvad, a mountain biker from Denmark and a new friend.

* * *

Brad quietly changed channels; he was watching NFL preseason football's Hall of Fame Game, the annual kickoff of the new season, and at the same time flipping back and forth between various

Olympic events taking place down south in Brazil. He had the twins with him, one asleep on the couch, the other one playing video games. They were upstairs in the game room, which was situated between their bedrooms. Brad liked hanging out in their play space when he had them to himself. The chance to be with his children alone, sadly, didn't come around as often as he would have liked. They hadn't been told about the trip to Brazil, so there was no reason to tell them that the trip was being delayed. Rachael was really good with Maddy and Mikey, now all of four years old. In the world of Bradley and Trisha Peterson, raising a family was definitely a village project, and the very reason they built their home right on the property of the Austin Day Care Center, soon to be known as the Austin Primary Day Care and Education Center. Rachael, who could not have children of her own, and who adored kids, had taken a different route in the fulfillment of her need to be with youngsters. Along with her husband, Adam, and with the help of the Roger Martin Foundation, they were building quite a future for themselves. The kids had eaten their dinner early, once Rachael had dropped them off, had had their bath, and were in their pajamas. Madison was already asleep and little Michael was fading fast. Still, once they had drifted into the dreamland of kids who never worry, Bradley kept them by his side letting them curl up with their dad.

Bradley allowed himself to drift. Here he was, living in a beautiful home that he and his wife had built together, and living the American dream, 21st century style. They both had incredible careers, the kids were fun, and he and his wife both got along with their respective families. Trisha's mother was great. She was so funny. Where would he be today without Trisha, though? Brad was a mess when he caught up to her a little more than four years ago. He wasn't sure if he would ever be able to practice medicine again. She had wanted him anyway. You see, that was the thing that turned him on about this girl. She cared not one whit about what he was, but was devoted to who he was. Brad wondered if Trisha was aware of how many people were alive today because of her and what she did for him . . .

"Brad, honey, what's the matter?" Things were still very new back then and if you look closely, anytime a brand new love kicks off, insecurity is the main ingredient in anything that goes awry. "Is there

anything I can do to help? You know, dear, this past few weeks have been the happiest of my life."

After their first night together, things had happened very quickly. Neither of them had ever spoken to anyone else of that night, but between them, the relationship had been born on very solid ground. They were engaged and Trisha had a ring on before the sun went down the next day. At first Brad had felt a bit guilty about the need to move quickly with the engagement, but all she did was laugh at him for it. They were married in just over a month, the amount of time that it took to pick a good date and get everyone invited to a party. By the time Becky had finished whipping up the show, it was totally out of control and there had been more than 250 people at the reception.

"Mine too, Trisha. Something has come up and I am handcuffed. I don't think I can go on like this. Do you know that kid with Down's Syndrome who coaches baseball over at Green Valley and also at College of Southern Nevada?"

"Mattie Boy Simpson is his name. Everyone knows him. He's the most popular kid in town, strutting all over the place for years like he owns it." Trisha smiled. "I admire that family."

"I don't envy them tonight, Trish. Mattie just had a brain scan and needs surgery for a tumor. The doctor who was to perform surgery was in an auto accident and there is no one around to replace him on short notice. It's tragic." He looked at his wife, seeming more like a rabbit caught in a trap than an accomplished surgeon.

Trisha didn't look worried, didn't blink, and did not appear to be sympathetic to his situation. She asked one question. *"Brad, do you still have your surgeon's license?"*

"Yes, I do. They didn't have the courage to take it away from me, but . . ."

"No ifs, ands, or buts, Bradley. I have some more questions for you. How did you find this out? Was it on the news or something?" The focus of her eyes, and the reality that she was deadly serious was a new side of her that he had not quite gotten to know yet. The reason that he had fallen so deeply for this girl was because she was such a big player in the game of life. It was like she had no fear and could get anything done.

"No, I haven't seen the news or anything. I got a call out of the blue. A surgeon's assistant that I worked with in Iraq, Margaret Ross, called

me. She and I last saw each other the night of the scorpion attack. She got bit and almost died. I've not visited with her since. By coincidence, she lives here in town now and was set to assist in surgery. She did not want to bother me and had not called, but today she did. Now I feel terrible. I wish there was something I could do, but I have no nerves. I would just butcher the child with any surgeon's tool, even the vacuum during the mop up job. I couldn't even . . ."

"Enough of that nonsense, Doctor." Trisha leaned forward. "Stop with the negative waves. Do you remember when Donald Southerland played the tank commander in Kelly's Heroes, that old movie with Clint Eastwood when he was younger?" Brad nodded, looking like he wondered where she was going with this. "Not another negative word out of your mouth, soldier. Now just listen, answer the questions, and perhaps we can help the big war hero on with his life. How well do you know this Margaret Ross?"

"Really well; I hand-picked her myself from the army pool I had access to. She's incredible. What of it? That still . . ."

"Stop, Brad," and Trisha started laughing. "You just can't help it. You have been through so much that you don't think your situation can resolve itself. I have been watching very closely and I think there is some method to the madness I have in mind, so if you will please just answer the questions." He smiled, nodding for her to continue

"Do you think you could work with her again?" The look on her face was animated. "In a minute, that is . . ."

"Ah . . . aht . . . , no, no . . . What if you could not hear her, but she could see and hear everything you say? Would you still be able to navigate the operation safely, even though you couldn't hear her? I mean, you could use a word pad to communicate or something if you had to, but you could not hear her with your ears. Could you do that?"

"Sure, I suppose. What's your hypothesis?" Brad was very interested. Trisha's ideas were always well thought out and it was a smart decision to listen when she was sharing. Brad listened.

"We go out running every day. Well, you run and I warm up. You keep telling me that you could perform surgery if only you could run in place at the table. You never shake when you are running. I have run with you several times and you do shake when you run . . . sometimes."

"I know. Things are getting even worse. I have been very worried . . ." She cut him off again.

"Silence!" This time Trisha raised her voice. "Things are not getting worse, Captain dodo bird. Good Lord. I can't believe you haven't figured this out yet. It's not the running, bean brain, but the iPod music. It is when you have the music on that the shakes completely disappear. How can someone so smart be so close to the problem and not able to see the solution? Have you been brainwashed by aliens or something? I wanted you to figure it out for yourself, but it is too late for that now. Put on the damn headset and go save that kid! Do you have any idea how special he is to so many people?"

Brad's mouth hung open. How could he have missed that? In a moment of clarity the epiphany was overwhelming. "Why didn't I think of that? You're suggesting that it is the music? You know, Trisha, you may be onto something there. Sometimes I have an attack while I am listening to music, but never when I have the iPod going. I wonder if the headset has something to do with it."

"Yeah, Doc, I am married to an alien abductee. The aliens have access to your brain through your ears. If you plug your ears, they'll not be able to interrupt your focus during surgery. Now, I notice that you don't seem to need earplugs to get you through bedroom rodeo activities. I think the aliens only want to stop you from performing surgery." In spite of how grave the situation was, Trisha always seemed to find a way not to take things too seriously.

Brad was already on the phone. He didn't even hear his wife and actually wondered why she was laughing. Did she not know how important this was? "Margaret, how is the situation down there?"

"Brad, the boy is slipping into a coma. Dr. Quint Burnham was supposed to perform the operation. He was in an automobile accident on the way over and he needs help too, your kind of help."

"I like him. What happened?"

"Another driver and I do not know his name, but you won't believe this either, he is also injured, needs help with severe head trauma and that makes three of them. This other driver was texting and driving at the same time. They found his phone and it was still on. He ran the light, the best we can tell, and hit Quinton right in the driver's side door. Brad, there isn't anyone around to help. I have three critical patients

who need emergency level intervention for head trauma or a tumor that is life threatening. What should I do?"

"You already got the ball rolling, Margaret. I feel like working today. The vacation is over. I want to make sure I understand correctly. You're at St. Rose Dominican up off of St. Rose Parkway, right?

"Yup, that's where we are."

"I will be at the surgeon's entrance in just a few minutes. Try to get three tables set up in close proximity. Let's do this triage style if we can. What have I got to work with?"

Trisha had disappeared and returned, dressed and ready to go. "Let's go. I am going to drop you off." With that, Brad, still on the phone, continued to bark out instructions on how he wanted things set up. He moved around the house, making sure, among other things, that he had a fully charged iPod including the charging plug and an extension cord. He quickly traded his Bermuda shorts and flops for some jeans and a pair of sneakers. Within just a minute or so they were out on Pecos headed straight for the hospital. Since the road became St. Rose Parkway just after crossing under the freeway, they didn't even have to turn until they were there. All the while, Brad was on the phone getting things organized. Trisha noticed that he was beginning to twitch already, now becoming concerned that he needed to get off of the phone and get the music therapy going. By the time they pulled into the hospital there was activity everywhere. All of the local television stations had mobile units set up, there were police, newspaper reporters and of course family members. Those were the ones Brad was concerned with.

"Lucky for me I don't have to deal with all of this today. Good luck, Doc, and Brad . . ." He looked back while getting out of the old Escalade he still had from before the war, "have fun today. You've earned this." He walked around the car, leaned in, planted a huge kiss on her lips, thanking the love of his life for saving his. She smiled and drove off back towards home.

Bradley Peterson had turned off the phone, turned on the music, and was working his way through the throng. "Captain Peterson, do you have time for just a word before you go in?" Fortunately, though he couldn't hear, he could read lips, so he understood the man thrusting a microphone in his face. Each minute was an eternity and so he just said to the one person who had made it over to him, "I'm sorry that

413

I do not have time for any comments right now . . . and with that he was in the door. Inside he pulled the plugs out.

"What was that all about?" Just like any doctor, any egomaniacal jerk, Doctor Captain Bradley War Hero didn't even acknowledge that he was talking to *a wonderful old friend.*

"Someone got word out the door that you were about to come in and perform surgery for the first time since before you were captured. We have no idea who or how. I'll tell you this, Captain, it wasn't me and I just found out myself when we were on the phone a few minutes ago."

"It had to be snoops that monitor the cell phones, Margaret."

"I can't believe it. They got here even faster than you did. Look out the window. The CNN guy just pulled up."

"Let's walk away from the door. First off, please forgive me for being so casual. The last time I saw you, we were in the middle of a firefight and the invasion of the killer scorpions. I thought we had lost you, and then after we revived your limp body, I never saw you again, and didn't know you had made a full recovery until after I got back to Landstuhl." Brad and Margaret had made their way into the bowels of the hospital when he turned toward his friend and gave her a big hug. "Thanks for making it, for being alive, and for calling me today. You have always been a great friend. I . . ."

". . . No, Captain Peterson, I'm proud to be here with you today. The best work I ever did was with you. We have a lot to do. I have everything set up just as you requested." As they walked the halls towards the surgery center Brad was greeted by others, "Hello, Doctor Peterson . . . Captain Peterson, welcome back to the hospital," and other supportive comments from well-wishers who seemed genuinely happy to see him.

Just before they walked into the operating room containing Matthew Simpson, Bradley put on the headset and turned up the music, full blast. "Margaret," he said, "don't ask and don't tell. I use these to keep the demons out. If you have any trouble following my lead . . ." and just like that the good Captain was back to work. In thirty-one hours he had saved three lives. It was just like old times.

Margret Ross had been by his side every working minute since. During the years in between, Bradley overcame the need to use the iPod, finally recovering himself. It was like the aliens had decided to leave him alone after that. He'd performed surgery all over the world, once again himself. His favorite assignment had been when he operated on Bob Hankle. It was the least he could do for the guy who had rescued him and had been the best man at his wedding. That he had to go all the way to Baghdad to perform that operation was cleansing. The crusty old soldier was still out in the field commanding troops. Brad had even performed surgery at Landstuhl a time or two, still doing favors for the Army. No matter how secretive and agenda driven the Armed Forces were, Brad never was able to learn how to say no. When they called, he served. Of what happened to him in Africa, he never spoke again to a single person except his wife. She knew everything.

Trisha Martin Peterson was his best friend in the world and now he had to sacrifice, even her, to work magic on this little genius kid, Billy Dace. The night before the operation, Brad was home alone with kids and dogs. In the moments he shared with the twins, there in the playroom while they slept, and even with the giant bulldogs curled at his feet, a wave of loneliness swept in and stole his joy. He missed his wife, terribly. He didn't want her here with him right now. What he really wanted was to be there with her. They were both working at the time, but she must be the one having fun and he wished he could get in on the action.

Mikey had curled up and placed his little head on Brad's lap. Madison was beginning to stir now and looked ready for bed. Brad gently lifted Mikey's head and placed it on a pillow, and guided his tiny little daughter into the bathroom. Lady Aubrey followed, but Sir Edward stayed behind to snore and fart with his legs in the air. Once the little bathroom trip was completed he carried her into the room and placed her on the bed, tucking her in, with Aubrey curled at the foot of the bed. When she smiled up at him, Maddy looked just like a miniature version of her mother, complete with hair to the waist, and so he choked up a bit. Then Captain Bradley Peterson, the renowned pediatric brain surgeon, sang lullabies until his little princess was sound asleep. He and the dog went back into the playroom and found his son still snoozing, trying to out-snore Edward; Michael was a little snorer. With the touch of a magician he lifted the little man into his arms and carried him softly into his bathroom, woke him for duties and then patiently read a Millie and Billy story called *I Wish* by Tony Murrell. The boy was fast asleep in two minutes.

Once Brad had straightened the playroom, he never left a mess, he meandered into his and Trisha's bedroom where he quickly showered and changed into comfortable pajamas, slipped into his favorite robe and then headed to his office at the bottom of the stairs. Brad shifted his focus a bit, picking up the two-ton folder containing the Dace charts, settling into his big green chair and began to review the data. Bradley was a bit old-fashioned in that he still fancied hard copy files where he could comfortably study pages of information in whatever order he pleased. His eyelids began to feel heavy. It wasn't even 9:00 yet. The next thing he knew, Rachael was nudging him awake. Somehow it had become 5:00 the next morning, he was as stiff as a board, and his head hurt, but it was time to go. The surgeon needed to be at St. Rose Dominican at 6:00 to begin the long day ahead with young Dace the Ace. He so wished that he had gone to bed for a proper night's sleep, but if wishes were fishes . . . Now it was time to greet the day and go to work.

9

Marathon

The bus rumbled towards a fate that had become the runner's destiny since a long ago challenge had changed her life. There were no word games being played this morning. The mood was not festive or all that pleasant. In fact, the silence was deafening. Three American athletes, all women, sat in quiet solitude dealing internally with the moment they had worked for their entire lives. Their coaches and other US Olympic officials visited in hushed reverence. For once, the driver of the bus knew enough not to make himself visible. The somber mood was one of anticipation mixed with a bit of fear. So much was on the line this morning. It was race day.

Stanley Burton, Trisha Martin's personal coach and trainer, had been sitting a few rows back with some of the officials, one of whom was on the phone. When he put the smart phone into his pocket they visited for just a few more minutes and then Stanley came forward and took his seat next to Trisha. He did not look at all happy. "We . . . uh, have run into a buzz saw, Trish. They're considering calling off this event. It seems that security types have uncovered problems that may compromise the safety of the athletes out on the course. It's these damn protesters. There are even rumors of planned violence somewhere along the way and their target may be the Americans. That's us in case you were wondering . . ."

"No way, Stanley, they can't give in to that crap." Tears of anger were forming in her eyes.

Trisha stared out of the window and noticed the crowd—building. They were almost there. She began to sense danger, real or imagined;

her stomach churned at the thought of being out on the open road in hostile territory. Securing the safety of athletic competitors at the Olympics was most challenging for the open road events outside of stadiums. It was only natural that the cowards would try to hurt them where they were vulnerable. "You go back there, get on the phone and tell them we're racing today. We've all worked too hard to get run off of the road by lunatics . . ."

"Hold on, kid. You know I'm just the messenger. Settle down and get back into mental preparation. The security folks down here have done a great job of keeping things under control so far, and they have the balls to go with this too. I am betting against them calling the race. They're just too proud to give in. You're in good hands, Trisha so don't let anything distract you." Stanley was clearly worried.

The bus had pulled into the parking lot and they were getting ready to disembark, the thumbs up for the race had been signaled to the runners and their coaches. Stanley continued sharing his final thoughts as they walked toward the front of the bus and Trisha's destiny. "You're my cheetah today, and not just because the cheetah is the fastest and sleekest creation in all of nature. You are certainly as beautiful as those cats are, but that is still not the reason."

Trisha was staring into his eyes, looking to get the glimpse of meaning behind his metaphor.

What is my coach trying to say?

"Every part of your body, much like the fast cat, contributes to your undisputed title as the best American long distance runner today. You have long slender bones in those pretty legs which give you great stride for distance and yet, much like the cheetah you're built for impact running. That's why you have the advantage of instant acceleration when you need it. You know what I think? Today, your history with weight becomes your best friend. You developed unknown strength carrying all that weight around. Now the fat is long gone, but the strength has been properly developed. You are going to win this race. Stay out of all the drama . . ."

They were outside of the bus; in fact they were not so far now from the starting line. Anticipation was easy to sense from the crowd up on the hill where the race would begin and their binoculars focusing on the tight knit group of Americans. The clicking of shutter lenses sounded like a swarm of Mormon crickets. Randy Moss and the NBC remote television crew approached. She had noticed them visiting with Kara Goucher and Shalane Flanagan. *I wish I could avoid the interview right now.* Instead she smiled.

"Welcome back to *Today on NBC.* I am live with Trisha Jean Martin. Good morning, Trisha. Are you ready to go?"

"Good morning to you, Randy. Yes, I'm ready. By the way, you look much safer than when I last saw you hanging out of a helicopter the other day." Moss openly laughed. "We, the three of us, are . . ."

* * *

Bradley was in the hospital room visiting quietly with his patient. *This kid is an amazing specimen. He should be asleep right now, not up watching television.* "Look! Captain Peterson. There she is, Trisha Jean Martin. Did you know she is from right here in Las Vegas! I love her. She is the most amazing runner in the world. We're going to get our own gold medal—just for us. How could anyone so pretty be so good at running? When she comes home I am going to find her and ask her to marry me. What do you think about that?"

There were tears running down the surgeon's face. She was being interviewed and the race was about to begin. He had wanted so badly to be there with her. If not for the fact that he had spent most of yesterday and half of the night in surgery with this boy, something of a miracle on his part for the tumor had been far more complicated than expected, he would have started laughing at the young lad's obsequious flattery. Instead he stared admiringly at the television and could not stop the tears of joy that flooded his heart. "She's not just spoken for, son, but is married with two adorable children, twins. I'm afraid you're out of luck. I know her husband and there is no way he'll ever let her go. You'll just have to find someone else, perhaps someone your own age that will be even more precious to you than our Las Vegas treasure there."

"How can you be so sure? Do you really know her? Everyone thinks they know these people, but no one ever does. How do you know her?"

"Oh, I don't know, Billy. Perhaps the fact that she and I went to Green Valley High School gives me an inside track, but that is not exactly how I know her so well."

The young patient looked into his doctor's eyes and noticed the pleading look of pride and his wet face. It was obvious he was telling the truth, but all politicians were natural skeptics and so he pressed on. "How then do you know her so well? Can you prove it?"

Bradley couldn't take his eyes off of her. It was all he could do to stay in the conversation with the child prodigy. He impulsively took the phone out of his pocket and hit the speed dial. "She is my wife, William Benjamin Dace. She is the World's and belongs not only to me, but to all of Las Vegas and today she is the United States of America. Let's see if we can get her on the phone. Would you like to wish her good luck?"

"Yes!" Billy seemed to forget that he had just survived brain surgery. "Oh, I can't even believe this. My doctor is married to the most famous person in the history of Las Vegas. Please get her to answer the phone, please . . ."

* * *

Randy Moss, in wrapping up his interview, had waited until the last moment to ask the hardest question. "Trisha, all of America wishes you the best today as you and your teammates undertake the grueling race. You're right, it looks hot and it's muggy. Perhaps we'll get a bit of rain to cool you off. I'm not sure you would like that or not. I can see you smiling, but with a great big thumbs down. Everyone, Trisha does not want rain." He and she were laughing. "What do you think about the security situation out here? No one is talking to anybody but there are all kinds of rumors about problems that may come up during the race. Are you worried?"

I am scared to death. Why do these guys always wait till the last minute to drop a bomb in an interview? "I'm sorry, Randy. I don't have any idea what you're talking about. Did any of the others know anything? We're just too focused on winning the event to get involved in things like security and politics. We trust the authorities and officials to take good care of us and up until now they have done a great job. I will venture this one thing and then I need to get going. You'd have to be stuck in a box not to know that along with all we are enjoying during these games, together, all of us, Brazilians, Americans, like minded folks from all over, live spectators and the athletes too; there is also too much hate and anger. You can see protesters from where we stand right now. I choose to let my love outweigh any negatives, not the corny kind of love, but what really binds all of us. I don't have a single ounce of energy for worrying about hatred today," *I wish anyway,* "and I am not going to allow them to interfere with what we're all about. My heart goes out to people who think the Olympics are a proper venue for their pain, an awful ache that must go to their core, that they would feel justified in trying to ruin this for everyone else. I don't know enough to push them down or judge their their cause. Whether they're justified or not, it is our turn and it is not their turn. Right now I would run through hell to win a medal for the United States of America, protesters or not."

"Thank you, Trisha. Once again, good luck in today's race. There are only about a hundred million of us watching live so don't worry about any pressure from our viewers." Trisha smiled, gave the broadcaster a hug and started walking away towards the top of the hill. "There you have the final word. All I can say is this. For someone who didn't have time to think things through, she gave us a pretty articulate answer." His smile was one filled with pride and respect for the athlete.

Trisha tried hard to focus on the race. There were so many things going through her racing mind. They would reach the check-in trailer in just a couple of minutes. Stretching would give her time to put the stupid threat out of her psyche. Stanley approached and he had her phone in his hand. *Now what?*

"Do you feel like saying hello to Bradley?"

Tears welled in her eyes. It was easy to see that the medicine she needed had just arrived as she took the phone from her trainer's hand. In one moment the runner was immersed in sights, sounds, and the smells of the big day. The screams of those that hate were being drowned out by deafening chants of USA . . . USA . . . . USA . . . Television cameras were whirling all over the place and the police were ubiquitous. The whole thing was chaotic. They had arrived at the staging area outside of the trailer. When she put the phone to her ear all of that disappeared and she could see through her heart to the one person who had the power to make her feel better, her husband. "Oh, Brad." She started to cry.

"Trish, look up and to your left. Do you see the television camera with the red light on?"

"Yes."

"You're beautiful, dear. I'm so in love with you. Good Lord, they are zooming in on you talking to me. Why are you crying? Is that thing Moss brought up bothering you?"

"No, yes, well yes and no. I need you. I mean no, I'm not emotional because of the crazed loonies out here. Screw them. I just needed you. You called at the perfect time. I love you, too. Can I take one minute off from all of this and think of you? How are the kids?"

"They're doing great. Rachael has been wonderful these past few weeks. I've had quite a bit of time with them myself. We're still planning on getting down there and hope to make the closing ceremonies. It's going to be a great reunion for the Peterson clan.

"I can't wait. Once the day is over, it is all I will be thinking about. Did your surgery on that young boy work out? Is he OK?"

Brad looked at his young patient. The television cameras had moved on and were highlighting other things. Trisha could be seen in the background, still on the phone. "Billy, do I have your permission to visit with my wife about your surgery?"

"By all means, Captain Peterson, tell her anything you like." Billy Dace was on top of the world. There was only the one big headache but that was from the operation. The tumor was gone and he was alive. He was more than alive. "I know you haven't been in the Army for a long time, but to me you will always be Captain Peterson, except from now on you will be the man who is married to Trisha Martin. Can I wish her good luck?"

Brad looked down at the bed where the kid was sitting up. He looked so silly with his head all wrapped up, even as he grinned from ear to ear. "Trisha, honey the operation was a complete success. I have never had a patient quite like young William Dace. He was under for such a long time and yet, just hours after surgery I came in to check on him and found the boy sitting up in bed watching the Olympics. His recovery is nothing short of a miracle at this point. I hated to bother you just before you run, but he challenged me to prove that I even knew you. Remember the name, William Benjamin Dace. He tells me that I just operated on a future President of the United States of America. He is hoping to perform his first official act as a candidate this morning. Is there any chance you would be open to letting him wish you good luck?"

"You can't believe how good this conversation is for me right now, Brad." *Where have all the heebie jeebies gone?* "Hand him your phone." An eager young boy was given the memory of a lifetime as he took the cell phone and put it to his ear. "Hello, young Mr. Dace. How are you feeling this morning? I am told that you've just survived quite the ordeal, and in fact I have been hearing about you for some time now."

"Thanks to your husband, Mrs. Martin, uh, or is that Mrs. Peterson?"

"Oh, I go by many names and Mrs. Peterson is one of my favorite. Not many folks know me that way, but you are one that does. You can call me Trisha, Trish, TJ, Ms. Martin, Trisha Jean Martin and there are others too, but my favorite name is Mrs. Bradley Peterson. Brad tells me you have some rather big plans. Is that so?"

"Yes, ma'am; I plan on getting into politics and I hope to become President someday. For my first official act as a candidate for President I would say on behalf of Americans all across this great country of ours; we wish you the best of luck in your quest to bring home the gold."

"Thank you very much, candidate Dace. There isn't much I would have been willing to forgo my husband's trip down here for, but it seems as though this sacrifice was well worth it. I will look forward to meeting you in person soon. Get well, get the proper rest, and do not let your mother catch you flirting with older women. Mothers have a problem with things like that. So long for now."

"I'll give you back to Captain Peterson, Trisha. You made my life this morning, and that is twice in one day from your family. I will never forget this moment." Billy handed Brad his phone and settled into a reclining position; his eyes were growing heavy and it was possible, just a bit possible that he needed to rest.

Bradley took just a second to look at the boy. It was amazing that he could find no swelling or other problems that were common in patients like him. "Thanks, Trish. You can't know how much this little time meant to Billy . . ."

"You can't know how much this little time means to me, Brad. All of a sudden I am ready to go. Just a few minutes ago my mind was all over the place and now I feel like running. Be sure to introduce him to me when we get back from our vacation at the end of the Games."

Brad, watching television in the boy's room, was astounded at the chaos as the story had switched to protesters and a screaming match underway with Olympic fans. The security presence was as intense as anything he had seen since coming home from the war. "I'd tell you to be careful out there, dear. Try not to run towards trouble, or to take any foolish chances, but, coming from me that might not mean much to you."

"Yeah, like I am going to listen to a fool war hero who put himself in harm's way like you." Trisha was laughing. "I feel so much better. You were just what I needed this morning. It is crazy out here. I can't believe this place. To tell you the truth, it looks like more fun to me. I'll talk to you on the other side. Wish me luck, honey."

"OK, lover. Good luck. I'll be watching." He barely got the words out before the call went dead. She was gone and suddenly he felt alone. There was something about being with Trisha that Brad never got enough of. Whenever they were together, even if they were just on the phone, her presence filled his life. That was one of the intangibles that kept their marriage interesting. He was known for the same thing in circles that he ran in, but the big secret in his life was that she was much bigger than he was. There was just something about Trisha . . .

Brad looked back at the television once more before making rounds and getting paperwork in order. The announcers seemed concerned. He was concerned. A kernel of fear jumped into his heart. The dread that he felt reminded him of a long ago nightmare he had somehow lived through. The worrying made him feel just a bit guilty for what he had put loved ones through while he recklessly took chance after chance when he served his country half way around the world. The camera shifted back to the trio of Americans warming up for the start of the race. Now it was his wife wrapped in the red, white, and blue of America's honor. Well, those skimpy outfits could not be considered much of a wrap. When the camera focused closely on Trisha, Brad let his mind wander in a different direction, if only for a few seconds. *How many men out there just saw her the way I did?* That brought a bit of a wince. *She belongs to me.* Brad hurriedly

424

moved to get things done so that he would not miss the race. His heart began to beat rapidly. *Olympic Gold!*

* * *

"Good morning and welcome back to Olympic Coverage on NBC's family of networks. I'm Bob Costas. We are paying close attention to the Women's Marathon today on NBC's flagship station. Three American hopefuls, flag bearer Trisha Martin, Kara Goucher and Shalane Flanagan promise to put up a strong effort in a field of 130 of the world's elite distance runners, all amid the strange chaos that envelopes today's event. There are all kinds of rumors about the safety of this race, yet Olympic officials and Rio security forces have assured us that everything is under control. There was some talk of cancelling this event. For more on this story, Matt Lauer is out at the starting line and has a special report. Matt, the scene out there looks wild. What is going on?"

"Good morning to you, Bob and to all of America. The women's marathon is about to get underway. There, near the starting line is Trisha Martin accepting well wishes from her family and support team. She seems in much better spirits now that the race is at hand. The other American runners, Shalane Flanagan and Kara Goucher are at the line, having accepted well wishes from their own teams. In addition to all the security and protesters, the mood of the crowd is festive and exciting. Trisha Martin has moved up to the starting line and we are set to go. There's the gun and they are off and running. Let's hope things go smoothly from here."

* * *

It's hot and muggy. I knew that would be a challenge. The course is flat almost all of the way along the beach. I wish there were hills so I could get some help from my climbing advantage, but that is not to be, either. I can't believe how fast this race started. I can't keep up with the leaders. It's all I can do to stay in the pack right now and I am so tired, so very tired. What is wrong with me? We're only five miles into the race and I feel as though I need to stop. The fatigue is excruciating. What's wrong with me?

Trisha had come off of the line flat and not able to get the early lead she'd planned. Worse, she felt terrible, almost like she hadn't been running these past six years. She had yet to find any wind, struggling to put one foot in front of the other and so she trudged forward looking for answers. At the moment she was running in the center of the middle pack. The leaders, Galana, the Ethiopian and Zhu of China, were at least a hundred yards out in front and looked very comfortable from way back where she was. To tell the truth, they were not the only runners way out in front. There were two others, a Cuban, Belmonte, and the Turk, Sultan Haydar, quite aways farther up and setting a grueling pace, but Trisha didn't expect either of them to finish that way. They were the quarter horses out to set a pace and figured to fade later on, especially in the blistering heat that ruled them all this lovely morning. When she began to feel pain in her lower back, real doubt set in. *Did I come all this way only to fail miserably?* Trisha's teammates, Flanagan and Goucher were running comfortably up in front about two thirds of the way between her and the leaders . . . right where they planned on setting up an attack when the one steep climb came into play at about 17 miles. She wished that she was at least up where they were.

When she arrived at the water station, up beyond the 6 mile mark, Trisha doused herself with two cups of water at the front table and took a drink from the end of the station. She was beginning to feel just a bit better. The leaders had gained even more ground. *I'd run through Hell to win a medal for the United States.* That single thought kept bouncing around in her head. It wasn't too long ago that she had uttered those exact words aloud in front of a national television audience. Was it true? Would she have to run through pain and Hell for any chance at a medal? As she moved away from the drink station she decided that it would be now or never. She would both fade and fail, or perhaps she would die trying. The pain in her back started up again. Her legs were throbbing. The sun was beating her down like never before. She was from Las Vegas for crying out loud. The heat should not have been a problem. There was only one way and that was forward. Trisha picked up the pace anyway. She passed a runner, then another, then another after that and found a new rhythm, something she could live with for a while. She may not gain on the leaders right now, but she was done falling further behind. In an effort to release the pain, the runner allowed her mind to drift to another time and another place, a happy place.

"Brad," Trisha was picking her husband up at Nellis Air Force Base. They had been married all of two and a half months and already the Army had him performing surgery out in the field again. Oh, long gone were the days of reckless adventure. These were specific assignments where only his particular talents were needed. This time he had been gone only a few days, but it had seemed like forever to her. They embraced and he nearly squeezed the life out of her. By the way he held her, it seemed obvious that he wanted more than just a family hug. When passion faded a their lips parted she smiled . . . nervously, "I have something to tell you."

"I'm not so sure I like the look of that smile, Barbie. There isn't anything wrong is there?" Brad could read Trisha's mind with ease. She just didn't do well in the concealment department. Hers had been an honest life. "The surgery was a success, and I am happy to work for our Armed Forces, not for the brass but truly for the kids who wear the uniform. I'm glad to be home, but they could have farmed this job out to someone else, too. I hope my being gone didn't cause you problems. What is it? Tell me, dear."

Trisha did her best to hide the story and deliver the punch line. She wanted to fool the master just one time. Perhaps today . . . "I went to the doctor. My splits have gone flat and for all that matters I am getting slower, so I went to the doctor. Brad, I have a growth. It's not malignant so don't worry. Sadly though, I will not be going to the London trials after all. I am out of the Olympics. The doctor says if I follow the treatment plan, get plenty of rest, and I have to curtail training, that everything will work out. I'll be back out on the road in less than a year."

"Oh, no. Oh, Trisha, I'm so sorry I wasn't here for you. What can I do to help? I am so sorry. I know how hard you've worked to make the Olympic team. Tell me more. I don't want to use any clichés, but I couldn't go on without you. Is this something life threatening?"

"People have died from this but it's very rare. Don't worry."

"What is the growth? Just tell me what it is. We can get through anything together. We have fought things like this already. What is it?" The look on his face was precious. He looked like a little boy about to lose his mother. It was pathetic. She played the card.

"I'm pregnant . . . with twins. You're a scoundrel. You've ruined my plans for London. Just look at you. Wipe that smile off of your face, mister. You got me pregnant!" Brad's wife melded her body to his and she kissed him again. Her emotions got the best of her and with her arms around his neck she spoke words of intimacy that young couples the world over dreamed of. *"We're going to be a real family. Can we get a couple of dogs?"*

The heavy thunder of a military helicopter jolted Trisha from her daydream. She could feel the cooling wind of the rotors as the security forces patrolled the race up and down the highway, roaring reassurance to the runners. At that moment she realized the pain was completely gone and decided to step it up again.

A small scooter pulled away from the side of the road and then a second one. The first one was obviously a television remote. On the back of the second one sat the broadcaster. Trisha's move was garnering some attention. "This is Chris Maddocks. We are back in the pack and it seems that at last Trisha Martin is making a move. As you know, she has not had the start she was looking for, struggling to keep pace with the front end of the field. Let's take a look at her current stride. In the past few minutes she has moved up from sixty second in the field and now finds herself in the top fifty. Here is a side by side view of her striding length now as opposed to just a couple of miles ago. She's increased the length of her gate by a full three inches. Even in marathon running inches make a world of difference. We'll keep an eye on her and see if this new level of energy gets her back into the race. Part of her situation is the result of the scorching pace of the entire group. She may be surprised to know that as it now sits, she is running one of the fastest races of her career. The problem is simple. So is everyone else."

All I have to do is run a measly 16 more miles . . . in pain from head to toe. This is the worst day of my life. What was it Michael said just before we boarded the plane in Colorado just a few weeks ago, something like it not being enough just to get here? He was right. I'm so miserable. I don't know if I am even going to finish. If I keep up this pace, perhaps I will get within shot of the leaders . . . in about a million years. The crowd is choking down on us. There are police everywhere. The screaming is getting worse, those faces look so angry. Look, now those others are real fans, real Olympic fans, and it's heartwarming to feel the support of enthusiasts who are not even American. Keep thinking, Trisha. Forget the pain. Americans! Look at that beautiful group of boisterous, noisy supporters all carrying American flags. That's more like it. Trisha, adjust your attitude. This is most certainly not the worst day of your life. You could be sitting on the couch rotting in front of a television at 275 pounds. No matter what happens I am an Olympian. This is most certainly not the worst day of my life. It is one of the best days of my life, even if I fall down and die out here. From this point in the race I am going to count my blessings instead of my troubles. When I walked into Club Sport Green Valley those years ago, into that friendly atmosphere, I knew I was where I belonged. It was there that I encountered people who had thought and felt as I had. At the Club I finally began to understand what I'd been searching for all of my life. Those doors opened to me and I walked back into my future. I was always a runner.

Now here I am trying not to feel sorry for myself. Trisha what are you most grateful for? Kara Goucher was right when she pronounced a comparison between running a hard marathon and having a baby. Gratitude, Trisha.

The runner, calling from deep within the well of self-determination, an inner place which only the most elite knew how to access, made the decision to pick up the pace again. Her stride was at its perfect gate so the job now was to move . . . faster. The first new step in the rhythm sent a shot of pain from her left foot up the backside of her leg, through the lower back and up into her neck. It was agonizing, and then just as if she had been touched by a magic wand, it was gone. She settled in at a new speed and this time her effort paid off. She was gaining ground on the entire field, closing the gap between her and the race leaders. She didn't know it yet, but others did. Some twenty minutes later she passed Ryoko Kizaki of Japan and moved into the top 40. For the first time in quite a while Trisha could see the front of the field. They were still way too far ahead for her to get excited about possibilities. She was in the race of her life, the culmination of her life's work, and yet because of physical challenges, she found comfort only in daydreaming, continuing to run on auto pilot.

"Rachael, grab my suitcase. Brad we have to go, NOW! My water broke. If you don't get going, Dr. Peterson, you'll be delivering this child, excuse me—these children—yourself in the back seat of that

girl catching bachelor car we decided to take to the hospital. First you deliver me to my own bed in that '57 Chevy and now we use the same car to go deliver the kids." Trisha was laughing as her sister and husband raced all over the place trying to make the hospital in time. They made it to the hospital. Trish couldn't remember who was the most excited. Bradley was the total male chauvinist, beating his chest with pride. Trisha was so happy to get the kids out of her and on their way, but Rachael, she was altogether in a different place. She couldn't have children of her own. What with Bradley traveling all over the world and Trisha living the life of a professional athlete, it was obvious to everyone that Rachael would assume a very special role in their lives. That's why Brad and Trisha had built their home next door to Adam and Rachael's place right there at the day care center. It takes a village. The kids delivered perfectly. When it was time to go home, Trisha surprised everyone by lacing up running shoes, squeezing into shorts and jogging two and a half miles back to the house, proving again that she was a runner. Only Rachael had been let in on the secret. Brad tried to stop her, but she felt fine and by the time she made it home, they were barely unloading the car. She hadn't missed a thing . . . Over the next few years her focus became the health, joy, and mentoring of the two people who meant more to her than life itself, her children. Brad quickly fell to sixth spot in her pecking order. He came after the twins, Rachael and the bulldogs. It wasn't really so, but it seemed to be. Theirs had been a happy life. Trisha had much to be thankful for.

The course took a sharp right hand turn, out towards the ocean. Crowds of race fans and others were crunching into the running lanes, sometimes leaving the athletes with just few feet or so of racing room. It was claustrophobic. Trisha had grown used to the deafening noise. Today was like none other, not only something she would never forget, but something she may never recover from. The pain was back again and this time it was worse than ever. Still she kept pace, moving ever so slowly through runners, one at a time. She had decided it was this pace or nothing. She had no chance to win at any other speed and Michael was right. Being here had turned out to be . . . just not enough. And then—déjà vu—who said lightning couldn't strike twice in the same place?

* * *

"Trisha."

I know that voice. The pain is so bad I'm losing my mind. We're barely half way through and already I'm suffering delusions. My mind is going to fail me because I am not giving in to the pain. I have young children and still I don't care. I don't care. I'll never give in. I'd rather die than quit this race.

"Trisha, you're not delusional."

"Tell me, Dad. How many of the girls out here are talking to their dead father? My mind is breaking down. Why else would I be in this conversation?"

"You don't remember the dreams, do you?"

"The dreams . . . what dreams? Dad, I dream about you all the time. I'd be a lot more affectionate right now, but I'm stuck in this brutal race. This nightmare is my dream. I want to win this race. Can you help? I'd be forever grateful."

"Mac tells me that you're receptive because you are phasing in and out of a waking trance. He has perfected how to implement my thoughts into your persona. This is a very special moment for me, little runner girl, and not just because you made it so far, but because we haven't been together like this for years. I can't run the race for you but I can help . . . just a little."

"Did you say Mac? Are you talking about Wise Mac, the second class angel? I am delusional. I remember him from dreams I had about you a long time ago. Are you really there, Daddy?"

"I sure am. Would you like me to prove it to you?"

"Thinking of you helps, yes, just thinking of you and how much I love you keeps me running without losing pace. That doesn't prove you are really there, though. You're just imaginary, right?"

"I said I'd prove it and I will. You're the engine of the Roger Martin Foundation if you haven't forgotten. Well, my name is Roger Martin. If I said I can prove it, I meant it. I agree about the affectionate part. I don't feel much like the lovey-dovey thing right now either. Let's get to work. It's your turn today and I won't let you down."

"Ok, Dad." Trisha chuckled, thinking herself a head case. She was in the middle of an Olympic marathon race, there were thousands of people right alongside the road and there was a global television audience watching, perhaps as many as a billion viewers. What was she doing? She was having a conversation with her deceased father.

How would that revelation play out in the post-race interview? She laughed again. At least she wasn't dwelling on the pain right now and she had clipped another mile off of the run. This would all be over in just 12 miles. *"What have you got for me, Father?"*

"Here we go, Trisha. In the beginning this is going to hurt, but only for a couple of seconds.

After that you'll feel like a million bucks. Are you ready?"

"You're the man, Daddy. Just give me the word."

"Slow down for just a second or so. Get an easy gate that leaves you in your most flexible state. Don't worry about falling behind; the maneuver will only take a few seconds."

This is ridiculous. Now I am to obey the commands of my dearly departed loving father and he wants me to slow down, even for a few seconds. "Do you mind if I kindly ask you and Mac what the strategy is? After the race they are going to ask why I slowed down."

Roger started laughing. "No they won't, Trisha. They will never know. Here is the strategy. Get ready to do an unexpected hurdle. Everyone else gets to run a flat course. If you want to win, you have to undertake a hurdle. Now do it, Kid-now!"

Trisha evened her pace and prepared for some kind of a jump. She did feel foolish . . . *good hell!* The dog leaped right in front of her, baring teeth as if ready to strike. She hurdled over the beast in perfect stride, using exact form as taught to her by a high school buddy more than two decades earlier, one Brad Peterson. At impact her entire body felt like it had been struck by lightning, but the pain meant nothing just like he had said. "Daddy, you . . ." He was gone, but her confidence zoomed. *Oh, Daddy . . . It's time to pick up the pace . . . again.*

* * *

"What just happened?" Becky Martin was glued to her seat along with her son, Michael, his wife, Janet, all three of their kids and sports agent David Giles. They had moved from the starting line of the race and were now in Olympic Stadium where the marathon would end in about an hour or so. There was a buzz all over because of what had just appeared up on the Jumbotron. It looked like Trisha had jumped something. "Did she just have to jump another dog, like when she was a child?" She was leaning forward, hoping to see the image again. When it did replay, the entire scene was so eerie. A dog had jumped in front of Trisha, she had cleared the animal, which turned and started to chase her, that is until it was subdued by security officials on the sight, like two seconds later. One of them looked injured, perhaps bitten. Then, off in the distance, police were chasing someone, catching him, and had him on the ground. "Was that an intentional act?"

"I don't know, Mom." Michael was troubled. His kid sister had been struggling the entire way. She looked gaunt, completely worn out, and yet her splits were the fastest of her life. He'd worked very hard to maintain a positive attitude and was feeling much better when she started moving up in the standings, slowly passing one runner at a time, but this, this dog thing had him paranoid. He knew that every athlete in that race was in danger of something terrible, something as yet unknown happening. He also knew that the self-confidence of the Brazilian security people bordered on arrogance. How could they control that mob out there? He feared for Trisha, and now this. "I just don't know, gang." *Get a grip on yourself, Michael. Think of something positive to say.* "Look at it this way. She hurdled over that beast like she had planned for it. That's our Trisha. It's like she detected the problem, made a decision, and cleared it like the professional she is. Her courage is contagious. I mean, all of a sudden my spine tells me that we . . . are backing the right horse. We need to wait and see what happens. Go, Aunt Trisha, go." The kids started cheering, Becky joined in, Mike smiled and David, well David was as white as a ghost. He knew better.

* * *

"Did you see that? I am amazing!" Imp Rogue, silicon, a sentient being, barely if you were to ask one of the Grays, was bursting with pride and patting himself on the back. "You can only imagine what the cute little racer girl is thinking now. I've been studying how the water-bag mammals think and this little trick is sure to, how shall I put it, mess her up. Now, all she will be able to think about is what happened when she was a pup. I even went with the same breed of dog that you used back then. Trust me. I have studied human psychology."

Stump Killer was sitting right next to his buddy. Together they had caused endless havoc in the lives of the humans, Brad Peterson and Trisha Martin. It was Stump who had personally set her back twelve years by prompting a little boy to lose control of his dog at one of her races when she was just emerging from an engaging childhood. No one had stepped forward to take credit for her father's demise a few months later. *People live and die all over the galaxy. It was just his time and the timing was perfect.* Unfortunately, the buoyancy of the young lady finally paid off and she recovered from her personal tragedies. "You did well, my friend. We are sure to be rewarded for our genius. We get to destroy this one, plus we get to wipe out the—how is it they call this celebration of their civilization—the Olympic movement—because of the actions of a few. It is the mammals own fault. They always destroy themselves. This experiment, the Earth project, has yielded a higher breed of mammalian intelligence, and they are very resilient, but in the end the result will be the same. We are sure to be rewarded for our creative plan. You know what we need to do? We need to make certain that Thiefdeamon doesn't get the glory. That fool steals credit for everything we do in the service of the Great Lord."

Stump Killer and Imp Rogue had, on their own, schemed up the idea of using pulse particle beams to agitate humans who were already prone to violence. They had traversed a small worm hole to get to the planet Mercury in a miniature anti-gravitational hover craft from their outpost near Polaris. To the best of their knowledge, no one even suspected they were gone yet, or so they thought. "OK, Imp. You had your turn. I even let you use my doggie idea. It was pretty good. You scared her for sure, but she jumped perfectly. Perhaps she remembered from the last time. What I liked about it, though, was what came after. I'll give you a . . . , a . . . , uh . . . , silver medal for that. Step away from the particle beam gun and let the gold medalist get ready." The tall, obsidian creature nestled into the seat and began the algorithm cycles that were necessary to his preparations. He started laughing boisterously, and then his friend did, too. They were having great fun.

* * *

Eric Finnegan had come down to the Laboratory this morning to run some simulations that had been downloaded overnight from Messenger, the only satellite to ever orbit the planet Mercury. The NASA mission was being spearheaded here at Johns Hopkins University's Applied Physics Laboratory in Laurel, Maryland. NASA had a good many high profile projects going on in the other direction, mainly to Mars, Jupiter, Saturn, and the recent flyby of Pluto, so Messenger's scientists had become the forgotten and neglected. Nobody seemed to care about Mercury anymore. As he studied the download, he noticed an anomaly. It seemed like there was a sudden flash of light and then something appeared out of the blue, just above the horizon on the night side of the planet. Messenger was orbiting around the other side at the moment and he decided to change the mission objectives and see if he could get a live look at the anomaly. The scientist worked the computer keyboard feverishly because the spacecraft was to swing back around in just a minute or so. In the meantime he multitasked, looking carefully at what he did have and could not believe his eyes. Because one of Messenger's primary objectives was to map Mercury's surface, he had only the one shot, but it was a beauty. He was looking at some sort of a UFO. It had to be. *Why are people always alone when they see something?*

His pulse quickened and he began to get sweaty palms. This, or something like it, had been the secret dream of his youth when he made the decision to devote his career to astronomy. Oh, he was smart enough not to tell anyone that he wanted to discover life in the cosmos; he would have been laughed out of the business, or worse relegated to the SETI Institute, but . . .

Messenger swung back out in front of the planet on its eccentrically elliptical orbit. Eric would have plenty of time to study the spot. Perhaps the object was still there. *I should call Faith. She would love this. Maybe I shouldn't call Faith. She can't be trusted to play this story close to the vest. If she sees this thing, she'll want to call Marilyn Lindstrom or anyone else at NASA in D.C. I am going to play this hand alone and then decide if there's anything to report. Right now there isn't enough to go on* . . . There was nothing. He used the telephoto lens so that he could take a look up-close and personal. There was still nothing. Finnegan turned every instrument Messenger had onto the spot. There was nothing, except . . . hold on, there was something. The magnometer was detecting a small magnetic disturbance just above the surface of the planet, right where his instruments were pointed. *What's that?* He intensified the view into an infrared radio picture and began to see the faint outline of something he just could not understand. *If I didn't know better, I'd say that's a cloaked Klingon Bird of Prey.* Within ten seconds Eric Finnegan's life changed forever. The object materialized into plain view. Messenger's radio antenna picked up a very strong particle beam directed right at Earth. At the end of another ten seconds, the beam stopped and the UFO became invisible again. The beam would hit Earth in less than six minutes, but since it took the same amount of time for his own signal come in from Messenger, it had already hit. *What the hell was that!* Eric pulled the phone from his pocket and dialed.

"MMT Observatory, how can I help you?"

"Good morning, this is Eric Finnegan at Johns Hopkins, may I please speak with Faith Vilas." *What an idiot I am. I shouldn't be calling her; she's a prig. Yeah, but you're in love with her. You can't resist. Like I said, what an idiot I am.* His colleague and friend picked up on the other end.

"Eric?"

"Faith, you're not going to believe what I have to show you . . . , hold on. I'm going to have to call you back." Something new had just popped up on his view screen, another bright flash of light. Eric, who had unceremoniously terminated the call, leaving his friend in the dark, looked intently at the screen. Now there were two of them, two Birds of Prey, sitting side by side. They both materialized into plain sight and then went into what he was calling the cloaked mode. About a minute later they both materialized again, and then in a simultaneous double flash they both disappeared, but not until after another particle beam was sent directly towards Earth.

The scientist, now more confused than ever, stared silently at his computer screen. Before he called Faith back, he decided to save the entire episode. He had the evidence that millions around the world craved and it was irrefutable. Unfortunately, when he tried to save the data in a second place, his computer froze. *What the hell!* He tried to restart and reboot, to no avail. He tried to reboot the machine in safe mode with no luck. He started to panic. After an hour of frantic software analysis he finally got the computer up and running only to find that everything he had observed in the past day was gone, completely gone. It was like the past day never even happened. He scanned every drive in the machine, looking for soft storage of the data in the temporary internet files, the hard disk, the deleted trash and several other places. It was gone . . . forever.

* * *

Slybrain Thiefdeamon was furious. "You idiots have no idea what you've risked, and for what; to play with some mice from planet Earth? Were you even aware they have a probe in orbit here? You've been in plain sight of trained scientists whose job it is to observe anything they can find on this molten rock! When Zama finds out what happened here, you're toast. I'm toast. It would go easier on you if I just sent you to the sunny side of this planet."

"Master Thiefdeamon," Imp was being as cautious as he could. "We would fry over there. We're too close to their star. Besides, we figured out how to rid ourselves of the girl. The Great Lord will be pleased. Stump and I worked it out. The particle beam would be coming straight out of their sun and would not be detectable from the any other normal radiation. We worked it out . . ."

"Silence!" Both underlings were cowering. Slybrain could taste their fear. "We need to get out of here. I have an idea. He signaled to the other ship that he would be returning with the wannabe heroes. Then he jumped into the firing seat, configured the variants, and then shot off another particle beam. In an instant both ships entered the wormhole and were on their way back.

"Instead of punishing you for this thoughtless adventure, I am going to try and teach you something. First of all, the girl is no longer of any importance to us. In case you haven't figured out the obvious, her lover, our real objective, has already performed his task with the young man who poses such a threat. We have failed. Second, and more importantly, these mammals are unlike any other we have encountered. Because some foolish Annunaki got too attracted to the females, about 3,000 earth cycles in the past, he impregnated one or more of them and a genetic mutation generated an exponential explosion in human intelligence. That is why they are so smart, so far advanced that if they get into the realm of Eternals, life as we know it could change drastically. Gratefully, they do not have the wisdom to match their intellect, and that is the problem with this boy. It has been determined that his leadership may just change that, too. I have heard from others that Didi thinkers believe the Earthlings are the smartest life form we have ever encountered." Thiefdeamon's eager students paid close attention. "Don't think that just because we have the ability to navigate space that we are all that smart. Do you have any idea how this ship works? I don't. Stop trying to outthink Didi! You are no match for these crafty humans. I think we can make this go away, that is if you can keep quiet, a real long shot as we both know. The particle beam I just sent will fix this. Now when we get back, you keep your silly mouths shut. We will report that you were on field reconnaissance studying a nebula just a few light years away and no one will be the wiser. Lurton Zama is nothing but a dumb lizard. He will never suspect us. Every time you ignoramus dimwits try something you put me on the chopping block. You are very lucky that I enjoy teaching . . . this time. Perhaps next time your fortunes will change. Of course, you could surprise me and spare me the necessity of a next time. We shall see."

* * *

". . . . is shaping up to be the fastest women's marathon in history. Our leader, China's Xiaolin Zhu, continues to draw the entire field forward at a torrid pace. Things look to tighten up just a bit though as she enters the only climb at the 17 mile mark, just a bit beyond 17 miles, actually. Zhu is not known as a great climber, but the runner behind her from Portugal, Marisa Barros, is and figures to make a move right here. Barros finished thirteenth in London just three minutes behind Gold Medalist Tiki Gelana, the Ethiopian who is speeding along just a few meters back and currently running third. One has to wonder how long the front runners can keep up the pace in this humidity and heat. If they do, then Paula Radcliffe's long standing world record, set in 2003, of 2:15:25 is definitely in danger of being broken today." The announcer, Chris Maddocks, was riding with the remote broadcast camera in the back of a very small, specially equipped Smart Car, able to navigate in and out of the running lanes. "Now let's take a look at the Americans. Kara Goucher and Shalane Flanagan are just a bit farther back in eighth and ninth at the moment. They will be heading into the hill in just a minute or so where rumors have it that they intend to attack. Both are very good climbers. Right now Goucher, who finished just behind Flanagan in London, is about 10 meters out in front of her teammate.

"One of the most interesting stories of this race has to be the effort put up by 36 year old Trisha Jean Martin. She has battled her way back from the middle of the pack and now holds onto fourteenth position. She has been running the fastest mile splits in the entire field for quite some time and is currently only a couple of minutes behind the leaders. Something has to give. At just over five minutes a mile, the pace she has kept since jumping that wayward dog, should give her time to catch the leaders before the end of the race. In case you think Trisha Martin is too old to win, think again. Marathoners compete longer than other track athletes. Romanian Constantina Dita won the gold in Beijing, setting an Olympic record when she was 38. She made the London games too but finished well back in the middle of the pack. Don't count Martin out of this race, not yet anyway, although as it stands right now, the race belongs to Zhu, Barros or Gelana. It's theirs to win or lose at this point. What's that? Oh my God! . . . No! . . . This can't be happening . . ."

* * *

"Get up and get going. We told you to expect this kind of trouble in your life. Get UP!"

Of course, she did as she was told. Her right leg was scraped raw and her right shoulder was bruised from landing on the pavement. The fetid smell of rot and feces was all over her body. She had also been hit by raw eggs in the back of the head and before she made it back to her running pace three runners had passed her. The shocked look on their faces and the fear in their eyes told her that the complexion of the entire race had changed. As she moved on the noise behind her had turned dark. There were fans, both American and from other countries as well, chasing the perpetrators down and police were descending from several directions at once. Two helicopters, not the television camera variety, but armed security types, converged behind her. Unbelievably, the race continued. Presently several broadcast helicopters also showed up. The lead

NBC crew that was on the scene already had captured the whole incident and broadcast it live.

Slowly but surely the runner collected her wits and swallowed fear. There was incredible encouragement from everyone as word of the incident moved forward like wildfire. Something began to change within her. Fear and doubt were being pushed aside by a powerful new emotion, cold hearted fury. She was damn angry. How *dare* those cowardly bastards! Her anger turned into rage. She began the climb up the hill, thrusting herself into a frenzied gallop. This was personal and for Trisha Jean Martin, there was a clear message to send and only she could be the messenger. The aches and pains were behind her along with the stench of whatever concoction had filled the water balloons heaved at her, at her! She decided to just ignore her bleeding leg. It wasn't all that bad. She had to remove the bands holding her hair in place so that she could pour water over her head at the next station and clean the egg off of her back and neck.

The three runners who'd made it past her, New Zeeland's Kim Smith, Hilda Kibet from the Netherlands, and Dailín Belmonte, the Cuban who was holding her own out there, quickly gave way to Trisha Martin's resurgent effort. The Cuban patted her on the back as she ran through and actually wished her well. No one out on the course wanted to win the race because of an incident like that, but they did want to win very badly.

Trisha crested the hill, went through the water station as planned and took stock of her situation. There were a measly eight miles left in today's race. The leaders were out there about 50 yards or so in front of her. She could see them now as the course flattened into a straight line. There were also six other competitors between her and them. Trisha had passed three more back on the hill, entering the top ten for the first time since the start of the race. She was closing on two who were still running together, Shalane and Kara, her teammates. They had become her next objective. Somehow the water balloon and egg incident had energized her. Could she hold out and keep this going for the next 40 minutes or so? It would take a miracle.

No one was running as fast as Trisha Martin. She had blazed from the middle of the pack to get into the top ten, achieving mile splits that seemed unreal. She felt the presence of a runner coming from behind, unable to surmise who could be creeping up, but Trish was determined to face forward and keep her focus on those ahead. When he caught up to her she nearly fainted.

To her, he was very real. Obviously to everyone else, he didn't exist. She wasn't spooked at all, but did consider herself delusional once again. Trisha couldn't explain how he was there to help her jump the dog, or to get up off the pavement when she fell. She was confused about how something like that could be happening inside her mind. The runner had found a second wind for the umpteenth time in this race. As long as she didn't get shot in the back, caught in an unseen trip wire, mowed out of existence by a flame thrower or fall victim to some other calamity, this marathon would become a personal record for her. Further, she had become the darling of the race. She was being given a wide berth by roaring fans every inch of the way; they were Olympic enthusiasts who felt personally responsible for her safety, for everyone's, really.

The crowd was huge. She had at least two television cameras on her at all times. *What is the media thinking about this? Why am I being singled out? I did nothing to enflame these crazies. If they wanted to light my fire and see me win, they couldn't have done a better job. "Dad, you know how I know that you are really just a delusion?"*

"Pick it up a little bit, Trisha. I didn't make this trip to see you lose. Quit worrying about how I got here and just . . . pick it up a little." She did and was now gaining precipitously on her next objective in the race. *"I'll stay with you for a while. You need the diversion. I know how you think. How is it that you know so much? How is it that you know I am just a figment of your imagination? Hold that thought. Here comes your trusty trainer with help."*

Stanley Burton, her coach and teacher, was himself sitting on the back of a large motorcycle. He wanted to spray something on her raw thigh. She evened her pace, slowing just barely, and let him take care of business. He looked terrible. *I'm the one stuck in this hell-begotten bad dream and it is Stan that I am worried about.* When the trainer was finished, it took all of three seconds; he smiled up at her and the bike began to pull away. She formed words on her lips, and then fell back into her mind where she was comfortable. At each turn the roar of race enthusiasts grew. Her enemies had created a monster; *to hell with them.*

"Dad, if you were real you would have worn the proper attire. You're wearing running gear that is, like, three decades out of place. You look like how I remember you which means that you are just a figment of my imagination, so there."

* * *

Stanley's scooter pulled ahead towards Olympic Stadium where he would be waiting at the finish. They passed the frontrunners one at a time. If he could speak with his student he would tell her that each of them was in pain, running along mostly on wits alone, striving for the unthinkable, an Olympic gold medal. They all looked shot. He could not believe that these people could still be running at such a relentless pace. Each woman seemed to be locked into some sort of a mental trance, everyone different from the others, all sunken into some inner place, a depth where heroes go when there is no way out. Not a single one seemed to be aware of the fact that the entire world was watching. Trisha's incident was being reported the world over. An Olympic event had become hard news, more than a mere athletic event. Stanley climbed off of the scooter and was walking to his place near the finish line. Trisha's phone rang. Stanley checked, smiled inwardly and then he picked up the call. "Bradley, I see you are watching the race."

"How is she and what did you just give her?"

"She's doing remarkably well, considering what she has been going through. To be quite honest, I have never seen courage like that. Your wife is the most amazing person I have ever met. I am watching on the Jumbotron right now and, as you can also see, she just passed Goucher and Flanagan. Did you see her encourage them to try and keep up? They tried, but they just can't. Right now she is threatening to break a five minute mile. I don't see how she can keep this relentless push up to the end, but if she does . . . , oh yeah, the medicine. I zapped her with a topical spray consisting of benzocaine to numb the pain a bit and some antibiotic clindamycin in case infection sets in."

"That's a pretty good choice, Dr. Burton."

"The Olympic types get the credit. They handed me the mixture and I just trusted that it would help some. She gave me a microsecond of herself to lip-sync a thank you and said she loved me. How are you?"

"I don't know. At first I was in total shock. Then I wanted to kill somebody, and then my phone started ringing. I took a call from a friend at the State Department and he told me confidentially that they have an idea who's behind all of this crap and that made me feel a little better. Then I took another call from an old friend, Bob Hankle. Bob is a Colonel, he's 68 years old now, and is still out there on active duty commanding troops in the field. The guy is ageless.

Anyway, he tells me that if the source of all this trouble is within reach, he and his boys intend to send them a thank you note. That made me feel a whole lot better. I love my army buddies. So, I would have to say that at best my feelings are mixed.

"By the way you're right about my wife. She just passed somebody named Tatyana Petrova Arkhipova, a Russian, and moved into sixth. I have never seen that look on her face. I didn't think she could get that angry. Someone picked a fight with the wrong girl. I hope my boys out there get the chance to make a return call."

Stanley felt the need to share. "Just so you are aware and don't say something you'll regret, you do know that we are not on a secure line. There are ears all over out here."

"I knew that, Stanley. That's why I said it. Let me repeat myself. My name is Captain Bradley Peterson of the United States Army. If you're out there and can hear me, know this; my wife is Trisha Jean Martin Peterson, the greatest marathoner in history. My friends and I are looking for you and we will find you." Bradley got off of the phone and allowed himself to be mesmerized by the race. Then rage stirred deep within him. He could feel it in his hands. *They are messing with my Trisha.* He started to shake. He felt fear, and then something very dark surfaced. Less than a day ago he had saved a boy's life. That deed had emerged from his good side. His hidden self then began to emerge from someplace he never knew existed until shortly after that plane crash changed his life. Now all he wanted was revenge, violent permanent revenge. *It's not about you, at least I think it is not about you, Brad. Try to let go of this poison.*

His dark mood began to improve. Trisha had just passed Kenya's Priscah Jeptoo. The race would end in just five miles. His soul mate had just improved her position again. There were now just four contestants between her and a coveted Olympic gold medal.

* * *

"Dear God Almighty, the One whom I serve. Please let me acknowledge the grandeur of your mighty creation of the heavens and the earth, for you are the succession of the night and the day, the One who has granted me insight to carry out your will. It is with purpose and meaning that you have created me for this one moment, to glorify your name. I have prepared my spirit, mind, and body to serve only you. I have not ceased my prayers, in hope that you will grant me, a humble and true believer, the reward I long for, glory in Paradise to inherit and abide in forever . . ."

The supplicant crouched low in a dingy building on a hill overlooking Olympic Stadium. He was dressed in a white thobe, his shaved head hooded, and his beard now fully grown. His face and hands were the only part of his holy body exposed. He was clean. Should God wish it, and allow him to continue his mortal service, he would survive the day. From his vantage he had access to the entire running track inside of the arena; it was almost a mile from where he had set up. The line of sight to his target though, once she ran beyond the local commercial area and into his shooting zone was still outside of the arena and would provide him the first of two shot opportunities. He only occasionally peeked out of the tiny window in anticipation of the deed he had been ordered to carry out. The marksman tried not to think of hunger which panged him physically. To invoke God's blessing he had fasted for three days, drinking only purified water to hydrate his nerves.

Once he had been a young boy, full of hope and joy. When his love of life had turned to hatred for the enemies of God, he himself a witness to the horrific nightmares inflicted upon his family by unbelievers, he began to look for retribution upon the infidels. He eventually found his way into al-Qaeda in Mesopotamia, where it was discovered that he had the uncanny talents of extreme marksmanship. The Olympics had been the gathering place of the finest marksmen on earth, yet his skill surpassed them all. Just a few days ago, he had competed as a marksman for his country, yet he purposely failed in his quest so as not to attract any attention to himself. That was how he had gained entry into the Olympic village. He could have easily killed the woman there, but had been ordered to wait until now, so that the world could witness the power of God and His greatness. Now his aim would be deadly and very public. Anticipation grew as the time for his first and best shot drew near.

There was irony in the tools of his trade, for he was the benefactor of weapons and communication devices created for him by his own enemies. The ultra-long range rifle, an Mk-15 50 caliber weapon, was mounted on a tripod set back from the window where it could not be detected. What seemed amazing to the shooter was how easy it had been to acquire the entire shooting package. It was a gun that was legal for private citizens to own almost anywhere in the United States, homeland of the Great Satan. *I employ the will of God Almighty using the tools of the Devil himself.*

The International Olympic movement of the entire civilized world would end forever the instant he squeezed the trigger. The only thing that meant more to him than knowing it would be his finger that God touched, was his target. He could only dream of the pain he would cause the instrument of Satan's hand, the mercenary surgeon who had saved so many of God's enemies, thereby staying the true hand of peace. There was but a single troubling aspect to his mission. In the past hour he had not received any updates from his masters. They had gone silent. The headset he wore underneath his hooded cloak screamed its silence. *What is wrong?*

* * *

The winner today will be the person that can keep this up from here to the end. Can I? "Dad, is it fair for me to have you as a shade to carry me through? I mean, isn't this cheating?" Trisha decided to keep up the charade of a two way conversation. Fortunately, she had the wind and had long grown used to the heat. That was the good news. There was other good news as well.

She had used the noise and focus of the crowd to buoy her spirits. Ever since the nasty attempt to take her out of the race, the entire world had been on her side. She was being pushed by the support of race enthusiasts from all over. It was like having an imaginary engine, well, as long as there was gas in the tank. If she ran out of gas that would be the end of this little run into history. Hers would then become a footnote of the real story, the tale of whoever survived to get to the finish line first. There were still runners ahead of her, too. There is always good and bad news. The bad news happened to be the pain, soreness and sharp jabs throbbing and pulsating from one end of her body to the other. When she had removed the hair bands, making it possible to clean the egg off, she worried that wind resistance would make a difference, but it hadn't. Her hair was flying behind her, something like that of a wild and wicked witch, but she didn't even notice. Besides, she was missing two things necessary to be a convincing witch, a black high-coned hat and the all-important broom. Would that she could fly in and take the race.

Roger Martin was distracted, almost missing her question. His daughter was in grave danger, he knew it, but could not warn her. *Of what use would it be for me to tell her that an assassin has a rifle and is out there trying to finish the job others had failed at this morning. "I'm not even here, remember. I'm just a figment of your imagination, created by you so that you can live with the unbearable pain. How do you know if all of the other leaders don't have secret training partners running alongside them? Keep your mind on business, Trisha. Take a look at that!"*

Jessica Augusto, Portugal's hope for a medal in this event, still in the race and running fourth, was faltering. Tricia, scooting smoothly along about twenty seconds back, began to notice a twitch in her gate and it was costing her time. She had both seen and experienced a very similar condition before. This was not good for the athlete, who was, in fact, one of Trisha's friends out on the running circuit. It didn't mean that she was finished or that she couldn't make it to the finish line, she had seen runners fight that sort of thing off before, but she was slowing perceptibly. *I hate to see it happen to someone I like so much, but . . .* "Except for the grace of God Almighty, Dad, there goes me too. Any part of me could cave at any moment. I'm sad for her." She decided to increase her pace again at the next mile marker, where fluids waited. *"Father, I would like to put you to another test."* Trisha felt like laughing, but refused to let it show on her face, the first and only time she let a television camera dictate a facial expression. She didn't want the viewing audience to think she was happy about Augusto's misfortune. If she had her way, they would've crossed the line one and two, just a millisecond apart, along with her American teammates. It wasn't going to happen. The twitch was growing and she was still slowing. *"Dad, see if you can tell me something, something uplifting, that I have never heard before. If you can do that, then perhaps I'll be convinced that you're real and I am being shepherded to the finish line by you and Wise Mac. Remember, Daddy, if you guys are breaking rules to get me a gold medal, you will be in trouble."* Trisha eased past Jessica Augusto. When she went by, there was eye contact, a reassuring token of love and respect, along with some verbal encouragement. The pain on her friend's face told the story, though, and Trisha now questioned whether she what it took to get to the finish line.

As quickly as Trisha moved on, Augusto dropped yet another position, falling into sixth as Sultan Haydar, the Turkish runner, sailed past. She was hanging right in there, perhaps the surprise of the day to this point.

Trisha approached the water station. Ever since her fall she had followed the exact same routine. She took water in open cups and drenched herself at the front and then took the drink at the end of the table. It was a one-race habit that was working wonders in this heat. Now it was time to pick up the pace . . . again. *I am not sure about the others up in front, but will Haydar notice and keep up? That is the question.* As for the other three, two of them were quite a ways out there yet, and there were just four miles to go in the race. Time was running out for the American.

"So, Dad . . ."

* * *

The swimming pools, both the outside and inside pools were empty, save for a few small children and their mothers who were playing in the kiddy pool. Certainly it was hot enough in the Las Vegas suburb of Henderson, Nevada at Club Sport Green Valley. Usually the pools were full. No one was playing racquet ball, hand ball, or squash. There wasn't a soul on the tennis courts indoors, in the bubble, or outside either. The usual hustle and bustle in the weight room was silent. The parking lot was full. There were cars parked all up and down the street. Across the way, a multi-level parking garage associated with the retail shopping center was full, but no one was shopping in this neighborhood today.

The baskets had been raised; temporary bleachers had been installed, as had a huge Jumbotron. There were literally thousands of club members and supporters jammed inside the basketball court area and they were going wild watching their hero, Trisha Jean Martin, fight her way into contention for an Olympic gold medal. When she had been attacked earlier in the race they had turned into a mob, ready to go down there as a group and find someone to lynch; it had been ugly.

When Trisha had jumped right back up and accelerated like the professional she was, they started into a wild and supportive chant. Could she catch the leaders? They would not get the blood they wanted, but could she catch the others and make a defiant statement for all of them?

April Keller and Greg Simpson, both longtime personal friends of Trisha's, sat together on the front row of the second set of chairs set up on the floor. They had a perfect view. April was currently employed at Club Sport. She had three jobs, actually, and had written a book. After graduating from UNLV, she was promoted into the management trainee program at Target, where she, Trisha, and Greg had worked together. Now she was a national buyer for Target and worked mostly. She was also a meeting leader at Weight Watchers. She and Trisha had lost all of their weight together. At Club Sport, April worked as a personal trainer. April's passions were health, fitness, and weight management. Greg on the other hand was a great guy, but incorrigible. He had fought off addiction problems, been fired from several jobs, had married and divorced, but finally seemed to have his life going in the right direction. He recently renewed his relationship with April Keller when he had joined the club. She kept smiling at him while he was completing the club membership application and he kept asking if they had ever met. When she finally told him who she was, he was stunned.

April watched over Greg like a mother hen, enjoying his little accomplishments like recently achieving three consecutive years of sobriety. He was in love and had no idea how to impress the beautiful woman at his side. He could only hope.

They were both overwhelmed by what Trisha was doing. Greg mused, "Who could have known where the three of us would end up? Do you remember that day we went to Applebee's and you two got me started on the road to recovery?"

"Hey, keep your hands to yourself, buddy. We're trying to win a gold medal here. Do I have to get molested in the process?" She smiled, turned, and kissed him full on the lips; it was more than just a peck. Her hands slipped around the small of his back. "What am I going to do with you, Greg? How can I ever trust you enough?"

"Bad boys need love too, April. In case you haven't noticed, I've been accepted to UNLV's Boyd School of Law, you know."

"So now I get stuck with a bad boy who's becoming a lawyer to boot. You're going in the wrong direction," she started laughing, but was suddenly distracted. The noise level in the room was metering up again. A frenzied tornado was beginning to stir. Something was happening. They both looked up at the Jumbotron. Trisha was gaining ground again. She and another runner following just a few yards behind were closing in on the next racer. It would only be a matter of time before she moved up. Trisha was flying like an American mountain cat in pursuit of its prey. Her long brunette hair was flowing wildly behind her and she had an intense look in her eyes. When April glanced at Greg, noticing tears welling from deep within his eyes, a new and exciting feeling began to flare up inside of her, something akin to forbidden desire accompanied by red flags. *Oh no, I can't be going there.*

* * *

The shade hadn't spoken in a while, running by her side effortlessly, though he looked serious, a comically concerned father outfitted in his old fashioned running gear. He was her conscience, a spiritual guide, her father. For years and years, Trisha had missed her dad. Due to some magical trick of the mind, he was with her now. He had saved her from the dog, a vicious beast. *How could that be?* At times during the past couple of miles his presence had sealed her off from the chaos of the screaming Olympic fans crowding in on their running space, the roar of helicopters overhead, noisy motorcycles, the heat, the dust and unrelenting fatigue. At other times she suffocated from all of the distractions, succumbing to agonizingly numb feet, rubbery legs, and an aching shoulder from the fall; she was suffering from dehydration and even blurred vision. The end of the race looked a hundred miles away. Trisha needed to get her mind off of the pain.

"So, Dad, inspire me. Tell me something I have never heard." *Are you really here?*

Her father looked like he wanted to tell a joke. *"If you want to lose weight and you're eating at home, you still need to dine like a queen. Set the stage and use a table cloth. Turn down the lights a bit, sing a little, be detail oriented with spices, herbs, perhaps a dollop of fat free yogurt. Whatever you do, don't eat out of the container. Sit down to eat."*

"You're kidding, right?"

"Starting your day with a healthy breakfast is vital to your weight loss journey. It fuels you up, especially if you focus on high fiber complex carbohydrates, lean protein, and just a bit of the right kind of fat."

"Father, you are a bit late with diet advice, Right now in my dehydrated condition, I bet I don't weigh a hundred pounds, so I am not feeling all that inspired. No matter what happens, when this is over I'm going to pig out. You have to do better than that. What else?" *Only my dad, or my brother, would take me so far off target. He has to be there.*

"I can sense your fear, Trisha. That is why I'm here to let you share it with me. In the end, fear is nothing but an illusion. When you share it with someone, it tends to disappear. You're right. I was just trying to distract you. I would love nothing more than to eat with you later today. We could stand on the corner, gorge on Chinese right out of the box, and laugh. We both know that isn't going to happen. You see, my little running companion, a child's life is like a piece of paper on which every person leaves a mark. You are my child and I am trying to leave you a mark to go on. You have helped so many. If you only stopped to count and could see, you would be amazed."

This, unbelievably, is working. The pain is gone again. It's like I really am with Daddy. This is the kind of stuff he always came up with. "Go on."

"Florence Shinn; have you ever looked into him? I bet not, so this will be something you may not have heard. Shinn was an American, an artist, a positive spiritual thinker in his day, and he lived a long time ago. He said, 'the game of life is a game of boomerangs. Our thoughts, deeds, and words return to us sooner or later—with astounding accuracy.' That, my dear is why you are in the conundrum you find yourself in, just minutes away from winning a coveted gold medal for the United States of America."

In any discipline, the great ones have certain traits, known only to themselves. They never talk about them, don't usually admit, even to the mirror in their bathroom, the existence of the hidden advantage. One of Trisha's was the ability to shut her mind to running, right in the thick of competition, and turn her body over to an auto pilot. During this part of this race, she had been lost in thought, perhaps daydreaming about some ongoing relationship with her long gone father, a delusional fantasy, or perhaps she just wanted to be away mentally. She checked back in to see consciously what was going on. The crowds were louder than ever. The humid heat was worse. The buzzing of television motorcycles was right there where they had been all along, just a few feet out in front. She began to feel the aches and pains again, but was lost. Something or someone was missing from her field of vision. *What's not right?* Then the answer to her question became obvious. *Where is Keitany?* Mary Jepkosgei Keitany, the Kenyan great was nowhere to be found. When last she checked, Keitany was running third comfortably ahead. Trish glanced back over her sore right shoulder. There was that pesky Turk, Sultan Haydar, and though she was hanging right in, she looked horrible. *How bad do I look, though?* When she checked to her left, she found the Kenyan.

Trisha had unknowingly passed her and was running, if the race finished right now, in the bronze medal slot. Her body experienced a blitzkrieg of emotion and Trisha wondered in awe at what it would be like to medal in a race of 130 of the fastest long distance runners on Earth. Then she saw Michael's face in her mind's eye. *Is it really enough just to get here?* The leaders, Galana, the Ethiopian and Zhu of China, beckoned ahead. They weren't all that far away. Was there anything remaining in her reservoir of energy? Could she call on her body to nudge itself just a bit and make a move on them? Without that nudge the whole race would show up as a big bronze penny to hang on the wall, and while it would be a treasured accomplishment, there was nothing golden about it. She dug down and increased her gait, smiling inwardly at the pressure she had just imposed on Haydar. *I like running with you. Stay with me, Sultan.* The pain was excruciating. *"Dad?"*

* * *

Some consider Mesopotamia, the land between two rivers, to be the cradle of civilization. Others disagree. This area had always been a battleground. First, Assyrians and Babylonians. Then Romans and Parthians later fought for control here even before the time of Christ. During the 7th Century, Arab Islamists conquered the Sessanid Empire. In recent times, Saddam Hussein launched the "mother of all wars" from this, the cradle of civilization. He would not succeed in his quest. Today, though the Olympics were being played out five time zones to the west, the future of the games was on the line right here in Baghdad.

"We've narrowed the source of communication down to one of those three buildings, Colonel." The war in Iraq, at least for America, had been over for years, well that was until ISIS gelled like a cancer from nowhere. If they were caught in this little clandestine adventure, the U.S. military would deny any involvement. The old man and his accomplice did not wear western garb, let alone a uniform. Their decision to wear a Shalwar Kameez, leaving their heads exposed, had been calculated as a strategy to hide in plain sight. They were bearded and wore sunglasses however, looking both high born and wealthy. Everything they needed would fit inside of a small pocket. Someone had been sending signals from this area directly into Brazil. They had finally decoded the messages and in the past few days had infiltrated the area. They wanted to decapitate the head of the monster. As far as the CIA was concerned, this was ground zero in war on terrorism. Colonel Bob Hankle had been chosen because he spoke semi-fluent Arabic. This time his age was a part of his camouflage. Who would pick an old man for a mission like this? His accomplice was a Shia, and fortunately, also a trusted ally. Within the past two hours, the signal had gone completely silent. Perhaps someone had tipped them off.

They were sipping coffee at a small café when Hankle's watch began to vibrate. He casually adjusted the triangulation and located the precise signal source. *We found them.* Unbelievably, they were in the building that housed the café itself. They paid the bill and walked across the street, but before they crossed, the young man pulled a small flying microdrone from his pocket, programmed the coordinates from his cell phone, and released the insect sized camera. The little device began a systematic flight up into the building, homing in on pre-programmed coordinates, taking advantage of open windows, doors, and moving people as it made way to its destination. By the time the two soldiers were in their vehicle, it had climbed four stories and was working its way down a dusty insect ridden hallway. The object would have been hard to identify, even if it flew right under someone's nose. It was difficult to distinguish from a common housefly . . .

Colonel Hankle and his partner, Gulzar Malik, began driving through the neighborhood with Malik at the wheel. Their nondescript late model black Dodge Obama granted them a measure of privacy because the tinted windows were treated with an invisible film to distort the optic of a camera or a rifle scope. In the vehicle they could speak English.. "In no way do I intend to offend, Colonel Hankle, but you may have tipped them off when you and your State Department called Captain Peterson. Perhaps that is why there has been silence since the call was initiated. One can only hope that our little flying compatriot will go undetected when it reaches the target."

"You make a good point, my young Iraqi friend. But silence can be deafening. We did find them. Now we shall see what they are up to if the good Lord wishes." Hankle turned on the view screen. It was built into the dashboard of the car. The tiny self-directed microdrone was close to the floorboards next to a door and was able to slip underneath and into the room, which was loaded with equipment. There were four men working quietly and a fifth. *What in the heck is that?* The fifth creature looked like a man but was far too tall to be human. He had a long Muslim style beard, was dressed in a hooded robe and he was the one doing all of the talking. His words came very rapidly, much too quick for Hankle to keep up, but that was what Gulzar was there for. Nobody, even the strange creature, seemed to notice a small fly in the room. As it had been programmed, it

453

kept distance from the people and to their backs as it scanned the equipment. Everything the two saw was being recorded and sent up the line, via satellite, to the war center inside of the Pentagon.

"The big one is presenting the how, the what, and the why, as to his command for pulling everyone out of Rio and the Olympic project, even now. He says that the racer girl has spoiled the day and poisoned the world against them, that nothing is to be accomplished. It is God's wish. Colonel Hankle, they are quitting the protest!"

"Are you sure, Malik? The big question is whether or not we let them broadcast the command or should we stop them. Are you really sure?"

"I only know what is being said. Perhaps they are performing for us; then again if you decide to take action, perhaps you will foil your own plans. It is an interesting turn of events, this new knowledge grants. The choice is yours, Sir."

Hankle made his decision quickly. He didn't get to be 68 years old and still alive in military service by being too cautious. He bet on himself and chose to wait. The four men spun into action barking commands all at once on different channels. They were very direct. When they finished, the men quickly started packing their equipment to leave. Hankle was very satisfied that the right decision had been made. Then something unusual happened. Just as they were driving back down the street in front of the building, the tall creature looked directly at the mechanical fly. He looked right into the camera and smiled. He knew! Without saying a word, he began to dissipate and then disappeared altogether. Hankle and Malik looked at each other in astonishment. In silent communication between them, this would never be discussed, but Bob Hankle knew what was going on. *One day we'll all have to come together and deal with those freaks.*

At just about the same time, Gulzar Malik slowed to a stop and popped the trunk. Before Colonel Hankle could go back and shut the trunk, 175 more microdrones hummed into the air heading straight up the side of the building, preprogrammed to home in on the signal they received from the first little flying bugger. They gathered in front of the window where the men were getting ready to leave. One landed on the glass and exploded, showering the sidewalk in a hail of broken shards. Moments before Hankle and Maik had driven off and were several hundred yards removed from the scene. Immediately all of the buzzing microdrones went inside the room and automatically dispersed to equal distance from each other, a sort of a metallic cloud. Terrified jihadists froze in their tracks. The explosive concussion broke no walls open and could only be heard as a muffled bang in the adjoining rooms. In the target room all of the equipment had been destroyed, and the occupants instantly killed.

Hankle had successfully beheaded the enemy in just minutes. It had taken the better part of a month to find them. *I can't wait to let Brad know that picking on his wife was definitely NOT a good idea. How many times do I have to save his bacon? Nah, I owed him one for removing that tumor and getting me cleared for service. Yes, Brad I owed you this time. Trisha Peterson, well she's worth it in any universe. I love that girl.*

* * *

"... We now return you to Olympic headquarters and Bob Costas."

"Good afternoon folks and welcome back to broadcast headquarters. Many of you just got through watching the U.S.A. basketball team defeat Argentina in yet another hard fought contest. It wasn't so long ago that the Americans were a lock to win virtually every game. There were the down years after the Dream Team in Barcelona introduced NBA style Olympic basketball to the world, and then the resurgence of American dominance when Mike *Krzyzewski* took the reigns; *but let there be no doubt about it, international basketball is here to stay. No game is a given anymore. We were just as lucky to get out of today's event as we were against the Brazilians the other day. Next up for the Americans is their old nemeses, Spain, in the gold medal round. Coach K and his team still have work to do if they want to repeat as Olympic champions.*

"The Americans are having a banner Olympiad this summer, medaling in many events for the first time in years. These games have also become known for the relentless protests which have marred an otherwise delightful time here in Rio. There is interesting news on that front as well. It looks to the naked eye as if things may finally be settling down. Across the spectrum, protesters have withdrawn and are leaving the area in droves. Of course it is far too early to tell, but at first glance it looks like they're throwing in the towel for right now. A

skeptic may argue that they are regrouping for something else, but a good deal of the credit has to go to local authorities down here. They've done a splendid job of keeping the peace. Rumors have also circulated that the incredibly nasty act committed against American, Trisha Jean Martin backfired and stole their passion. We are very happy that Martin's strong sense of determination rendered that act inert.

Not only did she weather the storm, but we need to send you back out to the Women's marathon and Randy Moss. Randy, is it possible that after more than 24 miles of running, we are still looking at a race that may go right down to the wire?"

"That's right, Bob. There is bedlam taking place out on the roads of Rio. The Women's marathon is shaping up to be the event of the entire Olympiad. What we are witnessing today is almost unprecedented. Usually by the end of a race like this, one and possibly two contestants remain in contention. Today we have no less than four runners vying for the gold medal and instead of spreading out and settling into their final positions, these women are bunching up. There is no way to tell what is going to happen. Let's set the table.

"The heat is unbearable. It is humid and dusty at the same time. A hot wind is brewing off of the landward side of the race. There is no breeze at all coming off of the ocean, so there is no relief for those courageous enough to try and win this thing. We have never seen a larger throng out for this event and the runners are being pinched by the crowd-swell. If the fans have their way it will be American flag bearer Trisha Jean Martin, the hero of the race since she got up off of the pavement and stayed in there.

"China's Xiaolin Zhu has led from early on. She took over the lead in the first five miles and has never given it back. Zhu has won marathons before, but has never medaled at the Olympics. She finished sixth in London. One has to wonder what is going through her mind as she and the others can now begin to visualize the end of this grueling event. I'll say one thing in her favor. She looks great, is running smoothly, and it appears she has plenty in the tank to carry this thing to the finish line. OK, that's three things.

"Tiki Galana, from Ethiopia, continues hanging in behind Zhu and has stayed right with her the entire way. Galana is no stranger to Olympic success. She won the gold medal in London. Many strategists out here see her as using Zhu to get her into the stadium where she will make her move on the lesser experienced athlete, somewhat of a gamble if she's really holding back. Galana is known for being strongest at the end of her races. At this point she may be the favorite to win, but we shall see. Galana has yet another advantage. She is from Bekoii, Ethiopia, perhaps the marathon capital of the world. What is Bekoii? It's a small town is southern Ethiopia which has produced a plethora of Olympic winners, like Fatuma Roba, the 1966 Champion, and others like Tirunesh Dibaba, Deratu Tulu and Kenenisa Bekele, all greats in their own right. These ladies have had the race to themselves, Dwight Stones, but not anymore."

"Not anymore is right, Randy. Of course, Trisha Martin has seen it all and is the American favorite in the Women's marathon. She was injured as a kid, lost her father, fought off obesity and made it from nowhere to the podium as a bronze medalist—that is if the race ended right now. It is hard to imagine that she's only been running professionally for six years. You can even throw a couple of kids into the mix. She and husband, former POW, Captain Bradley Peterson, have twins. We are told that Brad is home with the kids. They're just four years old. Her story today of jumping dogs, fighting her way back from the middle of the pack into contention, surviving garbage thrown at her by hooligans—resulting in that bad spill, is nothing short of amazing. How about Sultan Haydar, though? Haydar specializes in the 1,500 and 3,000 meter events, but has been running marathons of late. In London she finished a distant 72nd. She may be running for Turkey, but today she is running like an Ethiopian. I wonder if the fact that she herself was born in Ethiopia has anything to do with her skill. Like the other three in front of her, if she hangs with the leaders, she could wind up among the small group of runners who are about to shatter the world record . . .

* * *

He sat back against the wall on the floor of his dingy room, staring at the tripod with the mounted weapon, meditating. He prayed every few minutes, kneeling with his head to the floor and facing east. A timer would announce the one minute warning, for he was prepared in every other way to pull the trigger. There were roaches crawling in the walls, so many that he could hear them. He would watch each time one made its presence known to see where it would go. Sometimes it walked the space of the entire room, only to disappear into the wall on the other side. Sometimes the roach would climb the cabinet to the sink and disappear into the drain. *Theirs is an inspiring little society, all ordered from the chaos, each with a task to perform, all for the good of the body they are indentured to.* He held onto a fantasy of his own, a new future where mankind was ruled from above, also order out of chaos, which was the consequence of wicked and selfish people. It was time for the change to take place. His part in the future of mankind was but a tiny task, just like that of the roach tending to its own business.

Suddenly his receiver came to life! He began to hear garbled instructions, some definitely meant for him, some perhaps for others. What were they trying to tell him? At first he thought they gave him clearance to complete his honorable act, and then just as abruptly, unbelievably it sounded as though his mission was being called off. Why? What did become clear to him was that orders were being given to pull out of the area. Everyone was to leave immediately, but what about the girl? The sounds became somewhat garbled. What about the girl! Did they wish him to carry out the mission or was he being told to stay away? He couldn't tell for sure. There was something wrong with the message. He could not make out the words as the volume faded and became very difficult to understand. When urgently checking his equipment, his mistake, something that may just cost him his life, became very clear. The batteries were virtually dead. He had forgotten to change out for fresh batteries! The assassin worked as fast as he could and within seconds his signal strength was green again, but the message was lost; the transmission was completed and his receiver had gone silent again.

What should he do? He looked around the dimly lit room, eyeing torn furniture, wallpaper that was hanging loosely in several places and he felt lousy, just like the rest of the place that looked beautiful only minutes ago. Now he was awash in total fear. Dread replaced the quiet confidence he'd been enjoying. There were scant minutes, three at the most, until the target ran through the first of his two chosen kill zones, a vertex in the road course that would present a most likely opportunity. She would approach toward his position and then slow for the sharp turn, straight into his line of sight. When he glanced at the marathoners, they looked too close. He was not ready! *What—praise God Almighty—do I do now? If I kill her, and am not supposed to, I myself will be tortured and killed. If I do not kill her, and am required to, I will be tortured and killed as well.* He took the towel at his side, wiped his face and sweaty hands in an effort to settle jumpy nerves. He knelt once again and commenced uttering a short prayer to invoke help from God. Could He reduce or remove the butterflies which had invaded him. His decision was made.

* * *

Trisha Martin was beginning to see light at the end of the tunnel. There were still the two ahead of her, but they were close, oh so close. Up ahead she spied the crease in the course where the way kind of doubled back on itself, just a mile from Olympic Stadium. Sultan Haydar was right behind her. *What will she do when I kick in that little turn where I have decided to make my move? Haydar has run a better race than I have. She is so far out of her element, and yet has made no mistakes.* Zhu was still out in front and had been gaining some breathing room, creating separation between her and Galana. Trisha still figured Galana as the one to beat. *That one has been here before and succeeded.* Her father was still right there. He looked extremely concerned. "Daddy, now it's you who looks frightened. What is the matter?"

"I was just thinking about horse sense." *Let's see if she can follow me. Now I need to take my mind off of things.* "Do you know what I mean?"

"Not really, Dad. Tell me, ghost of my father, what do you mean?"

"You're almost home, Trisha. You have run a great race and there is nothing to be worried about. I was just lost in thought. Here's the thing about horse sense, something all of us could use a bit of from time to time. Are you aware of the legal betting line for this race, you know, like what the odds on you are?" *Please, God, don't let anything happen to my little girl. She has worked so hard for this.*

"I don't have a clue, Dad. I've seen them posted, but I've intentionally looked away. I didn't want to be thinking about the odds on any runners during the race. Getting involved in the guessing game would clutter my thinking, but where are you going with this?"

"Horse sense is what keeps horses from betting on what people will accomplish. They're smart enough to know that we are unpredictable. So, what I am talking about is destiny. Edwin Markham, a poet, said that choices are the hinges of destiny. I have just one piece of advice left to offer. I know what you want and that you are going to make your move at the next turn. I need to leave now, but I think you have what it takes to get this done. You have a unique choice in all of history. I'm looking for a fourteen letter word that begins with the letter 'p' if you can help me now."

Just like that, her father was gone. Zhu and Gelana had just made the turn right in front of her. She was almost there, just a few steps, the pivot off of her outside foot and . . .

* * *

"What was that, Cap? Did you see what I just saw up on the fortieth or forty-first floor, right up there on top in the northeast corner of the building?" Specialist Julio Dominguez, the spotter, had been watching the building for hours. There were several observation teams out in force, invisible CIA types, the Secret Service, even U.S. Army like these guys, looking for the shooter. Given the intelligence reports, most of them had clearance to be in the area, including these soldiers, but they did their work in secret, blending completely with the mass of people in the area. You wouldn't be able to tell one of these military guys from a typical spectator. Nobody knew they were there. "It was a white flash of light. I think someone just took a rifle shot out of there. I think we found what we've been looking for and I hope we're not too late." There was nothing to be seen now. The building had gone dark and there wasn't a single shred of observable evidence that someone had fired a weapon. This guy was good, real good. As quickly as he had shown himself, he disappeared again.

Captain Thomas Gerald was studying that area of the building as well. His team was positioned in another high rise, one not nearly as tall, across the street and down the way a couple of hundred yards. It had been impossible to get into that building since it was controlled by all the wrong people. Whoever was up there had the run of the place. "Hot Shot, get the infrared up on that part of the structure and see if you can find the source of that flash."

Master Sergeant Reggie "Hot Shot" Washington, the marksman on the team, moved to the second tripod in the room, the one with the infrared lens. There were heat signatures all over the place. He was looking for a lone personage bearing the signs of an assassin in action. He would be crouching down in a corner somewhere, or leaning over a gun mount and looking into a site scope. Unless he witnessed the rifle itself being fired, it would not be possible to see the actual weapon. Hot Shot was looking for a person, something akin to finding a planet orbiting a bright star, where it's the motion of the star that gives away the planet. Here, the motion of the man was supposed to give away the gun. That was the theory.

Dominguez pointed his binoculars down into the race area. They had been so busy, that no one had scanned the target area. *Did the shooter hit anything?*

* * *

Hassam Jabar sat back against the wall a few feet from his rifle, satisfied that he had done the right thing, carefully aiming his weapon and firing one round, close enough to the target, but deliberately missing the mark. He knew that he was being watched. If he had fired harmlessly into the air or in some other fashion, perhaps he would be noted as not being dedicated to the mission, a traitorous act sure to bring consequences, so in his deliberation he had found a way to buy the time necessary to invoke his masters to communicate. His prayers had been answered for he had discovered middle ground. If he was supposed to shoot, the message would be encouragement for the next try. If he was to stand down, he would be told such. Now fate lay in the hands of others and for the moment he felt safe. Jabar checked his equipment, making sure that it was all in good working order, and then settled in to reflect for a few minutes on his beloved Pishin Gan Sayedan, the village where he spent his childhood in Afghanistan.

On a beautiful spring day, many years earlier, before his entire family had been killed by Americans, he was walking with his father, tending orchards near his village southwest of Kandahar. *"Hassam," his father said, "when you pray to invoke the will of God, I am reminded of an old saying, that of the key and the lock. One who tries to use a broken key, damaged or partially damaged in some way, is thwarted and the lock does not open. Salat is the key to Paradise. In order for the door to open, the salat has to be properly made. If the salot is contrary to the ways of the Prophet Muhammad, then the key is upside down and will not work. One must concentrate and devote himself by completing prayers with the proper action. If not, that is the same as using a broken key, one with missing parts, which of course will not open the lock. Paradise is lost. Concentrate and devote yourself to complete actions that we may be joined in Paradise at the end, for this one loves his son"*

Jabar's earpiece remained silent and he began to shiver in fear. In spite of the reality that he had taken every action, had concentrated fully, been totally devoted to God, and had prepared his entire life for this moment, doubt had settled in. He prayed in earnest, hoping for a clear message from God. There could be no hell worse than not obtaining Paradise, for he would never be with his father again. Hassam Jabar had remembered many of the tales his father had used in his upbringing. He called upon them often and felt very close to the man he had not seen alive since he was but a boy. Why then, did he doubt this final action? Was the message from God to stop or to go forward? In the pit of his stomach, he knew no help would be coming. For some reason his masters were gone from the communication grid. Except from the answer to salat, he was totally alone. Scant minutes ago he had thought himself a true goshawk, the famous, lone bird of prey, and his nickname. Now he felt as if he were being changed into cowardly dog.

Did the marksman have the patience to listen to the voice of God as Allah had spoken? "And certainly, we shall test you with something of fear and hunger, some loss in goods, or lives, or the fruits, but give glad tidings to the patient. Who, when afflicted with calamity, say, Truly, to Allah we belong, and Truly, to Him we shall return." The words of Allah, spoken in the Qur'an, gave him his answer and he felt glad. "Say; nothing will happen to us except what Allah has decreed for us. He is our protector; and on Allah let the believers put their trusts."

Hassam had his answer. Gone were the jitters and fears for they had been lifted. He knew what to do. His actions, two bullets, one for the target and one from his sidearm for himself, would bring him both Paradise and the father he longed to be with, all in just a few minutes. Jabar was at peace with himself and set forth to undertake his final task in this life.

* * *

Trisha didn't dare look back over her shoulder. Sultan Haydar was so close now that it might be possible for her to clip the back of one of Trisha's running shoes. If not for the incredible noise, the chaos of screaming fans along the road just outside of Olympic Stadium, she would have been able to hear her breathe. The bedlam was supplemented by the vibrating blare of 80,000 waiting for them inside as the four leaders circumnavigated its entirety before heading through the tunnel and onto the track. Galana was right in front of Trisha. They were too close together, all of them. Zhu was still the leader—by less than a second, not even a half second ahead of Haydar, and yet one of these people would not even be getting a medal. The four of them were that bunched . . . kicking at an unbelievable pace.

It was obvious now that none of the usual factors would play a role in the outcome. This wasn't going to boil down to who wanted it more. They were all willing to die if need be. It wasn't going to be about conditioning. They were all in the best shape of their lives, and had the gas to make the end of the race at this pace. On the other hand, they were all running on wits alone, completely spent in every other way. This would not be about mental strength or will power, what country they were from, who got the better night's sleep or even about hydration.

For the first time since she won in the Trials, Trisha Martin considered the odds. *Whatever my chances were this morning before we got underway, they stand at one in four right now.* The group of runners made the final turn and was now heading straight into the tunnel, everyone's first break from the intense heat since they got off of the bus more than two hours earlier. *Don't jump the gun, Trisha. Let someone else make the first move.*

* * *

"They were bunched as tight as I have ever seen going into the tunnel, Randy. Have you everwitnessed such a competitive marathon in your lifetime?"

463

"No, Chris, none of us have ever witnessed anything like this. One can only imagine just how hard it is to be forced to kick if you want to win a marathon. This is an endurance race which has turned into a sprint . . . after more than 25 miles. Everyone inside of the stadium is on pins and needles waiting to see what happens, even the athletes have lined the track. Everything else in here has come to a complete stop. I have never seen anything like this in my life. All four of these greats will better the existing world record in the marathon, yet only three will medal. Here they come."

* * *

What is the right thing to do? I have no plan on how to win this race. Trisha was at a complete loss as to how she should try and get past the others at the finish line. She knew there was gas in the tank, but was not sure how much. The darkness inside of the tunnel, out of the sun's reach for the first time in the contest, felt so good, except . . . . *Is she going so soon? Can she carry the kick from here to the end? I just don't know. Wait, Trisha; just wait your turn, but do not wait too long. If you do you will regret it for the rest of your life.*

* * *

"Sultan Haydar has the lead!" Randy Moss had never been so animated. "Somewhere inside of the tunnel she made her final move and passed all three in front of her. For the first time since early on in the event, Zhu and Galana find themselves in pursuit of the leader!" Even though he was virtually screaming into the microphone, it was difficult to hear because of the noise of the crowd. They were going wild. "Zhu and Galana are kicking furiously to try and catch up with the unlikely surge of the Turkish hero. Martin has fallen back precipitously. Perhaps we are down to three contenders. Who knows? This story is yet to be told, Chris, as hard is as that statement is to believe at this point. There are two long trips around the track. I can't believe what I am seeing."

* * *

Inside of the James Joyce Irish Pub, in Istanbul, Turkey, at about 6:00 in the evening, the early crowd had swollen over to watch the race. When Sultan Haydar emerged from the tunnel in first place an eruption of bedlam could be heard two blocks away. Once it was determined that Haydar would be a contender, everyone nearby had converged, in much the same way all over the country to see if their girl could break through and win the big race. Now it looked like they would be rewarded as never before.

* * *

Hassam Jabar could see the man's face, in his mind's eye, while preparing to carry out his mission, the aging, full bearded Sheik and Palestinian founder of Hamas, Ahmed Yassin. He had been assassinated in 2004 during Israel's occupation, but lived on with the preservation of his words. "Sons of Islam everywhere, the jihad is a duty—to establish the rule of Allah on earth and to liberate your countries and yourselves from America's domination and its Zionist allies. It is your battle—either victory or martyrdom." *This time I will not miss, praise be to the only God.*

There were to be no messages from his masters. He surely knew that now. His target had entered the great arena of the Holy War. His time had come at last. The sidearm was loaded with one bullet and sat on the table next to his tripod. The rifle mounted on that tripod was trained on the finish line. He was scoping and tweaking the aim to account for the steady small breeze, the humidity in the air, and the trajectory of his shot, the new shot that would be heard around the world. Jabar slipped in behind the weapon and made ready to fire, thinking of his father, one last time. *I shall see you very soon, Father.* He thought he could feel his father waiting for him on the other side. *"Hassam, if you are being tested, seeming to go through hell, then keep on going. It is after the storm, when comes the calm. May God be with you, my Son, for we shall soon drink from the same cup."*

* * *

Dr. Peterson was sitting in a visitor's chair, inside of the critical care hospital room occupied by one Billy Dace, his patient. Every so often, he would notice a puzzled look on the face of someone, sometimes a hospital employee and at other times, patients, visitors, and volunteers, people like that. What would a doctor in a very busy hospital be doing just sitting there watching television in a patient's room while the child slept? It didn't make sense. Patients in hospitals wait hours to get a glimpse of their physician and when he or she finally comes in the door, they are gone again in just a few seconds, racing off to somewhere else. Not this guy.

Once the "incident" had taken place, Brad had not left the room. Billy had been asleep for almost the entire time. Fortunately, Brad had the DVR on at home and should things work out, he would have young Dace over for a BBQ to watch the entire event . . . should things work out. Right now, even though Trisha had drifted just a little behind once they were inside of the stadium, things were working out. Oh, he wanted the gold, more than almost anyone, but this race had been run . . . perfectly.

A senior citizen volunteer was staring at him from across the hallway. It made him want to shut the door, but he refused to. *I have given every patient I have in this hospital all the time in the world*, the handsome surgeon snickered to himself, daring to confront her with a look that suggested she may not know what is going on. *William Benjamin Dace is my only patient. I am where I want to be and thank you for caring, for I know that you do.*

Billy Dace came fully awake and spoke for the first time since the start of the women's marathon. "Captain Peterson, it itches."

"What, Billy the . . ."

"Forget that, Captain. Look at Trisha! She is running so fast. Who won the race?"

"We don't know yet, Billy. She is still in it. There are three ahead of her right now, and the race is going to be over in just a short minute or two. Tell me, though, about . . ."

"It doesn't itch any more. Come on, Trisha! Run faster! Oh, I love her so much! Run! We're going to win our own gold medal . . . ."

* * *

Trisha had made her move and was gaining ground quickly on the other three. *I hope I am not too late . . . breathe, breathe smoothly,*

Trisha, accelerate your kick. And I don't think I'm too late. Adrenalin had effectively killed any pain. She was not winded. Her sprint to the finish line would be just under two laps, not even a half of a mile. Galana, the Ethiopian was her first target, just a few yards ahead. *She's struggling, big-time.* Trisha passed her easily. When she went by the favorite, certainly the most experienced runner left in the race, Trisha noticed that she was favoring her left thigh. The courageous woman was fighting what surely looked like muscle cramps. Today would not be her day. The pain on her face, though, was emotional, not physical. When Trisha rounded the next turn she could see the tunnel where they had come in and the next runners through were the Americans, Shalane Flanagan and Kara Goucher. *I'm glad to see them next in the stadium. They look great and are running very fast.*

The track was lined by screaming athletes. Everything else had come to a complete stop. All eyes were on the race. It was chaos inside of the stadium. The screaming was louder than anything Trisha had ever experienced in her short professional career. She had watched every Olympic marathon for as long as she could remember and had never seen anything like this. Trisha indulged herself with one short look at the Jumbotron and the cameras were trained on her. It was a bit disconcerting, especially since she had all but forgotten that her hair was flying loose, and she quickly looked away to focus on her next target, the two frontrunners going head to head, side by side, still several yards in front of her. They were certainly not hurting and were a formidable challenge. She kicked again, this time into an all-out sprint.

Trisha . . . remember what I asked of you . . .

* * *

"Here comes Trisha Martin! Can she become the first American champion in this event since Joan Benoit in 1984 at the Los Angeles games?" Chris Maddocks was beside himself, an unbelievable witness to sports history in the making. "There are now just three left in contention. Gelana has fallen back and it is obvious she's hurt. Not only is she out of medal contention, it now looks like Americans Shalane and Flanagan will pass her, putting three American women in the top five. Sultan Haydar, the flying Turk and Xiaolin Zhu of China are trying to hold off the American, Trisha

Jean Martin. She is closing fast from the back of the group. It looks like she timed her kick perfectly. Let's see if she can get it done. What a story that would be, especially considering all the problems she has encountered during this grueling race. Someone is going to smash the world record! How do you see it, Randy?"
"Lightning strikes like this only once in a lifetime, Chris. There are no less than three contenders, all at world record pace, inside of the stadium in an all-out sprint to the line. Will we have a photo finish? There is the bell. They are on their final lap. It'll all be over in just one minute. How are they doing this? From up here it looks like the last lap of the 1,500 meter run.
They are flying. What we are witnessing is utterly unprecedented. How deep can an athlete dig to pull out victory?"

* * *

Up in the stands, Becky Martin, her son, Michael, his wife, Janet, the three kids, David Giles, and Becky's sister Betsy who had surprised them, were screaming their heads off. The fact that the noise level was off of the charts meant that they could barely hear themselves, let alone each other. The family heroine had made her move and was almost there. It looked like she was a sure bet—she pulled even with the other two with just a half of a lap to go . . . and then she cleared into the lead. The race was hers. For the first time today, after more than 26 grueling miles of pain, Trisha was alone at the front of the pack and pulling steadily away. Now she was a few yards out ahead of the other two. Pandemonium rocked not just in front of every television all across America, but all over the free world.

* * *

Hassam Jabar could smell the slight breeze out of the southeast, just as he had expected. He fine-tuned his aim two clicks to the right, accounting for the velocity and distance of the shot, watching the runner galloping straight towards him. There were three headed to the finish line. He was never surer of himself in his life. Deep within himself, though, a tinge of doubt set in. He was watching the most prolific athletic event in his life and was about to destroy it for everyone. *Am I really doing God's will? It will be as God wills it. He would certainly send the sign if it was not to be.* The marksman let go of his doubt and set himself to fire. He wanted the target within just seconds, right at the finish line. Jabar calmed his nerves one last time, *just a few seconds, Father,* it would be a head shot after all, the kind of an assassination that would bring the most shock. He watched as the runners approached the line and . . .

* * *

The air never smelled sweeter; it was more than that. The air was fresh and sweet. She did not notice the blimp up high in the air, could not see television cameras buzzing up the side of the track recording her every move. Trisha was not thinking about her family going mad up in the crazed stadium. She had lost all connection with the athletes and officials pushing in on the running lanes. There was no heat, no humidity, no pain, nothing between her and the finish line. Still there was something amiss. On the one hand she felt great joy. She had effectively won the race. It would be over in just a few steps. *Paraprosdokian . . . What is the best way to beat them in this race? How can I beat THEM in this race? It all depends on who THEY are. I can beat THEM by offering myself in a different way. All I have to do is give up sole possession of my gold medal and we beat THEM. That is the paraprosdokian; "Dad I know what to do!"*

* * *

. . . and he squeezed the trigger. The shot was away. Bingo! With a twinge of sadness in his heart—the mayhem and cacophony taking place down on the track sent shivers throughout his body. His business had made all of that possible. *War is so terrible,* he thought with mixed emotions . . .

* * *

Stanley waited just off of the track at the finish line, not in disbelief at what he was looking at; it's just that he could not believe it either. His protégé had the race in her pocket. It was over . . . , over, all except for the last few seconds. Trisha was comfortably ahead of the other two racers, well a few steps anyway, and could not be caught. They had won a gold medal. He glanced at the clock to note the time. He had been looking at that clock for a long time, or so it seemed. The splits were unbelievable. Not only was the gold medal theirs, but so was the world record. He had coached the girl who had just run the fastest marathon in history. The only thing left to be discovered was what the formal race time going into the books would be.

What the hell is she doing?! Trisha! Why in God's name are you slowing down? Stanley's stomach was falling to the ground. It looked like Trisha Martin was about to throw the race. She was slowing down—letting Haydar and Zhu both catch her. In just two seconds his countenance went from glee to horror. And then back to a mixed version of glee again. Trisha took the hand of each runner, the flying Turk, Sultan Haydar on her right and Xiaolin Zhu from China to her left. All three of them crossed the line hand in hand. The race had ended in a tie. For some incredibly strange reason, his girl, Trisha Jean Martin, had changed her life's dream from winning the gold medal at the Olympics into sharing the victory with the other two, a tie. *How can they have a tie at the Olympics? Who ever heard of such a crazy thing? Trisha. She has changed history.* Stanley couldn't wait to get inside the head of his runner. Warmth he had never known engulfed him. Considering all that had gone on this morning, this felt . . . right.

Stanley looked at the race clock; it read 2:13:10. They, the three of them, had shaved more than two minutes off of the world record. By the time he looked back at Trisha, he found her on the ground in a pool of blood . . . Oh, God, no. He was panic stricken. Stanley jumped the fence and . . .

* * *

Something was wrong; he was confused at first, and then things started to change. Hassam Jabar was disoriented. Had he pulled the trigger or had he not? *I think I hit the girl and then took matters into my own hands. I remember the flash of light and then everything went to black, but now I think, therefore I am. Is this death?* The Jihadist could now begin to see the dingy room and his own body on the floor in a crumpled heap of blood and twisted flesh. He glanced at the table where his final weapon of choice was to be used on himself and the gun was not there. It was on the floor beside his head. The room began to brighten beyond his ability to clearly make anything out and he was immersed in white light; there was no music, no sound of any kind and yet a portal of some sort began to open before him. *This is different than I imagined. Those who experienced the near death experience tell over and over again of feeling a secure peace, but I remain confused. What is this place? Why do I feel the way I do?* Hassam could feel only loneliness, a hollow shell of separation. *Where are my loved ones? Father, where are you?*

"I am here, my son. Come forth."

Hassam began to experience the transference between day and night, life and death, mortal existence and what comes after. Even though he had heard his father's voice, he felt very unsure of himself. *Where is the God that I have served my life to be with? Is my father with Him?* Out of the white light there appeared a dark tunnel . . . beckoning him with an uncontrollable urge, though he did not feel it was the path for him. Slowly, inexorably, Hassam Jabbar started to move, not really of his own accord, but as if he were being carried along a predetermined path.

Once enveloped inside of the tunnel, moving pictures began to appear, some to his right, others to his left, and above him as well. He saw a little boy playing at the feet of his mother, a joyous and happy child. For the first time since he had entered this stasis, he felt the warmth of love and acceptance. The boy was him. After a short while his mother turned from the little boy who had disappeared and whispered a lonely cry. *"Why didn't you come to see me?"* And then he saw the tears of desperation as she faded into the past, leaving him with a forlorn sense of abandonment. *But I loved you just the same, Mother.* She was gone.

Hassam thought again of his final act of service. *I cannot remember exactly what happened.* Mortality was no longer his concern; his life was finished in that place. As hard as he tried, he could not focus or remember how his final performance had played out.

The young man drifted further into the tunneled motion picture of the life he could see, the one played for him by others. He saw a young boy working with his family in the field. The boy was taking instruction from his father who was showing him the Muslim way of truth and love. *"Hassam, according to Allah, men and women are the equal of each other, lest you ever forget. Their roles may be different, but they are both to be respected and loved always. Though men are the protectors and maintainers of women, they are not superior. In the community they are most valiant in God's sight."* I have forgotten. I became smothered in my piety and have lost my mother in the process. *Did my mother abandon me or was it I who left her.* Tears of loneliness rendered him powerless to fix things. Where the love of his mother was concerned, he had embraced the poverty of arrogance. He moved forward . . . again.

His mother was grieving. The moving picture now reminded him of the days shortly after his family, save he and his mother, had been killed during the misplaced strike in his home village. This had become the turning point in his life. *Why did I leave you in your hour of grief, the woman who gave birth to me? It was my duty to step forward and protect you, but instead I drowned in hatred and sought comfort elsewhere. Oh, Mother, please forgive me. What have I done?*

While traversing the wormhole-like tunnel, Hassam Jabar watched in petrified grief how the remainder of his years had been lived, always hating, never allowing himself the joy of a loving life, seeking only vengeance on his enemies. At times he seemed to forget, even now, the lessons of his youth, the beautiful teachings of Allah, purified, not by hatred but by love. He had lost all sense of time and place and he watched decisions he had made unfold, leading him to the place of his death. Unfortunately, he remained confused. Perhaps he did not realize that he had not arrived at the resting place of his next life, but was being tested one more time. If he had come to understand the simple truth of this journey and its importance, perhaps he could have thought more clearly. Perhaps he was too far gone to remember why he had lived his life and all the good things he had accomplished. Perhaps it still wasn't too late.

There was a fork in the tunnel ahead. The moment of his final decision was arriving. *What is the definition of heaven and what does hell mean? Though I have struggled these many years, toiling in everlasting pain, I still don't know if I am evil or good. I have never killed anyone, at least not until today . . . I think.*

Once again, Hassam heard the voice of his father. *"I know you, Son. You are not evil. This is the moment of your liberation. You can be free at last, but you must choose wisely. Come to me at the pathway ahead. Choose the right. You are a good man."*

Hassam had arrived at the place where he was to decide. *Which is the correct path?* To the one side, all that had been promised him awaited. He was to be rewarded for his deeds. He saw young, pure women, all calling for him to come and be with them. They were festooned with fine cloth and all manner of riches. The pathway was golden and bright. He was infused with a . . . different kind of warmth. It seemed the way to go, but a tiny kernel of doubt enshrouded the inviting beauty. *Am I being shown the way, or am I deceived?* There was an old man down by the wayside, encouraging him to move forward and join with him. *Is that my father? It seems so, but I am not so sure of it.*

The other pathway was quite different, at first a hilly climb up into mountains along a rocky trail. There was rugged beauty that way. The azure blue sky did invite the soul's sincerest desire. That path, however, bore none of the signs of any promises that were made to him as he had worked through his adult life and it looked strange to him, but felt wholesome and good. It looked the hard way to go. He could see problems along that road, there would be much to do and many things to change. Hassam himself would need to change if he were to find comfort in that direction. He could see no women, nor any riches, but plenty of wheat to harvest when the fields were ready. The road did not look well traveled. He could see footprints, Muslim footprints, though some of those footprints were from the sandals of Christians and even Jews. In the end, before he made the decision and marched on, Hassam Jabar was given one final chance. *"The only God is God."*

He trudged on towards his destiny. Presently everything in sight vanished. The girls and all that came with them disappeared with the onset of a cold and dark wind. His father, *or is it,* approached and then he changed, too. Jabbar had been deceived. The man grew stranger and more foreign than ever. It was not his father or anyone he had ever seen.

"Welcome to heaven, stupid boy. Come and receive your reward." The smile on his face, it was pure evil, and the tone of his laughter, confirmed that he had not chosen correctly.

Hassam turned to run back, but when he looked, the opening had shut, barring the way out; it was just gone, and instead he fell into the abyss. *Father, please help me.* Hassam still had much to learn. He would never find out that heaven is not only a place of rest. There was always work to do and things to worry about, a lesson just learned by his own father. Hassam would not be able to return to his original home; that was gone now. He would still gain profound knowledge, but unfortunately it would be skewed by the bondage he had placed himself in. He was in hell and now began to understand its definition. He was to be separated from all that he loved. It wasn't fire and brimstone, but loneliness and separation that defined his hell, and he could never leave.

Along the other path and out of sight, his father grieved a pain he had never known. So much was lost. He slowly began to traverse the pathway back to his wife and other family members, who by now were surely aware that their Hassam was gone forever.

* * *

Specialist Julio Dominguez could see the tiny opening in the wall where Hot Shot's rifle had bingo'd the terrorist. A quick glance through the infrared high resolution scope on the tripod revealed a very eerie looking glow of the body on the floor. At first it was twitching, but slowly the twitch stopped, and there was something else, too. They already knew he was dead. The signature was fading as the body no longer supported the heat of life. They would be inside of the room in just a few minutes to take a look around, electronically speaking, that is. "Reggie," said Julio, "no one has entered the room yet. Right now it looks like you did the trick and no one was the wiser."

Hot Shot wasn't convinced. "That's possible, Dom, but it's just as likely no one has the balls to go in there. Would you?"

"Hell no; I wouldn't be going in that room. Who's to say I wouldn't be next?"

"Exactly, no one is going in that room anytime soon, but it's still a good bet no one is the wiser, either. Reggie, here comes Captain Gerald. Can you see him coming down the road?"

Once the shot was off and there was a confirmed hit, the man in charge, Captain Tom Gerald, had driven away in the little black Brazilian Chevy Sonic they had been issued. It was equipped with tinted windows, had local plates, and would blend in with anything out on the road. Without looking through binoculars, neither Hot Shot Washington nor Julio Dominguez would have been sure it was him; it was him. The plates confirmed it. He barely slowed when he passed in front of the subject building, releasing the n-bot, a small little flying camera, equipped with precision GPS locater software, accurate to within one inch, and a bunch of other nifty goodies that made for devastating surveillance—incognito.

In less than a minute, the little thopter, no larger than an eraser on the back end of a pencil, including its wings, had found the hole in the wall created by Hot Shot and it was inside of the room. The two, Julio Dominguez and Hot Shot Washington were watching on their computer as the boys back at Langley in Virginia, toggled around the room looking at the panoramic view. It was like snooping around and spying on a crime scene. Dominguez could clearly tell that Hot Shot was hurting. Killing a man was something he dreaded, even when it was necessary and today's necessity weighed heavily on his mind. If this guy had gotten his shot off, and they still weren't sure if he had or not, he could have done serious damage to the International Olympic movement, perhaps even destroyed it. Hot Shot should have been celebrating, but he was a bit of an empath and was not able to take any pleasure, he just couldn't. As far as Hot Shot was concerned, this misguided boy still had family somewhere and they had just lost a son, or a brother, or a father, or whatever. He felt a little better when they spied the handgun near his head on the floor. Obviously, he had knocked it off of the table when he fell after being shot. It also looked obvious that he planned on killing himself after his kill. In effect, he would have died anyway and so Hot Shot began to take solace from the knowledge that he had not caused a death, but instead had prevented someone else from being shot to death. This guy was a dead man walking. *I do not pity you, coward.* Master Sergeant Reggie Washington was no longer emotionally involved in the kill. He had done his job and knew it. But there was more to follow.

The rifle, ironically, *or not,* the same type of weapon he had used, was still mounted on its tripod and pointed directly at the track. The sight down the barrel as shown by the little flying, movie making buzzer, which was now hovering just beneath and to the left of the sighting scope, revealed what the shooter wanted. He sought one or more of the runners right while they were in the race; actually it was obvious that he wanted them at the finish line. "Hot Shot, look what you did. You saved the Olympics, man. One of those little girls down there is alive because of you. You're a hero." The computer screen went to its coded home page, a very innocuous web page that anyone in the world would recognize as just another advertisement. The page, which changed daily, was indeed a standard commercial webpage, but it sent a clear message; the show was over.

By the time Captain Gerald walked back through the door, they had packed all of the equipment and were ready to leave. The mission had been a success; the race had been a success because an American had won the gold medal. Hot Shot was not sure what her name was. He lived in a different universe and wasn't even a fan. His only interest that week had been in the shooting events. Nevertheless, he was very happy for her and for everyone. Maybe he would take a look at the race later and see just whose life had hung in the balance. If all went according to plan, the trio would be on a chopper out of the country within an hour. He may be a hero, but his would be of the unsung nature. This was a clandestine mission. What he wanted most right now was to go home.

* * *

Nothing in thirty-six years of life could have prepared Trisha for the events of this, the 19th of August, 2016. The race itself had been the hardest two-plus hours of her life—by a lot. The weather was hot and muggy, the crowd was incredibly supportive and yet she had been attacked and knocked to the ground, but first there was the dog! And still she had won the race. She had won the race in world record time. Somehow, Trisha Martin had pulled herself from the depth of fatigue, overcome obstacles that would have been unforeseen by anyone under any circumstance, to win the gold medal in world record time. *The clock doesn't lie.*

At the finish line, Trisha, Sultan Haydar and Xiaolin Zue twirled in a three way tear filled group hug. The two who were with her, drunken with joyous exhaustion were so profusely grateful, thanking her over and over again for coming back for them. She told them only that they deserved this just as much as she did and she wanted to share what had just happened with the entire world, their victory over the protesters. It was to be everyone's; it was not for her alone. She also told them not to worry about telling others that she had come back, but that the whole thing was the spontaneous result of athletic coincidence, and something that the three of them had decided in the special moment . . . together. The crowd noise made it impossible for her to know if they had heard and understood what she had said, but she was delirious with joy and dizzy from dehydration and the spinning of their embrace. It was then that she recognized American Hammer Thrower, Kibwe Johnson, a massive man, trying to reach her with an American flag. The chaotic atmosphere was over the top. She decided to run to him and get the flag, but tripped just off of the track and fell to the ground. She fainted, losing consciousness and landed in wet grass that had been painted red . . .

Trisha was only unconscious for a few seconds and when she came to, Stanley Burton, her trainer was standing over her, guarding against onlookers who had gathered around. He looked to be as white as a ghost with worry. The entire stadium had gone silent with shared concern. Trisha smiled up into his face, regaining her dignity, told him she was fine and had him lift her up, squeezing her tightly. He then offered her a cold bottle of Gatorade, which she took a sip of while at the same time everyone around began to applaud. And then the roar of the fans throughout the stadium erupted once again to a fever pitch. *I did it! They wanted me to train for a run at the gold medal here in Brazil and I did it!* Johnson arrived and handed her the flag with a huge smile on his face. She took it, gave the giant hammer thrower a big hug, opened the flag, holding the top as high as she could, for it was almost as big as she was, and then abruptly took off again in a victory lap around the stadium to the delight of the spectators who had witnessed history. *I did it! I can't believe this happened.* The runner noticed her two compatriots, Flanagan and Goucher crossing the finish line as the next competitors to complete the grueling run, and then she saw her fellow gold medalists with their own flags and felt the warmth of love and true friendship. Her decision had been the right one.

Trisha Jean Martin had lost 175 pounds, put on her running shoes, and climbed to the top of the world in six years. Where once she had not even been on a date, she married the man she had loved all of her life, gave birth to two beautiful children, and now this. *Where is my family? Where is Michael? Mikey saved my life. Oh, Daddy, we did it.*

There were adoring fans everywhere. After Trisha had completed a circuit of the track, she noticed race officials calling her to the athlete's tunnel where she would exit the stadium. She waved a final goodbye to the crowd, sensing the twinge that comes at the end of any moment like this and found Stanley waiting for her. He was holding her bag; it contained all of her belongings. He had to shout in order to be heard. "You need to go in and clean up quickly, because there's a helicopter waiting to take us to Olympic headquarters. You only have a few minutes, Trisha. Everyone wants a piece of you now!" The cacophony of everything made it impossible, or almost, to hear what he was saying.

Where is my family? I want to see them before we leave. She found them inside of the tunnel waiting for her. Trisha took just a second to put on the warm-up suit, folded the flag, tucking it into her bag and then went to her mother first. Before she could reach her, however, a very happy Randy Moss jumped in and started asking questions. Amidst the dissonance of the moment she was at a loss for words . . . in the beginning, but as her thoughts developed, her smile widened, and with the support of her loved ones, she was able to settle her nerves and speak gratefully of the crowd support after the incident, a hidden reserve which propelled her forward, and of how close she felt to her father in the last half of the race.

When Trisha reached her mother's arms, she started to cry. They had been through so much together during years of world travels. David smiled, hugged and kissed her, and whispered into her ears. "I know that it isn't the most important thing to you, dear Trisha, but you just made the Foundation millions of dollars. I knew it the moment you walked into the office that day. I spent my entire life getting ready to meet you."

"Oh, David; you are the one who made the money. I just ran along for the fun of it. We were lucky to meet each other."

Trisha hugged and kissed the rest of the family; the kids were the most excited, and then there was Michael. She looked up into his eyes, rested her head on his chest, "I don't know how, Mikey, but we did it. Here we are and we have the gold medal you signed me up for. It's an impossible accomplishment. Thank you. I'll be forever indebted to you and the Foundation for getting me going again. I don't know how I will ever be able to pay you back."

"Think of it this way, TJ. You still work for Dad, but I work for you now."

She stepped back, a bit startled, not even noticing the hundreds of flashing cameras still popping by the second. "How's that?"

"You are the new Chair of the Roger Martin Foundation. It's your baby now. The implications of what has happened today are . . . unimaginable. Obviously, Dad bet on the right horse. I am at your disposal, TJ. I belong to you now." Trisha couldn't even process what he was saying, but was shocked through to her bones. *The Foundation . . . and I'm the Chair. What does that mean?*

She was drawn away from her family, prodded by Stanley because they needed to get going. Stanley, her only trainer, the most important member of her team, was still working, guiding his world champion through the busiest day of her life. He forced her to hydrate at every opportunity, striving to get fluids into her drained body.

This would not be the day to cramp up. When they had made it to the locker room, he guarded the door so that she could shower and clean up in peace.

Once she got her tired and worn body underneath hot steaming water, Trisha had the time to reflect in private for the first time. *I'm going to take a long hot shower. I don't think they would leave without me,* she chuckled inwardly to herself. *I wonder if I can run the hot water down.*

Once she was clean, and that meant washing her hair more than once to get all of the grime and . . . icky stuff out, she moved one of the plastic chairs underneath the flowing water and let her mind empty. For the first time in a long time, her bruised shoulder made its presence known. She was so tired, so very tired. Very much like the worn out mother who seeks solace in a hot bubbly tub, Trisha drifted into a catnap.

"Mac and I are so proud of you, Trisha. Tag is too. You have proven yourself worthy . . ."

479

There was a knock at the door and Trisha was ushered back into reality. Before relaxing she had turned down the lights, hydrated yet again, and now the knocking door screamed that any privacy would be a rare commodity today. There would be precious little of it, then again; *how many times in my life will I be given the chance to celebrate Olympic gold medals and world records?* "I'm coming, Stanley. Tell them to be patient." Trisha was courteous in her quick reply. She and Stanley had, among other things, secret knocks that identified just who was calling and why. This one called for expediency.

What am I supposed to do with the Foundation? Trisha giggled while she was drying her hair. She had recently signed a promotional contract with Sedu, noting to herself that she only supported products she actually used. Her hair was dry in just a couple of minutes—no small accomplishment considering her hair. She emerged from privacy in less than thirty minutes looking like a brand new person, wearing a white cotton button-down blouse emblazoned with a remarkably simple but elegant TJM patch. This outfit just happened to be the breakout piece of the brand new *Trisha Jean Martin* collection, designed by her and friends at Ralph Lauren. It was complimented by a knee length matching skirt that had flair and grace, a large red, white, and blue belt, and finished off with white leather sneakers. The thin gold chain with an American flag around her neck, her wedding ring, a gold watch, and tiny matching ear loops made the whole ensemble complete. Her makeup was very conservative, but it perfectly enhanced the color of her skin and the clothing she wore. When she emerged the crowd noise from everyone inside of the room erupted again and the cameras were whizzing at breakneck speed. It was time to jump back up on the roller coaster. *Was I really a shy person? Please God, do not let this stuff go to my head.* The helicopter ride to the top of the broadcast center took just a minute or so, a much safer mode of transportation considering all of the crazy attention she was getting.

Trisha Martin walked onto the set and back into the lives of American television viewers. She was all smiles. Al Michaels, someone she didn't even know was in town, was the first to speak. "I thought we were going to get to interview the actual Trisha Martin? Who is this imposter, this, this, beautiful woman? Certainly, you are not the lady who set a world record in the marathon less than an hour ago?"

There was laughter all over the set, including cameraman and other technicians who were listening in just like the viewing audience. Stanley wasn't laughing. He was crying tears of joy, and dutifully standing aside, ever the protector of his protégé.

* * *

On the inside of a hospital room a surgeon and his patient watched, mesmerized by the sight of the beautiful runner, wife, lover, friend, and helpmate. "Billy . . ." Brad looked at the kid with the big white surgical turban. The boy-genius looked back. "She is mine. She was always mine and I am never going to let her out of my world. Your job is to pay me back by protecting my wife. You make President . . . you make me proud and you look after my wife no matter what. Agreed?"

"Agreed, Captain Peterson." He actually believed what he was saying. *I am going to be President because of her.*

Over at Club Sport Green Valley the crowd had finally broken up, the party was beginning to wind down and there were two who embraced romantically. It seemed the natural conclusion to the greatest day of their lives. In the background, up on the big Jumbotron behind them, a most beautiful person was answering questions of several interviewers. The two looked into each other's eyes, one hopeful that his life was finally going to work; the other was lost in a newfound love that she thought could never exist. "April, I am ready for this. I won't let you down."

Around the world, the beauty of the moment, the time when competitors came together and made their stand against the wrongness that had plagued the games, resulted in optimism that began to grow. Something had gone right in the human race for a change. A paradigm of civilized answers to questions began to take the place of crazy and disruptive anger. Things were changing.

* * *

The runner was thoroughly enjoying her moment in the sun. Today was her day. Randy Moss had a rather wicked smile on his face. "Now comes the time for our trivia question of the day. We have had a great deal of fun highlighting the personal lives of our great athletes. On the big screen behind him four pictures appeared.

Trisha's heart sank and she fell into shock. *I am going to KILL my mother!* Two of the pictures were obviously of her running in previous races. One was of a very pretty girl who looked almost exactly like her. *How did they get that shot? She is a dead ringer.* The fourth picture was one of a huge woman sitting astride a brand new bike. No one could have concluded who that was unless they knew. "Which one of these pictures is not Trisha Jean Martin?" Once the truth came out . . . on live global television, Randy Moss apologized profusely for embarrassing her.

Gratitude, Trisha. Gather yourself. Problems are just opportunities and I do not intend to miss this one. "No matter what your situation is, whether you are strangled by addiction, are morbidly obese; no matter how deep you are into trouble, there is usually a way out and this proves it. That's me. My mother took that picture on the day I purchased the bike. You have to remember though, by the time I got on that bike, I already had a professional team guiding my transition. You may not have that. You may not make it to where I am, but you can come back if you really want to. That is the lesson of the photograph. Life isn't about falling down. Everyone falls down, some more than others. Life is about getting back up again and heading off in the right direction.

My example proves that. If you are down and want to change, then get back up and try again. You will be glad that you did."

"Trisha," it was Bob Costas' turn, "today, you are America's pride and joy. Thanks for getting back up. Before we let you go I would like to take this opportunity to present you with this framed picture which was just handed to me. It is the working original of the *Sports Illustrated* cover in their edition set to hit newsstands tomorrow morning." The large glossy photograph was decoratively framed and professionally set in laminate, and it included the original autograph of the photographer who got the shot. It depicted three women crossing the finish line, hand in hand with their arms extended over their heads, all smiling and grinning from ear to ear. The title in huge bold letters read, "*Paraprosdokian!*" The subtitle said quite frankly; "*Trisha Martin sends protesters packing.*"

* * *

Epilogue

The old woman had finished her story. So many decades had passed since those wondrous days had transformed her into Trisha Jean Martin, the runner. Just thinking about how it had all happened, who the players were, and the magic of the entire journey left her with mixed feelings. It was a joy to share her experiences with these young people and that was true. She also missed old friends anew and her heart sank in loneliness. Except for Billy, she was the only one left, still climbing out of bed each day, promising herself to carry on until the end, the main ingredient that constituted her legacy. Slowly, amidst the ache of loss, and yet having basked in the sun of a beautiful midday Las Vegas winter breeze before coming inside, Trisha pulled a hanky from her pocket, wiped tears from her eyes, and then smiled. "Let's go run a race. What do you say? It is time for us to get this done. We have work to do."

"Excuse me, Mrs. Martin," The voice of the quiet one, an older runner, still quite young by Trisha's standard, perhaps she was in her mid-fifties, caught her by surprise. She had spoken not a single word the entire time. "How old were you when you knew that you wanted to keep this up your whole life?"

Mature runners are my favorite. It's a statement on aging for me to consider someone more than forty years younger than me to be mature. "Before I was even thirty five years old I met the most amazing person. We were at a track meet. I can't even remember where it was, but a young runner just out of college, what was her name . . . oh, yes, it was Whitney Gipson, a long jumping specialist; I think she won the NCAA's, and anyway she had us guessing the age of one of the contestants in the race that day. After watching *her* for a few minutes I guessed that she was in her late sixties. Her name was Olga Kotelko. One of the things I factored into my guess was that she moved so fluidly, was sturdy, and she spoke articulately. Except for the lines on her face I would have thought she was even younger. Turns out she was 94! I couldn't believe it. Right then and there I knew I would be running forever. OK, folks, let's get going.

* * *

Somewhere amidst the backdrop of the American way of life, late 21st century style, a young mother entered her kitchen through the side door. She had been out on her morning hour-long run, was the type of athlete who liked looking good and loved to work out in top-of-the-line TJM running clothes. Like millions of middle class mothers, her attention shifted to getting breakfast on the table for the kids. A huge in-wall television was on in the background. It was just another typical day. Something on the television distracted her, she looked, and her heart sank. *Oh, no.*

"We have sad news to report this morning," the newscaster held the choke of personal feelings aside as best she could. "Trisha Jean Martin, America's runner, passed away in peaceful sleep during the night. Unbelievably, she had just completed her 100th marathon at the age of 98, a new world record, and the 42nd time she found a way to put her name into the record books. Martin was perhaps the most prolific lifelong athlete in American history, winning gold in consecutive Olympics, 2016 and 2020. Her contributions as Chair of the Roger Martin Foundation enabled her to be a positive influence in countless lives. She will be terribly missed, leaving behind numerous friends and family members. Fortunately for all of us, our Brenda Williams spent several hours with Trisha just yesterday.

"Here is a very short video clip from yesterday's race." It was taken, obviously from a helicopter. "Note the woman at the head of the little pack. As the camera zooms in, you will see the final steps taken by Trisha Martin in a foot race. Her style and grace are impeccable, she is maintaining a full running gate, and it is obvious that she can still fit into the same outfit she wore when she won her first gold medal. She is all decked out in red, white, and blue. As the camera moves in, looking closely, you can see the TJM body-tard she wore to protect her skin. Look at her face. When you get a peek behind those stylish sunglasses, only then can you see the aged facial features. She never cut her signature, waste length hair. She smiles, wears makeup tastefully, and so looks decades younger than her years. One of the most amazing aspects of this last run was how it ended. No less than twenty runners, two of them world class athletes who decided to stay with her, are all holding hands at the finish line in celebration of her amazing run to the gold way, way back in 2016.

Please join us later this evening for a two hour special celebrating the life and times of Trisha Jean Martin. It is something you will not want to miss."

* * *

Sleep would come easily this evening. Trisha felt very good as she soaked in a hot frothy bath, recouping strength from an amazing day out on the road. *My goal of running the entire race without walking didn't happen; but then again I only had to stop and stroll a few times. I want to run one when I'm a hundred . . . if I live that long.* It was customary for Trisha to eat huge after a run and in that she did not fail. The after dinner party at The Palm out on the Strip was a treat she would long remember. More than twenty family members and friends had shown up. *I love to pig out, still.* "What do you think about that, Buster?" The sleepy bulldog at the side of the tub raised just his left eye and then showed teeth in the bulldog smile that she loved so much. She climbed from the tub, dried herself, applied her favorite lotion from head to toe, put on her favorite pajamas and climbed into bed, but not until she had helped her companion up the little steps he needed to make it onto their shared mattress. Trisha took time to meditate spiritually, making *conscious contact* as she liked to put it, and then fell asleep immediately. She dreamed, or so it seemed.

Trisha was resting comfortably but her eyes came open and then she seemed to float above the bed. She looked down upon herself and noticed that Buster was awake and looking up right at her. He was whining—sorrowfully. The room went black and she drifted into the vortex of what at first looked to be a dark cave, but then it came alive with white light. She pleasantly remembered many moments

485

from her long life as they played like a movie all around her. The feelings she had were reassuring and happy. She was so happy.

At length she came to a fork in the way. She had to make a choice and it seemed a simple one. Her father waited with open arms and she went to him. He was inside of the way, just a few yards more and she would be in his arms. The other path looked very hard. She saw climbing gear alongside an icy sloping cliff. "Oh, Daddy, am I finally there?" He smiled, but said nothing, waiving her in to where he was. Something felt very strange and Trisha looked beyond him so as to see as far as she could. There was nothing out of the ordinary. *Why doesn't he come to me?* "Daddy," she smiled with love and hope, "come over here so I can see you better." He didn't move, but instead beckoned her forward. She studied him as closely as she could and began to notice little things that were not right. *This is just another trick . . . .*

The wind blew sharply; it was bitter and cold. She was climbing a wall of ice up on the side of a cliff, very high up in the mountains, and she was young. The air was crystal clear. Each time she slammed the pick—there was one in each hand—into the face of the cliff, shards of ice sprayed into her face. It was exhilarating. She would pull herself a little higher, bite her spiked boots into the wall and then lift herself just a bit higher, again. At length she tried to hoist herself up onto a ledge, but couldn't quite reach. Fortunately the cliff wasn't straight up, so no ropes were needed, but still she was having trouble at this spot, when all of a sudden strong hands reached downward, took a firm grasp under her arms at the shoulder and lifted her up. He felt very familiar, but she could not see him underneath his protective clothing. He threw his hood back and just like that, Trisha Martin Peterson was looking into the eyes of the man she had loved all the days of her life. Brad's eyes betrayed him as he wept with joy. Trisha had been reunited with her husband. He lipped simple words that could not be heard in the biting wind. "Welcome home, Trish." There were no other words necessary as they both chose to communicate a bit more intimately, wrapped together like two polar bears rolling along the ground in a wrestling match. Before they could get up again, two became four as a couple of bulldogs crashed into them. The dogs, both fully grown and healthy, looked silly in their artificial fur overcoats.

This was a family reunion. Trisha laughed with joy. "Matilda, is that really you? Buster! I thought I left you on the bed. What are you doing here?"

"Ole Buster just showed up a bit ago. It seems he died of a broken heart at about the same time you went to sleep. I only knew him as a little puppy before I made the journey, but it seems we're all together again. I cannot believe how happy 'Tilda is to have him back. They've been rolling around fighting and wrestling from the minute they got together. You should have been there when we put their coats on."

"You get to keep your dogs in this life?"

"All dogs go to heaven, honey." Brad had always loved having dogs. "I'm not sure how it works, but I think you get the dogs you died with. I haven't seen any of the others."

Trisha's heart was swelling with happiness. She took a look around. They were in a place she remembered well. Once, a long time ago, she had walked this path. Trisha removed the spikes from her boots, and walked the narrow path alongside Brad, holding him, stopping intermittently to press her young, strong body against his and instinctively knowing the way. Watching the dogs play with each other only made things better. They crossed the beautifully decorated wooden bridge, engaging in of all things . . . small talk. "Did I ever tell you, little runner girl, how glad I was that you came to Frankfurt and saved my life?"

"Oh, you think I went there for you? I was in training for Madrid. It was pure coincidence."

She giggled, looking out of side-slanted eyes at him, grinning slyly."

This is my girl. I have my Trisha back. "Anyone can see that you aren't aware of enhanced penalties for fibbing on this side of the veil. I'm sure you will get some newcomers grace, though.

Let's take a look at the situation. You finish 22nd in Los Angeles, train like crazy, head to Europe and blow Frankfurt like an out of shape club runner; then you go to Madrid, finish third, and get your picture on the cover of *Runner's World* Magazine. That's one hell of a pure coincidence, fib wife, or it's the greatest comeback in running history."

Trisha was laughing. *Am I really young again? Is this real? This time I hope I don't get to wake up.* "Did you just swear? They let you get away with gutter language like that in these parts? What kind of afterlife is this going to be?" Trisha was beginning to get excited at the chance of a brand new future. "I confess, Brad. I wanted you to see me. I went there for you, and that is true." *I could never get away with lying, not to Brad, pretty much not to anyone. He looks awfully good in this reality, so strong and handsome. Please, God, let this be real.*

"You finally admit it then. Well, you ran and ran as fast as you could. I didn't catch the gingerbread man, but I did catch you, and I knew that I would." Their lips touched and the dogs started barking.

After another length of time they arrived at the wooden door, opened it and went into the mountain. The runner knew that it would be warm inside and once the door was shut she removed the heavy clothing that had kept her warm and safe on the outside. Brad was wearing simple clothing meant for a spring day. They had the dogs' coats off quickly and moved on. Of course she glanced back at where the door was and saw that once again it had disappeared. They made their way down the long and winding steps, through the well decorated, ambient lit tunnel and then out onto the patio overlooking the most beautiful valley anyone had ever seen. When she and Brad emerged, Trisha Jean Martin Peterson found them one and all. They were waiting for her, clapping like a huge family would for the return of a long lost sister. A young and handsome Stanley was the first to embrace her. He held her long and hard. One by one, Trisha squeezed her mother, hugged and kissed Michael, clasped hands with and stared into her sister, Rachael's eyes, sucker punched, and then kissed David Giles; and there were others she had not seen in many decades. This was not at all like any dream she had ever had. This was different. The group parted and there was her father, lighting a candle on top of a lovely cake. Standing next to him was Wise Mac. He was handling the ice cream, plates and other party favors. This was to be a celebration. Trisha's mother, young again and very beautiful, whispered into her ear, "We get to eat here and we don't gain weight. It's heaven."

Roger brought the cake forward and she blew out the candle. He set the cake back on the table, turned and hugged his daughter.

It was the sweetest moment she had ever had. "Welcome home, Trisha . . ."

For quite some time, the entire group mingled, reminiscing the lives they had lived. Trisha took time to visit with each and every one of them. There was laughter, music, friendship, love and much more.

Later, as the sun slowly drifted to the west and began its descent to the horizon and sunset, Trisha's father and his buddy, Mac, approached. It was Mac who spoke first. "Trisha, look out to the south. Do you see them?"

Trisha looked into the reddening sky, finally noticing two tiny dots dancing amid silver lined clouds of fire set against the deepening blue of encroaching twilight. "There they are, Mac. What are they?"

Her father smirked, coughed, and then spoke, rather sardonically, "Why, Trisha, you are about to witness the rarest of life forms in the known universe, the Giant Bald Ego." Mac started laughing and Trisha was just a bit confused. As they approached a bit closer, others began to take notice.

Within just a couple of minutes, two huge eagles flew into the patio area, setting down on the ground. They changed into men. Their transformation looked something like a transporter scene from *Star Trek*. Roger smiled. "They are among the very first humans to become Eternals," he said. And then he whispered quietly into Trisha's ear, "How those bloated ego types got in first is beyond me." She recognized one of them as Bob Hankle, the man who had rescued her husband during wartime. He was with, who was it, oh yes, Tag Peterson, her husband's grandfather. Tag gave her a quick hug, smiled, welcomed her and then stood back. "Folks, I hate to break up a family reunion like this but I have serious news to report. We have to get going now! It's those damned Deceivers again."

The End.

* * *

Enjoy this preview of Lloyd Wendell Cutler's next adventure, *End Game*, Book I of his soon to be published trilogy, THE ETERNALS.

End Game

Death, you come
on a black cat night,
no white clouds
nestled under your skin.
Wise Mac

October 20, 2064

Outside one could enjoy fluffy sporadic clouds and a fresh breeze on an otherwise sunny and pleasant day; the temperature was in the mid-50s which was normal for the middle of the afternoon. Inside, Na moved silently in dark and forbidding corridors, clutching a satellite telephone in his left hand, his right reassuring himself that the gun he had hidden behind his back was ready to fire should he need to take the life of the man he stalked, or even to use on himself to protect a deeply guarded secret. He and his allies wanted an end to the long dominance of the North's repressive control of his beloved Korea. Although it was a very dangerous assignment, here in the port city of Sinuiju, he had long wanted to find the source of influence that emboldened the seemingly common laborer he was tracking. Kyung Na hated being this close to the Chinese border in a small city full of loyal troops, immersed in their blind ideology.

He had followed the man on the train from Pyongyang, North Korea's capital, knowing that he was a key player in something that was planned, something terrible beyond imagination. Just tracking him on the old rickety electric train out of Pyongyang was terrifying. The noisy, rough ride amidst the clickety-clack of uneven tracks didn't bother him. He was used to that. North Korea had become a more open place than in the past and he felt some reassurance from the presence of tourists, even Americans who were on the train. He would've liked for the passenger load to be a bit heavier; there were enough people for him to hide in plain sight. Most of those not asleep were enjoying the rural countryside of dirt roads, pastures, and farm land. It looked somewhat like the foothills in Montana, until one looked a bit closer at the sparse number of vehicles and people along those roads. What terrified Na were the eyes; they were everywhere. During the trip he navigated to the same car that his target was in, almost bumping right into the boiler. When he got past that, he looked directly into the attendant's cabin and straight into the eyes of a red capped sentry visiting quietly with the steward. He was sure they were watching him, or at least that is how he felt. From that moment on, it was all he could do to keep his demeanor stable until at last, he departed the train and followed his mark into the old building.

Now he was moving like a ghost in an old burned out warehouse towards the manager's office where a tiny light signified the presence of life. *What is he doing in this godforsaken place?* CIA agent or no, Na was terrified of the man he followed. Thankfully, the floor was cement and not wooden, lest he make any sound and give himself away. Na slithered between broken benches, shards of glass, an infestation of rats, and positioned himself just outside of the office, not believing what he was seeing and hearing. He had already placed the remotely operated lens, a tiny device that hovered and flew about on his command, so that whatever happened could be captured and sent down the line. It looked sophisticated when viewed through a magnifying glass. Otherwise it was very hard to see, being about half the size of a gnat and even quieter. To the best of Na's knowledge, the little stealthy black bug was virtually undetectable.

Just before he entered the old factory, Na had witnessed and photographed strange bright lights just over the building and now he trembled with fear of what could not be understood. The man he had followed inside was conferring with the strangest creature he had ever seen, a black-bearded personage, whose head was the shape of an elongated egg, and he had to be twice as tall as any normal human being. Although he looked homo-sapient, the creature most certainly was not like anyone or anything he had laid eyes on. The terror behind what he heard, saw, and recorded shook him to the core and into a state of panic. *Was this to be the end of all?*

Kyung Gog Na had made not a sound, not even a breath exhaled could have been detected, and so he was caught completely off guard when they both turned sharply to where he was, hidden outside the open doorway of the office. Trembling now, he ran, zigzagging, bumping into tables though he did not get halfway back to the front of the building before he was snared in a net, its shards of thread so tiny that he could not see them with the naked eye. Kyung fell into broken fragments of glass splayed on the floor face down, instantly becoming a bloody mess. Fortunately he had some use of his hands and only two tasks left to perform before his part in the long struggle for freedom would come to an end.

* * *

"Where am I?"

"You're dreaming, Billy. I know it's been a while, but do you remember me?"

"You are a doctor, but I cannot remember your name. Didn't you fix me?" the young boy asked the handsome man. He was disoriented, but only for a second. *"Captain Peterson! You saved my life."* The confusion had to do with the age, his and Captain Peterson's. He was a boy and the doctor was young and healthy. His memories of Brad Peterson were of an older man, an old friend who had passed some years earlier, not as a young and handsome war hero. Now he remembered—all of it. This was what Trisha Peterson's husband looked like when they first met, at least mostly. In his current state he looked . . . ethereal, angelic. This dream seemed different, real in some way, not real the way that dreams fooled him, but really real. He was talking to him as he was . . . someplace, somewhere a long time ago.

"I did, young man. You had a tumor the size of a golf ball inside of your head and I removed it for you. Do you remember now?"

"You're Doctor Peterson. Of course I remember. I went to the hospital with terrible headaches and you made me better. I was just a boy then and now I am old, but now I am young all of a sudden. You were young then too, and yet you are, we are. Where are we?"

493

"My Earth life is over, but yours goes on. You're asleep in your bed on the second floor of the White House, Mr. President. I am with you now, just as I was then, only in a different way. Your purpose is now about to be fulfilled. You are the reason I was granted leave with special gifts to practice medicine. A great and marvelous work is about to be fulfilled, but your responsibilities are to become overwhelming, even for one such as yourself. When you awaken, the eternal destiny of the human race falls . . ."

"Mr. President, wake up."

"Ignore the voice for a minute, young President Dace. I need to give you important tidings . . ."

"President Dace."

"Billy. Move firmly, but be cautious in your quickness. Do not under any circumstances use nuclear weapons . . ."

"Mr. President! You must wake up this minute. Something is happening that needs your immediate attention."

This time Dace the Ace slowly emerged from a deep sleep. He had been dreaming and now could not quite remember . . . It had something to do with Captain Peterson and nuclear weapons. "What's going on?" As he sat up in bed, William Dace, President of the United States, noted several people in the room. His wife, Jackie, was not with them, and then he noticed someone moving in the bathroom with the light on. That had to be her. He was staring up into the face of his White House Communications Chief, Barnard Meacham. "Barney, what are you doing here at this hour?"

* * *

Printed in the United States
By Bookmasters